THE AUKMONDI

CURSE

OF THE

UNINSPIRED

H.D. HIGGINS

CITI OF BOOKS

CITIOFBOOKS, INC.
3736 Eubank NE Suite A1
Albuquerque, NM 87111-3579
www.citiofbooks.com

Hotline: 1 (877) 389-2759
Fax: 1 (505) 930-7244

Ordering Information:

Quantity sales. Special discounts are available on quantity purchases by corporations, associations, and others. For details, contact the publisher at the address above.

Printed in the United States of America.

ISBN-13:   Paperback   979-8-89391-757-4
            eBook   979-8-89391-758-1

Library of Congress Control Number: 2025912483

BOOK DESCRIPTION

The Curse of the Uninspired is death. When the curse is placed upon the Aukmondi people, there is nothing anyone can do about it except bury their dead.

During the mid-eighteenth century, in East Africa, the peaceful and idyllic life of the Aukmondi people is shattered when Mfalme Abul-Gwan, a tribal chief and successful entrepreneur in the animal products trade, visits the Aukmondi Valley. He brings with him his beloved mate, Abul-Tess, and a powerful Vodun houngan (Voodoo Priest), Onu-Vey. Abul-Gwan wants to hunt animals in the local area, but the barbaric Wabanga tribe members hamper his efforts. He asks Mfalme Ramuza Ncobba of the Aukmondi Tribe to help rid the area of Wabanga. The Aukmondi people, however, hold a high regard for life – all life. Out of principle, Ramuza refuses Abul-Gwan's request. Abul-Gwan is obviously disappointed, but he accepts Ramuza's decision. He prepares to move on. But before he leaves the Aukmondi Valley, his mate, Abul-Tess, is killed in a tragic mishap. Abul-Gwan, whose mood is already dark, falls into a crippling depression. He turns angry and vengeful, blaming the Aukmondi for the dismal prospects of his business in the area and the death of his mate. He wants retribution. Abul-Gwan asks the powerful Vodun houngan to get rid of the useless Aukmondi people. He wants them all dead.

Onu-Vey is reluctant but complies. He performs one of his darkest rituals to summon the Loa of Death, a spirit whose focus and sole purpose is to take the life of the Aukmondi people. Death, in physical form, roams the Aukmondi Valley killing dozens, upon dozens, of people in its wake. Whole kraal communities are wiped out. Ramuza makes an angry and impulsive effort to confront Abul-Gwan and the Vodun houngan. The loa killed him. Kharaambi, Ramuza's third mate and leader of the Aukmondi Army, reacts. Several regiments and prominent regimental commanders of her army are killed with only a wave of the loa's hand. Ramuza's only son, the little prince Adaulah, is now the new Aukmondi Mfalme. Despite his inexperience, he also makes a desperate and valiant attempt to stop the killings. His approach is insightful, but his effort is unsuccessful. More warriors die, and the killings continue.

The Aukmondi people questioned the core of their spiritual strength. Kon-Shambique, the brilliant spiritual leader of the Aukmondi, can offer little advice. He is too spiritually broken, as the love of his life also lies among the dead. Even the Supreme Spirit, known to walk among the Aukmondi, seems to have abandoned the helpless people. Can anything stop the Loa of Death?

The Aukmondi: Curse of the Uninspired is a page-turner that will leave you with a provocative and different perspective on life and death.

Other Books by H. D. Higgins

The Aukmondi: Secret of the Yululu Bone

H. D. Higgins Jr. was born and raised in Little Rock, Arkansas. After graduating from Little Rock Central High School and studying psychology for two years at the University of Arkansas, he enlisted in the U.S. Air Force during the Vietnam War. He served for more than twenty years in military intelligence, received training in Russian, and completed tours of duty in England, Turkey, Italy, and Japan. He retired from the Air Force in 1995 and has since lived in Baltimore, Maryland, where he works as a technical writer. *The Aukmondi: Curse of the Uninspired* is his second novel in the Aukmondi series. Other work includes *The Aukmondi: Secret of the Yululu Bone*, published in 2009. H. D. Higgins is currently at work on a third.

DEDICATION

To my sister Fareedah (Rita) Muhammad,
who made immortally very real,
from the other side of the river.

CONTENTS

The Aukmondi:
Curse of the Uninspired Characters

The Royal Family

RAMUZA KONEHENI NCOBBA – Mfalme of the Aukmondi Tribe: Soft-spoken, level-headed, and a proven leader, Ramuza has created an idyllic place for all to live. But when influences beyond the valley rim threaten to upset the peace and tranquility of the Aukmondi Valley, Ramuza loses control of it all.

RWUVA AZINTI NCOBBA – First of Ramuza's three wives: Rwuva is the Principal Mate and a tribal elder. So loved and respected by all, Rwuva's opinions can become tribal laws. When Rwuva decrees one of her opinions into law, a deliberate transgression with dire consequences may be the only way to save lives.

OLABISI SHEETSWA NCOBBA – Second wife of Ramuza and caretaker of the Sacred Temple: Olabisi arranged for hundreds of people to find solace in the Sacred Temple. But hundreds never get a chance to enter the temple. Olabisi is overwhelmed as the sadness and devastation spread. She can barely comfort the royal family as it crumbles around her.

KHARAAMBI NYOKA NCOBBA – Third wife of Ramuza: Kharaambi is the Gray Warrior, leader of the entire Aukmondi Army. Kharaambi knows the army is the obvious answer to confront the deadly threat to the valley. She soon learns that the obvious answer is also assured death for all her warriors.

ADAULAH AZINTI NCOBBA – Ramuza's youngest child (8) and his only son: Adaulah is inquisitive, energetic, and destined to become the next tribal Mfalme. He thinks he knows how to stop the deaths in the valley, but no one believes him. Adaulah risks his life to prove himself right. His failure only causes more to die.

Ramuza's Nine Daughters (and their ages)

Omari Azinti Ncobba (19) Mother: Rwuva	Yejide Azinti Ncobba (18) Mother: Rwuva	Kunto Azinti Ncobba (17) Mother: Rwuva
Audi Azinti Ncobba (16) Mother: Rwuva	Akwate Sheetswa Ncobba (13) Mother: Olabisi	Akuako Sheetswa Ncobba (13) Mother: Olabisi
Zindzhi Nyoka Ncobba (11) Mother: Kharaambi	Baako Sheetswa Ncobba (10) Mother: Olabisi	Alaba Sheetswa Ncobba (10) Mother: Olabisi

The Spiritual Support

KON-SHAMBIQUE – The tribal healer and spiritual teacher: Kon-Shambique's late grandmother taught him most of his medical skills. His spiritual guidance comes from the heart and a divine link with the Supreme Spirit. When his heart and divine link are broken, Kon-Shambique cannot give anyone spiritual guidance when the people need it the most.

TONGDA LENG – Unofficial mate of Kon-Shambique and his closest medical assistant: Tongda pays the ultimate price, but not before revealing a horrible premonition, written in blood. All will be dead in two days!

The Chinchigwe

AMEH JOBABWE – Mfalme of the Chinchigwe Clan of the Aukmondi: Ameh is one of Ramuza's closest advisors and the infant's grandfather, Tutapona. As one of the highest authorities in the Aukmondi tribe, Ameh realizes he can do nothing to save the people of the valley. He makes one desperate effort to save his grandson.

LOBARRA GENDEYANI – A Chinchigwe and mother of Tutapona: Lobarra is a reputable farmer. On a return trip from a farmers' conference in a neighboring village, Lobarra is unaware of all the deaths in the valley. Her greatest concern is the fretfulness and irritability of her infant son. What is Tutapona trying to tell her? Will she have time to learn?

TUTAPONA JOBABWE – Infant son of Lobarra and grandson of Ameh Jobabwe: Tutapona carries a name which means, "We will recover". Tutapona once embodied hope for the Chinchigwe people. Now, his name and the hope he offered are hollow promises for the Chinchigwe and the Aukmondi.

The Warriors

QUAZZI GEMBALO – The Brown Warrior, Foremost Lieutenant of the Aukmondi Army: Quazzi is Ramuza's best friend and Kharaambi's second in command. Quazzi's best effort to support them turns out to be mass graves, dug to bury the dead. He knows. No one gets out of this alive.

NIONU VOGAMA – A Royal Warrior, the youngest in the Aukmondi Army: Nionu has a sharp sense of humor and is often whimsical. His tactics are impulsive. Yet, he is one of the army's most brilliant warriors. But after confronting the greatest adversary of his life, Nionu's mood turns dark. He goes into seclusion as his brilliance fringes on madness.

OBE BENDABE – One of two Blue Warriors in Nionu's army: Obe stands over two meters tall. His imposing figure makes him an intimidating warrior. Obe is confident and level-headed. He takes his last stand against an enemy that lifts him off his feet.

DABETE EHKILI – The second of two Blue Warriors in Nionu's army. Dabete is a brilliant strategist and tactician. He and his regiment can often execute a mission while others still plan what to do. The best of plans can fail.

TUSHEMA MADULI – A Green Warrior in Dabete Ehkili's regiment: Tushema is a "no-nonsense" warrior. He and his detachment of warriors must escort a group of farmers from a neighboring village back to the Aukmondi Valley. Tushema is in a race with the forces of nature to keep the farmers safe. Tushema does not know that the faster he leads the farmers across the wilderness, the sooner they will all die.

WEMA MWEZZI – An Orange Warrior in Obe Bendabe's regiment: Wema is tasked by Mfalme Ameh Jobabwe to intercept the returning farmers. He must warn the farmers of the danger awaiting them in the Aukmondi Valley. Although fast on his feet, Wema discovers too late that the danger is no longer confined to the valley.

ROTHO TAUNZA – A Red Warrior in Obe Bendabe's regiment: Rotho is assigned to guard the Chinchigwe royalty, Lobarra, and

Tutapona. Day after day, Rotho develops a special bond with Tutapona. He does not understand how special it is until he reaches the valley and manages the bodies of the dead.

NIENKO CHERUNDI – A Red Warrior in Obe Bendabe's regiment: Nienko is Wema's friend and trainee. The two must deliver the warning to the returning farmers. But when their mission seems doomed to fail, Wema convinces Nienko that it is still salvageable if one of them is willing to face death.

UPENDA MUSHWALA – A White Warrior in Obe Bendabe's regiment, and Tongda's cousin: Upenda is inexperienced but highly dedicated. She gives more than what is needed from her, which is an inspiration in itself. Despite her inexperience, circumstances always put Upenda in crucial positions that make all the difference.

The Mangoni

ABUL-GWAN – Mfalme of the Mangoni Tribe: Abul-Gwan is an entrepreneur who trades animal products to European, Asian, and Colonial American merchants. The success of his business continues to grow, spreading across central and eastern Africa. Abul-Gwan needs help from the local tribes to protect his hunters from the deadly Wabanga people. His business takes a turn for the worse in ways he never imagined.

ABUL-TESS – Mate of Mfalme Abul-Gwan: Abul-Tess has always wanted to travel, meet others, and experience various cultures. As Abul-Gwan's mate, she can finally do those things. When Abul-Tess went with Abul-Gwan to the Aukmondi Valley, she thought she had experienced the best of everything. She was wrong.

ONU-VEY – The current High Priest or Mangoni Vodun Houngan (Voodoo Priest): Onu-Vey performs incredible miracles with his dark magic. And his words are as dangerous as any knife or spear. After arriving in the Aukmondi Valley, Onu-Vey performs his darkest magic ever. The damage goes beyond his control and is irrevocable.

GOH-JUMAANE – Leader of the Mangoni warriors: Goh-Jumaane, a hardened warrior, believes in standing by his Mfalme. His belief and loyalty remain strong, even when his Mfalme becomes a leader who is impossible to follow.

PROLOGUE

Many harvests ago, near the village of the Balba clan…

Mama Kinsi sat alone on the bank by the mountain stream. She listened to the babbling water as it flowed by at her feet. She envied the birds that sang and fluttered from tree limb to tree limb over her head. It was a peaceful moment. She savored it with each precious breath that she took. She felt the darkest hour was coming. Unlike the birds that sang their courtship songs or built their nests with the expectation of new life, her time was ending. Mama Kinsi no longer wondered what to do about it. She had done all that she could. She could not alter destiny.

The twig snapped behind her, drawing her attention away from the carefree birds. She turned to see her son, Onu-Vey, approaching. He was a tall, skinny boy who was fast approaching maturity. His chest was bare, and his youthful muscular development just barely hid his boyish rib cage.

Onu-Vey carried a spear in his hand – an unbecoming sight. Even worse, he wore a knife belted around his waist. When he spotted his mother sitting on the bank of the stream, he rushed to her side.

"Mama, we have to go. Enemy warriors are coming."

"I know." The news did not surprise Mama Kinsi. She looked up at her son. Her eyes made a sweeping assessment of the spear and the knife that he carried. "Get rid of those. They will make matters worse."

"But Mama," Onu-Vey started to protest, but thought better of it. He looked down at the spear and the knife at his side. He made his reassessment. Onu-Vey was no warrior. The weapons did not feel right. His mother's suggestion made him admit that the weapons made him uncomfortable. He tossed the spear to the ground. He untied the knife belt around his waist and dropped it to the ground. Weaponless, he still felt secure. He had much more faith in his mother's wisdom and powers.

"Mama, you are the High Priestess. People of all the clans respect you. Can you do anything to end this fighting and killing?"

"I have done all I can. I can do no more."

Rival clans fought for the ultimate leadership of the tribe. Tension among the clans was commonplace. Harvest after harvest, the tension increased. Fathers turned against sons. Sons turned against fathers. And brothers turned against brothers. There were betrayals, treachery, assaults, assassinations, and all-out war. After so many harvests, no one could say where the legitimate tribal leadership belonged. It had come to the simple fact that tribal leadership belonged to the ultimate victor.

"The peace they want will come after the war they must have. Do not fear the darkness, my son. The light will soon show what we must see." Mama Kinsi took her son's hand and stood. "Come. Please, walk with me."

Mama Kinsi's insistent behavior spoke more clearly to Onu-Vey than any words. His wisdom and maturity compensated for his skinny stature. He stopped walking and took his mother by the shoulders. "Mama, what are you about to do?"

Mama Kinsi stroked her son's face. "When the warriors come today, Mfalme Pal-Fomi, the head of our clan, will die. It is his destiny. Kold-Johan, the ruthless leader of the Mangoni clan, will gain power over us. It will be his final act to solidify his leadership of the tribe. As High Priestess of all the clans, I must serve him."

"But Mama, Kold-Johan is a jackal among men. He is aggressive and evil. You cannot serve him. If you serve him, he will have you doing evil things too."

"As High Priestess, I must serve him."

Onu-Vey sighed as he accepted the tribal protocol. He had no choice. It was what must be. He embraced his mother. "Your magic is too good for him, Mama. Serve him, if you must. Like a poison in his body, your magic will destroy him. What he must have, but cannot control, will consume him."

Mama Kinsi smiled again. The statement made her proud of her son and told her that he was ready for what she was about to do.

*****

Mama Kinsi led her son, Onu-Vey, deeper into the forest. She led him deep into her private enclave, where her strongest magic is born. A cove of congested rocks, trees, and twisted vines created the enclave. So secluded, Mama Kinsi and Onu-Vey were the only two to have ever seen it. People who approached it chose steps that led them away from this den of magic. To reach it, Mama Kinsi thoughtfully took steps known only to Mama Kinsi.

To unfamiliar eyes, a jumbled mess cluttered the entire place. Bags, gourds, calabashes, baskets, and crates filled the area. Huge, string-tied bundles of herbs, leaves, and dried grass filled many decayed and tattered baskets and crates. Many once-used items seemed forgotten and were never to be used again. The original purpose for all of it seemed incomprehensible.

Several bags hang by strings or ropes from tree limbs, and others are discarded haphazardly on the ground. A few of the gourds held smelly liquids of various putrid colors. Other gourds and calabashes lay overturned, abandoned, and the liquid inside long ago spilled or leaked out and dried to a crusty deposit.

Despite the clutter, the area was Mama Kinsi's home. Mama Kinsi knew every inch of it. She led Onu-Vey along a pathway that was not so readily visible. The pathway meandered around the baskets and crates toward the enclave's center.

Onu-Vey followed his mother faithfully. He mimicked her steps. He ignored the clutter as best he could. His steps did not falter until they reached the center of the enclave. When his mother stepped aside, Onu-Vey's steps slowed. He almost froze, startled by what he saw ahead.

A huge black serpent lay coiled on the ground before him. The serpent flickered its forked tongue twice and then raised its head.

Onu-Vey continued his approach, causing the serpent to hiss with its mouth agape, neck expanded, and fangs dripping with venom.

Onu-Vey said nothing, nor did he back away. He finally stopped his approach as he studied the serpent. Although unusually black, Onu-Vey recognized it as an Egyptian cobra. It did not frighten him. He had seen many things conjured by his mother. The cobra appeared less frightening than most conjuring. And if his mother had anything to do with it, Onu-Vey knew she would explain sooner or later.

Mama Kinsi placed her hand on Onu-Vey's shoulder, prompting him to kneel. Then, ever so slowly, Mama Kinsi also knelt before the serpent. With steady fingers, Mama Kinsi reached toward the serpent. The serpent hissed again; its coils tightening. Its hooded head angled, as if selecting a new target to strike. Mama Kinsi's fingers touched the ground. She slid them forward, plowing through the dirt toward the serpent.

Despite her focused effort to reach toward the serpent, Mama Kinsi was aware of her son. She knew that he was holding his breath. "You must remember to breathe, my son. The serpent feels what you feel. It can sense your tension."

Onu-Vey took a deep breath and forced himself to relax. He watched his mother move her fingers closer to the serpent. He watched his mother's mature and wrinkled fingers. Those fingers once brushed the tears from his cheeks when he was younger. Now they plowed through the dirt toward something never imagined.

Mama Kinsi did not stop until she had reached beneath the serpent's coils. The serpent continued to hiss. With mouth still agape, the serpent continued to angle its head for a prime target, but it seemed oblivious to Mama Kinsi's intrusion.

Mama Kinsi smiled triumphantly and slowly withdrew her hand from beneath the serpent's coils. She had recovered something. She sat back a moment, as if to catch her breath. Then she rose to her feet again and stepped back. With the object clutched in her hand, she turned to her son.

"Onu-Vey, you may stand and face me now." She waited until Onu-Vey rose to his feet and turned toward her. "May all the Laos bear witness to what I do here now. At this moment, I will open your eyes to see your gift. You see it for the first time. But it has always been yours."

Onu-Vey looked down at his mother's hand. He watched her uncurl her fingers. In the palm of her hand lay a crystal, oblong in shape and about the size of a large okra pod. One end of it was brilliantly clear and sparkled with a magical radiance. The other end was abysmally black as tar. It was the strangest crystals that Onu-Vey had ever seen.

Onu-Vey studied the crystal. He tried to reason out its purpose. Since the crystal came from beneath the serpent and was now in his mother's hand, Onu-Vey understood it was more than an oblong, oddly-colored crystal. He had to ask. "What is it?"

"It is whatever you want."

Onu-Vey frowned. He studied the crystal closer. At first, it held no relative meaning to him. In his confusion and effort to piece together his fragmented thoughts, he turned to look down at the serpent at his feet. To his amazement, the serpent had turned to stone. Its coils, raised and hooded head, gaping mouth, and fangs were still there, but now, solid stone. Onu-Vey kneeled to get closer. But before his knees touched the ground, he saw the serpent morph again. Before his eyes, the stone serpent magically dissolved into a fine powder. From the ground up, the powder rained down upon itself. When the rain of powder stopped, the dust pile morphed once more into a puddle of clear sparkling water.

More fascinated than ever, Onu-Vey leaned forward. He needed to get a closer look. The shimmering puddle was the strangest thing he had ever seen. Not trusting his eyes, he reached out to dip his finger into the water. Instantly, the puddle morphed again. With a sudden poof, it had changed into a raging flame. It snapped and crackled as it flared.

Onu-Vey sat back, startled. He could feel the intense heat of the flame on his face. Onu-Vey rose to his feet again. By the time he stood fully erect, the snaps and crackles of the flame had grown silent. Onu-Vey watched as the flame transformed into a spiraling column of air. The column stretched upward, over his head, into a whirlpool. It became a wobbling eddy of energy and then disappeared in a whisper.

Onu-Vey turned to his mother again. "Mama, your magic… it confuses me."

"This is not my magic, Onu-Vey. This is your magic."

"My magic? I have no magic."

"My son, we all have magic. It is time you realized that." Mama Kinsi turned to one of the wooden crates at her side. Several empty gourds and calabashes covered the top of the crate. Mama Kinsi searched beneath the gourds and calabashes, knocking many of them to the ground. She searched until she found the leather cord that she had placed there. Mama Kinsi took the cord and began to tie it around the crystal in her hand. She fashioned a necklace and hung it around Onu-Vey's neck.

"This is your *azima*," she said. "It characterizes your magic. It helps to focus your will, your magic. You can misplace it, but you can never lose it. You can forget that you have it. It will always serve you. You may never give it a single thought. Yet it will work for you constantly."

"So, how should I use it?"

"Use it as you see fit. Do with it as you please. It will draw to you whatever your heart and mind embrace, good or evil. Just beware, whatever you embrace, you must live with all it brings. Both good and evil bring forth unforeseen consequences. It is the nature of this *azima*."

Onu-Vey sat down on another crate near him. He reached up to examine the *azima* that hung over his chest. Overwhelmed and fascinated by the gift, he turned the crystal over and over, from side to side, looking at each end.

"Why are the ends so different?" Onu-Vey never took his eyes off the crystal.

"Magic, like all existence, must have balance," Mama Kinsi explained. "The crystal's ends symbolize the balances you must always consider. We cannot appreciate the light until we know the darkness. We cannot appreciate the heat until we know the cold. We cannot enjoy the silence until the noise assaults us. We cannot value love until we have known loneliness."

Onu-Vey understood the concept. He had heard it many times. He joined in with a few examples to show his mother his understanding: "We cannot appreciate familiarity until we have been lost. We cannot appreciate peace until we have experienced war. We cannot know life until we…"

"No, Onu-Vey." Mama Kinsi spoke softly, but sharply enough to stop her son's words. She knew where he was going with that last example. "Death is but a moment in life, Onu-Vey."

Hearing this, Onu-Vey stopped his close examination of the crystal. He turned to look up into his mother's face.

"Life… is eternal." Mama Kinsi smiled at her son. She stared into his face long enough to realize he understood her meaning. Then, satisfied with what she saw, she took three steps back. She bowed her head and morphed into a solid pillar of stone.

"Mama?" Onu-Vey panicked. "Mama?"

Onu-Vey stood up and rushed toward his mother. He reached out to embrace her. Just as his hands touched what used to be his mother's shoulders, the pillar of stone magically dissolved to a fine powder. The powder rained down upon itself into a dusty pile. Onu-Vey stepped closer as the pile of dust morphed into a huge puddle of clear water.

"Mama?" Onu-Vey stepped back, more horrified than ever. The puddle covered an area larger than the puddle made by the serpent. And like the serpent's puddle, Onu-Vey knew what would happen. He took several more steps back. Sure enough, with a poof, the huge puddle of water exploded into a column of flames. The force behind the explosion threw Onu-Vey back. Onu-Vey fell across the wooden crate he had sat on earlier, smashing it. He fell to the ground, hitting his head. Onu-Vey lost consciousness.

— **1** —

I CAN TELL YOU THIS ONLY ONCE

Onu-Vey's village sat in a hilly region just southeast of the Great African Lake (Lake Victoria). On a tree-filled mountainside, the village had grown to a population of 125 people. Most lived by harvesting and trading the precious timber that grew on the slopes north of the village. A two-kilometer-long cliff bordered the entire southern edge of the village. The villagers called this infamous cliff the Jabali. From the Jabali, and 75 jagged and rocky meters below, the Balba villagers could see one of the many tributaries that raced toward the Great African Lake.

After losing consciousness in his mother's enclave, Onu-Vey woke up several hours later. He realized someone had dragged him down from the mountain into his village. He lay on the ground, bruised and lacerated. A huge gash stretched across his forehead. His lower lip was bleeding. A short stake in the ground held his bound hands behind his back. Onu-Vey opened his eyes and struggled to sit upright. He made it up halfway. Blood from the gash and sweat from his brow ran down into his eyes, stinging painfully. Through blurred vision, he saw that enemy warriors now occupied his beloved village.

Onu-Vey looked back over his shoulder. He blinked and focused on several bodies scattered between the huts and inside the animal corrals. Balba villagers and village warriors, people he had known for most of his life, had tried to defend the village when the enemy warriors came. They died as a result. Onu-Vey realized that his mother was right. He would lie among the dead if he had held on to his spear and belted knife.

Onu-Vey tried again to blink the blood and sweat from his eyes. With blurred vision, he looked to his right. He recognized his nearest neighbor, an old woodsman whose name was Moh-Maamuni. Moh-Maamuni stood comforting his mate, Moh-Amina. Onu-Vey had known the couple for as long as he could remember. Only nine harvests ago, Onu-Vey's mother had helped Moh-Amina give birth to the couple's young son, Moh-Saalim.

The little boy, Moh-Saalim, stood between his parents. He held the rope handle of a huge bucket of water at his feet. Onu-Vey assumed that Moh-Saalim had used buckets and buckets of water in a futile effort to extinguish a fire that had destroyed the family's hut. The hut now stood as a smoldering pile of rubble and ash behind Moh-Saalim and his parents.

Despite his bindings, Onu-Vey managed to sit upright. Several meters before him, he saw the last of the village warriors. Six of them, beaten and subdued, stood at the edge of the Jabali. Onu-Vey realized with horror that enemy warriors were forcing each of the village warriors, one by one, to jump from the Jabali, 75 meters to their deaths.

Onu-Vey looked away. Over his shoulder toward his right, a small gathering of villagers stood nearby. They stood in a tight group. Unfortunately, they could not turn away. Enemy warriors stood among them and forced them to watch the executions. Onu-Vey saw beneath the looks of hopelessness that each villager wanted to do something to stop the atrocity. But they were helpless. Enemy warriors, with knives and spears held ready, threatened them with death if they looked away.

Onu-Vey had seen enough. He needed to stop or at least disrupt the executions. He looked around anxiously. Three enemy warriors stood at his left. They laughed with amusement whenever an enemy warrior forced a village warrior to jump from the Jabali. Onu-Vey forced himself to sit more erectly. He looked up at the three warriors.

"Water," Onu-Vey's voice sounded weak and hoarse.

The warrior who stood in the middle was huge. His frame was a mass of intimidating muscles. He waved his powerful arms to coach or cheer on the executions. His laugh and voice were unforgettably heavy, dominating the halfhearted cheers of the other two enemy warriors standing on his side.

When the huge warrior heard Onu-Vey, he stopped laughing. He held up his hand. The simple gesture caught everyone's attention. It suspended the executions and spared the lives of the last two village warriors. The whole area fell silent as everything stopped.

The huge enemy warrior smiled wickedly at the two standing beside him. He walked toward Onu-Vey. A long, broad-blade knife in a scabbard hung at his side. He angled the blade back to kneel on one knee. The wicked smile on his face broadened as he leaned in close to Onu-Vey's face. "You want water? Then water you shall have." He looked around, looking for a way to fulfill Onu-Vey's plea.

With evil intent still in his eyes, the huge warrior spotted the little boy, Moh-Saalim. The boy stood half-hidden between his parents, a bucket of water conveniently at his feet. The warrior pointed at the bucket. "Bring that to me."

The boy's father, Moh-Maamuni, stood rigid, almost paralyzed by fear. Yet, he managed to reach out and embrace his mate and son. He averted his eyes from the enemy warrior, trying to pretend he did not hear the warrior's command. But fear forced him to sneak a peek at the enemy warrior. He realized he could not ignore the warrior's command. He tried to hide the fear and the resentment on his face. Moh-Maamuni stepped in front of his son and his mate and reached down to take the rope handle of the bucket.

"No!" The enemy warrior barked. "Not you. I want the boy to bring it."

Moh-Maamuni stood back. He looked down into his son's face. He could see that his son was too young to show strong resentment, but fear was visible. "It is alright, my son. Go ahead. Take him the water."

Moh-Saalim peeled away from his mother's embrace. He took the rope handle of the water bucket and strained to lift it from the ground. The bucket held nineteen liters of water, almost too heavy for the young boy to lift. Moh-Saalim found it more difficult to carry. Water splashed about in the bucket. Water flew out of the bucket as Moh-Saalim waddled toward the enemy warrior.

The enemy warrior found Moh-Saalim's struggle humorous. He could not help but laugh. "What is this? No great warrior shows such weakness. You do want to be a strong warrior. Do you not?"

Moh-Saalim did not answer the enemy warrior. He set the bucket of water down to catch his breath. Somehow, the buckets did not seem so heavy when he was helping his father battle the fire that burned their hut. He flexed his fingers and shook his tired and cramped hands. He strained to lift and carry the bucket again. Answering the enemy warrior, at the moment, was a low priority.

The enemy warrior stopped laughing. The expression on his face turned sour. "I asked you a question, boy. When I ask a question, I expect an answer. You want to be a strong warrior! Do you not? Like me?"

"No." Moh-Saalim finally managed to say. "Not a warrior. I am a woodsman, like my father."

"You are … a what?" The huge enemy warrior found Moh-Saalim's response amusing. The simple ambition to be a woodsman was ridiculous. He laughed loud and hard. He looked back at the two enemy warriors who had flanked him earlier as he pointed at Moh-Saalim.

When Moh-Saalim made it close enough to the enemy warrior to set the bucket of water down, his fingers had given out. He dropped the bucket. The bucket hit the ground with a thud. By chance, the bucket did not fall over, but a liter of water flew from the bucket and splashed onto the enemy warrior's foot.

The huge enemy warrior stopped laughing. He looked down at his wet foot. He raised his leg and shook his foot as if to throw off the excess water. When he put his foot down again, water between his foot and his sandal bubbled out repulsively. With disapproval, he raised his eyes to Moh-Saalim and pointed at his foot. He spoke with an angry sneer. "Look what you did! Clumsy little runt. You could never be a warrior, not in my service. No. You deserve to be a useless woodsman."

The enemy warrior stood up and looked at his wet foot again. Enraged, he struck Moh-Saalim's face with the back of his hand. He knocked the young boy to the ground.

The boy's father, Moh-Maamuni, took an impulsive step toward his son.

The enemy warrior pointed at him. "Stop! Take another step and you will be a dead woodsman."

Moh-Maamuni froze. With undiminished concern for his son, he stepped back. He realized he could do nothing for his son. Instead, he turned to give a comforting embrace to his mate, Moh-Amina. The tears streaming down her face told him she needed his support just as strongly.

The enemy warrior's explosive anger stunned all the villagers. No one dared move. Even Moh-Saalim, out of sheer fear, continued to lie on the ground where he had fallen. The stillness and dead silence that followed confirmed the enemy warrior's ultimate power.

The huge enemy warrior studied all the pathetic faces around him. He turned in a slow circle. He savored every moment of his abusive power. When his angry scrutiny reached the two warriors who had stood at his side, it had transformed into a wicked smile again. The huge enemy warrior enjoyed himself.

"Water," Onu-Vey repeated, breaking the silence and spoiling the enemy warrior's moment of joy.

The enemy warrior looked at Onu-Vey as if the plea for water intruded on his control. He angled his knife again and kneeled. With his hands cupped together, he reached into the bucket of water at his feet. He flung water into Onu-Vey's face.

The sudden splash wasn't what Onu-Vey wanted or expected, but it did serve a purpose. The water washed the blood and sweat from his eyes. He blinked several times. When his vision cleared, he recognized the enemy warrior kneeling before him. "Kold-Johan."

"You do not refer to me as just Kold-Johan," the enemy warrior said. "I am Mfalme Kold-Johan, of the Mangoni. Your clan leader, that pathetic Pal-Fomi, another useless woodsman, is dead. Do you know what that means? It means I am Mfalme of all the clans – all of them. It means I am your Mfalme."

Onu-Vey showed no visible response to Kold-Johan's declaration. As he stared back into Kold-Johan's eyes, he realized that his lower lip was still bleeding. He chose that moment to lean over and spit blood from his mouth. The spittle of blood landed on the ground just centimeters from Kold-Johan's wet foot.

Kold-Johan took the natural act as a deliberate affront. He didn't like it. He struck Onu-Vey hard across the face, just as he had done to Moh-Saalim. The assault drew more blood and knocked Onu-Vey over to the ground.

Kold-Johan stood up and stepped back. He made a quick and angry gesture to the two enemy warriors who had stood at his side earlier. "Sit him upright!"

Abul-Gwan, one of the enemy warriors, started to do as Kold-Johan had ordered. He stopped and moved closer to Kold-Johan instead. He leaned close to Kold-Johan's ear to speak to him confidently. "Mfalme, do you want to do this?"

"You have something to say, Abul-Gwan?"

"Mfalme, you finally have the leadership you have been looking for. Be satisfied with that. Do you not know who this person is? This is the son of Onu-Kinsi – Mama Kinsi. You do not need Mama Kinsi or her son working against you."

"No, I do not. That is why I intend to fix all of that, Abul-Gwan." Kold-Johan pushed Abul-Gwan aside and pointed at Onu-Vey. "Now, sit him upright! I must find out where that wrinkled, old crone is hiding."

A mild reluctance made the enemy warrior Abul-Gwan hesitate again before responding. He tossed his spear and shield to the ground. He kneeled next to Onu-Vey. Abul-Gwan was also a boy with fast-approaching maturity. He did not appear to be much older than Onu-Vey. But unlike Onu-Vey, the young enemy warrior was much heavier and had well-developed muscles. He took Onu-Vey with both hands and yanked him upright.

Kold-Johan watched as Abul-Gwan braced Onu-Vey so he would not fall over again. He waited until the other enemy warrior, Kosi-Jawma, rushed over and pulled Onu-Vey's head back to appear to be giving Kold-Johan due respect.

Kold-Johan extracted his long, broad-blade knife from its scabbard. He held the knife with the clear intent to use it. He moved closer to Onu-Vey and kneeled. "I am your Mfalme. I am entitled to more respect. Disrespect me like that again … and I will kill you. Do you understand me?"

Onu-Vey said nothing. He only looked into Kold-Johan's eyes.

"I said … do you understand me?"

Onu-Vey suppressed his anger and resentment. "What I understand, Kold-Johan, will amaze you."

"Good. Now, tell me. Where is the High Priestess, Mama Kinsi?"

The answer to Kold-Johan's question was too painful to put into words. Onu-Vey had seen countless smiles on his mother's face. The last vivid memory of his mother was the smile she gave him just before she turned to a pillar of stone. He would never see her smile again. Onu-Vey closed his eyes as if to block the pain of loss and savor the now precious memory of his mother.

When Onu-Vey closed his eyes, Kold-Johan took the act as another affront. He saw it as another sign of blatant disrespect. The ill-tempered Mfalme held his broad-blade high, ready to strike. "When I ask a question, I expect an answer."

Onu-Vey opened his eyes. He saw the knife. Still, he said nothing.

The silence touched a nerve. Kold-Johan angrily hacked the blade of the knife across Onu-Vey's bare chest. He intended to cause enough physical damage to make Onu-Vey answer him. But the crystal hanging over Onu-Vey's chest blocked the blade's sharp edge.

Sparks flew in all directions. The blade's powerful impact on the crystal caused it to chime loudly. The unexpected event made the two enemy warriors, Abul-Gwan and Kosi-Jawma, flinch, release Onu-Vey, and move back.

Onu-Vey's crystal shattered into two. The dark half continued to dangle on the cord. The clear half flew to the ground. It landed in the dirt next to where Moh-Saalim continued to lie.

The sparks that flew from Kold-Johan's knife and the unusual chime of the blade astonished everyone. No one, except Moh-Saalim, saw where the clear half of the crystal fell. Moh-Saalim experienced astonishment too, but only briefly. As he lay there, with the crystal just centimeters from his fingers, the crystal overshadowed all he felt. He did not know the crystal's true significance. He only knew that it belonged to the son of Mama Kinsi. That alone made it special.

Moh-Saalim looked at the people around him. He had to see if anyone else had seen where the crystal had fallen. No one did. Moh-Saalim took advantage of the moment. He reached out and closed his fingers around the crystal. He drew the crystal toward him and hid it beneath his clothing.

Kold-Johan had not yet recovered from the strange way his knife blade had chimed. He had made the knife many harvests ago, when he was a young warrior. Until this day, the knife blade has never made such an unnatural sound. Kold-Johan stared at the blade. He flipped it repeatedly, from one side to the other. Seeing no damage done to the blade, Kold-Johan shrugged. He dismissed the strange occurrence. The oddity subsided as his anger at Onu-Vey repossessed him. "I asked you. Where is the High Priestess, Mama Kinsi?"

Onu-Vey looked into Kold-Johan's eyes. He forced the answer out through clenched teeth. "Mama Kinsi … is dead."

Kold-Johan experienced mild surprise and sat back with disbelief. He focused on Onu-Vey's face, trying to read his expression. He turned to Abul-Gwan. "Can this be true? Is he lying to me?"

Of all the Mangoni warriors, Abul-Gwan and Kosi-Jawma were the warriors closest to Kold-Johan. They knew his strengths, his weaknesses, and all that he was capable of doing. They knew, if Kold-Johan ever got close to Mama Kinsi, one way or another, it would be a very dark day for all the tribal clans.

Until this day, neither Abul-Gwan nor Kosi-Jawma expected Kold-Johan to get this close to Mama Kinsi. In their opinion, Mama

Kinsi was much too crafty, powerful, and elusive. Abul-Gwan and Kosi-Jawma were wise enough to keep that offensive opinion to themselves. But if it was true that Mama Kinsi was dead, then they didn't have to worry about offending Kold-Johan with the futility of his efforts to find her.

When Abul-Gwan answered Kold-Johan, his answer came more so from wishful thinking. "It is no lie, Mfalme. If she were here, we would have found her already. Besides," Abul-Gwan looked at Onu-Vey, "I can see it in his eyes. Mama Kinsi is dead."

"I agree, Mfalme," Kosi-Jawma added. "Never again must we waste more of your precious time searching for her."

Kold-Johan accepted the opinions of his warriors with reservations. He put the tip of his knife to Onu-Vey's chin. He used the knife to turn Onu-Vey's head toward him, to look him in the eyes and judge for himself. It took a moment, but Kold-Johan saw it too. Mama Kinsi was dead. Kold-Johan's own opinion seemed more convincing. He knew Mama Kinsi always behaved much too arrogantly. She seemed so confident of her powers. To hide from anyone was not in her nature.

"Well good riddance." Kold-Johan chuckled. He reinserted his knife into its scabbard. "It is no great loss. I never liked that old woman anyway. The funny thing is… I might have spared her life."

This statement made Abul-Gwan and Kosi-Jawma glance at each other. It came as a revelation to them. Both of them felt that Mama Kinsi would never be caught. If caught, they knew that Kold-Johan would kill her, unleashing the darkest days for all the tribal clans. It never occurred to either of them that, if Kold-Johan caught Mama Kinsi, he would spare her life.

Kold-Johan saw Abul-Gwan and Kosi-Jawma looking at each other. "What is wrong with you two? You look surprised. The two of you act as though I am incapable of mercy?"

"You are a huge man, Mfalme," Abul-Gwan said, "but in all honesty, a merciful bone exists nowhere in your whole body."

Kold-Johan laughed. "One of these days, Abul-Gwan, I will prove you wrong." Abul-Gwan and Kosi-Jawma laughed too, but with less conviction.

Moh-Saalim chose this moment to get up from where he had fallen. The laughter of the enemy warriors suggested that this was a safe moment. He got to his feet and began to walk toward where his parents stood.

"Where are you going, little woodsman?" Kold-Johan snapped.

Moh-Saalim turned to face Kold-Johan. He did not speak. He pointed toward his father and mother.

"Speak! When I ask you a question, I expect an answer. Where are you going?"

Moh-Saalim still did not speak. At that instant, the resentment that he was too young to show matured. He leaned over and spat on the ground like Onu-Vey had done.

Kold-Johan reacted with sudden anger. His eyes bulged. His nose flared. He stood up and stormed toward Moh-Saalim. Abul-Gwan knew what was about to happen and tried to grab Kold-Johan's arm. Kold-Johan flung him away.

After two thunderous steps, Kold-Johan caught a handful of Moh-Saalim's clothing. With one powerful hand, he lifted Moh-Saalim off the ground. Moh-Saalim kicked and screamed. He pulled and pried at Kold-Johan's hands. His efforts were no match for the huge warrior's powerful grip.

"You useless little wood-rat! I am your Mfalme. Shall I show you what happens when you disrespect me?" Unaffected by the young boy's kicks and squirms, Kold-Johan carried Moh-Saalim toward the Jabali. Everyone knew what was about to happen.

Moh-Saalim's mother, Moh-Amina, was the first to scream. It was an agonizing scream and plea to spare her son. She cried too hysterically to talk with any understanding. Moh-Saalim's father, Moh-Maamuni, dared to step forward despite the earlier warning.

"Kold-Johan … Mfalme," Moh-Maamuni said. He used the term 'Mfalme' in hopes that it would show the highest respect. "Please, Mfalme! Have mercy!"

Kold-Johan walked to the edge of the Jabali. He dangled the wiggling Moh-Saalim over the cliff as he looked back at the distraught couple. "Mercy?" He looked toward Abul-Gwan and Kosi-Jawma as he recalled his promise. He looked into Moh-Saalim's face. And then he smiled. "Yes. Yes… I will show mercy… I will show mercy. But not today."

Kold-Johan flung Moh-Saalim over the Jabali. The little boy's scream faded to silence as he fell 75 meters toward the rocks and the tributary. Kold-Johan edged forward. He looked over the Jabali as if to make sure of the Moh-Saalim's death. He wiped his hands together, as if to clean them.

Kold-Johan did not care about what he had just done. He turned and pointed to Moh-Amina, who had fallen to her knees, screaming and crying hysterically. "Shut that woman up before I cut out her tongue."

Moh-Maamuni cried too, but in silence. Tears streamed down his face. He stopped crying when he saw Kold-Johan reaching for his knife and began walking toward his mate as if to follow through with his threat. Moh-Maamuni had just lost his son. He would lose his mate too if he did not intervene. Moh-Maamuni rushed over to embrace and protect his mate. He managed to save her life by burying her face against his chest and muffling her sobs. He endured the pain of her fingers that clawed into his arms.

"That is better." Kold-Johan walked back from the Jabali, hearing only the stifled cries from Moh-Amina and other stunned villagers. The enemy warriors, Abul-Gwan and Kosi-Jawma, looked at each other as Kold-Johan kneeled again at Onu-Vey's side.

"Now, what were we talking about earlier? Oh yes, Mama Kinsi. So, tell me, how did she die?"

After witnessing Moh-Saalim's execution, anger and grief enveloped Onu-Vey like a dark cloud. He did not hear what Kold-

Johan was saying. His eyes had also welled up with tears. His vision blurred. And he was holding his breath.

Kold-Johan took Onu-Vey by the chin and yanked it, demanding Onu-Vey's full attention. "What is wrong with you people? Are all the Balba people like this? How many times must I tell you? When I ask a question, I expect an answer. How did Mama Kinsi die?"

"What do you care how she died?" Onu-Vey snapped.

"I do not care. I am only curious. Up there in the mountains, where we found you, we saw the aftereffects of a big fire. The whole area looked like it had been burning for days. Did Mama Kinsi die in that fire?"

Onu-Vey looked up at Kold-Johan's eyes, and like his mother had told him, he remembered to breathe. "No. She did not die in that fire. Mama Kinsi… *was* that fire?"

A flare of restless voices created a disturbance when everyone heard Onu-Vey's response. The village people knew the response was no play on words. Kold-Johan seemed unimpressed. Instead, he showed annoyance at the mumbling voices around him. With a warning stare, he waited for the mumbling to subside. He continued to kneel but shifted his weight from one leg to the other. He settled into a comfortable position and redirected his attention to Onu-Vey.

"Well, that fire has burned itself out. All that remains is charred timber and ashes, blown all over the area. Anyway, you look at it, and I guess Kosi-Jawma is right. I need not waste any more time looking for Mama Kinsi."

The enemy warrior Abul-Gwan knelt on the other side of Onu-Vey. Although Mama Kinsi was dead, a new concern just occurred to him. He got Kold-Johan's permission to speak. "Mfalme, may I?"

Kold-Johan made a quick, permissive gesture and sat back.

Kosi-Jawma forced Onu-Vey to sit upright as Abul-Gwan turned Onu-Vey's head to look at him, face to face. "Tell me," Abul-Gwan began. "Did Mama Kinsi happen to ordain anyone to take her place before she… before she burned away?"

Onu-Vey stared back into Abul-Gwan's eyes. As he did, he remembered the last thing Mama Kinsi did was open his eyes to his gift. Through tribal protocol, he was now the legitimate heir to Mama Kinsi's authority and powers. He was the Tribal Houngan. He looked down at the crystal hanging around his neck. He experienced a moment of panic when he discovered the crystal broken beyond repair. Only the dark half of the crystal remained.

To add to the shocking disturbance, blood from the gash on his face had run down his neck and chest and onto the crystal. The dark half of the crystal now dripped with his blood. Onu-Vey felt it was an ominous sign, but he wasn't sure what to make of it.

"What is that?" Kold-Johan saw Onu-Vey looking at the crystal.

"It is … it was my *azima*."

"Your *azima*? Does it mean that Mama Kinsi ordained you to be her replacement? Are you supposed to be the Tribal Houngan now?"

Onu-Vey said nothing.

Kold-Johan would have taken the unanswered question as another offensive sign of disrespect. But the crystal distracted him. Curiosity pulled him closer. He took the blood-covered crystal into his fingers to examine it. His fascination subsided when he saw the ugly, black crystal, which looked broken and incomplete. The broken and jagged end suggested it was only half what it should have been.

Kold-Johan dismissed the jagged end and the incomplete look as artistic design and foolish nonsense. He dropped the crystal back against Onu-Vey's chest. "Is that how it should look? It looks to me like your little *juju charm* is broken."

"Broken or not," Onu-Vey accepted the charm as it was, "the charm is still… my *azima*."

"If you say so." Kold-Johan chuckled at Onu-Vey's persistence. "Do you think that a toy like that is what makes you a Vodun houngan?"

Kold-Johan waited for Onu-Vey to answer. All the villagers who stood around huddled closer to hear Onu-Vey's answer. The answer could make a profound difference. Even the two enemy warriors who held Onu-Vey upright waited to hear what Onu-Vey had to say.

Onu-Vey remembered to breathe. Despite circumstances, he relaxed, allowing his physical pains to ebb away. He raised his head and looked around at all the Balba villagers. He looked to his right and left at the enemy warriors, Abul-Gwan and Kosi-Jawma. Onu-Vey finally looked into Kold-Johan's eyes. "No. The '*toy*' does not make me a Vodun houngan. I am… a Vodun houngan."

When everyone heard Onu-Vey's response, a rumbling commotion of restless voices erupted again. Despite their oppression by enemy warriors, the excited villagers spoke among themselves for the first time since the warriors invaded their village. The two enemy warriors who held Onu-Vey upright let him go. Each of them moved back out of fear, respect, or caution.

"A houngan with a broken *azima*," Kold-Johan laughed. It was a hardy, belly laugh. He laughed until he was almost breathless. He drew everyone's attention again when he extracted his long, broad-blade knife. His laughter died away when he turned to Onu-Vey and put the sharp edge of the blade against Onu-Vey's throat.

"Alright, houngan, let us see how powerful you are. I am your Mfalme. Your life is in my hands. I want to show Abul-Gwan and Kosi-Jawma that I can be merciful. I am going to ask you a question – a question that I might have asked your mother."

"Ask your question," Onu-Vey said. "I will answer your question. And when I do, you will not doubt that I am a Vodun houngan."

"Alright, houngan." Kold-Johan leaned in closer to Onu-Vey. "My question is this. If I let you live… can you be the Tribal Houngan? Can I expect loyal service from you?"

Onu-Vey looked into Kold-Johan's eyes again. He glanced over at Abul-Gwan. After another long moment, a revelation became clear to him. A twinkle of a smile almost cracked Onu-Vey's face. He turned back to Kold-Johan. "Listen to me, Kold-Johan. You must listen to me closely, for… I can tell you this only once."

"I am listening."

"I will serve you, Kold-Johan… until the day you die."

With this, the two enemy warriors, Abul-Gwan and Kosi-Jawma, looked at each other again. Their thoughts were similar. They felt that Kold-Johan would never catch Mama Kinsi, and a moment like this would never happen. The powerful and evil alliance that they feared came to life anyway. If Kold-Johan got complete control of a houngan's powers, there would be no end to his ruthless behavior and darker days for all the tribal clans. Abul-Gwan and Kosi-Jawma wanted no part of such an alliance.

Another weighted glance between two warriors acknowledged their thoughts. Without a word, Kosi-Jawma took another discreet step back. He knew what was about to happen. Abul-Gwan casually picked up his spear from the ground. Unexpected by everyone except Kosi-Jawma and Onu-Vey, Abul-Gwan drove his spear deep into Kold-Johan's stomach.

— **2** —

WE SHOULD HEAR THE TALKING DRUMS

orty harvests later…

The Aukmondi people look forward to a special event called 'The Daily Celebration of Life' every day. Every day, families, friends and loved ones come together. After completing the chores and tribal work, and just before sunset, almost everyone works his or her way down the north and south slopes. They find their way into the Royal Kraal; into the huge celebration area, out in front of the four huts of the Ncobbas and the royal dais. The people gather to bring a natural and fitting end to the passing day.

With the preparations for this evening's celebration underway, Ramuza exited his hut and stood for a moment. The tropical breeze had cooled the air down to a comfortable, pleasant temperature. Ramuza took a deep breath. It felt good. Magical energy hung in the air. He could tell the coming evening would be a special one.

Ramuza noted the long shadows that stretched across the ground. The sun would set in an hour, signaling when he would keep a longstanding tradition. He would take his position on the royal dais and announce the official start of today's celebration. For now, Ramuza enjoyed a few extra moments of time. He looked forward to spending that time as he always did. He walked out into the celebration area to mingle with his beloved people.

All evening long, most adults engaged in lengthy conversations and storytelling, which were the most common social events of the evening. One moment, the topics of conversation and stories were humorous. Each evening, Ramuza could look forward to outbursts of laughter here and there. The next moment, the topics may be serious, passionate, and sometimes controversial. Ramuza could also expect an argument or two to occur.

Ramuza had to bring his casual stroll to a sudden standstill when a Young Creation almost ran into him. The little boy stopped before a collision occurred. He was thoughtful enough to apologize to the Mfalme. Ramuza accepted the apology with a smile and watched the Young Creation run off to join his playmates.

If not captivated by the exchanges among their seniors, young children scatter to play their games. They frolic about the area like a litter of kittens or a herd of young gazelles. They play simple, carefree games of chase, tag, hopscotch, or marbles made with hardened clay. Throughout the area, they ran through dust clouds kicked up by their feet as they played more traditional games of *mamba* or *kululu*. Older children, with more competitive spirits, took their sporting games of hoops or kickball to serious victories, prompting fan cheers or jeers from opposing sides.

The smell of baked bread breezed past Ramuza. The inviting aroma almost brought Ramuza's casual stroll to another standstill. He took another deep breath. The delicious smell of fresh bread forced another smile to his face.

Families, friends, and loved ones spend most of their time preparing food in this free-spirited atmosphere. Food preparation is the second most common social event of the evening. It results in the biggest and most pleasurable meal of the day. Almost everyone takes part, from the oldest family patriarch or matriarch to the youngest able-bodied toddler.

They cleaned and cut fresh vegetables and fruits amid the conversations, stories, and games. Ramuza saw people setting up various-sized campfires all over the area, depending on what they were cooking. He saw others setting up kettles of water to prepare rice, soups, and stews. Some heated small kilns and hot plates for bread and vegetables. As the evening progressed, people would produce other inviting smells of foods, sending them swirling into the air and reaching out beyond the boundaries of the Royal Kraal.

As Ramuza continued his stroll, he realized that, of all the events during the daily celebrations, the most fun comes from the third most common event: the singing and dancing. Pockets of vocal and instrumental music sprang up all across the celebration area. People often respond to music by singing and dancing. Sometimes they responded in cascading waves of entertainment, one behind the other. Sometimes they responded in simultaneous or heated volleys of competition, all for the sake of fun. Each music, singing, and dancing period led to more laughter, conversations, and increased appetites.

Ramuza considered the Daily Celebration of Life his favorite time. Without a doubt, all the Aukmondi people felt the same. There is no greater pleasure than talking, sharing a meal, playing, singing, dancing, and just passing time with grandparents, fathers, mothers, sisters, brothers, aunts, uncles, cousins, mates, friends, and all other acquaintances. The Daily Celebration of Life is one of the Supreme Spirit's most precious gifts. During good times, the Daily Celebration of Life reminds people why life is worth living. When times are bad, it has the divine power to hold everything together.

Ramuza stopped one more time to study the people and their activities. He expected several gatherings during this time of day. But he noticed most of the people today were from the Motobo kraal. The Motobo kraal, on the opposite side of the valley, high on the south slope, is one of the valley's warrior kraals. Many warriors and their families lived there, including the Royal Warrior Nionu and his army. People from the Motobo kraal came to the Royal Kraal this evening for a special reason.

Most common events during the daily celebrations need no forethought. Conversations, storytelling, music, singing, dancing, and playfulness are spontaneous. But a few major events require extensive preparations. These include bulk food preparations, large musical performances, and choreographed dances. Each day, the responsibility for many major preparations rotated from one kraal community to the next. Ramuza realized that today's responsibility belonged to the people of the Motobo kraal.

Ramuza enjoyed the simple pleasure of watching these beautiful people and the efficient way they worked together. As warriors and their mates, efficiency was part of their nature. Groups brought huge baskets of food and set them up in various places. Other groups create scattered piles of dry timber, brushwood, and other kindling to support cooking fires and bonfires. Ramuza looked to his right, in front of the hut that belonged to his third mate, the Sacred Woman Kharaambi Nyoka. Ramuza saw more Motobo people setting up wooden marimbas, bow harps, *Kayamba* rattles, and *Ngoma* drums of various sizes.

An infectious community spirit washed over Ramuza. He walked farther out toward the center of the celebration area. The medley of voices and laughter about him put him in a good mood. The smoky smell of precooked foods continued to fill the air and added to Ramuza's euphoria.

During Ramuza's stroll, he saw the Sacred Woman Rwuva Azinti, the first of his three mates. As the mother of Ramuza's only son, Rwuva held the regal honor of being his Principal Mate. By default, she was also a tribal elder and the tribe's Official Hostess. She oversaw most public events in the valley, especially those within the Royal Kraal.

Ramuza stood for another moment, enjoying Rwuva's elegance as she talked with two of his twin daughters, Akwate and Akuako. Akwate and Akuako Sheetswa, his fifth and sixth daughters, born of his second mate, the Sacred Woman Olabisi Sheetswa, were sociable girls. Although they were just past their thirteenth harvest, the little girls were often Rwuva's closest aides in coordinating public events. To see the three of them working together was a common sight. As Ramuza watched, he knew the three were discussing the events scheduled to occur this evening. A mild curiosity forced him to walk in their direction.

When Akwate and Akuako noticed the Mfalme approaching, they rushed toward him.

"Great Creation," the energetic Akuako spoke first. She took her father's hand and led him to where Rwuva stood. "We need your permission."

"You do? For what?"

"People from the Motobo kraal want to dance this evening," Akuako began, "but the Sacred Woman Rwuva said they could not do it."

"The Sacred Woman said the dance is forbidden," Akwate added to her sister's answer as if to clarify it.

Ramuza looked at Rwuva, who stood with her arms folded. Her expression suggested that her mind was not about to change. Ramuza looked down at his daughters again. "If the Sacred Woman says the dance is not allowed, my permission will only complicate matters."

"But Great Creation, we already told the dancers it was alright. It was before we talked with the Sacred Woman Rwuva." Akuako explained.

"And these dancers have been practicing for days now," Akwate added. "They will be so heartbroken if they cannot perform."

"So, tell me, why are they not allowed to perform?"

Rwuva unfolded her arms and stepped closer. "As Akwate said, the dancers have been practicing for days. They have been secretly practicing up there in the Motobo kraal. There is a reason. I went up to the Motobo kraal this morning. I saw their performance. Great Creation, we are not ready for this dance. It will not take place in the Royal Kraal this evening."

Ramuza imagined the unseen dancers. He looked at his mate and made an easy assumption about the dancers. He looked down at his daughters again. They were children. Yet they promoted a performance that Rwuva had declared forbidden. How was this possible?

"You have seen these dancers perform?" Ramuza had to ask his daughters.

"Yes, Great Creation."

"And you thought they were worth seeing?"

"Yes. We thought they were wonderful. We think everyone should see them."

Ramuza looked at Rwuva again. He wondered how these strong differences of opinion developed. Is a compromise possible? He looked down into the innocent faces of his daughters. He had no good answer for them. "Rwuva is the Official Hostess here. I am afraid it is her decision."

"But what should we tell the dancers?" Akuako asked. "They will be so disappointed."

"Tell them, they can perform their dance at another time." It was the best answer Ramuza could give. He added a temporary solution. "Tell them that such a dance deserves a special occasion. But not at this evening's celebration."

Akwate sighed. "So be it, Mfalme." Her shoulders slumped. She took her twin sister by the arm and led her away.

"Thank you, Great Creation." Rwuva watched the girls walk away. "They grow up so fast."

"Yes, they do." Ramuza turned to his mate. "So, tell me about this dance performance. It must be something special."

"Oh yes, it is. You should see it." Rwuva smiled. "No, seriously. You must see it. As an entertaining performance, it is wonderful. But it is different. Maybe, a little too different."

"Different enough to be forbidden?"

"I have seen nothing like it." Rwuva took a sweeping look at all the surrounding people. "It is a change that, I feel, is too sudden. All of us may not be ready for it. We dare not force such a dance on them."

Ramuza had told his daughters the dancers could dance at another time, for a special occasion, to appease them. But hearing Rwuva's comments, he tried to think of a special occasion.

Ramuza set aside his thoughts when he noticed the Brown Warrior Quazzi and two subordinate warriors nearby. The three struggled to carry a large *Ngoma* drum. The drum, made from a hollow log, stretched almost 125 and 90 centimeters in diameter. Its size and shape made it awkward to carry. Ramuza excused himself and rushed over to help them.

Ramuza made himself useful by getting a firm grip on one end of the drum. With his added strength, the four carried the drum over to complement another *Ngoma* drum already set in place. The two drums made a set much larger than usual.

"Why such large *Ngoma* drums this time?" Ramuza asked as he dusted off his hands.

The Orange Warrior Lujaami, one of the subordinate warriors, extracted a baton from the side of one drum. He struck the drum's center with one hard stroke to test it. The resonant sound, like thunder, rumbled throughout the Royal Kraal. "These are not just *Ngoma* drums, Mfalme. These are Bendabe *Ngoma* drums."

"Bendabe? Like the Blue Warrior Obe Bendabe?"

"Yes, Mfalme. He created these things. We will make enough music, loud enough for the people of the Kiwane Village to hear it."

"Oh?"

"Do you not know?" Quazzi asked.

"Know what?"

"The news is everywhere, Mfalme. Everyone is talking about it. These drums will support a special dance performance this evening. Rumor has it that people from the Motobo kraal will dance in a performance you will not soon forget."

"Rumor?" The Brown Warriors' use of the term surprised Ramuza. "Quazzi, Great Creation, you are the warriors' Foremost Lieutenant. Have you not seen the dancers perform?"

"No, Mfalme, I have not. My brown cloak provides me with many privileges. Yet the Motobo dancers have kept their performance a guarded secret, even from me."

Ramuza could only stare at Quazzi and the two subordinate warriors. They seemed so excited. Ramuza hated telling them that such a performance would not occur this evening. He was about to tell them to set aside their expectations when Quazzi tapped him on the shoulder and pointed toward the center of the celebration area.

Ramuza turned to see his daughters, Akwate and Akuako, standing among several dancers. The dancers, about ten or twelve young warriors, were impressive-looking. They wore free and revealing garments. Their sleek, firm, warrior bodies now stood out as the bodies of born dancers, ready to dance. But the expressions on their faces told a different story. Akwate and Akuako had just told them the sad news.

"That does not look good," Quazzi commented.

"It is not good, Great Creation. There will be no special dance performance this evening."

"There will not? Why? How do you know this?"

Ramuza did not have time to answer. At that moment, the distinctive sound of a sentry drum high on the north rim filtered down into the valley. The sound echoed throughout the valley and demanded everyone's attention. A sudden quiet fell over the celebration area as everyone stopped whatever they were doing and listened. All eyes in the area turned toward the highest authorities now in the Royal Kraal – Ramuza and Quazzi.

"Now there is a timely interruption." Ramuza looked at Quazzi. "What could it be this time?"

"We should hear the talking drums in a moment, Mfalme," Quazzi answered.

Sure enough, the sentry drum stopped. A series of hollow and irregular knocks replaced the sound of the sentry drum. Both Ramuza and Quazzi translated the knocks. According to the signal, an urgent situation had developed on the valley's north rim. The situation demanded that someone above the rank and cloak of a Royal Warrior respond. Four people in the whole Aukmondi Valley fit that description: Ramuza, Kharaambi, Mfalme Ameh Jobabwe of the Chinchigwe clan, and Quazzi.

"I will go up to the rim, Mfalme," Quazzi began. "Mfalme Jobabwe is in the valley depths, talking with the historian, the Great Creation Bakha. The Sacred Woman Kharaambi is still up in the Motobo kraal. I will go up to the rim."

"I have nothing else to do. We will both go up to the rim." Ramuza started across the celebration area toward the exit of the Royal Kraal.

Before Quazzi started, he turned to the Orange Warrior Lujaami. "Find a talking drum set, Great Creation. Respond to the message from the valley rim. And make sure the response is loud enough to reach the Sacred Woman Kharaambi and Mfalme Jobabwe."

The Orange Warrior glanced at the huge Bendabe *Ngoma* drums they had just set into place. "Has anyone ever made *Ngoma* drums talk?"

When Quazzi heard the question, he had to look at the Orange Warrior. "Do not be ridiculous." He sounded annoyed. "But since we will not use them as intended, you are welcome to try."

3

JUST SHORT OF SUPERNATURAL

Mfalme Ncobba and the Brown Warrior Quazzi climbed the Pahoma pathway on the north slope up toward the valley's north rim. They continued to enjoy the spirit of the evening even though they walked beyond the boundary of the Royal Kraal and the festive atmosphere there. Who or what they might find on the valley rim did not concern them.

Ramuza had assumed, but dismissed, his original idea that an armed traveler wanted to cross the valley. Ramuza, himself, had decreed the normal procedure in such a circumstance. The Royal or Blue Warriors on the valley rim would confiscate all the travelers' weapons. The warrior would have the traveler escorted across the valley and then return the traveler's weapons on the other side. Rarely did this procedure need the approval from someone above the rank of Blue Warrior.

Although the call to the north rim was unusual, Ramuza and Quazzi expected nothing important. As they climbed the last few meters of the slope, they focused their attention elsewhere – the forbidden dance. Quazzi had just learned about Rwuva's decree.

"You mean, the Sacred Woman Rwuva completely banned it? After all the rumors I have heard, I was looking forward to seeing those dancers, Mfalme."

"Curiosity got the best of me, too."

"Tell me. Was the Sacred Woman Rwuva firm? Do you think she might change her mind?

"No, I think not. In her own words, Rwuva said that a change is taking place. It is too sudden. She suggests that we are not ready for what we might see."

"Was that her only reason? Do you think the Sacred Woman is considering the children?"

"It is possible. Until I learn more, it is the only other reason I can think of. But you know what confuses me – my daughters, Akwate and Akuako. They have already seen the dancers perform. They are but children themselves. How did that happen?"

"Those two daughters of yours, Mfalme, as young as they are, are remarkably sociable. They have friends and acquaintances that may rival your own. It may not be what we think if they have seen the dancers and are willing to promote their performance."

"Maybe. I have to accept Rwuva's judgment."

Quazzi thought for a moment. "The Friendship Feast is coming up soon. The Friendship Feast is a special occasion. Perhaps the dancers could perform then."

"Children will attend the Friendship Feast, Quazzi. The Sacred Woman Rwuva will probably continue her ban."

Quazzi thought for a moment more. He considered the anniversary of his birth. "I have a Personal Day of Creation coming up soon. It is my day. I can celebrate as I please. I will hold a special celebration. No children allowed."

"You would do that?"

"To see these dancers, I might."

Ramuza smiled at his friend's determination. "To see those dancers may demand such a conviction, Quazzi. If we do not find another occasion before then, I may champion your Day of Creation myself."

As Ramuza and Quazzi approached the crest of the valley rim, they could see through the trees a small cluster of people up ahead. Most of them were Aukmondi Green Warriors; Sentinels who had come out of concealment and converged in the clearing just beyond the sentry line. They detained a small caravan of travelers.

From a distance, Ramuza's tactical mind had already counted ten people in the caravan. Also, among the people, he estimated about twenty to twenty-five pack animals, including oxen, donkeys, goats, sheep, and a beautiful, pale gray Arabian stallion. The horse, oxen, and donkeys each carried a load of baskets and gourds on their backs. The people and animals have completed several kilometers of travel recently.

Ramuza found himself revising his original assumption. Maybe these travelers did wish to cross the valley but needed a night's rest. Royal and Blue Warriors on the rim could also grant such an appeal. Yet something had prevented them. The call to the north rim became a deeper mystery.

When the Royal Warrior Npatuzi Dawa, the ranking warrior on the sentinel line, saw Ramuza and Quazzi coming, he rushed up to meet them. He greeted them and told them that he had decided to send for a higher authority than himself.

"We have some unusual visitors, Mfalme."

Ramuza and Quazzi studied the travelers from where they stood. Nothing about the travelers seemed unusual.

"Show us what you have, Great Creation," said Quazzi.

Npatuzi walked out beyond the sentry line. He waded through knee-deep grass and led Ramuza and Quazzi toward the caravan. He took them to a Hefty Creation who stood in the forefront of the caravan.

"Greetings." The Hefty Creation said. "With whom do I have the pleasure of speaking?"

"I am Ramuza Ncobba, Mfalme of the Aukmondi. Who are you and your people?"

The Hefty Creation displayed self-confidence. His manner was informal but polite. He smiled when he learned Ramuza's name. "So, you are the reputable Mfalme Ncobba. I have heard much about you and have longed to meet you." He bowed. "I am Abul-Gwan, Mfalme of the Mangoni."

Ramuza studied the face of the Creation and then also bowed. He had heard of Abul-Gwan. Each Mfalme knew the other by name and history, but neither had met the other until now.

Ramuza knew Abul-Gwan as more than the Mfalme of the Mangoni. This Successful Creation led a huge and wealthy empire that had grown steadily over the past forty harvests. Many business transactions up and down the whole East Coast of Africa are related to the name 'Abul-Gwan' in some way.

"Your fame precedes you, Mfalme Abul-Gwan," Ramuza said. "To meet you is a historic occasion. Welcome to the Aukmondi Valley."

"Thank you." Abul-Gwan turned to introduce a woman standing behind him. He smiled proudly. He forced her to the forefront with noticeable pride. She was a tall woman with an elegant and regal manner about her. "This beautiful woman is my mate, Abul-Tess."

Abul-Tess and Ramuza exchanged greetings. Ramuza and Quazzi bowed to her in unison, impressing her respectfully. Abul-Tess reacted with a broad smile.

Abul-Gwan did not introduce the other members of his group, as if it were not necessary. Ramuza took the liberty of walking past Abul-Gwan and Abul-Tess. He began to inspect the other members, which was his right. Three things struck him significantly as he moved down the line of people.

The first was the Tall Creation, who had stood behind Abul-Tess. This Creation was also impressive looking. He wore the clothing and adornments, which Ramuza recognized as that of a Vodun houngan – a Voodoo Priest.

With a dark complexion and gangly stature, the houngan stood a few centimeters taller than Ramuza. His clothing and adornments were comparable to Abul-Gwan's—two average-sized pouches made of animal skin and fur hung by straps across his shoulders. A third pouch hung on a rope around his waist. A huge black crystal hung prominently on a leather string around his neck like an amulet or charm. On his head, he wore a cap made of animal skin. Two horns protruded from the forehead section of the cap. Like ram's horns, they arched back over the Creation's head.

All the while, the Creation stood working on an unidentified wooden figure with a long, narrow carving knife. He never looked up from his work. His attitude was distant and cold. He seemed unmoved by Ramuza's presence or by Ramuza's interest in him.

Ramuza, a Modest Creation, usually did not let something like this bother him. But this particular time, he was annoyed by this Creation's flagrant and disrespectful nature. When people meet, they should look each other in the eye. Ramuza felt offended. What is worse, the longer he stood there, the stronger the feeling grew. Ramuza forced himself to rise above the feeling. He dismissed the offense and continued to move down the line of people.

Before Ramuza reached the next person in the line, he walked past the second thing that caught his interest – a large basket made of wicker and mesh. He did not notice the basket at first; not until he suddenly heard a series of frantic and guttural birdcalls – *argh-argh-argh!* Ramuza stopped and looked down at the basket.

The basket, about one meter in diameter and a meter and a half deep, sat unsteadily, warbling on the ground. Something alive thrashed about inside the basket. Ramuza could see about seven or eight fan-tailed ravens through the spacing between the wicker straws and mesh. With wings flailing, beaks agape, the ravens thrashed about in reaction to Ramuza's approach. In the cramped space within the basket, the birds struggled to regain their comfort zone or escape the basket.

Ramuza stepped back, hoping it would calm the disturbed birds. It did no good. The ravens continued to caw. Argh! Argh! Argh! The basket continued to rock from the birds' frantic movements.

Ramuza looked back toward the Vodun houngan for an explanation. The Vodun houngan stopped his carving, but he never looked up. A brief pause showed his irritation. He reached for one of the rope handles on the side of the basket. He pulled the basket of birds to a new position behind him. The squawking birds fell silent. The Vodun houngan stood up again. He finally glanced at Ramuza and then resumed his carving.

Ramuza looked at Mfalme Abul-Gwan, hoping an explanation would be forthcoming. The Mangoni Mfalme smiled and shrugged. For now, the disarming smile was enough for Ramuza to dismiss this incident, too. Once again, he suppressed his offensive feelings and continued down the line of people.

The remaining seven members of Mfalme Abul-Gwan's group were all Mangoni warriors. They all carried spears, shields, and knives, a necessary precaution when traveling in this part of Africa. Two warriors each held the horse's guide ropes, oxen, and donkeys, carrying the travelers' baskets and gourds. Another warrior seemed responsible for Abul-Gwan's small herd of sheep and goats. Finally, four other warriors, including the Mangoni lead warrior, stood at the four corners of a sizable wooden cage.

This wooden cage was the third thing that stood out significantly to Ramuza. For inside the well-guarded cage was another person – an injured, maltreated Wabanga tribesman.

The Aukmondi had tried many times in the past to make peace with the barbaric, bizarre, and unreachable Wabanga people. Peace had no meaning to the Wabanga. Each try for peace ended in various degrees of failure, including death. The Aukmondi learned long ago that the Wabanga had no wish to communicate with outsiders. To them, all outsiders were as inferior as the lowest animal. Peace, to them, probably meant the freedom to hunt and kill all living creatures indiscriminately.

"Mfalme Abul-Gwan," Ramuza began, still looking into the cage at the spiritless Wabanga, "what is the nature of your visit here?"

"I would like to speak with you at length, Mfalme Ncobba, about a matter of great importance to me. I am confident; it will prove very worthwhile. All tribes in this region will benefit."

"This matter concerns what?"

Abul-Gwan smiled. He had seen Ramuza's reaction to the caged Wabanga. He had to continue strategically slowly. "Mfalme, we have journeyed far. Please. Invite us into your valley. Let us sit and talk. I come with a simple offer that I wish to discuss. I seek your approval, your acceptance, and your support."

Ramuza considered Abul-Gwan's appeal as he peered into the cage again. "Why the Wabanga?"

"Are you familiar with the nature of the Wabanga people?"

"Yes, I know the Wabanga."

"These people are treacherous," Abul-Gwan explained anyway. "They are sly, cunning, unpredictable, and deadly. Their aggressive behavior is just short of supernatural."

"I know the Wabanga," Ramuza repeated.

"Good." Abul-Gwan was still smiling. "Then the task before me may be easier than expected. I had the Wabanga captured because I assumed I would have to show their savage nature to you. I must convince you of my need."

"Mfalme Abul-Gwan, if you want my help, you only need to ask. I see no need for a… demonstration."

Ramuza kneeled beside the cage to study the Wabanga closer. He could see the tribesman still wore the large white markings across his face and shoulders, a camouflage worn during their killer hunts. The Wabanga's eyes were half closed; the irises rolled back. His lips were dry and cracked from dehydration. His breathing was shallow. He lay semi-conscious in an uncomfortable position.

The Mangoni warriors had tied ropes around the Wabanga's wrists and ankles. The bindings held so tightly that the Wabanga's wrists and ankles began to swell and bleed. Also, a bloody cloth on his upper arm covered a recent knife wound.

"You have him caged," said Ramuza. "Why do you also have him bound so tightly?"

"If you must ask that question, Mfalme Ncobba, then you do not know the Wabanga as well as you should. Even in his present condition, that 'beast' can still attack and kill all of us."

Ramuza knew the destructive skills of the Wabanga very well. He had seen what a Wabanga tribe member could do on several occasions. There was nothing new about the Wabanga's behavior that Abul-Gwan could show in any demonstration.

"Mfalme," Quazzi stepped forward. "For safety's sake, I recommend removing the Wabanga from this area. There is no reason whatsoever to hold him here."

"Yes. I must agree, Quazzi." Ramuza stood up and faced Abul-Gwan. "Mfalme, under normal circumstances, the Creation in his cage needs medical attention. But you said it yourself, he is still capable of killing us all. Lives are at risk here. Therefore, I cannot and will not allow him into my valley."

"Mfalme Ncobba, it is fortunate that you are already familiar with the nature of the Wabanga. But as I continue my journey northward, I believe others are not as knowledgeable. I cannot release him just yet. I may need him for future demonstrations."

"Mfalme," Quazzi spoke again to appeal to Ramuza's better judgment. "Is there anyone unfamiliar with the Wabanga? Because he is here, he is a danger. To hold him is foolish and not worth the risk."

Ramuza knew that Quazzi was right. He turned to the Mangoni Mfalme. "Abul-Gwan, I am afraid, I must insist."

"What if I insist on holding the Wabanga, Mfalme Ncobba? Do you withdraw your welcome and dismiss my urgent need to talk with you?"

"I look forward to talking with you. My welcome to you still stands. But I will not allow the Wabanga into my valley."

"So be it." Abul-Gwan sighed. He took a moment to survey the local area. "I am a man of business. I know the power of compromise. May my warriors set up camp here, outside your valley?"

Ramuza looked into the cage at the Wabanga. He glanced at Quazzi as he considered Abul-Gwan's compromise. His decision came with reservations as he faced the Mangoni Mfalme. "I go against my better judgment, but that is acceptable. If you must hold the Wabanga, he must be under constant watch, day and night."

"But of course, Mfalme." Abul-Gwan bowed to show his gratitude.

Hearing this agreement between the two Mfalmes, the houngan, standing behind Abul-Tess, stopped working on the wooden figure. He looked at the two leaders. He had taken an acute interest in development. With a look of concern on his face, he addressed Abul-Gwan. "Mfalme."

Abul-Gwan knew what the houngan wanted. He nodded his approval.

The houngan put the wooden figure into a pouch at his side. With his carving knife still in his hand, he walked past Abul-Tess and Abul-Gwan toward Ramuza and the wooden cage. He looked into Ramuza's eyes before kneeling to the caged Wabanga. With unshakable confidence about what he was doing, he reached into the cage and pulled the Wabanga closer to him.

With the carving knife, he cut free a small patch of the Wabanga's hair and stuffed it into the same pouch as the wooden figure. He reached into the cage again and pulled the blood-soaked cloth from the Wabanga's arm. It, too, went into the pouch. He stood up and glanced into Ramuza's eyes. He gave Quazzi the same cold scrutiny and then walked away. The houngan took his original position behind Abul-Tess.

Ramuza watched all this with curiosity. He watched until the houngan extracted the wooden figure from his pouch and began carving on it again. Ramuza turned toward Abul-Gwan again for an explanation.

There was a friendly smile on Abul-Gwan's face. The Mangoni Mfalme almost shrugged. "I think that was only a protective precaution, Mfalme Ncobba."

"I see." Ramuza was thinking of taking his precautions. He signaled the Royal Warrior Npatuzi to come closer.

"Yes, Mfalme?"

"Great Creation, the Mangoni will manage the Wabanga. While the Wabanga is here, I want your sentinels extraordinarily vigilant. Post your guards if you feel it necessary."

"So be it, Mfalme."

Ramuza looked down into the cage again. He noticed a constant tremor in the Wabanga's hand. He turned to Quazzi. "Great Creation, if Mfalme Abul-Gwan insists on holding the Wabanga, then I must insist on providing the Wabanga with some medical attention. It is only right."

"Ramuza, please. Under the circumstances, even that gesture is not wise."

"No, probably not. But the Supreme Spirit knows, it must be done. I will escort Mfalme Abul-Gwan and his people into the valley. Please send for the Great Creation Kon-Shambique. Ask him to do what he can for the Wabanga."

— 4 —

NOT ALWAYS WISE

In the spacious work area between the huts of Rwuva and Olabisi, the core of the Mangoni travelers sat with their Aukmondi hosts. Abul-Gwan, Abul-Tess, and the Vodun houngan sat on comfortable pillows before Ramuza, Rwuva, Olabisi, and Kharaambi. Everyone sat in relative seclusion, despite the growing and curious crowd just outside the work area. Several Aukmondi Orange, Red, and White Warriors, as well as two Mangoni warriors, held the crowd back as the visitors and the Aukmondi talked. The Brown Warrior Quazzi periodically helped the other warriors while trying to listen to the conversation between the Mangoni visitors and the Ncobbas.

Soon after meeting the Mangoni on the north rim and settling the conditions for entry into the valley, Ramuza arranged for the Mangoni to refresh themselves after their long journey. Since most of the Mangoni remained on the valley's north rim, settling the Mangoni's core into the valley went quickly.

Just moments ago, Ramuza led the refreshed visitors into the Royal Kraal. This is when the crowd outside the work area began to grow. Preparations for the Daily Celebration of Life were almost complete. Several bonfires burned throughout the celebration area. Groups of people talked, laughed, played, and cooked food in various locations. When the people noticed the Vodun houngan among the visitors, they began to gather nearby. Reactions became so chaotic that Kharaambi had to use available Aukmondi warriors to help the two Mangoni warriors hold the growing crowd back.

The warriors parted the crowd enough to allow Ramuza and the visitors to continue unimpeded across the celebration area toward the four huts of the Ncobbas. Normally, Ramuza entertained guests at the royal dais. But because of the chaotic energy in the crowd, Ramuza decided that privacy was necessary. He led the visitors past the dais into the work area.

"Mfalme Ncobba, did we come at a bad time?" Abul-Gwan asked as he settled beside Abul-Tess on his pillow. "It seems your people are amid some great celebration."

"No, Mfalme. This is not a bad time. It is our Daily Celebration of Life. It is how we spend most evenings. You would honor us if you, your mate Abul-Tess, your aide, and your warriors join us after we have completed business."

"Thank you. We will consider it."

"Mfalme Abul-Gwan," Kharaambi addressed the Mangoni, "you must know, one reason for that curious crowd out there is your houngan. Most people have never seen a Creation known to have such a raw and powerful ability to influence."

Everyone in the area looked toward the Vodun houngan. The houngan had resumed work on his wooden figure. In his typical cold manner, he never looked up from his work. Splinters and shards of wood flew in all directions as the houngan continued.

Abul-Gwan chuckled. "Yes. I would imagine so. People with his abilities are rare. I do not know what I would do without him."

"Great Creation," Kharaambi addressed the houngan. "How are you called?"

An awkward silence hung as everyone waited for the houngan to respond to Kharaambi's question. The houngan froze. The splinters and shards of wood stopped flying. But the houngan said nothing.

Abul-Gwan broke the silence. "Kharaambi, I am afraid, you will find my aide not very conversational. He is…"

To everyone's surprise, including Abul-Gwan's, the houngan interrupted. "Mfalme?"

Abul-Gwan nodded, giving his permission to the houngan to speak.

"Onu-Vey," the houngan finally said. He put away the wooden figure and the carving knife. "I am called Onu-Vey. Mfalme Abul-

Gwan was about to tell you that I chose not to speak. People listen too closely when I do. It is… not always wise."

Abul-Gwan chuckled again. "Nonsense, Onu-Vey. People are curious about you. I see no harm in that."

"Mfalme, respectfully, I do not wish to distract from your mission here. Please, allow me to remain… in the background."

Abul-Gwan looked at Ramuza and Kharaambi. He gestured toward the houngan. The gesture suggested that Onu-Vey had said it all. No further explanation was necessary.

"Great Creation Onu-Vey," Kharaambi addressed the houngan again. "Do you see that crowd out there? As word of your presence spreads, so does that crowd. Your wish to remain in the background is almost impossible. You must know that."

"I am a Vodun houngan. Often, I am known for doing the impossible." The houngan ended his talkative stint by pulling the carving knife and wooden figure from his pouch. He held a captive audience as he resumed his work. Splinters and shards of wood began to fly again.

"Mfalme Abul-Gwan, what is your mission here?" Ramuza asked.

Abul-Gwan was about to answer when the noise from the crowd out front changed. Quazzi interrupted his intermittent period of listening. He went to help the warriors again. He found the Mangoni warriors were holding the crowd back, while the Aukmondi warriors were trying to create a small opening. Everyone in the work area, except the houngan, watched curiously.

The Aukmondi warriors worked with the crowd enough to allow the Great Creation, Mfalme Ameh Jobabwe, to work through the people. Ameh rushed into the work area with his ever-present walking staff supporting his steps.

"Mfalme Ncobba, forgive me for being late." Ameh paused to catch his breath. "It is a long walk from the Great Creation Bakha's hut in the valley depths. I came as soon as I could."

Ramuza and all the Aukmondi present knew that Ameh had recently spent considerable time talking with the Great Creation Bakha and Bakha's history students. Since the surviving Chinchigwe people merged with the Aukmondi, Ameh spearheaded the effort to preserve Chinchigwe history. In the oral tradition, Ameh recalled as much history as possible for Bakha's students' ears.

"You need not apologize, Great Creation. We understand what you are doing. It is important for generations to come." Ramuza welcomed Ameh into the area. He offered him a seat beside him as he introduced Abul-Gwan, Mfalme of the Mangoni. Then, with a sense of pride, he introduced Ameh to Abul-Gwan. "May I present one of my closest and trusted counsel of advisers, the Great Creation, Mfalme Ameh Jobabwe?"

"Greetings." Abul-Gwan spoke for the Mangoni. As he bowed, a perplexed look appeared on his face. "You are also called Mfalme?"

Ameh smiled, showing his modesty. "Yes. I am called Mfalme, too. The Great Creation, Mfalme Ncobba, and the Aukmondi people have entrusted me with the authority to speak for all the Aukmondi people. But I am Mfalme only to the clan of Chinchigwe, Mfalme Ncobba's 'adopted' children."

In the next few minutes, Ramuza took a few moments to explain to Ameh who the Mangoni were. He reintroduced Abul-Tess, the mate of Abul-Gwan. He reintroduced the Vodun houngan as a close aide to Abul-Gwan. Finally, he gave Ameh a detailed account of developments from the Mangoni's arrival to the present moment.

Ameh followed Ramuza's introductions and detailed account as best he could. But when Ramuza introduced the Vodun houngan, Ameh's eyes and attention kept returning to the houngan and the wooden figure. The figure was beginning to take form. The image was a human figure now. Ameh stared, so distracted that he barely heard Ramuza redirect attention to the Mangoni Mfalme.

"Mfalme Abul-Gwan," Ramuza said, "was about to tell us the reason for his visit here."

"Yes. I have a problem. I need the help of the local tribes to solve my problem."

"If it is within my power, I will do what I can."

Abul-Gwan hesitated a moment. He chuckled. "Mfalme Ncobba, you seem so willing. I must admit, I am surprised. I have already gone to other tribes in the area, the Rimoza and the Kiwane in particular. My appeal for their help fell on deaf ears. They showed reluctance. I had that Wabanga captured to show what I was up against. They still refused to help. I get the impression that they are waiting to see what you do. What is your influence over these tribes?"

"We are but neighbors, Mfalme Abul-Gwan. The reasons for what they do are their own. I do not control them."

"Well, it seems so. As you already know," Abul-Gwan continued, "I am an entrepreneur. My business ventures cover most of central and eastern Africa. I sell various commodities to Asian, European, and Colonial American merchants."

The word 'merchant' touched Ameh's nerves and demanded his full attention. He broke away from the houngan's work and focused on Abul-Gwan. "Mfalme, when you say commodities, what exactly are you talking about?"

"I am talking about various natural resources, animal pelts, bones, and other parts. I also include some special vegetation. All my commodities are indigenous to Africa. Many of them are in high demand almost everywhere."

"You provide for your people like this? Merchants trade for these things?" Kharaambi frowned with amazement.

"Oh yes! The things that merchants will make a trade for may surprise you."

"Like what?"

"The list is endless. I have based my business on four main categories. First, there is vegetation, mainly wood from the Mpingo ebony and Muhugu tree. Merchants love these woods for all sorts of durable carvings. The demand is great. I trade the timber from these trees as fast as I can find and cut them down."

"Both those trees are becoming harder and harder to find."

"Making them more and more valuable." Abul-Gwan missed Kharaambi's point. He continued, showing pride in his business. "Second, there is 'bushmeat'."

"Bushmeat? What is this bushmeat?"

"It is food, of course. It is the flesh of certain animals. This category includes antelopes, impalas, monkeys, turtles, snakes, and birds. 'Bushmeat' also includes wild sheep, goats, and cattle."

"Great Creation," Kharaambi sat back. Since she grew up in an environment of vegetarians, she could not believe what she was hearing. "Do you mean, people *eat* these animals? You cannot be serious."

"I am quite serious. Customers of Asian, European, and Colonial American merchants enjoy eating these beasts. They do it, not for the taste, but to say that they have eaten an African animal."

"That is madness."

"Maybe. But this is only half of it. My third category is what I call the trophy commodities. These include the tails, heads, and sometimes the carcasses of lions, cheetahs, baboons, mountain gorillas, and buffalo."

"Why? Unless you are some scavenger..." Kharaambi paused to suppress her disgust. She did not succeed. When she spoke again, she still sounded offended. "Dead animals and animal parts... they serve no purpose."

"If you consider them trophies, they do. It all depends on how you see it, Kharaambi." At first, Abul-Gwan had made his appeal to Mfalme Ncobba, but now found himself addressing the Gray Warrior. "These trophies boost and preserve the great accomplishment that many visitors experience when visiting our land. Merchant hunters return to their homelands, filled with pride, taking some of Africa back with them for all to see."

"I still say, it serves no purpose. Forgive my naivety, but I do not see it."

Abul-Gwan shrugged. "Well, sometimes, neither do I. But the demand is there. I have built a profitable business by supplying whatever the merchants find necessary. My greatest profits come from the fourth and final category, the specialty items. These include such simple things as the talons of eagles and falcons, the teeth and claws of the big cats, rhinoceros horns, hands of the gorilla, and elephant tusks."

"Great Creation, no doubt, you have a huge army of hunters to go out, harvest, and supply all these things for the various merchants?" Ramuza asked.

"Yes, Mfalme. My warriors do most of the hunting for me. But many able-bodied people of my tribe supplement my warriors. I can say, if there is a demand for it, I can supply it."

"What about people?" Ameh asked sharply. "Do you harvest and trade African people as well?"

Abul-Gwan smiled. "There are merchants who trade for people. But I have my limit, Mfalme Jobabwe. I do not deal in the slave trade."

"Why not? There is a demand for it." It was Ameh's turn to feel offended. Unlike Kharaambi, he did not try to hide it.

Abul-Gwan felt Ameh's offense. He thought a moment. "Mfalme, I believe harvesting and trading people is wrong. It is inhumane. I will not do it."

"Mfalme Abul-Gwan, I am certainly pleased you feel that way." Ameh's sarcasm suggested that his offense might have been premature.

"Speaking of inhumane," Ramuza began, "after your demonstration to the Rimoza and Kiwane, why do you find it necessary to continue holding the Wabanga?"

"As I said, I have other tribes farther north to visit. I may need the Wabanga. As my business ventures expanded northward, my hunters faced more and more Wabanga. In central Africa, my hunters do a fine job flushing out the Wabanga. But in this area, Mfalme Ncobba, the Wabanga's extraordinary stealth gives them an overwhelming advantage over my hunters. Like the savage animals that they are, the Wabanga kill my hunters; senseless beheadings, mutilations."

"We know the Wabanga."

"In one such case," Abul-Gwan continued, "I lost the former leader of my warriors and dearest friend. I have known him since childhood. His name was Kosi-Jawma. He was leading a hunting party not far from here. A Wabanga ambushed him. Within seconds, the Wabanga managed to sever Kosi-Jawma's arm. Kosi-Jawma escaped, but he died before other warriors could help him."

Until now, Abul-Tess sat quietly at Abul-Gwan's side. When she heard the fate of the warrior Kosi-Jawma, she closed her eyes as if to suppress the pain she felt. A barely audible grunt was an added effort to force the pain away.

Everyone in the area noticed Abul-Tess's reaction. Ramuza finally held his hand, signaling Abul-Gwan to stop his graphic account.

"Great Creation, we are sorry to learn of your warrior and friend, Kosi-Jawma. Please spare us the details of his death. In the present company, details of his death are not necessary. I must repeat. We are familiar with the nature of the Wabanga."

Only now did Abul-Gwan realize the impact he was making. He noticed the disturbed faces of Rwuva, Olabisi, and his mate, Abul-Tess.

"Please, forgive me." He initially spoke to everyone but turned and spoke directly to Abul-Tess. He lovingly placed his hand on top of hers. "I am sorry. I did not mean to upset you."

Abul-Tess sat with her head bowed. She accepted Abul-Gwan's apology with a gentle nod.

Abul-Gwan looked up at Ramuza's mates. "Rwuva, Olabisi, please accept my apology. I am sorry. When I feel so strongly about something, my passion takes control."

"Please continue, Great Creation." Ramuza did not give his mates a chance to accept the apology. "What were you saying about your hunters?"

Abul-Gwan did not resume talking at once. He dropped his head in thought. He reconsidered his approach. When he raised his head again, he spoke with a more businesslike appeal. "I recognize many resources in this area of Africa. The Wabanga are preventing me from harvesting these resources. My hunters need a greater degree of protection."

"Let me understand this clearly. Are you asking me to provide warriors to help protect your hunters in this area? Or are you asking me to send warriors out, to flush out the Wabanga and rid the area of them?"

"I would value either of those actions. If agreed, I will gladly share my earnings from the merchants, whatever you feel is proper, with you, the Kiwane, and the Rimoza."

Again, the work area was silent. All the Aukmondi looked toward Ramuza as they waited for him to think about the offer and respond. Abul-Gwan sensed that a hasty response would not be in his favor, so he broke the silence.

"Mfalme Ncobba, hunting has brought the Mangoni people a long way. We have grown from groups of warring clans to a single unified tribe. I must say, we are quite successful. We are in a position where we can share that success. Please, take your time. Do not make a hasty decision. Think carefully about what you, the Kiwane, the Rimoza, and others stand to gain. The unique and natural resources in this area can help all of us."

"I need no time to think, Mfalme Abul-Gwan. If I decide to support you, it will jeopardize the true wealth of the Kiwane, the Rimoza, the Aukmondi, and the Mangoni."

"What are you saying, Mfalme?"

"I am saying, the varied life forms around us, your commodities, are more valuable to us alive than dead. The Aukmondi are not inclined to support your business, Mfalme Abul-Gwan. I will discuss your proposal with my council of advisers and tribal elders. They will judge if my decision is premature. But I can tell you now. Support from the Aukmondi is not favorable."

"But why? I can promise you that compensation for your support will be substantial. Very substantial. You will not regret it."

"Great Creation, you must understand, to support you, the Aukmondi must ignore one of our most basic principles – our respect for life, all life, that of even the Wabanga. We cannot compensate for this. We cannot support your business."

"But Mfalme, the Kiwane and Rimoza will follow your lead."

"As I said, I cannot speak for the Kiwane and the Rimoza. They make their own decisions."

"Mfalme Ncobba, you represent the solution to solving my problem in this region. Please. I am willing to make compromises. What must I do to change your mind?"

"I am sorry, Great Creation. There is nothing you can do."

Abul-Gwan tried hard not to show his dissatisfaction. He sat still, trying to think of a different approach. When nothing came to mind, he began to gather his things. He rose to his feet, forcing everyone else in the area to stand too. "Mfalme Ncobba, I thank you for your hospitality. And I am afraid I must decline your invitation to celebrate with you this evening. There is much I must reconsider. Abul-Tess, my aide, warriors, and I should return to camp on your north rim." He turned to his mate. "Abul-Tess, come. We must get some rest."

At this point, the Sacred Woman Rwuva touched Ramuza's arm, automatically gaining permission to speak to the Mangoni Mfalme. "Great Creation, please stay. There is no reason to hurry off. At least stay, and feast with us this evening."

"Thank you, Rwuva. It is a kind offer. Unfortunately, I must make new plans tonight. Under the circumstances of Mfalme Ncobba's decision, I intend to continue our travels early tomorrow morning. I must prepare my warriors."

"You still must eat something. Please stay, if but a short while?"

"Thank you for the offer, but no."

"Then, allow the Sacred Woman Olabisi and me to take some food up to your camp for you and your warriors."

"That is thoughtful of you, Rwuva. It is an offer that I can accept."

"Mfalme Abul-Gwan," Olabisi spoke, "Maybe the Sacred Woman Abul-Tess can stay long enough to help select some of the foods to take to your camp?"

Abul-Tess turned to her mate and smiled. She spoke for the first time. "I would like that."

Abul-Gwan bowed to Rwuva and Olabisi. "So be it."

Abul-Gwan then turned to Mfalme Ncobba, Kharaambi, and Ameh. "I am sorry for wasting your time."

"You have done no such thing, Mfalme," said Ramuza.

Abul-Gwan bowed to Ramuza. He turned to Kharaambi and gestured toward the crowd out in front of the work area. The gesture was his silent way of asking the Gray Warrior to escort him out.

5

A CALL TO HEAL

Halfway up the slope to Nagorda Peak, in the kraal of the Favored Tribesman, the Great Creation Kon-Shambique and his unofficial mate, the Sacred Woman Tongda, prepared to go down to the Royal Kraal. They intended to join the Daily Celebration of Life as they do most evenings. Kon-Shambique struggled to lift a huge barrel onto a small cart. The barrel, filled with a special drink he had brewed, was too heavy. Kon-Shambique knew that if he and Tongda were to get the barrel down to the Royal Kraal, they had to get it onto the cart.

The drink was an herbal tea that Kon-Shambique's grandmother had taught him how to make. The popular tea directly affects the body, mind, and spirit when consumed. The herbal mixture cleans the body of most toxins. When heated, the aroma of the tea causes a peaceful, euphoric attitude and feeling. Finally, in one of the most popular effects of all, the tea clears the mind of clutter and confusion.

"Did you make enough this time?" Tongda asked as she tried to help the Favored Tribesman lift the barrel onto the cart.

"It is never enough, Tongda. As always, people will drink every drop moments after we arrive in the Royal Kraal."

Kon-Shambique found the barrel still too heavy, even with Tongda's help. Both Kon-Shambique and Tongda stood back. They looked at the barrel and considered other ways to get it onto the cart. Nothing came to mind.

Kon-Shambique shrugged. "Maybe I did make too much. Next time, I will brew the tea in more than one barrel."

"Maybe next time, you will wait until you reach the Royal Kraal before you brew the tea."

Tongda had offered a logical solution to a simple problem. Kon-Shambique smiled at his oversight. "What would I do without you?"

Just then, Kon-Shambique and Tongda noticed someone walking through the kraal entrance. They recognized him as the Green Warrior Zabiba.

"Great Creation," Kon-Shambique gave the warrior a welcoming smile and wave. "Your timing is perfect. Here. Help me lift this onto the cart."

The Green Warrior dropped his shield and spear to the ground and rushed over to add his strength. Tongda held the cart steady while Kon-Shambique and Zabiba managed to position the barrel onto the cart, spilling only a small amount.

"Thank you, Great Creation," Kon-Shambique said triumphantly. "What brings you to my kraal?"

"I come from the north rim. The Brown Warrior Quazzi sent me. Mfalme Ncobba has summoned you."

"To the north rim? For what? Is something wrong?"

The Green Warrior related the sudden arrival of the Mangoni visitors. He ended his detailed account with the astonishing news that the Mangoni visitor had brought a caged and injured Wabanga tribesman with them.

"Mfalme Ncobba has forbidden the Wabanga from entering the valley," Zabiba explained, "which is why he must remain on the north rim. Nevertheless, the Mfalme requests, since the Wabanga is here, that you give the Wabanga medical attention."

The request surprised Kon-Shambique. He looked at Tongda and then at the Green Warrior Zabiba. "He wants me to help a Wabanga? Are you serious?"

"Yes, Great Creation."

"A Wabanga?" Tonga could hardly believe it herself. She addressed the Favored Tribesman. "Are you going to do it? Are you going to help him?"

"Of course I will help, Sacred Woman." Kon-Shambique wrapped his mind around the request. "This comes from the Mfalme. It is also a call to heal. I have to help."

Kon-Shambique rushed back toward his hut. He beckoned the Green Warrior Zabiba to follow him. "Tell me more, Great Creation. What is the condition of the Wabanga? How is he injured? I must determine what to take up to the rim."

Kon-Shambique led Zabiba into the hut as he listened to the Green Warrior describe the Wabanga's condition. Kon-Shambique gathered relative herbs, elixirs, bandages, and medical cleansers based on what the warrior said. He threw everything into a pouch and threw the pouch over his shoulder. He rushed back out of his hut.

Tongda met him at the entranceway. "Great Creation, you must know, I am coming with you."

"Tongda, I am going to treat a Wabanga. It may not be safe."

"As I listened to the Green Warrior Zabiba describe the Wabanga's condition, the Wabanga is in bad shape. He is caged and in bindings. How dangerous can he be?"

"Sacred Woman, he is a Wabanga."

"I am coming with you," Tongda repeated.

Kon-Shambique thought for a moment, but he did not argue with Tongda. He picked up one last item. It was a small ladle. As he walked past the barrel of tea, he scooped a ladle full and drank hardily. He handed the ladle to Tongda. "Here. Have some. You may need it."

— **6** —

LONG ENOUGH TO BOND

After meeting with the Mangoni visitors, Ramuza and Ameh came from the work area and went directly to the royal dais. As usual, the two spent their entire evening there. By longstanding tradition, it was also where Ramuza always announced the official start of the Daily Celebration of Life.

Long before Ramuza left the work area, he noticed that a festive spirit had already taken hold of the people in the celebration area. Still, he had to uphold the tradition. Almost an hour and a half later than usual, Ramuza took his position on the dais. He announced the start, but it was unceremonious and brief. He ended with his usual words, 'let the celebration begin'. Ramuza stepped back to his chieftain's stool and made himself comfortable.

"Mfalme," Ameh began as he eased himself onto his chieftain stool, "I have not been among the Aukmondi for long. But I have heard several announcements. That had to be the shortest Celebration announcement ever made."

Ramuza smiled. He nodded toward the people in the celebration area. "Look at them, Ameh. They perform the various chores of their passing day to reach this time of day. Once they begin to celebrate like that, any words I speak would be in their way."

As Ramuza and Ameh made themselves comfortable, various aides began to place huge bowls and platters of food and gourds of drinks around the edge of the royal dais. It was a routine and well-choreographed procedure. Within moments, Ramuza and Ameh had several choices of foods and drinks within easy reach. The pleasant aroma of baked tomato and olive bread prompted the two Mfalmes to reach toward the basket of bread simultaneously.

Ameh surrendered to Ramuza's superiority. "Allow me, Mfalme." He lifted the whole basket and offered it to Ramuza.

Ramuza took a small piece and broke it in two. He put a piece into his mouth and began to chew. He sat back as he savored the salty and oily flavor of the crusty bread. Ameh broke himself off a piece as he replaced the basket. Before he put his piece into his mouth, he leaned over and dipped it in a nearby bowl of thick sauce.

In the past, Ramuza had seen many varieties of drinks and foods placed around the dais. He did not recognize the sauce. He leaned over to study the sauce closely. "What is that?" He asked.

"It is a special condiment, Mfalme. I had it made from one of Sacred Woman Lobarra's recipes. It is one of her specialties. I love this stuff." Ameh lifted the bowl of sauce and offered it to Ramuza. "Here, try some."

Ramuza gingerly dabbed the other half of his bread into the sauce and bit off a piece. The hot, spicy flavor surprised him and made him smile. He closed his eyes to savor the delicious flavor. He nodded with approval, "This is good."

"I am glad you like."

"You say, it is one of Lobarra's specialties?"

"Yes, Mfalme. She calls it harissa or something like that. She says the recipe came from some region in the far north where it is common. I asked to have some made for this evening's celebration." Ameh dipped his bread into the sauce again and put it into his mouth. He took a moment to relish the flavor, too. "This batch is good, but… it does not have Lobarra's special touch."

"Oh, but this is delicious. I cannot imagine it tasting any better." Ramuza reached for another piece of bread. This time, he hardly dipped it in the sauce. He did not say another word until he chewed and swallowed. "Speaking of the Sacred Woman, how is she? And your grandson, Tutapona? I have not seen either of them in several days now."

"Mfalme, I thought you knew. Do you recall that group of farmers visiting the Kiwane a few days ago for the farmers' *mkutano*?"

"Yes."

"Lobarra was among them."

Ramuza recalled that two weeks ago, a small group of Aukmondi farmers left the valley to visit the Kiwane. They attended an agricultural farmers' conference, supported by the Aukmondi, Kiwane, and Rimoza tribes. The purpose was to share the successes and hardships that each tribe had experienced in recent harvests. The farmers' conference was one of the fastest ways to learn if any new or unusual trends had developed, positive or negative.

Ramuza also recalled that five of the eleven farmers who went were Chinchigwe. When the Chinchigwe people came to the Aukmondi Valley, most of them were farmers. When the elders selected the farmers to attend the *mkutano*, they included several Chinchigwe. Ramuza had just learned that Lobarra was one of them.

After Lobarra came to live among the Aukmondi, Ramuza soon learned that Lobarra was a reputable farmer. Farming was one of Lobarra's many skills. If the elders selected her as one of the farmers, it came as no surprise to Ramuza. But one thing did surprise him.

"She took Tutapona with her?"

"Yes, she did." Ameh sighed with a perturbed look on his face. "I tried to talk her out of it. I told her several aides and I would watch Tutapona for the fifteen days she would be gone. But no. She would have it no other way."

"Did you ask her not to take Tutapona?"

"Several times."

"As the Chinchigwe Mfalme, you could have insisted."

Ameh shrugged. "I almost did. She claims that she and Tutapona were still bonding. She carried that *little pup* in her belly for nine moons. I consider that long enough to bond. But no, Lobarra says it is a continuing process. How could I argue with that?"

"Do not be too concerned, Great Creation. We have taken part in the farmers' mkutano for the fifth or sixth harvest. The journey between here and the Kiwane Village is short, with few chances of falling into danger. Not to mention, I understand, the Green Warrior

Tushema Maduli is escorting the farmers, there and back. I know Tushema well. He is one of the most dedicated warriors I know. He is exceptional."

"So, I am told. Quazzi, Nionu, and Tushema's regimental commander, the Blue Warrior Dabete Ehkili, all speak highly of him."

"Rest assured. The farmers are safe. Tushema leads a detachment of eight warriors. They will not allow anything to happen to the farmers."

"Nine," Ameh corrected Ramuza.

"Nine?"

"Yes, Mfalme. Since I could not talk Lobarra into leaving Tutapona here with me, I asked the Brown Warrior Quazzi to assign an extra warrior to Tushema's detachment; a warrior whose sole responsibility is to guard and aid Lobarra and Tutapona."

Ramuza smiled at the Old Creation. "You have planned not to worry about Lobarra and Tutapona while they are gone."

"Yes, well, I tried. My plan did not work. I still worry day and night. I have not slept soundly since the day they left the valley. Mfalme, I have been counting the days like a pregnant elephant." Ameh sighed as he dipped another piece of bread into the harissa sauce. "But it does not matter now. It is almost over. They will be home soon."

"Yes," Ramuza recalled what he knew about the well-planned trip. "If I am not mistaken, we should expect the farmers to return in about four days."

"Exactly three and a half days, Mfalme. If everything goes as planned. By midday of the fourth day, Lobarra, Tutapona, and the rest of the farmers will return to the valley. Then, I can stop worrying. I can finally sleep."

— 7 —

WHAT DOES HE KNOW ABOUT HOME

One hundred sixty kilometers away, in the Kiwane Village, all but two of the farmers and warriors had gathered around a central campfire near the edge of the village lake. The farmers and the warrior escorts, so used to their Daily Celebration of Life, had gathered to spend the evening socializing with food, drink, and conversation. When not entertained by their Kiwane hosts, they did this every evening since arriving in the Kiwane Village.

The farmers consisted of six Aukmondi and five Chinchigwe. All eleven farmers had several harvests of experience behind them. The six Aukmondi farmers were tribal elders. Many had worked the soil and crops for most of their lives. They knew almost everything about farming, and their collective knowledge was invaluable.

The five Chinchigwe farmers had not achieved the status of elders, but their knowledge and skills were comparable. Each had gained unquestionable respect. Someday, each will be addressed as an 'elder'.

Several meters away from the gathering, in a semi-isolated spot, the Sacred Woman Lobarra Gendeyani paced. She had retreated to the spot to avoid disturbing the other farmers. She carried her infant son, Tutapona, against her chest. Tutapona cried, and he would not stop. Lobarra tried jostling the infant, which worked most of the time. But not this time. She had just fed him only a short while ago. He was not hungry. She had tried singing him his favorite lullaby, one of Tutapona's most soothing pacifiers. That didn't work either. No. Something else was wrong.

The Red Warrior Rotho Taunza stood at a discreet distance, nearby. Rotho was the extra warrior specifically tasked with the safety of Lobarra and Tutapona. When Lobarra left the gathering of farmers, Rotho followed her. This was the second time today that he watched the Sacred Woman do everything she could to quiet the infant. He could easily see frustration in her behavior. Out of concern, he approached Lobarra.

"Can I help, Sacred Woman?"

"No, I do not think so. Thank you." Lobarra shifted Tutapona from her chest to cradle him in her arms. She felt relief when Tutapona's crying subsided to a series of whimpers. "He has been so fretful lately."

"Do you think that he may be sick? I have recently learned that the Kiwane have a wonderful healer. His name is Ngo Wenfundi."

"Have you met him?"

"No, I have not. I only heard of him earlier today. I understand that Ngo Wenfundi travels a lot. He has just returned from a visit to the Kisumu Village, north of here, on the shore of the Great African Lake. I am told that Ngo is a Wise Old Creation with the blessed healing skills of our own Kon-Shambique. He may be a little tired from his travels. But, if asked, I am sure he will examine Tutapona for you."

"If Tutapona does not improve, I may ask him to do so later. Right now, it may not be necessary. When Tutapona is not fussing, he is alert, active, and strong, and his appetite is as healthy as a horse's. I do not think he is sick."

Rotho leaned forward to get a closer look at Tutapona. The innocent, tearful face that stared back at him made him smile. "Then, if you ask me, I think the Little Creation is just homesick. He wants to go home."

Lobarra looked into Tutapona's face. "What does he know about home?" She smiled. "But you could be right. His fretful behavior started shortly after we arrived here."

"If that is his problem, Sacred Woman, then his troubles will end soon. We have only one more day here. And I have heard talk among the other warriors. They say the Green Warrior Tushema would like us to begin our journey home even sooner, if possible."

Lobarra looked up into Rotho's face. The news surprised her. "Why? What is the rush?"

The Red Warrior shrugged. "I do not know. We missed the announcement and its reason after leaving the discussion earlier today."

Lobarra recalled that earlier today, during one of the gatherings, Tutapona became restless. At an untimely moment, he began to cry. His crying became such a disruption that Lobarra got up and left the gathering. She left abruptly with no time to apologize for the disturbance or for leaving. She missed all that happened after she left. When she quieted Tutapona and returned to the gathering, the day's session had ended.

"So, what else did I miss?"

Rotho shrugged again. Of course, when Lobarra left the gathering, as usual, the Red Warrior dutifully followed her. Everything that Lobarra missed, Rotho missed as well. He had gleaned bits and pieces of information from the other warriors. None of it was enough to give Lobarra the information she wanted. "I can find out for you."

"No, Great Creation. I will find out." Lobarra turned toward the group of farmers. Elder Zekke Okendai, the senior farmer and leader of the Aukmondi group, sat in the middle of the group. "I must speak with the Great Creation, Elder Zekke, anyway. I have yet to apologize to him for Tutapona's disruptive behavior today."

8

A FORCE OF NATURE

After the meeting in the work area, Rwuva, Olabisi, and Abul-Tess followed Ramuza and Ameh out of the area and toward the royal dais. They watched Ramuza take his usual position on the royal dais to announce the start of the Daily Celebration of Life. Rwuva and Olabisi invited Abul-Tess to listen to the usually inspiring words that Ramuza was about to give. But the announcement ended before they realized it. They heard no words of inspiration. Rwuva and Olabisi looked at each other with surprise and apologized to Abul-Tess for the unfulfilled expectations.

When Ramuza and Ameh settled into their usual positions on the royal dais, the people's interest in the vicinity shifted. Rwuva, Olabisi, Abul-Tess, and the two Mangoni warriors who shadowed them became the new center of attention. They drew a crowd around them as they strolled past the royal dais. The farther they walked, the larger the crowd grew, eventually becoming slightly inconvenient. But it also provided the women with an unexpected advantage.

The curious people overheard the plan to gather food and take it to Abul-Gwan's camp on the north rim. Word spread fast. Rwuva, Olabisi, and Abul-Tess had walked a few meters into the celebration area when people with platters of food approached Abul-Tess.

"Your people are most generous." Abul-Tess looked at all the food coming in her direction. So overwhelmed, she stopped walking. "This is more than we will need."

"Excuse me, Sacred Woman." Two young girls had walked up to Abul-Tess. Though they were but girls, both of them stood as tall as Abul-Tess. The taller of the two girls stepped closer to Abul-Tess. "Just how much food will you need?"

Before Abul-Tess could answer, Rwuva felt compelled to introduce the young girls to Abul-Tess. "Sacred Woman, Mfalme Ncobba has nine beautiful daughters. These two are Kunto and Audi Azinti."

After the girls completed the proper greeting, Abul-Tess tried to answer Kunto's question. Abul-Tess mentally counted the people in Abul-Gwan's camp. "There are ten of us. No, wait." Abul-Tess realized that she had not counted the Wabanga. For a moment, she wondered if the strange tribesman would eat anything. As a humane gesture, she counted him too. "Eleven. We will need food for eleven people."

"Thank you, Sacred Woman," Audi said. "We will gather food and drink for your people. May we borrow your warriors to help select what foods they want to eat?"

Abul-Tess looked at the Mangoni warriors standing behind her. Guarding her seemed to be an idle responsibility at the moment. Abul-Tess felt she could make better use of them. "Since they are the ones who will eat most of the food, I suppose that would be fitting."

"Please feel free to mingle with the people here while we gather the food," Kunto said as she and her sister moved away. "We will also arrange to take it up to the north rim for you."

"Thank you." Abul-Tess turned to Rwuva and Olabisi. "They are so thoughtful. That goes for all your people. Since I have been traveling with Abul-Gwan, I must say, I have met few people as generous and thoughtful."

So, Abul-Tess could enjoy the people, Rwuva and Olabisi led the Mangoni woman on a leisurely stroll about the celebration area. The three women talked among themselves as they watched Kunto, Audi, and the Mangoni warriors gather samples of food here and there.

"How long have you been Mfalme Abul-Gwan's mate?" Olabisi asked.

"Not long enough. In a few days, it will be one harvest now. But in that short period, I have already seen so many beautiful things and have visited so many interesting places. But I must say, I think, your valley is by far the best of everything."

"All the more reason, you should try to talk Mfalme Abul-Gwan into staying longer."

"I wish I could, but no. It would be fruitless. I know him well. He is a very determined person. I could tell the moment Mfalme Ncobba rejected Abul-Gwan's request that he would move on. He wastes no time. He stops for nothing. At least, as I travel with him, I see people and places I have only dreamed of seeing before."

"So, what did you do before you became Mfalme Abul-Gwan's mate?" Rwuva asked.

"Before I was Abul-Gwan's mate..." Abul-Tess hesitated, wondering if she should relate such a personal side of her life. "Before I was Abul-Gwan's mate, I was the mate of Kosi-Jawma."

"Kosi-Jawma?" Olabisi looked into Abul-Tess's eyes as she realized what the Mangoni woman was saying. "Do you mean the same warrior that Mfalme Abul-Gwan spoke of earlier? The one killed by the Wabanga?"

"Yes."

"I am so sorry, Sacred Woman. Now I understand why you became so upset when Mfalme Abul-Gwan told us about the incident earlier."

"Yes. I lost Kosi-Jawma almost three harvests ago. To this day, reminders are still painful. The love of Abul-Gwan has helped me to heal."

Rwuva gently touched Abul-Tess's shoulder. "You are fortunate, Sacred Woman. To find love again so soon after the death of your mate is unusual."

"You understand only half of it. I was a widow with children. Widows like me are not so fortunate. But I found the love I needed in Abul-Gwan. Please do not misunderstand me. I loved Kosi-Jawma. He was my first love. To this day, I still love him. But Abul-Gwan has given me the love and support I thought I had lost."

"How long were you Kosi-Jawma's mate?"

"Ten harvests, most of my adult life. I have known him even longer. I met both Kosi-Jawma and Abul-Gwan at about the same time. The two of them came as a pair, as bonded friends. At one time or another, each of them asked me to be his mate. After several harvests and much indecision, I chose Kosi-Jawma first."

"Why did you choose Kosi-Jawma instead of the Mfalme Abul-Gwan?"

Abul-Tess shrugged as she collected her memories. "I do not know. I was a restless, young girl then, unsure what I wanted. Over time, I grew to love both of them. Although Abul-Gwan was already Mfalme, Kosi-Jawma seemed more exciting to be with then. His stories of travel and adventure always thrilled me. Also, I was unsure if I could be a Mfalme's mate. There were too many demands and responsibilities. I did not think I was ready. I had no idea what I was missing."

"Do I detect a hint of regret in your voice?" Rwuva asked.

"Oh no! Kosi-Jawma has helped me to live a full and happy life. It was Kosi-Jawma that first inspired my dreams and helped me to fulfill most of them. Kosi-Jawma and I have had four wonderful children together. I regret none of it. If there is any regret, it is not being fully aware of Abul-Gwan's love for me until after Kosi-Jawma's death. Abul-Gwan has helped me to love and be loved again."

"*Nguvu ya asili*," Rwuva began, "*haiwezi kusimamishwa.*"

"What?" Rwuva's sudden switch to Swahili caught Abul-Tess off guard.

"A force of nature," Rwuva repeated, "cannot be stopped. The love between you and Mfalme Abul-Gwan seems to be a force of nature. Like any natural force, nothing can stop it – absolutely nothing. Such love will always manifest. And it will endure, no matter what."

"It would explain why Mfalme Abul-Gwan never gave up on me," Abul-Tess said in hindsight. "Abul-Gwan, Mfalme of the Mangoni, could have had almost any woman in the Mangoni tribe. Yet he wanted me. He withheld his feelings for me because of his bonded friendship with Kosi-Jawma. He waited patiently for over twelve harvests. He endured my union with Kosi-Jawma until he could finally ask me, in clear conscience, to be his mate."

Just as the three women completed their leisurely circle within the celebration area and returned toward the royal dais, Kunto and Audi met them. Behind the girls stood an Aukmondi Red Warrior, a White Warrior, and the two Mangoni warriors. The four warriors supported a pallet filled with various foods and drinks on their shoulders.

"Sacred Woman," Audi began. "We have gathered food and drink. May Kunto and I take them up to the north rim for you?"

"No, you may not," Rwuva answered at once. It was a motherly response.

"But Sacred Mother, we do not mind."

"I am sure you do not. But I do. Olabisi and I will escort the Sacred Woman up to the rim."

— 9 —

I WILL DO WHAT MUST BE DONE

The Green Warrior Zabiba, the Favored Tribesman Kon-Shambique, and the Sacred Woman Tongda stepped off the Pahoma pathway, just this side of the Pahoma Garden. The sun had set over two hours ago, taking with it the golden evening. Visibility was impossible for untrained eyes. Because the area was so close to the sentry line, the Green Warrior Zabiba led Kon-Shambique and Tongda through the darkness without any torchlight. They continued carefully through the trees and bushes toward the north rim.

The Green Warrior had no trouble finding his superiors. He found his regiment commander, the Blue Warrior Muusitu, and his army commander, the Royal Warrior Npatuzi, standing in a secluded area just inside the sentinel line.

"Welcome to the north rim, Sacred Woman." Npatuzi greeted Tongda first. He greeted Kon-Shambique with a direct question. "Great Creation, have you ever treated a Wabanga tribesman?"

Kon-Shambique thought for a moment. Treating a Wabanga would be a well-remembered experience. Kon-Shambique gave his answer with certainty. "No, Npatuzi. This evening will be my first time."

"Have you ever met one before?"

"Yes. Yes, I have. Fortunate for me, the Poor Creation was dead."

Npatuzi smiled. "Have no doubt. That is when a chance meeting is safest. Come. You are about to provide aid to your first live Wabanga. I need not tell you, be mindful of him. If he gets the chance, he will kill you, for the sheer sport of it."

The Blue Warrior Muusitu remained in the secluded area. Npatuzi lit a torch and led Kon-Shambique, Tongda, and the Green Warrior Zabiba beyond the sentinel line. They emerged from the cover of the forest. With wide steps, they waded out through knee-deep grass and into the clearing.

Once in the clearing, Kon-Shambique and Tongda looked at the area that had become Mfalme Abul-Gwan's provisional camp. Mangoni warriors had set up a large tent in the area. As the only tent out here, it belonged to Mfalme Abul-Gwan and Abul-Tess. Beyond the sentry line, the tent was set in the center of the clearing. Kon-Shambique realized this was a protective strategy against the constant threat of prowling lions, leopards, or hyenas. For the same reason, Mangoni warriors corralled the Mangoni pack animals and caged birds beside the tent.

On the other side of the tent, pack animals and caged birds, about three-quarters of the way across the clearing, a small campfire burned. Four Mangoni warriors and the Vodun houngan sat around the campfire. The four warriors talked among themselves. The houngan, as usual, continued to work with focused diligence on his carving. Further out, in an isolated area on the far side of the clearing, a single Mangoni warrior stood guard next to the wooden cage.

The Aukmondi were not paying a social visit. To avoid disturbing Abul-Gwan, they made a wide arch across the clearing. They tried to avoid the tent, pack animals, caged birds, and campfire.

Mfalme Abul-Gwan heard the Aukmondi approaching and came from the tent. As the Aukmondi walked by, he acknowledged their presence with a gentle nod. He knew why they had come. The smirk behind his smile suggested his opinion about what they were doing.

The four Mangoni warriors who sat around the campfire abruptly ended their conversation. They rose to their feet when they saw the Aukmondi approaching. The Vodun houngan remained seated. He made a brief and indifferent glance at the Aukmondi but never broke the rhythm of his carving.

As Kon-Shambique and Tongda drew closer and closer to the wooden cage, its mysterious content demanded all of their attention. Tongda had never been this close to a Wabanga, dead or alive. She was as curious as she was fearful. The light from the torch that Npatuzi carried was weak. At first, neither she nor Kon-Shambique saw anything discernible. Nothing moved inside the cage. Tongda squinted as she tried to make out anything recognizable.

Npatuzi stopped about two meters from the cage. The single Mangoni warrior who guarded the cage blocked his approach. Npatuzi waited for permission to pass. A nod from Abul-Gwan to the Mangoni guard signaled that permission. The Mangoni guard stepped aside.

Npatuzi, Zabiba, Kon-Shambique, and Tongda stepped closer and peered into the cage. Npatuzi held the torch closer to the cage to cast a better light. They saw a lifeless, battered human form scrawled out on the bottom of the cage.

"Great Sacred Spirit," Kon-Shambique said. The Wabanga lay curled up in a fetal position. "How long has he been like this?"

"The Mangoni brought him here like this. Can you do anything for him?"

"I must try. I need to clean his wounds first." Kon-Shambique slipped the strap of the medical pouch that he carried from his shoulder. He set the pouch on the ground and removed most of its contents – a small metal bowl, strips of cloth, medical knives, and various powders and ointments. "I will need some heated water."

Tongda responded. She took the metal bowl and propped it securely on several stones. She filled the bowl with water from a small bladder that she carried. Finally, she stuffed the underside of the bowl with grasses, twigs, and other kindling. The Green Warrior Zabiba saw what she was doing and helped her.

Kon-Shambique paused and took a deep breath before he gave his next instructions to Npatuzi. "Alright, Great Creation, open the cage. I must go inside."

The Royal Warrior handed the torch to Zabiba and kneeled. He cautiously untied the bindings that secured the wooden latch that closed the cage door. After another visual reassessment of the Wabanga inside, Npatuzi removed the latch and slowly opened the cage door.

At this point, the Vodun houngan stopped his carving. With his eyes locked on the unfolding events, he rose to his feet. As if expecting imminent danger, the houngan took two steps toward the cage. He looked at the Aukmondi with an uncharacteristic look of concern.

Kon-Shambique entered the cage. He reached out to touch the Wabanga's neck to judge the Wabanga's heartbeat. He studied the Wabanga's body from head to toe with caution at the forefront. The knife wound on the Wabanga's arm was still fresh, but it had stopped bleeding. Tight bindings on the Wabanga's wrists and ankles had caused the Wabanga's hands and feet to become severely discolored and swollen.

Kon-Shambique's first medical instinct was to loosen the bindings. After considering the safest approach, he started with the ankle bindings. The ankle bindings had cut so deeply into the Wabanga's skin that they made permanent markings. Kon-Shambique watched the Wabanga closely and pulled the bindings free. He threw the bindings aside.

By this time, just outside the cage, Tongda had ignited a fire under the water bowl. Several strips of medicinal cloth were already soaking and heating up in the water. Kon-Shambique reached for one of the strips. He intended to wash away the blood on the Wabanga's arms and ankles. When he returned to the Wabanga to clean one of the ankle wounds, Kon-Shambique hesitated. He sat still, as if rethinking his medical approach. Then he dropped the cloth and backed out of the cage. His sudden and quick exit was so awkward that he tripped over the water bowl. The water from the bowl spilled, putting out the fire beneath it with a loud sizzle and a thick cloud of smoke and steam.

"Great Creation?" Tongda reacted to Kon-Shambique's unexpected behavior. "What is wrong?"

"Close it!" Kon-Shambique told Npatuzi. His voice quivered from panic.

The sudden instructions caught Npatuzi by surprise. He hesitated for a second.

"Close the cage, now!" Kon-Shambique demanded.

Npatuzi slammed the cage door and held it closed. Zabiba quickly slipped the latch into place. He retied the binding, securing the latch and the door.

Kon-Shambique stood up and took two steps back. "Great Creation, that Wabanga… is much healthier than he looks."

Npatuzi looked into the cage. He, too, stepped back. "If he is healthier than he looks, then he is every bit as dangerous as we expect him to be. We must get him out of this area."

As the ranking Aukmondi on the north rim, Npatuzi turned to face Mfalme Abul-Gwan. He knew what must be done. With determination in his stride, he waded through the tall grass back toward the center of the camp. He walked past the four Mangoni warriors and the Vodun houngan. He approached the Mangoni Mfalme.

"Great Creation, Mfalme Abul-Gwan," Npatuzi was respectful but blunt. "Please. Instruct your warriors to take the Wabanga into the wilderness."

Mfalme Abul-Gwan at first took the Royal Warrior's demand lightly. He chuckled. "I will do no such thing. Why? Has your medicine man changed his mind about helping him?"

"The Wabanga needs no help from us. We must release him into the wilderness. At the least, we must remove him from this area at once."

"No. I cannot do that. I may need him."

"Please remove him, Mfalme. Or I will have it done."

For the first time, Abul-Gwan realized the Royal Warrior was serious. As he did, a volatile edge in his manner appeared. His expression turned rigid. He raised his voice. "Do you dare speak to me that way, Aukmondi?"

"Mfalme, please. It is not safe. With all due respect, I will not stand here and argue with you. The Wabanga is an unquestionable danger. I will do what must be done. If you object to my actions, please speak with Mfalme Ncobba."

Hearing this exchange, the four Mangoni warriors and houngan moved toward their Mfalme. Kon-Shambique, Tongda, and Zabiba moved toward Npatuzi. The Blue Warrior Muusitu came from his secluded area behind the sentinel line. Even from a distance, he could see tension developing. Stepping broadly through the tall grass, he walked briskly across the clearing toward the center of the camp.

Everyone heard the Sacred Women, Rwuva, Olabisi, and Abul-Tess inside the sentinel line at this untimely moment. The women and the four warriors delivered the pallet of food and drinks to Abul-Gwan's camp. In contrast to the tense development in the camp, everyone heard the women talking and laughing as they approached the north rim.

Muusitu was about to help the Royal Warrior when he looked across the camp toward the wooden cage. The Blue Warrior froze, chilled to the bone by what he saw by the light of the Mangoni campfire.

The body of a Mangoni warrior lay on the ground in front of the wooden cage. The door to the cage he had guarded hung wide open, and the cage was empty.

"The Wabanga!" Muusitu shouted. "The Wabanga is loose!"

Npatuzi reacted. He turned to the Green Warrior Zabiba. He pointed toward the sound of the approaching women – Rwuva, Olabisi, and Abul-Tess. "Great Creation, stop those women. Get them back into the valley! Now!" Npatuzi himself herded Kon-Shambique, Tongda, and Mfalme Abul-Gwan together. He forced them back across the clearing toward the sentinel line almost tactlessly, with pushes and shoves.

Meanwhile, the four Mangoni warriors and the houngan rushed toward the wooden cage and the body of the slain warrior. The Blue Warrior Muusitu joined them. As everyone gathered around, the Vodun houngan knelt by the slain warrior's body. He examined the knife wound with his fingers.

"The wound is from the warrior's knife. He foolishly came too close to the cage. The Wabanga managed to grab the knife, kill the warrior, and free himself."

"The knife is gone." Goh-Jumaane, the Mangoni lead-warrior, visually searched the nearby dirt and grass. "We must assume the Wabanga still has it."

Another of the Mangoni warriors made a broader visual search of the area. Despite the Wabanga's deceptive health, he was not in the best condition to move about. He could not have gone far."

"Because of your campfire, he is hiding." Muusitu nodded toward the campfire, where the houngan and Mangoni warriors had sat earlier. The Blue Warrior did not know if the Mangoni knew the Wabanga's strange inclination. He explained anyhow. "Wabanga avoid fire religiously. As long as it is burning, he will try to hide. But make no mistake. He is near. And healthy or not, he still intends to kill as many of us as he can."

Goh-Jumaane stood. He turned in a circle to search the clearing. "If he is hiding, he must be hiding in this tall grass. Out here, it is the only place he could hide."

The Mangoni lead-warrior's speculation was partially correct. He had overlooked another place where the Wabanga could hide. The warrior spotted it by accident.

"There! With the pack animals!"

Sure enough, everyone saw the Wabanga crouched in the center of the pack animals. As Muusitu said, the Wabanga hid, obscured by the horse, oxen, donkeys, and sheep. A more able-bodied Wabanga would have found hidden refuge in the surrounding forest. This one could only make it to Mangoni's animal corral.

The Wabanga uses the knife with remarkable dexterity to cut the bindings around his wrists. When the bindings snapped loose, the Wabanga clamped the bloodstained blade of the knife in his teeth. He massaged his wrists as he stared back at the Mangoni warriors from beneath the belly of a donkey.

With spears held ready, the Mangoni warriors rushed toward the Wabanga. When the Wabanga saw them coming, he stood erect. For reasons known only to the Wabanga, he took the knife from his teeth and swung wide, gracefully.

The knife ripped a wide cut in the belly of the donkey. The poor animal brayed and bellowed, bucked and kicked wildly, and frightened the other pack animals. The pack animals broke loose from their tethers, as if the Wabanga had expected the result. The animals scattered in every direction.

The guide ropes on one of the oxen hung free enough to drag the ground—the free end of one of the ropes caught and tangled in a lanyard on Abul-Gwan's tent. As a result, the whole tent collapsed. The ox dragged the tent behind it as it fled. Unfortunately, the ox ran toward the Mangoni campfire. The collapsed tent continued to trail behind it. When the tent traversed the campfire, it caught fire. Now the frantic ox, more frightened than ever, created a flaming path of destruction as it ran through the tall grass.

The four Mangoni warriors and the Vodun houngan dodged the ox and the other frightened animals as best they could. In the chaos and growing flames that followed, they lost sight of the Wabanga. No one saw which way the Wabanga had gone.

Once again, the Wabanga disappeared.

— **10** —

LET IT BURN

A solid line of flames stretched across the clearing along the north rim. Over one hundred seventy Green Warriors had come out of concealment from behind the sentinel line to battle the flames. Almost an entire sentinel regiment used their shields, cloaks, and whatever else they could find to try to beat the flames out. They did their best to ignore the heavy smoke, the flying embers, and the stinging smell of burning grass that filled the air.

The Blue Warrior Muusitu, four Mangoni warriors, and the Vodun houngan found themselves trapped in the center of Abul-Gwan's burning camp, surrounded by threatening flames that rumbled and grew with intensity. Muusitu and the Mangoni warriors could not follow the example of most of the pack animals, which had fled into the forest behind them. They had no choice but to use their cloaks and shields in the same manner as the Green Warriors. They had to clear a pathway through the flames back toward the sentinel line and to safety.

Despite the desperate situation, the houngan did not fight the flames like the others. Instead, he devoted his energy to rummaging through the remnants of the camp. At first, it appeared that he was frantically looking for salvageable items. In truth, he searched for his pouches, particularly the pouch holding the wooden figure. He threw aside baskets of clothing and other valued items that Abul-Gwan and Abul-Tess had collected during recent travels. He showed complete indifference to the smoke and raging fire around him. Even when his cap, adorned with the ram horns, fell from his head and began to burn, he ignored it. Nothing seemed more important than finding his pouches.

Muusitu and the Mangoni warriors on this side of the flames and several Aukmondi Green Warriors on the other side finally made a safe passageway. It was only a matter of time before the flames reclaimed their solid line across the clearing. When the passage became clear, Muusitu ensured that all four Mangoni warriors ran through first. As he ran through, he watched the last of the four warriors skip and dodge the hot spots and persistent flames. When the final warrior had reached safety, Muusitu looked back for the Vodun houngan. To his dismay, he saw him still scouring through the camp.

"Great Creation," he shouted to the houngan, "you must hurry! Whatever you are looking for, leave it!"

The houngan ignored the Aukmondi Blue Warrior and the smoke burning his eyes. He was about to tell the Blue Warrior to forget about him, to leave him. That is when he finally found his pouches. He fell to his knees to gather them. Since losing his adorned cap, the houngan had nothing on his head. The reddish glow of flames reflected brightly off his bald head as he pried open the primary pouch and dug into it with both hands. He ensured the wood carving and other contents were still there. Only then did he allow himself to join Muusitu.

The Vodun houngan ran toward the Blue Warrior, clutching his pouches under his arms. As he did, he happened to run past the basket of Fan-tailed Ravens. He heard the ravens inside the basket cawing and screeching louder than ever. He looked to see that half of the basket had caught fire and was burning strongly.

The houngan stopped. He secured his pouches tightly under his arm and kicked over the basket. Another powerful kick forced the basket to roll onto its burning side, smothering most of the flames. The Vodun houngan used his bare hand to snuff out the rest of the flames. Amid this crisis, the houngan took the time to set the basket upright and visually assess the damage done. Thick smoke from the basket prevented the houngan from making a good assessment. The sounds of the screeching birds within the basket seemingly convinced him that the basket and the birds inside were still salvageable. He grabbed one of the basket handles and began to drag it behind him toward safety.

The Blue Warrior Muusitu watched the whole incident. When the houngan risked his life to find the pouches, Muusitu thought it was not very smart. Muusitu's attitude and opinion about the houngan softened when he saw that the houngan was also risking his life to save the basket of birds. With the passage rapidly closing, the Blue Warrior rushed back to help the houngan. He grabbed the other handle of the basket. Muusitu and the houngan lifted the basket and leaped through re-surging flames to safety.

Through thick, blinding smoke, Muusitu managed to escort the Mangoni warriors and the houngan out of the clearing. It was dark now, but the intense red glow of the burning clearing was enough for Muusitu to see. He successfully led everyone behind the sentry line. They joined the Royal Warrior Npatuzi, Kon-Shambique, Tongda, and Mfalme Abul-Gwan there.

The thick smoke from the clearing hampered everyone's breathing. Everyone coughed uncontrollably. Their eyes and lungs burned. Everyone had collapsed to the ground, struggling to catch their breath. Even Mfalme Abul-Gwan crawled on his hands and knees, desperately trying to recover.

When the Royal Warrior Npatuzi saw Muusitu, he suppressed his coughing spasms to speak to him. "Great Creation… call your warriors back! Get your regiment from the clearing!"

"What?" Muusitu seemed confused by the order. He knew that every available warrior was needed to fight this fire. "The clearing, Great Creation… it is burning out of control!"

"Let it burn, Muusitu! Because of the Wabanga, your warriors must not abandon their posts. Call them back! Get them back to the sentry line!"

The order was clear this time. And it made good sense. Even though Muusitu had not fully recovered, he returned to the clearing. Still coughing and rubbing his eyes, he disappeared into a cloud of smoke as he went to pull back his regiment.

Npatuzi turned to the group of people scattered around him. "Is everyone here alright?" Heavy breathing and coughing continued. But no one complained. Npatuzi was about to ask Kon-Shambique to escort everyone safely back into the valley when Mflame Abul-Gwan found his voice and struggled to speak.

"No, wait! My Abul-Tess! I heard her. Where is Abul-Tess?"

Npatuzi looked to his right as if to visually find Abul-Tess. The pathway on which the women approached was over thirty meters away. Even with the strong, reddish glow, visibility was poor. The smoke was too thick. Npatuzi turned back to the Mfalme and made a reasonable assumption.

"She should be safe, Mfalme." When the Wabanga escaped, Npatuzi sent the Green Warrior Zabiba to intercept the women. He assumed that, if everything went as expected, the women would be well down the valley slope by now.

He was wrong. From that thirty-meter distance, a woman's scream pierced the smoke-filled forest area.

11

DEAD IS DEAD

Moments ago, the Green Warrior Zabiba managed to intercept Rwuva, Olabisi, Abul-Tess, and the four warriors carrying the pallet of food and drinks. He met them twenty meters from the sentinel line with a torch burning to light his way. He stopped them and put an end to their cordial mood and merriment.

Just as he explained the situation in the clearing, everyone heard a rustling of bushes nearby. They turned to see what was making the noise. Zabiba stepped between the group and the noise with a heightened sense of responsibility. The Green Warrior knew the Wabanga had escaped, but he was unaware that a fire had just started in the clearing and that all the Mangoni pack animals had fled. Zabiba held his torch higher to project its light. To the surprise of the entire group, the light showed one of the Mangoni oxen. The ox had tangled in the thick bushes and struggled to break free.

One of the Mangoni warriors carrying the pallet of food recognized the animal as one of their own. He felt it was his duty to rescue the valued animal. The warrior forced the others to ease the pallet of food to the ground.

"Great Creation," Zabiba spoke to the warrior. "Please, leave the ox. Other warriors can capture it later. We must get down into the valley."

"It will take but a moment," the Mangoni warrior said, ignoring Zabiba. The ox seemed more important.

After the pallet was down, the Mangoni warrior walked toward the trapped and frightened animal. He made it to within two meters of the ox when a dark shadow flew from over the ox's back. It was the Wabanga, the knife held menacingly in his hand. Like a huge tree monkey, with all four limbs sprawled out, the Wabanga landed on the Mangoni warrior. The savage killer planted the knife into the warrior's chest, killing him.

Olabisi screamed.

"Go! Go!" Zabiba herded Rwuva, Olabisi, and Abul-Tess back down the pathway. He pushed the Sacred Woman roughly without the gentleness that comes with respect. His actions were so forceful that he stepped into the center of the pile of food on the ground as he pushed the women ahead. Nothing was more important than getting the women to safety.

The other Mangoni warrior raised his spear and charged the Wabanga. He saw the Wabanga hop up off the body of the dead warrior. He saw the Wabanga pull the knife from the warrior's chest and stand ready for another challenge. But before the Mangoni warrior could reach the Wabanga, he saw the Wabanga duck behind a nearby tree. The Wabanga disappeared into the surrounding darkness.

The Aukmondi Red and White Warriors started over to help the Mangoni warrior, but Zabiba ordered them back. "Mbinga, Jafa! No! Stay with us! We are on the sentinel line. Let us take the chance to see if the sentinels will soon find and subdue the Wabanga. We must get these women back down into the valley."

Zabiba was unaware that most of the Aukmondi sentinels in the area were fighting a raging fire out in the clearing. He continued to nudge Rwuva, Olabisi, and Abul-Tess ahead. With his torch held high, Zabiba moved in front of the women to offer more lighting and lead the way.

Rwuva, Olabisi, and Abul-Tess huddled together. They followed Zabiba along the pathway. The Aukmondi Red Warrior Mbinga and the White Warrior Jafa brought up the rear. Everyone visually searched in every direction. They knew that, since the Wabanga was near, he could reappear out of surrounding darkness at any moment.

The group had gone a few meters when, suddenly, the body of the second Mangoni warrior dropped from a tree. He fell to the ground in front of the warriors Mbinga and Jafa. The Mangoni warrior was dead, his throat cut.

The Green Warrior Zabiba turned when he heard the thud of the warrior's body hitting the ground. He looked up into the tree. Sure enough, by the flicker of his torchlight, he saw the eerie image of the Wabanga perched on a limb, looking down on the group. Zabiba hurled his spear at the Wabanga. Zabiba, like all Aukmondi, held the highest respect for life. But the Green Warrior's unwavering intent was to kill. He aimed for the Wabanga's heart. Because of the poor lighting, his spear was off target by a few centimeters. He planted his spear to the left of the Wabanga's heart and solidly in the Wabanga's shoulder.

Atypical of his nature, the Wabanga appeared surprised by the spear in his shoulder. He looked at the spear briefly, but he showed no pain. The spear still had its effect. The Wabanga fell from the tree. Unfortunately, he fell behind the huddle of Rwuva, Olabisi, and Abul-Tess, and just close enough to knock all of them to the ground.

The three women screamed. They scrambled to get to their feet and away from the Wabanga, who miraculously struggled to stand, too. Zabiba, Jafa, and Mbinga rushed toward the chaotic pile of people. As Jafa and Zabiba focused on rescuing the three women, the Red Warrior Mbinga saw an opportunity and tried his best to end the situation.

With a wide kick, Mbinga swept the Wabanga off his feet. The Wabanga fell onto his back. Mbinga lunged at him with his spear. Even though Zabiba's spear still protruded from the Wabanga's shoulder, the Wabanga rolled out of the way. He followed through with a deadly thrust of his knife into the Mbinga's stomach. The Red Warrior fell dead.

The Wabanga stood up triumphantly. With a hint of anger or rage on his spotted face, he reached up and yanked Zabiba's spear from his shoulder. Now, besides the knife he had stolen from the Mangoni warrior guarding his cage, the killer Wabanga had a new weapon – Zabiba's spear.

As the Green Warrior Zabiba forced Rwuva, Olabisi, and Abul-Tess farther down the pathway, the brave and inexperienced White

Warrior Jafa turned to face the Wabanga. He learned, too late, that stealth and deception were one of the Wabanga's strongest tactics. The Wabanga had disappeared.

Jafa searched in all directions. He made a frantic, three hundred and sixty-degree turn before he found the Wabanga. He saw the Wabanga had bypassed him and was preparing to assault the Green Warrior Zabiba, Rwuva, and Abul-Tess. Zabiba had managed to huddle two women against a large tree and shielded them with his body. The Sacred Woman, Olabisi, stood alone, desperately lashing at the Wabanga with a large tree limb to no avail.

Before Jafa could raise his spear, the Wabanga viciously jabbed with the spear. The spear penetrated Zabiba's back and through his right shoulder. It grazed Rwuva's left arm. It plunged through Abul-Tess's left side and stuck in the tree behind them.

Olabisi continued to lash at the Wabanga with all her might. She grunted with each hysterical stroke. The White Warrior Jafa raised his spear to lob it at the Wabanga but changed his mind. The Sacred Woman Olabisi now stood in his line of sight. He lowered his spear and decided to bodily charge the Wabanga instead. The decision proved strategically sound. The Wabanga held his stolen knife in his hand again and turned on Olabisi. At the last second, Jafa tackled Olabisi instead, knocking her to the ground and saving her life.

The White Warrior rolled over just in time to see the Wabanga ready to bring the knife down with deadly force. But then, he saw the Wabanga freeze. The Wabanga looked off to the side. As far as the White Warrior Jafa could tell, the Wabanga had heard someone coming. An impulse to hide made the Wabanga crouch down, swivel around, and run for cover.

*****

The Royal Warrior Npatuzi finally came running into the area with several Green Warriors trailing behind him. Npatuzi assessed the situation and sent most Green Warriors into the nearby surroundings. They already knew their sole purpose was to find and subdue the Wabanga. Npatuzi singled out one of the Green Warriors and gave her different instructions. He ordered her to find a set of talking drums to alert the Royal Kraal and call in reinforcements.

Three Mangoni warriors came running into the area as the Green Warriors scattered. The Vodun houngan, Kon-Shambique, and Tongda followed close behind them. Mfalme Abul-Gwan and the Mangoni lead-warrior, Goh-Jumaane, brought up the rear. Goh-Jumaane supported Abul-Gwan, who continued to wheeze and cough from the smoke. Almost everyone rushed toward the carnage pinned to the tree. As a group, they peeled the injured people away.

The Royal Warrior Npatuzi and Kon-Shambique pulled the semiconscious Zabiba loose and eased him to the ground. Zabiba's spear still protruded, front and back, from his shoulder. Kon-Shambique broke the protruding ends off and threw them to the side. Olabisi and Tongda helped Rwuva to her feet and led her a few steps away. Olabisi cleared a place on the ground for Rwuva to sit as Tongda tore a strip of her wrap loose to tie a bandage around Rwuva's bleeding arm.

The Mfalme Abul-Gwan pushed people aside and forced his way to Abul-Tess's side. He hesitated from the shock of seeing Abul-Tess slumped against the tree and blood covering her left side.

"Abul-Tess?" The Mangoni Mfalme took Abul-Tess into his arms and eased her to lie flat on the ground. "I am here. It will be alright now."

"Abul-Gwan," Abul-Tess opened her eyes. She reached up to touch Abul-Gwan's face. Her hand trembled. "I … I am so sorry."

"What?" Abul-Gwan looked into Abul-Tess's face, wondering why she was apologizing. He dismissed her apology as mild delirium. He took her hand to stop it from trembling. As he did, he noticed the severity of her injury for the first time. He put his hand on Abul-Tess's side. It was a futile effort to stop the bleeding. He looked up, searching the people behind him for the houngan. "Onu-Vey! Where are you? Onu-Vey, you must help her!"

The Great Creation Kon-Shambique settled beside the Mangoni Mfalme and Abul-Tess. Because Abul-Tess's wound was the most severe, he had turned his full attention to her. He touched Abul-Gwan's shoulder. "Mfalme … please, allow me to help her. I can stop the bleeding."

Abul-Gwan, still searching for Onu-Vey, did not initially see Kon-Shambique next to him. When he did, he began to panic. He pushed Kon-Shambique away. He turned in a desperate effort to find the Vodun houngan. "Onu-Vey! Please, I want you to help her!"

Kon-Shambique turned to the Royal Warrior Npatuzi. "Great Creation, please move the Mfalme aside. I must get to the Sacred Woman to help her."

"Do not touch me!" Abul-Gwan snapped. Visibly angry, he glared at Npatuzi and Kon-Shambique. He pointed to Zabiba and Rwuva. "Go help your people."

Despite Abul-Gwan's demand, the Royal Warrior reached down to move the Mangoni Mfalme. As he was doing so, a firm hand caught his shoulder. Npatuzi looked back to see the Vodun houngan standing over him.

"Please," the houngan said calmly. "Stand aside."

Npatuzi abandoned his attempt to remove the Mangoni Mfalme. He stood up and moved back.

The Vodun houngan knelt at Abul-Tess's side. Without touching her, he studied her from head to toe. Time stood still. The houngan took forever before doing anything. After an unbearably long time, he touched the black crystal hanging at his chest.

Abul-Gwan had seen the houngan do this simple gesture many times. It was always an ill-fated sign. "Onu-Vey!" His voice, filled with horror, simultaneously sounded like a plea and a warning.

Onu-Vey stood. "I am sorry, Mfalme. You must … let her go."

"What? What? What are you saying?" Abul-Gwan became frantic. He stood up, too. He placed his hand on Onu-Vey's shoulder to force the houngan back down to Abul-Tess's side. "Onu-Vey, you have done nothing."

"I can do nothing for her, Mfalme." The houngan stepped away. He looked at Kon-Shambique as he walked past him. "No one can."

Just then, Abul-Tess moaned, forcing Abul-Gwan to kneel at her side again. With a trembling hand, she touched the Mfalme's face again. Her voice was barely audible. "Abul-Gwan, Mfalme, it is alright."

"Abul-Tess, please, do not talk. Save your strength."

"Thank you … for waiting for me. I am sorry. Our time together has been short. We had no time to bear a son together. I am so sorry. Our life together … has come to this. Know that I have always loved you. And my children … please tell my children that I … that I …" Abul-Tess's hand stopped trembling and slid from Abul-Gwan's face. She released her last breath, closed her eyes, and died.

Mfalme Abul-Gwan cried. Unbecoming of a tribal Mfalme, his gentle sobbing became one steady wail. He buried his face against Abul-Tess's shoulder, muffling the sorrowful noise deep inside him. He took her body into his arms and squeezed it, as if the act would force the life back into her. The Mangoni Mfalme would have sat there forever had not Kon-Shambique put his hand on the Mfalme's shoulder to console him.

Abul-Gwan put a sudden end to his sorrow. He stopped crying. He raised his head from Abul-Tess's shoulder. With her blood on his fingers, he wiped away his tears, smearing blood and tears across his cheek. Angrily, he pushed Kon-Shambique aside and sprang to his feet. Abul-Gwan rushed toward the Vodun houngan. He caught the houngan by the arm and spun him around to face him. He pointed at Abul-Tess and spoke through clenched teeth. "Fix this!"

"She is dead, Mfalme."

"Onu-Vey, you are a Vodun houngan. You can make her live again."

"No." Onu-Vey was still calm, but insistent. "You are mistaken, Mfalme. Dead is dead."

Abul-Gwan stared at the Vodun houngan. There was bitterness on his face. "Why are you here, Onu-Vey?"

"I am here to serve you, Mflame."

"Then serve me!" He pointed at the body of Abul-Tess again. "Fix this!"

Onu-Vey stared back into Abul-Gwan's face. Time stood still again as the two locked eye contact. Who would blink first? The sudden sounds of Aukmondi talking drums broke the tension in the air. That is when Onu-Vey turned and walked away from Abul-Gwan.

The Vodun houngan left the area to be alone. He did not go far. He walked to a semi-secluded area and stopped. The houngan stood in near darkness, illuminated by the nearby torches. After quickly scrutinizing the area, he found the location acceptable. He reached up to his chest and clutched the black crystal hanging around his neck. He closed his eyes and mumbled. Everyone heard him, but no one understood a word he said.

When Mfalme Abul-Gwan ordered the capture of the Wabanga, Onu-Vey knew there would be trouble. He did not know what kind. He just knew the Wabanga meant trouble. Assuming the Wabanga would be the cause of that trouble, Onu-Vey took precautions. He carved out the wooden figure of the Wabanga. He knew he would need it at some time.

That time had come. Onu-Vey's unintelligible words gradually grew louder and louder. The Aukmondi talking drums echoed in the background. The irregular knocks of the drums accented whatever he was saying. Onu-Vey's eyes remained closed as he spit the words out in a rolling, repetitive chant. Just as he had done at the start of all his powerful rituals, he raised the broken black crystal, clutched in his hand, to his forehead. Then he dropped the crystal, allowing it to dangle over his chest.

Onu-Vey reached into one of the pouches that he carried. He pulled out a handful of fine white powder. Still chanting, his eyes closed, he threw portions of the powder in every direction. With the last of the powder gone from his hand, Onu-Vey stopped chanting. He lowered his arms to his side and opened his eyes.

Onu-Vey took a deep breath and reached into the pouch again. This time, he came out with the bloody cloth that he had taken from the Wabanga's arm. He delicately peeled away the four corners as he held the folded cloth in the palm of his hand. Inside was the wooden figure he had been carving. The figure was complete now. It was a voodoo doll of the Wabanga, complete with the hair of the Wabanga attached to the head of the doll.

Onu-Vey replaced the bloody cloth in his pouch. Then, with both hands, he ceremoniously raised the voodoo doll over his head. With his thumbs placed in the center of the doll's back, Onu-Vey spat out one more unintelligible word. Then, with a loud snap, he broke the doll in two. He lowered his arms and tossed the broken doll to the ground.

Ironically, the Aukmondi talking drums stopped when the broken halves of the voodoo doll hit the ground. Onu-Vey looked down at the pieces. He wished that he had destroyed the doll earlier. Abul-Tess would still be alive. Onu-Vey stood still for a moment. He put his regret into perspective. He sighed as he recovered from what he had just done. Onu-Vey left the semi-secluded area and rejoined the rest of the people. He came to stand in front of Abul-Gwan again. "Mfalme, for what it is worth … the Wabanga is dead."

Everyone stood speechless after seeing the houngan's ritual and hearing his report. The Royal Warrior Npatuzi rose above the stunning moment. Feeling that everyone's safety was his responsibility, he was the most skeptical. He turned to Kon-Shambique. "Great Creation, I must insist that we get everyone down into the valley as soon as possible. Until my warriors tell me otherwise, the Wabanga is still at large."

Onu-Vey overheard Npatuzi's suggestion and comment and took offense. He looked at the Aukmondi Royal Warrior and repeated tersely, "The Wabanga … is dead."

This time, Npatuzi and the houngan locked eye contact. Another battle of will followed, with the decisive moment decided by who would blink first. Time stood still. At that moment, a Green Warrior came running from the surrounding area. He stopped next to Npatuzi as if to get his attention.

Npatuzi responded to the Green Warrior without looking away from the houngan. "Yes, Kodwana?"

"We found the Wabanga, Great Creation. He is dead."

Npatuzi blinked. He glanced at the warrior who delivered the news. "Are you sure?"

"Yes, Great Creation. He tried to elude us by climbing a tree. In his weakened condition, he fell. He fell across a log. He broke his back."

Npatuzi turned back to face the houngan. When he did, he saw the houngan had walked away.

— 12 —

DAYS THAT HAVE ENDED A LOT WORSE

Meanwhile, back in the Kiwane village:

"Some days just do not end as they should," Lobarra said as she sat among the other farmers. She had rejoined the gathering after Tutapona had fallen asleep. The infant slept snugly in a kanga – a baby sling on Lobarra's back. Conversation in the group had flowed until Lobarra felt compelled to express a nagging concern. "I must admit. I am glad this day is over."

Everyone in the group looked at Lobarra. Elder Zekke asked the question on everyone's mind. "What would make you say such a thing, Sacred Woman?"

Lobarra shrugged, embarrassed that she had expressed a negative and personal concern. All day long, she had battled Tutapona's periodic bouts of fretfulness. It had almost reached the point where she could not focus on her purpose for attending the farmers' *mkutano*.

In the beginning, Lobarra felt accepted as one of the farmers. But she was the most junior. This was her first time taking part in the farmers' *mkutano*. During the discussions over the past few days, Lobarra has tried very hard to contribute in any way she can. She tapped her heart, soul, and experiences to offer thoughtful insights and suggestions. Lobarra did her best to keep the discussions moving smoothly and productively. She was hoping that she had made a good impression. But after today, she wondered if she had put all her accomplishments at risk by bringing Tutapona to the *mkutano*.

"The Great Creation, Mfalme Ameh Jobabwe suggested that I leave Tutapona with him," Lobarra explained. "Did I make a mistake by bringing the Little Creation with me?"

Elder Zekke gave one of his crooked smiles. "You do not expect us to answer that. Do you?"

"Well, yes. This *mkutano* is important. Should I have taken Mfalme Jobabwe's advice?"

"Ameh Jobabwe is the Chinchigwe Mfalme. He is the infant's grandfather. I am sure he has some powerful influence on that decision. But you are Tutapona's mother. That carries notable weight too."

"What we hope to achieve here has no place for infants. If the truth is known, I think I am ruining everything for everybody."

"I do not see how. This *mkutano* is one of the best. And I will be honest with you. That may not be just my opinion." Elder Zekke looked around at some of the other faces. "Does anyone feel differently?"

Lobarra glanced at the faces around the campfire, too. She heard nothing but positive comments from several of the people who responded.

Lobarra smiled with relief. She felt better. "Thank you. And thank you for inviting me along. If I am ever invited to attend another *mkutano*, I am sure Tutapona will be older. I should have no objection to leaving him with his grandfather. But I still owe all of you an apology for the disruptions."

"Apology accepted, Sacred Woman," Elder Zekke said. "If you must know, you impressed us with your accomplishments long before we chose you to join our group. Tutapona's behavior will not change that."

"I am fortunate to have your understanding. I have it because… all of you know me." Lobarra thought for a moment. "I may not be so fortunate with Mfalme Menda of the Kiwane or Elder Sanba of the Rimoza. They suffered disruptions, too. Their opinions might be different. At the least, I owe them apologies too."

"Offer them your apologies if you wish, Sacred Woman. As for their opinions, I do not think they are much different from ours."

"Do you think so?"

"Well, we must wait and see." Elder Zekke rose to his feet. "Do you want my opinion about this day's end? I will say it has ended well. At my age, I have seen many days come to a terrible end. Compared to this day, some days have ended a lot worse. If there is any complaint about this day, it is the simple fact that we must end it early."

"Why, Great Creation?"

"Back home, our Daily Celebration of Life has already started. People are talking, laughing, singing, and dancing. The gaiety will last into the night. Unfortunately, our little gathering here has a few more restraints. We cannot celebrate into the night. The last day of the *mkutano* discussions will begin at sunrise tomorrow morning. I highly recommend that we attend. This means we have an early day tomorrow. We should all get some sleep."

13

JUST OUR NATURE

That assumed gaiety that Elder Zekke spoke about died soon after Kharaambi and Quazzi escorted Abul-Gwan to the north rim and returned to the Royal Kraal.

After that unproductive meeting between Ramuza and Abul-Gwan, the warriors Kharaambi and Quazzi escorted Abul-Gwan back up to his provisional camp. The two were aware of Abul-Gwan's disappointment. They could not help but notice his restrained behavior. The Mfalme said almost nothing during the entire climb to the north rim. Once there, Kharaambi and Quazzi respectfully saw to his comfort and immediate needs. They offered the Mfalme an open invitation to return to the valley. They asked him to send words down into the valley if there was anything else that he might need.

When the two warriors left Abul-Gwan's camp, they tried to put Abul-Gwan, his business, his current mission, and his disappointment behind them. But as they followed the meandering Pahoma pathway down the north slope, the topic of their conversation changed. They began to discuss Abul-Gwan, other merchants like him, and the merits of their business, which profited from Africa's vast resources without regard. Kharaambi and Quazzi had not given much thought to the topic until today. Neither of the two warriors had realized how strongly they felt.

At first, Quazzi tried to find comfort in the knowledge that Mfalme Abul-Gwan was finally leaving; that he was taking his destructive business elsewhere. Kharaambi, who seemed more sensitive to the issue, saw a broader perspective. She pointed out that such businesses affected everyone, everywhere. She clarified that such businesses' damaging impact would last for generations. When Kharaambi and

Quazzi reached the bottom of the slope, their indifference developed into strong feelings and heated opinions that others would hear about soon.

But once Kharaambi and Quazzi walked into the Royal Kraal, the magically festive atmosphere caused their heated opinions and feelings to subside. They began to enjoy the simple pleasures of walking across the celebration area. The groups of people, the talking, the singing, the dancing, and playing together overshadowed all their concerns. They forgot about Abul-Gwan and his business until they reached the royal dais.

Kharaambi and Quazzi were not the only ones expressing opinions about Abul-Gwan's visit and questionable business. As they approached the royal dais, they had to work through a small crowd. People sat and listened to Mfalme Ameh Jobabwe's perspective about Abul-Gwan's business. Twese Merende and Embabi Tende sat among several people who listened so attentively that Kharaambi and Quazzi had to get their attention verbally to move through the crowd.

Once at the dais, the two warriors found Ramuza, most of Ramuza's daughters, and the young prince Adaulah; all sitting in their usual places, listening to Ameh, and hanging on to his every word. Ameh was talking about a neighbor who once lived near him in the old Chinchigwe village.

"I thought my good neighbor was crazy at first," Ameh said. "We argued almost every day. You would not believe how we argued. He tried to convince me that people, wherever they lived, no matter what they did, destroyed the land and waters around them. He tried his best to sell me that crazy idea. According to him, it was just our nature. He gave examples of how the land became so abused that crops failed. The waters got so dirty that they became unsafe for most purposes. That Poor Creation felt people only take from the land. They take and they take! They take until nothing is left."

"Mfalme Abul-Gwan's business is a perfect example," Ramuza commented. "I am sure you know that Abul-Gwan's business covers most Central and East Africa. And he is not alone. There are others. Such business is popular, and it is constantly spreading. Your neighbor, Ameh, was not too far from the truth."

"Yes. Well, in those days, things were different. I did not agree with my neighbor. I understood what he was saying, but did not want to believe him. I assumed people had more common sense than that. I grew up as a farmer. I learned long ago to care for the land and the surrounding waters. Yes, my family and I took from the land and the water, but we never took more than we needed. And we always gave something back. That was all that I knew. In doing so, everybody and everything thrived."

"You sound like you have changed your opinion about your neighbor, Mfalme." Quazzi joined in the conversation. "Have you finally bought his crazy idea?"

"I suppose my neighbor was ahead of his time. He saw it coming and tried to warn us." Ameh nodded toward Ramuza. "The Mfalme made a wise decision when he rejected Mangoni's request. I guess he has a profitable business. But it is just not right. Mfalme Abul-Gwan is taking his people in the wrong direction. He says he does not deal in the slave trade. I do not care. That Creation bears watching. As resolute as he is about exploiting Africa's natural resources, he will eventually find a reason to trade a person or two. Heed my words. Abul-Gwan, as a person, I think, is a Decent Enough Creation. But his judgment," Ameh shrugged, "I do not know. I think he is misguided."

"Mfalme," Kharaambi addressed Ameh, "the Great Creation, Quazzi and I were discussing a similar topic. Mfalme Abul-Gwan is not 'misguided'. He is blatantly wrong. He has a business that is hurting all of us. But … his business is his business. What are we to do about it?"

Ameh shrugged again. "There may be nothing we can do, Sacred Woman."

At this point, all the gaiety of the evening abruptly ended—the distinct knocks of talking drums from the north rim filtered down into the Royal Kraal. People on or near the royal dais stopped talking. People in the celebration area stopped doing whatever they were doing. Everyone listened. All other sounds died away to silence as the talking drums continued.

The translation of the talking drums brought Mfalme Ncobba to his feet and a frown on his face. Almost in unison, he, Kharaambi, Quazzi, and everyone else who translated the irregular hollow knocks began to look back. They looked up toward the north rim, but the nearby trees on the north slope blocked their view. The people began to step down from the dais and walk out into the celebration area to gain a better vantage point.

Ameh had not been among the Aukmondi long enough to master translating the talking drums. He understood only fragments of the message. His brow knitted with confusion.

"What? A fire?" He asked. "What about a fire?"

Ameh used his walking staff to force himself to his feet. Because everyone else did so, Ameh also stepped down from the royal dais. He walked out into the celebration area. Still prompted by the behavior of others around him, he began looking toward the north rim.

Ameh and everyone who looked toward the north rim saw an unmistakable red glow across the whole horizon. It was most unnatural. The glow and Ameh's inability to fully understand the message forced him to turn to the Brown Warrior. "Quazzi, Great Creation, what is happening?"

"The clearing on the north rim," Quazzi clarified, "is burning out of control. And … the Wabanga… the Wabanga has escaped!"

Without a word, Ramuza turned and ran out across the celebration area. He knew the Sacred Women, Rwuva and Olabisi, were on the north rim. Suddenly, nothing else mattered. He needed to get to the north rim. The crowd of people respectfully parted as Ramuza rushed toward the exit of the Royal Kraal.

Kharaambi left almost as quickly. Before she broke into a strong run, she dutifully gave a series of orders to the Brown Warrior. "Quazzi, Great Creation, find the two most available armies. Send one up to the north rim to augment the sentinels. Use at least a regiment of the other army to keep everybody in the valley. I do not want anyone on the north rim without a reason to be there."

"Understood, Sacred Woman."

Kharaambi took advantage of the parted crowd that Ramuza had made. She easily ran across the celebration area, quickly disappearing beyond the cloud of dust raised by her feet.

The little prince Adaulah slowly started walking out across the celebration area without saying anything to anybody. With his head bowed as if to appear inconspicuous, he walked briskly and determined. Just as his walk became a run, he heard someone call his name.

"Adaulah!" It was his oldest sister, Omari. "Where do you think you are going?"

Adaulah stopped and turned to face Omari. At first, he said nothing, only pointed toward the north rim. When Omari shook her head negatively, Adaulah finally spoke: "But the Sacred Women Rwuva and Olabisi are up there."

"Yes, I know, Little Creation. All of us feel as you do. But you heard the Gray Warrior."

"But Sacred Woman…"

"Get back here, Little Creation."

"Omari, please," Adaulah begged.

Omari said nothing. She only waved Adaulah back.

"Adaulah," Ameh called out to the young prince. He also waved him closer. "Come. Why do the two of us not sit on the royal dais and prepare to answer questions? Soon, people will come to the Royal Kraal seeking answers. Let us keep them calm about … whatever is happening up there."

Adaulah's shoulders slumped as he surrendered to Ameh's suggestion. "Yes, Mfalme."

14

BY THE GRACE OF
THE SUPREME SPIRIT

The Pahoma Pathway was one of the main north-south pathways on the north slope. It stretched from the north rim to the bottom of the valley. From the rim, the pathway trailed past the beautiful Pahoma Garden, a 300-meter garden of wildflowers that filled the local area with a wealth of aromatic scents. The renowned garden was also where the pathway adopted its name.

One and a half kilometers south of the garden, the pathway came to the first of two major junctions. A small trail came out of the east and into the junction. The trail originally mimicked the serpentine turns of a stream that originated north of Nagorda Peak. When the stream turned southward, down the north slope, the trail turned southward, creating the junction at the more dominant Pahoma Pathway.

The Pahoma Pathway now mimicked the small stream. The Pahoma and the stream paralleled each other on the direct route down the slope for just over half a kilometer. The stream naturally continued southward, but the Pahoma Pathway veered westward. It opened to a large, dirt clearing, surrounded by trees. People of the valley knew this popular clearing as the Gongeri Junction.

The Gongeri Junction was a major intersection, the second of two junctions along the pathway. It connected all points on the north slope, north, south, east, and west. From the Gongeri Junction, another small pathway branched off to the south but doubled back and turned due east. It again met with the small stream on its southward journey down the slope. This smaller pathway crossed the stream, by way of a log-bridge, and continued eastward. As one of the major east-west passages on the north slope, it trailed past the Pogobi kraal and toward other points farther east, including Kon-Shambique's kraal on the south side of Nagorda Peak. It ended, six kilometers away, at Nagorda Peak's summit.

From the west side of the Gongeri Junction, the Pahoma Pathway resumed. It branched one more time. One branch continued westward. But the main pathway turned southward. This southernmost trail stretched to the bottom of the valley.

Ramuza came from the southernmost trail, already breathless. He sprinted toward the Gongeri Junction just in time to meet the line of people coming down the pathway from the north rim. He had climbed the north slope much faster than he should have. His chest pumped vigorously as he struggled to catch his breath. But catching his breath was the least of his concerns. He studied the approaching procession of people, looking for his mates, Rwuva and Olabisi.

The first person Ramuza met in the line was the Royal Warrior Npatuzi. Ramuza took one last gulp of air into his lungs before addressing the warrior. "Great Creation, where are the Sacred Women?"

"They are behind us, Mfalme. The Sacred Woman Rwuva received a minor injury on her arm, but she and the Sacred Woman Olabisi are both safe." Npatuzi swallowed hard before he continued. "Unfortunately, Mfalme, the Sacred Woman Abul-Tess, did not survive. I am sorry."

"What happened?"

"It was the Wabanga. He escaped. He managed to subdue and kill the Mangoni warrior who guarded the cage. The Wabanga was healthy enough to ... do as Wabanga do. He caused the fire on the north rim. As far as I know, it is still burning out of control. While most of the sentinels were fighting the fire, the Wabanga took the opportunity to continue his killing spree. Besides Abul-Tess, the Wabanga killed two Mangoni warriors and the Red Warrior Mbinga."

The information was painful. Ramuza instantly closed his eyes, forcing his mind to accept and confront the problem. "What about the Wabanga himself?"

"He is also dead, Mfalme."

Ramuza sighed with relief. At this point, he did not care how the Wabanga had died. He took comfort in knowing the Wabanga was dead, and the senseless killings would stop. "Was anyone else hurt?"

The Royal Warrior gestured toward the people pouring into the junction behind him. "The Green Warrior Zabiba was the most severely injured of the survivors."

Ramuza looked toward the small group behind Npatuzi. Two Green Warriors carried Zabiba on a makeshift litter. The Great Creation Kon-Shambique walked beside the litter, treating Zabiba as best he could.

"How is he?" Ramuza asked Kon-Shambique as he approached.

"He has lost a lot of blood, Mfalme. As you can see, he still carries part of his spear on his shoulder. If I can remove the spear without causing further damage and remain still for a few days, I think he has a good chance of recovery."

Just then, the semi-conscious Zabiba coughed. He sat up as if to roll off the litter. Kon-Shambique reached down for Zabiba's shoulders. He forced him back onto the litter and held him still. "Do not move, Great Creation. You will be alright."

Kon-Shambique faced Ramuza again. "Mfalme, I must get him to my kraal. Timing is important."

"Of course." Ramuza stepped back to allow the group to continue through the junction.

The next group coming into the Gongeri Junction consisted of Mangoni visitors. A single Mangoni warrior led the way, holding a torch in one hand, a scorched shield, and a broken spear in the other. The Vodun houngan and the Mangoni lead-warrior, Goh-Jumaane, followed. They supported Mfalme Abul-Gwan, who walked between them. Ramuza almost gasped when he saw Abul-Gwan. In bloodstained clothes, Abul-Gwan walked with his head hanging. He looked physically and spiritually defeated.

Ramuza stepped forward as the three approached. "Mfalme Abul-Gwan, Great Creation, I am so sorry."

Abul-Gwan did not acknowledge Ramuza's apology. He paused for an instant, never raising his head. With wide, reddened eyes, he stared blankly at the ground. He never spoke a word. Only the Vodun houngan glanced at Ramuza as he walked by, supporting Abul-Gwan. Ramuza showed respect by stepping aside and allowing them to pass.

Two more Mangoni warriors came next. They entered the junction, carrying another makeshift litter. On this litter was the body of the Sacred Woman Abul-Tess. She looked to be sleeping peacefully, lying on her back, her arms folded across her chest. Her bloodstained garments suggested the true horror of the situation and clashed with the Sacred Woman's serene beauty. Mfalme Ncobba closed his eyes again as he struggled to accept the reality of what he saw.

The last group entering the Gongeri Junction consisted of Rwuva, Olabisi, and Tongda. Olabisi and Tongda supported Rwuva as they walked three abreast. All three of them had been crying heavily. When Ramuza saw the three, he rushed up to give spiritual support and embraced all three of the women.

During that long, heartfelt embrace, the Gray Warrior Kharaambi ran from the western branch into the junction. She, too, labored to catch her breath. Like Ramuza, it did not matter. She composed herself and joined the embrace with her loved ones. Then, she and Ramuza focused on Rwuva. Rwuva's condition demanded their attention.

"Sacred Woman, are you alright?" Kharaambi asked.

"I am fine." Rwuva wiped the tears away from her face.

Ramuza touched the bandage that Tongda had put on Rwuva's arm. Rwuva put her hand on top of Ramuza's. "This … this is nothing."

"It should not have happened."

"By the grace of the Supreme Spirit, I am fortunate." Rwuva nodded ahead toward the body of Abul-Tess. "I am grateful they are not carrying me on that litter."

Ramuza embraced Rwuva again.

"You still need to rest, Sacred Woman," Tongda added. "You are free to return to your hut. But I recommend spending a day or two at the Favored Tribesman's kraal, where he can watch you and replace your bandages regularly."

"Thank you, Tongda. So be it."

After another round of embraces, Ramuza and Kharaambi stood back, allowing Rwuva, Olabisi, and Tongda to continue across the junction. Walking three abreast again, the women rejoined the line of people heading toward Nagorda Peak and Kon-Shambique's kraal.

The Brown Warrior Quazzi had finally made it up the north slope. While the Ncobbas comforted one another, Quazzi had worked his way past most of the people of the procession. He spoke to a few and gathered bits and pieces of what had happened.

"This is turning out to be a sad day in the Aukmondi Valley," Quazzi said to Ramuza and Kharaambi as he watched Tongda, Rwuva, and Olabisi move away. "We will need the Supreme Spirit's healing touch to get through this."

"No doubt." Ramuza agreed. He turned northward. "But now, we must do what we can for ourselves, starting with the north rim. Come. Let us extinguish the fire that is burning up there. We will need more warriors."

"Help is already on the way, Mfalme," Quazzi said. "I have called up the Kigire Army to augment the sentinels."

15

FIRES AND RUMORS

On the north rim, the remaining warriors of Npatuzi Dawa's Sentinel Army and the double-regimented Namla Kigire Warrior Army battled the raging grass fire. They worked to beat the flames down with their shields, cloaks, and green branches. Some of the warriors, working as relay teams, hauled baskets of dirt to various places to smother the flames. Other teams worked to rob the fire by destroying grass in the path of the flames, giving the fire nowhere to burn.

When the Kigire Army first arrived, it was a losing battle. The fire burned relentlessly. As everyone feared, the flames crept across the clearing and threatened the valley. The fire moved toward the sentry line itself. But the joint forces of Dawa and Kigire armies fought the fires with skill and persistence. The brave warriors soon pushed the fire back, putting out most of it.

The penultimate military tier of Ramuza, Kharaambi, and Quazzi fought the fire with the Dawa and Kigire armies. Although they were the Aukmondi's highest authorities, they risked their health, safety, and lives to defeat this raging fire.

The danger did not become clear until one of the burning trees fell. Ramuza's back was to the tree, and he did not see it falling. The tree fell on top of him, pinning Ramuza's leg beneath it, and flames leapt at him on all sides.

Kharaambi, Quazzi, and the Royal Warrior Namla Kigire saw the whole incident. They rushed over to rescue the Mfalme. Quazzi and Namla strained to lift the burning tree from Ramuza's leg. Namla received a first-degree burn on her arm. Quazzi got second-degree burns on the palms of his hands. Kharaambi called up strength she didn't know she had and pulled Ramuza free alone.

"You should not be here, Mfalme. " Namla bent over, catching her breath. It is too dangerous."

Ramuza brushed debris from his leg as he stood. "When danger threatens my valley, where should I be, Sacred Woman?"

"Not here, where you could get yourself severely injured … or even killed."

"You should be at the Favored Tribesman's hut," Kharaambi suggested. "The Royal Warrior is right. See about the Sacred Woman Rwuva. You should be at her side."

"Rwuva is sleeping."

"How do you know this?"

Ramuza pointed at a Red Warrior a few meters away. The young warrior was not one of Npatuzi's sentinels, nor did he belong to either regiment of Namla's army.

Kharaambi recognized the warrior as Gengu, one of Rwuva's aides and personal guards. Up here on the valley rim, he had volunteered to help carry a huge basket of dirt toward the fire line.

"I asked Gengu to bring me news about the condition of Rwuva and the others," Ramuza said. "The Red Warrior has already done so. He tells me that Rwuva is sleeping. The Sacred Woman, Olabisi, is there at her side. If I were there, I could only stand by, idle. You must agree, I can be of better use here."

"I suppose." Kharaambi looked at Quazzi and Namla. Namla finally stood erect after catching her breath. Quazzi was flexing his hands to suppress the pain of his burns. "What about the two of you? Both of you should visit the Favored Tribesman for treatment."

Quazzi dropped his hands to his side as if to dismiss his pain. "The Red Warrior Gengu also brings word. The Great Creation Kon-Shambique has his hands full, Sacred Woman. As we speak, he is working on the Green Warrior Zabiba."

"As for me," the Royal Warrior Namla waved her hand toward the clearing, "I have a fire to fight. My injuries are minor. As the

Great Creation Quazzi suggests, I, too, would be in the Favored Tribesman's way." After a quick nod toward Ramuza, Namla excused herself and returned to the fire line.

"What about you, Great Creation?" Kharaambi turned to Quazzi again. "You chose not to visit the Favored Tribesman, but your burns are more severe. You need treatment."

Quazzi looked at the reddened blisters on his hands. "For now, I will treat them myself. I will visit Kon-Shambique later, when he is not busy."

"Great Creation," Ramuza spoke, "your hands limit your ability to help here. May I suggest you help put out a fire on a different front?"

"What do you mean, Mfalme?"

"I have no doubt. Mfalme Ameh Jobabwe has been detained in the Royal Kraal, besieged by questions about what happened this evening. I am sure. He could use your help."

"So be it, Mfalme."

Kharaambi was still trying to secure Ramuza's safety. She turned to him. "Mfalme, please. You should go too."

"No, Sacred Woman. It is my original intent to help fight this fire."

"Can I suggest anything to get you to safety?"

"No. I believe the safety of this valley is my highest priority. I must do this, Kharaambi. When I leave here, I will go to Rwuva's side. Say no more to change my mind."

"It is no wonder the Great Creation Tanake calls you the ram. Your head is indeed as hard as the ram's horns."

In the Royal Kraal, the royal dais centered the other chaotic front that Ramuza mentioned. The royal dais was always a central source for information. People often found the details of most events in the valley at the royal dais. News of all the tragic incidents on the north rim proved the exception. As the incidents occurred, news spread rapidly throughout the valley. And like the child's game, when a child whispers a phrase into the ear of the next child, the phrase continues down the line of children. The phrase becomes distorted. When the phrase reaches the end of the line, the last child voices a phrase that is nothing like the original. News of the horrible incidents on the valley rim gave birth to rumors and strange stories that filtered down into the valley.

Ameh Jobabwe was the highest authority left in the Royal Kraal. To preserve calmness, Ameh struggled with untangling the half-truths and killing the wild rumors. Adaulah and three of Ramuza's oldest daughters, Omari, Yejide, and Kunto, sat around Ameh, providing him with moral support. Ameh also had several warriors from the Bendabe Regiment to help hold the crowd back and keep order. But the task of appeasing the crowd proved confusing and frustrating. Ameh did the best he could with his limited information.

When the Brown Warrior Quazzi finally entered the Royal Kraal, he found the front of the celebration area almost empty. Abandoned campfires and bonfires had burned down to smoldering embers. The people in the kraal had stopped socializing and crowded before the royal dais, seeking answers to their questions and trying to learn the details of fragmented stories.

Quazzi walked around the abandoned fires and across the celebration area with ease. Almost none of the people in the Royal Kraal saw him coming. The difficulty of getting through began at the rear of the curious crowd.

"Stand aside, please. Let me through!" Quazzi was polite but spoke with stern authority. He met strong resistance at first. He made his demands several times before the people finally recognized the Brown Warrior and respectfully gave way.

The crowd eventually parted wide enough to give Quazzi a clear passage up to the dais. But in the final stretch to the dais, people in the crowd overwhelmed Quazzi with question after question. Quazzi could barely believe some of them.

"Quazzi, Great Creation, is it true? Is it true that the Favored Tribesman untied the Wabanga and released him? Did the Wabanga kill all the Mangoni Warriors? Someone said the fire was burning down the north slope, into the valley. Is that true? Quazzi! Quazzi, someone said the Wabanga killed the Sacred Women, Rwuva, Olabisi, and Abul-Tess. Is it true? Did the Vodun houngan kill the Wabanga with magic? Is it true that Mfalme Abul-Gwan has gone insane with anger and revenge?"

Quazzi did not respond vocally to any of the questions. He stopped walking several times, stunned by a couple of them. He forced himself to ignore them and continue walking. The perplexed frown on his face showed his amazement at the people and some of the questions they yelled.

Quazzi greeted everyone on the royal dais, including a respectful nod toward Adaulah and the Sacred Women Omari, Yejide, and Kunto. He greeted Ameh by title. "Mfalme, where did such distorted notions come from?"

"You tell me." Ameh also frowned. He relaxed his look of exasperation when he nodded toward Adaulah, who sat at his side. "The Little Creation and I are getting a mighty heavy dose of what it is like to be a tribal Mfalme. It is not easy. Great Creation, we are glad you could join us."

"Mfalme Ncobba assumed this would happen." Quazzi looked back at the crowd again. "I did not realize it would be this bad."

"We have been trying our best to calm everyone. Unfortunately, we know little more than they do. It is almost impossible." Ameh replaced his moment of relief with a serious look of concern. He leaned closer to Quazzi. "So, what is the truth? What is going on up there?"

Quazzi stepped closer to the royal dais. He lowered his voice so only the people on the dais could hear his response. "To make a long story short, Mfalme, some of it is true. The Wabanga escaped. He caused the grass fire on the north rim. And in the short period he was free, the Wabanga managed to kill three of the Mangoni warriors, the Red Warrior Mbinga, and the Sacred Woman Abul-Tess."

"Oh, Great Sacred Spirit!" Ameh dropped his head as he adjusted to the horrible news. "This is bad. Some of the worst rumors are true."

"Yes, some of them."

"Mfalme," the Sacred Woman, Omari got Ameh's permission to speak before turning to Quazzi. The regal young woman spoke with fear knotted in her throat. Tears welled in her eyes, on the verge of running down her face. The question that she asked only paraphrased what she was thinking. "Someone said … the Wabanga … hurt our mother. Is that also true?"

"The Sacred Woman Rwuva is fine, Omari. The Green Warrior Zabiba and Rwuva both indeed received injuries. But please, relax. I understand that Rwuva is recovering. I understand that she was sleeping at Kon-Shambique's hut. The Sacred Woman Olabisi is with her. Olabisi suffered no physical harm. As for the Green Warrior Zabiba, the Favored Tribesman is still working on him. I do not know his condition yet."

"What about Mfalme Abul-Gwan?" Yejide asked. "That Poor Creation; to lose a mate so tragically. I could tell that he loved her. I feel so sorry for him. Can we do anything for him?"

Quazzi shook his head. "I do not believe so, Sacred Woman. I am told that Mfalme Abul-Gwan and all the Mangoni are secluded on Nagorda Peak. By choice, they want solitude, which is understandable."

"Great Creation," Ameh nodded toward the crowd before him. The people need to know the truth. You heard some of their questions. Their guesses and speculations have created misleading stories and rumors. With your help, I must stop them before they spread."

"I will do what I can, Mfalme."

Before facing the crowd, Ameh leaned closer to Quazzi and gave him one more taste of what he faced. "Rumor has it the Vodun houngan deliberately broke the figure he was carving in two, killing the Wabanga."

Quazzi shrugged. "The houngan performed some ritual. And yes, he broke the figure in half and tossed it to the ground. But the truth is the Wabanga fell across a log and broke his back."

Ameh looked at Quazzi with his characteristic frown. "Did I not just say the same thing in different words?"

"The houngan is a Powerful and Influential Creation, Mfalme. I cannot explain some of the things he can do."

"The crowd's curiosity is a direct result of his power and influence."

"Maybe so, Mfalme. But I agree with your earlier statement. Providing them with the truth should keep their distorted stories and rumors from spreading."

When Quazzi turned to face the crowd, the Sacred Woman Omari noticed Quazzi's hands. "Great Creation, your hands! You are hurt!"

Quazzi looked at his palms as if seeing them for the first time. Some of the reddened blisters had swollen and were turning white. "This is nothing, Sacred Woman. It can wait."

"Nonsense!" Omari reached for Quazzi's arm to better look at one of his hands. After a brief visual examination, she spoke to Adaulah. "Little Creation, there are bandages in a small basket against the far wall in Rwuva's hut. Please get them for me."

"Yes, Sacred Woman." Adaulah sprang to his feet. He ran off to do as asked.

"I assure you, Omari, this can wait." Quazzi tried again to postpone his treatment. "Both fires and rumors can cause serious damage if left uncontrolled. The sooner we douse them, the better."

"Allow the Sacred Woman to treat you." Ameh forced himself up with his walking staff. He walked toward the center of the royal dais. "Under the circumstances, out of respect for Mfalme Abul-Gwan and the Mangoni, the first thing I must do anyway is end this evening's Daily Celebration of Life."

16

NAGORDA PEAK

On the summit of Nagorda Peak, the Mangoni visitors spent most of the early part of the night setting up a new camp. It began when the Vodun houngan asked Kon-Shambique for the most secluded location in the Aukmondi Valley. Two places came to the Favorite Tribesman's mind. One was the valley depths, a sparsely covered, almost barren area located several kilometers deep in the eastern half of the valley. The other was Nagorda Peak. Nagorda's summit is one of the most beautiful places in the Aukmondi Valley. Although Nagorda Peak stands in the geographical heart of the valley, few of the Aukmondi people ever visited it, discouraged by the steep hillside climb.

The houngan considered the two alternatives. He chose the summit of Nagorda Peak for the new Mangoni camp without asking Abul-Gwan for approval. Since Abul-Tess died, Onu-Vey knew he had to assume leadership of the Mangoni visitors. He saw Mfalme Abul-Gwan falling deeper and deeper into depression. The Mfalme grew incapable of making any wise decisions.

Nagorda Peak's seclusion turned out perfect for Onu-Vey. He wasted no time getting up to camp. Onu-Vey led the four remaining Mangoni warriors to the perfect spot on the summit and told them where to build their campfire if they wanted one. He selected an isolated spot, beneath a cluster of acacia bushes, to store the bodies of the three Mangoni warriors killed by the Wabanga. In the Mangoni tradition, he covered their eyes with goatskin veils. He crossed their arms across their chests so their spirits would not wander away before receiving a proper burial.

Onu-Vey cordoned off a small area to corral the remaining pack animals in another out-of-the-way spot. After the disaster on the north rim, Aukmondi and Mangoni warriors managed to recapture only a quarter of the animals. Onu-Vey tethered the horse, ox, donkey, goats, and sheep to a single lanyard. He made a thorough assessment of his basket of birds. He learned that only four of the original eight Fan-tailed Ravens survived the fire. Onu-Vey left the four dead ravens in the basket with the live ones. He knew that fan-tailed ravens were a rare species of scavengers that would not eat their own. He knew the dead birds would still serve a purpose, if but only to keep the live ones agitated.

With great care, Onu-Vey selected a spot to place the body of Abul-Tess. He did not put her body beneath the acacia bushes with the bodies of the three slain warriors, nor did he cover her face with a veil of goatskin. Instead, he chose a spot under a large Marula tree, the only sizable tree on the summit. He arranged her body on her burial litter where the Marula tree could shade, protecting it from the African sun most of the time. For Abul-Gwan's convenience, Onu-Vey placed Abul-Tess's body where Abul-Gwan could view it. He also made Mfalme Abul-Gwan comfortable, where the Mfalme could rest his back against the Marula tree as he sat in constant vigil over Abul-Tess's body.

Just as Onu-Vey expected, by the time the new camp setup was complete, he saw Mfalme Abul-Gwan spiral so deep into depression that he refused to talk; he refused to eat; he refused to sleep. As the night wore on, Abul-Gwan sat unmoved, staring at Abul-Tess's body, lost beneath his crippling thoughts.

*****

About a kilometer down the hill, in the adjacent chamber of Kon-Shambique's hut, the Favored Tribesman and Tongda prepared to remove the spear sub from Zabiba's shoulder. Their first task, and one of the most difficult, was to calm the Green Warrior. Fully conscious, Zabiba squirmed almost continuously from the pain. Kon-Shambique and Tongda could do nothing for the Green Warrior until he stopped moving.

In the rear chamber of the hut, the Sacred Woman Rwuva rested on her back on a small cot. Her bandaged arm rested across her stomach. The Sacred Woman, Olabisi, sat at Rwuva's side to keep her company, but neither woman talked. They could hear Zabiba's agonizing moans from the adjacent chamber. Worry and concern dominated the moment. The two women sipped a strong, aromatic tea Kon-Shambique had provided to ease their tension.

In front of Kon-Shambique's hut, Olabisi's guard, Refuri, and Rwuva's guard, Gengu, sat around a campfire. They talked with four other warriors. They were Zabiba's four younger brothers and closest living relatives. Since Kon-Shambique had barred anyone from entering the adjacent chamber at this grave moment, Zabiba's brothers waited outside the hut for the result of the horrendous procedure. Refuri and Gengu did their best to help ease the warriors' apprehension with divergent conversations.

Just after midnight, Kon-Shambique and Tongda had quieted Zabiba. Removing the spear stub from Zabiba's shoulder went quickly and successfully. They left the Green Warrior sewn up, heavily bandaged, and asleep in an adjacent chamber.

Kon-Shambique and Tongda later entered the rear chamber to find Rwuva and Olabisi sleeping peacefully. They took a moment to tidy up the chamber. Their gentle steps about the chamber to reposition tapestry, clay pots, footstools, brooms, and other furnishings did not disturb the sleeping women. Even when Tongda removed Rwuva's drinking gourd from her fingers, Rwuva did not move. Tongda noticed that Rwuva's drinking gourd was empty. Olabisi's drinking gourd seemed barely touched.

Outside the hut, Kon-Shambique gave Zabiba's four brothers the answers to some of their questions and concerns. He approached their campfire with a gentle smile on his face. That smile alone assured the four brothers. Still, Kon-Shambique told them that Zabiba should make a full recovery. All the Green Warrior needed now was constant, undisturbed rest.

17

TOO MORALLY CRIPPLED

In the front chamber of Kon-Shambique's hut, the Sacred Woman Tongda woke with the golden light of the morning sun shining through the entranceway. Tongda had helped the Favored Tribesman for most of the night. It was late last night, or early morning, when she finally fell asleep with the exhausted Kon-Shambique at her side. As a ray of sunlight warmed her face, she rolled over. She discovered Kon-Shambique already up, dressed, and moving about the chamber. During one of those divine moments of love, she lay there momentarily, watching him stuff various herbs and medicines into one of his medical pouches.

Tongda sat up and rubbed the sleep from her eyes. "Good morning, Great Creation. You are up early."

"Yes, Sacred Woman. I did not sleep well last night."

"Are you concerned about the Green Warrior Zabiba?"

"No. Zabiba's recovery will come with the healing power of time." Kon-Shambique tied his medical pouch closed. "My greatest concern has turned to Mfalme Abul-Gwan for most of the night. I am worried about him. I am going up to Nagorda Peak to visit him."

"At this hour?"

"Yes. The Mfalme is hurting. He needs help. I can feel it. I must do what I can for him, as soon as possible."

"Do you need me with you?"

"No, Sacred Woman." Tongda's willingness to help always brought a smile to Kon-Shambique's face. "You have done enough. I appreciate your help last night. I could not have successfully helped the Green Warrior Zabiba if it were not for your help."

"It is one of the many reasons I am here, Great Creation."

"Rwuva and Olabisi are still sleeping in the rear chamber. Stay here with them." Kon-Shambique hung the strap of the medical pouch over his shoulder. "I suspect the Mangoni do not feel sociable right now. If my suspicion is correct, I will return shortly."

*****

Kon-Shambique endured the final steep kilometer stretch up to the summit of Nagorda Peak. The Favored Tribesman was one of the few who visited the summit. He did it often. Kon-Shambique knew what to expect physically. He knew how to pace himself during the strenuous climb. The climb never discouraged him. He found the spectacular views from the summit across the northern plains of the Serengeti to be an ideal setting to think and meditate. Such extraordinary views and the inspirations they gave birth to always made the climb to the summit worthwhile.

The pathway on which Kon-Shambique walked took one last turn to the left before ending a few meters short of the summit. That last few meters of the pathway trailed right through the heart of the new Mangoni camp. As Kon-Shambique rounded the turn, he could see Abul-Gwan up ahead, to the right of the pathway. In a forlorn stupor, Abul-Gwan sat slumped against the trunk of the Marula tree. The body of the Sacred Woman Abul-Tess lay on her back in front of him.

Kon-Shambique slowly entered the new camp. Only one Mangoni warrior stood guard on the pathway. Three other Mangoni warriors sat in a group off to the left. A few meters beyond the Marula tree and near the summit, Kon-Shambique could see the Vodun houngan, sitting alone and facing the awesome view across the Serengeti. As far as Kon-Shambique could tell, the houngan sat perfectly still, unaware of the Favored Tribesman's approach.

Kon-Shambique continued up the pathway. He focused his attention on the pathetic Mangoni Mfalme. He found it significant that Abul-Gwan sat with his back toward the Serengeti, his chin resting on his chest. The view across the Serengeti did not interest him. Although Abul-Gwan sat staring at the body of Abul-Tess, Kon-Shambique knew that all Abul-Gwan saw was the chaos in his head. Even from a distance, Kon-Shambique could see that Mfalme Abul-Gwan had changed. A heavy and painful loss masked the Mfalme's face.

With all his attention on Abul-Gwan, Kon-Shambique forgot about the Mangoni warrior standing guard on the pathway. As he continued up the pathway, the Mangoni warrior stepped suddenly before him. Kon-Shambique felt the shaft of the warrior's spear placed against his chest. He stopped walking. He expected resistance, but not like this.

"Please," Kon-Shambique said to the warrior. "I wish to speak with your Mfalme."

The Mangoni warrior said nothing. He held his spear in place.

Kon-Shambique frowned, confused by the warrior's unreasonable resistance. He considered ways to appeal to the warrior's understanding.

"Let the Aukmondi pass." The Vodun houngan's voice filtered down from the summit. Although Onu-Vey was still a few meters away and his back was toward the Favored Tribesman, the houngan was aware of Kon-Shambique's approach. When the Mangoni warrior withdrew his spear from across Kon-Shambique's chest, Onu-Vey finally stood up and turned to face the Aukmondi visitor. He studied the visitor briefly before walking down from the summit toward him. He made a compulsory glance at Abul-Gwan and the body of Abul-Tess as he walked past them.

Kon-Shambique stepped past the Mangoni warrior and moved toward the summit to meet the houngan halfway. The Mangoni guard followed him. Kon-Shambique ignored the warrior's protective precautions as he addressed the houngan. "Good morning, Great Creation. I hope you do not mind my unannounced visit. I came to see about your Mfalme. How is he?"

"My Mfalme," Onu-Vey paused. He looked back at Abul-Gwan again. He was searching for the most fitting description of what he wanted to say. "My Mfalme is not well. He is … grieving."

"His grief is my concern, Great Creation. May I speak with him?"

Onu-Vey took another step closer to Kon-Shambique and looked him in the eyes. "No. Abul-Gwan wants to have some time alone."

"I understand. But, if I can talk with him briefly, I think I may be able to help him."

"No, Aukmondi. You can do nothing for him. I have already given him all the help that he can manage. If he needs more later, I will give it to him."

Kon-Shambique looked past the houngan at Abul-Gwan. Abul-Gwan's wrinkled clothing suggested that Abul-Gwan had sat in the same position the whole night. The Mangoni Mfalme needed more than what Onu-Vey could ever give him.

"Please," Kon-Shambique pleaded with the houngan. "I will not be long."

Before Onu-Vey could respond, both he and Kon-Shambique heard Mfalme Abul-Gwan stir. Onu-Vey swiveled toward the unexpected sound. Kon-Shambique craned to look past the houngan again. They saw Abul-Gwan tugging at the blanket draping over his shoulders to fit more snugly.

"I do not want you here, Aukmondi," Abul-Gwan spoke for the first time since coming to Nagorda Peak. He raised his head and looked at Kon-Shambique. Even in the distance, his reddened, bloodshot eyes showed prominently. There was bitterness in his raspy voice. "Go away."

Onu-Vey seemed surprised by Abul-Gwan's effort to speak. "Mfalme?"

"I want no visitors, Onu-Vey." Abul-Gwan dropped his head and settled into his original position. He tugged at the blanket again to shield himself against the chill of the gentle morning wind. "Send him away."

"Mfalme …" Kon-Shambique stepped forward. The Mangoni guard jumped in front of Kon-Shambique. He blocked his advance by laying his spear across Kon-Shambique's chest again, with a slight shove.

Kon-Shambique stepped back. He leaned to the side to see past the Mangoni guard and the houngan. "Mfalme, please accept my condolences. Allow me to help."

"Abul-Tess is dead, Aukmondi. How can you help her?"

"Mfalme, it is you that I wish to help."

"I do not need your help." Abul-Gwan leaned forward and delicately brushed away a charred leaf that had fallen on Abul-Tess's face. "Onu-Vey has told you. You can do nothing here. Nothing. Why is that so hard to understand? Go Away! Just go away. Do not come back."

"Mfalme …"

Onu-Vey turned to Kon-Shambique and spoke with finality: "You will leave, Aukmondi. Mfalme Abul-Gwan has spoken."

It was as Kon-Shambique had expected. Before entering the new Mangoni provisional camp, he did not expect to reach the Mfalme. When the Mangoni guard stood his ground before him, Kon-Shambique yielded to circumstances. He craned his head again to see the Mfalme. He offered what he could. "I speak for Mfalme Ncobba and all the Aukmondi people. If you need anything, please ask."

Kon-Shambique got no response from Abul-Gwan. He turned away and started back down the pathway.

The Vodun houngan watched the Aukmondi medicine man descend the hillside. He watched until Kon-Shambique rounded the turn in the pathway and disappeared. At that moment, he heard Abul-Gwan call his name again. Onu-Vey swiveled around. Eager to help, he rushed back and kneeled in front of Abul-Gwan. "Yes, Mfalme?"

Abul-Gwan was staring at Abul-Tess's body. The bitterness that he felt behind her loss distorted his face. "Someone must pay for this."

Even though Onu-Vey kneeled before Abul-Gwan, he moved back as if to avoid the negative energy coming from his Mfalme. He sensed more bitter words to come.

"They are … a useless people. They are more useful … dead. I think … if my Abul-Tess cannot live, then I want them dead, Onu-Vey. I want them all dead."

Onu-Vey slowly stood. He stepped back as if more distance would give him a clearer perspective of his Mfalme's attitude. Onu-Vey understood the anger. He could not understand the bitterness. Onu-Vey looked at the body of Abul-Tess as he composed his thoughts. He kneeled again and looked into Abul-Gwan's eyes. "Mfalme, please. Do not express your grief like this."

"Abul-Tess is dead, Onu-Vey." Abul-Gwan stared blankly at the chaos in his head. He shrugged. It was a lifeless gesture, full of hopelessness and surrender. "I have nothing left – just grief, and sorrow, and all the pain that comes with it. Someone must pay."

"With death? And why the Aukmondi?"

"Before we came here, the Rimoza and the Kiwane told me what I was up against. They told me it would be difficult to convince the Aukmondi to support me. I listened to them. I thought I came prepared to face the Aukmondi. I did not expect the Aukmondi to be such a stubborn and uninspired people. After Mfalme Ncobba rejected my offer, I admit I was initially angry. After all that I had done, even after realizing the Aukmondi were just a waste of time, I prepared to cut my losses. I prepared to move on."

"You still can, Mfalme."

Abul-Gwan's blank stare finally refocused. He looked into Onu-Vey's eyes with confusion. He seemed surprised that Vodun houngan did not understand. "Move on? Move on to what? Do you not see? I have done more than waste my time, Onu-Vey. I have lost my Abul-Tess. I cannot walk away from this loss."

"And you think that death to the Aukmondi will compensate?"

"No. Nothing can compensate. At least, I can hold the Aukmondi accountable." Abul-Gwan looked down at his hands, thinking. In his chaotic mind, he saw the Aukmondi as the most proper place to direct his anger. "In their ignorance, they do not see what we could have had. They hold no hope for better things. They do not dream, as we dream. These people sit idly on their wealth, too morally crippled to use it to their advantage. Now … now, because of their simple complacency and rigid inability to change, we have lost it all. They are uninspired. No one can work with uninspired people. I think … they are better off dead."

"Mfalme, you offered the Aukmondi a hope for better things. But you cannot force your hopes and dreams on them."

"Do you see flaws in my hopes and dreams?"

"No, Mfalme"

"Then what is it?"

"Your hopes and dreams belong to you, Mfalme."

"Well … it is not fair." Abul-Gwan looked over at Abul-Tess's body. "It was Abul-Tess that gave my hopes and dreams value. I made her happy. All I did and did not do was because I always dreamed of a day to make her happy. I knew the day would come. So, I waited for her. With the patience of all the godly spirits, I waited. Even throughout her union with Kosi-Jawma, I waited, loving her from a distance. Then, when I could finally achieve the dream of making her happy, the Loa of Death took her away from me. She would still sit beside me if it were not for stubborn, ignorant people. I must lay the blame somewhere. I blame the Aukmondi."

"The Aukmondi have done nothing, Mfalme. The Wabanga killed her. The Aukmondi tried twice to convince you to take the Wabanga into the wilderness and release him."

"So, what are you saying, Onu-Vey? Is all of this … my fault?"

"You must answer that question yourself, Mfalme. Is it grief that you feel? Or is it guilt?"

Abul-Gwan sat back. A fresh tear rolled down his face. "Call it what you wish. A huge, ugly black hole grows in the pit of my stomach. I need to fill it with something. I want amends. I want the Aukmondi dead."

"Mfalme," Onu-Vey sighed, "time is a great healer. Please allow some time to pass. Give yourself time to grieve before asking for something you will regret."

"Since I became Mfalme, you have advised and served me well. Do not stop now. I said I want them dead."

"Please, Mfalme. Please do not ask me to do this. I beg you."

"I want them dead, Onu-Vey."

Onu-Vey took another step back. For a moment, he stared down at Abul-Gwan. He tried to wrap his mind around Abul-Gwan's demand. Without a word, he turned away and slowly walked back toward the summit where he had been sitting. When he reached the summit, he did not sit. Instead, he stared out across the Serengeti. He stood thinking for several long moments. The task before him would be one of the most devastating of his entire lifetime. He preferred not to do it. But his Mfalme had spoken. He had no choice.

Onu-Vey sighed heavily. For the dedicated houngan, it was his last sign of reluctance. Anticipating some of his ugliest, darkest magic, he reached up and briefly touched the black crystal hanging around his neck. Then he turned and left the summit again. Still without a word, he walked past Abul-Gwan. He walked past the guard on the pathway. He walked out of the provisional camp. The Vodun houngan left the Mangoni warriors bewildered as he rounded the turn in the pathway and disappeared down the Nagorda hillside.

18

BEWARE OF THOSE WHO GRIEVE

About that same time, just after the morning sun broke free from the horizon, the Sacred Woman Tongda stood out in front of Kon-Shambique's hut. She stirred a small cauldron of beans, corn, and rice. Tongda was preparing breakfast for Rwuva, Olabisi, and the two warriors who guarded and aided the royal mates. As the soup simmered, she added measures of various herbs and spices. She tossed some ground black cumin seeds into the cauldron when she noticed Kon-Shambique returning to the kraal.

"Great Creation, you are back already?"

"As expected, my visit with the Mangoni was not fruitful."

"So, how is Mfalme Abul-Gwan?"

The expression on Kon-Shambique's face said everything. He slipped his medicine pouch from his shoulder and removed some of the items. "Not good. He needs serious spiritual support. I could not talk with him as I wished. He and the houngan told me to leave."

"Well, you tried, Great Creation. An unsuccessful attempt does not always fail. This is one of the many lessons you have taught the Aukmondi people. You have taught us to do our best. You have taught us to help if we can. If we cannot help; if we have done all we can, let it go. Stand back and just let it happen. You called it our willingness to accept the grand design when we cannot understand what is happening."

"Yes. It is blind faith in the Supreme Spirit. All of this is in Her hands."

At that moment, the Sacred Woman Olabisi poked her head out of Kon-Shambique's hut. She took a deep breath. "What is that cooking? It smells good!"

"It is breakfast, Sacred Woman." Tongda stirred the cauldron again. "I am surprised that you can smell it with the heavy odor of burnt grass in the air."

"Hunger has given my sense of smell a higher priority, Tongda."

"Did you sleep well, Sacred Woman?" Kon-Shambique asked Olabisi.

"I slept, but restlessly. After all that has happened, and not being in the comfort of my hut, I am surprised that I slept at all."

"Tongda and I noticed you did not finish drinking the tea I gave you last night. Had you finished the tea, you would have slept like a baby."

Olabisi came from the hut and stretched. "Is that why Rwuva is still sleeping? I do not think she turned over once the whole night."

"Yes. The tea had a purpose. The two of you needed to relax."

"Another of your grandmother's recipes?"

"Yes. I made it for the Green Warrior Zabiba to put him to sleep. While it was brewing, I realized it would not hurt to give you and Rwuva a little taste."

"A little taste? Rwuva drank only one gourd full and immediately fell asleep. I can only imagine what you gave Zabiba."

"Only what he needed."

"So, how is the Green Warrior doing?"

"He is doing fine. The procedure went well. When we finally pulled the spear stub from Zabiba's shoulder, he knew nothing about it."

"Good." Without asking, Olabisi moved over to stir Tongda's cauldron of soup while Tongda helped to put away some of the items in Kon-Shambique's medical pouch. "Forgive me for eavesdropping, but did I overhear you went to the Mangoni camp to visit Mfalme Abul-Gwan? How is he doing?"

"Now there is a different story. The Poor Creation has lost his reason for living. I am concerned for him. I am afraid he may not be the same Creation you met yesterday."

"After his loss, it is no wonder. Do you think he will recover?"

"It is hard to say."

Olabisi made the final stirs in Tongda's cauldron and decided the soup was done. She wrapped a cloth around the hot handle and removed the cauldron from the flames so the soup would stop cooking. As she was doing so, she glanced toward the kraal entranceway. In the distance, she saw Ramuza and Kharaambi walking up the pathway.

"Tongda, Sacred Woman, I hope you made enough of this."

Tongda and Kon-Shambique turned to see what had prompted Olabisi to make such a statement. When they saw Ramuza and Kharaambi approaching, they joined Olabisi and walked toward the kraal entrance to greet the Mfalme and the Gray Warrior.

With words unnecessary, Olabisi embraced her mate and co-mate. Kon-Shambique spoke for everyone and verbally welcomed them.

"Good morning, Mfalme. And good morning to you, Sacred Woman." Kon-Shambique looked at the two, up and down. Both of them looked disheveled. Burnt grass littered their clothing and hair. Blotches of soot and ash covered their faces. "You two look like you have fought a great battle."

"We have, Great Creation." Ramuza tried to wipe soot from his face. He only streaked more soot across his cheek.

Olabisi, so pleased to be in the company of her mate and co-mate, had barely noticed. She finally studied the two from head to toe. She sniffed at Ramuza's chest. "Yes, and you stink like an old kiln. Before you return to the Royal Kraal, please go by the lake. Take a good, long bath."

"We intend to, Sacred Woman. It is our next stop. We had to come here first when we left the north rim."

"Is the fire out?" Tongda wanted to know. "We heard the upper half of the north slope was burning."

"Where did you hear that?" Kharaambi found the news surprising. "The fire burned the clearing, but no more. It breached the sentry line, but the Dawa and Kigire armies pushed it back. The slope remained untouched."

"Everything is under control, Sacred Woman." Ramuza finally answered Tongda's original question. "I believe the armies will put it out shortly."

"Compared to the stories we have heard, that is a welcome relief." Kon-Shambique finished welcoming the guest into the kraal with a gesture. "We were just preparing to eat a morning meal. Will you join us?"

"It smells inviting," Kharaambi said as she looked at the cauldron. She could see it was not enough. "But no, thank you, Great Creation. We only dropped by to check on Rwuva and Zabiba. How are they doing?"

"They are sleeping," Olabisi answered instead. "Kon-Shambique knocked both of them out good with one of his medicinal teas."

"Both of them needed the rest," Kon-Shambique added. "The Sacred Woman Rwuva will be up and about as soon as she wakes up. The Green Warrior will need several more days of complete rest. He will lose the use of his arm for some time longer. Both of them are fine."

"Then, we will not disturb them. Let them continue to rest." Ramuza brushed a straw from his face. "How about Mfalme Abul-Gwan?"

"He and the rest of the Mangoni have set up camp on Nagorda's summit, Mfalme." Kon-Shambique filled Ramuza and Kharaambi in on everything that had happened since the Mangoni came down from the north rim. He finished with the recent assessment of Abul-Gwan's condition and the unsuccessful attempt to visit him this morning. "I tried to help. But I could do nothing for him. On your behalf, Mfalme, I left an open offer to help."

"Thank you, Great Creation. What about the bodies of the Mangoni warriors and the Sacred Woman Abul-Tess? Do you know when the Mangoni will release their spirits and surrender the bodies to the elements? Will we need to provide help to perform a proper burial?"

"I did not get that far, Mfalme. The Mangoni intention is unknown. I can only assume Mfalme Abul-Gwan and the houngan will take care of that in due time."

The Red Warrior Gengu, Rwuva's guards and aides, approached the group. "Mfalme," he interrupted to get Ramuza's attention. He pointed toward the kraal's entranceway.

Everyone turned to look in the direction Gengu pointed. They saw the Mangoni Vodun houngan standing on the pathway just beyond the entrance. He stared at the Aukmondi.

Kharaambi brushed dirt and straws from her forearms as she walked toward the kraal entrance. Her strong, confident strides took her out of the kraal and directly up to the houngan. She looked up into his face.

"Great Creation, is there something you need? Can we help you with something?"

"I must speak with your Mfalme."

Kharaambi quickly assessed the houngan and saw no reason to refuse him. "Come," she said as she turned and led the way back into the kraal.

Ramuza walked toward the two. Out of curiosity, Kon-Shambique shadowed him. They met Kharaambi and the houngan just inside the entranceway.

"He wishes to speak with you, Mfalme," Kharaambi said and stepped aside.

Ramuza assessed the Vodun houngan himself. After hearing about Mfalme Abul-Gwan's sad status, he hoped the houngan would ask for help. "Yes, Great Creation?"

The houngan said nothing at first. He looked at Ramuza in the eyes. But unlike the usual unsympathetic stare he had given in the past, there was a hint of concern on his face.

"I have come out of respect for you, Mfalme Ncobba. Mfalme Abul-Gwan does not know that I am here. I came to warn you."

"Warn me? Of what?"

"Beware of those who grieve, Mfalme. For better or for worse, there is powerful energy in their pain. You and your people must prepare yourselves."

"Great Creation, I am sorry. You must explain. What are you saying? What must we prepare ourselves for?"

The Vodun houngan said nothing else. He turned and walked away. He walked out of the kraal, never looking back. With his strong, confident pace, he took the pathway that led back up the hillside toward Nagorda Peak.

19

YOU SHOULD HAVE KNOWN BETTER

In the Kiwane Village:

Lobarra rushed along the bank around the edge of the village lake. She held the hem of her wrap up in order not to trip and fall. She could see, in the open field on the other side of the lake, the last session of the farmer's *mkutano* already underway. Last night, the Great Creation Elder Zekke had asked everyone to attend. Lobarra was already late. She increased her pace, determined not to miss the rest of the session.

Lobarra looked across the lake again. A huge crowd had already gathered, which was a complete surprise. Lobarra realized that she was among the few who had not arrived yet. She lifted the hem part of her wrap and changed her pace to a gentle run.

This last farmer's *mkutano* session was an open and popular event. It drew more spectators than ever. Almost every member from each group of farmers of the Kiwane, Rimoza, and Aukmondi tribes was present. All the Kiwane villagers, many of whom were not farmers, attended. The people sat in a huge circle, listening to one speaker after the next. Each speaker gave their final thoughts and comments about the *mkutano*. All included a multitude of praises.

Lobarra finished her run around to the other side of the lake. She slowed to a brisk walk as she approached the circle of people. She dropped the hem of her wrap and visually searched the circle, looking for the section where Elder Zekke and the rest of the Aukmondi farmers sat. Lobarra sighed with frustration when she saw no one from her group. She had to walk almost to the circle's other side before finally finding them. Someone called her name. It was Elder Zekke who saw Lobarra first and called out to her.

Elder Zekke and the rest of the Aukmondi sat on the ground, near the inner edge of the circle of people. When Elder Zekke called her name, Lobarra had to wade through the crowd, around other seated spectators, to reach the Aukmondi group. She felt extra fortunate. Despite being so late for the session, Lobarra was lucky enough to have almost a front-row seat. Elder Zekke had reserved an area for her next to him.

"I was beginning to think that you were not coming," Zekke said as Lobarra made herself comfortable.

"I almost did not. Forgive me for being late. It was Tutapona again. He seemed agitated this morning. I did not think I would ever settle him down."

"Is he still throwing his tantrums?"

"No, not since last night. He is less fussy than he has been. But he is still restless."

Elder Zekke had already noticed Lobarra was not wearing the kanga as usual. "So, where is the Little Creation, anyway?"

"I left him with the Red Warrior Rotho. Rotho realized how badly I wanted to attend this session. He offered to put up with Tutapona's restlessness for me. Tutapona did not object to Rotho's company, so I allowed Rotho to keep him."

"That is thoughtful of the Red Warrior to offer."

"Rotho has been wonderful. I do not know what I would have done without him." Lobarra looked around at the huge circle of people. Her eyes finally came to rest on the current speaker in the center of the circle. "So, what have I missed?"

"Not that much. Most of the morning, the speeches have been the same. All the speakers gave endless praise about the benefits of the *mkutano*. You came at a good time. There are only three speakers to go."

As did most of the crowd, Lobarra already knew who those three speakers were. These last three speakers were whom everyone was waiting to hear: Elder Sanba of the Rimoza, the Great Creation Elder

Zekke of the Aukmondi, and the *mkutano* host, Mfalme Menda of the Kiwane.

It was midmorning when Elder Sanba of the Rimoza walked out to the circle's center. He wore a bright blue, embroidered tunic with matching trousers, cap, and sandals. Elder Sanba waved back at the crowd with both hands amid cheers, applause, and noisy ovations. He slowly turned in a circle several times while waiting for a comfortable silence and addressing the crowd.

When Elder Sanba spoke, he touched on several things. He focused on the overwhelming, cooperative support that everyone had given. He felt most impressed by everyone's willingness to tackle some of the most difficult farming challenges. Elder Sanba, filled with emotion, stressed that he never wanted to see such a positive and productive attitude end. He felt that if we kept this up in time, Africa would soon have ample food for everyone.

Elder Sanba ended his comments by graciously thanking Mfalme Menda for hosting the *mkutano*. Cheers, applause, and noisy ovations erupted all around again as Elder Sanba left the center of the circle.

It was now the Great Creation Elder Zekke's turn to speak. With bowed legs, Elder Zekke had a notable rock to his walk. Since his arrival in the Kiwane Village, Zekke's walk had become a popular attraction. Everyone liked it. The cheers, applause, and ovations seemed louder as Elder Zekke, dressed in some of his finest garments, rocked his way out to the circle's center.

The Great Creation Zekke touched on several things, too, but focused on the quality of information exchanged. He had to admit that he had attended many farmers' *mkutanos* in his lifetime. But never had he learned so much valuable information in such a short time. The information flowed freely and endlessly. The experience left Elder Zekke with no doubt that the future of food production is promising.

Elder Zekke also thanked Mfalme Menda and all the Kiwane people for their gracious hospitality. When Elder Zekke finished, cheers, applause, and ovations erupted. He waved to the people as he rocked back to his seat.

"I did not realize that we had done so much," Lobarra said to Zekke as she moved over to allow him to resettle on the mat beside her. She had to raise her voice to talk over the noise of the constant cheers and applause.

Elder Zekke chuckled at Lobarra. "After that comment you made last night, Sacred Woman, I am surprised you would say such a thing?"

"I must apologize for that comment. Yesterday was a difficult day. Nothing went as planned."

"I suppose you had your reasons, but you should have known better."

"What do you mean, Great Creation?"

The crowd's noise was too loud for Elder Zekke to answer as he wished. Instead, he gestured toward the center of the circle of people. The next speaker walked up and prepared to speak. "Let us hear what the Great Creation, Mfalme Menda, has to say. Then, if necessary, I will explain."

Amid the cheers and applause, Modoffa Menda, the Kiwane Mfalme, waved to the people. Unlike Elder Sanba or Elder Zekke, Mfalme Menda had dressed casually. He wore no adornments typical of a tribal leader. The only implication that he was the Kiwane leader was the small royal scepter he carried.

The scepter was a half-meter staff made of polished Mpingo ebony. Intricate cultural drawings and other engravings covered the entire staff. A huge, potbellied bullfrog was most prominently carved at the top of the scepter. The potbellied bullfrog held such intricate detail that it looked almost alive. With webbed feet and long, well-proportioned legs wrapped around the scepter, the bullfrog seemed to cling to the top of the scepter.

Mfalme Menda bobbed the potbellied-frog end of the scepter at the crowd and gestured with his other hand to silence the cheers. He had to wait a short while until the noise reached a level where he could finally speak.

"Elder Sanba of the Rimoza, Elder Zekke of the Aukmondi, and all the speakers before me have said it all," Menda began. "They have said it well. I will not waste your time repeating what you have heard all morning. But what I will do … is this. I will wrap this wonderful event up by explaining why we agree it has been so successful."

A wave of cheers and applause interrupted. Mfalme Menda had to wait until the crowd quieted down again. He had a very noticeable habit of tapping the potbellied-frog end of his scepter in the palm of his hand. He walked in a wide circle, along the periphery of people, tapping the frog in the palm of his hand with each step. "I will get right to the point. I would say organization is one characteristic that made this *mkutano* so successful. From day one, the planning and arrangement of the discussion sessions allowed new and valuable knowledge to flow freely and productively to where it was needed. I have seen nothing like it. I have to say, someone knew what they were doing. Someone drew on their knowledge and experience as a farmer and showed remarkable organizational ability. That is what made all the difference."

Mfalme Menda continued his walk, closer to the sidelines, tapping the scepter with each step. "I have already discussed this with Elder Sanba and with Elder Zekke. We agree, which brings us to this moment. The person who made all the difference; the person I speak of …" he stopped directly in front of Lobarra and pointed at her with the scepter, "is Lobarra Gendeyani of the Chinchigwe clan of the Aukmondi tribe."

Lobarra's mouth dropped open as the cheers erupted again. The sudden, unexpected attention directed at her was both surprising and embarrassing. Lobarra covered her face with her hands. Lobarra finally dropped her hands away from her face when the cheers continued. There was a wide smile on her face and tears of joy in her eyes.

Elder Zekke leaned closer to her. "Sacred Woman, after all you have done, I say again, you should have known this was coming."

"I had no idea, Great Creation. I was so concerned about Tutapona's behavior that I did not realize what I was doing. I felt so distracted."

"Well, we may have a solution for that, too." Elder Zekke nodded toward Mfalme Menda. "Listen."

Mfalme Menda walked back toward the center of the circle. He waved his hand and the scepter again to quiet the crowd. He tapped the potbellied frog in his hand several times before speaking again. "In honor of Lobarra Gendeyani's contribution, I am pleased to announce the next host of the farmer's *mkutano* - the Aukmondi."

Lobarra turned to Elder Zekke. "Great Creation, you knew all along. Did you not?"

"Yes. I knew. I have known since midday yesterday. I am proud of you, Sacred Woman. We are all proud of you. And this is only the beginning. Wait until this news reaches the valley."

20

ALL THAT LIFE IS NOT

The Vodun houngan, Onu-Vey, did not want to summon the Loa of Death. He did not think it was necessary. If the Aukmondi were to blame for all that had happened, Onu-Vey knew of other ways to achieve justice with less severity. Inspired or not, these people did not deserve the curse of death placed on them. During this curse, Onu-Vey knew the Loa of Death, like an endemic disease or famine, could destroy the Aukmondi people, wherever they may be.

Onu-Vey worked on two long and hollow logs that the Mangoni warriors had secured for him on the summit of Nagorda Peak. He called the work the toning process. Onu-Vey hit the sides of the logs with a sturdy limb. He listened for the resonating sound. If the sound was incorrect, the houngan dropped one or two fist-sized stones into one of the logs. Then he would strike each log again with the limb. He wanted the resonating sounds at the right level and off-pitch from each other. He tested, adjusted, and retested his work several times. Several times, he emptied the stones from the logs and repeated the process until he got it right.

Onu-Vey thought about Abul-Gwan as he worked. The two had started as natural 'clan against clan' enemies. Onu-Vey's inherited position as Tribal Houngan, High Priest of the Mangoni people, had forced him to work with Abul-Gwan. After several harvests, Onu-Vey had grown to respect Abul-Gwan, not just as his Mflame, but as a friend. He felt that, of all of Abul-Gwan's claims, he deserved friendship the most. But loyalty to his Mfalme carried greater weight than friendship. Almost any appeal made by Abul-Gwan, regardless of its purpose, Onu-Vey felt responsible for carrying it out.

On occasions, when Onu-Vey disagreed with Abul-Gwan's inclinations, Onu-Vey tried to reason with him or suggest a different course. It is what a friend would do. But once the Vodun houngan saw that his Mfalme had made up his mind, Onu-Vey offered no more advice or resistance. If it was within his power, he became an obedient servant.

Onu-Vey now had one of his Mfalme's irrevocable requests - summon the Loa of Death. Onu-Vey did not like it, but he yielded to his responsibility. His last reservations died after he gave Mfalme Ncobba fair warning to prepare the Aukmondi people for what was to come. Onu-Vey set aside all his reservations when he returned from visiting Mfalme Ncobba at the medicine man's kraal. He began his task.

To summon the Loa of Death was a simple but strenuous ritual. The preparations were lengthy. Fortunately for Onu-Vey, he did not have to lay the groundwork. Onu-Vey knew he already held a strong interest of the Aukmondi people. They found his powerful abilities captivating. And whether they wanted to admit it or not, they did not doubt his powers. The well-timed death of the Wabanga had convinced even the skeptics among them. As the details of Wabanga's death spread, so did Onu-Vey's influence. The Vodun houngan was confident the Aukmondi people were vulnerable to his magic. He was ready for the next step in his preparations.

Of the four remaining Mangoni warriors, Onu-Vey chose two of the strongest and most fit. He took his time and selected them with great care. These two warriors would embody the ritual's endurance. Onu-Vey called the two selected warriors his vessel warriors. The longer these vessel warriors lasted under the physical demands, the longer the Loa would walk among the Aukmondi. From the moment Onu-Vey selected these warriors, he treated them specially all morning.

With the resonating sounds of the logs perfected, Onu-Vey worked to position them. The ends of the logs had to project their ominous sounds out across the Aukmondi Valley. As Onu-Vey wrestled to move one of the heavy logs into place, one of his vessel warriors, Makoso-Kin, tried to help by grabbing one end.

"No!" Onu-Vey shouted. The houngan dropped his end of the log. He rushed toward the helpful warrior. Onu-Vey pushed him away. "No, Makoso-Kin! When I need you, I will call for you."

The sudden rejection startled the young warrior. Makoso-Kin stood speechless and confused. He walked away, but an annoying thought made him turn back to face the houngan. "Onu-Vey, you have chosen two of us, Metwe-Ngu and me, as your vessels. Yet, all morning long, you task Goh-Jumaane and Kum-Bufu to do all the work. Why?"

"They are my workers," Onu-Vey explained as he continued to work.

Makoso-Kin looked at the two warriors. Goh-Jumaane, the Mangoni lead-warrior, and Kum-Bufu, the oldest of the remaining Mangoni warriors, enjoyed a rest, although they sat under the midday sun. Makoso-Kin felt Onu-Vey had asked these warriors for more than their respective authority and age should have allowed. He tried to keep that opinion to himself. The outspoken young warrior's opinion came out anyway, in different words.

"If Metwe-Ngu and I are your vessels, why must we stand by, idle?"

The Vodun houngan did not respond to the young warrior. He finished positioning his logs. He ignored the warrior as he gathered one of his pouches and several small bowls.

The vessel warrior, Makoso-Kin, watched the houngan and waited patiently for an answer to his question. He watched as Onu-Vey poured various colored powders into the bowls. Fascinated, he watched Onu-Vey measure off a heaping pile of red powder in one bowl, and then a pile of yellow powder in another. When Onu-Vey began to pour a greenish powder in yet another bowl, Makoso-Kin gave up waiting for the houngan to respond. The young warrior turned and resumed his original intent to walk away.

"Makoso-Kin," Onu-Vey finally said, almost startling the young warrior. He continued his work while waiting for Makoso-Kin to turn and face him. "Your questions and willingness to busy yourself tell me you battle your fears. Tell me, Makoso-Kin. Are you afraid?"

The young warrior took a couple of steps closer to the houngan. "I have seen your magic. If I am chosen for something special, I have … some concerns. I am not afraid."

"You have seen my magic, and it frightens you to be a part of it." Onu-Vey set his bowls of colored powders aside. His face looked serious as he finally stood up and approached the young warrior. "I can use that fear. The energy in it is powerful. Let it fester, Makoso-Kin. The stronger the fear, the better. Your Mfalme needs you."

Makoso-Kin looked back over his shoulder at Abul-Gwan. He could see Abul-Gwan, still sitting next to Abul-Tess's body, slumped over, almost unmoved since last night. Makoso-Kin wondered if Abul-Gwan had slept that way.

"Will the Mfalme recover?"

"If the Mfalme recovers, it will be his choice."

"Can you do anything to help him?"

Makoso-Kin received no vocal response from the houngan. However, when he saw Onu-Vey's piercing look, he realized he should not have asked that question.

"I am a warrior in his service, Onu-Vey. I want to help too."

"Then go and be afraid. There is reason to fear the worst. When I call you for your chosen task, I want you compelled by fear."

Makoso-Kin stood erect to prove to the houngan and himself that he was a warrior who could manage any fear. He tried to imply in his posture that, maybe, Onu-Vey had made a mistake in choosing him. But then, he admitted to himself that he was afraid. Confused by what lay ahead, Makoso-Kin finally turned and walked away.

As the young warrior had said, Onu-Vey had tasked the two worker warriors with most of the preparatory footwork. Earlier this morning, Onu-Vey had called these warriors together. He sat with them for a while and meticulously explained what they would do and what he expected from them.

Since early morning, Onu-Vey had sent his worker warriors on a series of quests, one after another. The easiest of these quests was to secure the logs and limbs that Onu-Vey had just finished preparing.

The two logs lay in place. Several sturdy limbs lay next to them. These limbs would serve as clubs to strike the prepared logs. Six larger, thicker limbs also lay nearby. These larger limbs would serve as the framework for a sturdy, three-meter-tall, wooden pyramid-like structure when fitted together.

Gathering various grasses and leaves was the most difficult task that Onu-Vey had the worker warriors do. The grasses and leaves had to be indigenous to the local area. This task proved difficult because Onu-Vey needed an ample supply, enough of it in quality condition. The worker warriors had to deliver the grass and leaves to the houngan within minutes of harvesting. The complexities of the task kept the warriors running in a constant and tiring process.

When the worker warriors returned with a batch of harvested grasses and leaves, Onu-Vey examined each batch. Each time, Onu-Vey found it necessary to toss aside a few specimens. Several times, he tossed out the whole batch. This continued for most of the morning.

By midmorning, the Vodun houngan finally had a satisfactory supply of grasses and leaves. He piled the grasses and leaves into another special bowl he had prepared. And just when the worker warriors thought they had completed their exhausting tasks, the Vodun houngan gave each of them grinding stones. Onu-Vey told them to pulverize the grasses and leaves as finely as possible.

By midday, Onu-Vey and the worker warriors had completed all the preliminary preparations. Onu-Vey called all the warriors, the workers, and the vessels together. He did not explain why he had called them together. Instead, he demanded they stand and watch him for several minutes.

Onu-Vey searched the surrounding ground, looking for something. He did not explain to the warriors what he was looking for or ask for their help. He left the four warriors standing dumbfounded around him as he continued his search. When Onu-Vey found a particular spot on the ground, the houngan kneeled over it. Ever so gently, he reached and touched the spot. With lips moving, he began a soundless chant for several minutes.

Without taking his eyes off the spot, Onu-Vey finally withdrew his hand. He reached into one of the pouches hanging at his side. He pulled out a small metal spade. With both hands gripping the spade handle, Onu-Vey dug into the ground. The four Mangoni warriors continued to watch. Onu-Vey dug a small hole, about 15 centimeters wide and 30 centimeters deep. He piled the dirt extracted from the hole to one side. He worked with precision as if accounting for each granule of dirt. Satisfied with his dug hole, Onu-Vey did not lay the spade on the ground. He put it into his pouch.

Then Onu-Vey reached up and removed the black crystal that hung around his neck. The Mangoni worker warriors and vessel warriors looked at one another. As long as they could remember, the Vodun houngan had never removed the black crystal from around his neck. This simple act told them this ritual was unlike any the houngan had ever done. It had to be one of Onu-Vey's most powerful.

Onu-Vey took the black crystal into both his hands. He held it delicately. Slowly, he raised the crystal and touched it to his forehead. He chanted some unintelligible words and dropped the crystal into the hole in the ground. Still chanting, he pulled the spade from the pouch again and scoped every granule of the extracted dirt on top of it.

Onu-Vey packed the dirt over the crystal. He used more effort than was necessary. He spat out strings of unintelligible words each time he pressed down on the dirt. When finished, he stood up and stepped back.

"Onu-Vey," Makoso-Kin dared to speak. He had many questions. He wasn't sure what to ask the houngan first. His jumbled thoughts could only produce an obvious statement. "You just buried… your *azima*."

Onu-Vey said nothing at first. He had worn that crystal around his neck, day and night, for the past forty harvests. He stared at the buried crystal as if he had given up his most valued possession. Onu-Vey sighed before turning to the young warrior. "It *was* my *azima*, Makoso-Kin. It is my *azima* no more. When the sun falls below the horizon, it will become… all that life is not."

Onu-Vey's answer made no sense to the four warriors. They looked at one another, more confused than ever about what Onu-Vey was doing. They watched as Onu-Vey reached into his pouch again. This time, he came out with a handful of white powder.

Onu-Vey slowly streamed the powder from his fist. He trailed a huge arch on the ground. The Vodun houngan went into his pouch several times, bringing out more handfuls of the powder. The arch became a huge circle, six meters in diameter and centered by the buried black crystal. Onu-Vey made the circle large enough to encircle all of his collected and prepared items: the logs, limbs, the crushed grasses and leaves, the bowls of colored powders, and his pyramid-like support frame. When done, he finally faced the four warriors and pointed to the circle.

"This is death's *veve*," he said. "Do not enter this circle unless I ask you to do so. Understood?"

The warriors answered the houngan with nods and unsettled looks at one another. Makoso-Kin was bold enough to ask. "What will happen if we enter death's *veve* without your permission?"

"The Loa of Death will touch you, Makoso-Kin. Believe me. You do not want that to happen."

Each of the Mangoni warriors looked down at the circle of white powder and reassessed its significance. Three of the warriors took precautionary steps back. Only Makoso-Kin, confronting his fear, dared to stand his ground.

"Now, find some shade," said Onu-Vey. He pointed to the sky. "Get out of the sun. I want you to rest. We have two more tasks to complete before we fulfill Mfalme Abul-Gwan's request."

To find some shade, the warriors had to find another shade tree. Upon Nagorda Peak, trees stood scattered. Mfalme Abul-Gwan, with the body of Abul-Tess, rested under the Marula, the nearest and largest tree. Because of Abul-Gwan's unchanged depression, this setup would not change soon. The four Mangoni warriors had to walk a short distance down the hillside to find another tree large enough to give enough shade and begin their rest.

About 200 meters away, the four warriors were comfortable under their selected tree. From a distance, they could still see the Vodun houngan working with an uncommon zeal within the circular *veve*.

He was arranging and rearranging all of his collected and prepared items. When the warriors saw the houngan make a slow, sweeping look at all the surrounding items, they could sense his satisfaction with all his preparations.

The Vodun houngan then left the *veve* and walked toward the corral of pack animals. He approached the corner of the corral where the large basket of fan-tailed ravens sat. The frantic caws from the birds began at once and echoed down the hillside toward the fascinated warriors. *Argh! Argh! Argh!* The caws became louder as Onu-Vey dragged the basket from the corral back to a point just outside the *veve*.

"What is he doing now?" Makoso-Kin asked. From his comfortable position, Makoso-Kin sat up to improve his view.

Goh-Jumaane, the Mangoni lead-warrior, had known Onu-Vey longer than any of the other three warriors. He watched the houngan pry the basket lid open just enough to study the condition of the squawking birds. "Onu-Vey has always used a bird or two in his rituals. This is his strongest ritual ever. It would surprise me if he does not use every bird in that basket."

"Does anyone remember how many birds are in the basket?"

"Onu-Vey allows no one in that basket but himself. Only Onu-Vey knows for sure. I would guess only four or five, maybe. I know several birds died when the basket caught fire last night. I could smell the charred feathers and flesh after the houngan rescued the basket from the clearing and placed it next to me."

The four warriors watched as Onu-Vey tied one end of a meter-long cord to the base of his pyramid-like support frame. They saw him yank on the cord to ensure its security.

The houngan tied three more meter-long cords to the base. He tested each one with a firm yank. With this done, Onu-Vey finally pulled the basket of birds into the *veve*. He opened the basket lid again, just enough to reach among the squawking birds. Onu-Vey extracted one of the frightened and angry ravens. He ignored the bites and pecks as he struggled to subdue the flapping wings. He held the raven secure enough to tie one end of the cords to one of the raven's legs.

When Onu-Vey released the bird, it spread its wings and took flight. It flew to the limit of the cord, which snapped it from the air. The bird fell to the ground. It cawed and squawked as it pulled on the cord that held it prisoner. Feathers flew as the bird continued to struggle against the cord.

Onu-Vey pried the basket lid open again and extracted another bird. Like the first, he tied the end of another cord to its leg and released the bird. Now, two birds struggled against their respective cords. Each bird tried to fly away but fell to the ground each time.

Earlier, Goh-Jumaane had guessed the number of living ravens in the basket. When Onu-Vey tied the fourth and final bird to the base of the pyramid structure, Goh-Jumaane realized that his guess was almost right. He was completely right when he guessed that Onu-Vey would use every bird.

The warriors watched as Onu-Vey dumped the rest of the ravens, all dead, into a pile inside the veve. Onu-Vey kneeled over the pile. He gave a short, unintelligible chant, then sprinkled some of his prepared pulverized grasses, leaves, and herbs onto the birds. Satisfied with his work, he moved the carcass of each dead bird, one by one, within reach of the live bird.

"What is he doing?" Makoso-Kin asked. "Does he expect the live birds to scavenge the dead ones?"

"No," Goh-Jumaane spoke with confidence. Ravens and crows are among the strangest of scavengers. They will eat anything, but they will not eat their own. I suspect Onu-Vey put the dead birds there to cause distress among the living birds. He wants those live birds to remain agitated."

Watching the Vodun houngan work has always been fascinating. The warriors' fascination reached its highest peaks when they saw Onu-Vey walk out of the *veve* and approach the corral of pack animals again. This time, the houngan's interest seemed focused on all the animals. After yesterday's disastrous incident with the Wabanga, various warriors captured only the horse, an ox, a donkey, goats, and sheep. The rest of the pack animals had scattered into the wilderness on the north rim and were now lost to the lions, leopards, and hyenas.

Onu-Vey walked among the animals. Again, he searched for something. For several minutes, he examined the animals. He stroked, poked, and assessed the animals like a merchant preparing to buy one. All four Mangoni warriors sat up when Onu-Vey finally selected one of the goats and walked it back to the *veve*. Because Onu-Vey was who he was, the four warriors knew what was coming.

Onu-Vey handled the goat with care and gentleness. He stroked the goat's back several times as if to calm it. He gave the goat fresh grass to eat and fresh water to drink. He groomed the animal, picking away or untangling clumps of matted hair. He talked to the animal as if it were a loving pet. Then, just as the warriors expected, Onu-Vey pulled out a knife and cut the goat's throat.

Death came suddenly. The goat did not utter a sound as it collapsed to the ground. It did not struggle. Onu-Vey tied ropes around the hind legs. He hoisted the animal up on the pyramid-like support frame in the center of the *veve*. As the goat hung upside down, blood from the goat's neck ran into a large bowl placed beneath its head, and Onu-Vey patiently allowed the bowl to fill with blood. Then, he replaced the bowl with an empty one. Onu-Vey filled several bowls in this manner until the steady blood flow became an occasional drip. With the last bowl in place, Onu-Vey finally sat back and waited.

With the sensitive insight of a Vodun houngan, Onu-Vey waited for and watched the last drop of blood to fall into the bowl. He set the last bowl aside. Then he hoisted the goat down from the frame and untied the hind legs. With the goat's head dangling, its mouth agape as if gasping for air, Onu-Vey lifted the carcass in his arms. He carried it 200 meters down the hillside to where the four warriors rested. All four of the warriors rose to their feet as the houngan approached. Onu-Vey handed the goat to his vessel warriors.

"This is yours," he said. "You may share it if you wish. But before the sun sinks below the horizon this evening, you must cook and eat as much of it as possible."

Onu-Vey had finally given his vessel warriors something to do. All morning long, they sat and stood idle. While the worker warriors had worked tirelessly, the vessel warriors had nothing to do but wonder what would come for them. Now, they finally had a task to complete; a most unexpected task.

Nervous fear forced Makoso-Kin to speak. He wanted to protest. "Onu-Vey, suppose we do not want…"

"This is not a request, Makoso-Kin. Feast before the sun sets. You will need it." Onu-Vey turned and walked back up the hill toward the *veve*. He did not look back.

With the help of the worker warriors, the vessel warriors scrambled to follow Onu-Vey's instructions. The vessel warriors worked together to skin and gut the goat, while the worker warriors built a fire and a strong spit to cook the goat.

Meanwhile, back up the hill, the Vodun houngan crouched near the center of the veve. He built his fire over where he buried the black crystal. The largest bowl of goat's blood, almost cauldron-size, sat in the middle of the fire. When blood sizzled and bubbles around the edges, Onu-Vey tossed measures of the grasses, leaves, and other herbal mixtures into the cauldron. He mumbled an unintelligible chant as he worked.

Onu-Vey used the same knife he had used to cut the goat's throat to scoop a tip full of the red powder. He sprinkled it into the sizzling mixture. Sizzling bubbles formed. They suddenly grew huge. Smoke – thick black smoke burst from the bubbles. Despite the smell of burnt grass, the black smoke spiraled up and dominated the air with its repulsive, sickening odor.

— 21 —

FRAGILE AND IMPERFECT SPIRITS

Since Ramuza and Kharaambi spent the entire night helping the Kigire and Dawa Armies fight the fire on the north rim, they slept most of the following day. Ramuza finally came from his hut late in the afternoon. He stood just outside the entrance, feeling rested if not completely refreshed. He stretched to remove some of the knots in his overworked muscles. Ramuza looked out across the celebration area and the Royal Kraal. He compared the calmness of the evening with the chaos of the previous evening.

The celebration area was quiet and unusually bare. On a typical evening, people from one of the kraal communities worked throughout the area, preparing for the Daily Celebration of Life. Ameh canceled the celebration out of respect for the Mangoni mourning period. Ramuza supported the cancellation. Instead of a large group, Ramuza saw a few people from the Motobo kraal cleaning the area from yesterday's shortened celebration. Some gathered discarded items and debris. Others were raking fresh dirt over areas where bonfires had burned.

Ramuza looked to his right. In front of Kharaambi's hut, he saw several children from the Motobo kraal and his six youngest children, Akwate, Akuako, Zindzhi, Baako, Alaba, and the young prince Adaulah. They were playing a game of *kipofu*. Each of the children wore a blindfold and a loosely tied sash around his or her waist. Each did his or her playful best to take the other players' sashes. The last child wearing a sash would win the game. They laughed and played as only children could. The sight brought a smile to Ramuza's face.

Out in front, on the royal dais, Ramuza saw Ameh Jobabwe. The Chinchigwe Mfalme was talking with the Brown Warrior Quazzi

137

and the Favored Tribesman Kon-Shambique, who sat on the ground before the dais. Before Ramuza lay down to rest this morning, news had reached him that Ameh and Quazzi had their hands full last evening. Even after Quazzi arrived to help Ameh, the two Creations answered questions and offered explanations about yesterday's events well into the night.

When Ramuza and Kharaambi returned to the Royal Kraal early this morning, they walked past the royal dais. Ramuza remembered seeing the dais empty of people. Ameh and Quazzi were fortunate enough to get a break and a short period of sleep. But here they were again. No crowd of questioners was standing before them this time, only Kon-Shambique.

Ramuza turned his attention to his left. In the work area between Rwuva's hut and Olabisi's, he saw his oldest children, Omari, Yejide, Kunto, and Audi. The four young women had just finished cleaning the work area and secured a bundle of debris onto a two-wheel cart. The Orange Warrior Refuri, one of Olabisi's guards, was hitching the cart to a small donkey. Ramuza's second mate, the Sacred Woman Olabisi, held the small donkey steady while the others worked. When Refuri finally led the donkey away, Ramuza began his late day by walking toward the women.

Olabisi noticed Ramuza approaching and greeted him with a smile and a playful touch of sarcasm. "Good morning, Mfalme."

"Good evening," Ramuza returned the corrected greeting with a warm smile of his own.

"We were wondering if you would sleep all day."

"I slept later than I intended."

"You and the Sacred Woman Kharaambi had good reason. When the two of you came by Kon-Shambique's kraal this morning, both of you looked exhausted. You needed the rest."

"Is Kharaambi still sleeping?"

"The Gray Warrior? Are you serious? No, Mfalme. She slept as you did, but her day started long ago. Kharaambi has returned to the north rim. She helped to put out the fire. Now she is helping with the clean-up and restoration."

"I am not surprised," Ramuza looked out across the Royal Kraal again. "Speaking of a clean-up, the people from the Motobo kraal have done a remarkable job, cleaning the celebration area. At this hour of the day, it looks empty."

"It looks … it looks wrong, somehow," Omari added. "But under the circumstances, it is understandable."

"Yes. As long as the Mangoni are among us and are in mourning, we will mourn with them." Ramuza dismissed the somber moment with a gentle sigh. He redirected his attention back to the woman before him. "With no celebration, how shall we spend the evening?"

Olabisi nodded toward the royal dais. "Kon-Shambique tells us the Sacred Woman Rwuva is ready to return to the Royal Kraal this evening. We were preparing to go to the Favored Tribesman's kraal to walk back with her. Will you join us?"

The news and the offer brought a twinkle to Ramuza's eyes. They forced out the last sensation of sluggishness from his afternoon sleep. "I think that I will."

"Good!" Olabisi led the way toward the celebration area. "We have already sent word that we are coming. She is not expecting you. If you come with us, it will be a pleasant surprise for her."

"I will come. But you go on ahead." Ramuza walked with his mate and daughters as far as the royal dais. "I will catch up with you shortly. First, I wish to talk with the Great Creations Ameh, Quazzi, and Kon-Shambique."

Ramuza stood for a few moments and watched his mate and daughters leave. He felt fortunate that the Supreme Spirit had blessed him with such beautiful and thoughtful women. He watched them until they had made their way into the celebration area.

Ramuza ended the cherished moment and turned to the three Creations around the royal dais. He waved his hand dismissively in response to their greetings and respectful rise to their feet.

"Did you sleep well, Mfalme?" Ameh asked.

Ramuza stepped onto the royal dais and eased his muscle-stiff body onto his chieftain stool, prompting Ameh, Quazzi, and Kon-

Shambique to return to their original positions. "We experienced some unfortunate events yesterday evening. Sleep seemed impossible at first. But because of fatigue, when I fell asleep, I slept soundly. How about you? I understand that you and Quazzi did not leave the royal dais until late last night."

"It was late. After I canceled the Celebration of Life, Quazzi and I found it comforting to sit and talk longer after all the people left. It is disturbing how everything turned upside down in just moments. One moment, we are celebrating life. The next moment, we are dealing with one misfortune after another. I guess Quazzi and I had to express some of our disturbed feelings before we retired for the night. When we finally left the Royal Kraal, I only slept briefly. I am an Old Creation who sleeps lightly anyway. Under the circumstances, I expect nothing better."

"I suppose I slept lightly too, but for a different reason." Quazzi held his hands out, both wrapped in fresh bandages. "My hands still pain me once in a while."

"Bear with it, Great Creation," Kon-Shambique said. "You will suffer pain for a while longer. Continue to drink the tea I gave you. The periods of pain will be less frequent and die away quickly. Try not to rupture the blisters. Your hands will heal much faster."

"Tell me something." Ameh paused for a moment to put his thoughts into words. "Since the Chinchigwe became part of the Aukmondi, I have learned a few new things. I have learned to see life and the Supreme Spirit differently. Most things seem refreshing and promising. But I need to know. Is the Supreme Spirit aware of our recent misfortunes?"

"I am sure She is, Mfalme. The Supreme Spirit has a hand in it somewhere." Kon-Shambique sounded confident in his reassurance. "The Sacred Woman Tongda and I discussed this subject this morning. All that has happened is part of the Supreme Spirit's grand design."

"Grand design?" Ameh sat forward. His brow knitted with confusion. "What grand design are you talking about, Great Creation?"

"*Her* grand design, Mfalme. As I understand it, it is Her way of raising and developing our young spirits. Her grand design, whatever it may be, is as great and as incomprehensible as the Supreme Spirit Herself. Our simple hearts and minds are just too young to understand it. And we will not understand it until our spirits grow mature enough to join Her, finally at Her side."

"That still does not explain yesterday's incidents. You say the Supreme Spirit has a hand in it somewhere. If so, I do not understand. The death of the Sacred Woman Abul-Tess; the deaths of the Mangoni warriors, the Red Warrior Mbinga, and even the Wabanga; not to mention all the injuries – Rwuva, Quazzi, and the Green Warrior Zabiba. Why did they happen?"

Kon-Shambique shrugged. He could not explain the mind and thinking of the Supreme Spirit, nor was he about to try. But he had his perspective. He shifted his position to face Ameh. "As callous as it may sound, given our fragile and imperfect spirits, we should sometimes expect injuries and death, like yesterday's. Because our spirits are so young, we naturally live with our share of faults and frailties – some of us, more so than others. Unfortunately, this sets us up for all kinds of misfortunes where even the innocent and pure in heart may fall victim."

"I guess I am in a denial frame of mind, Great Creation. That does not sound right. I am sure. The Supreme Spirit can create a better design than that."

"If you have any suggestions, offer them to Her, Mfalme. I am sure She is listening."

Ameh only grunted as he realized he could never imagine a design greater than that of the Supreme Spirit.

"I know all of this is something you are uncomfortable hearing," Kon-Shambique continued. "But, as I understand it, our spirits must grow. All that happens to us is part of the divine learning process to bring us closer to Her. We will all learn what we must learn. And as hard as it may seem to us sometimes, we have no other choice."

"So, what should we do meanwhile? Must we go through each day, putting up with these misfortunes? Should we hope we do not fall victim to our own or someone else's faults and frailties?"

"So, it would seem." It was Kon-Shambique's turn to fall silent. He sat, thinking about Ameh's question, but had no reassuring answer this time. He smiled when he finally spoke again. "I have my flaws too, Mfalme. I must yield to my faults and frailties here. I can say nothing that might justify yesterday's incidents. Yesterday happened because of the things we did yesterday. We can never change that."

"Kon-Shambique, we call you the Favored Tribesman because you have amazing gifts. We expect you to have special insights into things like this. Even in hindsight, are there no suggestions?"

"Only to do as you suggested. We must go through each day, putting up with our misfortunes as best we can. Each of us must exercise a little self-discipline. We must follow some sense of morality with a willingness to love and serve others. If we try to do the right thing, in blind faith, the Supreme Spirit will see us through to our proper ends."

Ameh grunted. He still had strong reservations about the Favored Tribesman's explanation. "Great Creation, I know the value of love and service to others. The rest of the Chinchigwe and I have seen and experienced the benefits of such things firsthand. Otherwise, none of us would be here. But, you must know, self-discipline and a moral conscience do not always mean the same thing to everyone. Sometimes, even when you do the right thing, it creates conflict and more misfortunes for others."

"Yes, but self-discipline and a moral conscience, whatever it means to you or anyone else, will keep things civil – most of the time."

"This 'blind faith' you keep mentioning; blind faith, sometimes, does not come easy, especially amid a struggle, when your heart is racing, and your mind is in chaos."

"Then in such cases, use your self-discipline, moral conscience, and love for others to hang on, Mfalme. And help others to do the same. We are all in this together." Kon-Shambique smiled at the analogy that popped into his head. "We are like flies that mindlessly rest on a donkey's tail."

Ameh looked at Kon-Shambique. The frown on his face deepened. He was not sure if he had heard what he heard. He repeated. "A donkey's tail?"

"Yes, Mfalme. As flies on the donkey's tail, we are moving along, completely unaware we are moving. As we move, we endure disturbing ups and downs and do not know why. The violent swings from side to side often knock us off our feet. Sometimes, as the donkey uses its tail to swat at disruptive flies, we may become dislodged. We are overwhelmed by various things that may fall our way as the donkey moves along. Despite these difficulties and distractions, we do not realize that the donkey still carries us to where we need to go."

Ameh leaned forward. "Are you saying just hanging on makes all these ups and downs, these swings from side to side, and the 'stuff' that falls our way less tragic?"

"No, Mfalme. I am only saying that hanging on is the simplest form of blind faith. Do what you must do to stay strong and keep that faith. Surround yourself with love and understanding. Do whatever is possible to help others do the same. Whatever happens, you must not let go. Never let go. Let no one else let go. The flies that hang on go where the donkey goes."

"And the flies that do not?"

"Those flies must get back on the donkey's tail before it is too late."

Ameh sat back. He looked at Quazzi and Ramuza to see if they were as unimpressed as he was. He turned back to Kon-Shambique. "What you say holds little comfort for us, the living, Great Creation."

"But think about it, Mfalme. You are still traveling on the donkey's tail. There is enough comfort in knowing you and those you love have all arrived in the same place. For us, the living, nothing else should matter."

"I suppose." Ameh fell silent as his thoughts jumped to one of the most tragic times of his life, when slave hunters invaded and destroyed the Chinchigwe Village. He and a handful of other Chinchigwe survived by helping one another hang on.

Out of that survival, the Sacred Woman Lobarra gave birth to Ameh's grandson, Tutapona. The infant, Ameh's closest living relative, was now one of the most cherished parts of his long life. Since Tutapona and Lobarra had gone with the group of farmers to visit the Kiwane Village, Ameh had naturally worried about their safety day and night. As a tribal Mfalme, Ameh wondered if he had done all he could to secure their safety. The extra warrior he had sent with the group did not appear to be enough.

Affected by Ameh's long period of silence, Kon-Shambique looked over at the Chinchigwe Mfalme. "What is wrong, Mfalme. Did you not like my donkey tail comparison?"

The question brought Ameh back to the moment. Ameh looked at Kon-Shambique as he considered the Favored Tribesman's question. "To be honest, no. And I believe I am not alone."

This time, Kon-Shambique looked up at Quazzi. He looked back over his shoulder at Ramuza. Each of the two Creations looked away.

"That is a horrible way to put it," Ameh finally added, "but I think I understand the essence of what you mean. But this donkey's tail we are riding on is swinging mighty hard. It may be all but impossible to hang on."

22

THE SMELL OF DEATH

Ramuza patiently waited for the 'donkey tail' debate between Ameh and Kon-Shambique to end. When he felt comfortable that the two had said all they could, Ramuza decided to put the idea into practical use. He leaned forward and addressed the Favored Tribesman. "Great Creation, it would be nice if we could help our visitors on Nagorda Peak hang on. Have you heard any more from them?"

"No, Mfalme. Not since the houngan paid us that strange visit this morning."

"Any idea yet what he meant by that warning, 'beware of those who grieve'?"

"No, not completely. As best as I can understand, Mfalme Abul-Gwan is the primary one grieving. Onu-Vey seems to imply that there are consequences to his grief."

"Like what?"

"It is hard to say. People grieve in different ways. With some, their grief stays hidden. Others become completely different people for the rest of their lives. They begin to think differently. They talk and behave like never before."

"Whatever the consequences of Mfalme Abul-Gwan's grief are," Quazzi said, "the Mangoni houngan was thoughtful enough to warn us. It cannot be good."

"Yes. He told us to prepare ourselves."

"Prepare ourselves, how? For what?"

Ramuza sat back. "We must find out, Great Creation. We will begin by visiting the Mangoni ourselves."

"Mfalme Abul-Gwan has placed his camp off-limits." Kon-Shambique spoke to Ramuza. "When I spoke with the Mangoni, Mfalme Abul-Gwan told me, in no uncertain terms, not to return."

Ramuza stood. "Yes, while on Nagorda Peak, they are within the Aukmondi domain. Quazzi, you and I will visit the Mangoni camp later this evening. Select a couple of warriors to go with us in case of trouble. And inform the Gray Warrior. She may want to go as well."

"Understood, Mfalme."

Ramuza and Ameh stepped off the royal dais to join Quazzi and Kon-Shambique. Together, the four Creations started walking out across the celebration area. Ramuza and Kon-Shambique were on their way up to the Favored Tribesman's kraal. Ameh and Quazzi headed toward separate places on the other side of the Aukmondi River. Once across the river, Quazzi intends to go up the south slope to the Motobo kraal. Ameh planned to turn eastward on the south bank pathway toward the guest kraal, where he lived. He and many of the Chinchigwe had settled permanently in the kraal.

At first, the four Creations walked abreast. But Ameh's pace began to slow. He seemed distracted. He closed his eyes, mentally trying to focus on something.

"Do you smell that?" He asked the others as he sniffed the air.

"Smell what, Mfalme?" Quazzi stopped walking. He turned to face Ameh. "Are you referring to the smell of burnt grass? Are you not accustomed to that yet?"

"Yes. But it is not the burnt grass that I speak of. There is another odor in the air."

Both Ramuza and Quazzi took deep breaths. Both of them shrugged. Ramuza admitted, "I smell only the burnt grass."

Everyone looked toward Kon-Shambique. He stood with his eyes closed, focusing. He sniffed, just as Ameh had done.

"Yes, a slightly pungent, sweet odor." He opened his eyes. "It is a disturbingly unpleasant odor."

"Yes, that is it!" Ameh's knitted brow deepened again. "What is that?"

"Mfalme Ncobba," Kon-Shambique almost smiled at what his sharp mind had just told him. "I think I now understand the nature of the Mangoni houngan's warning. I recognize that odor."

"What is it?"

"Well," Kon-Shambique resumed walking. "Believe it or not, some refer to it as the smell of death."

"The what?" Quazzi had never heard of it. "What is this smell of death?"

"Some people will confess," Kon-Shambique explained, "that sometimes, just before someone dies, usually after a long illness, a distinct odor fills the air. That odor is the smell of death. If you have ever experienced this odor, you can never forget it."

"What are you saying, Great Creation?" Ramuza asked. "There is no one dying."

"I am saying the Mangoni houngan has followed up on his warning. He is making" Kon-Shambique pause to consider the right word, "a suggestion."

"A suggestion? What kind?"

"For those of us who wish to hang on, it is a suggestion we should ignore, Mfalme."

23

SOSO-DOSAMDI

Onu-Vey stared out across the Serengeti from his vantage point on Nagorda Peak. As the sun sank toward the horizon, Onu-Vey took pleasure in the quiet and the incredible beauty of the golden sunset. He sat in death's *veve* and watched over his boiling, bubbling cauldron of goat's blood and herbs. He ignored the thick black smoke from the mixture, which continued to spiral skyward, carrying the smell of death across the Aukmondi Valley.

At that magical instant, when the golden orb of the sun touched the horizon, the Vodun houngan took a deep breath and sighed. He looked to the ground at his left, at the center of the *veve*. Beneath the cauldron of bubbling goat's blood, beneath the flames of his campfire, beneath the dirt was the vestige of his *azima*. It was about to bring forth the darkest days of his life.

Onu-Vey poured another ladle of fresh goat's blood into the cauldron. He tossed two more measures of yellow and greenish powders into the mixture and rose to his feet. With the last nagging pull of reluctance, he turned and stepped from the *veve*. He walked over to where Mfalme Abul-Gwan sat under the Marula tree.

Onu-Vey found Abul-Gwan asleep. Even when Onu-Vey called his name, Abul-Gwan did not move. It pleased Onu-Vey that Abul-Gwan was finally getting the sleep he needed.

Onu-Vey kneeled in front of his Mfalme and next to the body of Abul-Tess. He took advantage of the moment. He gently covered Abul-Tess's face with a thin veil. That is when he heard Abul-Gwan's soft and raspy voice.

"She is not coming back, is she, Onu-Vey?"

"No, Mfalme. She is not."

Abul-Gwan raised his head. He blinked the sleep from his eyes. He turned to look toward the Serengeti. Brilliant sunlight continued to illuminate the plain. Abul-Gwan lapsed into silence again as he stared at the awesome sight. He stared, but he saw none of it. He blinked several times as his eyes welled up with tears again. "She is gone, Onu-Vey." He spoke as if accepting the truth.

"Mfalme, you must be strong. Your people need you. Please, be strong for them."

Abul-Gwan dismissed Onu-Vey's words of support. He finally broke his stare toward the Serengeti and turned toward the houngan. "I guess, I sometimes expect too much from you, Onu-Vey. You worked your black magic with such confidence. You walk in the favor of all the loas and all the guardian spirits. From the moment I first met you, when you spoke those simple words that sealed the fate of the evil Kold-Johan, I knew you were special. When I became Mfalme, I think one of my wisest decisions … No, unquestionably, the wisest decision I ever made was to embrace you. I treated you like my own, flesh and blood brother. Onu-Vey, for over forty harvests, you were closer than few people have ever been. Yet, in all that time, I never realized that you … You have your limits, too. There are some things … you cannot do."

Onu-Vey did not enjoy disappointing his Mfalme. He took pride in serving Abul-Gwan. When Abul-Gwan showed disappointment with his service, Onu-Vey felt spiritually hurt. In this case, as always, Onu-Vey chose not to speak up in his defense. He closed his eyes and bowed his head to suppress the pain. He resolved to recover by doing all he could for Abul-Gwan, which included taking care of some of the simplest and most immediate needs. "Mfalme, you should eat something. You will feel better if you do."

"I am not hungry."

"The warriors have roasted a goat. There is plenty left. Please, eat something."

Abul-Gwan waved Onu-Vey away with a feeble gesture.

Onu-Vey rose to his feet again. Unlike himself, he made one last appeal to Abul-Gwan. "Mfalme, I am about to begin the ritual to summon the Loa of Death. I beg you. Please tell me that it is unnecessary. It is not too late. Once I summon the Loa of Death, I cannot dismiss it. I cannot stop it. I cannot undo anything the loa does."

Abul-Gwan removed the veil that Onu-Vey had placed over Abul-Tess's face. He folded it and laid it over Abul-Tess's chest. "She meant everything, Onu-Vey. How do I make you understand that? Her presence was the most beautiful thing I have ever experienced. And now, she is gone. Nothing else matters now. Either Abul-Tess will walk out of this valley with me, or the Aukmondi people, every last one of them, will walk into the afterlife behind her."

Onu-Vey did not say another word. He stared at Abul-Gwan for a long moment. Onu-Vey moved back when Abul-Gwan closed his eyes, showing cold indifference or fatigue. The poison energy coming from his Mfalme was the worst he had ever felt. Onu-Vey finally turned and walked slowly away.

This was it. There was no turning back now. Onu-Vey walked the 200 meters down the hillside to where the four Mangoni warriors rested. He found all four of them in a semi-state of slumber. All four of them seemed satiated by their fill of roasted goat. The houngan had to nudge Makoso-Kin's foot as he called his vessel warriors by name.

"Makoso-Kin. Metwe-Ngu. It is time."

As trained warriors, the vessels had a higher than average ability to turn slumber into full alertness. Both warriors got to their feet in seconds. They stood ready for Onu-Vey's next instructions.

"Leave your spears, knives, and shields," the houngan said. "You will not need them. Strip down until your chest and back are bare. Remove all garnishments from your head, arms, and legs. Remove your sandals from your feet."

"Onu-Vey," the nervous but outspoken Makoso-Kin said, "do you want us naked?"

"It is unnecessary, Makoso-Kin, but it would help. I must also add that you must empty all waste from your body. You will be unable to do it again soon. Then join me at death's *veve*."

Both warriors took care of personal matters and stripped down as instructed. They finally walked up the hillside, each wearing only a frontal loincloth. With a sense of mounting uneasiness, they stopped just outside the *veve*. The warriors found Onu-Vey already standing inside the circle. He faded in and out of view, obscured by the thick black smoke that bellowed up from the cauldron of bubbling goat's blood.

Onu-Vey picked up two small gourds half-filled with small pebbles. He shook them for brief periods, creating a wave of rattling noises. Onu-Vey also mumbled another series of unintelligible chants. He ended each chant by calling out the name, Soso-Dosamdi, in a deep guttural voice.

With one final shake of his rattles, he turned to the two warriors. "Soso-Dosamdi, the Loa of Death, allows you into its *veve*. Once you enter, you cannot leave until the ritual ends."

"How long will this ritual take?" Makoso-Kin asked.

"A day … two days, maybe longer. It will end … when all the Aukmondi are dead."

The two warriors looked at each other.

Onu-Vey saw the uneasy looks on the warriors' faces. "Is there a problem?"

Makoso-Kin threw a glance toward the slumbering Abul-Gwan. "Is this what the Mflame wants?"

"It is what he wants."

Makoso-Kin and Metwe-Ngu looked at each other again as they gave in to their Mfalme's wishes. They stepped into the circle.

Onu-Vey pointed with the rattle-gourds, showing the warriors where to position themselves. He positioned a warrior next to each hollow log he had prepared. "You may stand, kneel, squat, or sit. You may even dance, if you feel so inclined. Within the *veve*, you have but one task."

"Which is?" Makoso-Kin asked.

Onu-Vey pointed with the rattle-gourds again. "Strike the logs before you with these limbs. You may do it fast. You may do it slowly. It is your choice. But you must uphold three requirements. You must strike the logs one behind the other, with a strong rhythm. Once you start, you cannot stop. And finally, you must not miss a beat. Are these instructions clear?"

"The instructions are clear, Onu-Vey. But, what happens if we fail one of these requirements?"

There was a brief pause this time before Onu-Vey finally answered Makoso-Kin. The look he gave the two warriors was only half as chilling as the following words. "You will die. Do not fail the Loa of Death. Beware. The loa angers with ease." Onu-Vey took two steps back and pointed at the logs again. "You may begin."

The vessel warriors reached down and picked up one of the limbs beside them. With a final look at each other to signal their readiness, they struck the logs. With obvious fear, Makoso-Kin struck first, followed by Metwe-Ngu. The sound that emanated was a thunderous *boom-boom*. The warriors struck again, creating another *boom-boom*. Within seconds, the warriors had picked up each other's rhythm. An unending series of *boom-booms* filled the valley.

Boom-boom! Boom-boom! Boom-boom!

With the first stroke of the logs, the four fan-tailed ravens tied to the base of the pyramid-like support cawed in a screeching chorus. They tried to escape by taking flight. Each bird fell to the ground when they reached the limit of their cord. Repeated attempts to fly away resulted in the same sudden falls to the ground. Each failed attempt created more panic in the already frightened birds.

Onu-Vey ignored the birds. He knew that sheer exhaustion would soon quiet them. Onu-Vey focused his attention on his vessel warriors. Satisfied with the warriors' coordinated rhythm, Onu-Vey began another series of unintelligible chants. Just as he had done before, he ended each chant by calling *Soso-Dosamdi*. This time, when he called out the name, Onu-Vey searched the surrounding area with his eyes. He was looking for the Loa of Death. Onu-Vey rattled his gourds, as if the sound would attract the loa.

"Soso-Dosamdi!" Onu-Vey called out. He ran around the inner fringe of the *veve*, rattling, chanting, calling, and searching. Onu-Vey's eyes grew large with excitement. He took on a frenzy seen only during his strongest rituals. "Soso-Dosamdi!"

At one point, in the middle of one of his frantic runs around the inner fringe of the *veve*, Onu-Vey suddenly stopped. He stared down the hillside. He caught a glimpse of a dark and ominous shadow approaching.

Boom-boom! Boom-boom! Boom-boom!

Several meters away, a tall black spirit glided into view. It glided up the hillside, directly up to the edge of the *veve,* and stopped. The spirit stood 215 centimeters in height. It wore an all-black garment of unquestionable decay. Torn, tattered, moldy rags, strings, and ropes covered the garment. The all-black garment was a ground-length tunic with a large, oversized hood. The loa wore a cape of the same thick black material, covered with more decayed, rotting rags, strings, and ropes. The cape gently flowed and waved in a persistent wind.

No part of the loa's physique showed except its bony hands and face. Beneath the oversized hood was the face of death – a dry, chalky white skull with bare teeth and hollow jaws. In the eye sockets were large, living, piercing eyes. The eyes alone were alive, contrasting with the loa's dead appearance. They were clear and focused. With fleeting movements, they searched, studying everyone present, including Onu-Vey.

The Vodun houngan showed no fear. He continued chanting at the figure as if talking angrily with an old acquaintance. He even rattled the gourds in the figure's face as if to taunt it.

The two vessel warriors continued to strike the logs as told. Both of them were afraid. Their hearts raced with fear. As fear lodged in Makoso-Kin's throat, one of his strongest impulses was to back away from the figure standing just outside the *veve*. But one step meant breaking the rhythm. He did not want to die. Like the warrior he was, he fought the impulse to run. He succeeded, losing only a small cadence in his rhythm.

Boom-boom! Boom-boom! Boom-boom!

The Loa of Death became aware of Makoso-Kin's struggle. It looked at the warrior, angry with the warrior's feeble effort. It moved slowly around the outer fringe of the *veve* and stopped in front of Makoso-Kin. The tall figure slowly stooped to Makoso-Kin's level. Nose to nose, it looked at Makoso-Kin's face.

Makoso-Kin felt nauseous from the rot and decay of the loa's foul breath. He looked up to see a bony skull staring back at him from under the black hood. It was the face of death with naked teeth rooted into exposed jawbones. But the most unexpected feature about the face was those eyes. The eyes were large, liquid, and alive. Because they focused on him, Makoso-Kin almost panicked.

"When death looks at you, there is no greater fear." Onu-Vey interrupted his chants. "Are you afraid, Makoso-Kin? Death stands before you. In this moment, the loa knows only you. Are you afraid? Let the loa feel your fear. Strike the log with all the fear you have. The loa can feel it. It likes it. It feeds on it!"

Makoso-Kin averted his eyes from the loa. He focused on the log before him. He struck at the log as if each blow would kill the crippling fear that held him. Makoso-Kin was thankful that he led the cadence. Otherwise, he would have lost the rhythm long ago.

The other vessel warrior, Metwe-Ngu, could not look at the loa. He had already closed his eyes. He upheld the rhythm by sound alone, predicting and striking his log when he heard Makoso-Kin's strike. But the fear that drove him was just as strong. He also struck the log as if to kill the fear; each time holding his breath and striking with all his might. The thunderous *boom-booms* that resulted grew stronger.

Boom-boom! Boom-boom! Boom-boom!

"Your fear has given birth to death," Onu-Vey told his vessel warriors. "The fear of my birds gives the loa purpose. And the fear of the Aukmondi people will nourish the loa and make it grow!"

The Loa of Death hovered about its *veve* for several long moments, shifting from one direction to the next. It seemed both lost and agitated. It finally moved away, gliding about the camp, looking for something. The loa glided down from the summit toward Abul-Gwan and the body of Abul-Tess.

Abul-Gwan had already gotten to his feet, fascinated by the beginning phases of Onu-Vey's ritual. When the thunderous *boom-boom* from the logs began, Abul-Gwan took a few feeble but curious steps toward the *veve*. Abul-Gwan had to see the unfolding of this ritual. But when the Loa of Death appeared, Abul-Gwan suddenly grew fearful. He slowly retreated. He felt a need to hide, but knew there was no place he could hide.

Abul-Gwan's fascination turned to sheer terror when the loa's aimless wandering about the camp centered on him. Abul-Gwan turned to run. He found himself already blocked by the Marula tree. He pressed his back hard against the tree. Abul-Gwan turned his face away from the loa and closed his eyes, as if the simple and childish acts would make the loa disappear.

The Loa of Death made slow and wide circles around Abul-Gwan, the body of Abul-Tess, and the Marula tree. It watched Abul-Gwan with an intense stare. It sensed Abul-Gwan's terror and moved toward Abul-Gwan like a lion about to pounce on its prey. Round and round the Marula tree, it went. Each circle about the tree brought the loa closer and closer to Abul-Gwan.

At one point, Abul-Gwan opened his eyes. Just before it disappeared from view around the tree, he caught a glimpse of the loa. In a momentary panic, Abul-Gwan swiveled around to catch sight of the loa when it reappeared on the other side of the tree. Abul-Gwan edged forward, peeping. He suddenly saw the loa come almost directly in front of him. Abul-Gwan jumped back. He fell to the ground.

The loa stood over Abul-Gwan. It slowly leaned forward and offered its hand to Abul-Gwan, as if to help him. It reached with long, bony figures. The loa's fingertips came with centimeters of touching Abul-Gwan.

At that moment, the two Mangoni worker warriors came running up from the guard post. In a blind sense of duty, they came to protect their Mfalme. Their rapid approach suddenly drew the loa's full attention. The loa turned to face them and raised its bony hands to strike.

Like Abul-Gwan, they had approached the *veve* slowly when the loa first appeared, fascinated by what they saw. When the loa circled Abul-Gwan so hungry and threateningly, the warriors set their fascination aside. Almost in panic, they reacted like warriors. They came running with their spears and shields held ready. When the loa suddenly turned on them, they froze. Fear destroyed their protective instincts. The warriors stepped back. They knew they were about to die.

"Soso-Dosamdi!" From within the *veve*, Onu-Vey called out, demanding the loa's attention. When the loa turned to see who had called its name, Onu-Vey slowly kneeled next to the four tethered and frightened ravens. "Come, Soso-Dosamdi! My birds can lead you to what you want."

The loa gave the two worker warriors and Abul-Gwan another hungry look. It seemed reluctant to leave such easy prey. But, Onu-Vey's promise had a stronger pull. The loa turned away. It glided up to the summit and the edge of the *veve*.

Onu-Vey reached down. He selected one of the cords holding the four ravens with one hand. He looped the cord. In his other hand, he held his knife, the same knife he had used to slaughter the goat. He placed the blade of the knife through the loop in the cord.

"You live in the void of darkness, Soso-Dosamdi, where nothing is visible." Onu-Vey ignored the loa's impatient stare. "Here, among the living, the brilliance of the light blinds you. In darkness or light, you cannot see. Your eyes are useless. You have no choice but to go where the wind takes you. You go here and you go there. Near and far, you move by the will of the wind. My first bird will go forth. The first of my birds will guide you, Soso-Dosamdi." Onu-Vey cut the cord. "Now. See where you must go. Then take what you must have."

Boom-boom! Boom-boom! Boom-boom!

The raven took flight at once. It did not fall back to the ground this time as it had done so many futile times earlier. With wings spread out, the raven circled the area twice. It spiraled higher and higher in the sky toward a successful escape. With ceaseless caws that faded in the distance, the raven finally disappeared over the trees on the southwest horizon of Nagorda Peak.

The Loa of Death watched the raven until it disappeared. As if angered by the raven's disappearance, the loa swiveled around to Onu-Vey again. The houngan had expected this reaction. He had already selected and looped another cord holding one of the remaining three birds.

"As the Loa of Death, you do not discriminate," Onu-Vey continued. "You take the fortunate as easily as you take the unfortunate. You take the diligent and the mindless. Soso-Dosamdi, you take the good and the evil. You take the peaceful as quickly as you take the violent. My second bird will go forth. The second bird will give you preference, Soso-Dosamdi. Before all else, you will hunger for the people who call themselves 'Aukmondi'."

Onu-Vey cut the cord. The second bird leaped into the air. With repeated caws that expressed its new freedom, the bird circled the Mangoni camp. It finally came to rest in the Marula tree, several meters over Mfalme Abul-Gwan's head. It perched on a limb and assessed its surroundings. Once the bird realized it was free, it used its beak to prune away loose feathers.

With its living eyes, the Loa of Death watched the second raven as anyone would. From the moment the bird took flight to the moment it began grooming itself, the loa never looked away; not until Onu-Vey demanded its attention again.

"Soso-Dosamdi!"

The loa jerked itself around and looked down at Onu-Vey. It seemed annoyed by the houngan's interruption. It glided closer to the edge of the *veve*.

"You have patience, Soso-Dosamdi," Onu-Vey said. "You have too much patience. You know that all must die; if not now, then later. Yet, you sometimes waste your time listening to feeble pleas of reason. You sometimes savor the useless sacrifices or favors given to you. You sometimes accept compromises, allowing some to live beyond their appointed time—no more. There will be no reprieves.

The third of my birds will go forth and join the others. This bird, Soso-Dosamdi, will give you restlessness." Onu-Vey inserted his knife and cut the cord. "You will take what is yours without waiting."

Boom-boom! Boom-boom! Boom-boom!

The third bird wasted no time securing its freedom. It flew over the loa's head. It caused the loa to spin around to keep the bird in sight. The bird flew westward, toward the last of the evening sun. Within seconds, the bird disappeared in the brightness of the western sky.

The loa spun around again, toward Onu-Vey. The loa moved even closer. With signs of frustration, the loa came to the edge of the *veve* and stopped.

"If you have one mercy, Soso-Dosamdi," Onu-Vey almost smiled, "you walk with soundless steps. Many do not hear you coming. And even when they learn of your approach, you sometimes give them the illusion of hope; the illusion that you may only walk by. No more." Onu-Vey picked up the final cord and looped it. He inserted his knife into the loop. "My fourth bird will go forth. The fourth and final bird will herald your coming and announce the end of life. This bird foretells an imminent end with no reprieve, no mercy."

The fourth bird flew toward the Marula tree. With charged caws and squawks, it flew past the second raven still perched on the limb. That second bird stopped its grooming and took flight behind the fourth. Together, the birds circled the Mangoni camp and disappeared over the trees on the southern side of Nagorda Peak.

With all the birds gone, the Loa of Death became agitated. So anxious to follow the birds, the loa glided directly across the ritual *veve*. The fire beneath Onu-Vey's cauldron of bubbling goat blood died out briefly as the loa glided by and continued its pursuit. It glided across the camp and down the pathway from Nagorda Peak. It moved down the hillside with a purpose.

24

SOME DISTURBING SIGNS

One hundred sixty kilometers away, on the edge of the Kiwane Village, Lobarra Gendeyani kneeled on the ground just outside the one-room guest hut where she stayed. She folded one of her garments and crammed it into a basket with other garments. The basket held an excess of garments, with more to come. Lobarra realized the other garments would not fit. She sat back, frustrated. Rather than force the impossible, Lobarra admitted that she had to repack the basket.

The hardy giggle of her infant son, Tutapona, interrupted Lobarra's focus. She turned to see Tutapona playing on the mat behind her. Tutapona, already crawling now, showed a joyful determination to crawl off the mat. The Red Warrior Rotho played with Tutapona. Each time Tutapona crawled off the mat, Rotho grabbed the infant and placed him back in the center. Tutapona enjoyed all of it. He giggled with excitement each time Rotho lifted him off the ground.

Lobarra smiled. She sensed that Tutapona must feel better, at least for the moment. She turned her attention back to the task before her. Lobarra removed some garments from the basket, hoping to refold them tightly so more would fit. She had removed about half the garments when she looked up and saw someone coming up the pathway toward her hut. Even in the distance, Lobarra recognized the approaching person by his distinctive walk – that noticeable rock from one side to the other with each of his steps. It was the Great Creation Elder Zekke Okendai.

Lobarra felt good after the tribute everyone paid her at the final session of the farmers' *mkutano* earlier today. All had hailed her as one of the most valued contributors. And even though Elder Zekke knew all along the tribute was forthcoming, he said nothing to her. He waited until Mfalme Menda announced the news to everyone. Memory of the incident brought another smile to Lobarra's face.

Lobarra was repacking the basket when Zekke finally stepped off the pathway and rocked toward her hut. Lobarra stood up to greet the elder out of respect for him, a tribute usually reserved for an Mfalme.

"Greetings, Great Creation."

"Greetings to you, Sacred Woman. Are you still packing?"

"I am afraid so. Somehow, I have collected more than I brought with me."

"Well, you are not the only one. All of us are taking extra things back with us. It is a good thing the pack animals are among the Sacred Spirit's most willing creatures. Otherwise, we might hear a few grumbles and complaints along the way." Elder Zekke took a moment to look over some of the other garments and items that Lobarra had not packed away yet. He wondered if she would get it all packed. He had to comment. "You realize, we intend to leave before daylight tomorrow morning."

"Yes, I know. I will be ready, even if I must leave some things behind." Lobarra kneeled. She picked up a piece of clothing to resume her packing. "Great Creation, why are we leaving so early tomorrow?"

"It is the Green Warrior Tushema. He wants an early start. Would you believe? He wanted us to leave immediately after today's session, but I talked him out of it. Tushema tells me he has seen some disturbing signs. He believes the great zebra and wildebeest migration has started early. It takes three and a half days to walk back to the valley. He would like to get us across the Mara River before nightfall of our second day of travel."

"What is the hurry? Why must we cross the Mara by that time?"

"I am not so sure. But you know the Green Warrior's determination. I think it's just a matter of timing. The Green Warrior is not taking any chances of us getting caught on this side of the Mara. Once the migration starts, if we are on this side of the Mara, we cannot cross the river until sometime after the migration peaks."

"Well, we do not want that." Lobarra understood that once the great migration began, it would last for at least two full cycles of the moon. "Tutapona and I want to go home."

Elder Zekke ignored the resistance of his joints as he kneeled. He offered to hold the basket while Lobarra stuffed more garments into it. "I thought you were enjoying yourself," he said.

"I am, Great Creation. I have enjoyed my visit among the Kiwane. I have met so many wonderful people. I would love to visit again sometime. But, honestly, I am looking forward to returning to the comforts of my hut."

"I suppose such feelings are normal. You become used to traveling when you have done this for a while. Long visits away from home become normal. You learn to find little comforts of home wherever you are."

"Do you not miss home?"

"Yes, I do."

Lobarra tied the basket close as Zekke continued to hold it for her. She sat back. She thought for a moment. "Do you know what I miss the most? I miss those wonderful evenings in the Royal Kraal. I have grown used to those evenings since the Chinchigwe have become part of the Aukmondi. Such evenings can be the most rewarding part of a day."

"All of us miss such evenings. And that is the reason I came to see you. We have already come together for our last gathering by the village lake. You, Tutapona, and the Red Warrior Rotho are the only ones missing. Others question why you are not there."

"We intended to be there, Great Creation. But Tutapona has thrown us a little off schedule. I had to interrupt my packing to feed him. The Little Creation's fretfulness and restlessness come and go. It is unlike him. I have just learned that when he throws one of his tantrums, one of the few ways to settle him down is to feed him."

Zekke looked past Lobarra to the mat behind her. He saw the Red Warrior Rotho lying on his back as if exhausted. Tutapona lay on the warrior's chest, struggling to climb to the mat. Zekke laughed at the two. "He is enjoying himself now. He plays with energy enough to put a Red Warrior on his back. There is no wonder the Little Creation's appetite is so strong."

The specific task of guarding Lobarra and Tutapona belonged to the Red Warrior Rotho. Lobarra was grateful that the Red Warrior was doing more than guarding her and her infant. Otherwise, she knew she would be nowhere near completing her packing.

Lobarra studied the clothing and other items she still needed to pack. She pulled another basket closer. She removed the basket lid and looked up at Elder Zekke. "Give us a few more minutes, Great Creation. The Red Warrior, Tutapona, and I will join you shortly."

"Can I help with anything? I do not mind staying with you until you finish."

"Thank you, Great Creation." Lobarra shoved the basket closer to Elder Zekke. "Let us see what we can get into this one?"

— 25 —

NOT JUST ANY WARRIOR

Rwuva's guard and aide, the Red Warrior Gengu, pull back the curtain that separates the front and rear chambers of Kon-Shambique's hut. He poked his head into the chamber. He found Rwuva and Tongda sitting on a large mat in the center. Tongda was working on a fresh bandage on Rwuva's arm. Even though Gengu was only doing his duty, the intrusion made him uncomfortable.

"Excuse me." He apologized to the two women before speaking to Rwuva. "I have a message to relay to you, Sacred Woman. The Sacred Woman, Olabisi, and several of your daughters are coming here. They are coming to walk with you back to the Royal Kraal. They ask that you do not leave until they arrive."

"Thank you, Gengu. I look forward to returning to my hut, but am in no hurry. I will wait right here."

Gengu let the curtain drop and retreated from the doorway. With the task completed, he quickly crossed the front chamber. He seemed eager to resume his comfortable post outside the hut.

Rwuva smiled at his hasty retreat. "Gengu is such a Wonderful Creation. He is one of my most thoughtful and devoted aides. But he seems so nervous around me."

"The Creation finds you attractive, Sacred Woman. Is it not obvious?"

"I am old enough to be his mother, Tongda."

"So? That means nothing. He cares about you. He loves you. I think the Mfalme and your friends had better watch it. His dedication shows how special you are to him."

"I suppose. It explains his behavior."

Tongda finished tying off the bandage on Rwuva's arm. "There. You have another fresh bandage. One of your beautiful daughters can apply the next one."

"Thank you, Sacred Woman. I am grateful for all the help you and the Great Creation Kon-Shambique have given me."

Tongda was about to acknowledge Rwuva for her compliment when they heard a loud *boom-boom*. The thunderous sound echoed through the valley. Both Rwuva and Tongda jumped at the sudden sound. They looked at each other. When the *boom-booms* continued, both of the women frowned with confusion.

Boom-boom! Boom-boom! Boom-boom!

"What do the drums mean?" Tongda asked.

Rwuva shrugged. "I do not know. I do not recognize them."

"Are they some new talking drums? From the north slope sentry line?"

"No. The rhythm is too regular." Rwuva's frown of confusion deepened as she considered other possibilities. "Celebration drums? Are we celebrating this evening?"

"No. Mfalme Ameh Jobabwe announced yesterday that we will mourn with the Mangoni. He canceled this evening's Celebration of Life." Tongda tilted her head to focus on the rhythmic boom-booms. "I think the sound is closer. I think it is coming from Nagorda Peak. Perhaps the Mangoni are doing something."

"Yes, probably." Rwuva took a moment to listen to the attractive but haunting rhythm. Boom-boom! Boom-boom! Boom-boom! "It most likely has something to do with how they are mourning the death of Abul-Tess and their warriors. They are probably preparing to release their spirits and return their bodies to the elements."

"I can think of nothing else that it could be." Tongda used a small knife to cut away a hanging strip of bandage on Rwuva's arm. "It only makes sense."

Both women set the mystery aside for now, confident they would learn the true significance of the drums in time. With the fresh bandage applied, both women got up from the mat.

Rwuva gently touched her arm. "How long must I wear these bandages?"

"Judging by the wound, I would say five or six more days. The sooner you expose it to the air without worrying about infection, the better." Tongda put away her tools, unused bandages, and ointments. "A wound like yours will heal fast. You were lucky, thanks to the Supreme Spirit."

"Yes, and the Great Creation Zabiba. Had he not deflected that spear as he did, the Sacred Woman Abul-Tess would not be the only one dead. How is the Green Warrior doing anyway?"

"He is improving. His recovery will take a while. But he will recover." Tongda turned to face Rwuva. "He is awake now, in the adjacent chamber. If you like, you can thank him yourself."

"Please. I must do that."

Tongda led Rwuva from the rear chamber of Kon-Shambique's hut into the adjacent chamber. She stepped quietly in case the Green Warrior had drifted back to sleep. She smiled when he looked her way.

"Great Creation, do you mind a visitor?"

"No, Sacred Woman. I would welcome a visitor."

"Zabiba, Great Creation, how are you?" Rwuva asked as she stepped into the chamber. She found the Green Warrior lying on a low cot in the back of the chamber. Bandages wrapped most of his upper torso. Rwuva shockingly sensed Zabiba's pain when the warrior tried to sit up and grimaced.

"No, Great Creation!" Tongda rushed over to Zabiba's side. She gently touched his good shoulder and forced him back down. "Do not dare get up. You must lie still."

Zabiba finally suppressed the pain enough to answer Rwuva. "I am fine, Sacred Woman."

Rwuva studied the huge bandage and wrappings on Zabiba's chest and shoulder. The bandages and wrappings held Zabiba's right arm stationary. "That looks uncomfortable. Does it hurt?"

"No, not really. It only hurts … when I am awake." Zabiba, Rwuva, and Tongda all smiled. Zabiba's smile faded as his thoughts turned serious. "I suppose, my greatest discomfort and pain comes from my failure to save the Sacred Woman Abul-Tess. Great Sacred Spirit! I had just met her. I did not know her well. But in those short moments in her company, I could tell. She was a special woman. And I failed her. That hurts more than anything. I did not want that to happen. I feel so bad about it."

"You tried Zabiba. Your heroic effort honors you."

"If you say so. Any warrior would have done the same. Some may have been more successful."

"At that crucial moment, no other warrior was there, Zabiba. Fate put you there. And you are not just any warrior. You saved my life. For that, I promise you, I will always honor you."

"Thank you, Sacred Woman."

While Zabiba and Rwuva talked, Tongda moved about the chamber. She picked up various bowls, cups, and gourds and sniffed at each one before replacing it. This subtle and strange behavior became a distraction to Rwuva.

"Sacred Woman, I have to ask. What arc you doing?"

"What?" Tongda did not know she was causing such a distraction until Rwuva spoke to her. "Oh, it is nothing. There is a strange odor here. I am trying to figure out where it is coming from."

"I smell only burnt grass," Zabiba said. "Is the north rim fire still burning?"

"No. It is out, Great Creation, thanks to the Kigire and Dawa Armies."

"But it is not the smell of burnt grass I speak of." Tongda lifted the lid of a small gourd and held the gourd to her nose. "It is another odor. The odor is medicinal, or perhaps an herbal mixture that has gone sour."

"Yes. It is a pungent smell, like a sweet mildew." Rwuva suddenly realized the odor that Tongda described. "I have smelled that odor all evening. No offense, Tongda, but I thought it was this healing chamber. The odor is not normal?"

"No, Sacred Woman. The odor is not normal."

"It is the Mangoni again. The drums and the odor could be part of the same ritual."

"It has to be." Tongda set another scent-tested bowl on a small table in the corner of the chamber. She smiled. "The Great Creation Kon-Shambique says, we must trust the obvious. The obvious answers most questions."

Boom-boom! Boom-boom! Boom-Boom!

Just then, everyone heard a noise in the front chamber of the hut. Tongda, Rwuva, and Zabiba looked at one another. They knew that no one else was in the hut but them. Tongda rushed from the adjacent chamber and across the rear chamber toward the front chamber to find the cause.

She pulled back the curtain and saw the Red Warrior Gengu again. He had rushed into the front chamber in pursuit of something. In haste, the Red Warrior had thrown his shield and spear to the ground to free his hands. He was slowly circling the chamber, crouched, as if stalking something.

"Great Creation, what are you doing?"

"Please accept my apology, Sacred Woman." Gengu pointed to the far corner of the chamber.

Tongda had to step through the doorway from the rear chamber to see where Gengu pointed. When she did, she saw a frightened raven, huddled in the corner. "Oh my! Where did it come from?"

"I am not sure. I first saw it circling overhead outside. I watched it briefly as it flew about the area. Then suddenly, it soared right past me, into the hut."

Tongda studied the bird. It was almost 47 centimeters long and was all black with a hint of purplish-blue when viewed at some angles. It was a beautiful bird with a thick beak and rounded tail feathers. Tongda knew enough about birds to recognize it as a fan-tailed raven.

At this point, the Sacred Woman Rwuva came from the rear chamber, curious about the cause of the noise. At once, she saw the bird, huddled in the corner. "That is odd."

Suddenly, the bird took flight. It cawed loudly. *Argh! Argh! Argh!* It flapped its wings without reserve as it circled the chamber and searched for an escape. The wide wingspan of the bird and the noise from the flapping wings created the illusion that the bird was much larger than it was. Gengu, Tongda, and Rwuva ducked to avoid the bird's wings. Both Tongda and Rwuva threw up their arms for protection. They squealed as the bird flew over their heads and returned to its original corner for refuge.

The Green Warrior Zabiba, in the adjacent chamber, heard the women squeal. Although confined to his cot, Zabiba was still a warrior. "Is everything alright?"

"Everything is fine, Great Creation," Tongda yelled over her shoulder. "A wayward bird has flown into the hut. There is no reason for concern."

"It looks frightened to death," Rwuva said. "Do you think the three of us can, somehow, herd it back outside?"

"Well," Gengu moved closer to the bird. "I hoped to catch it first, to decide if it is alright. It looks like it needs help."

"Yes," agreed Tongda. "As it flew past me, I thought I saw a cord tangled about its leg."

Gengu, Tongda, and Rwuva each studied the bird. The Red Warrior untied his red cloak. He quietly slipped it from his shoulders. "I have an idea." He pointed to his left. "If the two of you move that way and draw the bird's attention, I will try to snare it with my cloak."

Tonga and Rwuva slowly moved together around the chamber. They moved as if they aimed to catch the bird themselves. Gengu unfurled his cloak, holding it by two corners. He prepared to use it as an impassable barrier. Just as the bird took flight again to escape the approaching woman, Gengu quickly raised his cloak and grabbed the bird from the air. The Red Warrior wrestled to gain control of the flapping wings. Despite the bird's panicky resistance, Gengu was gentle. Only a few feathers flew loose. Gengu used his cloak to muffle the bird's frantic caws and wrap it with only its protruding legs.

Rwuva came closer. "Look, a cord hangs from its leg. But it is not tangled. It looks as though someone tied the cord."

Tongda reached out to examine the cord. "It was, indeed, tied on. This bird has escaped captivity from somewhere. Who would hold such a beautiful creature?"

"No one among the Aukmondi." Rwuva thought for a moment. The answer to Tongda's question came in an instant. "It must be our visitors, the Mangoni. This bird must be one of Mfalme Abul-Gwan's … what was the word he used? One of his commodities."

"Well, I hope Mfalme Abul-Gwan will forgive me," Gengu untied the knot that held the cord on the bird's leg. "I am about to set this little commodity free."

Tongda and Rwuva watched as Gengu loosened the knot and pulled the cord from the bird's leg. He then peeled his cloak from around the bird. Tongda gathered the warrior's cloak in her arms as Gengu focused on holding the bird's wings to prevent them from flapping again. He finally raised the bird for a final inspection.

"There. You look to be alright now." Gengu took the bird to the exit of the hut and released it. He watched it until it flew up and away from view.

"Thank you, Great Creation." Tongda handed the warrior his cloak.

"You do not have to thank me, Sacred Woman. It is my duty to serve."

Rwuva picked up the Red Warrior's shield and spear from where he had thrown them on the ground. She waited until the warrior secured his cloak over his shoulder again. She stepped forward to give him his gear. "I want to thank you, too."

"My pleasure, Sacred Woman."

Rwuva smiled. She thought about what Tongda had told her earlier. "So," she said teasingly. "With Tongda, it was your duty. With me, it is your pleasure. Why the difference, Great Creation?"

Gengu did not realize he had made that distinction. He smiled, embarrassed. "There is no difference. I suppose, in this case, my duty is my pleasure."

The Red Warrior Gengu returned to his post outside the hut. Rwuva and Tongda returned to the adjacent chamber. They found the Green Warrior standing beside his cot as they entered the chamber. Despite his pain, he got up when he heard the commotion out front.

"What happened out there?" Zabiba eased himself back onto his cot.

"Of all things, a raven flew into the hut," Tongda explained. "The Sacred Woman Rwuva and I helped the Red Warrior Gengu set it free."

"A raven?"

"Yes, Great Creation, a fan-tailed raven. We think it may have been a captive of Mfalme Abul-Gwan."

At that moment, everyone heard a loud crash again. As before, the sound came from the front chamber of Kon-Shambique's hut. It was louder this time. Tongda and Rwuva looked at each other. Zabiba's warrior instinct prompted him to sit up again. A stabbing pain rewarded him for his effort and forced him to lie back down. Once again, Tongda rushed across the chamber to discover why this noise occurred.

"Gengu, Great Creation, is that you again?"

Tongda got no answer. She continued across the rear chamber toward the front chamber. Puzzled by the noise, she pulled back the curtain at the doorway. There stood the Red Warrior Gengu again. This time, he stood in a defensive posture. Tongda realized something was wrong.

Gengu backed his way into the hut. He knocked over a small cauldron of water as he inched toward the chamber's center. The horrified warrior held his shield and spear ready, trying to hold off an intruder. Gengu jabbed his spear at the intruder, trying to force the intruder back. It was no use. The intruder, just outside the entranceway, kept advancing.

As Gengu moved back, the Loa of Death stepped inside the hut. Tongda screamed. She had never seen death in such a physical and aggressive form in her life. But the moment she looked at the loa, she recognized it as deadly. The creepiest feeling washed over Tongda. She screamed again.

The Sacred Woman, Rwuva, ran from the adjacent chamber and rushed to Tongda's side. She froze when she saw the thing standing in front of Gengu. The impulse to run made her step back. She pulled Tongda with her.

The Loa of Death stood well inside the entranceway of the front chamber. The tall figure hunched forward. It was too tall to stand erect in the chamber. It stood staring at the Red Warrior Gengu. As Gengu continued his feeble defense, the loa slowly reached out with one bony hand to take Gengu's spear. The Red Warrior saw this and jerked his spear back. Unfortunately, the act left the warrior vulnerable. The loa used its other hand to grab Gengu by the neck. It lifted the Red Warrior off the ground.

Gengu's feet dangled like strings. His arms fell limp at his sides. His shield and spear slipped from his hands and fell to the ground. All life left his body. The Loa of Death turned and tossed the dead warrior outside the front chamber like a bundle of trash. When it turned back, it focused its eyes on Tongda and Rwuva.

The Green Warrior Zabiba heard the commotion in the front chamber. As a hardened warrior, he had an overwhelming impulse to react. The pain in his shoulder shot through his entire body. Zabiba closed his eyes, clamped his teeth, and ignored the pain. He planted his feet on the ground and forced himself to stand up anyway.

Zabiba's first steps demanded more strength than he expected. His knees buckled. He caught himself, but not before stumbling against the small table in the chamber. He fell so hard against the table that two legs snapped off, causing the table to collapse. Zabiba remained on his feet, but he ruptured his spear wound. When he reached the rear chamber, his wound had begun to bleed freely. Zabiba looked down at his chest to see his bandage already soaked with blood. He ignored it. He staggered two steps to take a defensive position before Tongda and Rwuva. He looked up and saw the Loa of Death standing in the front chamber.

Zabiba did not save the Sacred Woman Abul-Tess. It was one of his greatest pains. He refused to let it happen again. Zabiba wasn't sure what stood before him, but he did not recognize the loa as a demon of death. He only saw the gruesome figure as an intruder – one he needed to stop.

Zabiba turned to Rwuva and Tongda. He began to unwrap the bandage that bound his right arm. "I will distract this … this thing. When I do, you must run past it to freedom. Try to call for help."

"Zabiba, Great Creation," Tongda protested. She touched his blood-soaked bandage. "You are in no condition to …"

"Sacred Woman, please! Do as I ask." A sharp pain shot through Zabiba's shoulder as his right arm fell free. The Green Warrior clamped his teeth together and ignored the pain.

Both Rwuva and Tongda looked at Zabiba as if they already realized the sacrifice he was about to make. Neither of them could hold back the tears. Rwuva held Zabiba's arm. She reluctantly let Zabiba's arm slip from her fingers as the warrior turned to face the loa.

The Green Warrior moved slowly around the front chamber. His right arm hung uselessly at his side. He hoped to get the creature's full attention. He hoped to lure it closer and away from the two women. His plan worked almost at once. Zabiba could see the creature's skull-like face recessed in its black hood. Large, living eyes stared back at him.

Boom-boom! Boom-boom! Boom-boom!

Zabiba was a more experienced warrior. He knew his advantage would improve if he could lure the intruder outside the hut. Zabiba continued his movement around the chamber. The intruder matched his movements, just as he hoped he would.

At one point, Zabiba saw Gengu's shield and spear lying on the ground. He thought the spear might give him another advantage.

When he moved within reach of the spear, he slowly reached down with his good arm to retrieve it. He never took his eyes off the intruder. He ignored the pain radiating from his shoulder and upper torso. As Gengu had inched into the hut, the Green Warrior strategically inched his way outside. He had to do it if Rwuva and Tongda were to find their opportunity to escape.

The demon moved around the chamber as if sizing up the Green Warrior. When Zabiba inched through the exit to the outside, the demon slowly followed him. The demon followed the warrior as far as the exit and stopped. Zabiba waved at the creature to challenge him, hoping it would continue to follow him. It would not. The loa only stood inside the exit, watching this insolent warrior.

Zabiba realized the only way to give Rwuva and Tongda their opportunity to escape was to engage the creature. He had no choice but to force the confrontation outside the hut. With a loud yell from deep in his stomach, he nullified the pain in his shoulder, bolstered his courage, and charged the loa.

The Loa of Death reached out with its bony hand and caught Zabiba's head. The impact was like running into a stone wall. Zabiba's yell died away suddenly. The Green Warrior collapsed. His entire body went limp, held up only by the loa's powerful grip. Just as he had done with the body of the Red Warrior Gengu, the loa lifted Zabiba by his head. Zabiba's legs, arms, and entire body dangled. Gengu's spear slipped from his hand and fell to the ground. Blood seeped through the warrior's shoulder bandage and streamed down his side. The loa tossed Zabiba's body on top of Gengu's. Then it turned from the exit. It locked its eyes on Rwuva and Tongda again.

The Sacred Women retreated across the rear chamber and into the adjacent chamber. They huddled together against the back wall. Each stood for the other's only source of comfort and security in this crisis. When the loa of death poked its hooded head into the chamber, the women screamed over and over again.

Boom-boom! Boom-boom! Boom-boom!

In desperation, the Sacred Woman Tongda reached for one of the table legs, which broke off when Zabiba crashed into the table. She threw the leg at the demon. The demon caught the leg and threw it aside. In a final but hopeful act, Tongda grabbed the broken table. She slid the table before the demon with her hands stained with Zabiba's blood. She hoped the table would work as a protective barrier for Rwuva and herself.

Tongda and Rwuva huddled down, against the wall and behind the table. The protective table barrier only gave a brief illusion of safety. The women had a few precious seconds to catch their breath. But then, just when they thought they were finally safe, they saw the demon's hooded face rise from behind the table. Its living eyes stared down at them.

It reached its bony hand over the table's edge toward the frightened women. In its hand, the demon held a dying and withered plant stalk. The demon offered the stalk to the women as a gift.

"Who are you? What do you want?" Rwuva asked, despite her crippling fear.

The demon thrust the plant stalk forward, as if insisting that one of the women take it. Both women refused. They moved back, but the wall behind them blocked their retreat. They could only huddle together. The demon finally dropped the stalk to the ground. Two fresh green flower buds fell loose from the withered stalk when it hit the ground.

Tongda looked down at the stalk and the flower buds. By now, the stalk had withered so dry that Tongda could no longer recognize it as a plant stalk. But the two flower buds defied nature. They stayed fresh, green, and full of life. She easily recognized them as the buds of two daylilies.

26

THIS CANNOT BE

The Sacred Woman Olabisi and four of Ramuza's oldest daughters followed the meandering pathway across the valley's north slope. Ramuza and Kon-Shambique walked a few meters behind them. All of them were on their way to Kon-Shambique's kraal, halfway up the Nagorda hillside. Although Ramuza and Kon-Shambique left the Royal Kraal several minutes behind Olabisi and the daughters, they walked with a stronger pace. They finally caught up with the women as they passed the Pogobi kraal.

As Ramuza and Kon-Shambique drew closer to the women, they could overhear a heated discussion. Two of the daughters, Audi and Kunto, insisted that a strange odor was in the air. Olabisi, Omari, and Yejide did not smell it yet. They could smell only the burnt grass.

"I do not know why the three of you cannot smell it," Kunto said. "It stinks. It smells like wet grass and is getting stronger by the minute."

"I admit that my sense of smell is not what it used to be," Olabisi responded. "But I know the odor of burnt grass when I smell it."

"Yes, Sacred Woman, the odor of burnt grass is there. But there is another smell on top of it. It is different. Can you smell it?"

Olabisi took a deep breath. "No, Kunto. If there is a different odor in the air, I do not sense it yet."

At that moment, Olabisi and the four daughters noticed Ramuza and Kon-Shambique closing behind them. Desperate to prove her point, Kunto dropped back to walk with her father.

"Great Creation, do you smell anything strange? An odor hangs in the air, something other than burnt grass?"

Ramuza and Kon-Shambique glanced at each other. They suspected the truth about the odor. Ramuza considered how he would tell the women the truth without alarming them. Kon-Shambique was already one thoughtful step ahead of his Mfalme. He hoped to deflate the situation with a half-truth.

"Yes, Kunto," Kon-Shambique admitted. "Other than the burnt grass, a subtle odor hangs in the air. I believe it is part of a ritual performed by the Mangoni."

The women were ready to accept that. They would have dropped the matter. But just then, the rhythmic and continuous boom-boom sound rumbled down from the north. Boom-boom! Boom-boom! Boom-boom! Everyone stopped walking. They listened. All the women looked toward Ramuza for an explanation. Ramuza and Kon-Shambique looked at each other again.

"I assume those drums are part of the ritual, too," Olabisi said. "So, the Mangoni are performing another ritual. To do what?"

The half-truth might have postponed the truth had not the drums started. But now, just knowing the Mangoni were performing a ritual wasn't good enough. It did not satisfy the women's curiosity.

Omari looked at Ramuza, expecting an answer. She waited for Ramuza to respond. Her patience ran out before he did. She jumped to her conclusion. "It is the Vodun houngan. He is doing something again. Is he not?"

"What do you mean, again?" Ramuza moved up to walk beside his oldest daughter.

"The news is everywhere, Great Creation. Mfalme Jobabwe and the Brown Warrior Quazzi tried to explain the incidents last night, but they danced around the questions like nervous gnats. They did not explain everything, especially how the houngan killed the Wabanga."

"The Wabanga fell across a log and broke his back, Omari. What else is there to explain?"

"The houngan killed the Wabanga with magic."

Kon-Shambique quickly moved up to walk on the other side of Omari. "Sacred Woman, you should know better. Do not surrender your mind to that."

"But Kon-Shambique, Great Creation," Olabisi objected, "you have taught us to embrace the truth, always. And the truth is, the Vodun houngan performed one of his rituals. Several people saw it. Remember that little wooden figure he was carving? It was a Voodoo doll. During the ritual, he held the doll in the air and snapped it in two. By some strange coincidence, the Wabanga fell from a tree and died of a broken back. How do you explain that?"

"If you believe that is how it all happened, Sacred Woman, then I cannot explain it."

"It is Vodun magic," Kunto insisted.

"The Vodun houngan has some influential abilities," Kon-Shambique explained. "He has insights into some of the Supreme Spirit's most protected secrets. But I assure you, his abilities are not magic. He cannot work against the forces of Her nature."

"Great Creation, are you saying the Supreme Spirit would allow him to use some of Her most protected secrets to kill with? I mean, he killed the Wabanga by snapping a Voodoo doll in two."

"Answer me this, Kunto." Kon-Shambique composed his question in his head before he asked it. "For whatever reason, would the Supreme Spirit allow the houngan to kill the Wabanga with, let us say, a knife or a spear?"

"If there were a reason, I suppose, She would allow it to happen." Kunto realized that a deadly weapon is still a deadly weapon, and whether she understood it to be a weapon or not made no difference. "But he used a Voodoo doll to kill with. How is that possible?"

"You believe he used a Voodoo doll to kill with. Your belief, Kunto, is the houngan's true power."

"So, what is the Vodun houngan doing?" Audi, the youngest of the four daughters, asked. "This strange odor and those drums, are they weapons too?"

Again, Ramuza and Kon-Shambique took too long to answer the question raised. This time, Olabisi assumed what she felt was the obvious. She turned to Ramuza. "He is! Is he not?"

Ramuza was still reluctant to admit the truth. He did not want to cause any undue alarm. Instead of answering any questions, he resumed walking up the pathway toward the Favored Tribesman's hut. Everyone else fell into step behind him. He walked silently for a few steps as he prepared to confront the truth.

"So, how do we fight such powerful influences?" He finally asked Kon-Shambique over his shoulder. "Do we stop believing what we think he can do?"

"Yes, more or less."

"It will not be easy. A Wabanga with a broken back and a Voodoo doll deliberately snapped in two; those make a convincing coincidence."

"Ignorance is our greatest threat here, Mfalme. The power of the houngan can only be successful when we replace common sense with ignorance. The houngan can do some amazing things. But make no mistake. He draws his power from the same source that everyone does, the Supreme Spirit. If we strengthen our minds with common sense, the skilled houngan may influence us, but he can do no serious harm unless we let him."

Ramuza glanced at the Favored Tribesman before continuing along the pathway. "Tell that to the dead Wabanga."

Boom-boom! Boom-boom! Boom-boom!

That is when everyone heard the faint screams echoing down from the Nagorda hillside, about a two-kilometer distance stretched between where the group stood on the pathway and Kon-Shambique's kraal. But even at that distance, Kon-Shambique recognized Tongda's distressed voice. He and Ramuza took off running.

*****

Ramuza and the Favored Tribesman saw the bodies of the warriors Gengu and Zabiba long before they entered Kon-Shambique's kraal. Because of Ramuza's stronger sprint, he reached the bodies first.

Zabiba's body lay in a messy heap on top of Gengu's body. Ramuza remembered Zabiba's near-fatal injury. He gently rolled the Green Warrior over and off Gengu. Both warriors lay soaked with blood. It never occurred to Ramuza that all the blood was Zabiba's. He easily assumed that some brutal slaughter had occurred to both warriors.

Thinking as a warrior himself, Ramuza grabbed up Gengu's spear. With urgency and caution, he approached the entrance to Kon-Shambique's hut, the spear held ready. Ramuza felt that whoever did this may still be inside the hut.

"Rwuva!" He called into the hut. "Tongda!"

Ramuza got no response. He braced himself against the outside wall and peeped into the hut. He saw Gengu's shield on the ground and the overturned water gourd in the front chamber.

By this time, Kon-Shambique had reached the bodies of Zabiba and Gengu. He kneeled between them, quickly trying to examine both of them at the same time. He looked up at Ramuza, horrified. "Mfalme, they are both dead!"

"Rwuva! Tongda!" Ramuza called into the hut again. He still got no response.

On the verge of panic, Kon-Shambique stood up from his kneeling position and headed toward the hut's entrance. Ramuza raised his hand to stop him. The Favored Tribesman battled an overwhelming urge to rush into the hut anyway. He slowed his pace, but he did not stop.

Ramuza had to grab Kon-Shambique's arm to prevent him from entering the hut. "Great Creation, whoever did this may still be inside. It may not be safe."

"Tongda!" Kon-Shambique called out desperately. When he got no response, he appealed to Ramuza. "Mfalme! They may be hurt, unable to answer?"

Kon-Shambique's statement made Ramuza realize he needed to get inside the hut now. With the spear held ready, Ramuza charged inside. He saw blood and chaotic disarray everywhere in the front chamber, but no sign of Rwuva or Tongda. Ramuza rushed toward the rear chamber. With just a measure of caution, he yanked the curtain aside and disappeared into the rear chamber.

With Ramuza's restraint gone, the Favored Tribesman finally crept into the hut. He took a moment to study the chamber. Kon-Shambique stepped around Gengu's shield and the overturned water gourd. He followed a clear trail of blood spattered from the outside and to the rear chamber. That is when he heard Ramuza's cry.

"Rwuva? Tongda?"

Kon-Shambique froze. Ramuza was not calling their names. He cried their names. And one of the most agonizing moans of loss Kon-Shambique had ever heard in his life followed Ramuza's cry. A horrifying chill physically enveloped Kon-Shambique's entire body. He rushed toward the rear chamber.

Kon-Shambique pulled the curtain aside. When he saw no one, he hurried across the rear chamber to the adjacent chamber and peeped through the entranceway. He found Ramuza sitting on the ground. The Mfalme cried as he held the bodies of both Rwuva and Tongda in his arms. Rwuva and Tongda, still huddled together, appeared dead. The expression on Ramuza's face showed total helplessness.

Kon-Shambique dropped slowly to his knees. He struggled to deny what he saw. "No. No, no. This cannot be! Sacred Spirit! Great Sacred Spirit, this cannot be!"

"They are dead, Great Creation. Both of them."

"No." Kon-Shambique raised his hands to his head, as if his mind would explode. Like Ramuza, he cried without shame. "This just cannot be."

"What happened here?" Ramuza forced himself to regain his composure. He looked up at the Favored Tribesman again. He fought hard to swallow the grief that had knotted so hard in his throat. When Kon-Shambique did not answer him, Ramuza spoke again through clenched teeth. His words came out wrapped in rage and anger. "Kon-Shambique! Talk to me! How can this be?"

Kon-Shambique slowly slid his hands from his head. Before Kon-Shambique answered Ramuza, he had to learn the answer himself. He slowly crawled over to where Tongda lay. He gently took Tongda's body into his arms. When he looked into her face, he cried again. The answer did not seem so important at the moment. The thought that he would never see her beautiful amber eyes again overwhelmed him. It almost tore his heart out when he realized he would never hear her laughter again. Kon-Shambique buried his face in Tongda's shoulder when he realized that never again would he share Tongda's precious, sweet, and secret moments of mischief.

"Great Creation," Ramuza had regained his composure. Only a hint of his rage and anger remained. "I must know what happened to them."

Kon-Shambique wiped the tears from his face. He studied Tongda's body from head to toe. He physically examined her head, neck, back, and stomach. His examination brought a frown to his face. "There are no wounds." He reexamined her head to learn if her hair hid an unseen injury. He quickly did a visual examination of Rwuva. "Mfalme, there are no wounds, anywhere."

"Then why are they dead?"

"I do not know, Mfalme. They are just … just dead."

"Great Creation, no one is just dead. There has to be a reason."

Kon-Shambique touched Tongda's face. He slid his fingers gently across her lips. Her lips were still moist and giving. "I have no answers, Mfalme."

Ramuza searched the chamber with his eyes, looking for clues about what had happened here. He noticed the underside of the table Zabiba had fallen on and collapsed. There, written in Zabiba's blood, was a chilling message. *All dead. Two days.*

The message unleashed Ramuza's anger again. He gently removed Rwuva's body from his arms. He got quickly to his feet and grabbed up Gengu's spear again. Ramuza kicked a wooden stool out of his way as he stormed out of the chamber.

From where he sat, Kon-Shambique saw the message too. The message's meaning naturally alarmed him. But, at the moment, Ramuza's anger and reaction alarmed him more. Kon-Shambique removed Tongda's body from his arms, ever so gently. He got up and went after Ramuza. He did not catch him until the Mfalme had crossed the front chamber and exited the hut. Kon-Shambique grabbed him by his arm and held it.

"Mfalme, what are you doing?"

"All dead. Two days." Ramuza quoted the message written on the table. He had taken it as a threat. He pointed back into the hut. "It takes no magic to write that. The Mangoni know what has happened here. They will answer for this."

"Mfalme! Wait! Please! Do not go up there like this."

"Release me, Kon-Shambique." When the Favored Tribesman hesitated, Ramuza jerked his arm loose from Kon-Shambique's grip and stormed ahead. He stopped only briefly to look down at the bodies of the fallen warriors, Zabiba and Gengu.

The Orange Warrior Refuri, one of Olabisi's guards, had entered Kon-Shambique's kraal. He was examining the bodies. He looked up at Ramuza. Refuri opened his mouth to speak, but the bitter expression on Ramuza's face was enough to freeze the words in mid-thought. He realized he did not have to tell the Mfalme what he already knew.

Ramuza said nothing. With powerful, angry steps, he left Kon-Shambique's kraal. He held a serious grip on Gengu's spear as he climbed the hillside toward Nagorda Peak.

Boom-boom! Boom-boom! Boom-boom!

"Refuri!" Kon-Shambique called the Orange Warrior's name. He called his name twice before the warrior finally responded.

"Yes, Great Creation?"

"Get the Gray Warrior, please. Quickly!"

— 27 —

YOU HAVE MY CONDOLENCES

Ramuza was only a quarter of the way to the summit of Nagorda Peak when he realized that Olabisi and his four daughters had finally reached Kon-Shambique's hut. At that distance, he could only hear the events that unfolded there. The heart-wrenching cries of Olabisi and his four daughters echoed up through the trees on the hillside. The wails of sorrow, against the ominous boom-boom of the drums from the peak, brought fresh tears to Ramuza's eyes. His grip on Gengu's spear tightened. His pace up the Nagorda hillside grew stronger, fortified by raw anger. The strenuous incline meant nothing.

Ramuza ignored the fan-tailed raven that flew down and landed on the pathway about ten meters ahead. He glanced at the raven and heard it caw three times before it flew away. But like the strenuous climb, the bird meant nothing. Lost in anger, Ramuza never gave the raven a passing thought. He had no way of recognizing the raven as the same one the Red Warrior Gengu had released earlier. And it never occurred to Ramuza that the bird was one from the basket of birds so protected by the Mangoni houngan up on the north rim yesterday.

Further up ahead, on the pathway, Ramuza encountered the two Mangoni worker warriors, Goh-Jumaane and Kum-Bufu, standing guard. The two looked as though they expected a visit by the Aukmondi. Ramuza could tell by their expressions that they did not expect the Aukmondi Mfalme himself. When the two warriors took defiant stances to block his approach, Ramuza prepared to give them another unexpected surprise. He leveled Gengu's spear toward them.

Boom-boom! Boom-boom! Boom-boom!

"Stand aside," Ramuza ordered. He did not stop walking. "I will speak with Mfalme Abul-Gwan and the houngan."

"You are forbidden here," Goh-Jumaane said. He shifted his position to stand in Ramuza's way. "You must leave, Mfalme Ncobba."

Ramuza stopped walking. "Get out of my way, Mangoni." He spoke, struggling to control his anger.

Both Mangoni warriors repositioned their shields, blocking the spear Ramuza held. They lowered their spears and angled them toward the Aukmondi Mfalme's chest.

Ramuza ignored the spears and tried to step around the warriors. Kum-Bufu placed the tip of his spear against Ramuza's chest. Ramuza stopped again. He looked down at the tip of the spear. He looked into Kum-Bufu's face and eyes, offended by this flagrant show of disrespect to a tribal Mfalme.

Ramuza sighed. The expression on his face softened. He lowered his spear arm and finally stepped back. He slowly turned away, as if to leave. But suddenly, with anger at it highest, he jabbed the butt end of Gengu's spear into the Kum-Bufu's stomach. The warrior doubled over in pain. Ramuza turned toward Goh-Jumaane. He grabbed the head of Goh-Jumaane's spear and yanked it. The sudden force pulled Goh-Jumaane toward him. Ramuza followed through with a powerful blow to Goh-Jumaane's face, knocking him to the ground. He ended his onslaught by kneeing Kum-Bufu in the face. Kum-Bufu remained bent over from Ramuza's first jab. The knee to the face flipped Kum-Bufu backwards, onto his back, and on top of the Goh-Jumaane.

Ramuza ignored the defeated warriors. He stepped over them and stormed ahead. Ramuza rounded the turn in the pathway and walked into Abul-Gwan's camp. He held Gengu's spear ready, expecting more resistance.

After a few steps closer, Ramuza noticed the Vodun houngan and the two Mangoni vessel warriors in the distance near the summit. Ramuza did not expect such a rigorous ritual, which is still underway. He stopped only a moment to assess the situation. The houngan and vessel warriors seemed preoccupied. Whether they noticed Ramuza coming, they showed no sign. As far as Ramuza could tell, they ignored him.

Ramuza focused his attention on Mfalme Abul-Gwan. He stepped off the pathway and stormed toward him, with no more resistance between him and the Mangoni Mfalme.

Abul-Gwan raised his head briefly. He saw the Aukmondi Mfalme's assault on his guards. He watched Ramuza's approach with complete disinterest. Despite Ramuza's threatening appearance, the Mangoni Mfalme resettled into his comfortable slump.

"Abul-Gwan," Ramuza began, "there is death in my valley. Are you responsible?"

"Death in your valley? What a surprising development." Abul-Gwan slowly raised his head again. He looked up at Ramuza with red and weary eyes. "What makes you think I would be responsible?"

"Are you responsible?"

Abul-Gwan did not answer at first. His brow knitted with a pretense of confusion. "Is that anger in your voice? What? Did someone close to you die? It hurts. Does it not? Well … what can I say? You have my condolences."

Ramuza tossed Gengu's spear aside. He reached down with both his hands and yanked Abul-Gwan to his feet. "I asked you, are you responsible?"

Abul-Gwan did not fight Ramuza. He was like a lifeless marionette in Ramuza's grip. "Abul-Tess is dead, Mfalme Ncobba. Onu-Vey says … he says, she is not coming back. She is gone. Gone … gone from my life, forever. I do not ... know what to do." Abul-Gwan looked into Ramuza's face. His eyes pleaded with tears. "What am I supposed to do without her?"

"What?" Abul-Gwan's question surprised Ramuza. He realized the Mangoni Mfalme suffered more than a loss. It was a crippling loss. To his surprise, Ramuza felt empathy for more reasons than one. He loosened his grip, but he did not let the Mfalme go. "Abul-Gwan, what have you done?"

"She is dead. Someone has to pay. Yes, Mfalme Ncobba. There is death in your valley. I have asked Onu-Vey to call up the Loa of Death. My Abul-Tess will not enter the afterlife alone."

Boom-boom! Boom-boom! Boom-boom!

By then, the two defeated Mangoni worker warriors had recovered from Ramuza's onslaught. Unseen, they grabbed Ramuza from the rear. They restrained his arms and forced Ramuza to release the Mangoni Mfalme.

"Mfalme!" Ramuza appealed to Abul-Gwan. "My mate, Rwuva, the mother of my only son, is also dead. Believe me. I know the loss you feel. Do you think the Sacred Woman Abul-Tess wanted this?"

Abul-Gwan sat and fell back down to where he had sat. He took a moment to readjust his clothing and recover his composure. He reached out to smooth away wrinkles in Abul-Tess's clothing. "Abul-Tess is dead. What she wanted does not matter now."

Ramuza, still restrained by Goh-Jumaane and Kum-Bufu, looked down at Abul-Gwan. The shock and stress on Abul-Gwan's face spoke louder than any words. Reasoning with the Mangoni Mfalme was useless. Ramuza looked up toward the summit at the houngan, Onu-Vey.

Boom-boom! Boom-boom! Boom-boom!

Onu-Vey sat unmoved in the center of death's *veve*, almost obscured by a thick column of black smoke. Entranced, his eyes seemed locked on Ramuza, but glazed over, seeing nothing. Onu-Vey and the two vessel warriors dripped with sweat. Onu-Vey chanted an unintelligible phrase. In rhythmic unison, the two vessel warriors continued to pound on the logs.

Boom-boom! Boom-boom! Boom-boom!

Nagorda's crosswind suddenly increased. It caused Mfalme Abul-Gwan to glance past Ramuza. When he did, his body tensed. He made a frantic effort to move back. The tree behind him blocked his retreat. The two worker warriors holding Ramuza's arms saw Abul-Gwan's reaction. They looked back over their shoulders to see what the Mangoni Mfalme saw. Their discovery caused them to release Ramuza's arms. They took defensive positions in front of Abul-Gwan, their spears held ready.

Ramuza turned. The towering and ragged Loa of Death stood less than a meter before him. Ramuza had to look up to see the bony, skull-like face, recessed under a black hood. Large, living eyes looked down on him.

Ramuza stepped back. But long skeletal fingers suddenly grabbed his neck and stopped his retreat. Ramuza's consciousness went dark as his feet left the ground.

28

INFESTED WITH GNATS

Several meters out and beyond the entrance of the Royal Kraal, a bridge stretched across the Aukmondi River. It was one of several bridges that connected the north and south slopes of the valley. Mfalme Ameh Jobabwe and the Brown Warrior Quazzi stood midway on the bridge. After leaving the Royal Kraal, they never reached their respective destinations. Since Quazzi had become the Brown Warrior at Ameh's appointment, the two had bonded into a strong friendship. They continued their conversation about recent events as they watched the calming water of the river flowing beneath the bridge.

The two had heard the intrusive Mangoni ritual drums. Like most everyone at first, Ameh and Quazzi assumed the drums supported some ritual to mourn the deaths of the Mangoni warriors and the Sacred Woman Abul-Tess. They ignored the drums as best they could.

Ameh watched Quazzi toss small pebbles into the water. The Brown Warrior did not seem hampered by his bandages. Ameh had to comment. "Your hands seem better by the minute."

Quazzi flexed his fingers several times. The hint of a smile on his face suggested the lack of pain surprised even him. "Yes. They do not hurt as much. Kon-Shambique's medicinal tea has amazing healing effects." He tossed another pebble into the water.

Ameh studied the cascading ripples made after the pebble plopped into the water. The water's currents quickly erased the ripples away. Ameh wondered if the turbulent ripples in the valley would wash away as easily.

"You know. To hang on is one thing." Ameh continued to stare at the flowing river. "But, in times like this, I have to wonder, where is the Supreme Spirit when we so desperately need Her?"

Quazzi shrugged. "I do not know, Mfalme. My heart and mind have not grown wise enough to answer a question like that."

"How much more of this must we endure before She intervenes?"

"I wish I knew." Quazzi tossed another pebble into the river. "As I understand it, there should never be any question about Her intervention. We must realize She is always present. Once in a while, I suppose, we must struggle through difficult moments to learn the lessons we must learn quickly. During such times, as the Favored Tribesman explained to us just moments ago, we have no choice but to ride it out, take our lumps, and hang on."

Ameh and the rest of the Chinchigwe knew, first hand, how to take their lumps and hang on. The Chinchigwe had gone through a difficult time and learned some of life's hardest lessons, painfully fast. Ameh recalled that horrible day when slave hunters, in just a matter of hours, destroyed the original Chinchigwe village and most of its people. Ameh and twenty-three others learned to survive that day by surrendering to fate and the graces of Her Supreme Spirit.

In his opinion, Ameh felt things had turned out well despite the Chinchigwe tragedy. He felt grateful. However, despite his continued efforts, he felt he could never show the Supreme Spirit enough gratitude.

Ameh turned to his right. He raised his eyes to look up through the trees, high on the south slope. The sun had already set, and it was getting dark. Ameh could easily see the brilliant torches burning in the Sacred Temple gardens. Flickering reflections off the golden temple doors also filtered down through the trees.

Ameh turned back to Quazzi. "You still intend to visit the Motobo kraal?"

"Yes, Mfalme. Why do you ask?"

"I will also force this old body up the south slope to visit the Temple. I have not been in a while. Will you come with me?"

"It would be an honor."

Boom-boom! Boom-boom! Boom-boom!

The two resumed their walk toward the south end of the bridge. Just then, Quazzi looked back toward the north bank pathway. Quazzi saw an Orange Warrior running along the pathway toward the Royal Kraal among the usual traffic of people coming and going. It was unusual. As the warrior drew near, Quazzi recognized him as Refuri, one of Olabisi's guards.

The warrior's urgent sprint made Quazzi stop walking. He got Ameh's attention. The two turned around and walked back toward the north slope end of the bridge instead. When Quazzi stepped off the bridge, he called the warrior by name and waved him closer.

"Refuri, Great Creation. Where are you going in such haste?"

Refuri interrupted his intent to reach the Royal Kraal. He veered off the pathway and ran up to Quazzi and Ameh. Breathless, he wasted no time with respectful greetings. "I must find the Sacred Woman Kharaambi."

As Refuri drew closer, Quazzi saw tears had trailed down the Orange Warrior's face. This was unusual. "Kharaambi is up on the north rim, Refuri. What is wrong?"

Boom-boom! Boom-boom! Boom-boom!

"Great Creation … the Sacred Women, Rwuva and Tongda, and the warriors Zabiba and Gengu … are dead."

"Dead?"

Refuri took a moment to suppress the hysteria that overtook his body. He struggled to hold back fresh tears. He had to force himself to speak. "Something happened at Kon-Shambique's kraal. They are all dead, Great Creation!"

Quazzi stood speechless for a moment. He stared at the Orange Warrior. "Does Ramuza know?"

"Yes, Great Creation. The Mfalme knows."

"Where is he?"

"When I left the kraal, he was heading to Nagorda Peak to speak with the Mangoni. And he was angry. Great Sacred Spirit, he was angry! The Mfalme was angrier than I have ever seen him before. He thinks the Mangoni are responsible. He believes the Mangoni houngan is performing some … death ritual."

"A death ritual?" The frown on Ameh's face deepened. Ameh stepped forward. "Refuri, there is no such thing."

"Maybe so, Mfalme. But I briefly overheard Mfalme Ncobba and Kon-Shambique arguing about it."

"Those drums we hear are they part of this so-called death ritual?"

"I think so, Great Creation. The Mfalme seems convinced the Mangoni houngan is performing a ritual – one that will kill all of us. I heard him tell the Favored Tribesman that we will all be dead in two days. Rwuva, Tongda, Zabiba, and Gengu are only the beginning."

"Kharaambi is up on the north rim, Refuri," Quazzi repeated. "Go! Hurry!"

"Is this some nightmarish dream?" Ameh asked Quazzi as the two watched Refuri run up the pathway past the Royal Kraal. "Can this be happening?"

"I wish it were a dream, Mfalme. Even so, we must wake up to end this nightmare."

"As I said earlier, we can use the Supreme Spirit's intervention right now."

"Yes, I would have to agree, but ..." Quazzi paused for a long, awkward moment. The reality of the moment, the deaths of people he had known most of his life, suddenly hit him hard. He suppressed an overwhelming wave of emotions and rubbed the sorrow from his own eyes. When he finally took his hands away from his face, he stood erect, as if to bolster his inner strength. "But even at the worst of times, we cannot force Her hand. We must ride this donkey out."

"It is not fair, Quazzi. It is just not fair! I think this donkey is mangy. It is smelly and infested with gnats. How can we hang on under such conditions?" Ameh did not expect an answer from Quazzi. He turned slowly and walked back toward the south end of the bridge. "Each of us must hang on as best we can. As for me, I need Her reassurance right now. I am going up to the Temple."

Quazzi had planned to visit the Temple with Ameh. But since Refuri delivered the devastating news, Quazzi now had more urgent business at Kon-Shambique's kraal. Quazzi stood and watched the Old Creation slowly walk away. Something in Ameh's behavior made Quazzi call him back.

"Mfalme, will you be alright?"

For several days, Ameh had worried about his grandson and his grandson's mother. For several days, he had not slept soundly. The stress of it all showed. Recent tragedies in the valley added to that stress. And Ameh felt many more unavoidable tragedies were ahead. It was almost more than he could bear. His stomach physically churned from all the anxiety. The last time Ameh felt like this was when slave hunters destroyed the Chinchigwe village. He paused, closed his eyes, and tried to tap his inner strength. He swiveled on his walking staff to look back at Quazzi. Ameh did not answer the Brown Warrior's question. Instead, he asked a question of his own. "Do you think there is anything to this curse the Orange Warrior Refuri just mentioned?"

Since Quazzi met Ameh, Quazzi had considered Ameh to be a Wise and Levelheaded Creation. He expected Ameh to be the last person to give value to the houngan's magic. The question caught Quazzi by surprise. He took a moment to dismiss his surprise before giving his answer. "Of course not, Mfalme."

"I saw that carving of the Wabanga doll myself. The houngan carved that doll with a purpose. Now, the Wabanga is dead. The Vodun houngan knew what he was doing all along."

"So, it would seem."

"And now the houngan has turned his magic against us. Are we doomed to die, like Refuri said? Can we expect all of us to be dead in two days?"

"How can that be, Mfalme? Think about it. An entire valley of people, dead in two days? It is just not possible."

"I do not know. Today's experiences tell us that we have underestimated the houngan's power. The deaths of the Sacred Women, Rwuva and Tongda, and the warriors, Zabiba and Gengu, have convinced Mfalme Ncobba. If he is right, if the curse is real, how do we fight this? How do we survive such power?"

Quazzi stepped back onto the bridge and walked toward Ameh. He tried to think of words of encouragement. "Whatever the truth is, we will survive this, Mfalme."

"Yes. We will." Ameh had gotten into the habit of comparing low moments with the lowest moment of all – the destruction of the Chinchigwe Village. That tragedy ended with promising results for the survivors. Could this crisis be any worse? "Whatever happens, there will always be a few survivors. Or will there?"

"What do you mean?"

"Forgive me, Great Creation. I was thinking of Tutapona, the Sacred Woman Lobarra, and the rest of the farmers. I had hoped that they would survive all of this."

"Mfalme, this so-called smell of death and those ritual drums have to have their limits. If there is anything to this ritual, which I doubt, the range cannot go beyond the valley rim. We should not worry about the farmers. They are far enough away to be safe."

"That is what I thought at first. You must realize the farmers are due back here in about two and a half days. The farmers will walk into a dead valley if we are all dead in two days. They will come within range of the smell of death and the sound of those ritual drums. They will fall victim too."

Quazzi's unsuccessful attempt to console the Chinchigwe Mfalme left him speechless. As he wrestled with what to do next, he looked into his bandaged hand. He still held a handful of small pebbles. A touch of frustration made him toss the whole handful into the river. "The Great Creation Kon-Shambique said we must hang on. He said that we must help others hang on if we do nothing else. Since you asked me to find another warrior to go with the farmers on their journey to the Kiwane village, I could easily see how worried you were. Your concerns have continued since the day the farmers left the valley."

"I tried to keep my concerns to myself."

"You failed, Mfalme. But please find comfort in this. If we cannot save ourselves, we can still do something to save the farmers."

"What are you suggesting?"

"Send warriors out with a message to alert the farmers. Instruct the farmers to stay away from the valley. After we resolve whatever is happening here, we can send word that it is safe to return."

Ameh stared down into the river water, considering Quazzi's suggestion. The irony of one of his thoughts made him smile. "I was telling Mfalme Ncobba, just yesterday, that I was counting the days until the farmers returned. Under the circumstances, I would like them to stay away just a little longer."

"It cannot hurt. At least, it will ease some of your worries. It might give you the strength you need to hang on."

"Thank you for your thoughtfulness, Great Creation." Ameh could already feel some of his anxiety and tension ebbing away. "I would like to make it so. But, first things first. Go up to Kon-Shambique's kraal. See what you can do there."

"So be it, Mfalme. But I think we can do both tasks. Do you still intend to visit the Sacred Temple?"

"Yes."

"Then, may I ask you a small favor?"

"Name it."

"Go by the Motobo kraal first. Find the Royal Warrior Nionu. Tell him I will need his services. Send him to meet me at Kon-Shambique's kraal. And when you find him, tell him to select another warrior or two to go out, meet the returning farmers, and deliver your message."

"Consider it done, Great Creation." Ameh turned and headed toward the south slope. There was more energy in Ameh's steps.

Quazzi watched Ameh until the Old Creation stepped off the south end of the bridge and started up the incline of the south slope. He experienced only a hint of his original concern for Ameh. Quazzi finally turned and stepped off the bridge himself. He started up the north bank pathway and focused on what he would find at the Favored Tribesman's hut. His pace slowly developed into a slow and steady run.

29

WHAT DO YOU MEAN, DEAD

The Gray Warrior Kharaambi had spent all the preceding night helping to fight the fire on the north rim. When she returned to her hut, she slept all morning. By midday, she had returned to the north rim and spent the rest of the day just beyond the sentry line, out in the blackened clearing. As darkness settled, she and several other warriors were putting the final touches on the day's work, spreading wheatgrass straws over various spots. Grounded wheatgrass was part of the Aukmondi food stock. However, under these circumstances, the straws of the wheatgrass served as an ideal means to achieve restoration. Kharaambi and several warriors sacrificed bunches of the wheatgrass for the clearing.

Kharaambi held a huge bunch of wheatgrass in her hands. She stopped working when she saw the Orange Warrior Refuri's strong approach toward her. Refuri walked across one of the areas covered by the straw. At first, his direct approach seemed disrespectful of the work completed by Kharaambi and the other warriors. But the Refuri's strong strides had purpose behind them. Kharaambi could tell that something was wrong.

"What is it, Refuri?"

"Sacred Woman," Refuri's eyes watered as a stinging knot lodged in his throat again. "An incident at Kon-Shambique's kraal demands your presence. The Sacred Women, Rwuva and Tongda, and the warriors Zabiba and Gengu are dead."

Kharaambi stared at Refuri. She took several moments to wrap her mind around the devastating news. "Dead? What do you mean, dead?"

Refuri only stood speechless. He had no words to make it any clearer.

In a moment of weakness, Kharaambi stepped back. She almost stumbled as she continued holding the wheatgrass in her hands. Refuri and another warrior felt it was necessary to help the Gray Warrior. They rushed to her side.

Kharaambi looked helpless for only a moment. She looked down at the bunch of wheatgrass in her hands as if wondering what to do with it. Anger took control. She tossed the bunch of wheatgrass to the ground. Without a word, she pushed the two warriors aside. She stormed past them and headed toward the sentry line and the north slope. She left the clearing running.

Boom-boom! Boom-boom! Boom-boom!

*****

On the opposite side of the valley, Ameh Jobabwe negotiated the rocky pathway high up on the south slope. The well-traveled pathway lay ahead. But anyone who climbed the south slope along the pathway had to be mindful of the rocks and the twists and turns. Ameh was grateful for his walking staff. Without it, he knew he would have lost his balance several times.

When Ameh and the Brown Warrior Quazzi left the bridge between the north and south slopes, it was Ameh's original plan to visit the Sacred Temple. He wanted to find a few moments of quiet and solitude. But before Ameh could enjoy those moments, he had to go by the Motobo kraal first, to find the Royal Warrior Nionu. He had a twofold mission for Nionu – one for Quazzi and one for himself.

For Quazzi, Ameh had to send the Royal Warrior to the kraal of the Favored Tribesman, where the deaths of Rwuva, Tongda, and the two warriors had occurred. The Brown Warrior Quazzi needed Nionu's special services. Ameh knew Nionu to be the youngest Royal Warrior in the Aukmondi Army. He was lighthearted and always fun-loving. Also known for his relentless determination, there were few other warriors like Nionu. If anyone could find out what happened at Kon-Shambique's kraal, Nionu could.

For himself, Ameh had to ask Nionu to assign one or two more warriors to go out and deliver an urgent warning to the returning farmers. Ameh's closest loved ones were among those farmers. If the unsubstantiated rumor the Orange Warrior Refuri had told was true, if a curse was placed on the Aukmondi, then Ameh hoped he could spare the returning farmers. He was hoping to get word to them to stay away from the valley until it was safe to return.

When Ameh finally reached the Motobo kraal, it did not take long to find Nionu. The simple fact that Ameh had climbed the south slope was news. News of Ameh's feat and impending visit spread quickly throughout the kraal. The news reached Nionu long before Ameh stepped inside the kraal.

"I found it hard to believe at first." The Royal Warrior Nionu came out to greet Ameh at the kraal entrance. A smile of amazement covered his face. "But it is true. Someone told me a sure-footed mountain goat has wandered into our valley. People have seen this mountain goat leaping among the rocks of the south slope."

Ameh was too breathless to respond verbally. He gave the Royal Warrior a weak smile.

"I know this visit is not a social one, Mfalme. How may we serve you?"

The weak smile disappeared altogether from Ameh's face. He wasted no time relaying the devastating news to Nionu. "The Sacred Women, Rwuva and Tongda, are dead – killed in uncertain circumstances. The same uncertain circumstances have also claimed the lives of the Green Warrior Zabiba and the Red Warrior Gengu. Quazzi needs you at Kon-Shambique's kraal."

Like a chameleon changing its colors, Nionu set his lightheartedness aside. He turned serious. He flung his royal cloak across his shoulder. The simple act signaled a White Warrior to bring him his shield and spear. The same act also called his Blue Warriors, Obe Bendabe, and Dabete Ehkili to his side instantly.

In their determination to get to the Favored Tribesman's hut, Nionu and his Blue Warriors left at once. They had almost exited the Motobo kraal entrance before Ameh could ask Nionu his second favor. Ameh had to call Nionu back.

Nionu stopped his hasty exit. His Blue Warriors shadowed him as he walked back into the kraal. "Yes, Mfalme?"

"Before you leave, I also need the services of one or two of your warriors – someone with the ability to travel great distances, quickly."

Nionu's natural response was to ask why. But an Mfalme had requested the services. 'Why' wasn't important. Instead, he reviewed the skills of his double-regiment army's warriors. Almost at once, the noted skills of the Orange Warrior Wema came to mind. He turned to his Blue Warrior, Obe Bendabe, to confirm his choice. "Wema?"

"Yes, Great Creation," Obe nodded. "The Orange Warrior Wema is perfect for the task. I will also suggest his trainee, the Red Warrior Nienko."

"Then so be it. Send for them." While Obe sent for the selected warriors, Nionu turned to Ameh again. He seemed eager to leave but did not want to appear disrespectful. "Is there anything else, Mfalme?"

"No, Great Creation."

When Nionu saw the Blue Warrior Obe returning with the selected warriors, he pointed them out to Ameh. "I have known the Orange Warrior Wema and the Red Warrior Nienko for a long time. They are good warriors, dedicated, and fast on their feet. They are yours. Tell them what you need. They will not disappoint you."

"Thank you, Great Creation."

With this, Nionu and his Blue Warriors turned and ran from the Motobo kraal. Like mountain goats themselves, they disappeared down the south slope, jumping over the treacherous rocks along the pathway.

— **30** —

WE DO NOT RECOGNIZE YOU

The Gray Warrior Kharaambi descended the north slope, running all the way. She ran through the darkness without a torch to light her way. She knew the pathway well. With the surefooted steps of an agile and sleek serval cat, she easily negotiated the twists, turns, and other obstacles in the pathway. Kharaambi felt the sooner she arrived at Kon-Shambique's kraal, the more likely she could do something to make the devastating news less tragic. The irrational idea drove her faster along the pathway.

The pathway on which Kharaambi ran meandered down from the north rim through a small forest area and past the Pahoma Garden. About two kilometers past the garden, she entered the Gongeri Junction. With a choice of branching pathways before her, to the south and the west, she took the southern pathway. She knew the pathway would double back, cross a narrow bridge over a small stream, and lead toward the east.

A fallen tree log served as the bridge that Kharaambi crossed. It was just wide enough to walk across without falling. Kharaambi's pace never slowed. She ran across the bridge with only a wobble to keep her balance. After another quarter of a kilometer along the pathway, Kharaambi ran past the entrance of the Pogobi kraal. The Pogobi kraal is one of the largest kraals on the north slope, second only to the Royal Kraal.

*****

Over one hundred fifty people lived in the Pogobi kraal. Most were dairy farmers and their families. During the evening, several people gathered around a central campfire in a clearing near the center of the kraal. The gathering was larger than normal. The canceled

Celebration of Life in the Royal Kraal gave the people no place else to go, so they socialized among themselves in their own kraal.

Despite the number of people, the Pogobi kraal was quiet. There was no dancing and little music. Only the casual interactions that result from everyday conversations occurred. No one in the kraal had heard about the deaths at Kon-Shambique's kraal yet. An atmosphere of calmness covered the kraal. That all changed after Kharaambi ran past the kraal entrance.

The Old Creation Najube Pembe, the kraal elder, stood near the entrance. He talked with several other kraal residents while waiting for his mate, the Sacred Woman Ingza. Two of their dairy goats had broken free earlier today and wandered out of the kraal. Ingza went to bring them back. It was getting late, and out of concern, Najube waited for her return at the kraal entrance. His wait and conversation with the other residents stopped when two beautiful fan-tailed ravens settled on the fence, just meters from where they stood.

The ravens perched on the fence just long enough to get comfortable. The sideways glance, typical of most birds, suggested they were watching Najube and the others. Their interest seemed just as strong as the interest they caused. Suddenly, each of the birds cawed loudly and flew away. Something had frightened them away. Seconds later, the Gray Warrior Kharaambi ran past the kraal entrance.

All attention jumped from the ravens to the Gray Warrior. Kharaambi's presence on the north slope, running by so quickly, was a curious oddity. Najube and the others moved closer to the kraal entrance. They had to get a better look. They watched until the Gray Warrior disappeared down the pathway into the darkness. All the while, they wondered what had prompted that strange event.

Elder Najube and the others who saw the ravens and Kharaambi's brief appearance were also the same ones to behold another strange occurrence. A tall, dark figure came out of the forest from the opposite side of the pathway. Once again, everyone's attention shifted, from the Gray Warrior to this stranger from the forest. They watched in awe as the stranger glided smoothly across the pathway toward the kraal.

The stranger appeared to be a Dark Creation with an unusually tall stature. He carried a huge load of firewood in his arms. The stranger entered the kraal and glided past Elder Najube and the others as if his behavior was common. The load of firewood in his arms was so large that pieces of the wood fell to the ground. The stranger ignored the lost pieces. He seemed focused on reaching the campfire at the center of the kraal.

"Ah, Great Creation?" Elder Najube raised his hand and called out to the stranger. In the darkness, Najube could not discern the stranger's face. He only saw a tall, dark figure he did not recognize, moving across the clearing. When the stranger did not stop, Elder Najube grew concerned. He excused himself from the others. He hastened his pace to catch the stranger. "Who are you, Great Creation? I am sorry, we do not recognize you. May we help you with something?"

The stranger ignored Najube.

Another piece of the firewood fell from the stranger's load to the ground. Najube noticed it had fallen. The Old Creation stooped out of kindness to pick it up for the stranger. The simple act served as Najube's last act of kindness. The moment Najube touched the wood, he stumbled. His knees buckled. Najube fell to the ground – dead.

The others, who had stood and talked with Najube, rushed to the Old Creation's side. They approached without any idea what had just happened. They knew that Elder Najube was in good health. Death was the last possible reason the Old Creation had fallen.

Several of the people rolled Elder Najube's body over to examine it. One of the Sacred Women who had rushed to Najube's aid reached for the wood still in Najube's hand. The moment her fingers touched the wood, she fell over dead on top of Najube. Two other people touched the piece of firewood, not knowing its deadly effect. They, too, fell over dead.

Others, who never made it to Najube's body but saw the collapse of those who did, stood back. Stunned and confused, they stared at the pile of bodies. They never saw the stranger dump his load of firewood onto the central campfire. They did not see the overload of firewood smother the healthy flames of the central campfire. None saw the column of thick and physically heavy black smoke rise and spread across the Pogobi kraal.

Those who finally realized something was amiss panicked and ran. Many gathered their families and ran toward their huts seeking refuge. A few thought it was time to call for the Favored Tribesman to get help for the fallen ones. Others intended to run for the Royal Kraal or the Obentawni kraal near the north rim to get help against this strange and aggressive intruder.

None of the people found refuge in their huts, and none of those who went for help made it past the Kraal entrance. The thick, black, and heavy smoke moved fast. Some of the smoke crawled across the ground like a creeping, hungry serpent. All touched by the deadly cloud fell dead.

Within minutes, the entire population of the Pogobi kraal lay dead. Not a living creature stirred. Even the dairy cattle and goats in the rear corrals had collapsed. After a short while, only the Loa of Death moved. To ensure the thoroughness of its deadly deed, it glided through the kraal, peering into each hut, the gardens, and the animal corrals, looking for survivors.

Elder Najube's mate, the Sacred Woman Ingza, had found their errant goats outside the kraal. She used a long, narrow branch to help herd the goats up the pathway toward the Pogobi kraal. But long before she entered the kraal, she noticed the thick black smoke oozing beyond the kraal's boundaries. It was an eerie and frightening sight. Even the goats were sensitive enough to turn and flee in fear. Ingza turned too. She dropped the branch she was carrying. "Great Sacred Spirit!" Ingza followed her goats in a panic.

Ingza looked back at the oozing smoke only once. She ran down the pathway for help. The Sacred Woman Ingza was a mature woman. By the Supreme Spirit's good grace, she still remembered how to run. But, unlike the agile Gray Warrior Kharaambi, she had no skill for running in the darkness. On the winding pathway of the north slope, her steps were not as sure as the Gray Warrior's. Ingza lost her footing. She fell to the ground, hitting her head against a huge stone beside the pathway. Ingza's cry for help just barely made it past her lips as she lost consciousness and grew silent.

31

IF BABIES COULD TALK

One hundred thirty-one kilometers away, in the Kiwane Village, down by the village lake, the infant Tutapona screamed. He screamed because he felt something was wrong.

About an hour ago, the Sacred Woman Lobarra completed her packing with the help of the old farmer Elder Zekke. Lobarra, Zekke, Tutapona, and the Red Warrior Rotho finally joined the rest of the farmers down by the village lakeside. In true Aukmondi tradition, Lobarra, the rest of the farmers, and all ten Aukmondi warriors enjoyed themselves as they sat around a huge campfire. For almost an hour, they talked; they laughed, ate, and sang together. It was their attempt to experience what they had missed since leaving the Aukmondi Valley. It was their way of doing what they do most every evening in the Royal Kraal.

A detachment of ten Aukmondi warriors, headed by the Green Warrior Tushema, had security responsibilities for the farmers. The warriors protected the farmers with the highest priority. But as long as the farmers were within the borders of the Kiwane Village, basic security for the farmers fell to the Kiwane warriors. This gave the Aukmondi warriors a few moments of leisure time. The Green Warrior Tushema gave the Aukmondi warriors the rare opportunity to socialize with the farmers.

The Red Warrior Rotho sat next to the Gold Warrior Oghani in the circle of people. The two warriors took advantage of their relaxed duties and engaged in a spontaneous duet. The lyrics were a volley of whimsical limericks. By the time the two warriors had finished, everyone was laughing so hard that tears of joy flowed.

The Aukmondi farmers and warriors laughed so hard that most of them did not notice the Kiwane villagers approaching. The Kiwane Mfalme, Modoffa Menda, and his staff of five dedicated aides approached along a nearby pathway. Tushema, the ever-vigilant Green Warrior, was the first to see the Mfalme and his small staff coming. When he saw them step off the pathway and walk toward the Aukmondi, Tushema rose to his feet. He suppressed his laughter just enough to announce their approach.

The rest of the Aukmondi let their merriment slowly subside as they rose. The Great Creation Elder Zekke, still chuckling at Oghani's and Rotho's performance, wiped the tears of laughter from his eyes. He rocked his way out to welcome the Mfalme.

"Mfalme Menda, I hope our noise has not been too much of a disturbance."

"No, no, Elder Zekke, it has not."

"Would you like to join us?" Zekke ushered the Mfalme closer.

"Thank you, but only for a moment." Mfalme Menda's staff stayed back as Modoffa Menda followed Elder Zekke into the circle of Aukmondi. As usual, he carried his royal scepter. He waved it toward the people who stood around him. It was his way of telling everyone to relax and return to their seats.

"As I approached," Mfalme Menda began, tapping the potbellied fog-end of the scepter in the palm of his hand, "I could hear you laughing several meters away. You are having a wonderful time. The idea to join you crossed my mind."

"Then you are welcome. We have plenty of food and all the banana beer you can drink."

"No, Elder Zekke. Thank you for the kind offer. You continue to enjoy yourselves. I only came to say goodbye. I understand that you will begin your journey back to the Aukmondi Valley before sunrise tomorrow morning."

"Yes, Mfalme." Zekke nodded toward Tushema. "Our Green Warrior suggests that we should start back as soon as possible."

"Then, I will probably not see you again before you leave. Thank you, Elder Zekke. Please relay my thanks to all the Aukmondi. I can only describe your generous contributions to this *mkutano* as remarkable." Mfalme Menda included a special nod and smile toward Lobarra. "This was the best we ever had."

"Thank you, Mfalme. It has been a rewarding pleasure for us, too."

"I would like to wish all of you a safe journey home and ..." Mfalme Menda did not finish his sentence.

It was at this point that the infant Tutapona screamed. Tutapona had sat in his mother's lap, fascinated by all the joy and merriment around him. But then, he squirmed. Something was suddenly wrong. Tutapona's restlessness and fretting quickly transformed into crying, and then one steady scream. The scream faded to silence as the scream pulled all the air from his tiny lungs. The infant's arms and legs trembled with spasms as those same lungs hungered for more air. With eyes closed, Tutapona sucked in one huge gulp of air and cried loudly and without restraint.

Everyone turned toward Tutapona. They watched as Lobarra lifted the infant from her lap. Lobarra placed Tutapona against her chest, with his head on her shoulder. She rose to her feet again. To calm him down, she jostled the infant. It worked. Tutapona's crying slowly subsided. Lobarra continued to jostle him and turned in a slow and patient circle.

It was an awkward moment as everyone continued to watch Lobarra do what only a mother could do. Mfalme Menda was the first to return things to normal. Tapping the bullfrog-end of his scepter in his hand again, he walked toward the mother and child. With a gentle smile, he playfully and gently stroked Tutapona's chin and cheeks with his finger. "Oh, such an awful, awful fuss! What is this all about? Is all of that necessary? What has upset you so?"

When Lobarra heard Mfalme Menda talking to Tutapona, she suddenly realized she had turned her back on the Kiwane Mfalme. She quickly turned around to face the Mfalme again to correct her mistake. She felt she owed him a twofold apology, for Tutapona's sudden outburst and her rude behavior.

"I am so sorry, Mfalme," she said.

"No need. I understand. I have seen my share of babies. I know they can be demanding sometimes. And if babies could talk, their innocence and honesty would probably make them the most outspoken people among us."

"After such an outburst, I wonder what he might say." Elder Zekke stepped forward. "Is he alright, Sacred Woman?"

"I think so." Lobarra gently lowered Tutapona from her shoulder. She cradled him in her arms. Seeing that Tutapona had stopped crying, Lobarra brushed the tears from his cheeks. "I wish I knew what troubles him."

"Is it an illness?" Mfalme Menda asked. "If you like, I can send for my healer, Ngo Wenfundi."

"No. Thank you, Mfalme. I do not think it is necessary. My son has just been so restless. At first, I thought it was hunger. When I feed him, it calms him down for a while. But …"

"Do you feed him each time he seems restless?"

"Yes. It works most of the time."

"Well, there is your problem, Sacred Woman." Zekke chuckled. "I suspect he is only suffering from a little indigestion."

"Great Creation, an infant seldom gets indigestion from his mother's milk. No. I think it is something else."

"As I told the Sacred Woman yesterday," the Red Warrior Rotho walked over and joined the group standing around Tutapona, "He is homesick. I think he wants to go home."

"An infant is often sensitive to its surroundings. You could be right. Infants know more than we realize," Mfalme Menda commented. "How long does it take you to reach the Aukmondi Valley?"

"Just over two days, I believe." Zekke glanced over at the Green Warrior Tushema to confirm his response. "Yes, about two and a half days."

"Well, that is not too long. The little one will be home soon." Mfalme Menda took the liberty of stroking Tutapona's chin again.

The baby's innocence charmed him. He smiled. "He is a healthy and handsome young man. Look at him. He seems fine now."

Tutapona had calmed down completely. As Modoffa leaned over him, Tutapona's bright eyes caught sight of the Mfalme's royal scepter. Tutapona could not take his eyes off the potbellied bullfrog. Fascinated by what he was looking at, Tutapona reached out.

"Oh, you like that?" Modoffa held the scepter with the bullfrog-end closer. He spoke in an octave higher than his normal voice, typical of most people teasingly talking to infants. "You like that? You like that, do you not? You want that ugly thing? Yes, you do. You want that?"

"Mfalme?" Lobarra was not sure of Mfalme Menda's intent. As far as she could tell, he seemed serious about giving Tutapona the scepter. "Mfalme, please, we cannot take your scepter."

"It is alright," Modoffa spoke to Lobarra as he continued to wave the bullfrog back and forth over Tutapona's face. "Is he not a prince of the Chinchigwe Clan of the Aukmondi?"

Still awed by the offer, Lobarra opened her mouth to answer, but Elder Zekke answered instead. "He is, Mfalme. He is the grandson of Mfalme Ameh Jobabwe."

"Then, if you do not mind him having it, I do not mind giving it to him."

"Mfalme, we cannot," Lobarra repeated.

"Oh, it is alright, child. I have others. Besides, this scepter stands among several of my oldest. Over many past harvests, I have replaced it a forgotten number of times." Mfalme Menda held the bullfrog up to his face. "But, occasionally, I miss this old bullfrog's company. I select it from among many, again and again. A few days ago, after hosting visitors, I dug it out again. I needed this old bullfrog's company one more time."

"Then, without doubt, it must be special, Mfalme."

"No. I have others far more special."

"But it is so beautiful. The handiwork is remarkable." Elder Zekke leaned in closer. He marveled at its complex detail. About

50 centimeters long, it had intricate carvings over the whole shaft. Painstaking attention to detail went into the frog's webbed feet, the pictures, and the symbols etched into the wood. Elder Zekke wanted to touch the scepter, but restrained himself. "May I ask who made it for you?"

Mfalme Modoffa Menda shrugged. He smiled with embarrassment. "I do not know. I received it over thirty harvests ago, when I became Mfalme of the Kiwane. It lay among the many gifts I received during my coronation."

"Then, it is a keepsake," Lobarra finally found her voice.

"I have kept it long enough. I offer it now as a gift to the prince, Tutapona."

"Thank you, Mfalme."

"My pleasure." Mfalme Menda lowered the scepter to within Tutapona's reach. Tutapona finally wrapped both of his tiny hands around the bullfrog-end of the scepter. He pulled it, as babies do, toward his mouth. Lobarra gently pulled it away but held it playfully over Tutapona's face. Tutapona's fascination continued. Unlike moments ago, he giggled and kicked with excitement.

"Well, I wish you a good night." Mfalme Menda turned to face Elder Zekke, Tushema, and the rest of the Aukmondi. "As I was about to say, I wish you a safe journey home. Please give my regards to Mfalme Ncobba and Mfalme Jobabwe. I hope to see all of you next harvest, if not sooner."

32

WE WILL GET THROUGH THIS

The Gray Warrior Kharaambi and the Brown Warrior Quazzi arrived at Kon-Shambique's kraal about the same time. They found that a huge crowd had gathered out front. Three Aukmondi warriors held the crowd back at the kraal entrance. Kharaambi and Quazzi worked their way through the crowd. It was a chilling experience. The crowd was quiet, but almost everyone in the crowd cried.

After seeing so many disturbed people, Kharaambi and Quazzi saw their second evidence of the tragedy after they entered the kraal. On the ground just outside Kon-Shambique's hut lay a huge bloodstain. The bodies of Zabiba and Gengu no longer lay outside Kon-Shambique's hut. Kon-Shambique had hoped moving the bodies inside would prevent undue alarm among all the gathered people. It did not help. The huge bloodstain still created its share of alarm.

Even in the darkness, the bloodstain was clearly visible by the light emanating from inside Kon-Shambique's hut. Kharaambi and Quazzi stood over the stain, staring down at it. They looked up at each other as the gravity of the moment took root. They took careful steps around the stain to enter the hut.

Inside, the two found the front chamber still in complete disarray. They stepped between more blood trailing from the hut entrance to the rear chamber. The chamber's water gourd still lay on its side. Spilled water had soaked into the ground, creating a messy mud-puddle. Gengu's shield lay on the ground in the center of the chamber. The bodies of the warriors Zabiba and Gengu lay out of the way, against the right wall. The uniform position of the bodies was the only neat arrangement in the whole chamber.

Kharaambi and Quazzi found Kon-Shambique sitting on the ground against the back wall of the front chamber. He sat with his knees drawn up, his arms wrapped around his knees. To complete the fetal position, his head rested on his knees. Kharaambi and Quazzi ignored the disorder in the chamber. They rushed over and kneeled at Kon-Shambique's side.

"Great Creation, what happened here?" Kharaambi asked.

Kon-Shambique raised his head and looked at the Gray Warrior. His eyes were red. He had been crying heavily. When he finally spoke, he spoke just above a whisper. "I do not know."

Kharaambi and Quazzi looked at each other again. Neither had ever seen their enlightened and most gifted spiritual adviser so broken. Quazzi turned to Kon-Shambique and gently placed his bandaged hand on his shoulder.

"Great Creation, are you alright?"

Kon-Shambique did not answer. He closed his eyes as if to suppress his pain.

"Where are Rwuva and Tongda?" Quazzi asked.

Kon-Shambique gestured with a nod of his head. His words were barely audible. "Their bodies … are in the rear chamber."

Kharaambi and Quazzi rose to their feet and moved toward the rear chamber. They could hear the girls, Kunto and Audi, crying before they entered. As the two pulled aside the curtain and entered the rear chamber, they saw Kunto, Audi, and Yejide huddled on the left side of the chamber. The three of them were sobbing. On the right side of the chamber, the bodies of Rwuva and Tongda lay on cots, side by side. Omari sat at Rwuva's side. Olabisi sat at Tongda's. Omari and Olabisi were not sobbing; tears rolled freely down their faces.

Everyone in the chamber, so oppressed by sorrow, remained silent. Kharaambi and Quazzi both stood and stared at the bodies of Rwuva and Tongda. Rwuva and Tongda looked to be asleep, their arms neatly folded across their chests. The dead women and all their surroundings did not seem real. As the reality settled in, the eyes of both Kharaambi and Quazzi welled up with tears.

Olabisi finally broke the silence when she wiped the tears from her face. She looked up at Kharaambi. "What must we do now, Sacred Woman?"

"What?" The question jolted Kharaambi back to the present. She blinked, forcing a single tear to run down her face. "We will … we will get through this."

"How?"

Kharaambi had no idea. She considered the question, tapping into one of her own sources of strength: "Where is the Mfalme?"

"I am told he is on Nagorda Peak," Quazzi answered. "The Mfalme thinks the Mangoni may be responsible for this."

"Then we will start with the Mangoni."

At that moment, the Red Warrior Zhanguta, another of Rwuva's aides, came from the adjacent chamber of the hut. He got Kharaambi's attention. "Sacred Woman, come. You must see this."

Still in shock at seeing the bodies of Rwuva and Tongda, the Gray Warrior had to force herself to move. She crossed the chamber and followed Zhanguta into the adjacent chamber. Quazzi followed her.

The Red Warrior Zhanguta pointed at the collapsed table in the corner. On the underside and written in Zabiba's blood, Kharaambi and Quazzi read the same message that had enraged Ramuza earlier. *All dead. Two days.*

"Oh, Great Sacred Spirit!" Kharaambi came closer to the broken table. She kneeled to get a closer look at the message.

"What is it, Sacred Woman?" Quazzi stood over Kharaambi's shoulder. He stared at the message. He could see that something about the message, besides the obvious, had piqued the Gray Warrior's interest.

"I recognize that handwriting. It belongs to the Sacred Woman Tongda."

"What? But, how can that be? Are you sure?"

"Yes. The handwriting is Tongda's."

— 33 —

THE OBENTAWNI KRAAL

Nothing stirred after the Loa of Death finished with the Pogobi kraal. News of the devastation spread slowly beyond the kraal. Others learned of the devastation late in the night. It would be an hour before midnight when others learned the demon also visited the Obentawni kraal.

The Obentawni kraal is one of the smallest kraals on the northern slope. Located just inside the north rim sentry line, the kraal features five small, multipurpose huts built around a central open area. This small encampment served the sentinel warriors who stood guard on the north rim. At most, only ten to twenty warriors visited the kraal at any given time.

No one knows if the loa had visited the Obentawni kraal before or after the Pogobi devastation. But the devastation proved just as thorough. It began shortly after Sentinel warriors heard a wayward raven cawing restlessly. The raven flew in the darkness from tree to tree, up and down the sentinel line. At the same time, and unseen by anyone, the loa entered the Obentawni kraal through the unguarded rear. It found twelve Green Warriors sitting and quietly talking together in the open area. No torches or campfires burned since the kraal was close to the sentry line. The warriors sat and talked in complete darkness.

The vigilant Green Warriors always watched for danger beyond the sentry line. None of them ever expected danger to walk up to them from the rear. The loa quietly approached the twelve warriors. It stood behind them, in the darkness, for several long moments without drawing attention to itself. When one of the Green Warriors finally turned, wondering who stood back so antisocially, the loa opened its arms wide open.

The loa took seconds to move from one surprised warrior to the next. One touch with its bony hands was all it took. All twelve of the warriors lay dead. None of the skilled Green Warriors had a chance to sound warning drums.

Four other Green Warriors walked into the kraal at that moment. Suspecting nothing, they came into the kraal with their defenses down. Because of the kraal's nature and purpose, the peaceful silence gave the warriors no clue that something was wrong. The only sounds heard were the occasional echoes of a raven's caw somewhere overhead. When the four Green Warriors saw the bodies of the fallen warriors, they rushed over to see what had happened to them. They realized that an attack had occurred. The realization came too late. By then, the loa stood behind them. None of them escaped.

Normally, Green Warriors enter and leave the Obentawni kraal throughout the night. This night was different. Unsuspecting warriors continued to enter the kraal. None of them ever left. As other Green Warriors entered, the bodies continued to pile.

34

DO NOT UNDERESTIMATE THE LOA OF DEATH

The Gray Warrior Kharaambi and the Brown Warrior Quazzi continued the debate over whether Tongda wrote the message on the underside of the table. Quazzi was not comfortable with the notion that she did. Like Ramuza had done, he saw the dark message as a threat. It made no sense. Tongda would not write such a thing. Kharaambi had no doubt the handwriting was Tongda's, but she was at a loss to explain it.

The sound of Nionu's voice ended the debate. Kharaambi and Quazzi heard the Royal Warrior in the front chamber of the hut. The anger in his voice demanded their immediate attention.

Kharaambi and Quazzi rushed out of the adjacent chamber, around the litters of Rwuva and Tongda in the rear chamber, and back into the front chamber. They found the Royal Warrior Nionu kneeling over Kon-Shambique. Nionu's two Blue Warriors stood behind him.

Nionu looked up at Kharaambi and Quazzi with enough respect to recognize their presence. He said nothing to them. Instead, he resumed his pointed interrogation of the Favored Tribesman.

"Great Creation, talk to me." Nionu pointed to the bodies of Zabiba and Gengu. He was forceful and angry. There was no sign of his usual whimsical nature. "What happened to these warriors?"

"I … dare not say." Kon-Shambique still spoke above a whisper. He continued to rest his head on his knees. Since his head was down, his voice was barely audible.

Nionu leaned in closer to hear the Favored Tribesman. "You dare not say? What do you mean by that? Were you here when this happened? Did you see anything? You must tell me what happened here, Kon-Shambique. Who did this?" When Nionu got no more answers, he reached over and physically raised Kon-Shambique's head. "Great Creation, you must talk to me."

"Nionu!" The tone in Quazzi's voice was an indirect suggestion to the Royal Warrior to ease up on Kon-Shambique. Quazzi knew Nionu had an unstoppable drive when he wanted to get to the heart of a matter.

Nionu sighed. He eased Kon-Shambique's head back down to his knees. He stood up and backed away. With a hint of frustration, the Royal Warrior picked up Gengu's shield and laid it next to the Red Warrior's body. He stood back as Kharaambi came to kneel again at Kon-Shambique's side.

"Great Creation, we saw that message in the adjacent chamber. Is that why the Mfalme went up to Nagorda Peak?"

"Message? What message?" The driven Nionu stepped forward again.

"We found a message on the underside of the table in the adjacent chamber. Someone …" Quazzi paused, still reluctant to name Tongda. "Someone wrote the message with the blood of the Green Warrior Zabiba."

"And what is this message?"

"*All dead. Two days*. Somehow, the Mfalme thinks the Mangoni are behind this."

Kharaambi turned to Kon-Shambique again. "Could this be true? Is that why Ramuza went up to Nagorda Peak?"

Kon-Shambique finally raised his head from his knees. "It is one of the reasons."

"But, Great Creation," Quazzi paused. He glanced at Kharaambi before he finished what he was about to say. "The Gray Warrior thinks Tongda wrote the message. Could this also be true?"

Kon-Shambique did not act surprised. He closed his eyes. "Yes. It is also true."

"But why? Why would she write such a threatening thing? What does it mean?"

"It is not a threat." Kon-Shambique unwrapped one of his arms from around his knees. He held something in his fist. He slowly opened his fist. In the palm of his hand were two fresh and green flower buds.

"What is that?" Nionu asked. He kneeled again to get closer to the buds.

"These are the buds of daylilies," Kon-Shambique explained. "I found them on the ground between the bodies of Rwuva and Tongda."

"What have daylily buds got to do with Tongda's message?"

Kon-Shambique pointed to one of the buds. "This bud will bloom with the sunrise tomorrow. The other bud will probably not bloom until the day after tomorrow. Both buds should have died with the stalk they were on. Yet they continue to live. The Sacred Woman Tongda saw this oddity and realized what it meant. She tried to warn us."

"Warn us of what?"

"A daylily's bloom lasts but one day. It means we have two days to live."

"Great Creation, you do not believe that."

Kon-Shambique did not respond to the Brown Warrior's statement. He slowly got to his feet. He rubbed the fatigue and weariness from his face. The Favored Tribesman walked around the chamber as if to reacquaint himself with his surroundings. He briefly looked into the faces of each of the people as he walked past them: Quazzi, Nionu, Kharaambi, and Nionu's two Blue Warriors, Obe Bendabe and Dabete Ehkili.

"There is an odor in the air. Can you smell it?" Kon-Shambique asked. "I do not mean the smell of burnt grass. There is another odor. It is the smell of death and dying."

Kon-Shambique paused a moment to peek outside the hut. He saw a huge crowd standing near the kraal's entrance. Unready to face such a crowd, he ducked back into the hut. He turned back to face the people inside the hut. "Do you hear those drums – that constant boom-boom, boom-boom? That odor and those drums are all part of a ritual the Mangoni houngan is performing."

"What ritual?" Nionu asked.

"It is the ritual of death. The houngan has summoned a loa to our valley. As we speak, this loa walks among us."

"A loa? What is a loa?"

"A spirit. If I am correct, the Mangoni calls this spirit… Soso-Dosamdi. It is the Loa of Death."

Nionu looked at each of the other faces in the chamber. He had expressions of doubt and disbelief as he turned back to Kon-Shambique. "For real? You expect us to believe such a thing?"

"Great Creation, with that attitude, you might be the safest among us." There was a touch of frustration in Kon-Shambique's voice. He looked at Nionu and pointed at the bodies of Zabiba and Gengu. "Look there! What do you see?"

Nionu looked down at the fallen warrior. He opened his mouth to answer the Favored Tribesman, but no words came out.

Kon-Shambique took Nionu by the arm and pushed him toward the entranceway to the rear chamber. He yanked back the curtain and forced Nionu to look into the chamber at the bodies of Rwuva and Tongda. "What do you see? Now, you tell me, Great Creation. Is this for real?"

Seeing the bodies of Rwuva and Tongda had a greater impact than the sight of the two warriors. The Royal Warrior Nionu stepped back. His expressions of doubt and disbelief softened. His attitude was different. He felt apologetic. "Alright. So, what are we supposed to do? Are we to sit around, waiting for this loa thing to kill all of us in the next two days? Where can I find this loa?"

"Search for death if you wish, Great Creation. The Loa of Death comes to you on its terms. It often comes at a most inappropriate time for many of us."

"Just tell me. Where can I find it? I want to give it something inappropriate."

"Nionu, Great Creation, please do not underestimate the Loa of Death. It can wipe out whole villages and tribes with a wave of its hand."

"Yeah, well … let it wave at me."

"Nionu, Great Creation," Quazzi spoke. "I sent for you because we need you. But we need you alive. I am putting you in charge of finding out what happened here. We need your determination. This goes beyond anything we have ever encountered. Can you and your army do this without getting yourselves killed?"

Nionu looked at the commanders of his regiments, the Blue Warriors, Obe and Dabete. "Yes, Great Creation. Just point us in the right direction and turn us loose."

"Kon-Shambique," Kharaambi addressed the Favored Tribesman, "Ramuza went to Nagorda Peak to speak with the Mangoni. Did he know the nature of this ritual the houngan is performing?"

"Yes, Sacred Woman." It was Kon-Shambique's turn to look apologetic. "I told him about it earlier. But I also asked him to ignore it. I did not believe the houngan's magic could be so powerful."

"If I know Ramuza, he intends to stop the ritual."

"There is no question about it, Sacred Woman. When he left here, grief and anger drove him toward the peak. I doubt anything could have stopped him." Kon-Shambique inhaled lightly to sample the air. "Unfortunately, we still smell the odor of death. And we still hear the drums. We can only assume the Mfalme, so far, has not succeeded."

"The Mfalme is probably … negotiating." Nionu gripped his spear as if to make a point. He signaled to his Blue Warriors to follow him as he went toward the exit. "We are going up to Nagorda. All the Mfalme needs is a little force behind his negotiations."

At that moment, one of the warriors holding the crowd back at the kraal entrance rushed into the hut. He came for the Gray Warrior. "Kharaambi, Sacred Woman! Come quickly, please!"

Kharaambi rushed past Nionu toward the exit. Quazzi, Nionu, Kon-Shambique, and Nionu's Blue Warriors followed her out of the hut.

Out at the kraal entrance, the crowd was restless. With screams and panic, the crowd scattered. People on the fringes of the crowd ran in all directions, trying to escape whatever was making its way through the crowd.

When the crowd finally parted, the Loa of Death glided through the kraal entrance. The tall, ominous figure in flowing black garments stopped inside the kraal and stood momentarily, staring at the group that had come from Kon-Shambique's hut.

Once it realized that it was the focus of everyone's attention, the loa extracted from under its flowing garments the lifeless body of Ramuza. With one hand, it tossed Ramuza's body toward the group.

Ramuza's body hit the ground hard. It rolled, stopping at the feet of Kharaambi, Quazzi, and Kon-Shambique.

Boom-boom! Boom-boom! Boom-boom!

— 35 —

ASK FOR HER UNDERSTANDING

With Ramuza's body at her feet, Kharaambi fell to her knees. The unquestionably strong woman sat in shock. Bewildered, she gathered Ramuza's body into her arms. His head fell back, mocking her embrace. His arms hung limp at his side. There was no question about it. Kharaambi could see that the Mfalme was dead. The tears she had been struggling to hold back suddenly overflowed.

"Sacred Spirit, please!" Kharaambi pleaded. She rocked Ramuza's body in her arms. "Great Sacred Spirit, where are you?"

Kon-Shambique, with fresh tears on his face, kneeled and touched Kharaambi's shoulder. "Sacred Woman … let us move him inside."

Kharaambi forced herself to regain her composure. She surrendered Ramuza's body to Quazzi and Kon-Shambique. Even when they lifted Ramuza's body from the ground, Kharaambi could not take her hands off him.

"No! No! This ends now! Right now!" The Royal Warrior Nionu jabbed his spear into the ground and paced restlessly. He, too, struggled with overwhelming emotion. He expressed his painful sorrow with visible anger. Nionu stopped his pacing and looked out toward the kraal entrance. When he saw the Loa of Death retreating through the parted crowd, he took several hurried steps toward the loa.

"Hey, Ugly!" Nionu called out to the loa. When the demon continued to move away without looking back, Nionu searched the ground until he found a fist-sized stone nearby. He picked it up and hurled with all his might. He hit the loa in the back of the head with a loud thump.

The loa stopped. It slowly turned, as if searching for whoever threw the stone.

Nionu raised both his arms and waved them to draw attention to himself. He thumped his chest. "Are you looking for me? I did that - you foul-smelling maggot bag! Yeah, I did it! Come and get me! What makes you think you can come into this valley and kill my people without consequences? Then you kill my Mfalme! And think you can walk away? No! No, no! You have to answer for that. You do not belong here. I will send you back to that dark hole you came from, if it is the last thing I do!"

The loa stared at the arrogant Royal Warrior. After a moment, he looked down at the stone Nionu had thrown. With long, bony fingers, it slowly picked up the stone. With its living eyes, the loa studied the stone in its hand. The loa looked as though it was deciding what to do with it, whether to throw it back at Nionu. The decision was made, and the loa looked up again at Nionu. Without looking, it gingerly tossed the stone aside, toward the crowd at its left. Robuti, a Young Creation known throughout the valley for his beautiful metal sculptures, caught the stone. Robuti fell dead.

Nionu froze. The loa's unexpected power stunned him.

Dabete Ehkili, one of Nionu's Blue Warriors, rushed to Nionu's side. He took the Royal Warrior by the arm. "Great Creation, with all due respect! What do you think you are doing? That thing will kill you."

"Probably. But it has to catch me first, Dabete."

"What? Do you think you can outrun it?"

"Great Creation, I have outrun death more times than I care to think about."

"Did you not hear the Favored Tribesman? Do not underestimate that thing's power."

"Yeah … it is too late, Dabete. I already have." Nionu looked at the crowd. Several people had gathered around Robuti's body. They moved it out of the way. Among them, Robuti's mother wailed over the boy's body. "The Sacred Spirit knows … I did not expect that to happen."

"What did you expect?"

"I was trying to provoke it. I was hoping it would come after me."

"Is that wise, Great Creation?" Obe Bendabe, the other Blue Warrior, approached Nionu. "Are you asking to die?"

"I do not intend to engage it. I only want to distract it; to keep it busy for a while."

"You are employing your cat's tail offense." Obe was familiar with the tactic. It was one of Nionu's favorite battle tactics. Small cats often use their tails to catch the undivided attention of their prey. While the prey falls to the hypnotic movements of the cat's tail, the cat pounces for the kill with teeth and claws. Nionu had taught the tactic to all his warriors. "But, it is risky. What did you hope to achieve here?"

"While I distract it, I want the two of you to use the time to get up to Nagorda Peak. Finish the Mfalme's mission. Do whatever it takes." Nionu looked at both Blue Warriors to emphasize his words. "And I mean, whatever it takes, to stop that ritual."

"Should we use our regiments? We could overwhelm the Mangoni."

Nionu thought for a moment. "No. It might be best to do this quietly, on a covert level."

"Great Creation," the Blue Warrior Dabete showed concern for his commander. "Obe and I can get into the Mangoni camp unseen with no problem. But you should, at least, use our regiments to help distract the loa. Give it an entire army to chase. That should keep it busy."

"Yes. It only makes sense." The Blue Warrior Obe agreed.

"No." Nionu was insistent. "Kon-Shambique also said this thing can wipe out whole villages and tribes with the wave of its hand. It could wipe out both of your regiments just as easily. No. Warriors are not expendable. I will not throw away their lives on such a risky undertaking."

"Nionu, Great Creation." Kon-Shambique had come from his hut and overheard part of Nionu's plan. "Do you think you will succeed, where the Mfalme has failed?"

Nionu was still feeling the confident power of his anger. "Kon-Shambique, I intend to have that maggot bag struggling to kill homeless fleas."

"I do not recommend that you challenge death so lightly."

"There is nothing light about this. I am serious." Nionu looked at Kon-Shambique. He could see the Favored Tribesman's concern. "Can you suggest a better plan, Great Creation?"

"No. I cannot."

"Then summon me when you can. I am open-minded. I will listen to any ideas you may have." Nionu looked out toward the loa. The demon had turned. It continued through the scattered crowd and back up the pathway toward Nagorda Peak. "If I am to succeed, I must act before that thing gets away. Please help me by moving the crowd back. Call them over to the side. Talk to them. They need you."

"What can I tell them?"

"Are you asking me? You are the Favored Tribesman. You think of something. Tell them whatever you think the Supreme Spirit wants them to know."

Kon-Shambique looked toward the crowd. It had grown larger since the last time he had seen it. Kon-Shambique already knew the people had gathered at his kraal for two primary reasons. Some were curious about developing events, and all were seeking the comfort of his guidance.

"I will see what I can do." Kon-Shambique walked toward the crowd. To Nionu's advantage, the Favored Tribesman angled his approach toward the crowd to the far right. Sure enough, the scattered crowd flowed toward him as if he were a magnet. He lured them together and away from the kraal entrance. His willingness to talk with them now held their undivided attention.

The Royal Warrior Nionu used that moment as an opportunity to exit the kraal. He ran up the pathway toward the loa. He only looked back at his Blue Warriors once. Nionu could tell that they waited for their opportunity to move. He intended to create that opportunity. Nionu had no idea how he would hold the loa's attention. But whatever he did, it would be a careful balance between taunting the loa and staying far enough away to keep from getting himself killed.

When Nionu thought he was close enough behind the loa, he picked up another fist-sized stone. He hurled it at the loa with all his might. He hit the loa in the center of its back this time. And just as before, the loa stopped and turned to face the Royal Warrior.

Nionu pointed at the stone. "Do not bother to throw that back. I intend not to catch it."

The loa glided toward the Royal Warrior. Nionu turned. He ran down the Nagorda hillside, away from the peak. He left the pathway. The Angrenni Forest lay just south of the pathway. Nionu ran into the forest. He hoped to use the thick trees of the forest to his advantage. He felt satisfied when the demon continued moving away from Nagorda Peak. Obe and Dabete should have enough opportunity to fulfill their clandestine mission. His immediate hope was staying ahead of the thing now coming after him.

*****

Back in Kon-Shambique's kraal, Nionu's Blue Warriors marveled at the boldness of their commander. As Nionu and the loa disappeared into the trees, the Blue Warriors exited the kraal and raced up the pathway toward Nagorda Peak.

Just a few meters away, Kon-Shambique was so overwhelmed by the crowd he never saw the Blue Warriors leave. He hoped and prayed that their mission would be successful. The Favored Tribesman had fully accepted that the only way to stop the Loa of Death from walking the Aukmondi Valley is to stop the houngan's ritual. Kon-Shambique wished them well and turned his attention to the crowd before him.

At first, the sudden cascade of questions from the crowd came at Kon-Shambique in a jumble. There were questions about the deaths of Rwuva, Tongda, the warriors, and about the Mfalme. What will become of the Aukmondi, now that Mfalme Ncobba is dead? How did this happen? Why did this happen? Where is the Supreme Spirit? Why is She so quiet when death walks so openly among us?

Kon-Shambique held up his hands to quiet the crowd. "Please. Listen to me. I cannot answer any of your questions now. I must be honest with you. I am just as confused and spiritually broken as most of you seem to be."

"We suffer our greatest fears, Great Creation." A voice from the crowd yelled out. "That thing is not killing only people. It is killing our livestock, too!"

Kon-Shambique took a moment to gather his thoughts. "Our livestock enjoy many of the same feelings we do, whether it is fear, hope, expectation, or bonding love. There is no difference. Because they are animals, they only react differently, except in this case. Our livestock reacts to the houngan's demon just as we do. They die too."

"What are we to do?"

"I do not know. I can only suggest that you go to a quiet place. Pray. The Supreme Spirit… will comfort you. If She does not come before you physically and speak to you as the Sacred Woman Eledah, then as always, She speaks to you in spirit. In quiet places, She speaks to you through your thoughts and heart. Go to the Sacred Temple and pray."

"I just came from the Sacred Temple." Another voice yelled out. "The Temple Gardens are crowded. And the wait to go inside is long."

"Then find another place; the valley depths, Elephant's Ridge on the south rim. Anywhere! I like to go up to Nagorda Peak." Kon-Shambique smiled at the irony of the situation. "But, I understand, the peak has its special crowd now. It does not matter where you go. It could even be the central chamber of your huts. Just go and talk with Her. Tell Her what you are feeling. She is listening. She will answer you."

"You have taught us these things, Great Creation." Another voice in the crowd said. "We know how to pray. And we have prayed. But She has given us no answers yet."

"You must be patient. Do not force Her to speak to you. Just sit still and listen. An answer will come. She speaks to us more often through our hearts and minds than all the times She has walked among us as the Sacred Woman Eledah."

"Have you talked with Her, Great Creation?"

Kon-Shambique reacted to the question by looking down. He seemed almost embarrassed to answer the question. He shuffled a pebble on the ground with the toe of his sandal. "No. No, I have not." He felt he owed the crowd an explanation.

When he raised his head again, his eyes had welled with tears. "You must know the Sacred Woman Tongda … Tongda was very close to me. I … I cannot … get past that yet. And because we have lost several warriors, including Rwuva and the Mfalme, I find concentrating even harder now. I beg your forgiveness and understanding."

"Kon-Shambique," an Old Creation spoke in front of the crowd. It was the senior craftsman, Tanake. The Old Creation hated climbing the Nagorda hillside. Yet, here he was, in the forefront of the crowd. "Do you expect us to do something you, the Favored Tribesman, could not do?"

"You must try, Tanake. You may succeed where I have failed."

"If we prayed, asking Her to make things right …"

Kon-Shambique held up his hand to stop Tanake in the middle of his question. "No. Please. Please do not ask that of Her. None of us know Her grand design. Have faith in what She is allowing to happen. Go to your quiet places and ask Her for understanding. Ask Her to enlighten you. In time, She will tell you what you must know. She will guide you to where you need to be. She will give you what you need."

36

WE WILL FIGURE THIS OUT TOGETHER

The tract of land south of the Nagorda hillside was a thick, woody area known as the Angrenni Forest. It was one of the thickest forest areas in the whole Aukmondi Valley. It stretched unbroken from south of the pathway outside Kon-Shambique's kraal to the bottom of the north slope. The southern boundary of the forest, at the bottom of the valley, stretched across two and a half kilometers along the north bank pathway and the Aukmondi River.

The Royal Warrior Nionu weaved between the trees and stumbled over bushes and vines. He moved quickly through the forest, despite the thick vegetation. It was dark and Nionu fled without the aid of a torch. Visibility was almost nonexistent. To move with ease, he had discarded his shield and spear. He knew that any direct combat at this point would be futile, and the shield and spear hampered his movements. He relied heavily on his agility and skills as a warrior to keep moving at a steady pace.

His idea to evade the demon down this congested part of the slope was impulsive and unintentional. When he started, he ran without any idea where he was going. Nionu hoped to use the trees of the forest to help impede the demon's approach. But those same trees impeded his progress. And the demon had the advantages of supernatural abilities. Nionu wondered if he could make this flight last. His Blue Warriors, Obe and Dabete, needed the time to succeed in their mission to stop the ritual of the Mangoni houngan.

At one point, Nionu sacrificed a few precious moments to look back. Despite the darkness, the Royal Warrior could see through the trees that a tall and ominous silhouette still moved in his direction. Nionu held a comfortable distance between him and the demon. But, the darkness and density of trees worked against him. With each step, his advantage of distance shrank.

Nionu continued his run. He needed to keep moving. He realized that, no matter how fast he moved through the forest, his flight from the demon would end in one of two ways. Either the demon would soon get close enough to him to rob him of his life, or his Blue Warriors would succeed in their mission; stop the Mangoni houngan's ritual and send the demon back to wherever it came. It was just a matter of time. Nionu only needed to stay ahead of the demon. Every second worked to the advantage of his Blue Warriors.

At first, Nionu ran mindlessly through the forest. He saw no defining landmarks and had no idea where he was. The thick canopy of trees blocked his view of the stars overhead. The downward incline of the north slope gave him his only reliable sense of direction.

By chance, a huge log blocked his progress down the slope. Nionu reached out with both hands to touch the log. A smile spread across his face. He knew this forest well. He knew this log. Nionu knew where he was. He suddenly realized he had another advantage. Only six hundred meters, straight ahead, was the southern edge of the forest and the north bank pathway. An eastern flight along the pathway would give him an unobstructed trail into the expansive and unpopulated valley depths.

The log before Nionu was over a meter and a half thick. Nionu had to hop up on top to cross it. With the graceful agility of a leopard, Nionu mounted the log with no problem. The problem came when he slid off the log to the other side. His royal cloak caught on a snag. Nionu's first impulse was to remove the cloak and leave it. But if he did that, he felt he would waste precious seconds by untying the cloak from around his shoulders. Instead, the Royal Warrior grabbed the cloak and yanked hard with both hands. With a disheartening noise, his beautiful royal cloak ripped. A meter-long tear stretched down the middle. Nionu dismissed the unfortunate occurrence with a shrug. At least he was free and able to move again.

Nionu focused on his immediate concern. The time it took to climb over the log and free himself may have cut into the comfortable distance between him and the demon. He hastened his pace through more bushes and vines to reach the bottom of the slope and the north bank pathway. He had covered another hundred meters when he looked back again, to see how much the demon had gained on him. When he did, he saw no sign of the demon. Nionu stopped. He turned and searched the forest behind him.

"Alright, Ugly. Where are you?" He spoke to himself. Had he outdistanced the demon? Had the demon given up the chase?

Nionu grew more concerned. He had to keep the demon's interest if his cat's tail offense was to work. He had to keep the demon charmed long enough for his Blue Warriors to succeed. If he had lost the demon, then he had lost the charm. Could he recover the charm? Nionu walked back up the north slope in search of the demon.

Fully aware that the demon could step out from behind any tree, Nionu moved cautiously. He studied every shadow and movement around him in the darkness. He listened to every noise made by the crickets and small animals nearby. He had to sacrifice his comfort zone to recover the charm of his cat's tail offense. He backtracked his way up the north slope through more bushes and vines. He continued in this manner until he came within ten meters of the log he had climbed over just moments ago.

On the other side of the log, the Royal Warrior saw the gruesome Loa of Death. Nionu sighed with relief. He had not lost the demon. The demon stood there, staring back at him. This meant that his Blue Warriors still had time to complete their mission.

Nionu stared back at the demon. Something was wrong. Why had the demon stopped? Nionu reasoned that the log presented a problem for the demon. The log lay before the demon as an insurmountable obstacle.

"Hey, Ugly!" Nionu called out. He pointed to the log. "Is that thing in your way? Can you not get over it? Do you need some help?" When the demon did not respond and only stared back at Nionu, the Royal Warrior folded his arms across his chest. He leaned back against a nearby tree and made himself comfortable. "I will tell you what. You and I will figure this out together. We will stay right here, all night if we must. You relax. I will figure out something for you."

Nionu used words to antagonize the demon. He had to keep the demon angry enough to stay with him. But Nionu underestimated the demon's sensitivity. He overdid it. His words had touched a nerve. Nionu watched as the demon glided closer to the log. He saw the demon slap one of his bony hands against the log. What followed taught the Royal Warrior a quick lesson in what follows death - decay. The log, the remnant of a long-dead tree, decomposed rapidly. Nionu heard the sound of wood crackling and popping as it turned brittle, porous, and ash-like.

Nionu unfolded his arms. His recline against the tree was no longer comfortable. He had overplayed what he thought was his advantage. An acute and deadly situation was developing. Nionu pulled away from the tree as the demon pushed through the log, sending ash and dust flying.

"Great Sacred Spirit!" Nionu said to himself. He realized that if he had not come searching for the demon, he would be on the north bank pathway by now. Instead, Nionu found himself in a situation where he may be unable to escape. Nionu turned and ran with reckless abandon. After all his efforts, he put only twenty meters between himself and the demon. He had to move faster. He had to put that six hundred meters to the north bank pathway behind him.

Nionu stumbled and fell several times as he forced his way through the bushes and vines. He took some comfort in the fact that, at least, the demon still chased him. At the least, his cat's tail offense was still in full effect.

When the Royal Warrior finally stumbled out of the Angrenni Forest onto the north bank pathway, several cuts and scrapes covered his face and arms. As if to make a final assault on him, a vine caught his foot. Nionu fell to his hands and knees onto the pathway.

The Royal Warrior knew he had no time to nurse his injuries. He scrambled to his feet and turned eastward, toward the valley depths. Nionu broke into a strong and unobstructed run. He hoped to regain at least half his comfortable distance from the demon.

Suddenly, Nionu stopped running. He broke his run so hard that he slid across the dirt beneath his feet. He could see the Loa of Death coming from the forest up ahead and around a bend in the pathway. The demon anticipated his plan and moved to block him.

Nionu crouched down, hoping the demon had not seen him. He darted from the pathway and back into the forest to safeguard his concealment. From behind a thick bush, Nionu watched the demon take a superior position directly ahead. Nionu watched the demon turn. It stood there, waiting. The demon seemed confident that the insolent warrior would come from around the bend in the pathway.

"Go ahead. Waiting for me. And be patient. I will be there in a minute," Nionu whispered to himself. The Royal Warrior watched the demon through the bush. He did not intend to fulfill the demon's expectations. Instead, he evaluated his limited choices.

The Royal Warrior abandoned his original plan to go eastward up the pathway. That choice would lead to a confrontation. It would not only be a suicidal decision, but it would end his cat's tail offense. The Royal Warrior did not want to go westward either. The westward direction led back to a heavily populated part of the valley. A westward flight would put people's lives in jeopardy.

Nionu realized he had only two practical choices left. He could retreat into the Angrenni Forest. With the demon only meters away, that choice was another suicidal move.

Nionu looked across the pathway toward his final choice – the Aukmondi River. He took a moment to consider the advantages and drawbacks. But out of the corner of his eye and through the bush, he saw the Loa of Death moving again. The demon had given up its wait. Nionu saw the demon gliding rapidly toward the bend in the pathway, coming this way, looking for him.

Without a second thought, Nionu sprang from behind the bush. Still crouching low, he darted from the forest and across the north bank pathway. In hopes the demon still had not seen him, he went over the bank and, as quietly as possible, eased himself down into the river. Nionu sucked in a deep gulp of air, held his breath, and immersed himself just at the demon came around the bend.

From beneath the water's surface, Nionu could see the tall, dark, ominous, and now grotesquely distorted figure moving along the bank of the river. It slowly moved past the point where Nionu had immersed, as if searching for the Royal Warrior. But then it stopped and turned. It came back and stood directly over Nionu's head on the bank.

Nionu sank deeper in the water. He wondered if a demon could see him in the darkness and beneath the water. He wondered how much longer he would have to hold his breath. His lungs burned. The alarming fact occurred to the Royal Warrior that, being this close, the demon could easily dismiss his life with just a wave of its bony hand now. Nionu sank deeper in the water. The alarming fact also occurred to Nionu that his breath would soon give out. Drowning would leave him just as dead.

The Loa of Death stood on the bank of the river, looking down into the water. It knew the insolent warrior was there. Besides its acute sense of life and death, the demon noted another unanticipated giveaway. No matter how deep the warrior sank, his royal cloak billowed near the water's surface. The demon saw the royal fabric wavering gently beneath the water's surface.

The demon knelt and waited patiently for the warrior's lungs to beg for air. In the darkness, the demon watched the warrior's royal cloak. He waited. With the luxury of time, he waited. He watched and waited until he sensed no more life beneath that tattle-tell cloak.

The demon reached into the water and grabbed the royal cloak to pull the dead body to the surface. The demon could sense no life because the cloak hung free in his hand when he extracted it from the water. He held the dripping wet cloak up as if in disbelief.

"Hey, Ugly!" Nionu's voice echoed in the darkness, from somewhere on the other side of the river. "That belongs to me. But keep it, if you like. I have another one."

Nionu had touched another nerve. The loa stood. Feeling cheated and frustrated, the demon began a tight pace, flailing its arms. It finally whirled around, stormed across the north bank pathway, and glided back toward the Angrenni Forest.

"Wait! Wait! Do not leave!" Nionu shouted as he watched the demon disappear into the forest, still carrying his cloak.

"I guess I did it that time," Nionu said as he climbed out of the river onto the south bank. The charm of his cat's tail offense was over and not recoverable. His only hope was that his Blue Warriors stopped the Mangoni houngan's ritual before the demon reached them.

37

LET US FINISH THIS

The Blue Warriors, Obe Bendabe and Dabete Ehkili, entered Abul-Gwan's camp in complete darkness.

Mfalme Abul-Gwan woke from one of his rare moments of sleep. Something had disturbed him. He opened his eyes, expecting to see the body of Abul-Tess lying near him. Instead, two Aukmondi Blue Warriors stood over him. Each warrior now held a torch that lit up the nearby surroundings.

Abul-Gwan forced his weary body upright. "How did you get here?" He looked toward the guard post on the pathway. He searched for the Mangoni warriors who guarded his camp. In the darkness, he could see nothing.

"Are you looking for your warriors?" Obe asked. The Blue Warrior pointed to the other side of the Marula tree.

Abul-Gwan leaned over on his hands and knees to look around the tree. He found both of his warriors muffled and tied to the opposite side. Since he could do nothing about the predicament, he looked up at the Blue Warriors again. "What do you want?"

"We want your cooperation, Mfalme." Obe Bendabe took a moment to look over at Abul-Tess's body. He held his torch to brighten the dead woman's face. He turned back to Abul-Gwan and pointed to the body. "Great Creation, this is wrong. Is it not time to release this Sacred Woman's spirit? Please. Surrender her body to the elements."

"I … I, ah … cannot let her go." Abul-Gwan stared at Abul-Tess's face. For several long moments, he battled an overwhelming bout of sadness. Images of Abul-Tess in happier times filled his mind until he remembered the warriors standing over him. He looked up at the warrior who had just addressed him. He snapped. "Did you come to judge how I mourn my love?"

Obe Bendabe stared into Abul-Gwan's weary eyes. He felt sorry for him. He could see the Mangoni Mfalme needed help. Obe wondered how long the Sad Creation could continue like this. But, at the moment, it wasn't his concern. He finally rose above the sympathetic moment and answered Abul-Gwan's question. "No, Great Creation. That is not why we came."

Obe lifted his torch and looked toward the summit and the houngan's ritual area. He addressed Abul-Gwan again before walking away. "Stay where you are, Mfalme. Please do not make us bind you like we have done your warriors here."

The Blue Warriors began their approach toward Nagorda's summit. The two warriors negotiated the darkness around them in silence and the highest sense of caution. They walked toward the light that was the ritual *veve*. Just as the *veve* came clearly into view, something suddenly flew between the two warriors. With a flutter and a tailwind, it disappeared into the darkness as quickly as it had appeared.

"Great Sacred Spirit!" The Blue Warrior Obe turned in a circle, searching. He held his torch higher to light up his surroundings better. "What was that?"

"It was a bird of some type," Dabete answered.

"An owl?"

"No. It was smaller. It appeared to be a raven."

"A raven? Do ravens fly at night?"

"Ravens hunt with no respect for time, Great Creation. Daylight or darkness, it makes no difference to them."

Dabete's statement allowed Obe to ignore the strange fly-by of the raven. He returned his focus to their mission and lowered his torch. He angled it to project the light farther ahead.

The darkness and the thick smoke bubbling up from the houngan's bowl of boiling goat's blood hid the interior of the ritual *veve*. The fire under the boiling goat's blood cauldron caused the smoke to glow bright red, resulting in a thick and murky reddish orb of light. Only silhouettes of the vessel warriors and the houngan moved about like ghosts inside the orb.

"I can barely see them," Dabete whispered.

Two dark, almost formless silhouettes of the vessel warriors drifted about near the rear of the *veve*. The silhouettes pounded on the ritual drums. Boom-boom. Boom-boom. Boom-boom. Another silhouette, more distinct in form, sat on the ground in the forefront of the *veve*. The sound of rattling gourds and an endless ritual chant emanated from this silhouette.

"We can see well enough, Great Creation," Obe said. The glow from inside the *veve* was enough to find their primary target. Obe dropped his torch to the ground and put out the flame by stomping on it. Dabete did the same. Both warriors readied their shields and spears.

The Blue Warriors walked up to the edge of the *veve* and moved toward Onu-Vey's silhouette. Obe Bendabe kneeled. He could finally distinguish Onu-Vey's face despite the spiraling smoke before him.

The houngan showed no sign of being aware of the warriors' presence. His eyes were wide, bloodshot, and entranced. He continued his ritual chant. Obe waved his hand back and forth in front of the houngan's face. He got no response from the houngan. Obe looked at Dabete, amazed at how oblivious the houngan seemed.

Obe faced the houngan again and leaned in closer. "Great Creation, stop your ritual … now."

The Mangoni houngan showed no reaction to the Blue Warrior's demand. He continued to chant. His body jerked with disturbing spasms. Still, he shook his rattle gourds and tossed pinches of colored powder into a cauldron of boiling goat's blood. The flame beneath the bowl flared up and sparkled as some of the powder missed the cauldron and fell into the flame. The smoke and the reddish glow intensified.

"Onu-Vey," Obe raised his voice. "Can you hear me? You must stop your ritual. We will not ask you again."

Both Blue Warriors lowered their spears toward the houngan, a gesture to show that force would follow. But again, neither the houngan nor the silhouettes of the two vessel warriors showed any reaction. The Blue Warriors moved forward, preparing to subdue the houngan physically.

At that moment, Dabete Ehkili peered through the red glow at the silhouettes of the vessel warriors, naturally expecting them to defend the houngan. Another silhouette stood between him and the vessel warriors: a taller, darker, and ominous silhouette. Dabete grabbed Obe's arm. Both the Blue Warriors stood. The sight of the huge silhouette caused them to step back. They recognized the tall, dark, ominous specter as the Loa of Death.

It glided forward. It stopped near the center of the ritual *veve,* where it became visible. The bright red glow of the ritual fire contrasted with the bone and dark shadows on the demon's face. It stood watching the Blue Warriors. When the warriors raised their spears, the demon held its right hand. It held high the cloak of the Royal Warrior Nionu, suggesting it was a trophy and a remnant of a great kill. It stretched its arm and held the cloak's hem over the fire beneath Onu-Vey's bubbling goat blood cauldron. The still-wet cloak resisted the flame. Thick white steam and smoke billowed up as the cloak sizzled and ignited. Crackling flames worked their way up the cloak.

The two Blue Warriors recognized the cloak as that of the Royal Warrior Nionu. And when the cloak flared up, the offensive sight hit Dabete hard. He reacted, powered by sheer anger. He threw his spear at the loa. The loa caught Dabete's spear in midair. After one dramatic moment, it flipped the spear and threw it back at the Blue Warrior.

Dabete displayed a skill of his own. He flipped backwards. The spear just barely missed his shoulder and stuck in the ground behind the Blue Warrior.

Dabete went to recover his spear, but Obe grabbed his arm this time. "No, Great Creation! Remember the stone?"

Dabete froze. His fingers were just centimeters from touching his spear. He recalled how the Young Creation Robuti died when he caught the stone the loa had tossed. He took no chances that his spear was just as deadly. Dabete abandoned any further use of the spear.

With his anger no less intense, but more focused, Dabete redirected his attention from the demon to the Mangoni houngan. He spoke to Obe as he stormed toward the ritual *veve*. "Ignore the demon. Let us finish this."

The primary mission of the Blue Warriors, to stop the houngan ritual, has now become the highest priority. Nothing else mattered, not even the specter that stood in the center of the *veve* and twirled Nionu's burning cloak over its head. The warriors charged at the Mangoni houngan. The ritual would end, even if it meant killing the houngan. But before the warriors could enter the *veve*, the Loa of Death flung the burning cloak at them.

The Blue Warriors saw the mass of fire flying toward them. They raised their shields for protection. In a natural reflex, each of the warriors ducked and turned away. The shields took the brunt of the flaming assault. Burning strips of cloth rained past them to the ground. The warriors stood up and turned to resume their charge for the houngan. The moment they turned, the loa stood directly in front of them. They had no time to react before the loa laid its bony hands on both shoulders.

— 38 —

THE BEST DEFENSE IS NO DEFENSE

The Royal Warrior Jokere Gota raced through the evening darkness up the hillside toward Nagorda Peak. He was a Hefty Creation who shunned long-distance running. But he was a Royal Warrior, and neither the darkness nor the hillside of Nagorda Peak would slow him down. He expected no less from any of his sentinel warriors. The news he had was horrendous. He entrusted no one else to deliver it. It had to be reported to Mfalme as soon as possible.

According to Jokere's latest information, Mfalme Ncobba had gone to the Favored Tribesman's kraal. After learning about the devastation at the Pogobi kraal, Jokere left immediately to find the Mfalme. Since Kon-Shambique's kraal was close by, Jokere ran, almost non-stop, across the north slope and up the Nagorda hillside. He did not stop running until he reached the sizable crowd of people that stood outside the entrance to Kon-Shambique's kraal. The crowd came as a surprise. Jokere had no idea that the Mfalme had already fallen to the demon rumored to be walking the valley.

Jokere stood for only a moment, just long enough to finally catch his breath and assess the situation. A large bonfire burned on the other side of the crowd, just inside Kon-Shambique's kraal. It provided the only light in the area. The bonfire's light silhouetted the crowd, making it difficult for Jokere to see details about the people. He could hear Kon-Shambique's voice talking to the crowd on the other side. The Favored Tribesman spoke too softly for Jokere to make out what he was saying.

Jokere wondered if this crowd resulted from the news he had. He resumed his approach toward the kraal entrance. The people before him listened so closely to Kon-Shambique that even Jokere's royal cloak did not give him an easy passage through the crowd. He gently pushed his way through the crowd. "Let me pass, please. Coming through! Coming through!"

About half way through the crowd, Jokere could easily sense the heavy and somber mood of the people. He heard the voice of the Favored Tribesman somewhat clearer now. As far as he could tell, Kon-Shambique was trying his best to console this crowd. The Royal Warrior realized that something else was wrong here besides the horrendous news he was trying to deliver. He doubled his efforts to reach the kraal entrance. He found two Red Warriors standing guard there. They held the crowd back and prevented anyone from entering the Favored Tribesman's kraal.

"Great Creation," Jokere addressed one of the warriors. He nodded toward the crowd. "Why are these people here?"

"Have you not heard?" The warrior seemed surprised that Jokere did not know. "The Mfalme … Mfalme Ramuza Ncobba… he is dead. It was the demon of death."

Jokere stared back into the Red Warrior's face, speechless. He glanced to his left. He could see the Favored Tribesman now, standing inside the kraal. Jokere was close enough to see the reflection of a single tear that had trailed down Kon-Shambique's face. Jokere wondered who needed consolation more, the crowd of people or Kon-Shambique.

"Great Sacred Spirit!" Jokere spoke to himself. He still had to report the news to someone. He turned to the Red Warrior again. "What about the Sacred Woman Kharaambi? Do you know where she is?"

"She is inside, Great Creation."

Jokere's royal cloak allowed him to step unchallenged between the Red Warriors and into the kraal. Without another word, he hurried around the bonfire toward the entrance of Kon-Shambique's hut. His strong and deliberate pace slowed only three times. Once, when he walked around the bloodstain on the ground where the warriors Zabiba and Gengu once lay, once after he entered the hut and saw the bodies of the two warriors lying next to the right wall of the front chamber.

The body of Ramuza Ncobba lay next to the left wall. The sight of the Mfalme's dead body was enough to stop the Royal Warrior cold. He stood inside the hut, staring at the unreal sight before him.

Jokere saw the Sacred Woman Kharaambi sitting beside Ramuza's body on a mat. He watched her as she, almost ceremoniously, folded the Mfalme's arms across his chest. The Brown Warrior Quazzi kneeled next to them. The Foremost Lieutenant looked as though he was praying. Jokere stood back, reluctant to interrupt despite the news he needed to deliver.

*****

Quazzi ended his prayer and raised his head to speak to Kharaambi. "Sacred Woman, we must accept that this demon that the Mangoni houngan created is real. We must focus on the houngan and his demon. They have made a direct assault upon our valley, our people, and our Mfalme."

"I know, Quazzi."

"They represent a force we must confront … right now."

Kharaambi sat back and sighed heavily. She could hear the unspoken words. She understood what Quazzi was saying to her. "I know. As I sit here over Ramuza's body, you are telling me, we have no time to grieve."

"What do you want to do, Sacred Woman?" Quazzi waited for Kharaambi's answer. He got no response. "Should we wait to see what Nionu can suggest? The Royal Warrior has a strategic and tactical mind that has proven invaluable. Both of us are confident he can suggest a proper course of action. But, dare we wait?"

"No. We cannot wait. People …" Kharaambi finally broke from her stupor and looked at the Brown Warrior. "People are dying. We must take the offensive. As you said, we must fight this thing, right now."

At this point, Kharaambi noticed the Royal Warrior Jokere standing by the hut's entrance. She turned to face him. "What is it, Great Creation?"

Jokere hesitated before taking a step closer. "Sacred Woman, I am afraid, I am the bearer of more bad news. This demon you speak of has done more harm than you know. It has destroyed the entire Pogobi and Obentawni kraals."

"What?" Kharaambi got quickly to her feet. Her spear was leaning against the wall. She rushed over and grabbed it. "Destroyed? Destroyed how?"

"All the people; all the livestock, are all dead."

Kharaambi closed her eyes, trying to fortify her strength. The image of the message written in Zabiba's blood flashed in her head – *All dead. Two days.* Whether the message was a threat or a warning, it was coming true.

Quazzi wanted to strike out at something. He reigned in his anger by turning away in total frustration. He turned back to the Royal Warrior. "When did all this happen?"

"I am not sure, Great Creation. I would estimate only one to two hours ago. My army and I were on our way up to the north rim to relieve the army of the Royal Warrior Npatuzi. We found Elder Najube's mate, the Sacred Woman Ingza. She was lying on the pathway. She had fallen unconscious. We revived her. By the grace of the Supreme Spirit, she suffered no serious harm. She alerted us to the devastation in the Pogobi kraal. I immediately sent runners to alert and summon help from the nearest army."

Quazzi knew the nearest warrior community to the Pogobi kraal was the small kraal behind the sentinel line on the north rim. "The Obentawni kraal."

"Yes, Great Creation. When my runner arrived at the Obentawni kraal, he discovered the same devastation. The Royal Warrior Npatuzi and his entire sentinel army had fallen to this demon."

"Oh, Great Sacred Spirit!" Quazzi was so overwhelmed that his knees almost buckled. He sat down. But then, another unwelcome fact suddenly occurred to him. He stood again. "No sentinels stand guard on the north rim?"

"For a short period. My Botele Regiment has assumed posts on the north rim. But, Great Creation, my warriors are just as vulnerable as Npatuzi's. They lack the knowledge to fight this thing. If this demon returns, it is only a matter of time before they fall, too."

Kharaambi expressed her frustration by jabbing her spear into the ground. "Can this get any worse?"

The Favored Tribesman Kon-Shambique entered his hut just in time to overhear Kharaambi's question. He had finished talking to the crowd out front. Feeling angry and frustrated, he gave Kharaambi a snappy answer. "It already has."

Kon-Shambique suffered spiritual exhaustion. He went to the back wall of the chamber. He slumped against the wall and slowly slid down where he had sat for most of the early part of the evening. Kon-Shambique leaned his head back and closed his eyes as if to rest. "We do not understand what we face here. We are unprepared for this. Our situation may be worse than we know, Sacred Woman."

Kharaambi, Quazzi, and Jokere looked at each other. They understood Kon-Shambique's behavior, but it surprised all of them. Quazzi walked over and slowly kneeled next to the Favored Tribesman. "Great Creation, we expect to hear more hopeful words from you."

Kon-Shambique kept his eyes shut when he spoke again. He made no effort to temper the anger and frustration in his voice. "You asked the question. I gave you the answer."

Quazzi glanced over at Kharaambi again before turning back to the Favored Tribesman. "Kon-Shambique, your attitude is most unbecoming. We need your guidance here. At the very least, we need hope and encouragement."

"I can give you no guidance. I have given all my hope and encouragement to that crowd out there." Kon-Shambique finally opened his eyes. He raised his head and looked at Quazzi, Kharaambi, and Jokere. He seemed to realize that his attitude appeared sour. Kon-

Shambique sat forward. "I am sorry. I know I can do better. All this is happening so fast. I need time to think. Please, accept my apology."

"Apology accepted, Great Creation. You must know, in times like these, we often look to you for inspiration."

"In times like these, you must know, it is not always easy." Kon-Shambique slowly got back to his feet. He seemed to be trying to escape his downward spiral. He gestured toward the outside of the hut. "Just when I thought I was making some progress with that crowd out there, the Loa of Death returned."

Kharaambi grabbed her spear from the ground. She rushed to exit the hut. Quazzi and Jokere stepped behind her as Kon-Shambique called them all back. "Wait. There is no need. The demon is gone again. It came back only to … to return the bodies of Obe and Dabete. Both of Nionu's Blue Warriors … are dead."

Kharaambi threw her spear against the wall in a momentary loss of self-control. Quazzi and Jokere both peered outside the hut anyway. All three of them found Kon-Shambique's news hard to accept. Quazzi continued outside the hut in disbelief. When he saw only the two Red Warriors standing guard at Kon-Shambique's kraal's entrance, he returned inside the hut.

"The crowd is gone. Everyone is gone." He turned to the Favored Tribesman. "What happened out there?"

Kon-Shambique attempted to wipe the weariness from his eyes. He shrugged. "As I spoke to the crowd, the loa glided down the pathway from Nagorda Peak. It had the bodies of the Blue Warriors under each of its arms. When the people in the crowd saw this, most of them panicked and scattered. When the loa came close enough, it flung the bodies of the warriors into the crowd. Several brave people gathered around the warriors, hoping they could help them. But there was nothing they could do. The warriors were already dead."

The Royal Warrior Jokere peered outside the hut again. "What happened to the bodies, Great Creation? Where are they?"

"They are being taken to the Motobo kraal. After the demon discarded the warriors, it returned toward the peak. I asked the people to gather the warriors' bodies and take them home."

"We have to do something! This must stop!" Quazzi was angry.

"It will stop, Great Creation. And it stops right now." Kharaambi had regained her self-control. She walked over and picked her spear up from the ground. She turned to the Royal Warrior. "Jokere, summon the other Royal Warriors for me, please. We are going up to Nagorda Peak. We will stop the houngan's ritual once and for all; even if we have to use every army we have."

"Do that, Sacred Woman, and you will all die." Kon-Shambique did not snap this time. His words were softer but unquestionably direct. "I know my words lack encouragement. I know it is not what you want to hear. But it is the truth. When I say the houngan's demon can wipe out whole armies, I mean that literally. You will all die."

"Then how do we fight this thing?" Jokere asked. "Are we really that defenseless?"

"In most cases, when death finally comes for you, there is no defense."

"If we have no defense," Quazzi said, trying to think of a sound strategy, "then we must mount a strong and decisive offense."

"Like what?" Jokere asked.

"Might I suggest," Kon-Shambique began, "sometimes, the best offense is no defense."

"What are you saying, Great Creation?" Kharaambi wanted to know. "That makes no sense. No defense is not an offensive move."

"I felt comfortable with my unconcerned thoughts and attitude when this began. When we first learned of this houngan, his powers, and this demon of death, my first response was to ignore all we heard or saw. I continue to feel it is good advice. And it is the best advice I can give everyone."

"You must explain yourself, Great Creation."

Kon-Shambique got up and began to pace slowly. "Focus on defeating death, and you will bring death closer to you. Run in fear of death, and your path will lead directly to death. Look over your shoulder for death. You will see death as easily as you see your shadow. Death will be there behind you each time you look, walking in your very footsteps and coming ever closer. If we wrap our minds around this demon in any way, our minds will become its home. We will lose."

"Kon-Shambique, death and dying are all around us," Quazzi argued. He waved his hands toward the bodies of Ramuza, Zabiba, and Gengu. "How can we ignore this? You ask us to close our eyes and not think of a white elephant. It is impossible."

"So, it would seem, but it has to be done. Place your mind on death in any way, and death will become your focus. Our mind goes where we lead it. The Mangoni houngan knows this. It is how the demon kills. We stay alive by focusing on life and the living. We must drown ourselves in living life the best way we know how."

"Kon-Shambique, you might as well ask each of us to sprout wings and fly away. No. I think our approach must be both practical and realistic. We must confront this thing directly." Quazzi had heard enough. He turned to Jokere. "Summon the Royal Warriors."

"No. Wait." Kharaambi took a few moments to walk back over to the wall. She leaned her spear against it. She turned back to face Quazzi and Jokere. "Kon-Shambique is right. And, I think I understand what he means. Whatever the Mangoni houngan is doing, this so-called curse he has placed on us, all this death and dying, will no longer be our concern. We will not walk into his trap."

"Sacred Woman, that is no defense," Quazzi continued to argue. "What you are suggesting is not practical. People are dying. Over two days, death comes to all of us. We must reach the peak and stop the houngan's ritual before time runs out."

"We have tried that, Quazzi. Every attempt at a direct approach has ended in more death. We have just lost two of our best tactical warriors – possibly three. We have not heard from the Royal Warrior Nionu yet."

"Then what are you suggesting?"

Kharaambi walked over to a far corner of the chamber. Several small, cup-like gourds sat upon a table there. Kharaambi recalled that Kon-Shambique had placed the two fresh, green daylily buds into one of the gourds. She picked up the gourd and dumped the buds into the palm of her hand. Even now, the buds still appeared fresh, green, and ready to bloom and die within the next two days.

"From this moment forward, we will rise above the Mangoni houngan and his dark magic." Kharaambi walked over to the hut's exit. She leaned out just enough to toss the buds into the bonfire burning outside the hut. She turned back to face Quazzi and Jokere. "And, from this moment, I forbid anyone to go up to Nagorda Peak."

"But, Sacred Woman…"

"No one, Quazzi! As for the impossible, we will succeed. If we entertain any thoughts of death and dying, it will only be with the respect and honors we give to those who have already fallen."

"With all due respect, Kharaambi," Quazzi was persistent, "you cannot control how people think."

"The Mangoni houngan did." When Kharaambi saw that Quazzi had no response, she turned to the Favored Tribesman. "So, how is that for an offensive?"

"I like it, Sacred Woman. It is a good beginning."

39

DO YOU HAVE FAMILIES

High up on the south slope, in the Motobo kraal, Ameh Jobabwe spent the early evening talking and getting acquainted with the warriors Wema and Nienko. He found the Orange Warrior Wema Mwezzi to be an experienced warrior who was younger and more energetic than he looked. By contrast, he found Wema's trainee, the Red Warrior Nienko Cherundi, to be just barely an Adult Creation. Yet, he was a Red Warrior, with enough experience to win Ameh's confidence easily.

Ameh told the warriors what he wanted; an urgent message must be delivered to the returning farmers. The farmers must stay away until the valley is safe. Ameh could tell by the warriors' reactions that they understood his concerns. Both warriors seemed eager to help the Chinchigwe Mfalme as best they could.

As the evening wore on, Ameh, Wema, and Nienko sat around a small fire. They worked out the details of the urgent mission. Ameh learned that the Orange Warrior Wema was already familiar with the route between the Kiwane Village and the Aukmondi Valley. Wema had made the journey himself several times. Wema explained that it takes two and a half to three good days, at a slow to moderate pace, to walk from the Kiwane Village to the Aukmondi Valley. One advantage of their plan was that they did not have to reach Kiwane Village. They only had to reach the returning farmers in time.

Ameh also found Wema to be well acquainted with the Green Warrior Tushema Maduli of the Dabete Ehkili regiment. Wema knew significant details of Tushema's travel schedule to and from the Kiwane Village. He knew where the Green Warrior would stop for the night after each day's travel. Because of this knowledge,

Ameh felt that the Royal Warrior Nionu could not have selected a more qualified warrior than Wema. Wema had already proven to be invaluable.

According to Wema, the most crucial part of the plan was to meet the returning farmers before they stopped after that second day of travel home. Because of the high probability of congestion and blockage at the Kiboko Passage, it was always a wise and necessary goal for travelers to put the passage behind them. This holds whether the traveler is coming or going. Wema felt confident that the Green Warrior Tushema would bring the farmers across the Mara River and through the Kiboko passage as soon as possible. This meant their second day of travel could not end until after that crossing.

Mfalme Ameh Jobabwe wanted the farmers to stay away from the Aukmondi Valley until it was safe. No one knew when this would be. If their stay was long, the traveling farmers should not cross the Mara River. They could return to the Kiwane Village on the far side of the Mara. They would not have that possibility on this side of the Mara. For Wema and Nienko, timing was important.

"We will leave by sunrise tomorrow morning, Mfalme," Wema said. "That should give us plenty of time to reach the farmers before they cross the Mara."

Ameh nodded with gratitude on his face. He looked into the faces of Wema and Nienko. "Tell me. Do you have families?"

"Yes, Mfalme." Wema showed surprise at Ameh's abrupt mention of family. "I have a mate and a small son. The Red Warrior Nienko lives with and cares for his mother and young sister. Why do you ask?"

"I would like you to meet the returning farmers as soon as possible, but I also recommend spending some time with your families first." When Ameh saw the two warriors looking at each other, he offered them an explanation. "You may know that a rumor of a Mangoni curse spreads through the valley. This Mangoni curse says we will all be dead in two days. If the rumor is true, your families … may not be here when you return."

There was a moment of heavy silence as the thought took root. The Red Warrior swallowed to suppress this sudden and undeniable concern. He broke the silence when he thought of expressing his gratitude to Ameh. "Your thoughtfulness honors you, Mfalme. Thank you."

"Yes, thank you," Wema echoed.

"It pains me to ask you to make such a sacrifice, but if there is any truth to this curse, if any of us are to survive this, what I ask of you must be done."

"We understand," Nienko said. "We will deliver the message, Mfalme."

"Yes." Wema agreed but took a moment to recalculate the travel time. "However, to reach the farmers before they cross the Mara, we must leave on the morning of the day after tomorrow, at the latest."

Nienko almost smiled. "That still gives us a whole day with our families."

"If we knew we had only a day to spend with our families, how would we spend it?" Ameh asked only in wonderment. He did not expect an answer from the warriors. "I know you will spend it well."

Ameh gripped his walking staff and rose to his feet. His smile showed his complete satisfaction with the warriors Nionu assigned him. Confident that the warriors would fulfill their mission, Ameh felt better.

Although it was already late evening, Ameh intended to go to the Sacred Temple. But the plan changed. Just as the three were parting, Ameh saw the White Warrior Upenda walk by, headed toward her hut. She walked with her head down and her hands covering her face. She seemed to be in tears.

"Upenda," Ameh called to her. "Sacred Woman, what is wrong?"

"Mfalme, please forgive me. I did not see you." Even with great sadness in her voice, Upenda acknowledged Ameh with respect. "Have you heard?"

"Heard what, Upenda?" Ameh made a quick assumption. "Are you referring to the news about the Sacred Women, Rwuva and Tongda?"

"No, Mfalme." A tear rolled down Upenda's face. "I just heard that Mfalme Ncobba, and the Blue Warriors, Obe and Dabete, have fallen. I am told that they … they are all dead. As we speak, the bodies of the Blue Warriors are being returned to the kraal."

"Oh, Great Sacred Spirit! Great Sacred Spirit!" Despite the support of his ever-present staff, Ameh staggered. There was no strength in his legs. The strenuous climb up the south slope and sitting for such a long period with Wema and Nienko did not do Ameh's legs any good. He would have fallen had not Wema and Nienko caught him. They eased him down to where he had sat.

"Will you be alright, Mfalme?" Wema asked.

Ameh sat for a long, silent moment to recover. He bowed his head as if to hide his embarrassment after his moment of weakness. "For fifteen days, my stomach has been in knots, worrying about Lobarra and Tutapona. I cannot tell you how much sleep I have lost. Then the Mangoni show up with their Vodun houngan and killer Wabanga. Next, a destructive fire on the north rim was almost burning its way into the valley. People are killed: Mangoni warriors, Abul-Tess, the warriors Mbinga, Gengu, and Zabiba, and the Sacred Women Rwuva and Tongda. And now … and now, we have three more deaths that include the Mfalme himself."

Ameh looked up at Upenda and the two warriors. His eyes had filled with tears. "Earlier, I told the Brown Warrior Quazzi that I have been through worse times. When slave hunters destroyed the Chinchigwe village, it was a painful loss. But we saw that loss coming for a long time. The losses we are experiencing now, I feel, can be more painful. They are so unexpected, and we are so unprepared. How much more can we take? I must admit. I have never felt so hopeless."

Upenda sat down beside Ameh. Her sadness seemed secondary to his. She wanted to help. "Mfalme, would you like me to send for the Favored Tribesman?"

"No, no Sacred Woman. Please, do not trouble him. I know how close he was to the Sacred Woman Tongda. That Poor Creation … he is probably in worse shape than I am." Ameh looked up at Wema and Nienko again. He gestured, requesting help to his feet.

Wema, Nienko, and Upenda helped the Old Creation. Ameh leaned heavily on his staff and forced himself to stand more erect. He turned to Wema and finally answered the Orange Warrior's original question. "I will be fine, Great Creation. I need to rest for a while and settle my mind. I think I will return to my hut. I must try to understand what is happening here."

"Mfalme, it is dark," the Red Warrior Nienko said. "The trail down the south slope is tricky enough in daylight."

Ameh gave Nienko his usual weak smile. "What is it, Great Creation? Do you think this old mountain goat cannot negotiate a few rocks in the dark?"

"Even mountain goats know when to stand still, Mfalme."

"Yes," agreed Upenda. "Spend the night in the Motobo kraal. Despite the circumstances, all the warriors here would be honored, especially if you are here when the bodies of the Blue Warriors arrive."

Wema stepped forward. "Upenda is right, Mfalme. And if you must settle your mind, there is no better place than the Sacred Temple. You might as well stay since you are already up here on the south slope."

Ameh looked around at the Motobo kraal. The darkness hid most of it. He saw a few of the nearby warrior huts and corrals. But it took little to change his mind. "So be it."

— 40 —

DEATH'S WORSE ENEMY

Because of his chaotic state of mind and his enormous need for rest, the Great Creation, Mfalme Ameh Jobabwe, postponed his visit to the Sacred Temple. The Sacred Woman Upenda had promised him a comfortable cot in her hut for the night. She also promised to escort him into the Sacred Temple after he got a good night's rest. These were persuasive promises. Ameh accepted.

Ameh did not retire for the night immediately. He waited for the bodies of the Blue Warriors, Obe Bendabe and Dabete Ehkili, to arrive. The bodies arrived shortly after midnight. Almost everyone in the Motobo kraal gathered at the kraal entrance to pay their respects. Ameh Jobabwe stood in the forefront of the crowd. His presence alone seemed to be a fitting tribute to the fallen warriors.

If the people needed more of a tribute from the Old Creation, Ameh felt he would not have been able to deliver. At that late hour, anxiety and weariness had begun to affect him. He leaned heavily on his staff for physical support. Fortunately for him, the respective families of the Blue Warriors seemed to want and need some privacy. Ameh offered personal condolences to the families and then asked the mournful crowd to respect the families' wishes. He had just enough strength and mental fortitude to watch the families take the bodies away and the crowd of people disperse.

*****

Ameh found Upenda's hut and the cot she offered very comfortable, as promised. But during the night, he tossed and turned. He slept for brief periods. Even the quietness in the Motobo kraal provided no help. The somber atmosphere was oppressive. Sound sleep did not come until early in the morning. Ameh slept until just after sunrise. When he woke, he opened his eyes and sat on the edge of his cot.

Ameh sat for a long while, flooded with memories of recent events. He greeted the morning with the same weariness as when he lay down to rest.

Ameh continued to sit, not ready to face the day. He sat still and waited, hoping to feel the benefits of last night's rest. He hoped that some of his uncomfortable feelings had melted away. But the night came and went, leaving him without rest. The longer Ameh sat on the edge of his cot, the worse he felt. The sadness persisted with memories of yesterday's developments manifesting over and over in his head, and fresh tears welled up in his eyes. Ameh felt rescued when Upenda entered the hut and interrupted his chaotic thoughts.

"Good morning, Mfalme. Did you sleep well?"

"I … I slept, Sacred Woman." Ameh could not say he slept well. With modest discretion, he rubbed the tears from his eyes and forced a smile on his face. "Thank you for asking. How about you? Did you sleep well?"

"I will only say you, no doubt, slept better than I did." Upenda did not explain. "After you have freshened up, I have hot food waiting for you out front."

"Thank you, Upenda. I will be there in a moment."

Morning chatter among the warriors in the Motobo kraal brought Ameh confirmation of the sad news that Mfalme Ncobba died last night, a short while before the Blue Warriors did. As sad as this news was, Ameh learned of other incidents that overshadowed it. Warriors told the devastating news that, sometime during last evening, the houngan's death demon had killed all the inhabitants of both the Obentawni and Pogobi kraals. It also killed the Royal Warrior Npatuzi's entire Muusitu sentinel regiment.

Ameh remembered meeting many of the inhabitants of the Pogobi kraal when he and the rest of the Chinchigwe first entered the Aukmondi Valley. The memory stood out among the first impressions of the valley. Ameh remembered receiving three figs, a coconut chip, two daisies, and a dozen peanuts in one of the warmest greetings. Even though he was going through one of the darkest times of his life, that simple greeting was now a cherished memory. It would give great value in his golden years. It was a memory he would take to his grave. Ameh took the loss of the Pogobi kraal personally.

In front of Upenda's hut, Ameh and Upenda attempted to eat a small morning meal together. Neither talked, and a communal bowl of hot githeri was set between them. The spicy smell of the corn and bean mixture was inviting, but both took meager bites.

"So … has anyone heard from the Royal Warrior Nionu yet?" It was Ameh's attempt at conversation. "I am sure losing his Blue Warriors has been hard on him."

Upenda poked at her food. She looked to her left, toward a sizable hut several meters away. The hut belonged to the Royal Warrior. Tongda glanced down at her food again before she finally answered. "He is there, alone, in his hut. I have been unable to speak with him myself. One of his Gold Warriors told me he does not wish to be disturbed. I am told he returned to the kraal very late last night. He went to visit the families of Obe and Dabete. But then, he returned to his hut. He has not come out since."

Ameh glanced at the hut. "Perhaps I should speak with him. Maybe I will have better luck if I visit him."

"Yes, Mfalme. I think that you should."

If he ever finished, Ameh intended to go by and speak with the Royal Warrior after eating. But he, too, poked at his food.

"Thank you, Sacred Woman, for allowing me to sleep in your hut last night."

"You will always be a welcome guest in my hut, Mfalme."

"So, where were you? I did not see you after the warriors Wema and Nienko left. You disappeared. Where did you sleep?"

"I … I did not sleep, Mfalme. I went back down the valley, to the Favored Tribesman's kraal." Upenda scooped a measure of the *githeri* onto a piece of bread and tried to take a bite. It was still too hot to eat. She put the uneaten piece down. "The Sacred Woman

Tongda is … Tongda was my cousin. I have been spending much time at Kon-Shambique's kraal, helping to prepare Tongda to meet our ancestors."

That sad revelation seemed to end the mood for conversation. Ameh and Upenda sat for a moment more in silence. Since neither Ameh nor Upenda seemed to have an appetite, they finally pushed breakfast aside.

"But, what about the *githeri*?" Ameh asked as he and Upenda helped each other stand. "You went through the trouble of preparing it."

"Do not worry about it, Mfalme. This kraal is a community of warriors. I guarantee it will not go to waste."

At that moment, from that sizable hut several meters away, the Royal Warrior Nionu appeared. Nionu wore none of his warrior gear. Instead, he wore a beautifully printed cloth around his waist—the same material draped over one shoulder. Half of Nionu's chest, shoulder, and arms were bare.

The Royal Warrior glanced at the kraal as he slipped his sandals on. When he spotted Ameh and Upenda, he walked several meters toward them.

"Good morning, Mfalme," Nionu spoke softly. He acknowledged Upenda with a gentle nod.

"It is morning, Great Creation," Ameh responded. "It is not a good one."

"I cannot argue that."

"Nionu, Great Creation, I am so sorry about your Blue Warriors. I can only imagine the grief you suffer. In the short time I have known Obe and Dabete, they have impressed me as extraordinary."

"Thank you for the kind words, Mfalme. They were … extraordinary. But the pain of their deaths pales when we consider all the other deaths; those in the Obentawni and Pogobi kraals and Mfalme Ncobba's."

"And that, I cannot argue." It was at this point that Ameh noticed the cuts, scrapes, and lacerations on Nionu's face and arms. Most of them were clean and already healing, but noticeable. "So, what happened to you?"

Nionu knew why Ameh asked the question. He glanced down at the cuts and scrapes on his arms. "This? This is nothing. However, I do not recommend running through the Angrenni Forest at night, even with death nipping at your heels."

"Are you alright?"

"To be honest, Mfalme, No. But I will survive. I will be fine." Nionu paused. He closed his eyes as a primal urge for revenge tugged at his insides. "I will be fine, as soon as I run that foul-smelling bag of bones out of this valley. That thing does not belong here. I am just about ready to devote the rest of my life to becoming death's worst enemy. As the Supreme Spirit is my witness, that thing must face me again. And I will win."

Nionu's burst of anger came as a surprise to Ameh. Ameh had always seen Nionu as light-hearted and whimsical. He had never seen this side of the Royal Warrior's behavior. He glanced at Upenda. When Upenda only shrugged, Ameh accepted the outburst as normal. Then, his brow knitted again in response to another surprised revelation.

Since Ameh first heard of the Mangoni curse, he assumed that all the deaths in the valley resulted from the Mangoni houngan's magic trickery. He had no idea that there was a tangible demon walking the valley. "Such a demon exists?"

"Such a demon exists, Mfalme," Upenda said. "I have seen it myself."

"I have not only seen it," Nionu thumped his chest. I know how to rattle his rotting bones. I have done it twice. That thing will hate to see me coming from this moment forward."

"Nionu," Ameh began. "The demon seems to be no ordinary foe. It may be the last thing you do if you confront it."

"It will be worth it. Just give me the chance." Nionu seemed to realize that too much of his raw emotion surfaced, creating foolish notions. He calmed himself down by taking a deep breath and slowly releasing it. When he spoke again, his attitude had changed. "I am sorry, Mfalme. I … heard you spent the night here, in the Motobo kraal. I had to let you know. We have appreciated the honor of your presence. This comes especially from the families of the Blue Warriors, Obe and Dabete. I relay to you their special thanks."

Nionu's thoughtfulness impressed Ameh. He looked into Nionu's face. After all this warrior has experienced, he still needed to emerge from his self-imposed seclusion to deliver and express this honor and gratitude.

"You are the most thoughtful one," Ameh said. "But I thank you."

With this, Nionu turned and walked back toward his hut. Thoughtful or not, Nionu neglected to ask the Mfalme's permission to leave.

Before Nionu had walked too far away, the Sacred Woman Upenda called to him. "Great Creation." When Nionu stopped and turned to face her, Upenda gestured toward the bowl of *githeri.* "Would you like some breakfast?"

Nionu glanced down at the bowl. The rising steam suggested that it was still hot. Nionu still felt the agitation that comes from anger and revenge. He was not very hungry. He said nothing. Instead, he turned and resumed walking toward his hut. An afterthought forced him to stop again. He turned around and walked back toward Ameh and Upenda.

Nionu stooped. He picked up the hot bowl of *githeri.* When he stood up again, he faced Upenda. "This will do me good. I need it. Thank you, Sacred Woman." He turned to Ameh. "Please, excuse me, Mfalme." He turned and left again.

— 41 —

CONSIDER THAT A BLESSING

The Aukmondi Sacred Temple, found high on the south slope, was about five and a half kilometers from the Motobo kraal. When Ameh and Upenda reached the Temple, they found the temple gardens crowded with people. People stood throughout the network of trails and clearings between the gardens. Ameh and Upenda naturally expected to find many visiting people, but they did not expect such a huge crowd.

Most of the people wandered about the gardens and intermingled as they waited to enter the Sacred Temple. Interactions among the people ranged from brief greetings to lengthy, in-depth conversations. At one point or another, the people, as individuals or small groups, joined the long line of people that slowly filed into the Temple. The line stretched from the Temple doors and completely across the gardens.

The crowd of waiting people puzzled Ameh at first. He had been inside the Sacred Temple several times and knew that the many caves, caverns, and passages inside were vast enough to accommodate every person. As he and Upenda moved about the gardens, they soon learned that most people wanted more than to enter the Temple. Most wanted to visit the central chamber, the heart of the Temple.

Aides to the Sacred Woman Olabisi, the official caretaker of the Temple, had already arranged, under the circumstances, to regulate the people into the Temple and the central chamber. As one group finished its visit, an aide would invite another group into the Temple.

To get over the impact of so many people, Ameh and Upenda mingled too. They moved about the Temple Gardens without direction. They exchanged greetings and talked with various people here and there. Often, when Ameh and Upenda walked by the line of waiting people, they received invitations from various groups of people to join their group. Each time, Ameh and Upenda considered the needs of all the people before them. Each time, they declined the invitations. They were in no rush to enter the Temple. In each case, Ameh explained that his wish to commune with the Sacred Spirit was strong but no more special than anyone else's here. He could wait his turn. When he and Upenda finally decided to enter the Temple, they worked their way down the line of people to find their place behind the last group that had gathered.

The last group sat just beyond the entrance of Temple Gardens. The group consisted of five people sitting in a tight, socializing circle. They talked among themselves while they waited. Like the other groups before them, they interrupted their conversation and rose to their feet when they saw Ameh and Upenda approaching. They invited the two to join them.

Since this was the last group in the line, Ameh accepted. Ameh was already well acquainted with two people in the group. They were Chinchigwe. There was Twese Merende, Ameh's closest friend and supporter during the Chinchigwe escape from the slave merchant and their trek to the Aukmondi Valley. There was also Komu Ndizi. Not yet an adult, the Young Creation was big and strong. Despite his youth, Komu was now a White Warrior. He was the first Chinchigwe to become a warrior. His unique skill to forge metal had introduced sword-like spears into the Aukmondi warrior arsenal.

Kakito Arrona, one of the Young Creations in the group, sat perched on a small boulder. He offered Ameh his seat so that Ameh would not have to sit on the ground. Ameh accepted. The group resettled as Ameh made himself comfortable on the boulder.

Ameh glanced up the line of people and groups. "So many people! It looks as though we might be here awhile."

"No, Mfalme," Kakito responded to Ameh's apprehensions. "The wait is not long. Temple aides are moving the groups fast."

"Has a number such as this ever visited the Temple at once?"

"Never since I can recall. This is a number never seen before. And it is because we have experienced nothing like recent events. Did you hear about the people in the Obentawni and Pogobi kraals? The Royal Warrior Jokere found all of them dead yesterday evening?"

"Yes, I heard," Ameh recalled the confessions of the Royal Warrior Nionu and the Sacred Woman Upenda earlier this morning. After seeing all the spiritually hungry people here, Ameh finally accepted something he found hard to believe. "So, all these deaths are by an evil spirit that walks among us?"

"Yes, Mfalme," Kakito said. "I have seen it with my own eyes. And this demon is not finished. Without warning, it continues to show up here and there throughout the valley. It continues to kill. I am told that all of us will die within the next two days."

Ameh looked down at Kakito with a knitted brow. "Let us pray that is not true."

"What if it is true, Mfalme?"

Ameh could sense Kakito's fear. He tried to help by giving the Young Creation something else to consider. "I have not seen this demon yet. Am I the only one?"

"If you have not, then consider that a blessing, Mfalme," Upenda said. "Believe me. You do not want to see it. To see it is very unsettling."

"Yes," Twese agreed. "If you see it and survive, your life becomes different."

Ameh looked down at Twese. Ameh had known Twese since the Young Creation's birth. Twese had grown to be a Thoughtful and Considerate Creation. In the past, Twese tended to be pessimistic. He usually saw the worst things before the good fell into his lap. But since living among the Aukmondi, Twese has no longer allowed pessimism to dominate his life. Ameh hoped that Twese's sighting of the demon was not a setback.

"You have seen it too?"

"Yes, Mfalme. I have. It was yesterday evening, just after sunset. The Great Creation Joswabi and his mate, the Sacred Woman Inta, and I had just finished harvesting figs in the food orchard. Our basket, full of fresh figs, was set on the ground next to the fig bush. It was getting dark, so we were preparing to leave the orchard when we saw someone harvesting figs on the other side of the bush."

"The demon?"

"Yes, Mfalme. We did not know it at first. We went to the other side of the bush. The three of us were curious. We wanted to see who stood there. We walked upon this thing - this horrible, smelly thing, well over two meters tall, with a face of bones and naked teeth and living eyes. It was the demon of death, Mfalme. It stood there looking at the three of us, holding a single fig in its bony fingers. As if being helpful, it dropped the fig into our basket, then turned and glided away."

"Is that all it did?"

"There is more. The demon bewildered all of us. Its appearance and behavior made no sense to us. We just knew it was not normal. We knew we had to tell someone about it. When we recovered enough to move again, the Great Creation Joswabi went to get the basket of figs. Before he touched it, he stopped. He had seen something unbelievable and called us over."

"What did he see?"

"Mfalme, the whole basket of figs had withered, rotten, and foul-smelling."

"The three of you were lucky," Kakito commented, "especially the Great Creation Joswabi. He is alive because he did not touch the basket. Rumor has it that, sometimes, you could die by touching something the demon has touched. Did you hear what happened to the Young Creation Robuti?"

"Yes, when he caught that rock tossed by the demon."

Kakito sighed heavily in an attempt to overcome his sudden flare of anxiety. "Upenda and Twese are right. I see things differently now. I must admit that, since I have seen that thing, my attitude toward death has changed. Before seeing this demon, I never gave death much thought. Now, death frightens me. I think of it constantly. To know that I must die someday frightens me. And to think it will happen within the next two days, overwhelms me with fear. It affects almost everything I do now."

"Do not think about it, Great Creation." Komu offered his advice. "Death is natural. It is not to be feared. For most of us, if and when we die, we will not know it until long after death has come and gone."

"That is easy for you to say. You and the Sacred Woman Upenda are warriors – White Warriors, but disciplined warriors. The two of you have learned to respect death. You have learned not to fear it. For the rest of us, it is not so easy. This thing walks among us. Long before we are ready, it takes life from the young and the old. That is just not right."

"I hear something else in your fear, Kakito." Ameh's knitted brow showed his concern. "Death has taken someone close to you?"

"Yes, Mfalme. It was the Sacred Woman Mitma."

"That spirited little old woman who lives in the hut behind yours?"

"Yes. Like the White Warriors Komu and Upenda, she did not fear death either. She has always been a feisty, outspoken woman. Despite her rough edges, she was a sweet old woman. Since my earliest memories, Mitma was my closest neighbor. I grew to love her as dear as my grandmother. When this demon entered our kraal, she walked right up to it. With her hands planted on her hips, she confronted it."

Ameh smiled. "That sounds like something the Sacred Woman Mitma would do."

"She ridiculed the demon for not respecting the natural laws of the Supreme Spirit. She even shook her finger in the demon's face as she spoke. She made such a fuss like a mother hen protecting her chicks. You should have heard her. At one point, she commanded the demon to leave the valley. When the demon raised its bony hand to touch Mitma, she slapped its hand away. She collapsed the moment her hand touched the demon's." Tears welled up in Kakito's eyes. "I will never forget the look on her face when she realized she was dying. That sweet old woman tried to put the demon in its place. She died for her effort. She was an old woman. But I know, in my heart, she died before her time. She had more life left in her to live."

"How do we fight this, Mfalme?" Twese asked Ameh. "If death is natural, like the Young Creation Komu says, then is there a right way to fight this thing?"

"I wish I knew, Twese. That is why most of us are here at the Sacred Temple."

"How many of us must die before the Supreme Spirit steps in to help us?" Upenda asked.

"I have been asking that very same question myself, Sacred Woman." Ameh looked around at all the people again. He watched them for a very long, thoughtful moment, struggling with personal and shared miseries. He realized all of them had stories to tell. Many had stores as horrendous as the ones told by Twese and Kakito. All of them were here seeking comfort and peace of mind from the Supreme Spirit. And, like him, they knew nothing else to do.

Ameh recalled the strange analogy that Kon-Shambique had told early last evening about hanging on to the donkey's tail. Ameh detested the analogy at first. But he realized the decision to send warriors out to stop the returning farmers was a perfect example of the analogy. He created a chance for others to hang on in a hopeless situation. Ameh felt good about his decision. Maybe Kon-Shambique was right. Helping others to hang on was the Supreme Spirit's way of helping.

"Maybe she is already helping us, Upenda," Ameh began, "but not the way we expect. Things appear to have gotten so bad that we expect divine intervention. It is possible that the Supreme Spirit feels we do not need divine intervention yet."

"What do you mean, Mfalme? She has to do something." Twese almost pleaded. "We cannot get through this ourselves."

Ameh reached down and patted Twese on the shoulder. "Yes, we can. The Supreme Spirit is loving and merciful. Some of Her blessings come, not through divine intervention, but through each of us – through our families, friends, and neighbors. The Great Creation Kon-Shambique says all we have to do is hang on. We must do what we can to help others hang on. If the Supreme Spirit has not stepped in to help us, as bad as it seems, then it is probably unnecessary."

At this point, the White Warrior Upenda looked across the Temple Gardens. She noticed that the crowd of people had grown much smaller. The line of people to enter the Temple had grown thinner. Several groups of people were leaving the Temple Gardens and heading toward the south slope. "Where is everyone going?"

The White Warrior Komu rose to his feet. "Let me find out." He got Ameh's permission to leave and ran to catch a group heading toward one of the pathways leading back down the south slope. He stood and talked with someone briefly. When he finished, he ran back to where Ameh and the rest waited.

"What is it?" Ameh asked. "Where are they going?"

"The Sacred Woman Kharaambi has left the kraal of the Favored Tribesman, Mfalme. She is bringing the bodies of the Mfalme Ncobba and the Sacred Woman Rwuva back to the Royal Kraal. Everyone is going down to the Royal Kraal to pay their respects."

Ameh made another quick but thoughtful assessment of all the people in the Temple Gardens. All of them, without a doubt, had come seeking comfort in the Sacred Temple. Now, almost half of them were leaving. It seemed that due respect to the Royal Family outweighed their comfort. Ameh gathered his walking staff and forced himself up from where he sat on the boulder. "Please, excuse me."

Everyone sitting around Ameh sprang to their feet—Ameh's sudden intent to leave surprised everyone, but no more so than Upenda.

"Mfalme? Are you leaving too?"

"I think that I should, Sacred Woman."

Upenda's respect for the Mfalme prevented her from asking why. "But you have wanted to visit the Sacred Temple since last night."

"I know. And I must thank you for the time you have given me. I know you walked from Kon-Shambique's kraal back to the Motobo kraal this morning to prepare breakfast for me. When we did not eat it, you gave it away so graciously. You came with me to the Temple Garden. You waited to escort me into the Temple only to learn that I have changed my mind about going inside. Please know, Sacred Woman, I am grateful for all you have done."

"I am in your service, Mfalme."

"Your service has helped me to hang on. I am a Better Creation. Selfless service like that will see us through this." Ameh swiveled on his staff. He gestured toward the people still waiting to go into the Sacred Temple. "I am sure these people will find strength, comfort, and hope inside the Temple. The Supreme Nature of the Temple will give them enough hope to hang on."

Ameh swiveled the opposite way and gestured toward the groups of people that were heading toward the south slope. "But for those people, it is different. They will find nothing but despair in the Royal Kraal. When they see the body of Mfalme and his Principal Mate, their spirits will sink to one of the lowest possible levels. It is a level of despair very difficult to overcome. I know because, as a Chinchigwe, I have experienced it. I must go to the Royal Kraal, where I can do the most good."

— **42** —

THERE WILL BE NO HOLDING

Before sunrise that same morning, the Loa of Death visited two more kraals. First was the Butetwa kraal, found in a remote area on the north slope of the western half of the valley. The fifty-five people there made a quiet community of mat-makers, rope and basket weavers, and a few garment makers. The people usually got up before sunrise and spent most of the day supporting their crafts. For most, the highlight of each day came when one of their beautiful crafts reached completion. But as a community, the highlight of each day came at sunset. At sunset, most people migrate down the north slope. They headed for the Royal Kraal and the Daily Celebration of life.

But the past two evenings were atypical. In the middle of the first evening, Mfalme Ameh Jobabwe cut the Daily Celebration of Life short. That night, the people of the Butetwa community returned to their kraal. They brought back with them all the sad news that had occurred that evening: the escape of the Wabanga, the clearing fire on the north rim, the death of the Sacred Woman Abul-Tess, and the onset of bereavement in support of the Mangoni.

By the time the Butetwa community ended their day on the second evening, the sad news of Rwuva's and Tongda's deaths compounded their already dark mood. The unbelievable rumor of a death curse was behind the deaths of Rwuva and Tongda. The rumor became real when news spread that the same curse had also claimed the lives of Nionu's two Blue Warriors and Mfalme Ramuza Ncobba.

By nightfall, a heavy depression crippled the spirit of all the people in the Butetwa kraal. No one bothered to react even when a small gathering of noisy ravens invaded their rice granary late that evening. The frantic caws of the ravens drew almost everyone's attention. They saw the ravens darting in and out of the granary. But the job of running the ravens away and securing the granary was someone else's responsibility.

Most of the Butetwa kraal people didn't remember falling asleep that night. With all the oppressive sadness, many people only remembered sitting in mournful silence. During the night, each person closed their eyes for just a moment. In that moment, the loa appeared and touched each one of them. In a whisper, each person's life ended. The people of the Butetwa kraal didn't remember falling asleep. They did not remember dying.

*****

Shortly after sunrise, the Young Creation Wotabe approached the dead kraal. Wotabe lived in the Mempa kraal about a kilometer down the pathway from the Butetwa. At his young age, he had already become known as the primary supplier of reeds, straw, and raffia grass fibers for the Butetwa basket makers. Wotabe led his donkey, Jallapunda, up the pathway. The donkey had two large bundles of fresh straw saddled across her back. Wotable held Jallapunda's guide rope, although it was unnecessary. The donkey knew the morning routine as well as Wotabe did.

Wotabe sensed something was wrong in the Butetwa kraal long before he entered the kraal entrance. He could see through the cracks between the hewn stakes that made the fence around the kraal. It was much too quiet. No morning campfires burned. No one could be seen tending to their morning chores, cooking their morning meals, or preparing for their daily tasks. He saw none of the usual faces he always saw tending to their routines – routines that were as regular and reliable as the sunrise.

"Where is everybody, Jallapunda?" Wotable spoke softly to his donkey as he searched for signs of movement in the kraal. When he left the pathway, he knew something was wrong and led the donkey through the kraal entrance. Jallapunda stopped walking. Wotabe tugged on the guide rope. Jallapunda refused to move.

"You do not like this either. Do you?" Wotabe walked back and gave Jallapunda several reassuring strokes across her muzzle. He gripped the guide rope tightly and gave a strong tug. Jallapunda resisted just as strongly.

"You picked a bad time for one of your stubborn moments." Wotable dropped the guide rope. He knew that forcing the donkey to move never worked. Wotabe walked back to stand at the donkey's side. He gently stroked the donkey's neck. In moments like this, waiting until Jallapunda changed her mind was always easier.

Wotable was not as concerned about Jallapunda's stubbornness as he was about the stillness of the Butetwa kraal. He stroked the donkey's neck and made another sweeping glance of the kraal. The stillness was rapidly becoming alarming. The only movement in the kraal was a few ravens moving in and out of the kraal granary.

Suddenly, Jallapunda snorted and brayed twice. The donkey took several restless steps backward. She bucked and kicked. The two huge bundles of straw on her back fell to the ground. The twine that held one of the bundles together broke loose, and the bundle burst open. Reeds and straw were scattered. Frightened, Jallapunda turned and trotted from the kraal. She turned westward and panicked up the pathway, braying loudly.

Wotabe called out to the donkey several times. He took several quick steps to pursue Jallapunda, but the donkey quickly outdistanced him. At that same moment, he caught sight of the reason for the donkey's strange behavior. A very unfamiliar figure came from one of the nearby huts. The figure was so tall that it hunched over to exit the hut. Once free of the door, it rose slowly to stand fully erect. Wotabe knew everyone in the Butetwa kraal, including the Old Creation Mkuni who lived in that hut. The tall figure was not Mkuni.

Wotabe walked toward the figure, curious to learn what was going on. But when he saw the skull face beneath the hood, he stopped. He watched as the tall figure glided toward him with open arms, as if to welcome him to the kraal. Wotable slowly backed away. He stumbled over the unbroken bundle of straw and fell to the ground. The tall figure stood over him when he recovered from his fall.

"Who … who are you?" Wotabe asked. The bone-white face and living eyes that Wotabe saw beneath the hood almost paralyzed him with fear. "What do you want?"

The tall figure said nothing. Instead, he leaned toward Wotabe and slowly offered his bony hand to help Wotabe to his feet. Wotabe scooted back. His efforts were futile. The broken bundle had made a bed of loose reeds and straw beneath Wotabe's hands and feet. Wotabe had no traction.

"No! Please, no." Wotabe begged. "Get away! Do not touch me!"

The tall figure stood erect and withdrew its bony hand. It seemed almost disappointed that Wotabe had refused help. As if looking for another way to gain Wotabe's trust, the figure looked up the pathway to its right, left, and beyond the kraal entrance. The repetitive brays of Jallapunda, somewhere in the distance, caught its attention. It seemed to realize how important the runaway donkey was to Wotabe. With a gesture to Wotabe to stay put, the figure glided around Wotabe. It exited the Butetwa kraal in pursuit of the donkey.

At the moment, Wotabe did not know the tall figure's intentions. He didn't care. He was glad the Frightening Creation had lost interest in him and left. Wotabe got quickly to his feet. He ran toward Mkuni's hut. He intended to offer or seek help, whichever was fitting. The thought of asking permission to enter Mkuni's hut never crossed Wotabe's mind. He stormed through the doorway, only to find the Great Creation Mkuni lying in a fetal position in the center of the hut.

"Mkuni, Great Creation!" Wotable kneeled at the Old Creation's side and touched his shoulder. He rolled Mkuni's body over to examine it. Wotabe realized that Mkuni was dead. "Great Sacred Spirit!"

In shock, Wotabe backed his way out of the hut. He turned and ran. His immediate impulse was to seek help from the nearest neighbor. The nearest hut to the Great Creation Mkuni belonged to the Great Creation Ventu and his family. Wotabe panicked, calling the Great Creation's name all the way.

"Ventu! Ventu! Come quickly! Ventu!"

Wotabe ran with such reckless abandon. He could not negotiate a sharp turn around Ventu's weaving loom. He crashed into the loom, knocking most of it to the ground. Wotabe stumbled and fell himself. He ignored the damage and scrambled to his feet again. He continued directly through the doorway of Ventu's hut.

Wotabe found Ventu sitting just inside the entranceway. Wotabe noticed Ventu's defensive grip on two weaving needles. The Great Creation held the 35-mm, wooden needles as weapons. He looked as if he had fallen asleep guarding his family. But Ventu was not asleep. He was dead. Ventu's family: a mate and two little girls, appeared to huddle against the back wall of the hut. They were also dead.

The Young Creation Wotabe saw enough. The Mangoni houngan's demon of death had struck down the entire Butetwa kraal. To seek help here was useless. Wotabe ran from Ventu's hut. With reckless abandon again, he worked his way toward the exit of the Butetwa kraal. Wotabe's next instinct was to seek help in his kraal, the Mempa.

Wotabe ran from the entrance of the Butetwa kraal. Before sprinting down the pathway, he looked westward, up the pathway. A few meters away, he saw the tall, gruesome demon returning. The "helpful" demon, as if fulfilling a good deed, held Jallapunda's guide rope. It dragged the dead donkey along the ground, in the dust and dirt behind him.

Wotabe stood and stared at the shocking sight. His impulse was to go to his beloved Jallapunda's aid, but fear and panic forced the Young Creation to turn away. He began his sprint down the pathway. He looked back only once. The demon seemed determined to return Jallapunda to him. The sight made Wotabe run faster than he had ever run in his whole life. It would take him and Jallapunda about fifteen minutes on a normal morning to travel the pathway between the Butetwa and Mempa kraals. Wotabe covered the distance in three and a half minutes.

Wotabe called for help long before he reached the entrance of the Mempa kraal. "They are all dead! Help! Someone help! They are all dead!" He shouted.

His cries for help were so full of fear and panic that all who heard him came running. The people in the Mempa kraal poured from their respective huts, many blindly ready to give help and support wherever they could.

When the Great Creation Zendani, the kraal elder, heard Wotabe's cries, he came from his hut. He came running, holding a meter-long scythe, normally used to harvest grasses and reeds. Elder Zendani held the scythe with a different purpose in mind.

"Wotabe," Zendani caught the Young Creation by the shoulders. "Who is dead?"

"The people in the Butetwa. That demon, the Mangoni's demon of death, has killed them all!"

"The whole kraal?"

"Everyone, Great Creation. They are all dead."

Elder Zendani looked around, trying to decide what to do. He noticed that other Mempa villagers had gathered. Twenty-five people, almost a quarter of the entire Mempa kraal, surrounded him. All of them had come running with makeshift weapons in hand. They all stood ready to risk their lives to help others, even if that help was already too late. Zendani turned to Wotabe again.

"We need help from the Royal Kraal, Wotabe! Run as fast as you can. Get us help." Elder Zendani glanced at the surrounding people again. "We will hold this thing off as best we can until help arrives."

"But Zendani, Great Creation, this demon … I do not think it can be stopped. And it is coming! As we speak, it is coming down the pathway!"

Elder Zendani and everyone who stood around looked up the pathway. Sure enough, in the distance, the morning sunlight illuminated a tall, dark figure gliding closer and closer. It pulled the dead donkey, Jallapunda, behind it, dragging her by her guide rope.

"Go get help!" Zendani repeated.

"You do not know that thing's power, Great Creation. There will be no holding! Help cannot come in time. It will kill all of you."

"We have no choice, Young Creation. Please! Go quickly now. Get help."

— 43 —

JUST A PRECAUTION

By daylight that same morning, the traveling farmers and their warrior escorts had already covered over five kilometers in their 131-kilometer journey back to the Aukmondi Valley. They walked in a loosely formed column at a slow but steady pace. All were completely oblivious to all the death, dying, and oppressive sadness back home in the valley.

Several of the farmers walked, holding the guide ropes to their pack animals—the donkeys, cattle, and goats that carried their food, water, and other belongings. Others walked, balancing large baskets or gourds on top of their heads. Travelers who must cross the variable terrain of the African savanna always walk with a strong and determined pace, but the pace of the farmers was comparatively slow.

Five of the ten escorting warriors walked in front of the farmers. A single warrior walked on each side of the column, and three warriors brought up the rear. As strong and energetic people, the warriors could easily outwalk the farmers. But they allowed the elders of the group to set the pace. There was a schedule to keep, but it held a much lower priority than the health and comfort of these valued farmers.

The Sacred Woman Lobarra Gendeyani walked in the middle of the traveling column of farmers. Since she walked with Tutapona bundled in a kanga on her back, she enjoyed walking with no other load. Lobarra walked with her hands and arms free. As a result, after five kilometers of walking, and despite a short night of sleep, Lobarra still felt somewhat refreshed. But then, she was also the youngest of all eleven farmers. Lobarra wondered if it was a fair advantage. She wondered if the other farmers felt as energetic as she did or if she should offer to relieve one of the other farmers' burdens.

The two warriors who walked to the left and the right of the traveling column were the Red Warrior Rotho and the Gold Warrior Oghani. Oghani walked on Lobarra's immediate right; Rotho on her left. When Lobarra glanced in Rotho's direction, she saw a surprising sign of fatigue. Rotho yawned so hard he shook his head to break free of the natural reflex.

Lobarra veered closer to the Red Warrior. "Did you get enough sleep last night, Great Creation?"

"Excuse me, Sacred Woman." Rotho suppressed his embarrassment after the unreserved yawn. "If you must know the truth, I did not sleep last night."

"Why?"

"I stood guard outside your hut the entire night last night."

When Lobarra and Tutapona left the Aukmondi Valley, Mfalme Ameh Jobabwe ordered that Lobarra and Tutapona be guarded day and night until they returned. The Brown Warrior Quazzi assigned another warrior to Tushema's detachment to do that task. The Red Warrior Rotho was that warrior.

"You got no sleep at all?"

"No. Most nights, one of the other warriors would relieve me. But not last night." Rotho gestured toward the warrior who walked on Lobarra's other side. "The Gold Warrior Oghani has promised me a full night's sleep tonight. He has offered to stand guard in my place tonight."

"Then, no doubt, you are looking forward to tonight."

"I am." Rotho rubbed his face as if to remove the fatigue from his eyes. "What about you, Sacred Woman? Did you and the Little Creation Tutapona sleep well? Tutapona seemed quiet. The whole night, I heard no tantrums."

"There were no tantrums. Last night, I settled Tutapona down to sleep with no trouble. I was becoming concerned at first. But I think he is getting better."

"A mother's concern works wonders. The Little Creation cannot talk yet. But, if something were wrong, if he needed something, you would know it first." Rotho took a moment to peer into the kanga. He could see Tutapona sleeping peacefully and soundly. "Did you have to pacify him again with the scepter Mfalme Modoffa Menda gave him?"

"No. It was unnecessary. I nursed and sang him to sleep, like always." Lobarra recalled last night's easy attempt to put Tutapona asleep. Since arriving in the Kiwane Village, Tutapona had fallen asleep each night with difficulty. To Lobarra's frustration and dismay, none of the usual pacifiers worked. Last night was different. Tutapona fell asleep the moment he closed his eyes.

Lobarra almost smiled as she recalled the amazing occurrence. "Once he fell asleep, he slept through the night. But I packed the scepter nearby in case I needed it."

Lobarra gestured toward a donkey that walked just in front of her to show just how nearby she had packed the scepter. A tightly rolled blanket hung among the packs on the animal's back.

Rotho could see the bullfrog-end of the scepter protruding from the blanket. "And what about you, Sacred Woman? How did you sleep?"

"Me? I will only say I slept. And I did not fall asleep as fast as Tutapona."

Lobarra remembered spending the early night trying to understand Tutapona's recent restlessness. At first, she thought Rotho was right. According to the Red Warrior, Tutapona was only homesick. Something about the Kiwane Village made Tutapona restless. Yet, last night was different. What made Tutapona fall asleep so fast? The occurrences sent Lobarra's mind racing. Her most plausible explanation was exhaustion. Tutapona was too tired to fret.

Lobarra never came to a firm conclusion. She lost an hour or two of sleep before she fell asleep herself. "I suppose I got enough sleep to feel rested."

"You slept peacefully and soundly when I woke you this morning."

Lobarra focused so hard on thoughts of last night that she didn't notice a gradual change in the escorting warriors' positions. When she became aware of the change, she realized that only the Green Warrior Tushema headed the column of traveling farmers. Lobarra looked to the rear. Likewise, only one warrior kept his position at the column's rear. The Red Warrior Rotho was still on her left, and the Gold Warrior Oghani was still on her right. But all six of the remaining warriors had formed a new, parallel column a few meters to the far right of the farmers.

Puzzled by the change, Lobarra moved closer to the Red Warrior Rotho again. "Great Creation, what are the warriors doing? Why have they shifted positions?"

"It is just a precaution, Sacred Woman."

"A precaution? Against what?"

Rotho pointed with his spear toward the right, toward the crest of a small hill. It was a direction slightly askew of the morning sun. Lobarra had to shade her eyes against the intense glare. She could see what all the warriors had already seen. About a hundred meters away, five huge lions strolled along the hilltop.

"It looks to be a male and four females," Rotho said. "When they roam like that, they are hunting."

Lobarra continued to watch the lions. They were big, beautiful, and powerful-looking animals. Their graceful moments were not without purpose. "I thought lions only hunted at night."

Rotho almost smiled at Lobarra's naivety. "Lions will hunt any time, Sacred Woman. They hunt with heightened aggression at night."

"Are we in any danger?"

Rotho shaded his eyes to take another look at the lions. "No. I think not. They are upwind and have no interest in us. They seem to be moving away, trailing a small herd of zebras ahead. I think the herd holds their interest."

Lobarra looked ahead at the zebras. She had not seen the herd at first. But now, she saw about two dozen zebras on the horizon. They moved through a cloud of dust. Lobarra looked toward the lions and shaded her eyes again. She studied the lions at length with concern on her face. "Great Creation, if those lions are hunting, would we not make an easier prey than a small herd of zebras?"

"Yes, we would, Sacred Woman. But, please, do not be too concerned. I think the lions will move away." Rotho was trying to ease Lobarra's anxiety. "If the lions have never eaten oxen or goats, they have no taste for our pack animals."

"Our pack animals? What about us?"

"Lions rarely hunt people either."

"Rarely?" The word did not reassure Lobarra. "Suppose this is a rare moment when they do?"

"Then tonight will be another sleepless night, Sacred Woman. For all of us."

— **44** —

TAKE YOUR PLACE

Ameh came down from the Sacred Temple Gardens to the bottom of the south slope. Physically, he felt much better than after the walk up the slope. He took the bridge that crossed over to the valley's north side. Ameh's ever-present staff thumped at a regular interval against the bridge, echoing his steps as Ameh walked at a leisurely pace. He was in no particular hurry to reach the Royal Kraal. He seemed preoccupied with thoughts of recent events and all the deaths in the valley. Considering what he had just heard in the Temple Gardens, Ameh wondered how difficult it would be to put Kon-Shambique's suggestions into practice. What else could he do to help others hang on?

Half-way across the bridge, Ameh looked off to his left. He saw Adaulah sitting on the north bank. Adaulah appeared to sit in a stupor, staring down into the Aukmondi River. Ameh stopped walking. He stood for a moment, watching the Little Creation. The sight of Adaulah, sitting there alone, did not seem right. Ameh resumed walking. With a sense of concern, his pace was faster.

The Little Creation Adaulah sat so lost in his thoughts that he did not hear or see Ameh approach. When he finally heard the footsteps behind him, he turned to see who it was. He wiped the tears from his eyes to see.

"Mfalme." Adaulah scrambled to his feet when he recognized the Old Creation. "Forgive me. I did not see you coming."

Ameh nodded his head to show his forgiveness. He leaned on his staff. "Are you alright?"

"Yes, Mfalme."

"Why are you not with your sisters? What are you doing out here … alone?"

"I am … I am waiting."

Ameh already knew why Adaulah was waiting. He looked over his left shoulder toward the north bank pathway. The pathway was always heavy with travelers coming and going, but not now. It looks naked of people. The reason was somewhere in the distance, slowly coming this way.

"The Sacred Women Olabisi, Kharaambi, Omari, and Yejide are returning the Mfalme, and my mother Rwuva, to the Royal Kraal," Adaulah explained. "This is where they belong until we return their bodies to the elements and release their spirits so they may join our ancestors."

Ameh pivoted around on his staff in the opposite direction. He looked over his right shoulder toward the Royal Kraal. Soon, hundreds of people would visit the kraal to view the bodies of Ramuza and Rwuva. At the moment, two Aukmondi Red Warriors stood guard at the kraal entrance. The kraal appeared to be empty, closed to all visitors. A crowd of people, some of whom Ameh had seen earlier in the Temple Gardens, was already massing just outside the entrance.

Ameh turned back to Adaulah. "May I wait with you?"

"Of course, Mfalme." Adaulah stepped aside to make room on the rocky ledge.

The two settled on the ledge. They watched the currents and the fish in the river below as they waited. They did not have to wait long. Before Ameh could make himself comfortable or find the right words to comfort Adaulah, they heard a procession of people approaching on the north bank pathway.

With reluctance, Adaulah stood again. He seemed to be afraid of what was unfolding here. Regardless of his fears, he was still thoughtful enough to help Ameh stand. Ameh thanked him for the kind act, but Adaulah never heard him. So absorbed in his thoughts, Adaulah turned and took a few steps toward the approaching procession, but stopped. He stood, watching the long line of approaching people through the gentle glare of the morning sun.

Ameh stood behind him, admiring the Little Creation's bravery. He could tell that Adaulah was preparing himself for that moment when he would see his father and his mother for the first time since their deaths. It was a difficult moment for the Little Creation. Ameh had long ago gotten over the death of his parents, although, to this day, he still has realistic dreams about them. Ameh knew Adaulah would get over his parents' death. And dream about them too. By some means, Ameh had to reassure the Little Creation. He had to let him know that everything would be all right.

The Sacred Women Kharaambi and Olabisi led the procession down the north bank pathway. Quazzi walked behind the two women. The three of them walked slowly but with purpose. None of them talked. There were solemn looks on their faces as they set the pace for all the people walking behind them. The constant 'boom-boom' of the Mangoni ritual drums, echoing across the valley, accented the solemn mood.

Behind Kharaambi, Olabisi, and Quazzi, six Aukmondi warriors carried upon their shoulders a large, royally adorned burial litter with Ramuza's body upon it. Another six Aukmondi warriors followed them, carrying Rwuva's body in the same manner. Ramuza and Rwuva lay upon their backs, arms folded across their chests so their spirits would not leave their bodies too soon.

The four oldest Ncobba daughters, Omari, Yejide, Kunto, and Audi, walked behind the two litters. Kunto and Audi supported each other. Even now, the two continued to cry. The usual complement of guards and personal aides surrounded the four daughters.

Two Gold Warriors trailed behind the Ncobba daughters. They separated the royal family, the head of the procession, from the rest. The rest of the procession, the bulk of it, was an endless line of people that trailed back along the pathway.

As the head of the procession turned off the north bank pathway to take the short trail up to the entrance of the Royal Kraal, Adaulah continued to stand, watching. His impulse was to run out and intercept them. But he seemed hesitant, not sure what he should do.

Ameh watched Adaulah. He could only imagine the multitude of thoughts in the Little Creation's head. Ameh reached out and gently put his hand on Adaulah's shoulder.

Adaulah jumped as if startled. He had almost forgotten that Ameh was standing behind him. With tearful eyes, he looked up into Ameh's face.

Ameh nodded his head toward the procession. "Go and take your place, Little Creation."

"My place?"

Ameh pointed toward the front of the procession. "You belong there, in front. Lead them home into the Royal Kraal."

Adaulah watched the procession for another moment. After glancing up at Ameh, he slowly walked out toward the procession. His pace grew stronger as he overpowered his fears and embraced what he had to do. He intercepted the procession at the point between the two royally adorned litters.

Kharaambi looked back. When she saw Adaulah standing just off the trail, she stopped walking. The whole procession stopped. With just a nod from Kharaambi, the warriors carrying the litters slowly lowered them to the ground.

Adaulah stepped back as the bodies of his father and mother came slowly into full view. Crippled by fear, Adaulah wanted to break away and run. He would have bolted, but in some strange way, the sight of Ramuza and Rwuva did not seem real. Looking upon them was not as frightening as he thought it would be. He felt a tremendous void. It was painful. He felt something was wrong and impossible to fix. But it wasn't frightening. His fear was beginning to dissipate.

Adaulah moved closer to the litter where Rwuva's body lay. He kneeled at Rwuva's side and slowly reached out to take her hand. Adaulah delicately lifted Rwuva's fingers, one by one, into his hand. Since he was a toddler, he had held Rwuva's hand many times. But this time, the pleasure seemed stronger. He felt the spiritual bond he held with his mother. It was as strong as ever.

Adaulah wiped away a tear that streaked down his face. With unexpected comfort, he put his other hand on Rwuva's hand and held it for a few more pleasurable moments. He smiled gently. Adaulah could almost feel his mother's spirit smiling back at him. Adaulah replaced Rwuva's hand, folding her arms across her chest. Then he rose to his feet.

He walked up next to the litter where Ramuza's body lay. *The Great Ram* of the Aukmondi tribe was dead. How could this be real? No. This cannot happen. Adaulah brushed the last of his tears away as he kneeled next to the Mfalme's body. He reached out and took Ramuza's hand. He felt a void of pain, loss, and an overwhelming sensation that the whole valley was forever different now. But he still felt the spiritual bonds with both of his parents. He could feel them smiling at him. Adaulah responded with a broader smile. Since the first time after hearing of his parents' death, Adaulah felt better.

Adaulah rose to his feet again and stepped back. He waited as the warriors raised the litters back to their shoulders. Adaulah turned and walked toward Kharaambi, Olabisi, and Quazzi. He stopped and looked into their faces. He said nothing to them, but his silence was not disrespectful. His presence alone told them he was ready to take his place.

As Ameh had suggested, Adaulah proceeded to the head of the procession. He did not look back. He continued walking toward the entrance of the Royal Kraal. With his head held high, he walked with noticeable confidence. He seemed to know that those behind him would follow him.

Adaulah's approach toward the Royal Kraal parted the crowd out front. The sight of Adaulah's courageous approach moved most of the people who watched him to tears. His unexpected behavior surprised both Kharaambi and Olabisi. They looked at each other with a hint of a smile. An inspirational tear also rolled down Olabisi's cheek.

Only the Royal family, with their guards and aides, entered the Royal Kraal. Quazzi and the two Gold Warriors stopped and turned around at the kraal entrance. They joined the two Red Warriors who already stood guard there. The five of them stopped the rest of the procession from entering. As a result, the crowd standing out front quickly grew larger and larger.

Despite the oppressive sadness among the people standing at the kraal entrance, there was also a small surge of restlessness and frustration. Many people felt they had a right to enter the kraal too, at least, into the celebration area. The celebration area was seldom, if ever, closed. Still, Quazzi and the Aukmondi warriors refused everyone entry.

Ameh stood on the bank of the river until he thought the restlessness was becoming too chaotic. With his walking staff, he struggled against the gentle incline of the bank and made his way up toward the crowd of people. Because he was a Mfalme, the crowd gave way and calmed in his presence. Ameh took a position beside Quazzi and turned to face the crowd. He leaned on his staff and waited until the crowd grew silent.

"These are difficult times for all of us," Ameh finally said. "It seems a gruesome creature, a demon of death, walks among us. Whether you have seen this demon or not, it has touched each of us. We now carry an almost unbearable pain. You must realize that almost every pain we have experienced in the past few days has also been felt right here by the Ncobbas. Think about it. That is a large amount of pain. And it is made all the more difficult for them since they have lost loved ones too."

"Mfalme Jobabwe," an Old Creation at the head of the crowd, spoke up, saying how most of the crowd felt. "Please do not misinterpret our presence here. Yes, it is true. Many of us are here seeking comfort and reassurance. Our Mfalme and his Principal Mate have just died. But we mean no disrespect. Many of us are also here to show our support."

"That is good to hear, Great Creation. Good! For those of you seeking comfort and reassurance, if it is inside this kraal, I have no doubt, you will find it. The royal family will stand by us. But if you wish to give support, begin by giving the royal family time to mourn their own losses."

"Of course, Mfalme." The Old Creation nodded his head in total agreement.

"You can give your condolences later," Ameh added. "In the meantime, you can support the Ncobbas by supporting each other.

Where you stand, each of you can see someone who needs support, just as the Ncobbas. The Favored Tribesman, Kon-Shambique, told me just yesterday that one of the best things we can do is help each other hang on. Help each other get through this."

"How, Mfalme?"

"Any way you can. It could be as simple as sitting and talking together. Sometimes, a sympathetic ear can help more than you know."

Ameh got no argument from the crowd. He glanced at Quazzi, who praised him with a smile for managing the crowd. Ameh stood guard with Quazzi and the warriors until most people had moved back down the trail toward the north bank pathway or the bridge. Only about a quarter of the people continued to wander about the kraal entrance when Ameh himself prepared to leave.

"Great Creation," he said to Quazzi, "I think I have done about all I can do here. I am returning to the guest kraal and waiting until the Royal Kraal opens up again. Would you summon me when it does, if you do not mind?"

"So be it, Mfalme." Quazzi turned to resume his post next to the other warriors when he remembered to ask Ameh about one of his earlier concerns. "Did the Royal Warrior Nionu get you the warriors you asked about?"

"Yes, Great Creation, he did. He selected the Orange Warrior Wema and the Red Warrior Nienko. The two will spend today with their families. If all goes according to plan, they will leave the valley by daylight tomorrow morning."

"Good. I know both of them well. They are good warriors."

"The Royal Warrior Nionu said the same thing. It makes me feel good that both of you think highly of them."

Ameh had begun to walk away again when Olabisi's guard and personal aide, the Orange Warrior Refuri, came out of the Royal Kraal and addressed him. "Mfalme, Great Creation, excuse me."

Ameh slowly swiveled around on his staff. "Yes, Refuri?"

"You and the Brown Warrior Quazzi are wanted before the royal dais."

Ameh and Quazzi looked at each other. Had the Ncobbas' moment of privacy ended already? Ameh acknowledged Refuri with a quick gesture. He and Quazzi followed Refuri back into the kraal, wondering what was behind this unexpected summons.

45

A LITTLE PUSH

Under the canopy of the royal dais, the bodies of Ramuza and Rwuva lay as if on display. The Sacred Woman, Olabisi, and all the Ncobba daughters were putting the final touches on this solemn display. Even the five youngest daughters took part, adjusting bracelets on Rwuva's arm or a feathered crown on Ramuza's head. Each girl wiped away tears as she battled the overwhelming sadness and loss that saturated the moment.

As Ameh and Quazzi approached, they could see Ramuza's chieftain stool in the front center of the royal dais. It sat bare. Tradition forbids anyone other than the Mfalme to sit upon the stool. With the Mfalme dead, the stool seemed almost oversized to symbolize the great void.

The Sacred Woman Kharaambi and Adaulah stood out in front of the dais, talking with each other. Their conversation seemed passionate, as words volleyed between them. They stopped when they finally saw Ameh and Quazzi approaching.

Olabisi and the Ncobba daughters finished the decorative arrangements around the bodies of Ramuza and Rwuva. They had just settled down into their usual places, upon pillows and cushions, as Ameh and Quazzi approached. With respect, they rose to their feet again, but Ameh waved his hand so they could stay seated. Under the circumstances, he could overlook protocol. Besides, he was more concerned with what was happening between Kharaambi and Adaulah.

"What is the urgency, Sacred Woman?" He asked. "Why have you summoned us?"

"I summoned only the Great Creation Quazzi. It was the Little Creation Adaulah that summoned you, Mfalme."

Ameh looked down at Adaulah.

"Mfalme," Adaulah said, "I just wanted to thank you."

"Thank me? For what?"

"On the bank of the river, you stood behind me. You gave me a little push."

"It was a little push, Little Creation, because I felt you barely needed it."

"I might have behaved differently if you had not been there. I am grateful." Adaulah took a moment to consider his new responsibilities. "Ameh, Mfalme, will you continue to share your wisdom and guidance with me as you have done for my father?"

"Adaulah, the Sacred Spirit knows, you do not have even to ask."

Adaulah turned to Kharaambi, "And you, Sacred Mother. Will you share your leadership and protection with me?"

"Adaulah, you know I will. As the Gray Warrior, my life belongs to you. But, with more significance, you must remember. I am still one of your mothers."

Adaulah smiled as he looked up at Kharaambi and Ameh. "If you two will do these things…"

Just then, Baako, one of the youngest Ncobba daughters, leaned forward to whisper in the ear of her twin sister, Alaba. "Is he really the Mfalme now?" When Alaba nodded her head in the affirmative, Baako sat back. She spoke louder than a whisper: "But I do not want him to be Mfalme yet."

The feisty Zindzhi, who sat clearly on the other side of the dais, had overheard her sister's objection. She battled her fears and sorrow with a touch of anger. "You have no choice, little sister."

Everyone present overheard the exchange. Olabisi turned. She gently touched Baako, who sat behind her, and Alaba, beside her. She looked at Zindzhi and signaled respect and silence by putting her finger to her mouth. Olabisi finally nodded apologies to Ameh, Kharaambi, and Adaulah.

Ameh excused himself and took a few steps closer to the royal dais. He stood where he could easily see Baako, who sat toward the rear of the dais. "Little Woman, why do you object to Adaulah being Mfalme?"

Baako only shrugged at first. "I do not know, Mfalme. He knows nothing about being Mfalme. He is too young."

"Too young? How do you know?"

"Because… he just is. When we play together, he is my little brother. He is not an Mfalme."

Ameh smiled. "Little Woman, Adaulah may be your baby brother, but he is also your Mfalme now. Like it or not, let us give him a chance to earn the title he must carry."

Baako glanced at Adaulah. She suppressed a childish grimace and forced herself to accept what must be. "Well … so be it."

Ameh walked back to where Adaulah stood. "The truth of the matter is, Baako loves you. She has lost her father. She has lost the Principal Mother. Now, she is afraid that she is losing her baby brother too."

"She is afraid that we might not be able to play together as we have done in the past." Adaulah turned to his sister. "Do not worry, Baako. I still like to play. I promise. We will play together as we have always done."

"In the meantime," Kharaambi folded her arms across her chest, "I must maintain my promise."

Adaulah knew what the Gray Warrior meant by keeping her promise. He looked up into Kharaambi's face. "But, Sacred Mother, please…"

"Adaulah, I said no!"

"Do I detect another voice of dissent?" Ameh asked. He and Quazzi realized the passionate discussion between Adaulah and the Gray Warrior continued.

"I can explain, Mfalme. We are opening the Royal Kraal back up shortly so that the people can view the bodies of Ramuza and Rwuva and pay their tributes."

"So soon?"

"Yes, Great Creation. As you well know, death runs rampant through the valley. Entire kraals are dying overnight. Last night, the Mangoni demon of death killed everyone in both the Pogobi and Obentawni kraals."

"Yes, I have heard about that. And the deaths of the Royal Warrior Npatuzi, his entire Muusitu Regiment, and both of Nionu's Blue Warriors followed."

"Yes. We must surrender the bodies to the elements and release the spirits to their ancestors as soon as possible."

"That is understandable, Sacred Woman. So, what is the problem?"

"Before we begin, the little Mfalme here," Kharaambi sounded sarcastic, "wants to go to the Mangoni camp to talk with Mfalme Abul-Gwan."

Ameh was speechless. With a knitted brow, he looked down at Adaulah again. "Little Creation, what do you plan to say to him? What do you expect to gain?"

"Mfalme Abul-Gwan is angry. I must tell him that he has no reason to be angry. The spirit of the Sacred Woman Abul-Tess is still with him. Without anger, he would realize this. Without anger, Mfalme Abul-Gwan can do the right thing."

"Do the right thing?"

"Yes, Mfalme. Release the spirit of the Sacred Woman Abul-Tess to her ancestors. Mfalme Abul-Gwan is afraid to let her go. He does not understand that the spirit of the Sacred Woman will not go far."

"Little Creation, do you not think he will soon realize this alone?"

Adaulah shrugged. "He might. But since we will be burying our dead, I thought the Mfalme would join us to bury his people."

Ameh knew Adaulah's innocence kept the Little Creation from understanding. It was not as simple as that. The look of concern deepened on Ameh's as he glanced at Kharaambi and Quazzi. He looked at Adaulah, thinking of a way to open the Little Creation's eyes to the truth.

"That is very thoughtful of you, but I am afraid Mfalme Abul-Gwan wants nothing to do with us."

"He is just angry because the Sacred Woman Abul-Tess died too soon. He still has to give the Sacred Woman a proper release. When he does, he will feel better. He will not be so angry. And he will stop the ritual that is killing us."

"It is evident, Little Creation, that you have been thinking a lot about this." Ameh admired Adaulah's amazing insight. "But, to confront the Mangoni Mfalme is too dangerous."

"Mfalme Abul-Gwan only needs to know that letting the Sacred Woman Abul-Tess go is alright. The bond with her is still there. I have to tell him that. He needs to know."

"Why you? Listen to your Mother. She is right. If you feel this must be done, then send someone else to do it. You are too important to the Aukmondi. As your family's last male descendant, you are more important than your father was."

"Adaulah," the Brown Warrior Quazzi stepped forward. If you feel this is necessary, I will tell him for you."

"Everyone, stop!" Kharaambi unfolded her arms. "I am allowing no one up to the Mangoni camp. It is final. I will hear no more of it. Quazzi, Great Creation, I have a different mission for you."

"Yes, Sacred Woman?"

"Open up the Royal Kraal. Allow the people to pay their final respects to the Mfalme and his Principal Mate. Also, because of the number of people that have died, we should begin arrangements to bury our dead as soon as possible."

"So be it," agreed Quazzi.

"Under the circumstances, I think having at least two mass grave sites will be most appropriate."

"Mass grave sites? Is that the proper thing to do? Should we not consult the Favored Tribesman about this?"

"I will speak with Kon-Shambique. If he has any objections or if there is anything else he may need, I will let you know. But I suggest that you get started by finding two grave sites. We cannot afford to wait any longer. We may already be overwhelmed by the task before us."

"With so many deaths, do you have any suggestions where these grave sites should be, Sacred Woman?"

"I will leave that decision up to you, Quazzi. At least one should probably be in the valley depths. I think there is ample room there for a mass grave."

Ameh stepped forward. Another idea that popped into his head had merit. He offered it up for consideration. "If no one has any objections, may I suggest that the other grave site be closer to what is left of the Pogobi kraal? The people of the Pogobi kraal gave the Chinchigwe the warmest greetings when we first arrived. That place holds a special place in my heart. But after so many deaths there, even I would find it very difficult to re-settle there."

"Good suggestion, Mfalme." Kharaambi turned to Quazzi. "Great Creation, make it so."

"So be it, Sacred Woman. I may have to employ the warriors of two armies to do this. If we start now, we can finish by sunrise tomorrow."

"Finish paying tribute to the Mfalme and his Principal Mate, Great Creation. But get started as soon as possible and do whatever you feel is necessary."

— 46 —

WHAT WE MUST DO IS OFTEN LIMITED

Unlike earlier this morning, a large crowd filled the Royal Kraal. By mid-morning, several groups of people wandered about the celebration area. People filled the area from the kraal entrance, across the celebration area, and back to the four huts of the Ncobbas. Some of the people had already paid their respects to the royal family. They continued to linger, in no hurry to leave. Other people moved here and there, socializing with one another as they prepared to join the line of others filing past the royal dais.

Those who filed past the dais offered warm, heartfelt condolences to the royal family—Kharaambi, Olabisi, the Ncobba daughters, and Adaulah. Many of them paid long, tearful tributes to Ramuza and Rwuva. Some left gifts of flowers, food, precious stones, woodcarvings, and other items of personal value. The gifts piled so high that aides had to move them aside to make room for more gifts to come.

This uninterrupted tribute to Ramuza and Rwuva lasted until just before noon. The Young Creation Wotabe, from the Mempa kraal, finally walked into the Royal Kraal. He no longer showed his panicky, desperate behavior. Wotabe moved in a stupor, shocked by what he saw earlier this morning. He walked slowly into the Royal Kraal with his head down. He seemed in no hurry to find the urgent help he needed. The Broken Creation had walked over halfway across the celebration areas before drawing attention to himself. All who saw Wotabe knew he had not come to pay any tributes. A concerned crowd gathered around him.

The Gold Warrior Gabon, a warrior in Obe Bendabe's regiment, patrolled the celebration area nearby. He saw the chaotic crowd around Wotabe. It seemed to grow larger and noisier as he approached it. Gabon pushed through to learn the cause of this crowd. When he found Wotabe at its center, he could tell something unfortunate had occurred. He exercised his authority to ask the crowd to stand back. He took Wotabe aside. "Young Creation, what is wrong? What has happened?"

Wotabe finally raised his head. When he saw the Gold Warrior standing before him, he realized he stood in the Royal Kraal for the first time. "I need to tell the Sacred Woman Kharaambi about ..."

"Tell her about what?"

"I have seen ... that thing. I have seen the demon ... that walks our valley ... up on the north slope."

Even though the Gold Warrior had asked the crowd to stand back, some people stood close enough to overhear Wotabe's comment. They reacted with a new burst of noise and restlessness. Gabon needed to take Wotabe by the arm and quickly escort him away before panic gripped the crowd.

The Gold Warrior respected the solemn tribute to Mfalme Ncobba and the Principal Mate Rwuva. This new development had the potential to cause a major disruption. Gabon quickly escorted Wotabe toward the royal dais. But with forethought, he took the Young Creation directly past the royal dais and into the semi-secluded work area between Rwuva's and Olabisi's huts.

Just as the Gold Warrior Gabon had expected, only a minor disturbance erupted as he escorted Wotabe past the royal dais. And, as he had hoped, that minor disturbance was enough to cause the Sacred Woman Kharaambi, Mfalme Ameh Jobabwe, and the Brown Warrior Quazzi to grow concerned. They follow him into the work area.

Kharaambi led the trio into the area. The untimely interruption angered her. When she spoke, the irritation could be heard in her voice. "What is going on here?"

"Sacred Woman, we apologize," the Gold Warrior Gabon began, "but the Young Creation Wotabe says he has seen the Mangoni's demon, up on the north slope."

"Where, on the north slope?" Quazzi asked. Anger affected his voice, too.

"The Butetwa and the Mempa kraals." Wotabe spoke softly as tears welled up in his eyes. "The demon struck the Butetwa kraal … I guess sometime last night. I found everyone there … dead. I walked upon the demon, still there this morning. So, I ran. The demon followed me. It struck the Mempa kraal just a little while ago. I saw it all. My kraal, all the people are dead. The demon waved away their lives with just a flip of its wrist."

"Quazzi," Kharaambi turned to the Brown Warrior, "get me the most available army. We are going up there."

"No. Do not go up there! There is no hurry, Sacred Woman." Wotabe took a moment to wipe the tears streaming down his face. "There is nothing to be saved. I ran for help. But I had to hide to keep the demon from following me. I saw it all. They are all dead – everything and everybody. If you go there, certain death awaits you. After what I have seen, I believe no army can defeat that demon."

"Great Sacred Spirit!" Quazzi turned to Kharaambi. "Something still has to be done."

"I am open to suggestions," Kharaambi said, looking at the people around her. "Any ideas?"

"It is clear." Ameh leaned heavily on his staff. "What we must do is rid our valley of the Mangoni houngan and his demon. But that has proven to be … next to impossible. Sometimes, what we must do is often limited to what we can do."

"What do you mean, Mfalme?" Kharaambi asked.

"Well… until we figure out how to stop this demon, as you suggested, Sacred Woman, we must give our dead a proper burial. It is something we have to do. And, if we wait too much longer, we cannot do that either." He turned to Quazzi. "Great Creation, you made a guess earlier about how long it would take to dig two huge grave sites. In light of this news, maybe you should rethink your guess. We must now bury the people in two more kraals."

* * * * *

Moments ago, when the Gold Warrior Gabon escorted Wotabe into the work area, he had expected that Kharaambi, Ameh, and Quazzi would notice and follow him. He did not expect the behavior of the little prince, Adaulah, who also followed everyone into the area.

During Wotabe's work area revelation, Adaulah stood behind Ameh. No one saw him. The Curious Little Creation heard everything said. All of it affected him. The talk about two more dead kraals frightened him, and the talk about digging mass grave sites disturbed him.

Adaulah had heard enough. He quietly backed his way out of the work area. He agreed with the Brown Warrior Quazzi. Something had to be done. With unmistakable clarity, Adaulah knew what that something was, and it went beyond Ameh's suggestion of burying the dead.

In Adaulah's opinion, the Great Creation, Mfalme Abul-Gwan, had to stop being angry. There is no reason for it. Adaulah had to tell him so. He had to tell Abul-Gwan that the spirit of the Sacred Woman Abul-Tess is still with him. If Mfalme Abul-Gwan knew this, he would stop being so angry. He would stop the houngan's ritual. When the ritual stops, the deaths would stop. Adaulah wondered. Why wasn't this as clear to everyone else as it was to him?

Adaulah walked slowly back to the royal dais. As he walked in front of the dais to take his seat, he saw that people were still filing by, paying their tributes to Ramuza and Rwuva. Before he sat down, he glanced at all nine of his sisters and at the Sacred Woman Olabisi. All of them seemed preoccupied with the acknowledgements to the tributes being paid. None of them seemed to realize his brief disappearance.

Whenever the nine Ncobba daughters sat upon the royal dais, they always sat in designated places. If, for whatever reason, one of them was missing, it became noticeable at once. He held no designated spot on the dais. Adaulah sat anywhere he wanted. Since he was an infant, he had the liberty to move about, if he was on the dais at all. He was more apt to be playing nearby. Adaulah recognized an immediate advantage here.

Adaulah sat down on the front edge of the dais. He turned his attention to the people who filed before him. He realized that a vast majority of the people still recognized Ramuza Ncobba as the Mfalme. In their hearts and minds, the Powerful, Charismatic Creation, even in death, was still the Mfalme. Many were unaware that the title had already transferred to the young Adaulah. Even as Adaulah sat directly in front of the empty chieftain stool, Adaulah's new significance had not yet registered with many of them. Adaulah felt that here was another two-fold advantage he could use.

Under the circumstances, with everyone so focused on paying their respects to Ramuza and Rwuva, no one noticed when Adaulah got up from his seat again. Adaulah quietly moved to the side of the dais between the condolences and tributes. He stood there for a moment. Feeling his discreet movement was successful, he finally moved back behind the dais. It was a temporary refuge and a final confirmation that he could finish what he had in mind.

*****

Several minutes later, the Sacred Woman Kharaambi, Mfalme Ameh Jobabwe, and the Brown Warrior Quazzi came from the work area. They had sent a small detachment of warriors up to the Butetwe and Mempa kraals to investigate the situation. Kharaambi, Ameh, and Quazzi returned to their original positions on and around the royal dais to finish paying their tributes to Ramuza and Rwuva. Sure enough, all of them complied with all of Adaulah's advantages. Several minutes later, no one noticed that Adaulah was missing. Kharaambi was the first.

The intuitive woman got up from her seat. While receiving well-wishes and condolences, she searched from one side of the dais to the other. When she saw no sign of Adaulah, she quietly moved next to a Red Warrior who stood guard nearby.

"Great Creation," she whispered, "where is Adaulah?"

"He is back here." The Red Warrior led Kharaambi behind the dais. With confidence, he thought he could show Kharaambi where Adaulah sat. But to his surprise, no one sat behind the dais. "He was there a moment ago, Sacred Woman."

"Find him for me, please."

*****

Adaulah was skillful at disappearing when he wanted. His sisters, because of the sacred essence about them, always had guards and aides around them. Adaulah had them only on special occasions. He did not want the aides. And, as long as he stayed inside the valley, he did not need the guards. So, it was easier for him to find moments of solitude. It was easy for him to move about and mingle. It was easy for him to slip from one socializing group to the next.

Adaulah worked from behind the royal dais and across the celebration area. Yes, several people saw him. They all offered him their condolences, and Adaulah graciously accepted them. Some thought it was strange to find Adaulah wandering about the celebration area, but none of the people questioned him. In each case, the people dismissed and soon forgot their concerns. After only a few minutes, Adaulah took the liberty to walk completely out of the Royal Kraal.

Adaulah encountered fewer people once he got outside the Royal Kraal. He knew he would meet even fewer people if he avoided the north bank pathway. That well-used pathway paralleling the Aukmondi River toward the east was often busy. So, once he got outside the Royal Kraal, Adaulah started up the north slope instead. At this point, Adaulah realized he would meet no people if he avoided the pathways altogether. The Little Creation left the pathway. He took a northeast route, up the north slope, through the trees, bushes, and intermittent clearings.

Just over three kilometers up the north slope, Adaulah emerged onto a pathway, only a few meters from the Gongeri Junction. The unconventional route up the slope was slightly more difficult to make, but it had saved him over two kilometers. It had also ensured his disappearance from the Royal Kraal. Even if people discovered him missing now, it was too late to stop him. From the Gongeri Junction, Adaulah needed only a short time to reach Mfalme Abul-Gwan. He needed even less time to tell Abul-Gwan what he needed to know. To ensure his success, Adaulah broke into a comfortable run. From the junction, Adaulah took the pathway that would lead eastward toward the south side of Nagorda Peak.

47

THIS IS NOT SAFE

By midday, the traveling farmers and the escorting warriors had completed twenty-six kilometers on their journey home. Since leaving the Kiwane Village, the Aukmondi elders continued to set the pace, which was slow across the rolling savanna grassland. As the sun climbed higher in the sky, the elders could feel the gradual increase in heat and humidity. The walk grew increasingly uncomfortable.

The Green Warrior Tushema glanced back over his shoulder at the traveling caravan of farmers. In his opinion, their pace was too slow. Tushema had considered pushing them harder despite the heat and humidity. He thought he had a good reason. Days ago, he had seen some disturbing signs that it might be too late to get them across the Mara River. He hoped that he was wrong.

About halfway through the visit to the Kiwane Village, Tushema had seen the very first signs that the annual zebras and wildebeest migrations were beginning ahead of season. There had been brief periods of rain. This, in itself, was normal. At first, Tushema gave little thought to the rain's significance. But then, the frequency of rain increased and came with occasional downpours. Nature took a turn that Tushema did not expect. He grew concerned. He knew that there were still several days before he would lead the farmers back to the Aukmondi Valley. But, within those several days, there was ample time for the rains to nourish and replenish the savanna grasses, starting an amazing natural sequence.

Within days after the frequent and occasional heavy rains, herds of gazelle and zebras would move into the area. The fresh, new grass would draw the gazelle and zebras with ceaseless appetites. As the rains grew stronger in the Maasai Mara region, the animals would migrate northward in pursuit of taller grasses. They would leave behind only stubble; grasses gnawed down to a level now preferred by wildebeests. After several more days, massive herds of wildebeests would move into the area in their own northward migration. Herds of gazelle, zebras, and wildebeests overlapped as they fed on their share of the grasses.

In a short period, this annual migration of animals would peak with thousands upon thousands of ungulates moving through the area. It was one of nature's grandest spectacles. And one simple fact was the most awesome aspect of this grand spectacle. Each animal must cross the Mara River at one point or another. No one expected this cycle to begin for another half-cycle of the moon.

Tushema glanced back at the farmers again. In spite of the urgency of getting them across the river, he resisted the urge to force them to increase their leisurely pace. He could tell by their low level of conversation that their comfort level was already low. More than half of these farmers were tribal elders. They were elders not only in recognized authority but also in respected maturity. Tushema did not want to push them any harder than necessary.

Out of respect and consideration, the Green Warrior reconsidered the timeliness of the next scheduled rest stop. A planned mid-day stop was another two kilometers ahead. But judging by the farmers' appearance, Tushema felt the stop should be sooner.

Another unanticipated development made the thoughtful Tushema consider stopping early. He focused his eyes ahead. He could still see the five hunting lions through a gentle shimmer of quicksilver. All morning long, the lions had followed the small herd of zebras. When first noticed, they had walked about a kilometer ahead, on a parallel course with the traveling caravan. By midday, the lions had shifted their course to a disadvantageous position. They were now directly ahead of the farmers and only a half kilometer away.

When Tushema first saw the lions, he did not expect the lions to show much interest in the farmers or the pack animals. The small herd of zebras, which continued to travel about a kilometer ahead of the lions, still appeared to be the lions' preferred target. But the pace of the cats slowed. Tushema didn't like it. The distance between the lions and the herd of zebras grew larger. The distance between the lions and the farmers grew smaller. Tushema realized that the closer proximity of the farmers and the pack animals to the lions could instantly heighten the lions' curiosity and change their priority.

As the Green Warrior watched the three lions, he led the farmers by a knoll, not far off to the right. Across the rolling grassland, Tushema almost walked past this knoll. But a large and sturdy acacia tree stood on top. The shady area beneath the tree would offer an almost ideal spot for the group to escape the midday sun for a while.

With the planned rest stop still two kilometers ahead and after moving so close to the lions, the Green Warrior glanced at the tree several times. Each time the tree gained renewed value. A tree this size and an ideal opportunity like this may not come again before the lions moved on, or before exhaustion overwhelmed the farmers. Tushema turned to face the caravan behind him. He pointed to the acacia tree with his spear. It served as a welcome signal to the farmers and the detachment of warriors. The acacia tree was now the place for their midday stop.

Four of the warriors quickly surveyed the area for security's sake. It was a necessary precaution. The cool shade of an acacia tree in such an open area could attract more than exhausted travelers. Besides the hunting lions, other dangers could lurk in the area. As an added precaution, the four warriors found strategic positions at the base of the knoll to set up guard posts. They would stand guard for the duration of the stop.

As for the farmers, they understood this rest stop would be brief. Once Tushema gave the sign, the farmers wasted no time. They forced their weary bodies up the moderate incline of the knoll toward the acacia tree. The Great Creation, Elder Zekke led the way. The rocking motion of his characteristic walk almost disappeared in his efforts to push himself up the knoll's incline.

In their journey to and from the Kiwane Village, the farmers had set up camps many times. It was now a matter of routine. They knew what needed to be done and how to do it quickly. Each farmer had their designated task. Some senior farmers quickly corralled the donkeys, cattle, and goats together. They also provided the pack animals with a small ration of water they carried. Most of the junior farmers unloaded some of the heavy bundles, baskets, and other cargo that the animals carried to give the animals their own respite.

The Sacred Woman Lobarra was one of the junior farmers. During this stop, it was her responsibility to prepare food and ensure that everyone got enough to eat. Since the farmers and warriors were traveling, she knew beforehand that there would be no time for extensive food preparation during the morning or mid-day rest stops. As a well-organized person, Lobarra prepared and packed away food the preceding evening. Lobarra had little to do except find a central spot where everyone could eat and then arrange the food so it was accessible.

The Red Warrior Rotho quickly completed his own safety survey of the area. As Lobarra's guard and aide on this mission, he went to help the Sacred Woman. He found that Lobarra had already spread out a large mat under the acacia tree where most everyone would eat. Rotho volunteered to help her move the food basket and gourds of water to the mat. The Red Warrior carried two of the water pouches under his arms, while Lobarra, with Tutapona still bundled on her back, carried the barrel-shaped food basket to the mat.

Lobarra set the basket down, untied the lid, and pried it open. Beneath the lid was an inner cloth covering. Lobarra peeled it back to expose about four dozen vegetable samosas, kiln-baked pastries stuffed with seasoned potatoes. The ambient temperature of the day was high enough to keep the samosas warm. Both Lobarra and the Rotho inhaled as the earthy smell of cooked potatoes poured from the basket. It was a pleasant sensation that brought a smile to their faces.

"I do not know, Sacred Woman," Rotho said as he stared down at the samosas with a playful look of concern on his face. "If everyone is as hungry as I am, I do not think you made enough."

"There is enough, Great Creation. I made sure of it." Lobarra removed some of the samosas from the basket. One by one, she piled a dozen samosas on the basket lid as Rotho looked on.

"So, what are you doing?"

"If everyone is as hungry as you are, I am ensuring everyone gets some." Lobarra picked up the lid. "I am taking these to the Green Warrior Tushema and the warriors standing guard at the base of the knoll."

"That is very thoughtful of you." Rotho glanced around toward the outer boundary of the knoll. He studied the positions of Tushema and the four warriors standing around the knoll. Rotho considered Lobarra's intention from a security point of view. He saw nothing of any concern, but he kept his quick assessment to himself. Instead, he picked up one of the samosas from the lid and bit into it. He spoke with his mouth full. "I guess it would be thoughtful of me if I made sure their water pouches are full."

"Yes, Great Creation, it would."

The rest of the farmers and the remaining warriors gathered around the mat under the acacia tree to begin their communal meal. As they did, Lobarra and Rotho descended the north side of the knoll. Lobarra carried the lid full of samosas. Rotho carried one of the water pouches and a drinking ladle. They served the Red Warrior Berko first, who stood guard there. They left Berko with two samosas and two ladles of water; one to fill his water pouch and one to drink. To Lobarra and Rotho, Berko seemed grateful, although the Red Warrior had to eat and drink without the comforting shade of the acacia tree.

With the sun almost directly overhead, Lobarra and Rotho walked around to the knoll's west, south, and east sides. They patiently served each of the warriors who stood guard at these points: Ngosi, Wekesa, and Kibwe. By the time Lobarra and Rotho reached the White Warrior Kibwe, Lobarra looked forward to the shade of the acacia tree. Several times, she glanced up to the summit of the knoll, looking forward to the coolness of the tree. Serving the guarding warriors, however, was almost complete. They had one warrior left to serve.

Lobarra and Rotho found the Green Warrior Tushema the hardest to catch of the warriors at the base of the knoll. He moved about constantly. The Green Warrior moved from one guard-post to the next, coordinating some added precautions. At one point, just when

Lobarra and Rotho made a deliberate effort to catch him, they saw Tushema leave the knoll's base and wander across the grassland.

The Sacred Woman Lobarra and the Red Warrior Rotho followed him. They assumed that the Green Warrior was not going far; that he was scouting ahead. They wanted to ensure Tushema filled his water pouch and received his share of the samosas. But the Green Warrior continued walking eastward, too far. Rotho grew concerned.

"Wait, Sacred Woman." The Red Warrior stopped walking. "This is not safe. Let us not go any farther. We must stay near the rest of the group."

Lobarra stopped walking. She focused her eyes on the Green Warrior. "Where is he going?"

Rotho studied the Green Warrior. He looked ahead, trying to find the Green Warrior's focus. "It looks like he is concerned about the lions."

"So, what is he doing? Does he intend to run them away?"

"I would not be surprised. The Green Warrior has that determination. We must wait and see." Rotho turned. It was a subtle suggestion to Lobarra that she should turn too. "Come. Let us return to the knoll."

48

I SAID RUN

Halfway up the hillside to Nagorda Peak, the atmosphere had completely changed in the kraal of the Favored Tribesman Kon-Shambique. The frantic, chaotic activities of earlier this morning had settled to relative quietness. Most of the warriors had gone. Earlier, Kon-Shambique sent the bodies of Ramuza and Rwuva to the Royal Kraal, where they belonged. Likewise, he sent the bodies of the Green Warrior Zabiba and the Red Warrior Gengu to their respective warrior kraals, where family and friends could pay their proper respects.

At present, family and friends remained in Kon-Shambique's kraal to pay respects and a small tribute to the Sacred Woman Tongda. Tongda's body, dressed in all white, lay upon an adorned burial litter on display out in front of Kon-Shambique's hut. Considered as one of the most beautiful women in the Aukmondi Valley, Tongda looked almost angelic.

Tongda's family bracketed her body on three sides. The Favored Tribesman, considered by all as part of Tonga's family, stood on one side. He still looked somewhat weary from the loss of his love. Despite the fatigue in his eyes, he forced a small smile on his face as he accepted the condolences from the people who filed before him.

Tongda's aged father, Benwe Bomah Leng, sat upon a mat behind Tongda's burial litter. He sat still, with almost no expression on his face. Only red and watery eyes showed his pain. His sister-in-law Oraka Sameah Mushwala, Tongda's aunt and Upenda's mother, sat beside him. She held his hand tightly. It was impossible to tell if it was for their respective comfort.

The White Warrior Upenda stood on the other side of Tongda's litter. Upenda was Tongda's cousin and a binding cornerstone in the Sameah family. Through all the grief and sadness, Upenda coordinated all the preparations for Tongda's release, right down to the current display. She accepted condolences as she fluctuated between gratitude and sorrow. So many tears had streaked down her face that she had stopped wiping them away.

"She is so beautiful," one young woman said as she filed past Tongda's litter. "I know all her ancestors will welcome her. I know they have gathered, expecting her arrival. The whole Sameah family will feel their joy. And you, Upenda, will receive special blessings for all you have done for Tongda."

"Thank you, Sacred Woman." Upenda finally brushed away a tear that hung on her chin.

A growing distraction outside of the kraal caught everyone's attention. In the distance, down the hillside, the people saw Adaulah approaching on the pathway. The fact that he was running was a distraction in itself. Was he coming to pay a tribute to the Sacred Woman Tongda?

Adaulah took full advantage of his youth. He took the hillside with effortless strides. He had no idea that this amazing feat had captivated so many people. When he finally reached the entrance of Kon-Shambique's kraal, he stopped. He stood for a moment to study the people inside the kraal. He labored only to catch his breath. As his breathing settled, he realized what was happening inside the kraal. So obsessed with his intentions, Adaulah had completely forgotten about the events unfolding here. He took three steps back, as if the simple act would serve as an apology for his interruption.

When Adaulah did not enter the kraal, Kon-Shambique's sharp and observant mind alerted him to the unexpected. "Oh no," he said to himself. "Great Sacred Spirit, please tell me. Does he intend to do as I suspect?"

Adaulah turned. He continued his sprint up the hillside toward Nagorda Peak. His intention suddenly became obvious to everyone in the kraal. The somber atmosphere made another change, quickly turning into confusion and restless concerns.

"He has to be stopped!" Kon-Shambique said to Upenda.

Upenda reacted by wiping away the trail of tears on her face. She embraced her responsibility as a White Warrior and darted toward Kon-Shambique's hut. Her shield and spear lay just inside the entranceway. She took only seconds to retrieve them.

Kon-Shambique caught Upenda's arm as she ran past him. Although not yet related in family or blood, he loved her as if she were a relative. He knew what she was preparing to do. Kon-Shambique knew that, since yesterday evening, everyone who had gone up to the peak had died. He wanted to stop her. He also knew that Upenda was only doing her duty as a warrior. With the deepest concern on his face, he held Upenda's shoulders. The words he finally spoke were only a hint of how he felt. "Sacred Woman, please ... be careful. Come back to us."

A brief look into Kon-Shambique's eyes was Upenda's only acknowledgement. She gave the same cherished look to Benwe and Oraka, her uncle and mother, who stared back at her. The thought occurred to her. She might never see them again. The thought grew with her fear. Rather than face it, she forced the crippling thought from her mind. She broke free from Kon-Shambique's grip and ran toward the kraal exit. With only one more glance back, she matched Adaulah's sprint up the pathway toward the peak.

*****

Adaulah's youthful endurance finally gave out about a hundred meters down the hillside from where the Mangoni worker warriors stood guard. The Little Creation would finish the climb at a strong walking pace. The slower pace was acceptable. His goal was almost in sight. He could easily see the Mangoni warriors, standing guard 300 meters ahead.

Adaulah's new pace worked to Upenda's advantage. She continued her sprint up the hillside. After several minutes, she closed the gap between her and Adaulah. She suppressed her labored breathing. She came up behind the Little Creation without a sound as a tactical warrior. Adaulah did not know Upenda was behind him until she touched his shoulder.

"Little Creation, what are you doing?"

Startled, Adaulah jumped. "Sacred Woman! Where did you come from?"

"That is not important. You must come with me. We must go back down the hillside."

"But I must talk with Mfalme Abul-Gwan."

"That will not happen. Come with me."

"Sacred Woman, please! I have to do this."

"Maybe you do, but not right now; not like this. Come."

"Sacred Woman," Adaulah thought hard about what he was about to do. A couple of minor advantages had gotten him this far. He considered using his greatest advantage of all. He looked up, directly into the White Warrior's eyes. "Upenda, I am … Mfalme."

"Yes, you are!" Unfazed, Upenda shoved Adaulah back down the pathway. "That is one of the main reasons you are coming with me."

Adaulah protested, but both Upenda and Adaulah heard a rustle in the bushes just off the pathway. They turned to see what it was. It was only a fan-tailed raven, foraging for seeds or bugs in the bushes. It cawed several times and then flew away. Upenda and Adaulah continued down the pathway when they heard the rustle in the bushes again. It was stronger this time. They turned. When they did, they saw a most gruesome sight.

The Loa of Death stood watching them. Its large, black, oversized hood did not obscure its bony white face or living eyes. Minute movements in the huge eyes suggested the demon studied every detail about them.

Upenda assumed a defensive position and posture in front of Adaulah. She adjusted her shield, drew her spear back, and leveled it. She did not have to tell Adaulah to stay behind her. The Little Creation hid behind the White Warrior, hugging her leg like his life depended on it.

The last words that Kon-Shambique said to Upenda echoed in her head, *"Be careful; come back to us."* Is there any such thing as 'careful' when death stands before you? Death was coming. As

Upenda stared back at the demon, memories of the pleading looks of her uncle and mother were the only images she saw.

Upenda slowly inched her way backwards down the pathway. She could feel Adaulah pressing close to her leg in his position of refuge. The lump in her throat and the fear that filled her mind were paralyzing. Only the adrenaline that raced through her body kept her moving. The retreat seemed to be working. Upenda and Adaulah had moved back almost two meters when the Loa of Death slowly moved toward them. Death was coming.

"Run, Adaulah! Run!"

"What about you, Sacred Woman?"

"I said run!" Adrenaline made the command sound angry.

Adaulah turned. He ran, but with strong reluctance. He kept looking back over his shoulder out of concern for Upenda. Adaulah had run only a few meters when he finally looked ahead and saw the massive regiment of an Aukmondi army running up the pathway toward him. Out in front was the Gray Warrior Kharaambi. Adaulah's sprint finally became strong as he raced ahead. He took a new position of refuge behind his mother.

Kharaambi embraced Adaulah. She hugged him several times before her warrior mode resurfaced. She took Adaulah by the arm and shoved him toward one of the Gold Warriors behind her. "Gabon, Great Creation, take a detail of warriors and escort him back down to Kon-Shambique's kraal. Keep him in your sight."

"So be it, Sacred Woman." The Gold Warrior Gabon grabbed Adaulah by his waist, lifting him off his feet. He carried him under his arm.

Adaulah was just able to glance back at Kharaambi. "Sacred Mother," he yelled out as Gabon carried him away. "I am sorry. I did not mean this to happen."

"I know, Little Creation. Your intention was honorable. But I will talk with you about it later when I return." Kharaambi turned to help Upenda and faced the demon gliding down the pathway. "If I return."

— **49** —

LIONS IN OUR PATHWAY

Almost one hundred and five kilometers away, under the shade of the huge acacia tree, Tutapona screamed. He woke with several short whimpers from the slumber of a midday nap. He squirmed within the confines of the kanga on his mother's back. And then he screamed. Tutapona screamed because he felt something was still wrong.

*****

Several minutes earlier, Lobarra sat with the rest of the farmers under the acacia tree. She had just finished eating her own share of the samosas when she finally saw the Green Warrior coming up the side of the knoll. Without disturbing the sleeping Tutapona, she quickly adjusted the kanga and got to her feet.

Lobarra was surprised to see only three samosas left from the entire batch. She had just prepared enough. Lobarra gathered the samosas and placed them on the lid again. She called Rotho, prompting him to retrieve the water pouch, ladle, and follow her. Lobarra met Tushema just after he reached the top of the knoll. She offered him the entire lid.

"Thank you, Sacred Woman." Tushema took only one of the pastries. He held it in his hand, still too distracted to eat. He stared out across the grassland toward the lions. When he finally bit into the samosa, he chewed without savoring the food.

Lobarra watched the Green Warrior eat. With a gentle frown, she finally redefined his distracted behavior as anxious worry. "Great Creation, if you do not relax and eat as you should, you are asking for a bout of indigestion. And I am afraid. No one here is strong enough to burp you."

"Excuse me?" Tushema looked at Lobarra, pulling his mind away from his distraction. He seemed to realize the unhealthy way he was eating. Rather than continue, he replaced the once-bitten samosa on the lid.

"Your concern about those lions seems to grow," Lobarra said. "Is there anything wrong?"

"No, only that … Great Sacred Spirit, they will not move!" Tushema sounded frustrated. "We have waited here too long, Sacred Woman. We have been here much longer than I had planned."

"Great Creation," Rotho began. "You are trying to get us across the Mara. We have a day and a half. Can we not recover lost time before nightfall tomorrow?"

"Each second we wait, herds will likely block the Mara. We cannot recover lost time. I fear we may be too late already if you must know."

Tushema made another anxious glance toward the lions. He recalled the irrational and faulty assumption he had made just moments ago. Since it's unusual for lions to hunt people, the disinterested lions should move on if approached. When Tushema tried it, the lions only watched him get closer and closer. They did not move.

Tushema's impatience had blinded him to something he and every other Aukmondi warrior knows. A lion runs away from nothing. He made a dangerous and foolish oversight. It did nothing but jeopardize his safety and made him angry with himself.

Tushema sighed. He picked up his unfinished samosa and took another big, hearty bite. "The lions are delaying our progress."

Lobarra attempted to focus her vision through the quicksilver. She saw only the head of one lion. She saw no sign of the zebras. "Where is the herd they were following?"

Both Tushema and Rotho looked toward the far horizon. Unlike Lobarra, the trained warriors knew where to focus. They could easily discern the herd of zebras through the distorted images. And even the less experienced Red Warrior Rotho could tell by the cloud of dust that the herd was moving eastward at a steady pace.

"The zebras are still there. At the rate they are moving, they will not be there for long," Rotho refocused his scrutiny on the lions. Three lionesses sat upon their hunches as they looked up and down the grassland. The remaining female and the male had stretched out and rested in the shallow grass. "The lions appear to be in no hurry to catch the herd. I think they have given up. It looks as though they are trying to decide whether to stay where they are or go hunt somewhere else."

"So, what does this mean? Will they come this way?"

"It is possible." Tushema made another quick assessment of the situation. He resisted second-guessing the lions. And he was not about to make another faulty assumption about them. "As long as they sit there, we cannot continue."

"As long as they sit there, our fate hangs in the balance." Elder Zekke got up from where he sat. He and the Gold Warrior Oghani had been talking together when they overheard Tushema's frustrated comments. He led the way over to where Tushema, Lobarra, and Rotho stood and addressed the Green Warrior. "When fate hangs in the balance like this, you must tip that balance in your favor."

"What do you mean?"

"If timing is important, then we must do something to continue."

The Gold Warrior Oghani agreed. He stepped forward to offer his suggestions to the Green Warrior. "Great Creation, I could take a small detail ahead. We could distract the lions, or," Oghani reworded a more deadly choice, "we could remove them."

As drastic as Oghani's suggestions were, they were still available options. The Green Warrior took a moment to consider them. Tushema knew that running the lions away would not work. He tried it already. As for Oghani's other suggestion – removing the lions, Tushema knew it meant putting his warriors in unquestionable danger or a needless killing of the lions. A safe and prompt crossing of the Mara River was urgent. But it did not demand such drastic action – not yet.

"No, Great Creation," Tushema finally said. He made a deliberate effort to readjust his attitude. "The Supreme Spirit put those lions there for a reason. Whether we like it or not, it seems to suggest we should exercise patience here. Let us wait a while longer. Sooner or later, the lions will move on."

"And if they do not move on?"

"We will wait. For safety's sake, we will wait as long as necessary."

"You wish to wait?" Elder Zekke turned to the Green Warrior in confusion. "We have a schedule to keep. Your schedule. You wanted to get us across the Mara before nightfall tomorrow."

"That was the original plan, Great Creation. The Red Warrior Rotho is right. We have a day and a half. As urgent as our schedule is, it is still somewhat flexible. It is not important enough for us to confront those lions so directly. I think we can wait."

"Then consider this, Great Creation." The Gold Warrior Oghani stooped down. He scooped up a fistful of loose dirt. He stood and held out the dirt, allowing it to drain slowly from his fist. A stream of dirt fell to the ground, but dust from the dirt blew eastward.

"Yes, I know. That is a concern, too," Tushema said. Once again, he looked toward the lions.

"What does the falling dirt mean?" Lobarra asked.

"The dust from the falling dirt means the wind has changed directions, Sacred Woman. The new direction works to our disadvantage. It now carries our scent directly toward the lions. It may be the reason the lions have stopped following the herd."

Elder Zekke attempted to focus his vision on the resting lions. He chuckled about the new wind direction. "Fate plays funny games with us sometimes. It seems the balance of fate has tipped in the wrong direction."

Fate was not through playing its 'funny' games. As if to show Zekke his oversight, it was at this point that the Little Creation Tutapona screamed. Until now, Tutapona had slept soundly in the kanga on Lobarra's back. Lobarra's ceaseless activities of distributing the samosas and trying to catch up with the restless Green Warrior did not disturb the sleeping infant. But at this quiet moment, Tutapona woke from the slumber of his sleep. Despite the snug wrap of the bundle, Tutapona squirmed and tried to stretch. His face contorted. Just as he had done the night before, Tutapona cried without reserve. The baby's cry echoed across the savanna.

The Sacred Woman Lobarra quickly removed the kanga from her back, lowered it to the ground, and unwrapped Tutapona. She lifted the squalling infant into her arms. Just as she had done the night before, she placed Tutapona against her chest and jostled him to calm him down.

Everyone under the acacia tree fell silent. They watched Lobarra try her best to quiet Tutapona. The jostling seemed to have only a slight effect. Tutapona stopped his wailing. But he continued to cry. By now, even the four warriors standing guard at the base of the knoll looked toward the group under the acacia tree.

"Sacred Woman, please." Tushema's voice was gentle and kind. There was also a touch of urgency in his voice. "Do what you can. Calm the Little Creation."

"Lobarra, Sacred Woman, is there anything I can do?" Rotho asked. He also felt the urgency and indirect responsibility to quiet the infant. He offered his help, knowing beforehand there was nothing he could do.

Desperate to offer help, Rotho considered the scepter. Since it had worked so well before, Rotho thought it was worth a try again. The scepter lay wrapped in the blanket, which was now lying on the ground next to the acacia tree. Rotho rushed over and extracted the scepter from the blanket. He rushed back just as quickly and offered it to Lobarra and Tutapona.

"No, thank you, Great Creation. That will not work this time." Lobarra lowered Tutapona in her arms to look at him. She studied the infant and made a quick, motherly assessment. "He has no interest in playing now. Tutapona is the only one among us who has not eaten yet. I think he is only hungry. Let me try to feed him first."

Lobarra walked away. She cradled Tutapona in one arm as she worked to free one of her breasts. Lobarra's instincts appeared to be correct. Before Lobarra had reached a semi-secluded spot on the side of the knoll, Tutapona had fallen silent.

Although Lobarra had her back to everyone under the acacia tree, almost everyone under the tree continued to watch Lobarra. Few farmers and warriors saw when the Gold Warrior Oghani tapped Tushema on the arm to get his attention again. Without a word, Oghani pointed in the opposite direction – eastward.

Tushema looked and focused his eyes. He saw the five lions on their feet again, two hundred and fifty meters away. All five had reversed their original course and strolled directly toward the knoll. Each of them seemed highly curious about what their acute senses of sight, sound, and smell had focused on.

"Great Creation?" The Gold Warrior Oghani stood ready. By addressing the Green Warrior, he asked if he should execute the drastic suggestion he had made earlier.

Tushema studied the approaching lions. He could see they walked with heightened purpose in their steps. Even now, he was reluctant to allow Oghani to confront the big cats. He sighed as he realized the safety of the farmers was at stake. Something had to be done. With a nod, Tushema finally gave Oghani the order that the Gold Warrior had expected.

The Gold Warrior Oghani took off running in an instant. In a wide sweeping run down the side of the knoll, he summoned together the four warriors at the base. They would serve as his detail in this dangerous task.

The four warriors had also expected this moment. Berko, Ngozi, Wekesa, and Kibwe quickly gathered with the Gold Warrior on the east side of the knoll and prepared themselves. Their basic intention was to do whatever they could to run the lions away, but they also prepared for a more deadly encounter if necessary.

Just as the warriors moved out toward the lions, with spears and shields held ready, the three lions suddenly stopped approaching. The big cats were not responding to the approaching warriors. They became aware of something else. All five, with heads held high and ears perked, focused all their senses southward.

Moments later, everyone became aware of what the lions had sensed. There suddenly came a massive rumble from the hills on the southern horizon. The volume of the rumble grew louder and louder. It became a continuous wave of thunder, loud enough to cause everyone to stop whatever they were doing.

Oghani and his warrior detail stopped their approach toward the lions. They looked southward. The farmers, who had already gathered to watch the Gold Warrior and his detail, also turned southward. They searched the horizon for the source of the rumble. The pack animals, corralled under the acacia tree, danced and shifted about restlessly, pulling against their tethers. Elder Zekke and several other farmers had to grab the reins and tethers in case the animals broke loose.

Tushema and the rest of the warriors moved toward the south side of the knoll. As trained warriors, they already suspected the cause of the rumble. As dedicated warriors, they assumed a defensive posture.

About two kilometers away, another much larger herd of zebras spilled over one of the hills on the southern horizon. The herd moved fast, already in a stampede. The galloping mass flowed on thundering hooves and raised a cloud of dust behind it as it rumbled nonstop. Fortunately for the farmers and warriors, the herd moved from the south toward the northeast.

"Oghani!" Tushema called out. With a wave of his arm, he signaled the Gold Warrior and his detail to return quickly to the knoll. The warriors stood in no immediate danger, but the Green Warrior took no chances. The course of the herd could change like the wind. As a precaution, Tushema ordered everyone to higher ground atop the knoll.

Oghani and his detail turned and darted back up the side of the knoll. They joined the farmers and the rest of the warriors under the acacia tree. Awed by this amazing natural spectacle, everyone watched in silence for several minutes as the herd continued to thunder across the savanna.

The thundering herd also affected the lions, who were recharged by the energy of the herd. As if of one mind again, the lions moved toward the herd, where preferred food thundered toward them. All signs of their characteristic laziness disappeared. At one point, their muscular and agile hunting prance suddenly burst into an all-out sprint to intercept the herd. Within seconds, they disappeared into the cloud of dust raised by the herd.

The farmers and warriors watched until the massive herd dropped from view over the hills on the northeast horizon. No one moved until the last rumble of thundering hoofs died away. When the last of the zebras disappeared and the cloud of dust behind the herd dissipated, the farmers and warriors realized the zebras had taken the lions with them. There was no sign of the lions.

Elder Zekke held tightly the guide ropes to several restless cattle and donkeys. He gave one of the donkeys a reassuring pat on its neck to calm it down. He chuckled as he addressed the Green Warrior. "What was I saying about fate? I am unsure which is the greater blessing, the lions or the zebras."

"A blessing? What do you mean?"

"On the one hand, the stampeding zebras have solved our lion problem. But, on the other hand, if those lions had not stopped us in the first place, we would have continued our travel. The timing would have placed us in the middle of that stampede."

Tushema walked over to help settle the pack animals. He glanced southward. "Let us hope that fate," he corrected himself, "the Supreme Spirit's grace continues to work in our favor. We may need it, because I am afraid we have a bigger problem."

"What?"

"That herd we just saw may be only a small example of what we are against. More herds, many of them much larger, will come soon. Our crossing of the Mara may already be blocked."

"But, how can that be? Did we not plan this trip ahead of the peak migration season? You and I sat down together. We considered all the signs. What happened? Where did we go wrong?"

"We made our travel plans, Great Creation. But, somehow, we did not notice what Mother Nature told us. The size of that last herd suggests either the peak season has come early, or the migration will be much stronger than normal."

"So, what does that mean for us?" Elder Zekke asked. "Do we return to the Kiwane Village to wait out the migration?"

"We may have to, but I hope not."

Zekke regarded the Green Warrior as a Creation with proven leadership ability. "What do you think we should do?"

"Let us try to reach the Mara first before we make that decision." Tushema addressed all the farmers and warriors. "Everyone, gather your things. If we hurry, we still have time to reach our next camp before sundown."

50

COUNCIL OF ADVISORS

When the Gold Warrior Gabon delivered Adaulah to Kon-Shambique's kraal, the Little Creation stood on his own feet again. He walked into the kraal with Gabon close behind him. He held his head down, ashamed of what he had done. When he heard the people inside the kraal cheering and voicing their joy at his safe return, Adaulah raised his head only briefly. He acknowledged their joy without a smile.

Adaulah walked with his head down until he came directly before Tongda's burial litter. The shock of seeing the body of this beautiful woman made his shame seem so insignificant. He stood for a long moment, staring. Tongda was such an intrinsic part of the valley and its people. Adaulah found it very hard to accept that she was dead too. Just like seeing his own parents, his heart and mind told him, this cannot be real.

Adaulah raised his hand to reach out and touch Tongda. He remembered his comforting relief when he took his mother's hand. But he stopped. He suddenly became aware of the Great Creation Benwe Bomah Leng and the Sacred Woman Oraka Sameah Mushwala, Tongda's father and aunt, sitting behind the burial litter. Adaulah was not family. To touch Tongda's body may be looked upon by them as an intrusion. Adaulah abandoned his attempt to re-bond with her. He dropped his hand back to his side.

Adaulah walked around to the other side of the litter. He stood before the Great Creation Benwe and the Sacred Woman Oraka. "I am sorry for your loss. I will miss her."

Tongda's father acknowledged with only a gentle nod of his head. Tongda's aunt forced a smile on her face. Grief allowed only a soundless 'thank you' from her lips.

"And I am sorry for the confusion I caused earlier," Adaulah added. "The Supreme Spirit knows, I did not mean to disrupt the tribute being paid here for the Sacred Woman Tongda."

"Adaulah." Kon-Shambique, who stood off to the side, called the Little Creation's name. He beckoned him to come closer. The Favored Tribesman knew something else that had not yet fully occurred to Adaulah. The Little Creation had done more than disrupt Tongda's tribute. Kon-Shambique called Adaulah over before the Little Creation rubbed salt into an open wound.

Adaulah had to step around the Gold Warrior Gabon to approach the Favored Tribesman. "Yes, Great Creation?"

Kon-Shambique took Adaulah gently by the shoulder. Before he spoke again, he ushered Adaulah into his hut to speak in some privacy. He gave up complete privacy when he learned that the Gold Warrior Gabon was told not to let Adaulah out of his sight. The warrior took it literally.

"Little Creation," Kon-Shambique began slowly, "you have expressed your condolences to the Great Creation Benwe and the Sacred Woman Oraka for losing their daughter and niece. For now, it is best to leave it at that."

"What do you mean, Great Creation?"

Kon-Shambique paused as he considered a tactful way to tell Adaulah what he had done. "Did you know, since the Mangoni ritual began, everyone who has gone up to Nagorda Peak has met the demon of death … and has died? This may now include Benwe's niece and Oraka's daughter, Upenda. This may now include your mother, Kharaambi, and a regiment of warriors who went up there to rescue you."

The realization formed like a sudden dark cloud in Adaulah's head. The tremendous damage he had caused was too much to bear. Adaulah's face slowly contorted with grief. Tears flooded his eyes.

"Great Creation, I am so sorry. This did not happen as I wanted. The Sacred Spirit knows, I meant things to happen differently."

Kon-Shambique took Adaulah by the shoulders to console him. "Yes. She knows. She knows your heart, Little Creation. Your intention was honorable. She knows your part in all of it. And I am sure She forgives you."

Adaulah pushed himself away from Kon-Shambique and wiped the tears from his face. "I wanted to do the right thing. I was so determined to speak with Mfalme Abul-Gwan that I did not consider the mistake I was making. Kon-Shambique, I do not want to be Mfalme anymore."

"Little Creation, with your father's death, you have no choice in the matter."

"I do not want to be Mfalme."

"May I ask, why not?"

"I cannot do it. It is too hard. I do not understand what I must do. I tried to help, and people died. My sister Baako said I am not ready to be Mfalme. I think … she may be right."

"An Mfalme's responsibilities are not easy. You must be willing to take responsibility for all you say and all you do. If you do and your heart is in the right place, then the Supreme Spirit will help you do what must be done, whether you understand it or not. Understand?"

"I … I think so."

"And, Adaulah."

"Yes, Great Creation?"

"The Supreme Spirit knows if you want to be Mfalme."

"And if I do not?"

"She will take care of that too."

Just then, more cheers of joy poured in from outside the hut. Kon-Shambique, Adaulah, and the Gold Warrior Gabon all peered through the exit to see what was happening. It turned out that the Sacred Women Kharaambi and Upenda had just returned.

"They came back!" Adaulah shouted to Kon-Shambique. Despite the tears still on his face, he smiled and repeated. "They came back!"

"Yes, I see." Kon-Shambique also smiled for the first time in a long while.

Outside the hut, Upenda was sharing very emotional embraces with Benwe and Oraka as Kharaambi attempted to offer her condolences. Under the circumstances, Upenda was more successful as her hugs and kisses seemed to dominate the moment.

Kharaambi had other things on her mind anyway. It was clear when she spoke briefly to one of the nearby warriors. The warrior pointed directly at Kon-Shambique's hut. Kharaambi handed her spear and shield to the warrior and walked toward the hut. There was anger in her steps.

Adaulah had seen Kharaambi angry many times, but she seldom directed her anger at him. This time, he was not so lucky. Before Kharaambi entered the hut, Adaulah backed away from the entranceway.

"I am sorry, Sacred Mother! I am sorry!"

"Not good enough, Little Creation," Kharaambi said as she entered the hut. She dismissed the Gold Warrior Gabon. She turned to ask Kon-Shambique for a moment of privacy.

"No!" Adaulah anticipated Kharaambi's intention. "Please. Can the Favored Tribesman stay?"

Kharaambi shrugged. "That is up to him."

Kon-Shambique glanced at Adaulah. As a compromise, he quietly moved over to the far corner of the hut.

"Did I not tell you, no one is to go up to Nagorda Peak?" Kharaambi asked Adaulah.

"You did, but ..."

"But nothing! Did you not understand me? Because you disobeyed me, twenty-five to thirty more warriors from Obe Bendabe's regiment just died at the hands of that demon. They died, Adaulah, so that we could rescue you. Those warriors would be alive right now had you obeyed me."

At first, Kon-Shambique stood back, allowing Adaulah to take his punishment. This was a moment of discipline between mother and son. But Kharaambi was not being at all gentle with him. He had to say something. "Sacred Woman, please. Is that not a little strong?"

"Is there a better way, Great Creation?" Kharaambi did not give Kon-Shambique a chance to answer. She paced. "He has to know the truth. He cannot escape the consequences of his behavior. One moment, Adaulah stands in the Royal Kraal convinced that Mfalme Abul-Gwan must do the right thing. The next minute, he runs off to do the wrong thing."

"I am sorry," Adaulah said softly. "I tried to help."

"You have every right to help. But what you did was irresponsible. What makes you so special that you can ignore what is right?"

Adaulah glance at Kon-Shambique. He was grateful for Kon-Shambique's counsel. It gave him the strength to answer finally. He turned to his mother and tried the same tactic he had used on Upenda earlier. "I… I am… Mfalme."

"What?" The statement produced the desired effect and caused Kharaambi to stop pacing. She turned to face Adaulah.

"I am Mfalme," Adaulah repeated softly, with more confidence in his voice.

Kharaambi looked at Adaulah. She glanced at Kon-Shambique before turning her attention back to Adaulah. Her stern look melted as a smile crept across her face briefly. "Yes. Yes, you are Mflame. As Mfalme, you must embrace all that comes with it. Little Creation, it does not allow you to do unwise things."

"I know. I made a mistake. I am sorry. I have learned my lesson."

"My Little Mfalme." Kharaambi kneeled and took Adaulah by his shoulders. She spoke without sarcasm or anger. "You do not ask me to share my leadership, or ask for the benefit of my protection, if you intend to abuse it. As Mfalme, you have a broad council of advisors. Your advisors can help you make wiser decisions. They help you do what is right."

"They do?"

"Yes, they do. Your sister, Yejide, holds more knowledge than anyone else in the valley about other tribes and other peoples. There is Bakha, the historian. He can give you the most brilliant insights as to why the Aukmondi do what we do or do not do."

"And there is the Favored Tribesman," Adaulah added.

"Yes. There is the Favored Tribesman. Do you know anyone else who can read the hearts and minds of another as easily as Kon-Shambique?"

"No." Adaulah's eyes gleamed as he realized the priceless value of the people he knew. "And do not forget Mfalme Ameh Jobabwe."

"Yes. Ameh Jobabwe, too. You do not ask Ameh for his wisdom and guidance if you do not intend to use it. Mfalme Jobabwe has lived a long and experienced life. He knows enough to teach you about almost every aspect of life you will ever encounter. Your father always consulted each of these advisors before deciding on most matters."

"Yes. I have seen him talk with them many times."

"You must learn to talk with them too."

Adaulah shrugged. "I guess I am learning the hard way how important they are."

Kon-Shambique sensed that Kharaambi's disciplinary talk with Adaulah was ending. He moved closer. "Little Creation, I am curious. You tried to talk to Mfalme Abul-Gwan. What did you intend to tell him?"

"Mfalme Abul-Gwan is using the Vodun houngan to kill our people. The Mfalme is doing it because he is hurt and angry. I wanted to help him stop hurting. I was hoping to make him stop being so angry."

"Help him, how?"

"Abul-Tess is still there. The bond with the Sacred Woman is still there. Even though he cannot talk with or hear her voice like before, her spirit is still here. And it is as strong as ever. Mfalme Abul-Gwan would feel much better if he knew that the Sacred Woman was still close to him. He must be told that he has not lost her completely."

"Where did you learn such a thing, Little Creation?" Adaulah's conviction fascinated Kharaambi.

"It happened when I took the hand of my Sacred Mother, Rwuva. I took her hand. I could feel her smiling at me. And then, I took my father's hand. Ramuza's spirit smiled at me, too. I knew they were still close, almost as if they never left."

Kharaambi rose to her feet. "That is very thoughtful and insightful. But, I am afraid, Mfalme Abul-Gwan is just a little too angry to feel anyone smiling at him, even the spirit of Abul-Tess."

"You do not believe me, do you?" Adaulah waited for Kharaambi to answer him. When she only glanced at Kon-Shambique, Adaulah shrugged again. "It does not matter if you believe me. For now, it is only important for Mfalme Abul-Gwan to believe me. He has to know."

"Maybe so. Just promise me you will not try to go to the Mangoni camp to convince him yourself."

Adaulah sighed. "Alright."

"Promise me."

"So be it, Sacred Woman. I promise."

"Anymore disobedience like that, Little Creation, and I will appoint a warrior to stand guard over you. A warrior, like the Gold Warrior Gabon, will stand over your shoulder day and night until you grow up to be a Great Creation. Understood?"

"I understand, Sacred Mother. There will be no more disobedience."

"Now, I suggest you return to the Royal Kraal where you belong. The people know that you are the Mfalme now. They need you there."

Adaulah thanked the Favored Tribesman for his help and darted from the hut. Kharaambi and Kon-Shambique watched him as he left. They saw more bounce in his steps.

It brought another smile to Kon-Shambique's face. "It is good you got that promise out of him. That Young Creation has his father's determination."

"I well know of his determination. I suspected he would try something. But it never occurred to me he would try to go up the Mangoni camp himself."

"So, what happened up there? I expected no one to return."

Kharaambi took a moment to review the horrific events that occurred. She sighed heavily before she spoke. About a quarter of the warriors of the Blue Warrior Obe Bendabe's regiment volunteered to honor Obe and the Blue Warrior Dabete Ehkili. They used Nionu's cat's tail offense by confronting the demon and drawing its full and undivided attention. They pulled it away. As a result, they caught the fatal wrath of the demon. They sacrificed themselves to give the rest of us the chance we needed to escape."

"Great Sacred Spirit!" Even Kon-Shambique had heard of Nionu's cat's tail offensive. He knew it had its advantages and disadvantages. "I suppose it achieved a desired result. But it was an exorbitant tactic, Sacred Woman. That is twenty-five to thirty more deaths."

"I know." Kharaambi paused briefly to put everything into perspective. "Under the circumstances, we had no choice. But that is only the beginning. You may not be aware of many more deaths, Great Creation."

"Many more? Do you mean more than the entire Pogobi and Obentawni Kraals and the Royal Warrior Npatuzi's Muusitu Regiment? Remember, I was here last evening when the Royal Warrior Jokere delivered the news."

"There are more, Great Creation. We just learned a little while ago that this demon has destroyed the Butetwa and Mempa kraals too, with countless other deaths scattered all across the north slope."

"When did all this happen?"

"Some time between last evening and earlier this morning."

This news was a new assault on Kon-Shambique's spirit. He stood speechless. He slowly sat down as if to devote all his strength to wrapping his mind around this new development.

"So, how do we keep this positive?" Kharaambi kneeled beside the Favored Tribesman. She pulled a nearby pillow closer and sat upon it. "In light of what you told us last evening, if deaths like this continue to occur, how do we push death out of our lives and focus on life?"

"I … I do not know, Kharaambi. I do not know." Kon-Shambique slumped. For the moment, his positive attitude had completely failed him. He sat for a very long moment before he finally spoke again. He forced himself to put his own words into practice. "We have to hang on. An answer will come. We have no choice. Hang on and do what comes naturally."

"Do what comes naturally until an answer comes to us," Kharaambi almost smiled. "You sound like Mfalme Ameh Jobabwe now. He said something quite similar earlier today. What we must do is often limited by what we can do."

"He is right."

"That brings up another matter I must discuss with you, Great Creation. The most urgent and natural thing we have to do right is bury our dead. We must give them the honor of a proper burial."

"Of course." Kon-Shambique sat more erect to bolster his spirit. "Since the bodies are piling up so quickly, it is an issue we must address very soon."

"The issue is already being addressed. I must apologize to you, Great Creation. I know you have been so busy assisting Upenda with the preparations for the tribute being paid to the Sacred Woman Tongda. We made a major tribal decision without consulting you. Time prevented us from talking with you earlier."

"What decision is this?"

"There have been far too many deaths for individual grave sites. Earlier this morning, Ameh, Quazzi, and I decided to have at least two mass grave sites for everyone. It was a hasty decision. I hope you will approve."

"Mass grave sites?"

"Yes, Great Creation. We will begin with at least two. We feel it is almost necessary."

Kon-Shambique closed his eyes. He reviewed the notion and morals of mass graves. He raised his hand and gently massaged his forehead, as if the thinking process was painful. It was a disturbing idea. He had never experienced an occasion requiring a mass grave. But, throughout his life, he had never learned a reason to forbid such a thing. He dropped his hand and opened his eyes. He chose not to resist the idea. "I have no objections, Sacred Woman."

"Good!" Kharaambi almost sighed with relief. She had sat, almost holding her breath as she waited for Kon-Shambique to respond. "That is very good to hear. I prayed you would not decide otherwise. As we speak, the Brown Warrior Quazzi has begun overseeing the preparation of the two sites."

"You have selected the locations of these grave sites?"

"Yes, Great Creation. Again, unless you have some objection, one site will be in some isolated valley depths."

"And the other?"

"The Great Creation, Mfalme Ameh Jobabwe, has suggested that the Pogobi kraal serve as the location for the other grave site."

Again, Kon-Shambique considered the situation. His response this time came even slower. He became so lost in his thoughts that Kharaambi had to ask him for an answer.

"Are these sites acceptable, Great Creation?"

"Oh, yes." Kharaambi's question jolted Kon-Shambique back to the present. "Yes, Sacred Woman. Under the circumstances, those sites are acceptable."

"But what?"

"I just realized that individual burial rituals must be performed over each body before placing it in the grave. All who have died deserve individual tributes."

"Individual burial rituals? That is a lot of rituals."

"Well … there are a lot of bodies."

"Can you do that?"

"Whether I can do it or not, it has to be done," Kon-Shambique recalled the stern lecture Kharaambi gave Adaulah. "It is the proper thing to do."

"Normally, you would have the Sacred Woman Tongda to help you. Can you do it without her? I mean, with two mass graves, is it possible?"

"The burial ritual is very important. Some extensive preparations are needed. The ritual itself is simple. I can do it." Kon-Shambique paused a moment to give the matter more thought. He knew that he could not be in both places at once. "I must devote time and energy to one place at a time. In which location will the Mfalme and his Principal Mate be buried?"

"Probably in the Pogobi kraal location, since it is closer to most people. That is one of the reasons Ameh suggested it. People in most of the valley can easily visit the royal grave."

"Then I will perform the first rituals in the Pogobi kraal. Tell the Great Creation Quazzi to focus his first preparations there."

"I will relay this suggestion to him. Is there anything else he should know?"

"No. Nothing else comes to mind at the moment. How soon do you think the Brown Warrior will have the sites ready?"

"If I am not mistaken, the Brown Warrior employs the entire Elka and Kdedi Armies. They intend to work throughout the evening and the night. If they focus on the Pogobi kraal, they will complete it first. Quazzi thinks the site will be ready by early tomorrow morning."

"Then, as soon as we finish the tribute to the Sacred Woman Tongda, I will prepare to perform the rituals. I will also be ready by early tomorrow morning."

— **51** —

THERE ARE NO ORDINARY SUNSETS

By late evening, the traveling caravan of farmers and warriors had completed their first day's journey back to the Aukmondi Valley. Four hours ago, they left the knoll and the shade of the huge acacia tree. They walked non-stop until they had put another nineteen kilometers behind them.

In some ways, the walk during the second half of the day turned out less oppressive than the first half. The African sun was at the travelers' backs now. The sun's glare no longer blocked their view ahead. And the heat and the humidity were less intense. The walk, however, was still somewhat grueling. The Green Warrior Tushema led the farmers across the rolling savanna grassland faster than he cared. He pushed the aged farmers to their physical limits.

Tushema's original plan was to get the farmers halfway to the Mara River by sundown. He was unhappy that the farmers had lost over an hour of travel time after the lions settled directly in their pathway and blocked their progress. He felt that the lost time was still recoverable. The determined Green Warrior did his best to salvage his original plan. He regretted having to walk the farmers so fast, but he felt the consequences of falling behind would be worse.

As he walked, Tushema held the guide ropes to some of the pack animals. It was his way of keeping everyone moving at the pace he felt was necessary. At regular intervals, he glanced back at the caravan. Each time, he wondered if he should slow the pace. He sacrificed a few precious moments out of guilt or concern to allow brief rest stops. Out of guilt or concern, these brief rest stops occurred more and more. During these stops, Tushema helped to manage the heavy pouches of water. He developed a personal responsibility to make sure everyone drank their ration of water.

*****

The most pleasurable part of the whole nineteen-kilometer journey developed after the Red Warrior Rotho glanced toward the infant Tutapona. As usual, Tutapona nestled piggyback style in the kanga. Only his head protruded. He rested the side of his face against his mother's back. Tutapona was not asleep this time. With the eyes of total innocents, Tutapona was watching the Red Warrior. Rotho could not help but wonder. What could the infant be looking at with such interest? He found the baby's stare so fascinating that it made him smile. When Rotho smiled, so did Tutapona.

The Sacred Woman Lobarra looked over at the Red Warrior. She saw the smile on his face. "You seem to be in a good mood, Great Creation. Walking at this pace, half of us can catch our breath. Yet, you find cause to smile. What is so amusing?"

"I wish I knew, Sacred Woman." Rotho gestured toward Tutapona. "You should see the Little Creation. He is showing both of his tiny teeth with the biggest smile you have ever seen."

"Good! I am glad to hear that. I think he is much better. He did not like the Kiwane Village. Since we left, his fretfulness has subsided."

Since the journey to the Kiwane village, the Red Warrior Rotho had strongly bonded with Tutapona. However, he was not yet close enough to the infant to notice increased or decreased fretfulness. He had seen only two or three crying tantrums and noticed nothing unusual about the infant's behavior.

If Rotho could name anything unusual about Tutapona, the big smile was second only to how the infant always reacted to the scepter that Mfalme Menda gave him. Rotho enjoyed the way Tutapona reacted to the scepter.

"Sacred Woman," Rotho began, "do you mind if I entertain the Little Creation?"

Lobarra did not have to ask Rotho to clarify himself. She knew what he had in mind. "Children never tire of playing, do they?"

Rotho smiled and shrugged with embarrassment. He knew Lobarra had him in mind with that comment.

"I do not mind, Great Creation," said Lobarra. "If it pleases Tutapona, then it pleases me."

Rotho looked toward the pack animals. He increased his pace and maneuvered himself to the donkey carrying the blanket with the rolled-up scepter. He could see how accessible Lobarra had packed it. Rotho pulled it from the blanket like a knife from a sheath.

Like Tutapona, Rotho found the scepter fascinating. He had seen and examined it many times since Mfalme Menda gave it to Tutapona. Each time, he studied the detail of the engravings that covered the entire length of the staff. Rotho easily understood why the scepter fascinated him. But Tutapona was much too young to appreciate such craftsmanship. Rotho concluded that the pot-bellied bullfrog at the top of the scepter held Tutapona's fascination.

Rotho tapped the bullfrog in the palm of his hand, just like Mfalme Menda always did. The balance of the scepter felt good. Rotho understood why Mfalme Menda enjoyed the strange habit. It amazed Rotho that the Mfalme would give away such a beautiful and well-crafted symbol of royalty.

Rotho maneuvered himself to walk beside the Sacred Woman Lobarra again. He glanced over at Tutapona and held the scepter up in front of the infant's face. And just as Rotho expected, the big, two-tooth smile reappeared. Rotho playfully bobbed the scepter up and down, as if the pot-bellied bullfrog was hopping. Tutapona giggled, squirmed, and buried his nose against his mother's back.

The Red Warrior Rotho was so thrilled by Tutapona's reaction that he laughed. He waited until Tutapona slowly raised his head and showed his face again. When he did, Rotho bobbed the scepter again. This time, he mimicked the sound of a croaking bullfrog. "Quark! Quark!"

Tutapona's giggle was stronger this time. Once again, Tutapona wiggled with excitement and buried his nose.

The Sacred Woman Lobarra could not see in the kanga but could feel Tutapona wiggling excitedly. The excitement was enough to make her laugh, too. She laughed each time Tutapona giggled, wiggled, and buried his face.

Everyone could hear Tutapona. His giggles were infectious. The baby's laugh had an almost magical effect. After several minutes of this, almost everyone was laughing, including the Green Warrior Tushema. For several long minutes, the hard-pressed and grueling walk across the open savanna became only a minor discomfort as everyone enjoyed the simple pleasure of a baby's laugh.

This moment of pleasure lasted until the Little Creation Tutapona giggled himself to exhaustion. The infant buried his face against his mother's neck, too exhausted to play anymore.

The Red Warrior Rotho watched Tutapona until he realized the infant was asleep. He smiled again. Knowing he had given the infant so much pleasure with such a simple toy felt good. Rotho studied the people of the caravan; the farmers and other warriors. Many of them were waiting for more. The pleasure, however simple and brief, had spread to everyone.

Rotho looked at the scepter in his hand. It was a symbol of royalty. And even though it was an infant's gift, it still had a value that Rotho could not explain. Instead of returning the scepter to the blanket roll on the donkey, Rotho stuck the staff of the scepter into a carry-pouch at his side. It was more accessible. Who knows when he or Tutapona might want to 'play' again?

*****

Just before the sun touched the western horizon, the Green Warrior Tushema ended the grueling walk. To the farmers' surprise, he darted up a hillside toward a small escarpment. At the top, he turned to face them and beckoned them to hasten their pace up the hillside.

Elder Zekke and several aged farmers looked at the steep hillside before glancing at each other. Their weary bodies could not justify any need to hurry. With no change in their pace, they tugged at the guide ropes of their pack animals and forced themselves to climb the hillside to join Tushema.

After the farmers gathered around him, Tushema pointed over the escarpment's edge. "We made it. We will camp tonight down there, in that nook."

Elder Zekke moved closer to the edge of the escarpment and looked over the edge. The escarpment sheltered a sizable but cozy-looking nook. Zekke leaned out farther and looked down. He looked for the bottom of the nook. It was over five meters straight down. Zekke stepped back and spoke to the Green Warrior. "It looks nice, Great Creation. But I must tell you, most of us farmers will not survive the jump. Is there another way down?"

Tushema smiled at the Old Creation's sarcasm. He beckoned everyone to follow him. He led the way around the edge of the escarpment. After only a few more minutes of walking, he descended a small incline that circled and trailed back into the nook.

"Now this is more like it," Zekke chuckled as he entered the nook. "It looks much better from this angle. During our walk, I was looking forward to the cool comfort of another acacia tree, but the escarpment wall provided ample shading from the setting sun. This is nice. It looks comfortable."

"I hope so." Tushema ushered Zekke farther into the nook. "Everyone deserves a little extra comfort after that grueling walk. Great Creation, I must apologize for pushing everyone so hard this afternoon. I am doing my best to get you across the Mara before it is too late."

"Apology accepted. We understand what you are doing. None of us realized how urgent the situation was. After seeing that last herd move through, we stand behind you. A herd that size was unexpected."

"As the migrating season progresses, we can expect more herds like that. But do not be concerned. Until we resume our travel tomorrow morning, we will be safe."

"You sound confident, Great Creation."

"It is one of the reasons I pushed you so hard to reach this nook. The escarpment wall will provide more shade than the afternoon sun. It will also protect us from any herds that may pass through.

If another herd comes through, it will come from that direction." Tushema pointed toward the back of the nook and the wall of the five-meter escarpment. "We reached the nook by going around the escarpment. Herds coming this way must go around the escarpment too."

Zekke gave one of his characteristic chuckles. "Great Creation, you deserve your green cloak."

"Thank you," Tushema smiled. He gestured toward the nook again. "The nook is yours, Great Creation. Make yourself at home."

Elder Zekke, the other farmers, and the warriors wasted no time setting up the new camp. As usual, they divested the goats, cattle, and donkeys of their heavy loads. Then they corralled, fed, and watered them. The camp would last throughout the night. The food preparers had more time to prepare food. Lobarra and some junior farmers foraged the small nook for firewood. They could cook a hot meal this time. They built a large, multipurpose campfire near the nook's heart.

While the farmers set up the camp, Tushema and his detachment of warriors secured the entire area. They surveyed the area for safety. Tushema decided that only two guard posts were necessary this time. He set up one post at the entrance of the nook and the other post on top of the five-meter escarpment at the rear.

By sunset, all the farmers and warriors had completed the tasks necessary to make the camp comfortable. Food was cooking, and the spicy smell of *chana batata* filled the air. Except for the two warriors standing guard, everyone sat around the campfire, conversing as they waited for the chana batata to finish cooking.

"This time tomorrow," the Green Warrior Tushema said, "we will be on the other side of the Mara. The most difficult part of our journey home will be behind us."

"Why is it imperative to get across the Mara, Great Creation?" Lobarra asked as she stirred the pot of *chana bateta*. "What I mean is, does it matter? I realize we could be trapped on this side of the Mara. But has it occurred to anyone? Massive herds are beginning to move through the area, moving from the other side of the Mara to this side. Danger exists on the other side, too."

"That is true, Sacred Woman. If the great migration has started, we will come across dangers until we reach the Aukmondi Valley. We will encounter many larger herds on the other side of the Mara. But for us, the actual crossing of the Mara is the most difficult and important."

"What do you mean?"

"The herds of wildebeests, zebras, gazelles, and many other animals migrate from southern regions to the moist wetlands of the Mara Triangle and the northern Serengeti. During their migration, all of them must cross the Mara River at some point. They can cross the Mara in many locations, up and down the river. For us, the locations where we can cross are limited. In this area, only one place exists."

"The Kiboko Passage," Elder Zekke knew the passage well.

"Yes, the Kiboko Passage," Tushema repeated. "As you may remember, during our travel to the Kiwane Village, the passage is shallow, narrow, and almost ideal for us to cross. To our misfortune, the migrating animals use that passage too. We will find the crossing impossible if they reach the passage before we do. After we cross the Mara, the congestion will be behind us. We may still meet herds of migrating animals, but we will also be more capable of avoiding them. And, as an added incentive, once we cross the Mara, we will be only five hours from the comforts of our valley."

"The comforts of our valley," Zekke chuckled. "That sounds so good. I cannot wait to get back home."

"Great Creation," Lobarra said, "you sound like you miss the valley. You told me, after a while, you get used to long periods away from home."

"Yes, I said that. But you misunderstood me." Elder Zekke smiled to himself. "I miss home the most, beginning at this hour. It is sunset. Our Daily Celebration of Life begins."

"Are you saying that our Daily Celebrations of Life make the sunsets so special?"

"Maybe so," Zekke shrugged. "And, maybe I should not say that. It is not true. After so many harvests, I have learned there are no ordinary sunsets, no matter where you are." Zekke looked toward the back of the nook and up at the top of the five-meter escarpment. It was his impulsive attempt to see the sunset.

The other farmers and warriors around Zekke saw him looking up toward the escarpment, and they looked up, too. The Sacred Woman Lobarra finished stirring the pot of *chana batata*. She turned toward the escarpment and looked up, as if to catch what was holding everyone's interest.

None of them saw the sunset. The escarpment blocked it. Instead, they only saw the dark silhouette of a warrior standing there. The bright sunlight behind the warrior made it difficult to see any of the warrior's distinguishing features.

"Is that the Red Warrior Rotho?" Lobarra asked.

"Yes, Sacred Woman." Tushema didn't have to recognize any distinguishing features. He already knew. "Since Oghani has given the Red Warrior the privilege of sleep tonight, it is his turn to stand guard until nightfall."

Lobarra studied the warrior's dark silhouette. The warrior's shield and spear enhanced his dedicated pose. With the setting sun directly behind him, rays of brilliant sunlight reached out in all directions, creating a brilliant aura around him. It was an inspiring sight.

Lobarra returned to the *chana batata* pot and poured a bowl of chopped potatoes into it. She picked up the spoon and stirred again. She smiled as she glanced over at Zekke. "Even when we cannot see the sunset, its light can still make all we can see beautiful."

52

MORE THAN JUST A BOND

Darkness enveloped the nook where the farmers and warriors camped. The evening's 'unseen' sunset was only a memory now. Flames from the central campfire had died down to half their original size but provided the only light in the area. The pot of *chana bateta* sat almost empty over the fire. Almost everyone had eaten their share. Just enough remained for the two warriors who had not eaten yet. One warrior still stood guard at the entrance of the nook. The other stood up on the escarpment.

Conversations had also died away. Only a few farmers and warriors continued to sit around the central campfire. They spoke softly, not to disturb the rest of the farmers and warriors. The rest of the farmers and warriors found comfort and privacy around the camp's periphery as they settled for a night's sleep.

The whole area was quiet except for the constant but gentle chorus of chirping crickets. Once in a while, the bellow of a lion or the frenzied whimpers of hyenas filtered into the nook from some distant place in the surrounding savanna. Within the nook, the snap or crackle of the campfire accented all the soothing sounds, as did occasional bursts of laughter from the farmers and warriors around the campfire.

The most predominant sound everyone heard was the lullaby that Lobarra softly sang. The Sacred Woman had moved to an isolated spot in the nook to feed Tutapona. Lobarra often sang the lullaby to Tutapona when she fed him. This moment was no exception. The effects of mother's milk and the lullaby often relaxed Tutapona to sound sleep almost every time.

Lobarra sat in a comfortable position that would allow her to lie down when she finished feeding Tutapona. She knew that after Tutapona got his stomach satiated, he would fall asleep. Once asleep, the two would sleep throughout the night. This time, she nursed the infant and sang the melody of his lullaby over and over, a forgotten number of times. Tutapona still looked up at her with bright, wide-awake eyes.

"Are you not sleepy, Little Creation?" Lobarra spoke just above a whisper. Her assumption that the Kiwane Village affected Tutapona was no longer valid. Puzzled by Tutapona's behavior, Lobarra smiled as she looked down at the infant cradled in her arms. "What thoughts continue to make you so restless?"

Lobarra rose to a different position. She tried rocking Tutapona, hoping the gentle motion would lull him to sleep. Lobarra rocked for several minutes. She almost rocked herself to sleep. Tutapona refused to close his eyes for the night. She was about to try again to sing him his favorite lullaby when she looked down into his eyes. Lobarra realized that Tutapona wasn't looking at her. He was looking past her, over her shoulder.

Lobarra turned her head to see if she could see Tutapona's interest. The campfire flames caused huge shadows to dance on the escarpment wall at the back of the nook. The effect was fascinating, and it caught her attention. But she realized that Tutapona was not looking at the shadows. On top of the escarpment, she saw two warriors talking. A replacement warrior had come to relieve the Red Warrior Rotho at his guard post. Lobarra could see Rotho sharing instructions as he prepared to leave the escarpment for the first time all evening.

Lobarra looked down again at Tutapona. The Little Creation unquestionably held his eyes trained on the Red Warrior. Lobarra looked back and forth between Tutapona and the Red Warrior. This continued during Rotho's long descent, down the escarpment along the periphery of the nook. To Lobarra's amazement, Tutapona watched Rotho almost every step of the way.

From her isolated spot in the nook, Lobarra studied the Red Warrior. She tried her best to see what Tutapona found so fascinating about him. Lobarra watched Rotho enter the nook and go directly toward the central campfire. He exchanged a few inaudible words with the farmers and other warriors there as he washed his face and arms in a water bowl. Lobarra smiled as Rotho seemed eager to get his share from the last of the *chana bateta.*

When Rotho settled around the campfire to eat his evening meal, Lobarra felt Tutapona squirm in her arms. She looked down at the infant. The Little Creation had lost sight of the Red Warrior. He was trying to reposition himself so he could see the Red Warrior.

This was so unusual. Lobarra had to learn why. To do so, she needed to speak with the Red Warrior. She did not call out to him in thoughtful consideration of the others sleeping around her. Instead, she rose from her sitting position to her knees. The movement was just enough to attract everyone's attention around the campfire. When Lobarra saw Rotho looking her way, she beckoned him.

The Red Warrior set his bowl of *chana bateta* down. He got to his feet and walked over to Lobarra. "Is there something you need, Sacred Woman?"

"Do you have a moment, Great Creation?"

"The Mfalme Ameh Jobabwe has asked that I serve you. All my moments are yours. Tell me what you need."

"Go get your bowl of *chana bateta* before it gets cold. I …" Lobarra looked down at Tutapona. "The Little Creation and I wish to talk with you briefly, if possible."

Rotho glanced at Tutapona, who continued to stare at him. "Of course."

While the Red Warrior returned to the central campfire to get his food, Lobarra made herself comfortable again. She knew Tutapona would want to keep his eyes on the Red Warrior. Lobarra also positioned him in her arms, where he could do so.

"I have discovered a most curious thing, Great Creation," Lobarra said as Rotho settled on the ground before her.

"Which is?"

"The Little Creation Tutapona holds a bond with you. I can only be described as unusual."

"What do you mean?"

"As his mother, I have noticed that he has been unusually fretful, especially during the first half of our visit to the Kiwane Village. At first, I thought the village affected him. But now, I think he becomes restless when you are not around."

"Me?" Rotho looked at Tutapona again, surprised. "Why?"

"I do not know. Since we have set up camp here, you have stood guard up there on the escarpment. I just learned that the Little Creation has watched you most of the time."

Rotho glanced up at the escarpment. The huge dancing shadows on the escarpment wall caught his eye, too. "Are you sure the shadows did not draw his attention?"

"I am sure, Great Creation. Tutapona seems to be more joyful and at peace around you."

"Sacred Woman, I cannot explain it. I am a warrior tasked with protecting and serving you and the Little Creation. I must admit that during this journey to the Kiwane Village and back, a bond grew between Tutapona and me. I find pleasure in being around him. Judging by what you have just said, the feeling must be mutual."

"I think it is more than just a bond between you and Tutapona. It is a special bond." Lobarra looked down to see another surprising effect of Rotho's presence. She smiled as she directed Rotho's attention toward the infant. "Look at him. I have tried most of the evening to put him to sleep."

Rotho looked down at Tutapona to find him soundly asleep. "You have succeeded, Sacred Woman."

"No, Great Creation. You did."

53

WELCOME TO THE POGOBI
GRAVE SITE

Back in the Aukmondi Valley, and long before sunrise the next morning, Kon-Shambique left his kraal. He began the long descent down the Nagorda hillside. At this early hour, he headed for the Pogobi kraal. He had several preparations to complete before sunrise. And the walk to the kraal would take him almost an hour.

The Favored Tribesman walked alone. In a huge bundle on his shoulder, he carried all the items he would need for the burial rituals. Because of the sacred nature of the rituals, Kon-Shambique could not carry the items on the back of a pack animal or a wheeled cart. Nor could anyone else help him carry the items. The Favored Tribesman had to carry everything by his physical efforts. He used one hand to steady the bundle on his shoulder. He held a burning torch in his other hand to light his way.

Normally, his love and closest assistant, the Sacred Woman Tongda, would go with him on this mission. Ironically, even if she were here, tradition would not allow her to carry anything he would use for the ritual. Yet Kon-Shambique felt her absence. He found it difficult to accept that she would never go with him again on any mission.

Kon-Shambique held the torch higher over his head to penetrate the surrounding darkness. His thoughts split between Tongda's absence and the persistent creepy feeling he got from the black void beyond the torchlight. Kon-Shambique admitted to himself that he had underestimated the power of the Mangoni houngan. The houngan's demon of death was very real. The powerful apparition could step out from behind any tree at any moment. Irony of ironies, Kon-Shambique was grateful for the persistent pain of Tongda's loss. Otherwise, Kon-Shambique knew that most of his attention would be on wondering where and when the demon would appear before him.

Kon-Shambique released a sigh of relief when he finally reached the bottom of the Nagorda hillside. Even though the Pogobi kraal was still several minutes ahead, he experienced the comforting illusion of other people nearby. Kon-Shambique could see hundreds of other torchlights in the distance. He knew that, under those torchlights, in the expansive pasture of the Pogobi kraal, the warriors of the Elka or Kdedi armies were still at work, preparing the huge grave site.

Kon-Shambique had learned long ago that most fears dissipate when confronted. To confront his nagging fears of running into the houngan's demon, Kon-Shambique extinguished his torch. He felt comfortable walking the rest of the way in total darkness. The distant torchlights would give him the guidance he needed. Sure enough, the Favored Tribesman forgot about an encounter with the demon. Most of his attention centered on putting one foot in front of the other along the winding pathway.

Kon-Shambique did not regret this decision to extinguish his torch; not until he finally reached the Pogobi kraal and walked through the kraal's entrance. Once inside the kraal, he stopped. He stood for a moment, looking to his left and right. Nothing stirred in what used to be a thriving community. There was total silence. All the huts were dark. All the gardens were empty. In this darkness, it was an eerie sight. Although hundreds of warriors worked out in the kraal pasture, the empty kraal made a chance encounter with the houngan's specter of death seem imminent.

Kon-Shambique adjusted his bundle on his shoulder and hastened his pace through the dwelling areas. He weaved between the empty huts, gardens, and animal pens. He did not stop again until he reached the back of the kraal and the entrance of what used to be a huge pasture of dairy cattle and goats. In the distance, in the center of the pasture, scattered torchlights illuminated a large, rectangular hole in the ground – the grave site.

About ninety-six meters this side of the grave site, Kon-Shambique saw the Great Creation Quazzi. He slowed his pace as he watched the Brown Warrior work. Kon-Shambique could see the physical toil in the Brown Warrior's appearance. Quazzi looked dirty, sweaty, and unlike the Foremost Lieutenant of Aukmondi warriors. Kon-Shambique watched Quazzi place the final few markers into the ground. The markers, sticks with a strip of black cloth tied at the top, sectioned off the ritual staging areas. Kon-Shambique waited for Quazzi to measure off one of the last markers before he called his name and approached.

Quazzi heard someone call his name and turned toward the call. He saw no one at first. He held his torch higher to search the darkness beyond his torchlight. From the void of darkness, he saw an individual approaching across the pasture with a large bundle on his shoulder. Quazzi realized that only Kon-Shambique would walk in total darkness like that with such a load on his shoulder. He beckoned the Favored Tribesman closer.

"Good morning, Great Creation. Welcome to the Pogobi grave site."

"Good morning, Quazzi." Kon-Shambique eased his bundle to the ground.

Quazzi waved his hand over the work before him. "I hope these staging areas meet with your approval."

Kon-Shambique took the liberty of borrowing Quazzi's torch. He studied the area next to where he stood. It was a square patch of ground, three meters wide and three meters long. One of the markers protruded from the ground at each of the four corners. Kon-Shambique held his torch higher. From what he could see, an endless row of staging areas stretched before him.

"The markers section off over 140 staging areas in six rows," Quazzi explained. "We are standing at the end of the sixth row. There are nine meters of space between each row. We dug the mass grave at the far end of the first row. You must look at it too, to see if it meets with your approval."

Kon-Shambique intended to do so, but he continued to marvel at the nearby staging areas. The number that Quazzi had just quoted overwhelmed him. "You have over 140 of these?"

"Yes, Great Creation. I believe 144 is the precise number. I estimate that to be about a third of the number of deaths that have occurred since the Mangoni death ritual began. The remaining two-thirds, and any new deaths that may occur, will have to be buried in the valley depths."

"This is remarkable." The incredible range of work done impressed Kon-Shambique. "You started this last evening?"

"Yes, the army of the Royal Warriors Anganyi Elka did. You see here that only half of the work is done. A somewhat larger grave site is being prepared in the valley depths by the army of the Royal Warrior Dodae Kdedi."

Once again, Kon-Shambique visually sized up the marked-off area next to where he stood. After a gentle nod of approval, he gave Quazzi his torch back. He lifted his huge bundle to his shoulder and walked slowly from the sixth row past the end of the fifth row. He continued walking toward the first row. Kon-Shambique glanced at the staging areas at the end of each row.

Quazzi followed Kon-Shambique. He held the torch for the Favored Tribesman. The Brown Warrior knew what the Favored Tribesman was doing, but he had to ask. "Do they meet your approval? Are they large enough, Great Creation?"

"These are fine, Quazzi. They are standard size." Kon-Shambique could hear a touch of concern in the Brown Warrior's voice. "You and the warriors have done a commendable job on such short notice."

"Thank you, Great Creation. I will pass the compliment on to the Royal Warriors and their armies."

When Kon-Shambique reached the end of the second row, he turned left. He walked down between the second and first rows toward the huge grave site. He shifted his huge bundle from one shoulder to the other as he inspected several more staging areas, on his left and right. That touch of concern he heard in Quazzi's voice made him study the areas with a different perspective. He reassessed the standard size of the staging areas himself.

Each of these staging areas would center the body of a dead loved one, lying upon a burial litter. Immediate family members would surround each body and the burial litter. Each family member would carry an item or two to be buried with the body. Kon-Shambique admitted that some of the areas would be cramped. In most, however, there would be ample room. It would all balance out.

At the far end of the first row, Kon-Shambique finally approached the huge grave site. He eased his bundle down from his shoulder and stood on the grave site's edge. It was a rectangular pit, 6600 cubic meters.

Kon-Shambique realized that Quazzi had followed him to the edge of the grave. "This is impressive, Quazzi."

"Thank you, Great Creation."

Kon-Shambique leaned out to see the bottom of the grave. It was over two meters deep. On this end of the grave, at Kon-Shambique's left, a dirt ramp led down into the pit. Several Elka warriors stood at measured intervals, relaying baskets of dirt up the ramp and out of the pit. Other warriors, down in the pit, continued digging dirt from the grave's back wall.

"They will finish by daylight," Quazzi said. "At that time, families are expected to arrive, delivering the bodies of loved ones to the staging areas."

"Then, I must get started." Kon-Shambique kneeled and pried open his bundle. He pulled out a large gourd and removed the lid. The gourd held a fine mixture of blessed herbs and spices. Walking to the first staging area, he reached into the gourd and got a handful of the mixture. Like a farmer planting seeds, he sprinkled a small measure into the staging area.

"May I help with that?" Quazzi asked.

"No, thank you, Great Creation. This is another part of the ritual which I must do myself."

Quazzi made a sweeping glance over the first row of staging areas. He looked back over his shoulder to see the five other rows. "You do realize, it may take you a while to do all these areas."

"Yes. It is the very reason I have come so early." Kon-Shambique moved over to the second staging area. He reached into the gourd for another handful of the mixture. As he did so, he caught a glimpse of the fatigue in Quazzi's face. He finished sprinkling the mixture on the ground. Once again, he took the liberty of reaching over and taking the torch from Quazzi's hand. He held it higher to get a better look at the Brown Warrior. "You look exhausted, Great Creation. Will you be able to attend the burial rituals?"

Quazzi looked down at his appearance. He brushed dust and dirt from his arms and hands. "A few more preparations are yet to be done. But I have time to freshen up and rest before the rituals start."

Kon-Shambique glanced again over the tremendous array of work. "I will ensure that the rest of the preparations are completed here. You get some rest. The rituals will probably not start until shortly after sunrise."

"Are you sure?"

"Yes, I am sure."

"Then, thank you. I will see you after sunrise."

Kon-Shambique watched the Brown Warrior walk away. Quazzi was still brushing dust and dirt from his face and chest. The Favored Tribesman didn't have the heart to tell Quazzi that fatigue would overwhelm him. He knew that Quazzi had been working nonstop since yesterday evening. He estimated that Brown Warrior could attend only the first few rituals. The first few rituals would include the rituals of the Mfalme and his Principal Mate. But beyond that, Kon-Shambique expected Quazzi to fall asleep standing up in the middle of one of the rituals.

54

THE SPIRIT AND THE INTENT

In the pasture of the Pogobi kraal, the Favored Tribesman sprinkled the blessed herb and spice mixture on the last few staging areas. He had fallen behind schedule despite his early start. He could see that the first influx of family groups had already entered the pasture, causing a minor distraction. Kon-Shambique had five more staging areas to complete before he finished. Yet, he did not increase his tempo. Instead, he focused his attention on what he was doing. Blessing the staging areas was important. He knew that in these areas, the families would give the physical bodies of their deceased loved ones the final goodbyes.

Thanks to his ability to concentrate, Kon-Shambique blessed the last staging area with the same heart and mind as the first. When he finished, he said a final prayer and dusted off his hands. He turned to look at his work. It was dark when he started. Now, in the morning light, it surprised him to see the size of the area he had covered; over 4,500 square meters.

With the preliminary phase of the burial ritual complete, Kon-Shambique sighed with relief. He stooped down to pack his empty gourds back into his bags. He finally surrendered some of his attention to the arriving family groups as he worked. He looked back through the lifeless village area of the Pogobi kraal and toward the pathway in front of the kraal. He could see many more family groups coming from both directions, up and down the pathway. They were entering the kraal at a regular interval now.

All his life, the Favored Tribesman Kon-Shambique had been a natural people-watcher. This moment was no exception. As he watched, he made a few comparative observations, unaware he was doing so. He could see that the arriving family groups varied. Only four or five blood-related people formed some groups. Huge crowds formed other groups, made up of extended families. However, small or large family groups, Kon-Shambique could easily see that circumstances had forced the bonds among them to draw all of them closer together.

Kon-Shambique also noticed that some of the people were dressed in elaborate clothing. They dressed for the occasion as an honor and final tribute to the deceased. Yet, other people dressed in simple, everyday clothing. Kon-Shambique reasoned that these people had not found it necessary to honor or pay tribute to the deceased. In some ways, this was understandable. It was a clear reluctance to acknowledge or accept the death of loved ones.

Kon-Shambique could see that most family groups seemed spiritually unprepared for the upcoming rituals. A lot of them walked into the pasture bewildered and lost. Warriors from the Blue Warrior Ukwatzi regiment greeted people at the pasture's entrance. The warriors ushered the people in and directed them to where to assemble.

Kon-Shambique could see that few people talked. Except for a few greetings, condolences, and well wishes here and there, the people said little else, even among their family groups. Their mood was quiet and somber – almost too quiet. The noise level in the Pogobi pasture should have grown as the number of people grew larger and larger. But it didn't. In a disturbing irony, the most prominent sound that Kon-Shambique heard throughout the pasture was the relentless 'boom-boom' of the Mangoni ritual drums. The drums seem to add to the somber atmosphere.

Kon-Shambique suddenly realized what he was doing and ended his people-watching. The main burial rituals were starting soon, and he still had to recover lost time. He poured water from a water bladder onto each of his hands to wash off the rest of the fine, dusty powder that had accumulated. After shaking his hands to dry them, he packed the water bladder into one of his bags. He flung the bag over his shoulder and began his walk toward the first row of staging areas.

A half-kilometer distance stretched between the sixth and first rows. To recover from his original schedule, he walked at a fast pace. It took him about four minutes to reach the end of the second row. But as he turned to walk down between the second and first rows toward the first staging area, Kon-Shambique stopped again to watch the people.

From where he stood and in the morning light, he could see the entire length of the first two rows. Many people had gathered, and most stood between the rows. They respected the boundaries of staging areas. Sacred, ritual rules forbid entrance into a blessed staging area. Once blessed, only family members, Kon-Shambique, and four consecrated warriors may enter the marked-off areas. Most of the staging areas remained empty. But Kon-Shambique could see people entering the first few areas, those near the huge grave.

Kon-Shambique resumed his walk. He spoke to as many people as time would allow as he walked past them. With sympathy in his smile, he tried to give each of them individual, heartfelt greetings. He knew these people would see their dead loved ones for the last time. He tried to leave them with a sense of hope and encouragement. They had to know that, after the burial rituals, the loving bonds with their loved ones were not as final as they seemed.

The tenth staging area was the first completely occupied area. In it, Kon-Shambique greeted the family of the Blue Warrior Dabete Ehkili. Dabete's father, mother, three brothers, two sisters, and both of his father's parents stood in mournful silence as they waited for the rituals to start. They surrounded the body of the Blue Warrior, which lay upon his burial litter and was dressed in full warrior's gear. Dabete's shield and best spear lay beside him. His family had prepared him well. Even in death, the Blue Warrior looked impressive.

Kon-Shambique had known Dabete Ehkili as a gentle, soft-spoken person. He considered the warrior a brilliant tactician. Dabete was such an efficient warrior that he could often complete most tasks while others were still making plans. Kon-Shambique believed the Aukmondi had lost one of its greatest warriors.

The family of the Blue Warrior Obe Bendabe, Dabete's closest friend, filled the ninth staging area. Obe's mate, one son, three daughters, and his mother bracketed the burial litter of the Blue Warrior. Obe's body lay also dressed in full warrior's gear. Even upon his burial litter, Obe held an exceptional stature. Kon-Shambique considered him one of the most imposing warriors he had ever seen. No one, including Kon-Shambique, expected this magnificent and charismatic warrior to lie among the dead so soon. And the fact that a dear friend was dead hit Kon-Shambique with renewed intensity. Tears welled up in Kon-Shambique's eyes.

Kon-Shambique looked back at the body of the Blue Warrior Dabete and at the body of the Blue Warrior Obe again. He approached the first eight staging areas and the gathered bodies and families. His heart suddenly grew heavy. None of this seemed right. Kon-Shambique felt an oppressive sadness regaining momentum. He felt a personal closeness with all these people. He wondered if he would have the emotional strength to impart the many blessings that would be needed from him.

At that moment, Kon-Shambique saw the Royal Warrior Nionu, slowly pacing nearby. He had not seen Nionu since the day before the deaths of the Blue Warriors Obe and Dabete. There was no doubt in Kon-Shambique's mind that Nionu had taken their deaths hard. The Favored Tribesman was pleased to see the Royal Warrior despite the present circumstances. It meant Nionu had ended his self-imposed seclusion and was finally out among the people again.

Kon-Shambique forced the sudden surge of his dark feelings aside. He walked up over to greet the Royal Warrior. "Good morning, Great Creation."

Nionu, also dressed in full warrior's gear, carried his ceremonial royal shield, which was larger than he usually carried. Nionu shifted the beautiful shield from one hand to the other before turning around to pace in the opposite direction. He looked up to see Kon-Shambique standing before him. He stopped his pacing. "Oh … Kon-Shambique, good morning. I am sorry. I did not see you."

"When heavy thoughts stand in your way, they can sometimes blind you. Great Creation, you are pacing like a caged animal. Are you alright?"

The Royal Warrior Nionu's mood seemed restless and edgy. With frustration clear, he looked to his left and then right. He appeared to be censoring his true answer. "Why do people keep asking me that?"

Kon-Shambique looked at the warrior with concern. Then he glanced behind him at the bodies of Nionu's two Blue Warriors, Obe and Dabete. He turned back to Nionu. "People have good reason to ask."

Nionu looked at the bodies, too. He sighed. "I am fine, Great Creation. I … I just. I want to bury my warriors … so I can move on."

"Move on?"

"Yes." Nionu shifted his shield to his other arm again. "There are things I need to do."

"Things? Like what?"

"Well … if you must know, I must break a few bones. I need to get rid of a maggot infestation I found. I want to give that dark spirit walking our valley a good, healthy dose of daylight. You know – things like that."

Kon-Shambique said nothing. He stood for a moment and watched the Royal Warrior. He wondered just how much truth there was in the warrior's sarcastic comments. The Favored Tribesman hoped this was not a subconscious death wish by the Royal Warrior.

Kon-Shambique would have asked Nionu to explain himself had the Royal Warrior not ended the conversation and walked away. Kon-Shambique did not press the issue. He watched as the Royal Warrior resumed his pacing. Besides, the Favored Tribesman had his own pressing agenda. He turned and continued his walk toward the first staging area.

The body of the Young Creation Robuti occupied the eighth staging area. Kon-Shambique saw Robuti's moment of death with his own eyes. Even now, as the horrible memory resurfaced, Kon-Shambique could not believe death could come from such a simple act. As Kon-Shambique greeted each of Robuti's relatives, he could only imagine how they must feel. Robuti's parents, both sets of grandparents, and several aunts and uncles stood around the

Young Creation's body, each holding one of Robuti's beautiful metal sculptures. Many more of his sculptures lined his staging area.

Of all the staging areas, the sixth and seventh were unquestionably the most royally adorned. For in these areas lay the burial litters of Mfalme Ncobba and his Principal Mate, Rwuva. In the seventh area, Ramuza's body lay dressed in the full gear of the penultimate military rank of Black Warrior, including feathery headdress, wrist, and ankle adornments. A huge black ceremonial shield and his spear lay at his side. Kon-Shambique stopped walking, awed. He stared at Ramuza's body. Nothing so impressive should lie so dead.

The burial litter of the Principal Mate, the Sacred Woman Rwuva, lay royally adorned in the sixth staging area. Rwuva's body lay beautifully dressed in all white. The golden light from the first rays of the morning sunlight enhanced her mature radiance. The peace and serenity on Rwuva's face seemed to belie the sadness of the occasion. Her inner spirit continued to shine.

Most of the Ncobba family surrounded the litters of Ramuza and Rwuva. The Sacred Woman Olabisi, nine Ncobba daughters, and a huge host of extended family relatives crowded in and around the staging area. The only family members missing were the Gray Warrior Kharaambi and Adaulah.

Kon-Shambique looked ahead, searching for the missing members. In the distance, near the first staging area, he saw Kharaambi and Adaulah. The two stood with the Chinchigwe Mfalme, Ameh Jobabwe, next to the huge gravesite. As the three highest officials in the tribe, they would take part in the burial rituals once they began. Kon-Shambique realized that they had already assumed their places and were waiting for his arrival.

Kon-Shambique had intended to exchange a few heartfelt greetings and further condolences with the Sacred Woman Olabisi and others in the sixth and seventh staging areas. But he dismissed that courtesy. He had already run out of time. The sun had already peeked over the horizon, and there were so many people in the sixth and seventh areas that they overflowed beyond the markers of the two areas.

Ramuza's feisty little daughter, Zindzhi, stood inside Rwuva's staging area. When she saw Kon-Shambique walking by, she stepped from the area and addressed the Favored Tribesman. "Good morning, Great Creation. Do you have a moment?"

Kon-Shambique looked down at the little girl. He glanced ahead at Kharaambi, Ameh, and Adaulah, who were still waiting for him. He looked back down at Zindzhi. "I will create a moment for you, Little Woman."

"We need to move," Zindzhi said, expecting no objection.

"Move? Why?"

Zindzhi gave a sweeping gesture toward the areas. "These are not big enough. Not all of us will fit in these tiny areas. Can we move Ramuza and Rwuva closer to the gravesite, where there is plenty of room?"

Kon-Shambique looked toward the gravesite. Zindzhi was right. There was ample space between the first staging area and the gravesite. But Kon-Shambique had to say 'no' to Zindzhi's suggestion.

"So, why not?"

Kon-Shambique could not help but smile at Zindzhi's resolve. Undoubtedly, the little girl was the natural daughter of the Gray Warrior Kharaambi. He stooped down to give Zindzhi a complete and thoughtful answer.

"We are born in a divine order," Kon-Shambique began. "We are all born by Her grace at the proper time to fulfill our purpose in life. We can assume that we must be released to the Supreme Spirit in about the same divine order as our deaths."

"Who made up that rule?"

"Well, it is how we cooperate with the Supreme Spirit's will. It is part of the burial ritual. For this reason, the bodies of Rwuva and Ramuza must occupy the sixth and seventh staging areas. They were the sixth and seventh to die. Understood?"

Zindzhi looked back at the staging areas. She studied the people gathered there. Although she had experienced only her eleventh harvest, she was intelligent for her age. She understood the reasoning behind the burial order.

"I guess so. Then, it is good that the Royal Family stands in the first row. Unlike the other rows, plenty of open space lay behind the first row. I guess, these areas will do."

"They will have to do," Kon-Shambique agreed.

"Thank you, Great Creation."

Kon-Shambique rose to his feet again. Zindzhi had brought a momentary smile to Kon-Shambique's face. He watched her until she stepped back into Rwuva's staging area.

The smile on Kon-Shambique's face did not last long. When Kon-Shambique finally came to the fifth staging area, he stopped walking again. The body of the Sacred Woman Tongda lay in the fifth area. Tongda's father, the Great Creation Benwe, her aunt, the Sacred Woman Oraka, and her cousin, the White Warrior Upenda, bracketed Tongda's body. Tongda's burial display held an eerie beauty. It captured Kon-Shambique's mind and spirit. As people paid tribute to her in his kraal all day yesterday, Kon-Shambique had marveled at Tongda's irresistible beauty. As unbearable as his grief had been, and despite all the pain that knotted so tightly in his stomach, Kon-Shambique recovered. By the day's end, he reached a point where he could move about like normal.

But suddenly looking upon Tongda again, laid out in the staging area, it was like opening an old wound. The love of his life was dead. Will of the Supreme Spirit or not, it seemed wrong. The impossible task of getting over her death loomed before him. Pain and grief flared up and suddenly hit him hard. Kon-Shambique's eyes welled up with tears again, this time so fast that a tear streaked down his face before he could stop it.

Kon-Shambique rushed ahead before his emotions incapacitated him. His remarkable ability to concentrate failed him. He had to stay focused for the burial rituals. The Favored Tribesman struggled so hard to suppress this new flare-up of grief that he did not remember walking past the last four staging areas. He walked right past Kharaambi, Ameh, and Adaulah without saying anything. He walked right up to the edge of the huge grave. Kon-Shambique stood, wondering if he had the strength to do what he had to.

Kon-Shambique stood for a long while staring down into the grave, watching the warriors of the Elka Army put the final touches on the site. The huge hole in the ground did not compare to Kon-Shambique's void in his stomach. He took several long minutes to recompose himself. He had to make sure his own heart and mind were spiritually ready. Kon-Shambique would have stood there longer had not Kharaambi, Ameh, and Adaulah walked up behind him.

"Great Creation," Kharaambi touched Kon-Shambique's shoulder. "Are you alright?"

"Yes. Yes, I am fine, Sacred Woman." It was a half-truth. Kon-Shambique surrendered his heart and mind to the will of the Supreme Spirit. He wiped away the tears with a quick and discreet brush. He turned to face the staging areas. "Is everyone ready?"

"I do not know what to expect," Ameh commented. "In the Chinchigwe tribe, our burial rituals were different. But, I suppose, I am as ready as ever."

"As I understand the Chinchigwe rituals, they were different. But, the spirit and the intent are the same, Mfalme." Kon-Shambique gave Ameh a reassuring smile. He looked toward the first row of staging areas to reassure himself and regain self-control, and focused on the burial procedures.

For a proper release and burial, Kon-Shambique had to enter each staging area and inspect the body of the deceased. His first task was to examine the body thoroughly. He then had to determine that the families had prepared the respective bodies. Once done, family members would be free to make final requests to the departed, usually special wishes whispered into the ear to be delivered to family ancestors.

After all the family requests, the Favored Tribesman's next task would be to give the final blessing. The ceremony would end with an appeal to the Supreme Spirit to grant the spirit of the departed permission to leave the body and enter the afterlife.

Kon-Shambique closed his eyes, took a deep breath, and sighed. He felt ready. He finally opened his eyes and turned to Adaulah. "Little Creation, as the new Mfalme, we follow your lead. May we begin?"

Adaulah wore the garments of a Black Warrior, except that he carried no shield or spear. He acknowledged Kon-Shambique with a small nod of his head. As it was his duty, he turned and ceremoniously led the Favored Tribesman to the edge of the first staging area. He invited the Favored Tribesman to step inside the area.

55

AS A MASK HIDES A FACE

Kon-Shambique took another deep, relaxing breath and entered the first staging area. As it turned out, he had to perform the initial burial ritual on the body of the Red Warrior Mbinga. Mbinga was not the first to die. Kon-Shambique recalled that when all the deaths in the Aukmondi Valley began, three Mangoni warriors and the Sacred Woman Abul-Tess were among the first to die.

The unfortunate Mangoni warrior who guarded the Wabanga's confinement cage was the first. The Wabanga stabbed the warrior to death with the warrior's own knife. Later, the Wabanga used the same knife to kill the two Mangoni warriors who had helped to carry the food pallet up to Abul-Gwan's first provisional camp. One received a fatal stabbing when he went to rescue one of the Mangoni pack animals. The other got his throat cut when he pursued the killer Wabanga alone into the darkness of the surrounding woods. And then, in what seemed to be a more profound tragedy, the Wabanga killed the Sacred Woman Abul-Tess with a spear through her side.

The Vodun houngan took the bodies of the three slain Mangoni warriors and the Sacred Woman Abul-Tess up to Nagorda Peak. Kon-Shambique assumed that the Mangoni houngan would take care of them. Unless asked, the Aukmondi were not responsible for giving them a proper burial.

The Red Warrior Mbinga was the first Aukmondi to die. The Red Warrior gave his life helping to protect the Sacred Women, Rwuva, Olabisi, and Abul-Tess. Kon-Shambique greeted Mbinga's relatives: his mother and two brothers. He made sure they were ready to continue with what lay ahead. As part of the ritual, he examined Mbinga's body from head to toe. Mbinga's family had done a beautiful job of sewing up his knife wound. Kon-Shambique found no open wounds. Mbinga's limbs were intact; no fingers or toes were missing. His body was presentable. Kon-Shambique declared Mbinga's spirit ready for release.

The Favored Tribesman stood back. He allowed several long moments for Mbinga's mother and brothers to each whisper their ancestor-bound messages into Mbinga's ear. This was, by far, the longest part of the ritual. Mbinga's mother had an endless string of messages she wanted delivered. Kon-Shambique stepped from the staging area and stood with Adaulah, Kharaambi, and Ameh. He waited patiently for Mbinga's relatives to finish.

After the whispered messages, Kon-Shambique stepped into the staging area again. He freed his heart and mind with a deep, relaxing breath to allow the Supreme Spirit to work through him. He offered a short prayer, then reached up and gently touched Mbinga's forehead. The touch reminded Mbinga to open his spiritual eyes and see his way into the afterlife.

Kon-Shambique then took each of Mbinga's hands. He held them close to his heart as he addressed Mbinga's spirit. Kon-Shambique commanded him to go forth and walk among all those relatives who had come before him. He commanded Mbinga to get to know his past relatives, see their faces, and remember their names. He commanded Mbinga to learn from where he had come. By doing so, only then could he protect the family he leaves. He commanded Mbinga to remember his living family for as long as they remembered him. Finally, still holding his hands, Kon-Shambique gently laid Mbinga's hands and arms to his sides. He did not fold his arms across his chest. Mbinga's spirit was free to go. The initial burial ritual for the Red Warrior was complete.

As Kon-Shambique stepped from the staging area, the four consecrated Aukmondi warriors entered. They lifted Mbinga's burial litter to their shoulders and took it down to the edge of the gravesite. They waited until Mbinga's mother and brothers gathered all the gifts and belongings to be buried with the Red Warrior. Mbinga's family and the consecrated warriors ceremoniously descended the dirt ramp into the huge grave.

With the first of many initial burial rituals complete, Kon-Shambique followed the tribal leaders, Adaulah, Kharaambi, and Ameh, to the second staging area. Surprised, the Favored Tribesman discovered that the second death, not the responsibility of the Mangoni, was that of the Wabanga. Since the Wabanga died in the Aukmondi Valley, the Aukmondi people had to give him a proper burial.

The Wabanga lay upon an unadorned burial litter. A few volunteers had cleaned and sewn up the knife wound and spear wound on the Wabanga's arm. They made the Wabanga's body presentable. No open wounds or bloodstains were visible. Unfortunately, no one knew what the painted markings on his face and shoulders meant. No one knew if the markings represented growth and goodness, or if they represented death and destruction. The volunteers left the markings untouched.

No family members were standing in the Wabanga's staging area. No one stood in support of the Wabanga's life. And no gifts or belongings lay beside the litter to be buried with the Wabanga. Kon-Shambique was not the only one to wonder about the Wabanga's ancestors, who may or may not come to welcome him into the afterlife.

The Favored Tribesman did his best to give the Wabanga a complete and proper initial burial ritual. He examined the body from head to toe. The body seemed to be intact. Kon-Shambique spoke all the right words. Since no family members could whisper messages into the Wabanga's ear, Kon-Shambique freed his heart and mind to give the last ritual prayer.

When the moment came to touch the Wabanga's forehead, Kon-Shambique hesitated. Would it do any good? Did the Wabanga want his spiritual eyes opened? The Wabanga people seemed to have no moral conscience. From Kon-Shambique's perspective, it was a blindness. It occurred to Kon-Shambique that the Wabanga's spirit could wander through the afterlife, lost forever because of this blindness.

Kon-Shambique tapped the Wabanga's forehead anyway. There was the hope that the Supreme Spirit might take the Wabanga's hand

and lead him to where he needed to be. The thought comforted Kon-Shambique to complete the ritual without too many reservations. He had no trouble commanding the spirit of the Wabanga to go forth and walk among his ancestors. He felt a touch of concern when he commanded the spirit of the Wabanga to bless the family he left. From some perspectives, such a blessing promised more harm than good.

Kon-Shambique laid the Wabanga's hands and arms at the Wabanga's sides. By then, the four consecrated warriors had returned. Kon-Shambique stood back and allowed the four warriors to carry the Wabanga's body from the staging area. He waited until the warriors carried the body to the edge of the gravesite before he stepped from the Wabanga's staging area.

"That was a memorable experience," Kon-Shambique said as he returned to join Adaulah, Kharaambi, and Ameh. "I have never performed a burial ritual for a Wabanga before. Their culture is so different and such a mystery. I wonder if I included all the Wabanga needed."

Ameh leaned on his staff. He looked at the four consecrated warriors as they descended the dirt ramp into the gravesite with the Wabanga's body. "As far as I can tell, you gave the Wabanga more than he deserved. You did fine, Great Creation."

"Appearances are sometimes deceiving. My words were hollow. And I felt nothing but sorrow for him. He may be lost forever if the Supreme Spirit does not take him. He will not reach the afterlife."

"Among the Chinchigwe, we bury those with evil or amoral character with a secure blind covering their faces."

"Why?"

"To ensure they stay lost and not find their way back among the living."

"Are you saying I should not have opened his spiritual eyes?"

Ameh shrugged. "If the Supreme Spirit does not take him, his savage spirit just might find its way back here with us."

"Let us hope not. It is out of our hands now. Let us hope, if and when his spirit returns, it can respect the sanctity of life." Kon-Shambique dismissed the experience and turned to Adaulah. He was ready to move on. "Little Mfalme, shall we continue?"

The body of the Red Warrior Gengu lay in the third staging area. Gengu had come from a small family. Gengu was an only child. His parents took his death hard. His mother, Zawadi, could barely attend the burial ritual. Since Gengu's death, her tears had not stopped flowing. Gengu's father, Gudwando, stood at the head of Gengu's burial litter, supporting his crying mate. He stared straight ahead, looking at nothing. He was straining to hold his emotions. There was no expression on his face. Neither of Gengu's parents acknowledged Kon-Shambique's greeting when he entered the area.

The first half of Gengu's burial ritual went smoothly. Difficulty began when Kon-Shambique stepped from the staging area to allow Gudwando and Zawadi to whisper their ancestor-bound messages into Gengu's ear. The Sacred Woman Zawadi could not do it. Even when the Favored Tribesman tried to help her, she cried so hard that she could not stand.

"It must be done," Kon-Shambique spoke to both Gengu's parents. "At this moment, your son is your strongest link with your ancestors. Do not let him enter the afterlife without carrying your wishes."

Kon-Shambique's words did not affect Zawadi. She continued to cry. Gudwando, however, finally broke his constant stare. He forced himself to do what was necessary. He slowly looked down at his son. The effort to hold in his emotions collapsed. Tears ran down his cheek as he lowered his lips to Gengu's ear. When his whispers began, they flowed like his tears for several minutes.

When Gudwando's whispered wishes stopped, Kon-Shambique strayed from the ritual process. He took a moment to console Gengu's parent. He led them aside. They needed his immediate attention.

"As strange as it may seem," Kon-Shambique began, "the most difficult moments have already come and gone. Let him go. Accept his death. You will feel his loss. Many things will be different. But you will recover. Can you do this?"

"We will be alright, Great Creation," Gudwando said. "Thank you for your thoughtful concern."

"He was … he was just so young." Zawadi finally spoke through sobs. "His life was so short; so empty. It hurts me to know that he never found anyone to love."

Kon-Shambique smiled. He did not want to seem insensitive, but the statement was surprising. "Is that your concern, Sacred Woman?"

Zawadi did not respond. Her mate, Gudwando, offered Kon-Shambique an explanation. "The Sacred Woman often asked Gengu if he had found a mate yet. Each time he visited us, she would ask, 'Have you chosen a mate yet?'. As his mother, I think it was one of her strongest wishes. But each time she asked, Gengu never gave her a direct answer."

Kon-Shambique wrapped his arms around the shoulders of Gudwando and Zawadi. He spoke to them in confidence. "The Red Warriors were only looking in the wrong place. It may be difficult to think that he found no one to love. Take comfort in knowing that Gengu greeted each day with a smile."

"How do you know this, Great Creation?"

"It is well known that the Red Warrior Gengu was one of Rwuva's best and most dedicated personal guards. There is a reason for this."

With a tear still hanging in the corner of his eye, Gudwando almost smiled. He already knew where the Favored Tribesman was going. "I suspected as much. In hindsight, I should have shared my suspicion."

"Probably. In this case, you suspected the truth. Zawadi would feel better now if she knew the truth. Gengu lived each day to be near the Sacred Woman Rwuva. He loved her from a distance. No, it was not an ideal situation. But please believe me. His life was not at all empty. He looked forward to every day. The Sacred Woman, Rwuva, was the magic in his life. He found the joy he wanted."

There was a hint of a smile on Zawadi's face. "As I recall, Gengu never complained about being lonely or alone."

"In his short life, he was happy." Kon-Shambique ended his affectionate embrace of Gengu's parents. "Let us finish this ritual and release him."

Gudwando and Zawadi resumed their positions at the head of Gengu's burial litter. The Sacred Woman Zawadi fulfilled her closure process by leaning close to her son's ear and whispering her ancestor-bound wishes. She took several minutes longer than her mate Gudwando had taken. Like her mate, tears were streaming down her face. Unlike her mate, she now held a gentle smile as she spoke.

Kon-Shambique was pleased to see Zawadi's smile, which made him smile, too. Although the Sacred Woman was saying her final words to her son, Kon-Shambique knew she felt better about doing it.

The Favored Tribesman waited patiently until Zawadi finished. When she did, Kon-Shambique reentered the staging area and took his place at Gengu's side. He gave the final ritual prayer, then touched Gengu's forehead to open his spiritual eyes.

When Kon-Shambique held Gengu's hands close to his heart, a gentle frown formed on the Favored Tribesman's face. He momentarily pulled Gengu's hands away and looked at them as if to reexamine them.

The frown on Kon-Shambique's face was so noticeable that Gudwando had to ask. "Is there something wrong, Great Creation?"

Kon-Shambique replaced Gengu's hands against his heart. "No. No, everything is fine." Just as he had done in the two earlier rituals, Kon-Shambique commanded Gengu's spirit to walk among his ancestors; to learn who his ancestors were so he may bless his family. He gently laid Gengu's hands and arms at his side. With reluctance, he let go of Gengu's hands.

Kon-Shambique stepped from the staging area and rejoined Adaulah, Kharaambi, and Ameh. He continued to hold the wrinkles of concern on his face. He watched the four consecrated Aukmondi warriors carry Gengu's body from the staging area to the gravesite. Kon-Shambique watched with a feeling that haunted him.

The body of Zabiba and the Green Warrior's four brothers were in the fourth staging area. Kon-Shambique stood for a long moment before he entered the area. He felt distracted, still thinking about the Red Warrior Gengu. Kon-Shambique massaged his eyes and focused on regaining his concentration. He could not enter Zabiba's staging area without being able to give the Green Warrior and his family his full concentration.

Adaulah, Kharaambi, and Ameh sensed Kon-Shambique's reluctance to enter Zabiba's staging area. Ameh turned to the Favored Tribesman. "What is wrong, Great Creation?"

"Nothing. I … I need to focus. Give me a moment."

"You have completed only three rituals," said Kharaambi. "Several dozen rituals are still to come. Are you up to finishing this? Who will do this if you cannot?"

Kon-Shambique looked to his right along the first row of staging areas. Families and their deceased loved ones occupied each of them. Kon-Shambique looked back over his shoulder. Half the second row was full, and more families and bodies continued to arrive. A tremendous task lay ahead, and his focus already faltered. Kon-Shambique realized he had better pace himself. Otherwise, the tragedies of recent days would grow worse.

"I will release the body of the Green Warrior Zabiba," Kon-Shambique said. He looked to his right, into the fifth staging area. The fifth staging area held the body of his love, Tongda. He remembered his flare-up of emotions when he walked past the area earlier. He knew he would need special strength to complete her ritual. "I will take a moment to refocus before I release the Sacred Woman Tongda."

"So be it, Great Creation. We are moving at your pace. Do what you feel is necessary."

Kon-Shambique started as he had planned. He entered the Green Warrior Zabiba's staging area. He greeted the four young warriors standing there: Zabiba's family. One Gold Warrior, two Orange Warriors, and a Red Warrior stood strong. Each showed unquestionable pride in their older brother, in the heroic way the Green Warrior died.

Kon-Shambique examined Zabiba's body. He had re-sewn the spear wound closed himself. He had no trouble declaring Zabiba ready for release.

As Zabiba's brothers imparted their ancestor-bound messages, Kon-Shambique, as usual, stepped aside. The whispered messages took a while. That is when Kon-Shambique lost his focus again. He looked toward the gravesite again and again. He was thinking about the body of the Red Warrior Gengu. Something about Gengu's burial ritual felt wrong to him. But the flaw eluded him. Several times, Kon-Shambique considered re-doing the ritual of the Red Warrior Gengu.

Kon-Shambique did not notice when Zabiba's brothers finished their ancestor-bound whispers. His mind was still elsewhere. His mind returned to the present only after the Sacred Woman Kharaambi lightly tapped him on the shoulder again.

Kon-Shambique apologized for his inattentiveness. He gathered his thoughts and reentered Zabiba's staging area. He used his remarkable ability to concentrate and refocused on what he was doing. Kon-Shambique freed his heart and mind to pray sincerely over Zabiba's body. After he touched the Green Warrior's forehead, he gave Zabiba's spirit the usual commands: learn who his ancestors were, watch over the family he leaves, and remember them for as long as they remembered him.

Kon-Shambique slowly took Zabiba's hands into his. He held them close to his heart. He held them there longer than usual. The strange feeling he got from Gengu was not there. Zabiba's hands felt just as he expected them to feel. This eased Kon-Shambique's concerns. The Favored Tribesman could complete Zabiba's burial ritual without distractions. He laid Zabiba's hands and arms at his sides. He stepped from the staging area and allowed the consecrated warriors to take Zabiba's body from the staging area to the gravesite.

"Great Creation," Kharaambi said. "The body of the Sacred Woman Tongda is next. It is understandable if you take extended time to prepare yourself. In consideration, we will wait until you are ready."

"Thank you, Sacred Woman." Kon-Shambique wanted to walk down to the gravesite. The edge of the huge gravesite was the only place in the immediate area where he could isolate himself. But before he left, he looked down at Adaulah. Seeing the Little Creation dressed as a Black Warrior made Kon-Shambique recall Adaulah's incident yesterday.

Kon-Shambique remembered how Adaulah tried so hard to reach Mfalme Abul-Gwan's camp. He realized it was not because Adaulah functioned as the new and inexperienced Aukmondi Mfalme. Kon-Shambique knew that Adaulah felt something undeniable; something he knew was right. And, according to Adaulah, that relentless push was all because he had taken the hands of his parents, Ramuza and Rwuva.

Kon-Shambique stood, staring at the Little Creation, thinking. He could sense a relationship between yesterday's incident and his haunting feelings at Gengu's side. As the facts and feelings came together like a gathering storm, Kon-Shambique felt a surge of spiritual energy.

Adaulah looked up and saw Kon-Shambique staring at him. "Great Creation, everyone has been asking you, what is wrong. I guess it is my turn to ask. You stare at me, but your thoughts are elsewhere. What is wrong?"

"Nothing is wrong, Little Mfalme. Nothing at all." Kon-Shambique experienced a moment of mental clarity. He took a dare and acted on his suspicions. Kon-Shambique walked around Adaulah. He walked past Kharaambi and Ameh.

Instead of taking a break, Kon-Shambique rushed ahead and abruptly entered Tongda's staging area. Out of courtesy, he greeted Tongda's extended family, Benwe, Oraka, and Upenda. Without disrespect, he took Tongda's hands into his. He held them close to his heart.

There it was.

"Oh, Great Sacred Spirit! Why did I not see this before?" Kon-Shambique spoke to himself. A smile spread across his face. He looked around, searching for Adaulah. When he found him, he beckoned the little Mfalme to come closer. "You were right, Little Creation. Great Sacred Spirit! You were right!"

"I was?"

"Right about what?" Kharaambi asked as she came closer too. Out of respect, she stopped behind the marker, at the edge of Tongda's staging area. "I thought you would take a personal moment before beginning the Sacred Woman's ritual?"

"It is unnecessary now." Kon-Shambique reached over and, without asking, took Kharaambi's hand. In violation of ritual rules, he pulled her into the staging area. He placed Tongda's hand into Kharaambi's.

There was a sudden chatter of disturbed voices from everyone. The Favored Tribesman had violated the rules of Tongda's initial burial ritual. Benwe, Oraka, and Upenda moved closer together. They held onto each other as they watched this offense in Tongda's staging area. What was Kon-Shambique doing?

Kon-Shambique held Kharaambi's hands and wrapped her fingers tightly around Tongda's hand. "What do you feel?"

Kharaambi looked down at Tongda's hand. She frowned, confused about what she should focus on. "I feel nothing."

"Yes, you do, Sacred Woman. Sometimes, the eyes and the heart fail to see what they have not learned to recognize." Kon-Shambique was beaming like a child. "How long has Tongda been dead?"

Kharaambi thought a moment. "About a day and a half now. What are you getting at, Great Creation?"

Kon-Shambique looked at the people standing near him. The White Warrior Upenda was the nearest. Again, without asking, he reached over and grabbed Upenda's hand. He pulled her closer and forced the White Warrior's hand into Kharaambi's. He forced Kharaambi to hold Upenda's hand tightly. "Now, tell me. What do you feel?"

"The same; I feel nothing." The Gray Warrior still had not understood what Kon-Shambique was trying to show her.

"Again, I ask, how long has Tongda been dead?"

Kharaambi's face lit up when the truth suddenly hit her. She looked down at Tongda again. "Her hand ... her hand feels the same as Upenda's. She is not dead, is she?"

"No, Sacred Woman, she is not. Her hands are just as flexible and warm as any living person's. This was true from the very beginning. But I could not see it. The houngan's ritual hid the truth as a mask hides a face. Life continued behind a mask of death." Kon-Shambique put his hand on Tongda's chest, directly over her heart. What he felt caused his smile to grow wider. He placed Kharaambi's hand over Tongda's heart. "Here! Feel this!"

Kharaambi thought she felt the unmistakable beat of the houngan's ritual drums: boom-boom! Boom-boom! She smiled when she realized the truth: "I have never known the dead to have a heartbeat."

"Or warm hands." Kon-Shambique looked toward the huge grave. "Excuse me for a moment, Sacred Woman."

Kon-Shambique stepped past Kharaambi and quickly left Tongda's staging area. He ran down to the gravesite. Kon-Shambique descended the dirt ramp into the huge grave to reexamine the four bodies placed there by the consecrated warriors. He already knew what he would find. He just needed to confirm his suspicions.

Kon-Shambique kneeled and gently took the hand of the Red Warrior Mbinga. He held it briefly before replacing it, just as gently, at the warrior's side. He moved over and took the hand of the Green Warrior Zabiba, holding it just long enough to remove any doubt in his mind. The Favored Tribesman kneeled at the Wabanga's side for thoroughness and took his hand. He held it long enough to reach a firm conclusion. Mbinga, Zabiba, and the Wabanga were all truly dead.

When Kon-Shambique kneeled next to the body of the Red Warrior Gengu, he took the warrior's hand in one hand. He placed his other hand over the warrior's heart. At once, Kon-Shambique recognized the signs of life; the signs he had overlooked so easily. He smiled.

Kharaambi, Ameh, Adaulah, and both of Gengu's parents stood at the forefront of a small crowd of people on the rim of the grave. All of them looked down at the Favored Tribesman. When they saw the smile on Kon-Shambique's face, they knew what the smile meant. All of them cheered. The Sacred Woman Zawadi, Gengu's mother, screamed and joyfully jumped. She cried tears of happiness.

With leaps and bounds, Kon-Shambique ran up the dirt ramp. He seemed eager to join those standing on the rim of the grave. He barely cleared the ramp before Gengu's parents warmly embraced him.

"Thank you, Great Creation," Gudwando said, unable to hold back his tears of joy. "Thank you so very, very much!"

"Do not thank me. I did nothing. Thank the Supreme Spirit. Show your gratitude to Her."

"We will." Gudwando gestured toward his son's body, down in the grave. "May we bring him back up?"

"No, not yet, Great Creation. The final burial ritual still has to be done over the bodies of the Mbinga, Zabiba, and the Wabanga. Until then, their bodies must not be disturbed. I will have the consecrated warriors bring Gengu up for you."

"Thank you, Great Creation."

Ameh, Kharaambi, and Adaulah walked over to where Kon-Shambique stood. Ameh gestured down into the grave. "So, the Red Warrior Gengu is still alive. Any hope for the others?"

"No, Mfalme. They are truly dead." Kon-Shambique looked back into the grave. "The Red Warrior Mbinga died of a very real knife wound. The Wabanga died of a broken back. And the Green Warrior Zabiba bled to death when he severely ruptured his spear wound."

"So," Kharaambi began, "since the Green Warrior Zabiba, no one else has died?"

"No, Sacred Woman, not a single person."

Ameh turned to look across the staging areas and all the burial litters and bodies, still in place. "That is wonderful news." He spoke without the joy that should have gone with such a statement.

Kon-Shambique looked at Ameh. Behind the Mfalme's characteristic frown, he could see genuine concern. "But?"

"I hate to be the bearer of bad news, but I think we still have a problem."

"What is that, Mfalme?"

Ameh gestured toward the litters with his walking staff. "You say all these people are alive. I must ask, what is wrong with them? Why will they not get up?"

Kon-Shambique glanced across rows of staging areas. He studied the bodies as if seeing them for the first time. "I do not know, Mfalme. I have not figured that out yet. For now, it seems they lack the will to escape death's hold. I would say, they suffer from … the curse of the uninspired."

"The curse of the uninspired? Is there such a thing?"

"Yes, there is. It is the prelude to death itself."

"How long can such a curse last?"

Kon-Shambique considered Ameh's questions. The answer that came to mind caused genuine concern: "An uninspired person can literally die before he or she ever wakes up."

"Then, it is just a matter of time before the houngan's illusion of death becomes real."

"We have to fix this somehow."

"Yes, we must, and soon." Kon-Shambique looked back toward the gravesite. "Final burial rituals are still necessary for the Red Warrior Mbinga, the Wabanga, and the Green Warrior Zabiba. Adaulah, Kharaambi, and I must take care of them first. Then I will figure out how to inspire the uninspired, before it is too late."

56

THE TIP OF THE SPEAR

On their second day of travel, just before dawn, the farmers and their escorting warriors left the cozy nook where they had camped. When the morning sun finally rose, the travelers could see that they walked across an expansive and rolling savanna. The view in all directions gave the illusion of an endless journey, impossible to cover. The view, however, was much more beautiful than discouraging. It motivated the travelers to keep a strong pace throughout the morning.

Sprawling patches of greenery covered the region where the farmers and warriors walked. Trees, bushes, and grasses stretched to the horizon in all directions. The passing rains in the north had forced the parched brown savannas to turn rich, thick, and moist. The natural cycle had occurred earlier than expected.

The Green Warrior Tushema, with the help of the Elder Zekke, had used knowledge of this cycle to plan the trip to and from the Kiwane Village. They intended to make the entire fifteen-day trip long before the rains came. But since yesterday's midday stop under the acacia tree, the Green Warrior Tushema had seen much more greenery than he had wanted to see. He found it harder to dismiss the sightings of two migrating herds of zebra. He knew small, fragmented herds were common and normal. But now, after seeing all the green grass, Tushema realized the recent herds meant more than they appeared to be.

Tushema maneuvered closer to the Gold Warrior Oghani as he continued to survey the surrounding area. "I am convinced, Great Creation, Elder Zekke and I have made a serious error in our travel plan."

"How so, Great Creation?"

Tushema made a sweeping gesture with his spear. "Look at all this. We should walk through much more brown grass than this. The rains in the Maasai Mara region have come as expected, but have come heavily. All this is just too green."

As one of the most experienced warriors, Oghani agreed. He glanced southward. He was also well aware of what all the greenery meant. "You suspect the herds cannot be far behind."

"Yes. We have seen two small herds already. I believe they are, but the tip of the spear. Many more herds are coming. And something tells me they are closer than we think."

"Great Creation, we have made good progress. We will reach the Kiboko Passage and cross the Mara as scheduled." Oghani attempted to sound encouraging.

"Getting through the Kiboko Passage before sundown today was according to our old schedule. I have the agonizing feeling we may already be too late. Those two herds we saw suggest a prelude to the animals soon to come across the Mara. Who knows how many herds are massing on the other side now? As we speak, the Kiboko Passage may be blocked."

Oghani turned to examine the traveling caravan of farmers walking behind him. They had completed a full day's journey yesterday. Today, there was still another full day's traveling ahead before crossing the Mara. If migrating herds blocked the Kiboko Passage, Oghani already knew the consequences. The farmers and warriors would have to abort their trip home. They would have to walk another two days to return to the Kiwane Village.

"Great Creation," Oghani began, "may I suggest you send a warrior ahead, to see if the passage is blocked?"

Tushema looked out across the rolling savanna. He considered Oghani's suggestion. The Kiboko Passage was still another sixty kilometers ahead. At the farmers' pace, it was an eleven-hour walk. Those eleven hours did not include the midday rest stop yet to come. Tushema also realized, in half the time, one of his detachment warriors could easily reach the Kiboko Passage. By the time the farmers reached the midday rest stop, the warrior could return with vital information.

"So be it," Tushema finally said. "If we learn it is necessary to return to the Kiwane village, it will save the farmers at least a half-day of walking."

"Unless … you are forced to decide now."

"Why would I make such a decision now, Great Creation?"

"That agonizing feeling you mentioned, it may be justified."

While Tushema and Oghani talked, they had crested another small hill. On the other side of the hill, about a kilometer ahead, another herd of zebras was passing through the area. Oghani was the first to see it. This herd was much larger than either of the earlier two herds. Oghani pointed at the herd with his spear.

"Oh, Great Sacred Spirit! That is not encouraging," Tushema said. "I regret seeing that, Oghani."

"So, what are your decisions, Great Creation? Is it worth the effort to send a warrior ahead? Or do we return to the Kiwane Village?"

The Green Warrior studied the herd. Even now, he still hoped this herd and the other herds were normal but rare occurrences. Tushema felt that if the travelers were lucky, they would see no more herds like this. He glanced back at the caravan of farmers again. He sighed heavily. "Let us send a warrior ahead. I would like to know, with certainty, what the Kiboko Passage looks like before I decide."

57

JUST FOCUS ON MY MISSION

Far on the other side of the Mara and eighteen kilometers beyond the north rim of the Aukmondi Valley, the Orange Warrior Wema looked back over his shoulder. He studied his friend and traveling companion, the Red Warrior Nienko. He wondered how Nienko felt after starting their very special mission. The two warriors left the valley before daylight. After an hour of walking, they emerged from the Bonjii Forest onto the open savanna grassland.

All day yesterday, they had spent as much quality time with their families as they could afford. The warriors ignored, as best they could, the news of recent events in the valley. They enjoyed the simple pleasures of conversation with their families. They shared precious memories. The Orange Warrior Wema, for example, learned things about his young son he had never realized. He saw his son for the first time through his mate's eyes. The things Wema's mate told him about his son made Wema realize his young son had developed traits much like his own, long-deceased and beloved grandfather. The infant had never met the grandfather. Yet Wema could see a link between the two. It had a magical effect on Wema, making him proud of his family.

Likewise, the Red Warrior Nienko and his sister learned more about their ancestry from their mother than they ever knew. Nienko's mother introduced the possibility of blood relatives living in the Motobo kraal. In fact, a close friend of Nienko, one he had grown up with, was a distant cousin. In one day, Nienko learned he had more relatives than he realized.

Leaving these precious families did not come easily. As warriors, Wema and Nienko often left their families when they set out on one mission or another. One of the hardest tasks any warrior must do is leave their family. No warrior ever gets used to doing it. But this time, for Wema and Nienko, it was especially hard.

Messages that the dead were not dead had reached the Motobo kraal just before Wema and Nienko left. As far as the warriors knew, the messages came with no proof. They amounted to unsubstantiated rumors. All the dead still lay upon their burial litters. There was far more evidence throughout the valley that the Mangoni houngan's demon of death still walked the valley.

When the moment came to leave their families, both warriors found it difficult. Believing they may never see their families again made leaving impossible. But the persistent, unsubstantiated rumors spread through the Motobo kraal, giving the warriors enough hope and strength to do what they had to do. As dutiful warriors, they said their goodbyes.

Earlier this morning, as Wema and Nienko set out on their mission, Wema's mate and young son stood with the Red Warrior Nienko's mother and sister. The group, with other well-wishers, stood just inside the entrance to the Motobo kraal, waving goodbye to the parting warriors. That image held strong in the hearts and minds of the parting warriors as they descended the south slope of the valley and crossed the Aukmondi River. They climbed the north slope with heavy hearts, exited the north rim, and set out across the wilderness. All along the way, neither warrior spoke until well after they had cleared the Bonjii Forest onto the savanna, eighteen kilometers north of the valley.

"If the rumors are true, they will be alright, my friend," Wema said to Nienko. The Orange Warrior could tell Nienko's heavy silence was due to the young warrior's concern for mother and sister. "We will see them again."

"I can only hope and pray so." Nienko made wide steps as he waded through the tall grass. He increased his steps to catch up with Wema. "My mother told me not to worry about her and my sister. Can you believe that? That is difficult to do."

"Yes, it is."

"My mother told me to just focus on my mission. She spoke like it was the most important thing I could ever do. She sounded like focusing on my mission would make me feel better."

"I have known your mother longer than you have, Great Creation. The Sacred Woman is wise and insightful. I think she gave you good advice."

"How can that be? If the houngan's demon of death wipes out all life in the valley, everything ends."

"Not so, my friend." Wema tried to put Nienko's mother's advice into practice. "If the demon wipes out our valley, at least the returning farmers will be safe. And your mother is already bursting with pride knowing her son fulfilled his mission and saved a few survivors."

58

COVER OUR EARS

By mid-morning, Kon-Shambique and the current Aukmondi leaders, Adaulah and Kharaambi, emerged from the huge grave site. They walked across the Pogobi kraal cattle pasture and the former staging areas. Just moments ago, they had finished the final burial ritual and ceremony for the warriors Mbinga and Zabiba and for the Wabanga—the only three people who had died.

*****

The final ritual was a short and simple ceremony. Like the initial burial ritual, the final ritual was also important. With the families of Mbinga and Zabiba looking on, Adaulah thanked the warriors for their service and ultimate sacrifice. He gave them their final honors. Adaulah called upon the Gray Warrior Kharaambi to summarize the heroic deeds of the warriors since she knew them best. Adaulah had Kharaambi's complete support through this part and for all phases of the final ritual, but he didn't need it. Despite his inexperience as an Mfalme, Adaulah had paid an official tribute to fallen warriors. Experience tempered his heart and mind. He knew what to do. He knew how to do it well. Adaulah's mature and thoughtful tribute to the warriors pleased both families.

The final ritual for the Wabanga was a different matter. No one knew the Wabanga. There were no final honors to bestow upon him. Adaulah was speechless when it came time to bless the Wabanga. After a long, silent moment, Adaulah glanced at Kharaambi and Kon-Shambique. All who saw this awkward moment thought Adaulah was looking for help. He wasn't. He was about to give the Wabanga a blessing that some might consider offensive.

"The Wabanga was just being the Wabanga," Adaulah began. "As he enters the afterlife, he probably does not have the heart to seek our forgiveness. But that is alright. Each of us probably has no strong desire to forgive him. If the Supreme Spirit does not take him, we do not have to forgive him anyway. But … we know that She will. And when She does, She will open his eyes and his heart. The Wabanga will realize all he has done. It will probably be very painful for him. Our forgiveness may be his only comfort. So, forgive him if you wish."

The statement caused Kharaambi and Kon-Shambique to glance at each other. They found the statement thoughtful, and Kon-Shambique also found it humorous. A smile forced its way onto his face. He was not the only one. When the Favored Tribesman looked toward the Zabiba and Mbinga family members, some were smiling, too.

After Adaulah finished his part of the final ritual, the Favored Tribesman Kon-Shambique followed behind Adaulah with his part. He did his part by offering another prayer to the Supreme Spirit. He asked the Supreme Spirit to bless the bodies as he sprinkled them with more of the powder he had used to bless the staging areas. The Favored Tribesman ended the ceremony by taking some of the dirt that would be used to cover the bodies. He gave each of the family members a handful of the dirt. He instructed them to take the dirt back to their huts and put it in a safe and secure place. It was a symbolic reminder that the fallen would always be near them. Kon-Shambique tossed a handful of the dirt used to cover the body of the Wabanga into the air. The dirt tossed in the air symbolized putting the dirt into the hands of the Supreme Spirit.

*****

In the Pogobi cattle pasture, family groups completely ignored the markers, which once defined the staging areas. Even though several burial litters continued to occupy many of the areas, people had begun to move about freely without any need to respect the marked-off areas. Conversations among the people naturally increased, and a more sociable atmosphere developed as the news spread that the dead only appeared to be dead.

The Chinchigwe Mfalme Ameh Jobabwe and the Blue Warrior Ukwatzi stood in the middle of the pasture. They talked with each other and watched the changing moods of the family groups around them. Ukwatzi had used warriors of his regiment to usher the family groups into the pasture and to help them file into the staging areas in the proper order.

Ukwatzi wondered if his warriors should be used to restore order in the area. He knew that Adaulah, Kharaambi, and Kon-Shambique were performing the final burial ritual in the nearby grave site for Zabiba, Mbinga, and the Wabanga. The noise of the energized crowd was inappropriate for the ritual, so he turned to Ameh for his opinion.

"Mfalme, should I use my warriors to usher the people from the pasture? They should, at least, be reminded that a sacred ceremony is being performed nearby."

Before answering Ukwatzi, Ameh leaned on his staff and made another sweeping study of the family groups around him. Ameh felt that, after the stressful events of the past two days, the families needed the freedom to release their worries and anxieties. Restraining them in any way seemed wrong. But the Blue Warrior had expressed a valid concern for the moment. If the noise level grew any louder, something must be done.

Ameh looked back toward the grave site. He saw Adaulah, Kharaambi, and Kon-Shambique coming. "Crowd control is unnecessary, Great Creation. The final ritual is already completed. Let the families enjoy themselves."

When Kharaambi, Kon-Shambique, and Adaulah came within speaking range, Ameh swiveled on his staff to speak with Kharaambi. "Sacred Woman, I hope the final ritual went well."

"It did, Mfalme. The families of Zabiba and Mbinga embraced the release of their loved ones with admirable respect." Kharaambi made her own sweeping study of all the people in the pasture. "Is this the same crowd from earlier this morning?"

"Yes, it is. But there is a noticeable difference. In a few moments, they transformed from a crowd of mourners to a crowd of revelers.

They did not disturb you. The Blue Warrior Ukwatzi wondered if his warriors should exercise a little crowd control."

"We could hear the crowd from the grave site. It caused a minor distraction. But it was not a disturbance. Although the families of Zabiba and Mbinga were the only ones to have actually buried loved ones, they did not seem to mind. They looked forward to sharing the triumph of life with the rest of the tribe. The joy they heard from the crowd gave them something to look forward to."

"Well, good." Ameh glanced at a nearby row of bodies, still stretched out upon their burial litters. "I only hope we are not getting ahead of ourselves."

"What do you mean, Mfalme?" Kon-Shambique heard a lingering concern in Ameh's comment.

"You said earlier that the bodies on the litters are suffering from the curse of the uninspired."

"Yes. It is the prelude to death."

"If we do not wake everyone up soon, they could all actually die?"

"Yes, Mfalme."

"I assume you have not figured out how to wake them?"

"No, I have not." Kon-Shambique glanced at one of the nearby family groups. The body that lay upon the litter in the center of the group was that of the Sacred Woman Mitma.

Ameh noticed Kon-Shambique looking at Mitma's body. "That is one spirited little woman. I am told that the Sacred Woman Mitma, the matriarch of her family, made a bold and deliberate stand before the demon. She walked right up to that thing when everyone else was running away."

"Yes, I heard about the incident."

"With such a spirit, she is far from 'uninspired'. Amazingly, she fell 'dead' in the first place."

Kon-Shambique approached the family of the Sacred Woman Mitma. He addressed the family as he gestured toward Mitma's burial litter. "May I?"

Four Strong Creations, Mitma's grandsons, stood near Mitma's burial litter. They had been the ones who carried her litter into the area. Busham, the oldest of the four grandsons, permitted the Favored Tribesman to approach. They stood back to give Kon-Shambique complete access to re-examine their grandmother's body.

Kon-Shambique kneeled, visually studying Mitma's body from head to toe. He sat thinking, but at a loss for what to do. He nudged Mitma's shoulder as if to wake her. A nudge seemed the natural remedy. Kon-Shambique had tried this approach with Tongda, Rwuva, and Ramuza several times. And like before, it failed. The Favored Tribesman leaned in close to see if he could hear Mitma breathing. He put his hand into hers, then leaned close to her again. He put his lips close to her ear. "Sacred Woman, can you hear me? Squeeze my hand if you can."

When there was no response from Mitma, Kon-Shambique sat back and sighed heavily. He gently stroked her hand. The warmth and flexibility of life still in her fingers felt good. He had overlooked this quality so many times. "Mitma's spirit is in this body. And she probably knows that we are here. But I cannot think of a way to reach her."

"The answer involves that houngan," the Blue Warrior Ukwatzi commented. He stood at Kon-Shambique's shoulder. "It is crucial to stop the houngan and his ritual. It is the most direct approach. We may fix all this if we stop him and his ritual."

Kharaambi could sense the warrior's intention. "Stay away from Nagorda Peak. We have tried that approach several times. We have enough dead."

"What about an indirect approach?" Ameh asked. He addressed the Favored Tribesman. "Great Creation, you must come up with, maybe, a ritual of your own. Perform a ritual that will overpower the houngan's."

"That sounds good, Mfalme." Kon-Shambique shrugged. "Unfortunately, I do not have the influential power the houngan has."

"I disagree, Great Creation." Kharaambi kneeled at Kon-Shambique's side. "You told us these people are alive. Those simple words stopped us from burying them."

"Sacred Woman, I cannot take the credit for that." Kon-Shambique nodded toward Adaulah. "The credit goes to the Little Mfalme. It was his insight and his influences that saved everyone from being buried alive."

Ameh turned toward Adaulah. "Well, Little Mfalme? Any more insights to share?" He sounded sarcastic, but he was halfway serious.

"No, Mfalme. I do not."

"Anything at all?"

"Well, I like the suggestion you gave the Favored Tribesman just a moment ago."

"What? That the Favored Tribesman should perform a ritual of his own?"

"Yes. One that is more powerful than the Mangoni houngan's."

"Is there such a ritual?" Kon-Shambique considered the idea. He looked down at the Sacred Woman Mitma again. He analyzed the Mangoni houngan's ritual and how it had affected Mitma and everyone else.

Kon-Shambique realized three characteristics of the ritual that directly touched everyone in the Aukmondi valley. First, there was the obvious influential power of the houngan. The houngan convinced everyone to accept his powers unquestioningly. Although the houngan's rituals were not always understood, everyone expected something to happen when the houngan performed a ritual. They looked for some magical occurrence.

Second, the smell of death wafted through the valley. It was a subtle odor but powerful enough to mask the smell of burnt grass. The odor reached everyone and had become commonplace. It was a constant reminder that death was in the air.

Third, there was the constant beat of the ritual drums. The drums had been beating nonstop since the ritual began. The drumbeat became an irritant. Like the odor, it was an unshakeable intrusion powerful enough to mask the heartbeats of everyone in the valley. Everyone found it difficult to relax or concentrate.

In one last desperate attempt to figure out what to do, Kon-Shambique used his hands to cover the ears of the Sacred Woman Mitma. He was trying to block, at least, the sound of the drums. He held his hands tightly over Mitma's ears for several seconds, watching for any sign of recovery.

It worked. Ameh was the first to notice.

"Great Creation!" Ameh got Kon-Shambique's attention and pointed to Mitma's right hand. "Her fingers! I saw them twitch."

Kon-Shambique would have tried other pragmatic approaches, but Busham and the rest of Mitma's family could not contain their joy. They huddled around Mitma's body, forcing Kon-Shambique to move back. He surrendered her body to them. Other pragmatic tests were no longer necessary. Kon-Shambique smiled with budding confidence. "I think I know what we must do."

"What? Cover our ears?" Ameh was being sarcastic this time.

"In essence, yes." Kon-Shambique was still firming up his presumption. He looked up at the Blue Warrior Ukwatzi. "You, Great Creation, and all the other warriors who tried or suggested we stop the houngan, were right all along. Stopping the Mangoni ritual drums would be enough to stop the houngan and his demon of death. But it was a direct approach. There is another way; an indirect way."

"What do you mean?"

"The houngan masked our living heartbeats with his ritual drums. Well … we will do something similar. We will mask his entire ritual. We can weaken his influence by focusing on something else. The houngan's smell of death can remain, but we do not have to smell it. The ritual drums can continue. We do not have to hear them. We can forget that the Mangoni houngan is even in our valley if our minds are preoccupied with something else."

"I like the sound of this already, Great Creation," Kharaambi said. "What do you have in mind?"

"We can cover his smell of death with our greatest and most inspiring smells. We can drown out his ritual drums with our own irresistible noises of pleasure. And we can do all of this easier than you might imagine. We do it all the time."

"Of course; in a Celebration of Life!" Kharaambi finally understood what Kon-Shambique had in mind.

"Yes. That is our ritual. We know it well. It is the noisiest, most sociable time of the Aukmondi day. It has all the ritual elements we need; family togetherness, the powerful smell of good food cooking, singing, laughter, music, dancing, all the simple pleasures of togetherness that are often remembered for a lifetime."

"Great Creation." Ameh gave Kon-Shambique a questionable look. "You figured all this out just by putting your hands over the ears of the Sacred Woman Mitma?"

"It was the beginning, Mfalme. The moment the Sacred Woman stopped hearing the Mangoni ritual drums, there were visible signs of life in her body again. I am confident that if we can celebrate life as we know how, we can push the houngan's influences of death completely from our minds."

"It is worth a try. So, when do we start?"

"We must start as soon as possible," said Kon-Shambique. "If we do nothing, our people could still die. If the uninspired fail to receive nourishment from the pleasures of life, then death's appeal grows."

"But… a Celebration of Life? At this hour?" Adaulah tried to remember a celebration starting before sunset. He could not. "Sacred Mother, it is not even midday yet! We have never done this before!"

"The sooner we get started, the sooner we will wake the dead." Kharaambi stood up and looked around at all the family groups. "We need to get everyone down into the celebration area."

Ameh looked at the Blue Warrior Ukwatzi and smiled at the ironic timeliness. "Now, Great Creation. Employ your warriors. Usher the people from the pasture."

"With pleasure, Mfalme." The Blue Warrior left at once to gather his regiment and give them new orders.

Kharaambi turned to Adaulah. She kneeled at his side. "And you, Little Creation, I need you to perform another of the duties of the Mfalme. Remember how you ran to reach Nagorda Peak and Mfalme Abul-Gwan?"

"Yes. I remember."

"You must run like that again. I need you to run ahead of us to the Royal Kraal. Take your position on the royal dais. And, like your father does every evening, I need you to announce the start of today's Celebration of Life officially."

"I can do that?" Adaulah asked.

"Well, I would do it," Ameh began teasingly, "but I cannot run as fast as you. Sure, you can do it."

Adaulah turned to leave but hesitated. "I will announce the start. But suppose people do not believe me? At this hour, they will think I am only playing. Will the people celebrate because I ask them to?"

"Adaulah," Ameh spoke with a touch of sternness in his voice. "As long as Ramuza lay upon his burial litter, you are not asking them to do anything. You are telling them. You are Mfalme."

Adaulah smiled. He turned and walked toward the exit of the cattle pasture. His steps quickly developed into a strong run.

59

WARNING SIGNS

By late morning, the warriors Wema and Nienko had reached the grassy plains of the northern Serengeti, southwest of the Mara Triangle. Even with constant walking across the open and gently rolling savanna, they had fallen behind in their planned schedule to reach the returning farmers.

"Let us pick up our pace, my friend," Wema said. He glanced at his shadow to judge the time. The sun was almost directly overhead, and his shadow only covered the area beneath his feet. "If we do not reach the returning farmers before nightfall and before they cross the Mara, Mflame Ameh Jobabwe may be very upset with us."

The Red Warrior Nienko ran a few steps to catch up with Wema and to walk at his side. It surprised him that the Orange Warrior was showing concerns about their progress so early in their journey. "Wema, Great Creation, do you doubt we will cross the Mara before nightfall?"

"We will make it, even if we must run the rest of the way."

The Red Warrior Nienko knew that the fifty-five-kilometer stretch to the Mara River was a short trek for the two able-bodied warriors. He had no doubts about covering the distance. Nor did the thought of running fifty-five kilometers distress him. He had the energy and stamina to do it. But as time passed, the young warrior focused on a different concern. It was the actual crossing of the great Mara River.

From its swampy source in northern Kenya, the Mara River flowed southward. Persistent rains over the swamps and five strong tributaries, including the Aukmondi River, kept the Mara flowing strong and alive. Once the Mara entered Tanganyika (now called

Tanzania), it meandered westward and emptied into the Great African Lake.

The river's water level changes with the seasons. During the long rains of the summer months and sometimes during the short rains of the winter months, the banks of the Mara would swell. But in between the rains, during the dry seasons, until about late August, sections of the Mara would become shallow.

If things proceeded as planned, Nienko knew that he and the Orange Warrior Wema would cross the Mara, not once, but twice – going to meet the farmers and coming back. That fact seemed to bother him. "Wema, I heard that big, ugly crocodiles infest the Mara. Is that true?"

Wema smiled at Nienko's almost childlike concern. "Maybe 'infest' is not the best way to describe them. Once we reach the Mara, we may see just a few more than we would like."

"A few? Just one is too many."

"One or two crocodiles pose no problem, Great Creation." Wema paused, teasingly adding, "If they are not hungry."

The light humor flew by the young Red Warrior without causing a smile. Nienko's concern still dominated his mind. "Crocodiles are always hungry."

Wema glanced at his traveling companion again. He offered a more serious answer. "This is supposed to be the end of the dry season, my friend. Many sections of the Mara are still shallow. If we cross at the right place, we will see none."

Nienko considered what Wema had just told him. Crossing the Mara at the right time meant crossing during the right season. He knew that the Green Warrior Tushema and Elder Zekke had planned the trip to and from the Kiwane Village for the tail end of the dry season. At that time, the Mara is most suitable for crossing. He looked up and down the savanna. Although he was a young warrior, he had enough experience to see the very same inconsistency that the Green Warrior Tushema had seen on the other side of the Mara.

Nienko shifted the travel pack on his shoulder. He waved his hand across the savanna. "Look at all this, Wema. You call this the tail end of the dry season? It looks unusually green to me."

"I said, it is supposed to be the tail end." Wema reassessed the surrounding area himself. "But you are right. The savanna is too green. It appears the dry season has ended a little early."

"So, what does that mean? Is the Mara River as shallow as it should be?"

"It should not be a concern. The water from the rains in the Maasai Mara region flows from north to south. We can probably expect the flow to be stronger. But the river should be shallow enough for us to cross." Wema looked at Nienko with a slight smile on his face. "You sound as if you have never crossed the Mara before?"

"I have crossed it, once – a long time ago. I was but a child. I was traveling with my parents. I do not recall the reason we were traveling. But I do remember making the crossing." Nienko's smile broadened at the pleasant childhood memory. "It was not so bad. It was fun."

"I cannot guarantee any fun. But, if we cross it at the right place, it will be uneventful."

Nienko looked ahead. Because of the beautiful panorama and his warrior training, he looked from left to right, from horizon to horizon. To his right, in the distance, he saw three hyenas moving about in a nervous scuttle. Their unique cackle seemed to show the urgency in their movements. They surrendered their precious hunting ground to a female elephant and her calf passing through the area. A flock of scavenger birds squawked overhead, waiting to see if the hyenas would abandon anything worthwhile.

To Nienko's left, the crest of a small hill fell away. Beyond the hill, Nienko could see a herd of zebras. With snorts and bellows, the animals grazed in the tall grass. The herd was larger than it should have been, but the young warrior missed this subtle fact. He did not realize that the herd size was abnormal until he saw Wema looking at the herd with a frown of concern.

"What is wrong, Great Creation?"

Wema gestured toward the herd. "That should not be."

"What should not be?"

"A herd that size is not due through this area for, perhaps, another half-cycle of the moon."

Nienko studied the herd again. The herd was large, but the density was thin. To him, it looked like a typical migrating herd. It stretched southward as far as Nienko could see. "The size of the herd is unusual? Has the dry season ended early, as you suspected?"

"I must surrender to what Mother Nature seems to say here. From harvest to harvest, a short dry season may happen occasionally. This may be one of those times. If so, it gives us another reason to quicken our pace. If we must warn the farmers to stay away from the valley, they cannot be caught on this side of the Mara."

Wema's strides became stronger as he descended the other side of the hill and headed out toward the herd.

Nienko hesitated before falling into step behind Wema. He glanced out across the herd. "Wema, is this safe?"

Wema looked back and smiled at Nienko's apprehension. "No. It is not safe. But we are warriors with a very important mission. You will not let a herd of grazing zebras stop you. Will you?"

"No." Nienko adjusted his backpack. He ran a few steps to catch up with Wema again. "Suppose they stop grazing? Suppose they start moving again?"

"Let us hope that does not happen." The Orange Warrior studied the herd. "We will proceed with a little caution. If the zebras move, they will probably move northward. We can easily pass through the herd if it does not move too fast."

Nienko looked ahead again, wondering if he and Wema could circumvent the herd by passing through it. He wondered what would happen if the herd became startled. The warriors would find themselves trapped, unable to do anything about it. Safety would be a major concern until they reached the other side of the herd. He focused his eyes on the horizon. "How much farther before we reach the Mara?"

"We still have a way to go, my friend." Wema nodded toward another hill directly ahead. "I can give you a better estimate once we reach the top of that hill."

The thin density of the herd allowed the two warriors to walk through the grazing animals without difficulty. They walked in silence until they reached the hilltop. The hill was a small escarpment that gave way to another grassy plain. They could see across the plain from their vantage point on the hill. The plain stretched ahead to the horizon. It was an inspiring view. It was a sea of golden and green grasses, with small patches of bushes, acacia, and baobab trees.

Scattered over most of the area were more zebra herds. For both of the warriors, it was an unexpected sight. Many of these fragmented herds were denser than the two warriors had just passed. These herds also included gatherings of wildebeests, gazelles, and other ungulates. It was another sign that the dry season was over, and the great migration was progressing faster than normal.

"I wonder if the Green Warrior Tushema knows about this," Nienko said as he studied the herds.

"I hope so."

"These herds must cross the Mara, just like us, Wema. It is not safe for us, and it is especially not safe for the returning farmers. There are just too many of them. If I know the Green Warrior Tushema, he will never risk bringing the farmers through this."

"If he knows."

"I am sure Tushema has seen warning signs."

"Just in case he has not, it is up to us to warn him." Wema turned to leave the escarpment. He moved with added urgency in his steps. "Come. We have to hurry."

Nienko fell into step behind the Orange Warrior. The two quickly found a sloping pathway that led down onto the grassy plain about fifteen meters below the escarpment. Their strong pace developed into a steady run across the grass. Their course meandered somewhat, to snake through the openings between the herds of zebras, wildebeests, and gazelles.

With most of their energy channeled into their steady pace, the two warriors did not speak again for another seven kilometers.

60

SOMETHING WE CAN DANCE TO

From the Pogobi kraal, Adaulah rapidly descended the north slope. He ran like a cheetah in pursuit of its prey. Unlike his unconventional route up the slope, Adaulah took the southern half of the Pahoma Pathway through the intermittent trees and clearings. It was unobstructed, downhill, and much faster.

Adaulah's chest pumped harder than ever when he finally entered the Royal Kraal. He had run so hard that he gasped for air. But thanks to his youthfulness, he recovered quickly. Despite the brisk and determined strut across the celebration area, his labored breathing had died away long before he was halfway across the area.

Adaulah drew the attention of all who saw him. That trek across the celebration area and the fact that he still wore the garments of a Black Warrior drew most of the people. By the time Adaulah reached the royal dais, several moments later, he had attracted a huge and curious crowd behind him.

Adaulah stepped up onto the royal dais. He turned and stood in front of Ramuza's chieftain's stool. The little Mfalme watched the crowd as it continued to grow before him. His ability to draw so many people, with his presence alone, surprised him. He smiled at the amazing phenomenon. He waited for the crowd to settle before he spoke.

"I just came from the Pogobi kraal," he began. "By now, most of you have probably heard that the dead among us are not truly dead yet. But we have to wake them up before it is too late. They will still die if we do not wake them. I bring word from the Favored Tribesman. He believes that one of the best ways to wake them is for us to celebrate. We have to celebrate, right now. So, for this reason, as Mfalme, I am officially announcing the start of today's Celebration of Life. Please. Let the Celebration begin!"

There was a rumble of voices as the crowd looked at each other and voiced their confusion. Except for a wave of interpersonal communication, no one made any effort to celebrate. The rumble of voices settled as the people looked toward Adaulah again. They stared at him, not sure how to respond.

"You may sing and dance." Adaulah waved his arms as if to urge them into action. "Go ahead. It is alright. You can start now."

"Adaulah," a single voice in the center of the crowd addressed the Little Mfalme. "So much has happened. You must understand. Under the circumstances, we are in no mood to celebrate."

"Yes," another voice yelled out. "And no one has made any preparations. We are not ready to celebrate."

"Then get into the mood to celebrate." Quazzi's voice shattered the resistance. The Brown Warrior forced his way through the crowd. He emerged and took a position before Adaulah and the royal dais. He turned to face the crowd. "If you are not ready to celebrate, prepare yourself as you go."

Quazzi had spent most of yesterday evening and the entire night before helping the Elka Army prepare the huge grave site in the pasture of the Pogobi kraal. He had done some of the digging and hauling dirt himself. He was spiritually and physically tired. He intended to get some rest, freshen up, and return to the Pogobi kraal in time for the burial rituals of Mfalme Ncobba and the Principal Mate.

Quazzi had stepped off the north bank pathway only a short while ago on his way back to the Pogobi kraal. He saw Adaulah racing down the Pahoma Pathway toward him. The very unusual sight had made the Foremost Lieutenant stop. When Adaulah gave him only a glance, continued down the pathway, and turned onto the north bank pathway, Quazzi called out to him.

"Adaulah! Wait! Where are you going so fast?"

"To the Royal Kraal, Great Creation," Adaulah never stopped running. He provided Quazzi with an explanation over his shoulder as he continued to run. "Kon-Shambique thinks he knows how to wake the dead."

This enticing bit of information made Quazzi hesitate for only a moment. With one thoughtful glance up the north slope, he aborted his intent to return to the Pogobi kraal. The burial of his Mfalme and Principal Mate was important, but the resurrection of the dead offered the potential to be more important. Quazzi turned and ran back along the north bank pathway toward the Royal Kraal, too.

Quazzi's progress along the pathway was slower than that of Adaulah's. Quazzi wanted to ask Adaulah several questions. But by the time Quazzi had decided to follow the Little Creation, Adaulah had already put a substantial distance between them. It wasn't until after Quazzi made his way across the celebration area and through the crowd that he caught sight of Adaulah again.

Quazzi had worked his way through the crowd to the front of the royal dais in time to hear most of Adaulah's announcement. Quazzi felt spiritually and physically rejuvenated by the details of what he heard. Even that energetic run along the north bank pathway to the Royal Kraal did not faze him.

Quazzi stood, facing the crowd of people. He tried to think of a way to motivate them quickly. He looked to his right and saw the huge Bendabe *Ngoma* drums sitting idly in front of Kharaambi's hut. An impulsive thought made him glance behind him at Adaulah. With a wild idea in mind, he started toward the drums.

Adaulah could tell what the Brown Warrior intended. "Great Creation, do you know how to play such huge drums?"

Quazzi shrugged. "I am no expert, Little Creation. But I think I can play something worth listening to."

"Something worth listening to? Great Creation, everyone needs to do more. They need to celebrate. They need to dance and sing."

"These are just drums, Adaulah." Quazzi extracted the batons from the side of the drums. "How difficult can it be?"

Standing at the edge of the crowd was the Orange Warrior Lujaami Dokae. Lujaami, who usually patrolled the Royal Kraal, was a warrior in the regiment of the Blue Warrior Obe Bendabe.

When he heard Quazzi's comment, he stepped forward to correct the Brown Warrior, and if for nothing else, to defend the honor of his regimental commander. "Great Creation, with all due respect, please. These are not just drums."

"They are not? Then, what are they … besides huge?"

"They are Bendabe *Ngoma* drums." Lujaami handed his shield and spear to a Young Creation standing beside him. He approached Quazzi and asked for the batons. "May I?"

Quazzi recognized Lujaami as one of Obe Bendabe's former trainees. And like the Blue Warrior, Lujaami had the talent and skills to beat the drums well. Quazzi surrendered the batons to him. "Alright, Young Warrior, give us something we can dance to."

Lujaami took the batons. He stood behind the drums and took a deep breath. Then he began. The resonant sound of the huge drums made Lujaami's first few beats thunder throughout the area. Lujaami's talent followed through with a moving and possessive rhythm that sent chills down everyone who heard it.

Lujaami's drumbeat moved Quazzi. The Brown Warrior smiled. He clapped his hands to the beat of the drums. "Good! Good! You might as well be dead if you cannot feel that." He moved toward the crowd. He waved his arms just as Adaulah had done earlier. "Sing! Dance! Summon the rest of your families; even those lying upon their burial litters. Let us all celebrate! We know how. Let us do it!"

A small group of Young Creations standing in the center of the crowd looked at each other. Without a word, they stomped their feet in unison. At first, they showed little enthusiasm. But once their steps echoed the beat of the drums, the excitement and the enthusiasm took hold, grew, and spread to others.

Quazzi clapped his hands again to cheer them on.

Adaulah smiled. He was grateful for the Brown Warrior's help. He called out to him. "Quazzi!"

Quazzi turned, still clapping his hands.

Adaulah had to yell over the rumble and rhythm of the huge Bendabe *Ngoma* drums. "Thank you, Great Creation!"

"My pleasure, Little Mfalme!"

— **61** —

DRUMS OF THE FORBIDDEN DANCE

A steady line of people, many families in a grand procession, stretched from the Pogobi kraal westward through a small wooded area. They moved through the Gongeri Junction and down the north slope incline along the Pahoma Pathway's southern half. This trek represented only half of the journey to the Royal Kraal. At the bottom of the slope, the procession of people turned right onto the north bank pathway. The grand procession walked another three kilometers parallel with the Aukmondi River. At the western end of the pathway, about one kilometer past the Katola Garden, the procession took a small trail that branched. It led up to the entrance of the Royal Kraal.

The families that walked along these pathways and trails were grateful that they were not burying their loved ones now. Inspired by the Favored Tribesman's assumption, each family group set aside its oppressive sadness. They gathered up their fallen loved ones and all the precious items they intended to bury with them. The families quickly filed from the Pogobi kraal at regular intervals. They followed the pathways and trails that would take them to the Royal Kraal. Once there, they hoped one of the greatest Celebrations of Life ever held would completely drown out the Mangoni houngan's ritual of death.

There was no particular order of families. Each family group left the Pogobi kraal as soon as they gathered and were ready to leave. But they allowed the Royal Family to lead the way out of respect. The Sacred Women Olabisi, Kharaambi, and all the Ncobba daughters escorted the burial litters of the Mfalme and his Principal Mate. They were the core of the largest family group in this long procession. As usual, their entourage of guards and aides surrounded them. Many of them carried gifts and trinkets that were selected to be buried with the bodies of Ramuza and Rwuva. Just under two hours after leaving the Pogobi pasture, the Royal Family group led the way into the Royal Kraal.

Not far behind the Royal Family, a few warriors from the rest of the Bendabe Regiment carried the litter of the Red Warrior Gengu. Gengu's father and mother, the Great Creation Gudwando and the Sacred Woman Zawadi, led the way. Gudwando still tightly embraced his mate. Neither of them talked. Motivated by the hope of Gengu's resurrection, Gudwando showed livelier expressions on his face, and Zawadi no longer cried.

The family group of the Sacred Woman Mitma came next. Mitma's oldest grandson, the Great Creation Busham, led this group. Before the group left the Pogobi kraal, Busham had tried to wake his grandmother by duplicating the pragmatic attempt used by the Favored Tribesman. Over and over, Busham placed his hands over his grandmother's ears. Each attempt was unsuccessful.

Busham became discouraged and frustrated. He suspected that the Favored Tribesman had made a hasty assumption. Other family members finally had to stop Busham from making any more attempts before his damaged spirit affected the rest of them. With reluctance, Busham quit trying but vowed to resume his efforts once the family reached the Royal Kraal.

The family group of the Young Creation Robuti walked a few meters behind Mitma's family. It was a good thing that Robuti belonged to a large family. Some of Robuti's metal sculptures lay on his burial litter beside his small body. It took several of his brothers, uncles, and his father to carry the heavy litter.

Behind Robuti's family, the White Warrior Upenda and several more warriors from the fragmented Bendabe Regiment carried the burial litter of the Sacred Woman Tongda. Tongda's father and aunt, the Great Creation Benwe and the Sacred Woman Oraka, walked in front of the litter. Despite the hope of Tongda's resurrection in the Royal Kraal, Benwe and Oraka still had not recovered enough to talk yet. They walked arm in arm as they listened to Kon-Shambique, who walked beside them offering emotional support. Kon-Shambique looked upon Tongda's family as his own. He walked with them because he felt this was where he belonged. And whatever he was saying to Benwe and Oraka, he successfully produced a smile or two on their faces.

About a quarter of a kilometer behind Tongda's family walked the second largest group in this procession. It included the families of the Blue Warriors, Obe Bendabe, and Dabete Ehkili. Since these warriors and their families were such close friends, their respective family groups walked together. The burial litter of the two fallen warriors, one behind the other, centered this double-family group.

Of all the family groups that walked the pathway toward the Royal Kraal, this huge group was one of the quietest and most reserved. Like everyone else, this group did not seem affected by the hopeful possibility of resurrections. The group's attitude was different. It was not because the people of the group had doubts about Kon-Shambique's beliefs or convictions. It was not because both Blue Warriors of the group had died, or because twenty-five to thirty warriors of the Bendabe regiment died in that sacrifice to save Adaulah. No. Something else directly affected the attitude of this group.

The Royal Warrior Nionu led the group along the north bank pathway. He walked alone. He seemed absorbed in thought as he stared at the ground. The usually whimsical and talkative Nionu had become obsessed with avenging his Mfalme, his Blue Warriors, and everyone else who had fallen victim to the demon of death. He had become so preoccupied that he seemed to be a different person.

Nionu's dedication to his warriors was still clear. Since their deaths, when he was not in quiet seclusion, he stayed near the bodies of his warriors. He did whatever he could to support the warriors' families and friends. But he had become so self-absorbed that he said very little to anyone. As a result, everyone around him reciprocated. Nionu's behavior had set the mood for everyone around him.

All of that changed after the family groups of Obe and Dabete continued along the north bank pathway and passed the Katola

Garden. As the scents of the aromatic wildflowers died away, the family groups experienced another torrent of sensations.

The Daily Celebration of Life in the Royal Kraal was going strong. Stimulating smells of cooked foods and the sounds of drum-based music traveled beyond the boundary of the Royal Kraal, 850 meters away, toward the approaching family groups. The smells and the sounds grew stronger and stronger as the family groups drew closer and closer.

In the Royal Kraal, the Orange Warrior Lujaami, as instructed by Quazzi, continued to beat the huge Bendabe *Ngoma* drums. Since the celebration started, Lujaami pounded out one attractive rhythm after another. He took only a few short intervals of rest. By midday, Lujaami had established a standard series of beautiful rhythms. He rotated through the series. Each time he took position behind the drums, all the other drummers and musicians followed his lead.

During one of his drum rotations, Lujaami broke from his established rhythm series. He pounded a rhythm he had learned from the Blue Warrior Obe Bendabe himself. Lujaami had learned the rhythm well. To honor his immediate commander and his mentor, Lujaami pounded out the rhythm with more heart and passion than Obe Bendabe would have ever expected.

The rhythm of the huge Bendabe *Ngoma* drums reverberated throughout the celebration area. The gripping vibrations radiated beyond the boundaries of the Royal Kraal and met the approaching family groups walking along the north bank pathway. Even as the Blue Warrior Obe Bendable lay upon his burial litter, the vibrations penetrated the shell of death around him. They reached deep into the recesses of Obe's mind.

In the darkness of his mind, the Blue Warrior Obe Bendabe felt spiritually touched. He felt the magic of something wonderful, something he had created. Filled with a surging pride, Obe could no longer feel the tight grip of the houngan's dark ritual. His mind pushed the darkness aside. Like the Sacred Woman Mitma, Obe's finger twitched. Obe forced his eyes open. He blinked twice. Upon his burial litter, the semiconscious Blue Warrior rose from his litter to sit erect.

The warriors who carried Obe's burial litter felt the warrior's movements. The unexpected movements startled them. They lost their grip on the litter and fumbled to keep the balance. The litter tilted, and Obe slid off the side. A few people who walked nearby saw the sudden and shocking developments. Some moved back in a panic. A few rushed to help. But all showed signs of total confusion.

With the ingrained skill of an experienced warrior, Obe Bendabe leaped from the litter before he hit the ground. Like a cat, the tall warrior landed on his feet. Obe looked around, ready to use his defensive skills to the fullest. His last clear memories were fiery strips of a royal cloak raining down upon him just before the demon of death placed its bony hand on his shoulder. Obe was prepared to defend himself. But then, he noticed family members gathering around him. He dropped his defensive stance as familiar embraces quickly moved in, pushing those lingering chaotic memories from his mind.

Obe relaxed. He dismissed the last of his confusion and surrendered to the warm embraces. He was surrounded by his mate, son, three daughters, and mother. Obe returned his family's affections with his embraces. He did not release them for several long moments until he saw the Royal Warrior Nionu, standing off to the side, staring back at him.

Obe eased himself free and approached his commander. "Nionu, Great Creation, we thought … we thought you were dead."

"I could say the same about you."

"What happened?"

"You tell me. Great Creation, I only ran from death. You … you died. I must hear your story first." The solemn expression on Nionu's face slowly transformed to an appreciative smile. He shifted his huge royal shield to his other arm and embraced his friend. "Welcome back, Great Creation."

Obe returned the embrace, but then he stepped back. "Welcome back? What do you mean I died? I did not die."

"What do you remember?"

Obe quickly reviews his last memories again. "I remember the Blue Warrior Dabete and I failed to stop the houngan. We did not expect the demon to show up so soon. I am sorry."

Nionu waved his hand to dismiss Obe's apology. "I may be to blame for that. I could not hold its interest long enough."

"It charged us before we could subdue the houngan. The next thing I remember was the irresistible pull of that *Ngoma* drum rhythm. That rhythm and those special drums are my creations, for which I am very proud." At this point, the Blue Warrior Obe saw his friend, still lying upon his burial litter. "Dabete? Great Sacred Spirit!" He rushed over and knelt beside the litter. "He did not survive the demon?"

"He did, Great Creation," the Sacred Woman Nanuufe, Obe's mate, came over and kneeled at his side. She embraced her mate one more time. "He survived, just as you did."

Obe Bendabe looked down at Dabete. "I do not understand. He is … he is dead."

"No." Nanuufe shook her head. "The Blue Warrior is not dead. The Favored Tribesman has discovered that no one touched by the houngan's demon of death has died … yet. He believes we can resurrect those touched by the demon."

"Great Sacred Spirit! Can this be true?"

Nanuufe smiled. "It is true. You are proof of it, Great Creation. The demon touched you, too. For a while, you lay upon your burial litter. But here you are."

Again, Obe studied the face of his friend. He put his hand on Dabete's shoulder as if to disprove what his eyes were telling him. His touch offered no answers. He looked up at his mate. "Sacred Woman, why have I returned from the dead and Dabete has not?"

"We are not sure. I can offer only a partial explanation, Great Creation." Nanuufe gently placed her hand on Dabete's chest, too. "The Favored Tribesman says that the houngan's ritual was powerful enough to make those touched by the demon believe that they were dead. The constant beat of the houngan's ritual drums and the mock odor of death have reinforced that belief. Because of the sound of drums coming from the celebration area, the houngan's ritual drums cannot be heard. And in this valley area, we no longer smell the odor of death. It has thinned to nothing."

Obe raised his head to sniff the air. Instead of the pungent smell of death, the smell of charred wood from the bonfires in the celebration area filled the air. The smell carried a mixture of pleasurable aromas of various cooking foods. He could not sense the mock smell of death. And as Nanuufe explained, he did not hear the boom-boom of the houngan's ritual drums either. He refocused on the drum rhythm emanating from the celebration area. That rhythm and those drums had pulled him from the depths of darkness. As he listened, his focus brought forth a pleasant revelation. He smiled.

"Is that the Orange Warrior Lujaami that I hear?"

Nanuufe listened for a moment. She smiled too. "There is no doubt. He honors you, Great Creation, with that rhythm. His unique cadence is unmistakable."

The smile on Obe Bendabe's face was only a hint of the pride he continued to feel. But he shook his head. "I am not so sure he honors me, Sacred Woman. Do you not recall what that rhythm gave birth to?"

"Yes, I do." Nanuufe looked down at Dabete. "It is the rhythm that gave birth to the dance created by the Blue Warrior here."

"Yes, the very dance that the Sacred Woman Rwuva has forbidden."

"But no one violates the elder's decree, Great Creation. We hear only the drums. No one is dancing the forbidden dance."

"No. They are not," Nionu said. He stood over Obe and Nanuufe, thinking. The exchange between Obe and Nanuufe had planted a seed in Nionu's mind. He stepped away as if to focus on his thoughts. "Not yet anyway."

Obe and everyone who heard Nionu's comment looked up at him. They knew the Royal Warrior well. They knew those words were a prelude to something unprecedented. Everyone waited for Nionu to say more.

Nionu stood for a moment before coming to a decision. He turned to face Obe again. "Tell me. Whose bright idea was it to wake the dead with the drum rhythm of the forbidden dance?"

Obe stood up to face his commander. "I believe the drum rhythm is unintentional, Great Creation. The Orange Warrior Lujaami is behind the drums. He may not be aware of what he is doing. I will send word ahead to stop him."

"No, Great Creation. Let the Orange Warrior continue." Nionu took a moment to listen to the inspiring rhythm again. He smiled. "Those drums and rhythm represent something I need."

Nionu recalled his horrendous flight from the demon in the darkness of the Angrenni Forest. During that flight, Nionu knew he had angered and frustrated the demon twice. Nionu noticed an emotional reaction when he teased the demon's progress after it came to that huge fallen log that blocked its way. Nionu could see pure rage when the demon pulled the royal cloak from the river, only to learn that Nionu was not wearing it. Each time, Nionu could see the demon vulnerable to assaults of frustration. For a day and a half, Nionu seemed obsessed with repeating similar assaults. He wanted to push the demon over the edge, to its breaking point. The effort was part of Nionu's vow to become the demon's worst enemy.

Nionu stepped closer to Obe. "You are the one who taught that rhythm to the Orange Warrior Lujaami?"

"Yes."

"Then, when we get to the Royal Kraal, I want you to join him. I want you to double the sound of those drums."

"Join him? To what end?"

"Is it not obvious? Look at you. You are proof that the Favored Tribesman is right. The spirit heard in the rhythm of those drums brought you back to life. It is what we need to wake the dead."

"Nionu, it pleases me that others can hear the spirit I intended in that drum rhythm. But others may not hear it as I do. It may not mean the same to others."

"I disagree, Great Creation. I am sure you created that rhythm to inspire others. You have done that successfully." Nionu paused a moment to consider taking his next step. "I suggest that we take this whole thing to the limit. Why do we not add the dance that goes with that rhythm?"

"But Nionu, Great Creation," Obe protested, "we cannot do that."

"Says who?"

"The Sacred Woman Rwuva. The dance is forbidden!"

"Well… it used to be forbidden. The Sacred Woman Rwuva … does not know it yet."

"Nionu!" Obe knew his commander well. He spoke his name as if it were a word of warning. He knew Nionu's relentless drive was about to take hold and not let go.

Nionu looked into Obe's eyes. "Great Creation, do I have your support?"

"You do. But you must know, we will lose our cloaks over this."

"Do not concern yourself with that. I have lost my cloak once or twice before." Nionu smiled. He adjusted the fresh, new replacement cloak on his shoulder. "If it is yours, you will get it back. I promise. Besides, I will take full responsibility."

Obe sighed. "So be it. What is your plan?"

"I understand that most dancers are from Dabete's regiment."

"Yes, Great Creation, some warriors and their mates."

"Then, get word to them. Tell them, they have permission to perform."

Obe hesitated. He looked toward the Blue Warrior Dabete, still upon his burial litter. He faced Nionu again to express a concern.

"Nionu, Great Creation, I am the Blue Warrior's closest friend. I know him and must speak in his defense. I have no doubt. Dabete will object to the misuse of his warriors. If he stood before you now, he would take offense."

"I am his friend too. And I think I know him well enough. Yes. He probably will object. But, I am also his commander. I need his warriors, Obe."

Obe sighed. He glanced at the surrounding people, looking for the dancers of Dabete's regiment. He wondered if any of them would ignore the decree of a tribal elder, knowing that Dabete might object. Obe knew that Dabete also held very high regard and respect for Nionu. This was the only reason Obe did not protest anymore.

"Most are here," Obe said. "A few may be up in the Motobo kraal. Those who are here must return to the kraal to prepare themselves. It may take a while."

"No matter, make it so. Summon them all to the Royal Kraal as soon as possible."

As Nionu and Obe talked, they stood over the body of the Blue Warrior Dabete upon his burial litter. Unknown to them, their words were audible to the Blue Warrior. When Dabete heard that some of his warriors and their mates were about to violate an elder's decree, Dabete took very strong offense. He had to say something. He struggled to speak. As hard as he tried, his body would not respond.

From beneath a heavy darkness, the Blue Warrior fought to remove an unrecognizable, oppressive mass that pressed against his will to see, move, and speak. To him, it was a very physical, all-or-nothing battle against an untouchable omnipresence. To those who stood over his body, it manifested as an almost inaudible moan and a gentle tremor in his hand.

The Royal Warrior Nionu heard Dabete's moan. He looked down just in time to see the tremor in the Blue Warrior's hand. Nionu threw his spear and shield aside. He kneeled and took Dabete's head in his hands. "Dabete! Dabete, Great Creation! Wake up! Can you hear me? Wake up!"

The touch of Nionu's hands against his face was all the Dabete needed to link with the help he needed and push the dark battle into his favor. Suddenly, he could easily distinguish between the darkness and the consciousness he had known all his life. He opened his eyes and took a deep, relaxing breath. He rolled over and struggled to stand.

Dabete's family descended upon him. Dabete's father and three brothers had carried Dabete's burial litter. In their joy, they lifted Dabete from the ground. They tossed him several times before planting Dabete on his feet. The three brothers surrendered Dabete to the father for a series of serious, heartfelt embraces.

"My son," Dabete's father began, "because of Kon-Shambique's wonderful discovery, I did not get a chance to whisper my wishes to our ancestors into your ear. I am ashamed to say that I would have asked them to find it in their hearts to send you back when the moment came."

"Then, it seems, our ancestors anticipated your intention, Great Creation."

"The Supreme Spirit knows that you are a warrior whose service among the living is incomplete. You have much more to do. She has allowed you to do it."

"I hope to show my gratitude to my ancestors and the Supreme Spirit by doing the right thing." Dabete turned to Nionu. There was a serious, confrontational look on Dabete's face. "Great Creation, what you intend to do with my warriors and their mates is wrong."

Nionu reacted with only a speechless stare at Dabete. He stepped closer to the Blue Warrior and frowned. "Do I have your support?"

Dabete returned Nionu's stare. "Do you want to do this?"

Nionu's frown deepened. It was not because Dabete seemed to show resistance. Nionu showed surprise at something else. "You could hear what we said?"

"Only parts of it, here and there. I could hear some of the words. I did not seem to regain control of my consciousness until I heard you and the Blue Warrior conspiring to defy the decree by the Sacred Woman Rwuva. You intended to use my warriors and their mates. I could not lie there and allow that to happen. I had to say something."

"What are you saying, Great Creation? Do you object?"

Dabete allowed a smile to melt away the serious expression on his face. "Please allow me to summon my own warriors and dancers to the Royal Kraal."

Nionu gave both of his Blue Warriors a prideful look and smiled. "So be it. Let us proceed into the Royal Kraal and wake the dead. I am eager to see old bone-face's reaction."

62

CONSIDER THE CONSEQUENCES

When the Favored Tribesman Kon-Shambique walked through the entrance of the Royal Kraal, he found the huge celebration area filled with people. So overwhelmed by what he saw, he stepped aside from Tongda's family group. He had to experience the initial impact of this crowd for just a while longer. He stopped and stood for a moment in awe of the large crowd. Everywhere that he looked, he saw people already fully absorbed in various events in support of today's most unusual and special Daily Celebration of Life.

The royal dais and the four huts of the Ncobbas sat recessed in the back of the kraal. Normally, across the celebration area, Kon-Shambique could barely see the canopy of the royal dais and the huts. But now, people have completely blocked Kon-Shambique's view from left to right. He could only see a dozen meters in any direction. Kon-Shambique could not recall seeing so many people in the area.

Throughout the area and around the campfires and several raging bonfires, Kon-Shambique saw countless groups of people talking, laughing, feasting, playing, singing, and dancing. The noise level emanating from each group was high and varied, depending on which way he turned or where he focused his attention.

For example, Kon-Shambique saw a small group of Boisterous Young Creations in the northwest corner of the kraal. They drew attention to themselves as they formed a huge circle. In a series of jumps and loud, thundering stomps, they stepped in unison with the Bendabe *Ngoma* drums that vibrated from across the celebration area. The Young Creations continued until three of them lost their coordination and fell to the ground, laughing. Kon-Shambique enjoyed their impromptu performance in spite of the chaotic end. Their laughter and joy seemed to be all that mattered.

On the opposite side of the kraal, a group of elderly women caught the Favored Tribesman's attention. It amazed Kon-Shambique to see how these highly respected women played like children. They had formed a line that weaved around crowds of cheering and chanting bystanders. They shuffled their feet, bobbed their heads, and clapped their hands in unison with the rhythm of bush harps, which complemented the *Ngoma* drums. Each one of the elderly women swiveled her hips, showing a personal pride in just how flexible and nimble her mature body was.

A small group of young girls, each with a hosha rattle or a Djembe drum in her hand, skipped directly in front of Kon-Shambique. Their chaotic movement showed their dancing inexperience. They danced as individuals with arms waving and feet kicking in every direction. Still, they shook their rattles or tapped their drums in unison with the *Ngoma* drum rhythm. Kon-Shambique had to move out of the way quickly. They seemed completely oblivious to his presence as a couple of the young girls skipped directly across his feet, stepping on his toes.

Kon-Shambique found it fascinating that each group had picked up the spirited rhythm of the Bendabe *Ngoma* drums. The groups used the rhythm as if it supported their performance alone. Each group seemed to know they were unquestionably the center of all attention. All of it was encouraging. Kon-Shambique smiled and nodded his head with approval.

The Favored Tribesman would have stood there longer, watching the people, but a small crowd of people suddenly surrounded him just moments after he entered the Royal Kraal. Kon-Shambique suddenly found himself the center of attention. It turned out that, despite the high spirits, there were several lingering concerns on the minds of most of the people who saw him. And only the Favored Tribesman could answer those concerns.

"Great Creation! Great Creation!" A Young Creation shouted as he rushed toward Kon-Shambique. "How soon will the resurrections occur? You said the people would rise from the dead if we celebrated! Do we have to do anything special? Is there some ritual you must perform first?"

Kon-Shambique struggled to keep his footing as the crowd of people swallowed him. He tried to answer the initial questions. The pushes and shoves prevented him from getting a single word out. The level of noise made it almost impossible to hear his own voice.

"Kon-Shambique, are you sure about this?" Someone else shouted. "The Mfalme, his Principal Mate, and the Sacred Woman Tongda have all arrived here in the Royal Kraal. The Mfalme and his Principal Mate have been here since midday. Yet, they still lie upon their burial litters. We have seen no change."

"Yes," another shouted. "Gengu, Mitma, and the Young Creation Robuti are still dead too, Great Creation! We saw them a little while ago as they passed. They showed no signs of recovery."

Kon-Shambique raised his hands to quiet the skeptical people nearest him and to make more room for himself. He quieted the crowd enough to speak without shouting. He had gained enough maneuvering room to turn in a slow circle as he spoke to the surrounding people. "This is new for me, too. I have no answers to your questions. In all honesty, I cannot say what will happen here. We have to wait and see. Please, exercise a little patience. I suggest continuing to do what you were doing. Enjoy yourselves."

"Enjoy ourselves?" A young woman shouted. "Great Creation, as you can see, we are truly trying. But it is not as easy as it may seem. It is so very strange to see burial litter throughout the celebration area. The litters of the dead are ... they are everywhere and so distracting. Do you really think this will work?"

"Well, I think so, Novana," Kon-Shambique began, suppressing his reservations. "First, we must build on the hope that it will work. We must give it a chance to work, with the greatest expectations. And we have to ..."

Kon-Shambique did not have time to finish what he was saying to Novana. At that instant, the Royal Warrior Nionu, flanked by his Blue Warriors, Obe and Dabete, walked through the entrance of the

Royal Kraal. It was a pivotal moment. When the people saw the Blue Warriors, they cheered loudly. The warriors represented the first positive proof that resurrections were possible. The center of attention shifted from the Favored Tribesman to the warriors.

Obe and Dabete stood together, still dressed in full warrior's gear, from head to toe. Nionu stood behind them, showing pride in his Blue Warriors. The three smiled and waved back at the cheering crowd. People surrounded them, but since the warriors still held their spears and shields, they did not seem to be as approachable as the Favored Tribesman had been.

The Royal Warrior Nionu moved up between his Blue Warriors to step triumphantly into the forefront. He had overheard Novana's question. He addressed the young woman as he walked up and touched Kon-Shambique's shoulder. "Novana, this Creation is called the Favored Tribesman for a reason. He speaks with the heart of the Supreme Spirit. How could you possibly have doubts about what he has suggested here?" Nionu stepped back, bringing his Blue Warriors to the forefront again. He anticipated the crowd's reaction.

Sure enough, cheers from the surrounding crowd erupted again. The noise lasted for several long moments and rose to a deafening level, almost erasing the rhythmic sounds of the Bendabe *Ngoma* drums.

The Favored Tribesman Kon-Shambique was just as excited as everyone to see the Blue Warriors. As the crowd cheered around him, Kon-Shambique rushed toward the Blue Warriors. He huddled them together despite their spears and shields. He ushered them farther into the kraal. Kon-Shambique and the Blue Warriors exchanged words, but no one could hear them. Nionu raised his shield and spear over his head to quiet the crowd and hear the exchange.

"Obe! Dabete! You are alive!" Kon-Shambique was saying. He continued to embrace the warriors by the shoulders. The pleasure of the embrace seemed to dispel his disbelief. The excitement in his voice showed his eagerness to learn firsthand what the first resurrected victims of the Mangoni houngan had experienced. "So, tell me. How do you feel? What was it like?"

"I feel fine, Great Creation." The Blue Warrior Obe shrugged. "It was almost like being asleep – but a dreamless sleep."

"Yes," Dabete agreed. "I knew nothing until shortly before I woke up. Whether we were dead or just asleep, I am truly grateful that you figured out how to wake us, Great Creation."

"Thank you for the compliment, but I cannot accept all the credit here. The Young Prince Adaulah provided the insight we needed. He helped me to focus my attention where it should have been. Otherwise, I would still be lost and confused, too, and you … you would be two meters underground. By the grace of the Supreme Spirit, we seem to be moving in the right direction now."

"We seem to be?" The Royal Warrior Nionu looked at Kon-Shambique. He found it hard to accept what he had just heard. "We seem to be? What do you mean, Great Creation? I can understand the Sacred Woman Novana's doubt. But you? Do I hear doubt in your voice?"

Kon-Shambique gestured toward Novana. "The doubt that the Sacred Woman expressed may be justified, Nionu. I hate to admit it, but there is room for doubt. This crowd will tell you. No other resurrections have occurred. So far, your Blue Warriors are the only two that have broken free of the houngan's magic."

"And that is not proof enough?"

"I am only saying this may not work for everyone. We still have to wait and see."

Nionu looked away, hiding his guilt. "Great Creation, I am afraid we cannot wait and see."

The sharp-minded Kon-Shambique heard the guilt in Nionu's voice. He looked at the Royal Warrior and studied his face. "What have you done?"

Nionu waved his spear toward the people in the celebration area. "Look at all of this. You and Adaulah have started something here. This begins a great victory. This is our 'comeback'. We are about to push this victory through to the end and force 'Old Ugly' out of our valley."

"Which reminds me," the Blue Warrior Obe Bendabe stepped forward. He worked his way between Nionu and Kon-Shambique and out toward the crowd. "Please, excuse me. I must make my way across the celebration area."

"So, where is he going?" Kon-Shambique asked Nionu.

"He is about to show the Orange Warrior Lujaami how to make those *Ngoma* drums come alive."

For the first time since stepping into the Royal Kraal, Kon-Shambique listened to the thunderous Bendabe *Ngoma* drums. He focused on identifying the drums' rhythm. Something very significant about that rhythm lay dormant in the back of Kon-Shambique's mind. With a brief focus on the right place, he made a shocking realization. Kon-Shambique turned to Nionu. "That rhythm … that is the drum rhythm of the forbidden dance!"

"It is impressive. Is it not?"

Kon-Shambique gestured toward the Blue Warrior Obe, who had already disappeared into the crowd. "So … he is serious? You mean, he intends to join those drums?" Kon-Shambique received no answers to his questions. He only got a smug smile. "Great Creation, may I assume you are responsible for playing that drum rhythm?"

"No, I am not," Nionu answered quickly, but changed his mind. "Well, yes. I guess, maybe I am."

"Which is it? Did you somehow ask Lujaami to play that rhythm?"

"No. I am told that he chose it on his own."

"And now the Blue Warrior Obe Bendabe will join him?" Kon-Shambique didn't wait for Nionu to respond. He smiled again. He wondered if he should tell Nionu something he already knew. "As the Royal Warrior of both Obe Bendabe and Lujaami Dokae, you can stop those drums."

"Yes, I know, Great Creation. And that is where I assume full responsibility. I did not stop Lujaami because that rhythm on those drums resurrected my warriors. It worked for them. I think if that rhythm continues, it will work for everyone else. I asked the Blue Warrior Obe to join Lujaami."

Kon-Shambique shrugged. "Maybe the transgression is not as bad as it seems. You have not truly done anything wrong. Only the dance is forbidden, not the drum rhythm."

"Yes, I ah … I know that, too."

Kon-Shambique still heard too much guilt in Nionu's voice. "There is more?"

"Great Creation," Nionu hesitated only a moment before confessing to the rest of his transgression. "I thought I could increase the magical effect of the rhythm by adding the dancers too."

"To perform the forbidden dance?" Kon-Shambique glanced at the Blue Warrior Dabete, who stood at Nionu's side. Dabete seemed to battle his share of guilt.

"Dabete has already sent word to his warriors and their mates," Nionu confessed. "I have authorized them to perform. If all goes as planned, the dancers will arrive here in the Royal Kraal as soon as they can prepare themselves."

During most of the conversation between Nionu and Kon-Shambique, the Favored Tribesman held a gentle, cordial smile. That smile almost disappeared, but Kon-Shambique allowed it to creep back on his face. It was a subconscious effort to take the edge off a very serious situation.

"Nionu, Great Creation, your determination is legendary."

"Is that a compliment? Or, are you telling me I am in a little trouble?"

Kon-Shambique placed his hand on Nionu's shoulder. "The Sacred Woman Rwuva is the Principal Mate. That makes her a tribal elder. If she says the dance is forbidden, then the dance is forbidden. You are not in a little trouble. You, my friend, are in plenty of trouble."

"I, kind of, exceeded my authority. Did I not?" Nionu waited for Kon-Shambique to respond. He grimaced when he saw Kon-Shambique nod his head to say yes.

"You are a Royal Warrior, Nionu. I suppose you did what you thought you needed to do. I am sure you did not decide lightly. But, tell me, did you consider the consequences of your actions?"

Nionu had to think for a moment. He glanced at the Blue Warrior Dabete before answering. "The possibility that my Blue Warriors and I could lose our cloaks came up briefly. We considered such a consequence a minor obstacle."

"And now?"

"And now, even in hindsight," Nionu thought for a moment, "if we are successful, I think it would still be worth it."

"I must commend you on the sacrifice you and your warriors are making."

"But, I am still in trouble. Any advice for me?"

Kon-Shambique considered Nionu's situation. To violate a decree by a tribal elder was very serious. Even if he got word to the dancers to revoke their permission to perform, Nionu would still be in trouble. He had already dishonored the decree. Kon-Shambique reasoned that the Royal Warrior had only one small recourse.

"You could appeal to the Sacred Woman Rwuva."

"Rwuva? But the Sacred Woman still lay upon her burial litter."

"If you are so confident about the Sacred Woman's resurrection, then I recommend that you be right there at her side, if and when that happens. As impossible as it sounds, you must somehow make your appeal to her before the dancers arrive."

Nionu attempted to look toward the royal dais and Rwuva's burial litter. But the huge crowd of people between him and the dais blocked his view. The Royal Warrior handed Dabete his shield and his spear. "Here, Great Creation. Please take care of these for me. I must also make my way through this crowd."

"Great Creation," Dabete took Nionu's belongings in his arms as he nodded toward the crowd. "Do you think you can make your appeal before the dancers get here? Most of them are warriors. They can get to the Motobo kraal, prepare themselves, and return to the Royal Kraal much faster than the average person. I would not be surprised if they arrived before you got halfway across the celebration area."

Nionu removed his headdress and gave it to the Blue Warrior. "Watch me. I ran from death through the thickness and darkness of the Angrenni Forest. I am sure I can work through a crowd in broad daylight." Without another word, Nionu moved quickly toward the royal dais. In an instant, he disappeared into the crowd.

420

— **63** —

YOU DO NOT NEED LUCK

The Royal Warrior Nionu made good progress toward the royal dais despite the crowd of people in the celebration area. As an experienced warrior, he usually had a strategy long before starting on the most difficult tasks. In this case, he followed Tongda's burial litter and her family group. Tongda is the unofficial mate of the Favored Tribesman and one of the many reasons the Aukmondi people held her in such high regard. Nionu knew Tongda's burial litter would be carried as close to the Royal Family as possible. This seemed to hold as the crowd gave the litter and the family group clear passage toward the back of the kraal. Nionu took advantage of the parting crowd.

Nionu had reached about a quarter of the way across the celebration area when the volume of the Bendabe *Ngoma* drums suddenly doubled. The vibrations echoed across the celebration area like rumbling thunder. This could only mean one thing. The Blue Warrior Obe had just joined Lujaami. Together, the two warriors pounded out one of the most inspiring rhythms Nionu had ever heard in his life.

Nionu saw the effect of the fortified rhythm on the surrounding people. Their noise level increased. Everyone seemed to be cheering, dancing, singing, and chanting in unison. They synchronized their tempo with the rhythm of the drums. Nionu felt a chill wash over his body. A good feeling, filled with magic, made him smile.

Nionu doubled his efforts to move ahead. He wanted to be somewhere in the vicinity of the Sacred Woman Rwuva if and when she woke. But then, it suddenly occurred to Nionu that he had no reason to hurry as he weaved between the groups and gatherings of people. Although he used the openings made by Tongda's burial procession and made good progress, he still had a couple more obstacles before him—obstacles he had no chance of overcoming.

In the first place, the Sacred Woman Rwuva still lay upon her burial litter. She must wake up first. And Nionu must wait until that happens. Nionu felt confident she would recover. His Blue Warriors represented proof of the possibility. He also felt confident that Rwuva's recovery had not happened yet. If she had, Nionu would know it almost at once. News of the Principal Mate's resurrection would move through the crowd much faster than he could.

In the second place, once Rwuva woke up, the Royal Warrior knew he would not be among the first to gain her attention. The Sacred Woman has nine daughters, one son, two co-mates, and a host of aides who held much closer privileges than he did. His royal cloak would offer some advantages. But no advantage would move him close enough to be among the first to speak with her.

Finally, what would he say if the Sacred Woman recovered soon and Nionu stood among the first to speak with her? What would be his defense?

"Sacred Woman, I am sorry." Nionu imagined a possible scenario in his head. "I gave the dancers permission to dance the forbidden dance. I know it was wrong of me, for it goes against your decree. But I did it for the tribe. I have proof that the drums and the dancing will resurrect the dead. I hope you understand. I hope you can forgive me."

Nionu also imagined Rwuva's probable response. "I am sorry, Great Creation. I forbid the dance for a reason. Tradition secures our survival. Yes. The dance raised the dead, just as you expected. Your intention is honorable. But I cannot dismiss your transgression."

The Royal Warrior had no urgent wish to hear that. He slowed his pace. At that moment, a small group of people moved in front of Nionu. At first, the Royal Warrior prepared to plow through the group, but he thought better of it. Instead, he stopped and waited. He allowed the group time to move past him and out of his way, at their pace. He greeted some of the people as they walked past them.

The first half of the group continued past him quickly. The last half aborted its progress. It quickly moved back, giving Nionu clear passage. Nionu thought that his royal cloak gave him the usual advantages. He did not think to check behind him. When he did, he learned the reason why the group moved back. He learned the reason for his overall good progress across the celebration.

Nionu saw that, from where he stood and back to the entrance of the Royal Kraal, the crowd of people behind him was rapidly parting. A spacious clearing opened wider and wider. People on both sides of the clearing continued to cheer, sing, and chant in tune with the rhythm of the Bendabe *Ngoma* drums. A line of dancers strutted around the campfires and bonfires down the middle of the clearing. They snaked their way into the kraal with graceful strides like charging warriors. In a short time, Nionu saw that the head of the dancing line had moved across the celebration area and up to only several meters in front of him.

The dancers stepped, shuffled, and hopped as individuals. But they held their flowing movements, struts and strides, in synchrony with the rhythm of the Bendabe *Ngoma* drums. Once in a while, in a well-choreographed performance, all of them would stop their struts and strides simultaneously. In a breathtaking instant, they would suddenly squat with knees wide apart in a shocking but beautiful sight.

In complete awe of the dancers, Nionu turned to face them. He bobbed his head, moving with the rhythm of the drumbeat.

These were the Motobo dancers. The Royal Warrior knew each of these dancers by name. Each of them was a warrior or a warrior's mate from his own Dabete Ehkili Regiment. He had seen each of these dancers dance many times before, but never like this. None of the semi-naked dancers wore the garments of a warrior. With bracelets of feathers on their wrists and ankles, each of them wore colored garments made only of filaments of ropes and woven grass. The garment covered the essentials of their bodies but left little to the imagination. The sleek, muscular trim of each of their bodies showed from head to toe.

Their dance performance did not appear indecent in itself. But it was taboo. For the first time, creations and women danced together in the same group, breaking from long-standing traditions not just within the Aukmondi tribe but across the entire African continent.

In the past, within the Aukmondi tribe, there had been countless dance performances during each Daily Celebration of Life. Some dance performances lasted for a long time, only after days of practicing and elaborate preparations. Other dance performances ended after getting started, the result of a few joyful impromptu steps. They lasted until the performers surrendered to the laughter and overwhelming cheers or jeers of the surrounding crowds.

Throughout the past, dances have always varied in creativity and entertainment content. Sometimes, singing inspires the dances. Sometimes, drums, harps, or rattles support unforgettable dances. Other times, the ruffles, swirls, and flow of colorful costumes give special meaning to the dances. On rare occasions, thundering feet on the ground and the laughter and cheers generated make the dance performances memorable.

In all cases, spectators sang, laughed, cheered, and sometimes jeered. For those spectators, this represented the welcomed but limited extent of participation in the many dances. However, for dancers throughout history, every dance performance included one exclusive gender at a time. This African cultural tradition remained unbroken.

Only Elderly Creations danced together. Only Elderly Women danced together. Only groups of young creations or groups of young women danced together. Children of one gender or the other always danced together. These groups may break down into tighter schisms of artists, warriors, farmers, or herders. But the genders never intermixed. The only exception might be when a mother danced while carrying her baby in her arms or bound in a kanga on her back. The mother always danced with other women, but the baby could be of either gender.

This rigid tradition represented the base of all dance performances throughout history. It reaffirmed community structure and social belonging. To support this rigid tradition is to guarantee the wealth of pleasures symbolized by dancing, which a strong and loving community deserves. To keep this rigid tradition is to guarantee stability. When any major difference occurs, even in a dance performance, tribal elders like the Sacred Woman Rwuva must review and approve it first.

Rwuva always considered herself open-minded. She believed that most cultures' rough and ragged edges would wither and fall away, like old leaves on a tree. She knew shallow, whimsical ideas would dry up and soon be forgotten.

Rwuva understood that this natural process usually took care of itself. The shallow and insincere, however magnificent, would not last. Quality and integrity, however simple, would endure. Still, the Sacred Woman Rwuva felt it necessary to nudge the process occasionally.

Rwuva had previewed the dance of the Motobo dancers several days ago. She enjoyed their performance. Like anyone who heard the addictive rhythm of the Bendabe *Ngoma* drums and saw the inspiring dancers, Rwuva bobbed her head. She clapped her hands with a wide smile on her face. She found the performance artistic and pleasing. However, creations and women dancing in the same group offered a characteristic she had never seen before. As the Aukmondi tribe's Official Hostess and the Principal Mate of the Mfalme, she knew that her opinion affected many people. This dance was too different, too sudden. Rwuva acted on the side of caution. She banned the performance. She declared the dance forbidden.

"Great Sacred Spirit!" Nionu saw the obvious break from tradition. He stopped bobbing his head. The prestigious Royal Warrior covered his eyes with his hand as if to shield his view or hide his face. "What have I done?"

"That is a good question, Great Creation."

Nionu took his hand down from his eyes. He saw the Brown Warrior Quazzi standing next to him. He stood erect. "Quazzi, I did not see you approach."

"I wonder why? Distracted by something else?"

Nionu opened his mouth to answer the Brown Warrior, but nothing came out. He stood speechless. To admit the truth would not help. The Royal Warrior faked his innocence. He tried to justify his predicament. Nothing came to mind except a temporary deflection of the issue. "Quazzi, Great Creation, you sound upset."

Quazzi nodded toward the dancers. "Are you responsible for this?"

"What?" Nionu pointed toward the dancers. "That?"

Quazzi turned and stared directly into Nionu's face. He seemed unyielding and stern. "Yes, that! Did you forget this dance is forbidden?"

"Forbidden?" Nionu glanced at the Motobo dancers and looked up into Quazzi's face. He saw no way out of this. He knew that faking innocence was much more damaging than the consequences of the truth. "No, Great Creation. I knew. But I authorized the dancers because…"

Quazzi held up his hand. "Stop! Give me no explanation. I do not want to hear it. Come with me, please." He turned and walked away.

Nionu sighed. He prepared to embrace his fate. He matched Quazzi's pace and fell into step beside the Brown Warrior. "Great Creation, how did you know I was responsible?"

"I just spoke with the Favored Tribesman."

"What? He told you?"

"No, he did not tell me."

"Then, what did he say that led you to me?"

"The Favored Tribesman and I were discussing this celebration briefly. He had to tell me about the recovery of your Blue Warriors. Their recovery is a significant occurrence. He found it difficult to keep the details to himself."

"That is understandable."

"Despite your warriors' recovery, Kon-Shambique still doubted this celebration would work for everyone. But then, in the brief time we talked, we witnessed four more resurrections with our own eyes."

"Yes! I knew it would work!" Nionu almost jumped with joy. But then he realized he showed a touch too much arrogance. He quelled his behavior out of respect for Quazzi. "You saw four resurrections? Really?"

"Really." The stern expression on Quazzi's face remained. "The Favored Tribesman had to admit that the resurrections were occurring and occurring even faster than he anticipated. He also admitted that this rapid recovery may be partly due to all happening here. He said all this is due to the insightful determination of one headstrong warrior. At first, I did not understand what he meant."

"But you figured he was talking about me?"

"Great Creation, I know only three or four warriors with enough determination to defy a ban set by the Principal Mate. Nionu, I suspected you first."

"Well," Nionu reflected on his two Blue Warriors. "The magical energy behind those drums got Obe and Dabete on their feet. That rhythm belongs to the Motobo dancers. I felt the people needed the drum rhythm and the dancers. The combined effect will resurrect everyone."

"You could be right, Great Creation. Yet … the dance … is forbidden."

"Yes, I know. So, what now? I suppose you want me to surrender my royal cloak?"

"If it were my choice, I would dismiss your disobedience with a strong reprimand. Unfortunately, this is serious. I am afraid, you must answer to an authority greater than mine."

Nionu could hear in Quazzi's voice that the Brown Warrior sympathized with him. But the situation was beyond Quazzi's control. Nionu showed complete understanding. He sighed heavily. "Alright, Great Creation. Do what you must do."

Quazzi walked away again, but he stopped. He had caught sight of something over Nionu's shoulder. Whatever he was looking at shattered his stern demeanor and forced a smile to his face. He nodded. "Look. There is another one."

Nionu turned and focused on the small group of people a few meters away. It was the family of the Young Creation Robuti. Robuti's family stood in the foreground, watching the Motobo dancers. Robuti, almost buried under several of his sculptures, lay upon his burial litter behind them. The dancers held the attention of the family members. None of them saw some of Robuti's sculptures fall away, and Robuti sat up on the litter. Quazzi and Nionu were among the few who saw Robuti slowly climb off his burial litter and stand.

"That is the fifth resurrection I have seen," Quazzi said.

In his usual playful mood, Nionu walked over and stood directly before Robuti's father. He greeted the Great Creation but got no immediate response because of the singing, cheering, and drums. Nionu waved his hand in the face of Robuti's father to get his attention. He succeeded and then pointed to Robuti. At once, Robuti's father and the rest of his family forgot about the Motobo dancers. They suddenly descended upon Robuti, surrounding him.

Nionu felt good about the strange occurrence. He walked back over to where Quazzi stood. "Okay. If that is my fault, I accept the blame for it. I am ready to accept whatever is coming to me."

Quazzi had to smile at Nionu's confidence. He pointed to another family group farther away. "Do you accept the blame for that, too?"

Nionu turned to see the family of the Sacred Woman Mitma. He saw a very inappropriate family confrontation between Mitma and her grandson, Busham. It was completely out of place with the joy and gaiety of the celebration. The elderly Sacred Woman Mitma had sat up from her burial litter. She angrily slapped Busham's hands away from her ears.

In a hysterical frenzy of total confusion and intense, residual anger, Mitma struck Busham across the face again and again. As her hysteria grew stronger and stronger, so did the force behind her assaults.

Nionu grimaced. He could almost hear the sharp, angry slaps despite the surrounding noise. He wondered if he should intervene. As a Royal Warrior, one of his many duties was peacekeeping. The

Brown Warrior Quazzi was thinking similar thoughts. The two of them rushed toward Mitma to stop the assaults.

Busham withstood several of Mitma's angry blows. The physical pain of the slaps across his face had caused his eyes to water. But the love for his grandmother and the joy of her resurrection overpowered every bit of the pain he felt. When Quazzi and Nionu made it halfway to Mitma's burial litter, Busham had finally caught his grandmother's hand. With total forgiveness and love, he embraced Mitma in his arms. The act seemed to suppress Mitma's hysteria and clear her confusion enough to recognize her grandson.

Quazzi and Nionu abandoned their impulse to intervene when they saw Basham holding and stroking the honored, wrinkled hand that had struck his face. They could tell that the tense situation had taken care of itself. Quazzi and Nionu looked at each other with relief. They turned to walk away.

At that moment, the line of Motobo dancers suddenly filed directly in front of them. The line stopped, blocking the two warriors. One of the female dancers, the Sacred Woman Kona, a Red Warrior, stood directly in front of Quazzi. With her knees wide apart, she suddenly squatted. The Brown Warriors admired the woman's sleek, beautiful, and toned body. He finally took a respectful step back. With a hint of embarrassment, he glared at Nionu.

Nionu covered his eyes as he had done earlier. The awkward situation lasted only a short while. Through the gaps in his figures, Nionu saw the Sacred Woman Kona rise to her feet again. He saw Kona smile at Quazzi as she moved away, never missing a step with the other dancers. Nionu did not drop his hand from his face until he saw Quazzi drop his reserve long enough to return Kona's smile.

Nionu tapped Quazzi on the shoulder to get his attention. He pointed at Kona and pretended to be upset by the dancer's disrespectful behavior. "Great Creation, if you ask me, I think she crossed the line just then. Do you wish me to reprimand her for that?"

Quazzi feigned seriousness again. He glared at Nionu, turned, and walked away, knowing the Nionu would follow him.

*****

The royal dais sat in the center of the cove at the back of the celebration area. Surrounded by the four huts of the Ncobbas and reserved for the royal family, it was a six-by-four-meter canopy-covered platform of logs and straws. Rugs, blankets, pillows, and other decorative and comfortable items covered the logs and straws. The royal dais represented the heart of the celebration area, the seat of tribal leadership, and the focal point for information on all major developments within the valley.

All the people permitted upon the royal dais and within the valley occupied their usual positions. This included all nine Ncobba daughters, the young prince, Adaulah, and Ramuza's two surviving mates, Kharaambi and Olabisi. This also included Mfalme Ameh Jobabwe. He and the infant Tutapona were the only two individuals not of the royal family but with the royal privilege of sitting upon the dais. Although the bodies of Ramuza and Rwuva lay on display upon their burial litters, all the people upon the dais sat indifferent to the bodies. They sat watching the people who continued to gather nearby. They sat, waiting for pending developments.

A massive crowd stood in the vicinity of the royal dais. People always gathered near the dais, even under normal circumstances. This time, circumstances were not normal. People gathered, anticipating the Mfalme's and his Principal Mate's resurrections. But they showed an added and heightened curiosity about what would happen to the very popular Royal Warrior Nionu. All the people seemed to suspect Nionu's fate was not good. Because of their curiosity, the number of people gathered grew. Available warriors had to hold the crowd back and keep a spacious and respectful clearing before the dais.

The Bendabe *Ngoma* drums continued to thunder nearby, and the chatter of joyous voices overflowed from the celebration area. The group on the dais and the crowd in the vicinity seemed unaffected. No one sang, clapped their hands, chanted, or danced. The group on the dais and the nearby crowd waited for the inevitable moment when Nionu would finally arrive, face his judgment, and meet his fate.

Besides the Brown Warrior Quazzi, four other individuals had the authority to reprimand Nionu for his transgression. There was the

Chinchigwe Mfalme, Ameh Jobabwe. There was the Gray Warrior Kharaambi. Mfalme Ramuza Ncobba could reprimand Nionu if he woke in the coming moments. If he did not, then by tribal succession, there was also the little Mfalme, Adaulah. With tension heavy in the air, Ameh, Kharaambi, and Adaulah waited for Quazzi to escort Nionu before the dais.

The Royal Warrior Nionu held his head high as he continued to walk beside the Brown Warrior Quazzi. Despite the huge and curious crowd, the two walked toward the dais through a space wide enough to move through without restriction.

Nionu studied the faces of the people as he walked past them. He noticed the Great Creation Gudwando and the Sacred Woman Zawadi standing in the forefront of the crowd on his right. The body of their son, the Red Warrior Gengu, lay upon his burial litter between them. Nionu waved at Gudwando and Zawadi. The rigid Gudwando acknowledged with a small nod of his head. A small, sympathetic smile appeared at the corner of Gudwando's lips. But his eyes expressed sorrow for Nionu.

Not far from Gengu's family lay the body of the Sacred Woman Tongda, still upon her burial litter. Tongda's family group, including her father Benwe, her aunt Oraka, and her cousin, the White Warrior Upenda, surrounded Tongda's burial litter. The Favored Tribesman Kon-Shambique stood between Tongda's burial litter and the royal dais. Nionu waved at them. Only Kon-Shambique waved back. Nionu expected, at least, a smile of encouragement from the Favored Tribesman. The look on Kon-Shambique's face, however, was solemn.

Quazzi and Nionu stopped directly in front of the dais. Quazzi greeted the royal gathering. He received a quick acknowledgement from the Great Creation Ameh and the Sacred Woman Kharaambi. Kharaambi slowly rose from her sitting position, her eyes locked on Nionu. Her expression was cold, almost angry.

"Shall I silence the *Ngoma* drums?" Quazzi asked Kharaambi.

"No. The Motobo dancers seem to need those drums." There was sarcasm in her voice. She never took her eyes off the Royal Warrior

Nionu as she stepped down from the royal dais and approached him. "I must hear your explanation, Great Creation."

Nionu opened his mouth to speak. He was prepared to use the same justification he had imagined using with Rwuva. But before speaking a single word, someone behind him suddenly yelled.

"Rwuva!"

It was the Red Warrior Gengu. Unseen by anybody, Gengu had gotten up from his burial litter. Blinded by his last clear memory, he came rushing toward the royal dais to fulfill his duty; to locate and protect the Sacred Woman. "Rwuva? Is the Sacred Woman alright?"

Gengu's father, the Great Creation Gudwando, was trying to restrain his delirious son. But Gudwando was no match for Gengu's youth and warrior skills. Gudwando lost his footing. He fell and trailed along the ground as Gengu struggled to reach the dais. The crowd of onlookers showed a mixture of emotions: elated that another resurrection had just occurred, but panicked by Gengu's hysteria and treatment of his father.

Kharaambi, Quazzi, and Nionu rushed over to help. Nionu caught the Red Warrior. He held him around his upper torso to restrain him. Quazzi helped Gudwando, who had completely fallen to the ground, back on his feet. Kharaambi took advantage of Nionu's restraints and gripped Gengu's face in her hands.

"Gengu, Great Creation." Kharaambi forced the young warrior to look her in the eyes. "Calm yourself down! You are a Red Warrior! Behave like one!"

Gengu seemed to realize what he was doing. He relaxed. He stood erect and displayed more self-discipline. "There was … There was this thing! This horrible thing … it was coming for us. I must get to the Sacred Woman, Rwuva? I must know that she is safe!"

"You need not be concerned anymore, Great Creation." Quazzi spoke with stern authority. "That thing … is gone. We have not seen it in a while, not since …"

"Not since yesterday," Kharaambi finished Quazzi's statement. She recalled the heroic sacrifice of the warriors from Obe Bendabe's regiment.

With some reservations, Gengu accepted what everyone was telling him. He seemed to settle down until he looked toward the royal dais again. The burial litters of Ramuza and Rwuva were easily visible. The litters did not fit into what everyone was telling him. His body tensed with renewed panic. He made an impulsive move to charge forward again, but others stopped him.

"It is alright, Great Creation." The Favored Tribesman had walked up and joined the consoling people around Gengu. He held the Red Warrior by the shoulders. He noticed the warrior's fixed stare upon the royal dais. "I assure you. It is alright."

"But …"

"Circumstances are not as they appear, Great Creation." Kon-Shambique wanted to explain, but he felt the complicated details could wait. Instead, he redirected Gengu's concerns. "Gengu, your family has missed you. At the moment, they need you more than the Sacred Woman Rwuva does."

Gengu suddenly realized that his father was standing next to him. He looked over and saw his mother too. Gengu saw the distress in their faces. He forgot about everything else and devoted all his attention to his parents. He embraced his father. Without letting go of his father, he embraced his mother too.

The crowd's cheers and chatter resumed and merged with the continuous rumble of the *Ngoma* drums. The noise level increased again, but another unexpected cry pierced the noise.

"Rwuva?"

This time, it was Tongda. Everyone turned toward the Sacred Woman, who had sat up on her burial litter. She looked around, searching, "Where is Rwuva?"

Tongda's father, Benwe, aunt Oraka, and cousin Upenda moved to console her. Tears of happiness were everywhere as everyone, all at once, tried to calm Tongda down.

The Favored Tribesman rushed to Tongda's side. He joined the huddle of Tongda's family. Even Kon-Shambique could not hold in his emotions. With tears of joy, he took Tongda into his arms. He felt the last of his doubts and reservations disappear. He could barely talk. "Sacred Woman … Great Sacred Spirit, you are back! You are back! I feel whole again."

Tongda accepted the embraces of the Favored Tribesman and her family with just a hint of her original distress. Her beautiful amber eyes were restlessly searching. There was still confusion on her face. Her concerns were elsewhere. "Where is Rwuva?"

"The Sacred Woman Rwuva is safe," Kon-Shambique finally sensed her anguish.

"But, did you see that thing? It was horrible! It was death! When it touched Rwuva, she collapsed. I saw her die! She …"

Kon-Shambique embraced Tongda to calm her down. "The specter you saw touched you and the Sacred Woman Rwuva. Both of you died. But we can undo all the damage done. Rwuva will recover, just as you did."

Tongda loved and trusted Kon-Shambique completely. She looked into his eyes with no reason to doubt his words. She settled down enough to finally bring her father, aunt, and Upenda back into her loving embrace. Tongda seemed relieved as happiness dominated her emotions. She pulled her family in closer, tighter. If her arms were long enough, she would have pulled everyone around her into her embrace.

By then, Kharaambi, Quazzi, and Nionu had gathered nearby. All of them were pleased and inspired by Tongda's resurrection. They stood watching Tongda and her family group for a long moment. Only when they heard the renewed cheers and felt the rising energy of the crowd behind them did they realize they were intruding on a private family moment.

Nionu, Kharaambi, and Quazzi backed away. As the three turned to begin their walk back toward the royal dais, something occurred to Nionu. "Tell me something. Have either of you noticed? When someone wakes up from the dead, they ask for Rwuva. Where is Rwuva? Where is Rwuva?"

"Since you have mentioned it, it seems to be a common occurrence," Quazzi looked back at the Red Warrior Gengu and the

Sacred Woman Tongda. He also tried to make sense of it. "It may be just a strange coincidence."

"It may be stranger than you realize," Nionu added. "When you came for me, out in the celebration area, I needed to get to Rwuva, too."

Kharaambi looked over at the Royal Warrior. "I think I understand everyone else's concern for Rwuva. Why did you need Rwuva?"

"I was hoping I could speak with her when she wakes up. I hoped she would lift the ban on the forbidden dance before the dancers arrived."

Kharaambi could see the Motobo dancers still weaving in and out of the nearby crowd. The dancers were moving closer and closer toward the dais. "Great Creation, the dancers are here. It is too late, in more ways than one."

Nionu heard a very disturbing seriousness in Kharaambi's voice. He stopped walking, forcing the Gray Warrior to face him. "Is it too late? What do you mean?"

"Kon-Shambique, your transgression is far more serious than you think. Speaking with the Sacred Woman, Rwuva, will do you no good. Whether she lifts the ban, it makes no difference. Her ban was in place when you violated it."

Nionu closed his eyes as the size of his problem seemed to grow. He sighed heavily. "So, what are you saying?"

"I am saying, your appeal to Rwuva would be a wasted effort."

"In stronger words, you are saying I must find a new usefulness. I can no longer serve as a warrior. I might as well surrender my royal cloak to you right now."

"I could take your cloak, Nionu. But taking your cloak may be the least of your problems. You must still answer to the Mfalme himself when he wakes up. You may keep your cloak until we learn the Mfalme's judgment."

Nionu glanced toward the royal dais. Even on his burial litter, the Mfalme Ncobba still represented the ultimate judgment. Nionu swallowed before turning to Kharaambi again. "May I still have your permission to speak with the Sacred Woman, Rwuva? She has a lot of influential power over the Mfalme. I must take advantage of that."

"If you wish, so be it, Great Creation."

"Thank you, Sacred Woman."

"I wish you luck, Great Creation." Quazzi gave Nionu an encouraging pat on the shoulder as he walked away.

Kharaambi also turned away to return to the royal dais. Her wordless departure disturbed Nionu. "Sacred Woman, are you not going to wish me luck, too?"

Kharaambi ignored Nionu. She gave Mfalme Ameh Jobabwe a respectful nod as she stepped up on the dais. Before she returned to her seat, she finally turned to the Royal Warrior. "Nionu, you do not need luck. If anyone can escape judgment, you can."

The moment that Kharaambi was comfortable, Ameh forced himself to his feet. With his walking staff in hand, he stepped down from the dais. It was his turn to speak with the Royal Warrior.

"I will be honest with you, Great Creation," Ameh said as he approached. He glanced around at Kharaambi, Quazzi, and several nearby opinionated people. A serious look was on Ameh's face as he finally stopped and leaned on his staff. "I have seen a cascade of resurrections taking place. After all I have just seen, I am grateful for what you have done."

"Really?" Nionu's surprise was genuine. "Mfalme, you and the Favored Tribesman are the only two to admit it."

"Yes, well, you made a serious mistake. Defying an elder's ban is wrong."

"Everybody keeps telling me that, too."

"When Quazzi and I first heard of what you did, the Great Creation tried to bring you before my judgment. He knew I would probably be lenient with you."

"But you refused?"

"I am sorry, Great Creation. The punishment I think you deserve is inappropriate for your transgression." Ameh looked back at

Kharaambi again. He turned and looked Nionu in the eyes. "The Sacred Woman Kharaambi is right. In a situation like this, you must answer to the Mfalme. Yes. The Brown Warrior Quazzi, the Gray Warrior Kharaambi, and I could all punish you. Even the little Mfalme Adaulah could levy an irrevocable judgment for what you have done. But once Mfalme Ncobba wakes up, if he thinks we were too lenient, you will have to answer to him anyway."

Nionu glanced at Ramuza's burial litter again. As long as he could remember, the Mfalme had always been brilliant and fair-minded, but strict. "I will take my chances."

"You may never know, Great Creation. Mfalme Ncobba can sometimes be lenient too."

"I cannot count on that." Nionu continued to stare at Ramuza's body. "I could lose more than my royal cloak."

— **64** —

DEATH WILL DO WHAT DEATH DOES

The Mangoni houngan, Onu-Vey, sat with his legs crossed near the edge of death's *veve*. His body slumped, and his chin rested on his chest. His eyes had glazed over, seeing nothing. He continued to chant just above a whisper. He suddenly stopped chanting as Nagorda's crosswinds stirred. His eyes cleared, and his vision came into focus. Onu-Vey broke from his trance and sat erect with a jolt.

The houngan slowly raised his head. The Loa of Death stood before him just outside the *veve*. Onu-Vey had to lean back to look up into the loa's face. The loa towered over him and stared down at him.

"Soso-Dosamdi?" Onu-Vey did not expect this visitation. It was as much a surprise as his raspy voice. His throat was dry. He thirsted for a swallow of water. But, Onu-Vey realized, water was one of the many things not to be found within the periphery of the *veve*. He cleared his throat before he spoke again. "Your mission, Soso-Dosamdi, is not complete. Why are you here?"

The loa began to pace slowly, back and forth; back and forth. It never took his eyes off the Vodun houngan. The loa seemed frustrated that the houngan would ask such a question.

Onu-Vey sighed. He forced himself to relax. He looked around at all the paraphernalia within the *veve*. His cauldron of bubbling goat's blood was only simmering now. The once-thick black smoke had thinned to a gray haze. His bowls of colored powders were near empty. He twisted around to look at his vessel warriors. The warriors continued to strike the logs before them, but their efforts were feeble, and their rhythm faltered. The counter-sounds from the Aukmondi

Ngoma drums resonated stronger, almost obscuring the constant boom-boom, boom-boom.

Onu-Vey turned around and looked up into the loa's face. "My ritual supporting you grows weaker, Soso-Dosamdi. And the Aukmondi have found a way to defy you. It seems, in their revelry, they have no time to fear you. You find it harder to approach them. What do you expect of me?"

The Loa of Death stopped its pacing for a moment. It stared at the houngan, offended by the question. Then, to show the houngan what he must do, the loa quickly glided around the periphery of the *veve*. With both of its bony hands raised, it stopped in front of the vessel warriors. The loa's obvious intent was to frighten the warriors. Fear would force the warriors to increase their efforts. Fear would also give the loa enough nourishment to continue his killing spree.

The vessel warrior Metwe-Ngu, as always, closed his eyes, but not out of fear. Metwe-Ngu suffered from exhaustion. He continued to strike the log before him with the last of his strength. He barely maintained his rhythm. The other exhausted vessel warrior, Makoso-Kin, looked into the loa's eyes. His anger eclipsed his fear. He stared back at the loa, daring the loa to go ahead and kill him. The way Makoso-Kin felt at the moment, death would be a relief.

"Soso-Dosamdi," Onu-Vey said, "do not fault my vessel warriors. They are giving you all they have. You cannot expect much more from them."

The loa turned to face Onu-Vey with a jerk. With its bony hands still raised and threatening, it quickly glided back around the *veve* to where Onu-Vey sat, this time, as if to directly intimidate the houngan.

Onu-Vey almost smiled. "Soso-Dosamdi, you will starve to death if you expect nourishing fear out of me. What is left of my ritual is all I have to give." Onu-Vey gestured toward an empty, bloodstained bowl that sat next to him. "I have given you my last bowl of sacrificial blood. The fire beneath the cauldron burns weakly. There is no kindling to replenish it. The remaining blood in the cauldron may never boil away."

The loa glided about in a tight circle again. It glided away from the *veve* twice and wandered through the Mangoni camp. Twice, it wandered through the Mangoni animal corral, down by the worker warriors' guard post, and then back to the *veve*. Each time it returned to the *veve*, it stood over Onu-Vey. Each time it returned, it came with heightened frustration, expecting the houngan to give him something.

Onu-Vey gestured toward the pathway into the Mangoni camp, a couple of meters behind the guard post where the two worker warriors, Goh-Jumaane and Kum-Bufu, stood. One of the fan-tailed ravens had just swooped down from the sky onto the pathway. The bird had a live gecko in its beak. It slammed the small lizard against the ground several times, killing it. The lizard's tail snapped loose. The tail continued to wiggle and twitch with a life of its own.

Onu-Vey waited for the loa to take note of the bird and turn back to face him. "The birds I have given you still fly over the valley. They are still yours. You must follow their lead and complete your mission."

The loa dismissed the raven with a back-handed wave of its bony hand. A visible current of frigid air rolled from the loa's hand toward the bird. The raven had pounced on the gecko's tail and swallowed half when the air hit it. From the impact of the air, the raven tumbled. Its wings flapped desperately, then stopped as the bird died. The gecko's tail wiggled as it hung from the bird's beak.

The assault on the raven by the Loa was a complete surprise to Onu-Vey. He sat back. His body tensed. He looked up at the loa. At this moment, Onu-Vey realized he had lost his influence over the loa.

The loa wandered away from the *veve* a third time. This time, it went directly toward the Marula tree. It circled the tree, the body of Abul-Tess, and the sleeping Abul-Gwan. Its behavior seemed agitated and threatening.

Onu-Vey's two worker warriors had watched the loa since it returned to the camp. The warriors abandoned their guard posts when the loa circled the Marula tree and Abul-Gwan. They ran up the hillside, ready to defend their Mfalme. They held their spears and shields ready, for all the good they would do.

Onu-Vey uncrossed his legs when the Loa stopped and leaned over the sleeping Abul-Gwan. His stiff and cramped legs resisted the effort with a wave of pain. Onu-Vey ignored the pain, overshadowed by the alarming loss of control over the loa. Onu-Vey called out. "Soso-Dosamdi!"

The loa looked toward the houngan. It looked to its left and right at the two worker warriors poised to defend their Mflame. The loa slowly stood erect as if the Mangoni warriors had a quelling effect on its original intention. It faced Onu-Vey again to hear what the houngan had to say.

"You are the Loa of Death, Soso-Dosamdi," Onu-Vey spoke calmly. With difficulty, he forced himself to stand. "I summoned you because I needed you. I knew beforehand that once you came, I could not dismiss you. I knew that, once you started, I could not stop you. So, to control you, I made you believe you were subject to the power of my ritual; subject to my will. I made you believe you needed to be nourished by fear. By doing so, I thought you would fulfill your mission quickly, completely, and then return to your dark realm."

The loa heard nothing of interest. It dismissed the houngan's babble and leaned over Abul-Gwan again. He raised his hand to touch the sleeping Mfalme. The two worker warriors moved closer to the loa. Both of them drew their spears back, poised to throw them.

"Soso-Dosamdi!" Onu-Vey demanded the loa's attention. When the loa looked up again, Onu-Vey stepped forward. For the first time since the ritual began, Onu-Vey stepped from the ritual *veve*. "You now realize, I have no power over you. I can delude you no longer. So, I ask you now, if you cannot finish the task I gave you, then please, by your own will, spare the Mfalme. Go back to the dark realm from which you came. Please."

The loa slowly stood erect again. He dropped his hand to his side. It looked down at the sleeping Mfalme as if considering Onu-Vey's appeal and this act of mercy. Suddenly, with the speed of a cobra, the loa grabbed the worker warrior, Kum-Bufu, by the neck. It lifted the warrior and drew the warrior toward him, face to face. Kum-Bufu's body went limp. His spear and shield fell to the ground. The loa flung the dead warrior aside. He turned to the other warrior, Goh-Jumaane.

Goh-Jumaane jumped back, beyond the loa's reach. As an afterthought, he rushed to examine Kum-Bufu, to see if he could help him. He could tell that Kum-Bufu was dead long before he blindly reached down and touched the body. He never took his eyes off the loa.

Goh-Jumaane's impulse to flee was strong, but his dedication to his Mfalme was stronger. He adjusted his spear and shield and took a defensive position between Abul-Gwan and the loa. In his panicky haste, he nudged Abul-Gwan's foot, waking him.

"What?" Abul-Gwan opened his eyes from his deep, depression-induced sleep. He pushed himself up from his slump. "What is this? What is going on here?"

"I am sorry, Mfalme." Goh-Jumaane stood with his back to Abul-Gwan. He held his shield to protect himself and the Mfalme. He held his spear ready to throw it. "The loa that Onu-Vey has summoned … something is wrong with it. It is … out of control."

Abul-Gwan rubbed the sleep from his eyes. He leaned over to peep around Goh-Jumaane. When he did, he saw, a few meters away, the body of the warrior, Kum-Bufu. He stared at the body. The death of the Mangoni warrior was almost as unbelievable as the death of Abul-Tess.

Abul-Gwan leaned over again. He had to lean out farther to see around Goh-Jumaane's shield. This time, he saw the loa pacing restlessly. As far as Abul-Gwan could tell, the loa seemed ready to strike out at anything. Abul-Gwan's heart almost skipped a beat when the loa glided directly toward him and Goh-Jumaane. Abul-Gwan scooted back. The Marula tree blocked his retreat. By chance, the body of Abul-Tess upon her burial litter blocked the loa's path. It was just enough to divert the loa's approach. The loa glided toward the animal corral instead.

Abul-Gwan twisted and rose to one knee to look around the Marula tree. When he saw the loa again, the loa had already lifted two sheep from the ground. Abul-Gwan watched the loa toss the sheep from the corral. The sheep hit the ground in successive thuds, like two heavy bags of grain. Both sheep were dead.

Abul-Gwan and Goh-Jumaane watched the loa spin around in the corral to face the other animals. It held a bony fist high over its head. When the loa brought his fist down, he struck the ox between the eyes. All four legs of the ox buckled, and the ox collapsed to the ground, dead.

All the while, both the donkey and the horse kicked and bucked. The animals' frantic noises were twice as loud as when the fire broke out on the valley's north rim. The animals could sense death's deadly proximity. Both animals broke the tethers that held them. They bolted from the corral and sprinted down the hillside. For the moment, only the horse, the donkey, and one sheep escaped death's rampage.

With a look of horror on his face, Abul-Gwan craned around toward the houngan. "Onu-Vey? Why is it doing that?"

"I am sorry, Mfalme. The Loa of Death is killing now … for the sake of killing."

"Can you not control it?"

"No." Onu-Vey glanced at the loa. He could see that the loa was enjoying its unleashed freedom. The loa waved its bony hand toward the fleeing donkey. A rolling ball of frigid air tumbled toward the donkey. When it hit, the donkey somersaulted as it fell dead. "I controlled the loa only by deception."

"Deception? Deception, Onu-Vey? You dare to control the Loa of Death with deception?" Abul-Gwan pointed at the body of Kum-Bufu. "But it is killing our people now. You must do better than that, Onu-Vey."

"I am sorry, Mfalme. We … I made the mistake of summoning the loa. The loa walks among us now. Death will do … what Death does."

"You need to stop it?"

"I cannot."

"Is there anything you can do?"

"No. My influence upon the loa has ended." Onu-Vey turned and stepped back into the *veve*. Without a second thought, he placed his foot on the rim of his cauldron of bubbling goat's blood. He pushed it, sending it tumbling. The blood in the cauldron spilled out. Some of it ran back into the fire and extinguished it with a loud sizzle and a cloud of black smoke.

Onu-Vey walked over and stepped between his two vessel warriors. He watched the warriors long enough to judge the frequency of their feeble strikes against the logs. Boom-boom! Boom-boom! Boom-boom! Onu-Vey grabbed each of the limbs they used. The boom-boom stopped. The vessel warriors collapsed from sheer exhaustion as if the limbs had been the source of their strength.

"Onu-Vey," Abul-Gwan called out. He struggled to stand. The worker warrior Goh-Jumaane had to help him to his feet. "If you cannot stop the loa, what are you doing?"

Onu-Vey tossed the confiscated limbs to the ground. "We are done here, Mfalme."

"Done? Done? All the Aukmondi are dead?"

"No, not yet. But they will soon be. And … so will we."

"What do you mean? What are you saying?"

Onu-Vey said nothing at first. He extracted the spade from one of his pouches and knelt near the center of the *veve*. He scooped aside the muddy mess of blood, ashes, and charcoal. Onu-Vey dug where his ritual fire once burned. He threw aside huge scoops of dirt, searching for the black crystal, his *azima*.

"In my arrogance," Onu-Vey finally said as he continued to dig, "I gave the loa guidance, to know where to strike and when. I gave the loa preference to favor the Aukmondi. I gave the loa restlessness, to complete his task quickly and to the end. In my arrogance, I gave the loa finality, so there would be no reprieve for what must be done. None of that was necessary. Death is a Loa who needs nothing. It will kill because it can. And now, it will kill us, all of us, because it is here."

Onu-Vey finally dug deep enough into the ground to uncover the black crystal. He sat back and stared down at the crystal in the hole. He felt sure he would never see it again. But there it was. He tossed his spade aside and reached into the hole. He delicately pulled the crystal from the ground. Onu-Vey did not bother to knock away the dirt and debris hanging onto it. Instead, he gently touched the crystal to his forehead.

Mfalme Abul-Gwan and Goh-Jumaane watched the Vodun houngan dump the contents of one of the pouches onto the ground. He sorted the contents until he extracted a small leather pouch and cord. Onu-Vey dropped the crystal into the pouch. He untangled the cord, secured the pouch, and ceremoniously placed it around his neck.

"Onu-Vey?" Abul-Gwan took a step closer to the *veve*. "What are you doing?"

Onu-Vey did not answer Abul-Gwan. Instead, he sat in a comfortable position and crossed his legs. He clutched the small leather pouch containing the crystal with both hands. He closed his eyes and bowed his head. He began a chant of unintelligible words. Onu-Vey had shifted so quickly into another of his rituals that, already, his body rocked back and forth with increasing intensity.

— **65** —

NO RIGHT TO ABUSE HER GRACE

The Royal Warrior Nionu sat on the ground before the royal dais while he waited for the Sacred Woman Rwuva's and Mfalme Ncobba's resurrection. He sat in a position where he could enjoy the performance on the huge *Ngoma* drums by the Blue Warrior Obe Bendabe and the Orange Warrior Lujaami Dokae. Once in a while, people moved between Nionu and the drums, blocking his view and creating minor distractions. Nionu tolerated the distractions. The thundering sounds from the drums continued to come through loud and clear. He enjoyed himself. He bobbed his head and clapped his hands in tempo with the rhythm of the drums. After a while, he almost forgot about his predicament.

Nionu had almost forgotten about the Motobo dancers, too. That is, until the dancers suddenly snaked their way into the area directly before the royal dais. Nionu got quickly to his feet. He and others near him had to move out of the dancers' way. Nionu gave up his prime position near the drums. He moved farther out into the celebration area. He did not mind the move. The drum rhythms came through as strong as ever. He resettled upon the ground in his new position, giving him an unobstructed view of the dancers.

All the Motobo dancers dominated the area within minutes before the royal dais. Numbering almost a full regiment of warriors, the dancers formed concentric circles that shifted from side to side in opposite directions. They continued with their unique strides, audacious struts, and other choreographed movements. Even after all this time, the wide-knee squats still caught everyone off guard. The awesome effect was a crowd-pleaser, although few would admit it.

Nionu looked past the dancers, toward the royal dais. He checked to see if the Mfalme and the Sacred Woman Rwuva had resurrected. He also checked to see how his superiors, Quazzi, Kharaambi, and Ameh, reacted to the dancers. Nionu was pleased to see Ameh and Kharaambi bobbing their heads with the beat of the drums. They swayed from side to side in unison as they watched the dancers. Quazzi, who stood before the dais, also enjoyed the dancers. Nionu could see the Brown Warrior clapping his hands without reserve with the rhythm of the drums. Nionu smiled. All he saw made him think that maybe his transgression was forgivable.

At this point, Nionu saw three fan-tailed ravens perched on top of the canopy of the royal dais. He saw the beautiful birds sitting in a row along the front edge of the canopy. They tilted their heads, typical of a bird's sideways glance. They appeared fascinated by the dancers and the crowd of people before them. With increasing concern, Nionu thought the ravens seemed strange. He knew that ravens are easily frightened away by people's proximity. These ravens seemed curious.

Whether or not his career as a warrior was in jeopardy, it did not matter. Nionu transformed into a dutiful and responsible warrior. The smile on his face disappeared as his concerns grew. He slowly got to his feet. He worked his way around several people beside him as he moved closer toward the royal dais. The Royal Warrior had to get closer to those birds. He had to investigate this strange phenomenon. Something about those birds was not right. For reasons he could not explain, Nionu saw them as an ill omen. If the birds had not seized his attention, Nionu would have been the first to see the tall, gruesome demon of death. The demon had emerged from the bank of trees behind the four huts of the Ncobbas.

Unseen by anyone, the demon glided smoothly into the work area between Ramuza's and Rwuva's huts. It stood for a moment. It assessed the crowd of people. The demon looked furious if a face of living eyes and bone could show anger. It finally locked its eyes on what may have been the immediate source of its irritation – the Bendabe *Ngoma* drums. When the demon moved again, it headed straight for the huge drums. It glided smoothly to a point directly behind Obe Bendabe and Lujaami Dokae. It moved so fast that the two warriors never saw the demon coming.

With one hand on each of the warriors, the demon lifted them and flung them aside. The beautiful rhythm of the drums stopped. Piercing sounds of screams and panicky chaos replaced the beautiful rhythm as the bodies of the now-dead warriors tumbled through the air. The screams increased when the bodies crashed into a crowd of nearby people.

The demon grabbed each of the huge Bendabe *Ngoma* drums, one in each hand, and easily lifted the heavy drums. Then, holding them high over its head, the demon threw them toward the Motobo dancers.

The drums crashed in the center of the dancers. Each drum broke apart when it hit the ground, but not before striking several dancers. All the dancers hit by the drums died. The rest of the dancers, warriors, and warriors' mates did not flee in panic. Instead, they endured the assault. With the benefits of experience and training, they scrambled to their feet again, battle-ready.

Their regimental commander, the Blue Warrior Dabete Ehkili, rushed up after the demon appeared. He had heard the Bendabe *Ngoma* drums suddenly stop. He heard the chaotic screams that followed. From somewhere out in the celebration area, Dabete ran up in time to witness the devastating assault by the demon on the Motobo dancers. He suppressed his reactions of anger and rage. With two or three quick orders, he rallied the remnants of the dancers. He had them standing in attack formation.

The Motobo dancers were no longer dancers. They were warriors now. Although weaponless, they stood ready with nothing to fight with except their bare hands. After another order from Dabete, they charged the demon with the Blue Warrior in the lead.

The demon saw them coming. With a gentle and dismissive wave of its bony hand, it sent a visible torrent of frigid air rolling forward and expanding in size. The air enveloped the charging warriors. All the warriors, including the Blue Warrior Dabete Ehkili, crumbled to the ground, dead.

"No!" The Royal Warrior Nionu screamed. He saw the whole assault. "Oh, Great Sacred Spirit! No!"

Nionu fell to his knees in anguish. Throughout his career, he had lost warriors. But witnessing the loss of his Ehkili Regiment hit the Royal Warrior hard. Nionu bowed his head and closed his eyes to suppress his pain and the rage that tore at his insides. Nionu was not completely successful. He endured the pain, but he lost all control of his rage.

When Nionu raised his head again, he locked his eyes on the loa. He got to his feet again. The energy of anger and revenge had completely crippled his rationality. He was also weaponless. He had no chance of defeating the demon. With both of his fists clenched tight, he walked toward the demon.

"Nionu!" The Brown Warrior Quazzi also saw the assault on Dabete and his warriors. He saw the Royal Warrior's reaction as he struggled to recover emotionally. When Nionu walked toward the demon, Quazzi knew the warrior's determination was out of control. He rushed over and caught the Royal Warrior's arm. "Nionu, Great Creation. No. That thing is too powerful. You are walking into certain death."

"I will get over it." Nionu yanked his arm loose from Quazzi's grip and continued walking toward the demon.

"Nionu! Stop!" Quazzi ordered.

The Royal Warrior stopped walking. He looked back at Quazzi. He seemed to realize what he was doing. Nionu looked at the demon again. "The Supreme Spirit knows we do not deserve what that thing is doing to us. The Supreme Spirit stands with us, Quazzi. She is with us! With that knowledge, I intend to face this thing. I will take it out."

"Yes, but not this way. Though the Supreme Spirit stands at your side, you have no right to abuse Her grace and act like a fool. Great Creation, we need your tactical mind to defeat this thing."

The Royal Warrior Nionu finally pushed his rage back to a more manageable level. He allowed the Brown Warrior to turn him away from the demon. The two moved back. As Nionu retreated with the Brown Warrior, he saw a fist-sized stone beside him. The stone's easy availability was enough to spark a final flare of revenge. Nionu picked it up from the ground. Without a second thought, he turned and hurled it at the demon.

The demon caught the stone in its hand, almost without looking. It hurled the stone back at the Royal Warrior so fast that Nionu never saw it coming. The stone hit Nionu in the chest with a sickening thud. Nionu fell to his knees. He fell forward on his face, dead.

66

I SHALL RUN NO MORE

When Kharaambi saw the demon appear behind the warriors Bendabe and Lujaami, she shifted into a complete warrior's manner. She stepped down from the royal dais with her spear now in hand. She made a quick and strategic assessment of the area. There were always a few warriors near the royal dais. With just a wave of her spear, Kharaambi worked some magic of her own. She signaled the nearby warriors to her side. Within moments, eleven warriors gathered. They stood around her, waiting for her instructions.

The Brown Warrior Quazzi forced himself to recover from the sudden and senseless loss of the Royal Warrior Nionu. Like so many times before, he set aside his grief. The current situation demanded that he focus his attention elsewhere. He made a quick reassessment of developments, too. The demon had made another sweeping wave of its arm, sending out another torrent of frigid air and bringing down a small group of people. The demon was circling now, looking for more victims. Quazzi realized that, in its hunt, it had turned back toward the royal dais.

"Sacred Woman," Quazzi ran over to join the small gathering of warriors around Kharaambi. "We are all that stands between that thing and the Royal Family."

"I know, Quazzi. We must do something. And we must do it quickly." Kharaambi looked toward the royal dais.

When the demon appeared, everyone on the dais naturally got up and huddled together on the far side. The Sacred Woman, Olabisi, had gathered most of the Ncobba daughters together. Ameh stood in front of them. The Elderly Creation held his staff like a weapon, ready to defend everyone. The little prince Adaulah, half frightened, half highly curious, hid behind Ramuza's burial litter. He peeped over the edge at the rampaging demon.

Kharaambi turned toward the demon again. She knew that the demon could wipe out whole armies. She saw a sample of the demon's capabilities yesterday when it destroyed most of Obe Bendabe's regiment. Kharaambi also knew the small group of warriors standing beside her had no chance against such a powerful foe. "We have a tactical dilemma. Our options are limited."

"We could try Nionu's cat's tail offense," Quazzi suggested. "I could take half the warriors here and draw the demon away while you take the rest to secure the Royal Family."

"Secure the family? Secure them where? How? It would take half the warriors here to move the litters of the Mfalme and the Sacred Woman Rwuva."

"With all due respect, Sacred Woman, the Mfalme and Rwuva are already dead. Let us do what we can to save the living."

Kharaambi focused on the bodies of Ramuza and Rwuva. To abandon the bodies seemed very wrong. But Quazzi was right. Kharaambi glanced at the huddle of Olabisi, the Ncobba daughters, and Ameh. She caught the fearful look on Adaulah's face as he peeped from behind Ramuza's burial litter.

"So be it."

Quazzi quickly selected five of the warriors. He did not wait for the small detail to gather around him. He explained what he expected of them. "We must capture and hold the demon's attention. We must do this without provoking it. If the demon attacks, we lose our usefulness. We aim to draw the demon away from the Royal Family."

Whether his instructions were clear, Quazzi wasted no time. He turned to face the demon again. He walked toward it with slow but committed steps. The demon had already moved toward the dais. Quazzi raised his shield and rattled it. He hoped that the noise would be enough to catch the demon's attention. The small detail of the warrior behind Quazzi did the same.

It worked. The demon turned to face the noisy warriors. The look in the demon's eyes was threatening. It slowly raised its bony hand to strike. Quazzi and his detail did not expect to draw the demon's attention so easily, so suddenly. They stopped rattling their shields. Each of them took precautionary steps back. The demon lowered its hand but continued to move toward the warriors.

"This way." Quazzi slowly moved to his right. He intended to lead the demon back between Ramuza's and Rwuva's huts. This direction would lure the demon away from the Royal Family. It would also lead the demon away from the multitude of panicky people still out in the celebration area.

"Quazzi, Great Creation," Momi, an Orange Warrior, whispered over Quazzi's shoulder. "The tree-filled north slope behind the huts is too steep. It will prove to be a major obstacle for us. We cannot stay ahead of the demon."

"Yes. I think it should make us a very appealing target." Quazzi's sarcasm showed he was already aware of the obstacle before them. "Did you expect to get out of this alive, Momi?"

Quazzi's true hope was to reach at least that tree-filled, steep north slope. The Brown Warrior did not anticipate the demon's impatience. Long before he and his warrior detail reached the huts' rear and the slope's foot, he saw the demon raise its bony hand. The demon flexed its fingers wide open. An ostrich egg-size orb of frigid air rolled out and expanded. By the time it reached Quazzi and his warriors, the orb had expanded large enough to envelope all of them. Quazzi and the warriors lost consciousness, collapsed, and died.

The demon, so confident in its deadly assault, did not even wait to see the warriors fall to the ground. It turned around and focused on where he had it before – the royal dais. If the demon could show surprise, it did at that moment. Its expressions of rage and anger faltered instantly when it saw the royal dais empty of living people. The demon dropped its bony hands to its sides. It stood erect. It looked from side to side, searching for the missing people.

The trickery only enraged the demon more. It stormed ahead, straight toward the royal dais. The demon stepped onto the dais and stood between the burial litters of Ramuza and Rwuva, still searching. It saw a sea of panicky, frightened people running away in the celebration area. The people had abandoned their campfires, bonfires, and other burial litters as they ran across the celebration area toward the exit of the Royal Kraal.

In a final rage, the loa raised its hands above its head. He threw his hands forward with a loud whoosh. One of the thickest and most visible torrents of frigid air rolled forward. It grew larger and stronger as it rolled out across the celebration area. People fell dead when the tidal wave of air rolled over them. Even the campfires and huge bonfires, one after another, died out when the air rolled over them.

*****

During the chaos, the Favored Tribesman tried to flee with the Sacred Woman Tongda and her family. But their progress was slow. In a last resort, Kon-Shambique fell back on his faith. He turned and stood his ground. He made one last appeal to the Supreme Spirit to show that Her grace and influences were much stronger than anything happening here. Kon-Shambique never finished his appeal. A strong gust of cold air hit him. It hit him so hard that Kon-Shambique spun around and fell to the ground, dead.

The family of the Sacred Woman Tongda died just as quickly. Benwe, Oraka, and Upenda died huddled together. At least none of them suffered the grief of seeing the Sacred Woman Tongda die a second time.

The Red Warrior Gengu saw the rolling torrent of frigid air coming. He had seen its effect just seconds earlier and knew its danger. The heroic warrior only did what came naturally. To protect his parents, Gudwando and Zawadi, he covered them with his shield. The torrent of cold air ripped Gengu's shield from his hand. It sent the shield tumbling as it swallowed Gengu and his family. Gengu, Gudwando, and Zawadi collapsed and died.

The Great Creation Busham also saw the torrent of air coming. He saw how it was killing everyone it touched. He and his three brothers tried to flee with their grandmother, the Sacred Woman Mitma, in tow. But because the old woman could not move as fast as her young grandsons, the whole family gave up trying. Busham took his grandmother in his arms. All of them turned to face the coming wind. They waited for the inevitable. Busham, his brothers, and the cornerstone of the family died together, embracing each other.

When the demon attacked and all the people ran toward the exit of the Royal Kraal, the chaos caused the Young Creation Robuti to separate from his family. Nothing seemed more important to Robuti in this perilous moment than finding them again. He fought against the powerful tide of people to return to where he thought they should be. The Young Creation located his father, only meters away, reaching for him. Just seconds before their fingers touched, the cold air separated them again, killing them.

In a matter of minutes, the entire Royal Kraal celebration area lay quiet, filled with dead people.

*****

The Gray Warrior Kharaambi kneeled in hiding among the trees on the steep north slope between Rwuva's and Olabisi's huts. Kharaambi and her small detail of warriors led Ameh and the remaining members of the Royal Family to the only refuge they could find. Several meters to the left of where Quazzi's small detail had lured the demon. They reached it just seconds before the demon struck Quazzi and his detail dead.

Ameh kneeled at Kharaambi's right. The little prince Adaulah was at her left. The Sacred Woman Olabisi and all nine Ncobba daughters were behind them. Kharaambi's detail of six warriors surrounded all of them. Everyone peered out from their hidden position. Their view through the trees and across the work area allowed them to see the royal dais and part of the celebration area. They watched the devastation unfold before them.

The demon stood on the royal dais with its back to those hiding. He looked out across the celebration area. Bodies of the dead lay scattered throughout. As far as Kharaambi and those in hiding could tell, the dead bodies stretched to the entrance of the Royal Kraal. And it was quiet. An eerie and heavy silence settled across the area. The only sounds were the caws of three fan-tailed ravens perched in nearby trees. The only movements were the spiraling columns of smoke from the destroyed campfires and bonfires, and the fidgety behavior of the demon on the dais.

A superficial end to all the devastation came when the demon seemed to realize all the people were dead. It stood on the royal dais between the burial litters of Ramuza and Rwuva. It looked out across the celebration area as if wondering what to do next. The demon grew restless and angry because it saw no more living bodies. It looked down at the bodies of Ramuza and Rwuva. In a final rage, it reached down and turned over the litters. The bodies tumbled from the litters and rolled completely off the dais.

Omari, the oldest daughter, perceived the act as a horrendous desecration. She covered her mouth to suppress a scream. But an agonized moan escaped just as Omari lost consciousness and collapsed. She would have fallen had not one of the nearby warriors caught her and eased her down to the ground.

The demon, out on the dais, heard Omari's moan. It whirled toward the source of the moan. It raised both hands, ready to strike, before identifying its target. The demon searched with its living eyes. It finally centered its sight, directly across the work area between Rwuva's and Olabisi's huts, and onto the very foot of the north slope. It saw none of the people hiding. But it sensed living people nearby. The demon slowly glided toward the work area.

Kharaambi turned to her warriors. She pointed to Omari. "Gather the Sacred Woman up. We have to leave!" She reached down to help Ameh to his feet.

"No, Sacred Woman." Ameh refused her help. "This hill behind us is too steep. Of the people here, I lack the capability of running. I … shall run no more."

"But Ameh, Great Creation, please," Kharaambi pleaded. "You are Mfalme. If I do nothing else, I must get you out of harm's way."

"Your responsibility demands that. It seems the proper thing to do." Ameh used his ever-present staff to force himself to his feet. He glanced out through the trees. He could see the demon still slowly approaching. Ameh turned back to Kharaambi and tried to smile. "But not this time. I will only slow you down."

"Ameh!" There was no compromise in Kharaambi's voice. "You are coming with us."

"Kharaambi, hear me. I speak to you now as the Chinchigwe Mfalme. I said no! My death will not end the Chinchigwe royalty. My grandson, Tutapona, will maintain that bloodline." Ameh finally smiled and nodded toward Adaulah. "Devote your efforts to the little prince. Save him for the Aukmondi."

"Ameh." Kharaambi's voice was softer but still pleading.

"Go! Before it is too late." Ameh barked his order again, "Go!"

'Too late' came when a Fan-tailed Raven flew in and perched upon a nearby limb. All those hiding looked up to see the unusually curious bird. The bird held their attention just long enough for a wave of frigid air to roll in and blanket them.

67

NOTHING HAS CHANGED

For most of the past seven kilometers, the warriors Wema and Nienko found the scattered herds easier to walk through than expected. They discovered that the cautious animals gave them clear passage long before they approached. The scattered herds, however, seemed endless. With wildebeests now the majority of the animals, the warriors heard constant, characteristic grunts and bellows from all directions.

Under normal circumstances, Wema and Nienko could have reached the Mara River in about three hours. However, several herds prevented them from doing so. On two occasions, the warriors encountered moving herds. The warriors had to stop their gentle pace and wait for the herds to pass.

Wema and Nienko took advantage of the situation and rested while they could. They sat on the ground and waited patiently for the first two herds to pass. However, while waiting for the second herd to pass, the Orange Warrior showed impatience several times. Twice, Wema got up and paced. He glanced toward available shadows, seeing almost two hours of precious travel time slip away.

Long before the tail end of the last moving herd passed through, Wema got to his feet a third time. He flung his travel pack across his shoulders. He gathered up his shield and spear as he addressed Nienko. "Come, my friend. Our wait must end. I am afraid we have no more time to spare. As I suggested, we will run the rest of the way."

Nienko quickly got to his feet. As he gathered up his belongings, he studied the herds. They were thicker now. The spaces between the herds were smaller. He felt that walking between the herds was difficult enough. Running between the herds would be next to impossible. "If we run, are you not afraid of frightening them, Great Creation?"

"It is a chance we must take to recover our schedule. Are you up for the challenge?"

"Of course, Great Creation. Shall I set the pace this time?"

Wema gestured ahead. "Lead the way, my friend."

*****

The regular 'swish-swish' sound of the grass beneath the warriors' feet continued for almost an hour. With Nienko in the lead, the warriors quickly covered another six kilometers. Their pace would not have slowed had they not encountered a herd too thick to continue. Nienko's pace slowed to a brisk walk.

"There are so many!" Nienko turned in a complete circle as he walked. "If the herds are so large here, imagine what we will find converging on the Mara banks."

"It does not appear promising, does it?"

"Do you think the Kiboko Passage is still clear?"

"We will soon find out. We are almost there." Wema pointed ahead. "Look there, on the horizon. That is the Mara River embankment."

In the distance, on the other side of the massive herd, the edge of the grassy plain gave way to a level horizon. From the far north to the far south, the horizon lined the bank of the Mara River. Four rocky gorges, several hundred meters apart, broke the horizon.

The Orange Warrior Wema pointed to one of the rocky gorges. "That second break from the left; that is where we must cross."

Nienko searched the horizon. One of the wide and jagged areas included a deep crevasse. The crevasse was the mouth of a small gorge easily visible across the five kilometers. "Is that the Kiboko Passage?"

"Yes, Great Creation. That is the Kiboko Passage."

The Red Warrior Nienko surveyed the stretch of land between where he and Wema stood and where the small gorge began. It was a five-kilometer stretch. A few scattered herds of grazing zebras and wildebeests covered the area, but, in Nienko's opinion, it looked as though the worst was behind them. Nienko glanced toward the sun. It was almost sunset. He smiled. "It looks as though we will make it before nightfall."

"If we do not run into any more moving herds."

*****

The Orange Warrior Wema led the way across the next three kilometers. But just as Nienko had done earlier, Wema slowed his pace. He came to a complete stop. And just like Nienko, he turned in a circle, searching.

As far as Nienko could tell, the Orange Warrior seemed suddenly alarmed. "What is it, Wema?"

"Listen. Do you hear that?"

Nienko took a moment to focus on the surrounding sounds. At once, he heard the gentle rumble of thundering hooves. Nienko turned in a circle, too. The sound was coming from over the rolling hills toward the south.

Suddenly, a massive herd of stampeding zebras and wildebeests spilled over the hill. Less than two kilometers behind the two warriors, the massive herd flowed like the rush of flooding water across the savanna. As more animals spilled over the hill, the herd grew larger and larger. The zebras and wildebeests peacefully grazing on this side of the hill reacted to the stampede. They stopped grazing and ran, too. It was just a matter of moments before the stampede would engulf the warriors Wema and Nienko.

"Wema, Great Creation!" Panic forced Nienko's voice to hang in his throat. "What are we going to do?"

Wema said nothing. He turned in several directions, searching for anything that might give them some chance of surviving this stampede. The Orange Warrior finally located the huge stump of a dead baobab tree several meters away. He pointed to the stump.

It was the only communication necessary. Nienko understood what had to be done. He and Wema raced toward the stump. They reached it with only seconds to spare. With their backs pressed hard against the north side of the stump, they stood motionless. The warriors closed their eyes. They held their breaths as they endured the rumble and thick cloud of dust that enveloped them.

The two warriors could do nothing to quiet the thundering hooves that roared past them. The rumbling thunder continued to grow louder and louder. There were moments when the warriors thought that even the baobab tree stump would not withstand the force that rolled past them.

The Red Warrior Nienko grimaced to endure the deafening noise around him. Sensing imminent devastation, he dared to open his eyes. He could barely see anything through the cloud of dust around him. Before the dust forced him to close his eyes again, he caught only glimpses of black and white stripes that continued to streak past him.

The noise of the thundering hooves peaked. It slowly died away. Both Wema and Nienko opened their eyes. Because of the cloud that lingered, nothing beyond three meters was visible. Neither warrior dared to move. They pressed tightly against the tree, waiting for a sure safety sign.

Nienko took his first breath in a while. He coughed to clear the dust from his throat. "Is it safe?"

Wema listened for more hooves. He heard only intermittent gallops around him. Wema slowly peeled away from the stump and peered to the other side. He forced his eyes to pierce through the dissipating cloud of dust. The Orange Warrior saw nothing discernible. He resumed his refuge against the stump just as he glimpsed something black and white lying on the ground. It brought a frown to his face. What he thought he saw made little sense.

Nienko noticed the frown on Wema's face. "What is it, Great Creation?"

Again, Wema said nothing. He heard no more hooves. He felt it was safe to peel himself away from the stump again. Wema slowly moved round to the other side. By then, the dust cloud had dissipated enough that Wema saw and recognized a nearby zebra.

"Nienko," Wema called back to his friend. "Look at this."

The Red Warrior, with just as much caution, came from behind the stump. He also saw the unusual sight on the ground. "What is wrong with it?"

Wema approached the zebra. He nudged it with the head of his spear. "It is dead."

"Dead?" Nienko came closer. "From what? Did the others trample it?"

That was Wema's initial assumption, too. He stooped and stroked the zebra's neck as if the brief examination would give him a better answer.

Wema stood back up, more confused. "I find no evidence that the others trampled it."

"Then, what killed it?" Nienko came closer.

An alternate possibility caused Wema to step back. He looked around the area. The cloud of dust around him had dissipated enough that Wema could now see several meters in all directions. The view confirmed his new assumption. "Oh no! Oh, Great Sacred Spirit! No!"

Nienko searched the area too. Stunned by what he saw, the Red Warrior fell back against the baobab tree. As far as he could see, in all directions, other animals lay dead. And it wasn't just a few unfortunate animals. The entire zebra, wildebeest, and gazelle herd lay dead around them.

"How can this be?" Nienko asked as the answer came to him. "The houngan's demon?"

"I believe so, Great Creation."

"But how? I thought the demon only roamed our valley."

"As did I. It appears we are wrong." Wema turned in a slow circle, taking in the sight of all the dead animals. He was also looking for any sign of the ominous specter. "This demon of death knows no boundaries."

"It followed us!" Nienko also turned in a circle, searching in every direction. "It is out here somewhere! Wema, that thing is out here!"

"These dead animals suggest so."

"So, what does this mean? What do we do now?"

Wema said nothing at first. He dusted himself off and adjusted the pack on his back. Preoccupied with his thoughts, he walked out across the savanna again, weaving around the carcasses of dead animals. He did not speak again until he heard Nienko's footsteps behind him.

"Nothing has changed, Nienko."

"What?" Nienko studied one of the fallen animals as he walked around it. "Great Creation, you do these dead animals. Do you not? If the demon is out here …"

"Nothing has changed!" Wema repeated with frustration in his voice. "Only two or three kilometers remain before we cross the Mara. We must still warn the Green Warrior and the farmers. And, we must hurry."

"But, Wema!"

Wema ignored his young friend's confusion. He resumed his run toward the horizon.

— 68 —

ONE LITTLE VICTORY

The Red Warrior Nienko did not agree with Wema when he said, 'nothing had changed'. In Nienko's opinion, the urgency of the mission had intensified. And if the houngan's demon was out here, it meant an unsuccessful mission.

For the next kilometer and a half, the steady run across the savanna was different, too. The warriors maneuvered around hundreds and hundreds of dead animals. Nienko missed the constant grunts and bellows of the grazing animals. All he could hear were the 'swish-swish' footsteps as he and Wema ran through the grass.

At one point, the warriors came upon a horde of scavenger birds that circled the sky a few meters ahead. The screeches and calls that the birds made broke the eerie silence. Nienko welcomed the sight and sounds of the birds. That is, until he and Wema drew closer. On the ground, the warriors came upon a badly mangled and contorted zebra carcass. The unfortunate zebra fell during the stampede. The other animals trampled it to death. The birds Nienko saw circling overhead were only a small part of the squawking birds that now covered and ravaged the zebra's carcass.

Nienko found the frenzy of the big birds fascinating. He stopped running and stood long, watching the bloody carnage. His face was contorted with disgust. He had never seen such a spectacle. He would have stood longer had not Wema called his name.

"Great Creation. We have no time for that."

"I am coming." Nienko never broke his gaze away from the carnage, awed by all he saw. He finally turned away and ran a few steps to catch up with the Orange Warrior. "I am sorry. I have never seen buzzards do that."

"They are buzzards. They will do as buzzards do."

"I understand the birds see the zebra's remains as food. But to pile on the remains of one zebra with such madness makes no sense to me." Nienko waved his hand over the sea of dead animals around him. "Look at this, Wema! There is enough for all of them."

"The buzzards start with the animals already mangled and torn apart. The rest of the fallen animals are not going anywhere. It is Mother Nature's efficient way of cleaning away all the messiest remains first."

"As these animals decompose, Mother Nature will clean for quite a while."

"She can do it. And the buzzards are not the only scavengers." Wema pointed to a small gathering of fan-tailed ravens. "Some may have to wait their turn, but each will have an exclusive part in the cleaning. Nature will get the job done."

Nienko studied the ravens. The birds seemed to be waiting so patiently for their turn at the zebra's carcass that they seemed indifferent, in Nienko's opinion.

"Come. We must hurry." Wema turned to resume his run.

*****

To reach the returning farmers before they crossed the Mara River, the Orange Warrior Wema and the Red Warrior Nienko held firm to their conviction. They ran the rest of the way across the grassy plain. Their progress had improved since their only obstacles now were the carcasses of the fallen animals. By the time the sun set, less than half a kilometer remained before they would leave the grassy plain and descend the slope of the Kiboko Passage. They had made it close enough to the Mara River to see that the returning farmers had not crossed yet.

"We did it, my friend," Wema said as he slowed to a strong walk. "If the farmers had crossed the river, we would see signs of them already."

"That is good. But we have yet to cross the Mara ourselves. And it pleases me, we do not have to cross in darkness."

"Does crossing the Mara still concern you?"

"Yes, a little."

"I am surprised, Great Creation. That is unbecoming of you. I knew you long before you became a warrior. I know that you have it in you to look forward to challenges like that."

"I do like a good challenge, Wema. You know that. I do not like crocodiles."

Just then, the Orange Warrior stopped walking. He suddenly stooped low to the ground to hide in the tall grass. Wema pulled Nienko down with him. He spoke in a whisper. "My friend, crocodiles are the least of our problems."

"What is it?"

Wema put his finger to his lips to silence the Red Warrior. He nodded to his right, suggesting the Red Warrior peek across the plain.

Nienko rose and peeped over the tall grass. His mouth fell open when he saw what Wema had seen. Nienko quickly stooped back down to concealment beside Wema. He had seen the demon of death, only three hundred meters away, paralleling their course toward the Kiboko Passage.

"It followed us!" Nienko spoke in an excited whisper. "Wema, Great Creation, that thing followed us. It knows about the farmers. It is going after them."

"Yes, it would seem so. And judging by its movement, it knows where they are located. It will probably get to them long before we do."

"So, what do we do now? Do you still say nothing has changed?"

"Nothing has changed, Great Creation. As your Sacred Mother told you, let us focus on our mission."

"Sure. We can do that." Nienko was feeling cynical. "Except now, we must stop this demon of death first."

With the demon past them and moving ahead, Wema slowly rose from concealment. He saw that the demon had already made it most of the way across the remaining half-kilometer stretch to the Kiboko Passage.

"Even if we caught this thing, I doubt the two of us can stop it." Wema tried to think of a plausible strategy. "Yet, somehow, the farmers must be warned."

"Wema, you make no sense. If we cannot catch that thing and if we cannot defeat it, then we have no hope of getting ahead of it and warning the farmers."

"We still have to try."

"Wema, knowing what we know, it is frustrating to hear you keep saying that."

"Come, my friend." Wema resumed his strong walk. "If we hurry, we can, at least, close the distance between us and the demon before it reaches the bottom of the passage."

Nienko matched Wema's pace. "Yeah, and if we are fast enough, we can grab old Bone-Face by its tunic and wrestle it to the ground. And then what?"

"There will be no grabbing, Great Creation. We will use a tactic that our commander, the Royal Warrior Nionu, likes to use."

"What? You do not mean the cat's tail offense?"

Wema nodded. "Yes, the cat's tail offense. Only once we get close enough to the demon will I engage it. I will draw it away. I will create the time you need to get past it."

"Wema, Great Creation, you know the cat's tail offense will not work; not in this situation." Nienko tried to explain.

"Nienko!" Wema silenced the Red Warrior by speaking his name. "Hear me! Mfalme Jobabwe has given us a mission. We have to honor his request somehow. Under the circumstances, and strategically, I think Nionu's cat's tail offense is the only option left to us."

"Yes, we must honor the Mfalme's request. But we need a better plan."

"Then, if you know one, please share it with me. I am listening."

Nienko searched his mind for other options. Though he was a tactical warrior in one of the best tactical warrior regiments, his tactical mind drew a complete blank. Instead of offering Wema an alternate course of action, he found arguing against Wema's plan easier. "Mfalme Jobabwe sent us out here to warn the farmers to stay away from the valley. We have just learned that Bone-Face is out here too, heading directly toward the farmers. That means, when he reaches them, they are dead. Our warning serves no purpose now."

"So, what should we do? Give up? Go back to a dead valley?"

The statement was enough to silence the young Red Warrior. When he found his voice again, he spoke softly. "I think our mission has failed, Wema."

"You are not thinking like a warrior, Great Creation. Get failure out of your head. Listen to me. As warriors, we must always do our best, even when it seems hopeless. Leave it to others to determine if we have failed or not."

"To reach the farmers, we must cross the Mara. The Kiboko Passage provides the only way to reach the Mara. With the demon descending the passage before us, it is like walking into a spider's web. That thing will easily snare and kill both of us."

"I realize that. That is why you will get to the Mara differently. You will not go through the passage."

"I will not? Do you know of another way?"

"Yes, over the river's embankment." Wema looked toward the rocky embankment that ran up and down the Mara River. He pointed with his spear. "You may go upstream or downstream. It does not matter which. Somehow, you must go over the embankment. It will be a long drop. It will be dangerous and impossible in some places. But you are a Red Warrior, Nienko. You can do it. You have to do it. Get past the embankment and cross the Mara. The farmers cannot be too far on the other side. Find them. And, for what it is worth, deliver the Mfalme's warning."

The Red Warrior Nienko always admired Wema. Several harvests ago, when Nienko asked the Blue Warrior Obe Bendabe for permission to join his regiment, Wema vouched for his qualities as a good warrior. Nienko vowed his allegiance to Obe Bendabe and never let Wema down for his support.

"So be it, Great Creation." Nienko set aside all his objections. He surrendered to his duties. He conducted himself like a Red Warrior. "What about you? What are you going to do? You have to know, if you engage the demon, it will kill you."

"Maybe. But please, my friend. Let me find a little comfort in, at least, thinking I can somehow out-smart this thing. If our timing is right, you will find the farmers and warn them before death finishes with me. For what it is worth, our mission will be successful."

"Wema, it is said this thing can drop whole armies with the wave of its hand. It will kill you. It will kill me. And then it will kill the farmers. Is that a successful mission?"

Wema shrugged. "It sounds hopeless. In times like these, the Great Creation Kon-Shambique has taught us to focus on the little victories, one little victory at a time. Little victories have the power to destroy hopelessness. One tiny victory can make a difference."

"One tiny victory? Wema, we will need a lot of tiny victories."

"Then, let us begin with the first."

"Which is?"

Wema shrugged again. "I would love to see death's mouth drop open with surprise when you get past it and reach the farmers."

Wema's statement caused a smile of inspiration to crack Nienko's face. Nienko looked in the Orange Warrior's eyes. He had known Wema for as long as he could remember. He cherished his bond with the Orange Warrior, his friend and his mentor.

Nienko took the initiative. He switched his strong walk to a slow run. "Come, Great Creation. You want to see the demon's mouth drop open with surprise? Then get ready to count every tooth in its bony head."

"Now there is the Nienko I know." Wema matched Nienko's pace.

— **69** —

A SHORT REST BEFORE THE CROSSING

Back on the north side of the Mara and just before sunset, Tutapona cried again. His discomfort did not qualify as a tantrum yet. He experienced enough irritability to squirm and stretch in the kanga on his mother's back as best he could.

Lobarra reached up to shift the kanga from her back to the front. Before she could cradle Tutapona in her arms, she knew the problem. It was feeding time. Tutapona's appetite was as strong and as regular as sunrise and sunset. But his periods of hunger did not correspond with the traveling farmers' rest stops. Tutapona's crying was his way of asking for what he felt he needed.

Lobarra tried to calm him with a few jostles. The jostling did not work, and Tutapona's crying grew stronger. As Lobarra walked, she freed one of her breasts and offered it to Tutapona. The infant quieted down and suckled. He took a few nourishing draws but pulled away in frustration. He cried again. Lobarra offered her breast twice more. Each time, Tutapona rejected it, as frustration dominated the moment. Lobarra recovered her breast and raised Tutapona, so his head rested on her shoulder.

Lobarra resumed the sometimes successful technique of jostling him back to sleep. Once more, countless times during the trip to Kiwane Village, Lobarra regretted not listening to Tutapona's paternal grandfather's advice. The Chinchigwe Mfalme, Ameh Jobabwe, had asked Lobarra to leave Tutapona with him. Ameh had offered to care for Tutapona while Lobarra was away. But Lobarra refused the offers.

Lobarra did not want to break the bonding process with her son. She felt that the process was at its strongest. As a loving mother, Lobarra did what she could to keep the process strong and healthy. But as Lobarra struggled to pacify Tutapona, she wondered if she had done all she could. In hindsight, the bonding process may have been better under different conditions.

The Red Warrior Rotho noticed Lobarra's distress and walked up beside her. "Sacred Woman, can I help?"

"Thank you, Great Creation, but no." Lobarra looked into Tutapona's face. Tutapona lay with his eyes closed, but he still squirmed. "He is hungry. I think nothing will satisfy him now but his mother's milk."

Rotho looked ahead and behind at the traveling caravan. "Our pace is slow, Sacred Woman. Can you not feed him as we walk?"

"I have tried, Great Creation. Recently, I learned that Tutapona does not enjoy his nourishment unless I am relaxed and comfortable."

The Red Warrior Rotho looked at Tutapona and smiled. "Even now, his mother's comfort must come first. It only means he will grow to be a Thoughtful Creation."

It was a compliment, and Lobarra accepted it with a smile. "When is our next stop? Will it be soon?"

Rotho glanced at the setting sun. "I think we have, at least, another kilometer to go before we reach the Mara River. If the Kiboko Passage is still clear, we will cross the river before we stop."

"Do you think we could stop on this side long enough for me to feed Tutapona?"

"I do not know. It will be the Green Warrior's decision. Would you like me to ask him?"

Lobarra looked toward the head of the caravan. The Green Warrior Tushema was among the seven warriors leading the way. "No, Great Creation. I will ask him. We have to stop on this side. I must feed Tutapona. He will not wait until after the crossing. If I ask Tushema to stop, the Green Warrior may be more understanding."

Lobarra broke from her position in the caravan and increased her pace. She drew curious looks from each farmer as she walked past them. She quickly moved toward the front of the group.

The Green Warrior Tushema made one of his frequent glances at the caravan behind him. Lobarra's break from her usual position easily caught his attention. When he saw her coming, he became concerned and slowed his pace. He dropped back to walk at Lobarra's side.

"What is it, Sacred Woman?"

"Great Creation," she began, "is it possible we may stop on this side of the Mara for a short while. I need to feed Tutapona."

The Green Warrior Tushema looked at Tutapona. The infant squirmed as he lay against Lobarra's shoulder. Just as Rotho had done, Tushema looked toward the setting sun to estimate the time. The sun was no longer a red orb. It had merged with the evening clouds and had become a brilliant red mass melting and spreading over the western horizon.

Earlier, Tushema instructed the Gold Warrior Oghani to send a warrior ahead to scout the Kiboko Passage to determine whether migrating animals had blocked it. Oghani selected the Red Warrior Berko, who left running.

Several hours ago, Berko returned with very good news. The Kiboko Passage was clear, and the news was enough to give the Green Warrior his final incentive to get the farmers across the Mara.

"Sacred Woman, I want to cross the Mara River before nightfall. Can you feed him after the crossing?"

Tutapona cried again. Once again, Lobarra jostled the infant. "I do not think so."

"We will reach the north bank of the Mara within minutes, Sacred Woman. I will allow a short rest stop before the crossing, but a very short one; just long enough to prepare the pack animals for the crossing. Will that be acceptable?"

"Yes, Great Creation. A short stop is all we need. Thank you."

— 70 —

A MOST UNUSUAL TRAVELER

Several meters of barren and sandy ground lay exposed on the Mara River's north and south banks, naked of greenery and life. Once covered by higher water levels, small boulders, driftwood, and other debris lay scattered up and down the banks. Here and there among the debris lay the dried bones of a few unfortunate animals; the flesh long ago washed away by the river water, baked dry by the African sun, and then picked clean by nature's efficient cleaners - the scavenger birds and bugs.

The Green Warrior Tushema led the caravan from the gassy plain, down the gentle incline of the embankment, and onto the sandy riverbank. He brought the farmers, warriors, and pack animals to a stop about midway between the plain and the river water. He instructed the group to wait a moment where they stood. The Green Warrior wanted to quickly survey the area before agreeing to cross the river.

Tushema, alone, walked down toward the unpredictable river. He studied the flow of the river as he approached. The rapid movement of the water always surprised him. He broke his focus when he walked around the bony remains of a small gazelle that lay nearby. His approach had frightened away three fan-tail ravens that pecked at the gazelle's bones and hunted for the bugs and the final, minuscule morsels of flesh.

Tushema looked down into the river water at the river's edge. He knew the river well. The water level was not as low as he expected. But, in his opinion, it was still safe enough for the crossing. The experienced warrior knew it was always formidable, even when the Mara looked safe. Its currents, even at half-meter depth, were sometimes strong enough to sweep the most agile Creation off his feet. The rushing water always held other dangers that were not so visible.

This section of the river was almost perfect. In total consideration of the farmers, the Green Warrior had chosen this section for the crossing for two reasons. This section of the river was only ten meters wide at its narrowest point, and its depth was about half a meter at its deepest point. Crossing the river, Tushema assumed, should not be too difficult for the farmers and their pack animals.

Tushema looked across the river to the opposite bank and toward the second reason for choosing this section of the river: the Kiboko Passage. The Kiboko Passage was a narrow incline trailed through the rocky embankment. It was a gorge, created over time by hippopotamuses entering or leaving the Mara River during the wet seasons. Migrating wildebeests, zebras, and other ungulates always seemed to know where this gorge was. They used it repeatedly, making it a permanent passage used by every living creature that passed through the area.

The Green Warrior Tushema saw footprints and droppings of migrating animals around him. He could tell that a few herds had already crossed the Kiboko Passage, crossed the river, and proceeded northward. But at the moment, the Kiboko Passage, on the south bank, was still clear and easily accessible, just as the scout warrior had reported.

The rest of the bank on the opposite side of the river was almost the same as the north bank on which Tushema and the farmers stood. Barren and sandy ground, several meters wide, stretched between the river water and the opposite embankment. But unlike the gentle incline of the embankment on this side of the river, the opposite embankment stood as a solid wall. It rose almost eight to nine meters straight up, impossible to climb. It stretched as far as Tushema could see, upstream and downstream. The Kiboko Passage, like a sizable crack in the wall, provided the only way through the embankment and up to the grassy plain on the south side of the river.

After Tushema had initially surveyed the crossing point, he turned and walked back toward the farmers. He singled out Lobarra. "Sacred Woman, as promised, you may have a few moments."

"Thank you, Great Creation."

As Lobarra walked away to find a semi-secluded spot, Tushema nodded at the Red Warrior Rotho. With that nod, Tushema reminded the Red Warrior to stay close to Lobarra and Tutapona. In this brief period, it would be his sole responsibility. Rotho acknowledged Tushema with a nod of his own. He set out to follow Lobarra at a discreet distance.

The Green Warrior Tushema selected and sent three warriors to scout the upstream bank of the Mara River. He sent three more to do the same along the downstream bank. It was a thorough and necessary precaution. He knew the Mara River drew animals from the open plains – lions, hyenas, cheetahs, baboons, giraffes, hippopotamuses, and elephants. Because of the Kiboko Passage, all the animals found it easy to cross here. And any of these animals, driven by their instinct to use the passage, could present a danger.

Since everyone had to wait for Lobarra to finish feeding Tutapona and for the warriors to secure the banks of the river, Tushema made use of those precious moments. He used the time to help prepare the rest of the farmers for the crossing.

"This is our return trip, and I know you have all heard it from me before," he said. "Please exercise caution. As we cross the river, expect the unexpected. I cannot overemphasize this warning enough."

"We can sense your concerns, and we are grateful. Elder Zekke chuckled at Tushema. "But do not worry about us. For most of us, this return trip is one among many. We have done this before, in deeper waters than this."

Tushema was helping another farmer secure baskets and gourds more tightly on one of the pack animals. When he heard Zekke's comment, he almost took offense. He stopped working and looked at the Old Creation. "Even though you have crossed the Mara many times, each time is a new experience. This river has no room for complacency."

"Yes, you are right, Great Creation. I stand corrected. Please, be assured. We will make this crossing with caution. It will be like our first."

"During the dry season," the Green Warrior continued, "the water is clear. In the shallow areas, you can see the bottom. I need not tell most of you that the clarity of the water makes no difference. It is still just as dangerous. If you do nothing else, watch your step. Watch the water at all times."

"As you said, you need not tell most of us. Experience counts for something." Elder Zekke nodded toward the downstream bank. The subtle gesture told the Green Warrior there was one among them who was less experienced.

Tushema looked in the direction Zekke had directed. Several meters away, he could see the Sacred Woman Lobarra. She had found an old log. She sat upon it, peacefully nursing Tutapona. Tushema could also see, not far away from her, the Red Warrior Rotho. Rotho walked near the river's edge as he guarded Lobarra and Tutapona.

"The Great Creation, Mfalme Jobabwe, was thoughtful enough to augment this trip with an extra warrior," Tushema said. "Lobarra and Tutapona have an extra set of eyes on the surrounding waters."

*****

The Red Warrior Rotho paced on the riverbank, only a few meters from where Lobarra sat. He noticed that Tutapona's crying had stopped. Against the running river water, he heard the soft, melodious lullaby that the Sacred Woman Lobarra always sang to Tutapona. Lobarra had relaxed enough to feed Tutapona with ease. Tutapona appeared to nurse with contentment. The lullaby and the beautiful sight of mother and child brought a smile to Rotho's face.

Rotho turned in a slow circle. With the eyes of a warrior, he kept a careful watch on the entire surrounding area. He looked along the upstream bank to see the rest of the farmers. The farmers huddled with their pack animals, preparing them for the crossing. Further along the downstream bank, Rotho saw the three warriors that Tushema had sent to survey the southern stretch of the bank. They had found nothing significant and were already on their return upstream.

The river where Rotho stood was wider, and the water seemed more turbulent as it rushed past. As he studied the area, he could not help but notice the rocky embankment on the opposite side. It seemed, at least, another meter or two higher.

Rotho noticed a lioness and three kittens walking along the top edge of the embankment. Rotho saw one of the kittens wobble near the ledge as they moved farther downstream. One of the kitten's paws slipped over the edge. But the young cat was agile enough to claw a firm hold. It followed the others as if nothing had happened. A fall, ten meters straight down, could be tragic. It made Rotho reassess how valuable the Kiboko Passage was, not just for the caravan of traveling farmers, but for anything crossing the Mara.

Rotho watched the lioness and her kittens until they disappeared from view farther down the embankment. By this time, Lobarra had finished nursing Tutapona. Rotho gave her a few more moments to re-wrap Tutapona in his bundle. When she got up, Rotho approached her.

"That was fast. Is he finished already?"

Lobarra looked down at Tutapona, cradled in her arms. "I am just as surprised as you are, Great Creation. He nursed strongly, but not for long."

The three warriors returning upstream were close enough now to overhear Lobarra's comment. The most senior warrior of the three was the Gold Warrior Oghani. He walked over in playful confusion. "Do you mean he only nursed briefly after all that fussing and fretting?"

"Yes, Great Creation. I suppose he was not as hungry as he thought he was."

"The Little Creation fooled all of us." Oghani peered into the baby bundle. He stroked Tutapona's cheek with his finger. He and Tutapona smiled.

Rotho and the other warriors huddled over Oghani's shoulder, peering into the bundle. Tutapona seemed aware of all the ogling faces and the attention he was getting. He gave all of them a broader, two-tooth smile.

"Are you ready to rejoin the others, Sacred Woman?" Rotho finally asked.

"Yes. The Green Warrior Tushema will be happy to learn that we did not need all the time he graciously gave us. There may still be daylight when we reach the grass plain on the other side."

Just then, the Red Warrior Rotho looked upstream to where the rest of the farmers waited. He saw an unmistakable sign that something was wrong. All the farmers had gathered about their pack animals in a tight huddle. The other Aukmondi warriors stood in an alert formation behind Green Warrior Tushema. Tushema, with spear and shield held ready, stared out over the Mara. On the other side of the Mara River, at the entrance of the Kiboko Passage, an unusually tall stranger stood, staring back at them.

"Who is that?" Rotho asked. "He is a most unusual traveler. Do any of you recognize him or his tribe?"

At first, no one answered Rotho. The traveler's odd appearance struck everyone speechless. Something about the stranger was not normal. The traveler stared back at the farmers and the warriors. His stare seemed aggressive and threatening.

The Gold Warrior Oghani stopped walking. He held his arms out of caution, signaling the others at his side to stop walking and hold back. "He is from no tribe I can recognize."

Just then, the strange traveler noticed the small group coming upstream. He slowly turned and looked in their direction. Over the distance, Oghani, Rotho, Lobarra, and the others could see no clear features of the stranger. But they caught a glimpse of the stranger's face, recessed under the oversized hood.

"Look at him!" Rotho's whisper was almost vocal. "His face is painted, like a Wabanga."

Oghani shook his head. "No, Great Creation. That is not a Wabanga."

"Where do you suppose he came from?"

"I do not know. I recognize nothing about him."

"Whoever he is or wherever he is from, I sense he means us no good."

"I have to agree." The Gold Warrior Oghani tapped Rotho on the shoulder. "Secure the Sacred Woman. Make sure she and Tutapona stay out of harm's way." Oghani addressed the other two warriors. "Come. I am sure the Green Warrior can use our help."

Oghani and the other two warriors rushed upstream to join the group standing behind the Green Warrior Tushema. In that ten-meter stretch across the river, they could now see what everyone else saw— what people in the Aukmondi Valley had seen over the past two days.

The strange traveler stood 215 centimeters in height. He wore an all-black garment of unquestionable decay. Torn and moldy rags, tattered strings, and ropes covered the garment, a ground-length tunic with a large, oversized hood. He wore a cape of the same thick black material covered with more decayed, rotting rags, strings, and ropes. The cape gently flowed and waved in the wind, where there was no wind.

Although the traveler's eyes could not be seen, its chalky white face was visible under the oversized hood.

"I do not know. His face is painted, like a Wabanga," Rotho insisted.

"Remove that thought, Great Creation." There was a touch of tension in Oghani's voice. "His face is not painted. That is no Wabanga."

"No, he is not." The Green Warrior had overheard Rotho and Oghani's debate. He took another step toward the river to focus on the stranger. Even though he and no one else could recognize who they were looking at, Tushema was still willing to make one more civil attempt to make peaceful contact. He called out to the traveler, "Great Creation! Are you lost? Can we help you? Is there something you need?"

The traveler did not answer. Instead, he slowly reached out with his right hand. With fingers of bone, it beckoned.

Lobarra stood with the other farmers. The traveler's face was just as bony as its hand. The shocking sight made her step back. "Great Sacred Spirit! What is that thing? It is … it is not human."

The Green Warrior took a more defensive posture. He adjusted his shield for more protection. He lowered the point of his spear toward the stranger. He gave a series of commanding orders without taking his eyes off the stranger. "Oghani, Rotho, move the farmers back. Look after them. The rest of you, flank me. We will learn how human our traveler really is."

"I got a bad feeling about this." The old farmer Zekke spoke, discomfort heard in his voice. "Tushema, Great Creation, do you think it is necessary to challenge him like that?"

"It seems to be what he wants. And if we are to cross the river by nightfall, it is inevitable." With another step, the Green Warrior stepped into the Mara River.

"No! Stop! Stop! Do not do it!" Nienko's voice suddenly echoed from a distance.

The frantic Red Warrior was about eighty-five meters away, downstream. He stood on top of the embankment in about the same place Rotho had seen the lioness and her kittens. Nienko stood tall, waving his spear and shield over his head as he yelled. He was desperately trying to get the Green Warrior's attention.

In his efforts, he too stood close to the embankment's edge. His foot slipped. Nienko fell. He desperately reached for something to hold on to. He clawed into the dirt and grass. The Red Warrior broke his slide for just an instant when he caught a root. But then, the root snapped. Nienko slipped completely off the embankment. Nienko yelled. His voice echoed upstream and foretold a sure tragedy.

The yell ended with abrupt silence when Nienko hit his head against the rocky wall of the embankment. Semi-conscious, Nienko made one hopeless tumble. He hit the sandy bank below with a solid thud.

When the demon heard Nienko yell out, it stopped beckoning. With almost a look of surprise, it swiveled around in the Red Warrior's direction. When the demon heard the resounding thud of the warrior's body hitting the bank, it glided smoothly and quickly downstream. Although several meters away, it reached for the injured Red Warrior, eager to kill with a touch.

— **71** —

YOU KNOW HIM TOO

Just a short while earlier, the Orange Warrior Wema and the Red Warrior Nienko had quickly crossed the final half-kilometer stretch to the Kiboko Passage. They peered down the rocky slope. The passage was a small gorge, centered by a well-trodden pathway. Boulders, nooks, and crevices lined the walls of the gorge. The carcasses of a few dead animals lay here and there along the gorge's slope.

Because the slope meandered, the warriors could see only a few meters into the small gorge. They knew that gorge's pathway ended on the bank of the Mara. They also knew the demon was somewhere on that pathway, between where they stood and the river's bank.

The Orange Warrior pointed to a large, nearby boulder, almost a meter and a half high. He spoke in a whisper. "I can still see most of the Mara's embankments from atop that boulder. I will wait there until you reach the embankment. Be mindful, I will not descend the passage and engage the demon until I see you go over. Understood?"

"Understood, Great Creation." The Red Warrior turned and left. But he hesitated. He looked back at Wema. In his opinion, Wema was making a heroic but deadly sacrifice. Nienko realized this may be the last time he would see his friend alive. Parting was difficult. It was second only to leaving his mother and sister in the valley.

"Wema." Nienko paused. His feelings were strong. To put those feelings into words came hard. "May the Supreme Spirit always be with you."

"And you too, my friend." Wema made sure he returned Nienko the smile of a true friend, one that would be remembered always. He leaped up onto the boulder and made himself comfortable. "I cannot promise everything will turn out well. But whatever happens, let us do our best to embrace Her will."

Without a word, Nienko turned away. He studied the distant embankments. The Red Warrior Nienko considered Wema's strategy and chose the downstream embankment. It offered the clearest and most unobstructed view from the boulder and the entrance of the Kiboko Passage. In a crouched and cautious run, he quickly headed for the embankment, about 223 meters away. His only obstruction came just before reaching the embankment. In an unexpected development, Nienko intruded upon a roaming lioness and her three kittens.

When he saw the lioness, Nienko froze. A lioness with kittens could be protective to the point of being aggressive. He readied his spear, just in case. He slowly stooped to the ground to avoid drawing attention to himself. The effort drew more attention. The lioness looked directly at him. She snarled at the intrusion. But she had other, more pressing things on her mind. She dismissed the warrior with a short, rumbling groan. She hastened her pace and led her kittens away.

Nienko watched the lioness and her kittens until they had moved farther along the embankment, downstream. After he felt it was safe enough, he belly-crawled the rest of the way to the embankment's edge. Near the edge, he slowly rose to see what he could see.

To his surprise, Nienko's first sight was the Red Warrior Rotho standing at the river's edge on the opposite bank. Rotho was staring across the Mara watching the lioness and her kittens farther down the embankment. A few meters inland, Nienko saw the Sacred Woman Lobarra sitting on a log. Lobarra cradled Tutapona in her arms. She looked as if she had been nursing him. Further downstream, Nienko also saw the warriors Oghani, Berko, and Wekesa. The three were walking back upstream to join Lobarra and Rotho. Seeing them all was a pleasant surprise. Nienko realized that he was closer to the farmers than he expected. And he saw no sign of the demon yet. He smiled.

Nienko crawled a few centimeters closer to the ledge. He slowly peered over the embankment. It was a noticeable drop, about ten meters straight down. As he considered ways to reach the bank, he remembered the plan of the Orange Warrior Wema. Wema would not descend the slope and engage the demon until he saw Nienko go over the embankment. It suddenly occurred to Nienko that he might not have to go over the embankment if he could get everyone's attention. Wema would not have had to make such a heroic sacrifice of himself.

When Nienko saw the Gold Warrior Oghani leading the others farther upstream, he stood. Nienko had to hurry. He had to get their attention before they moved too far away. But he stood up and saw the Green Warrior Tushema farther upstream. Tushema was standing in a noticeable defensive posture. Other warriors stood behind Tushema with spears held ready. Nienko knew the reason.

The Red Warrior leaned out over the edge of the embankment. He tried to locate the demon. He tried to improve his view twice, edging closer to the ledge each time. That is when he heard the Green Warrior Tushema call out to the demon on the opposite bank. *"Great Creation, are you lost? Can we help you? Is there anything you need?"*

From his vantage point on the ledge, the Red Warrior Nienko still could not see the demon. But he had no doubt Tushema spoke to it. When Tushema stepped into the Mara, Nienko realized a direct engagement was inevitable. The Red Warrior also knew those warriors had no idea what they faced. He felt he had no choice but to stop them–right now!

"No! Stop!" Nienko waved his shield and spear over his head as he shouted. "Stop! Do not do it!"

Nienko completely forgot about how close he was to the ledge. The soil beneath his left foot suddenly fell away. Nienko lost his balance and slipped over the edge. In a desperate effort to grab something to hold on to, Nienko dropped his spear and shield. His spear and shield tumbled twice, banging against the rocky facing of the embankment. They fell over ten meters before coming to rest on the bank. As the Red Warrior slipped farther over the ledge, he hung on to a thick root, but only for an instant. The root snapped.

Nienko fell backwards over the embankment. He tumbled only once, but the drop seemed like forever. The side of his head hit the rocky face, almost knocking him unconscious. Nienko barely remembered landing hard on the bank.

The pain in Nienko's leg was tremendous. It brought him back to full consciousness. The Red Warrior held his breath to prevent all unnecessary movements. With his lungs begging for air, he rolled over on his back and struggled to sit. To his dismay, he discovered his left leg was broken. He also realized blood from his injured head streamed down his neck onto his chest. That is when he looked up and saw the demon of death gliding along the bank toward him. The Red Warrior tried to stand but the crippling pain intensified. The demon continued its approach. Nienko looked around for his spear and shield. They lay on the ground only two meters away. The instant he located them, he realized they would do him no good against the demon.

Despite the pain, Nienko forced himself to stand on his good leg. He abandoned his shield and spear. He hopped downstream along the bank to escape the approaching demon. The foot of his broken leg never touched the ground, but his leg throbbed with each hop.

Nienko looked back. The demon was gaining on him rapidly. Nienko had no hope of hopping away from the demon. He made the impulsive decision to hop into the river. With the demon on his heels, he made it to the river in five painful hops. He fell into the water, hoping that he could swim away from the demon faster than he could hop.

The Red Warrior hit the water with a very ungraceful splash. Underwater boulders, rocks, and debris obstructed his first desperate swim effort. Nienko could feel the river bottom. Instead of swimming, Nienko grabbed rocks and debris to pull himself through the water.

Nienko's efforts to move seemed to entail strength and leverage from his broken leg. The physical pains continued to intensify. But he had to keep moving. He flipped over to move past a small boulder that blocked his way. Nienko looked back at the riverbank. He saw the demon standing on the bank. The demon had stopped chasing him and only reached for the Red Warrior. Nienko seized the opportunity to abate the pain in his leg. He flipped over and stopped. He rose to sit on the river bottom in the middle of the Mara.

By the time Nienko had wiped the water and blood from his eyes, the demon had returned and retrieved the Red Warrior's spear. The demon rushed back to the edge of the water. As if to rescue the injured warrior, the demon offered Nienko the butt end of his spear. Nienko refused it. The demon extended the spear further, suggesting that the warrior take it. Nienko refused it again and scooted away. In frustration, the demon tossed the spear aside. It paced back and forth, beckoning Nienko with both bony hands to return to the bank.

By this time, the Green Warrior Tushema and the other warriors had rushed downstream to help Nienko. Most of them had waded into the river water to come out and rescue the Red Warrior. Two warriors yanked Nienko up to stand on his good leg. Tushema and several other warriors took a defensive position before Nienko to protect him from the demon, their spears ready. Tushema drew his arm back, ready to whirl his spear at the demon.

Nienko saw the warrior's imminent strike. He feared that provocation would cause the demon to resume his deadly advance. Once again, he yelled out to Tushema. "No, Great Creation! Do not! That thing can kill you with a wave of its hand."

Tushema froze. He slowly lowered his spear and ordered everyone back onto the north bank. The two warriors who supported Nienko under his shoulders helped him hobble back to the bank. The rest of the warriors, their spears still held ready, never took their eyes off the demon. They slowly waded backwards until they had joined Tushema and the others on the bank.

Tushema could see blood still streaming down Nienko's face. He quickly led everyone back upstream to where the farmers and the pack animals waited. One of the pack animals carried all the medical supplies that Nienko might need. As Tushema walked, he threw curious glances toward the demon. Its appearance and behavior continued to fascinate him. In his long career, Tushema had seen nothing like it.

The demon had stopped his pacing and beckoning. He followed Tushema and the others upstream on the opposite bank until they set the Red Warrior down among the farmers and pack animals. As the curious farmers huddled around Nienko, the demon paced back and forth, stopping only to beckon.

The Green Warrior Tushema finally broke his fascination with the demon and worked to the group's center, huddled around Nienko. He kneeled beside Nienko and nodded toward the demon. "Do you know that Creation?"

"Yes. You know him, too. He is …"

While Nienko and Tushema talked, Elder Zekke did his best to clean and bandage Nienko's head. The Gold Warrior Oghani also examined Nienko's broken leg. He gently gripped Nienko's shin and then, completely unannounced, yanked the Red Warrior's leg.

Nienko cut short what he was about to say to Tushema. He yelled out in pain.

Oghani waited for Nienko to recover from his pain before he told him, "Sorry, Great Creation. Your leg is broken. It had to be reset."

"Great Sacred Spirit! At least, you could have warned me." Nienko snapped at Oghani. It was the pain talking. Tears from sheer pain welled up in his eyes and ran down his cheeks. Nienko closed his eyes and held his breath to overpower the pain. He opened his eyes and sighed heavily when the pain subsided. Nienko suddenly realized he had just shouted in anger at a superior warrior. He looked at Oghani and touched the Gold Warrior's shoulder. "I am sorry for yelling at you, Great Creation. I meant no disrespect. Thank you."

With a smile, Oghani accepted Nienko's apology as he continued to splint and wrap the Red Warrior's leg.

The Green Warrior Tushema had stood up and moved back when Nienko yelled out in pain. He looked down at the Red Warrior and waited patiently for him to recover. When he saw Nienko wipe away his tears of pain and look up, he spoke. "You were saying."

"My apologies to you, too, Great Creation." Nienko pointed. "That Dark Creation on the other side of the river is death."

"Death?" Tushema looked at the demon. He looked down at Nienko again. As a 'no nonsense' person, the Green Warrior's brow knitted with confusion. "How is that Creation 'death'?"

"That is no Creation. That is the spirit of death. If it touches you, Great Creation, you will die – literally. If you touch anything it has embraced, you will die. Challenge it. It will consume your every thought, overpower you, and take your life. That is death."

"How do you know all this?" Elder Zekke asked. "And why are you here anyway?"

"Since you and the other farmers left the valley, Great Creation, there have been several, horrible… very horrible incidents in the valley. Conditions are so bad that… everyone feels abandoned by the Supreme Spirit. It got to where Mfalme Ameh Jobabwe sent us to warn you. He wants you to stay away from the valley until … until whatever happens to us is all over."

"What is happening?" Tushema asked.

"People are dying, Great Creation." Nienko sighed. He considered the best way to explain recent events. "People are dying in great numbers. It all started two days ago when Mfalme Abul-Gwan of the Mangoni Tribe visited Mfalme Ncobba on business. He brought his mate, a Vodun houngan, and a caged Wabanga."

"A Wabanga?"

"Yes. Mfalme Abul-Gwan said that the caged Wabanga was necessary to demonstrate an urgent need. The Mfalme needed help from us and other tribes in the region. He wanted to create the freedom to hunt, kill, and sell various animal remains. To make a long story short, Mfalme Ncobba refused to help the Mangoni. Mfalme Ncobba explained. Our respect for life prevented any help. It was a matter of principle. Abul-Gwan did not seem to understand this, and it upset the Mangoni Mfalme. I guess the refusal changed Mfalme Abul-Gwan's attitude about us. He turned bitter. At first, he prepared to leave our valley."

"But? He did not leave?"

"No. Things turned ugly when, later, the Wabanga escaped. He killed the Sacred Woman Abul-Tess, the mate of the Mangoni

Mfalme. Abul-Gwan somehow blamed the Aukmondi people for wasting his time and causing the death of his mate. Out of grief and revenge, he asked his Vodun houngan to place the curse of death on all of us."

"The curse of death?" Elder Zekke sat back, bewildered. "Is there such a thing?"

"Yes. As unbelievable as it sounds, Great Creation, the curse is very real. Many people in the valley have already died from death's touch, including all the people of the Pogobi, Obentawni, Butetwa, and Mempa kraals. The deaths include the Mfalme Ncobba, the Sacred Women Rwuva and Tongda, and the warriors Mbinga, Gengu, and Zabiba."

"Oh, Great Sacred Spirit!" The news overcame Lobarra, and she could no longer stand. Rotho and several other warriors helped her sit on the ground.

"I do not have to tell you that the whole tribe is saddened," Nienko continued. "Even the inspiring spirit of Great Creation Kon-Shambique has turned dark. After Tongda's death, you would not believe how the Favored Tribesman is broken."

"Please tell me this is not true!" Zekke and everyone else looked at the specter across the river again. They looked at him in silence and awe. They saw the beckoning demon with a completely new perspective.

"Before we left the valley to warn you," Nienko continued, "we heard a rumor that the entire valley would die in two days. The rumor started almost two nights ago. If the rumor proves true, then by now, everyone in the valley…"

The Green Warrior Tushema gripped his spear. He turned and took several steps toward the river. Tushema was ready to confront this 'so-called' demon of death. He stopped only when he realized what Nienko had just said. He turned back to the Red Warrior. "You said *we*? You did not come alone?"

"No, Great Creation. To spare you and the farmers the touch of the demon, the Mfalme Ameh Jobabwe sent me and the Orange Warrior Wema to warn you."

"So, where is the Orange Warrior?"

Nienko pointed across the river. "He should be somewhere on the Kiboko Passage. From the grassy plain, we saw the demon enter the passage. The Orange Warrior went behind him to use the Royal Warrior Nionu's 'cat's tail' offense, to distract or engage him. He hoped to hold him back long enough for me to get past him, over the embankment. We hoped I could get to you first and deliver the Mfalme Jobabwe's warning."

"Is this demon aware that the Orange Warrior is coming down the passage?"

"That thing seems aware of everything." Nienko rubbed his eyes as if to massage away the hopelessness he felt. When his vision cleared, he saw Tushema looking at him. Tushema was waiting for a more professional answer. Nienko looked at the demon and gave Tushema a more thoughtful answer. "I do not think so, Great Creation. If the demon knew Wema was coming down the passage, he would go after him. That is how it works."

"If the Mangoni houngan called this demon to kill us," the Sacred Woman Lobarra said, "then why has it not come to finish us? Instead, he only stands there, beckoning."

The Green Warrior Tushema studied the demon at the river's edge. When he heard Lobarra's question, he looked down at the flowing river water. He realized something that everyone had overlooked until now. "It is the river. The river seems to be a natural boundary."

Elder Zekke stepped forward. "The Red Warrior Nienko says this thing can dismiss life with just the wave of his hand. Yet, you say the river bounds him?"

"Is it not obvious, Great Creation? Since the demon has appeared, he has only beckoned. I will say, the river limits the demon."

Zekke studied the demon. "It seems so. I think you are right."

"The river is one of the Supreme Spirit's natural boundaries. The demon cannot cross it, nor can its deadly influences. As long as we keep the river between us and the demon, we are all safe."

"We may be safe," Nienko added. "But what about the Orange Warrior Wema? He is still on the other side. Can we help him somehow?"

Tushema studied the beckoning demon again. He looked past him, into the inclining gorge that made the Kiboko Passage. He searched for any sign of the Orange Warrior coming down the passageway. There wasn't yet. It meant he had time to execute an idea.

Tushema turned to the group behind him. He pointed southward. "Everyone, let us move downstream. Hurry!"

"Great Creation," Zekke protested at the sudden order. He gestured toward the other farmers and pack animals as he lifted a basket from the ground. "You realize that we are not warriors. You must give us a moment to gather our things."

"Leave them." Tushema selected two warriors, then pointed to Nienko. "You two, assist the Red Warrior. He has to move too."

Elder Zekke set the basket back down. "To where are we moving, in such a hurry?"

"About a hundred meters downstream, Great Creation. Now, please, let us hurry."

"Why are we doing this?"

After moving just a few meters downstream, Tushema glanced across the river at the demon. He pointed. "That is why." As Tushema suspected, the demon mimicked the group, moving downstream on the opposite bank. "When the Orange Warrior Wema emerges from the passage, he must have enough room and time to get from the passage, across the bank, and to the river. We are moving the demon out of Wema's way."

72

DEATH WANTS ME DEAD

Several moments ago, at the edge of the grassy plain, the Orange Warrior Wema crouched on top of the boulder near the entrance of the Kiboko Passage. He waited and watched his friend, the Red Warrior Nienko, move quickly through the grass toward the downstream embankment. While he waited, he contemplated the deadly task before him.

The demon of death; what is the best strategy to engage it? Wema thought, should he taunt it? Should he call it out and confront it face to face? Should he try to sneak up on it and attack it from the rear? Wema thought about each of these strategies. He dismissed each one. All of them were only preludes to instant death. Wema realized that he had only one clear aim, to make death take as long as possible to finish him – the longer the better.

Wema ended his contemplation abruptly when he saw a lioness and her kittens crossing Nienko's path. The lioness represented the potential for a failed plan in more ways than one. Wema stood. He jumped from the boulder and prepared to run to Nienko's rescue. But by the Supreme Spirit's good grace, the lioness moved on.

Wema relaxed and returned to the boulder. But before he could climb back on top and wait again, he saw Nienko stand. He saw the Red Warrior, with his spear and shield in his hands, waving his arms over his head. Was this some signal? From across the 223-meter stretch, he heard Nienko yell to someone over the embankment. It was a desperate yell.

Something was wrong. Wema took several anxious steps toward Nienko. Did his friend need his help? Before the Orange Warrior could recognize the problem, he saw something completely unexpected: Nienko suddenly went over the embankment.

Wema knew that Nienko had fallen down the rocky embankment. The Orange Warrior turned to enter the gorge. He descended the meandering slope at a full run. Wema's original plan was to get to the demon quickly. He planned to create whatever situation he could to make death take its time about killing him. But that plan was the old plan. The demon's location became a secondary concern. Wema had to find Nienko. The Red Warrior could be hurt, if not dead.

The Orange Warrior ran, hopped, and jumped among the rocks and treacherous trails that made the Kiboko Passage. To keep his rapid pace, he had no choice but to step on the carcasses of some of the dead animals lying along the way. He had to reach Nienko as quickly as possible. If Nienko only suffered some injury and needed help, Wema knew he might be the Red Warrior's only chance for recovery.

Wema's heightened concern for Nienko made him almost forget about the demon. Halfway down the gorge, Wema suddenly realized the demon could lurk behind the next twist or turn. At any instant, Wema could round the next corner right into death's hand. He had to take that chance. But then he also realized that if Nienko was dead, he was now the only hope to warn the returning farmers. Wema's pace became more cautious, but it never slowed.

*****

To his surprise, the Orange Warrior Wema reached the bottom of the passage. Despite his reckless urgency, Wema successfully negotiated the rocks, crevasses, and animal carcasses along the pathway. It seemed to take forever. But here he was. He estimated he had completed over 200 meters of twists and turns without incident. Just over ten more meters remained before exiting the rocky gorge. He could see the bank of the Mara, straight ahead.

Wema sighed with some relief. He reached the bottom of the passage without seeing a single sign of the demon. And, if the demon had seen him, the Orange Warrior would know it. Wema felt lucky. He also knew that, with such persistent luck, it had to end soon.

That thought ended Wema's rapid progress, increasing his sense of caution. Wema stood still for a moment to reassess his surroundings. Only the overwhelming urge to reach and help his friend forced Wema to move forward again. He slowly walked the last ten meters toward the gorge's exit, looking behind each boulder.

"Well, how about that?" Wema said to himself when he finally exited the gorge. He had expected to encounter the demon long before reaching this point. Wema came to a stop again. He stood for a moment, then slowly leaned forward to look around the entrance walls of the gorge. Wema listened. He heard only the sound of the rushing river water. The Orange Warrior looked out across the bank of the Mara. He saw nothing. Wema took two steps forward and looked to his right, upstream. Again, there was nothing and no one.

With another cautious step forward, Wema turned to his left and looked downstream. He saw a group of people about sixty meters away on the opposite riverbank. It was the farmers and their escorting warriors. In the middle of the group, Wema also saw his friend, the Red Warrior Nienko. As far as Wema could tell, Nienko appeared well. He had survived the fall.

Wema smiled. He raised his shield to wave. He called out to his friend. "Nienko!"

In that same instant, everyone standing on the opposite bank caught sight of Wema. Because of Nienko's story, everyone expected Wema to emerge from the gorge at any second. Nienko reacted first. He called back to Wema. Despite the pain in his leg, Nienko raised to rest all his support on his good knee. He pointed to some obscure point on the opposite side of the river. "Wema, Great Creation! The demon!"

Wema walked farther out on the bank to see where Nienko was pointing. Wema saw the demon several meters away, just as the demon saw him. The Orange Warrior's mouth went suddenly dry. His heart seemed to leap into his throat the instant the gruesome specter glided toward him.

"Cross the river, Great Creation!" The Green Warrior Tushema shouted out. "Cross the river if you can! The demon cannot cross the river!"

Wema did not wait for an explanation. With a burst of energy, he sprinted toward the river. With peripheral vision, Wema could see the demon closing the distance on him with amazing speed; its deadly, bony hand was already reaching.

When Wema reached the river's edge, his momentum never slowed. He made three loud, splashing steps into the river. But then he stopped. He stopped so suddenly that he almost fell forward. The Orange Warrior turned. He headed back to the south bank. He ran out of the water as fast as he entered. There was a good reason. Only centimeters behind him, a huge crocodile emerged from the river water.

The crocodile came halfway out of the river to pursue the Orange Warrior. With armored, scale-covered skin, the mud-colored creature was almost four meters long. It quickly waddled onto the bank and finally came to a stop with its toothy mouth held wide open. It hissed loudly. One clawed foot slowly moved forward as if the crocodile was thinking of resuming his pursuit of the warrior.

With the heart and training of a warrior, Wema had turned to face his aggressive attacker. In a natural 'fight or flight' stance, Wema stood his ground. The crocodile lay still, but Wema knew this deadly creature could charge him any second. He held his spear high. He was ready to ram it right down the crocodile's throat. It was a perfect stand-off between the two, except for a third participant.

The demon now stood only three meters away from Wema. It had stopped its approach. It hovered as if entertained by the deadly stand-off between Wema and the crocodile. The demon's living eyes volleyed between the Orange Warrior and the crocodile. It seemed thrilled, expecting the deadly outcome of this stalemate. Would it be Wema or the crocodile?

By now, the Green Warrior Tushema and the other warriors on the opposite bank had raced upstream. When the crocodile destroyed Wema's opportunity to cross the Mara River, the warriors had no choice but to come rushing to his aid. All of them, with Tushema in the lead, waded into the river water. All of them held their spears, aimed at the crocodile.

"No. Stop! Go back!" Wema shouts. "All of you go back!"

"Wema, Great Creation," Tushema said. "We can stop the crocodile."

"Perhaps." Wema did not move a muscle. He never took his eyes off the crocodile. "But what about old Bone-face here? Can you stop him, too?"

Tushema looked at the demon. Tushema was close enough to see the living eyes in the demon's bony face for the first time. The demon looked back at him, waiting for the Green Warrior's answer. The eerie sight was frightening. Tushema felt a gripping chill when the demon beckoned him. He broke loose from the chill when he heard Wema speak again.

"All of you, please. Go back." Wema repeated. He still stood his ground. He was calm. "Whatever you do, come no closer. I still have an advantage."

"What might that be, Great Creation?"

"The crocodile … is only hungry," Wema said. "Death … wants me dead."

"How is that an advantage?"

"Just do not move. Wait. You will see." Wema fell silent. He stared at the crocodile, his spear held high and ready.

For several long moments, no one moved, no one said anything. The warriors stood ready, but they followed Wema's instructions. They stood still, watching Wema, the crocodile, and the hovering demon of death. Wema stood like a tree. The crocodile's mouth was still open, lying as still as a log. Only the demon of death fidgeted.

The demon eyed the Orange Warrior Wema, waiting. Some very tense moments passed. Just as Wema had assumed, the demon's urge to cause death grew stronger and stronger by the second. It slowly raised its bony hand toward Wema. The urge to touch the Orange Warrior was almost irresistible. Still, Wema did not move.

Then it happened. The demon suddenly gave in to its need. It moved toward Wema. And just as Wema expected, the crocodile grabbed the first thing that moved – the demon.

The fierce crocodile had no chance against the demon of death. Death caught the crocodile by its snout, killing it in an instant. The demon easily lifted the 400-kg reptile off the ground. Filled with anger, it flung the crocodile back. The crocodile arched through the air, tumbling. It hit the wall of the south embankment. The reptile fell to the bank below, landing belly-up, dead.

But that brief sequence of action was all that Wema needed. He knew the pivotal moment was coming. When it did, the Orange Warrior splashed into the Mara River. Death grabbed at Wema but missed touching him by just a centimeter.

73

INTO DEATH'S HAND

Tushema and the warriors had moved the farmers and pack animals farther downstream. The Green Warrior felt it was not safe to stay where they were, directly across the river from the Kiboko Passage. Too many creatures, large and small used that passage. Some, like the wildebeests and zebras, traveled in sizable herds. Tushema wanted the farmers clear when one of the herds came through the passage.

"Such a move is not necessary," Wema had said to Tushema shortly after the Orange Warrior had crossed the river.

"Why, Great Creation? It is a necessary precaution."

"I know you must be aware by now that the great migration has started much earlier than expected."

"Unfortunately, yes. We saw signs long before we left the Kiwane Village. It has started early, and it may be stronger than usual."

"Then, you also know that the Kiboko Passage should be crowed with migrating animals by now." Wema pointed across the river toward the passage. "But as you can see, the passage remains clear."

Tushema looked at the passage across the river. He realized that Wema was right. Herds of migrating animals should pour out of the gorge, but there were none. The Green Warrior suspected the reason. "The demon?"

"Yes, Great Creation. The Red Warrior Nienko and I encountered several herds in our journey to reach you. The demon did too. In its effort to reach you before we did, it destroyed all the herds in its pathway."

"All of them?"

"All we saw. Throughout the Kiboko Passage and all beyond, for at least five kilometers, not a single beast is standing."

The Green Warrior turned to face the demon. Even after seeing how the demon killed the crocodile, Tushema had a new respect for the demon's awesome power. He took two steps toward the river. He stared at the dark, pacing specter. Another chill washed over his body when the demon, once again, stopped pacing, looked directly at him, and beckoned.

"This thing is unnatural." Tushema spoke to himself. "Nothing, so unnatural can have such power."

"Nienko and I witnessed what this thing has done, Great Creation."

Tushema reconsidered what Wema had just told him. He sighed before concluding that the safety of the farmers still came first. The migrating herds were a force of nature, too. And more herds were due to come. "We are moving downstream anyway."

The farmers and warriors gathered their things. When they reloaded their gourds and baskets back onto the pack animals, it was dark. With the light from several torches, the farmers and warriors worked along the sandy bank over half a kilometer downstream. The demon of death, just barely visible on the opposite bank, followed them.

*****

Throughout most of the evening, as the farmers set up the new camp, the Green Warrior Tushema went to stand at the edge of the river. He stared across the water despite the darkness, trying to see the gruesome adversary on the opposite bank. He saw nothing except complete darkness. The Green Warrior held a torch in his hand. He lifted it higher with almost no effect. The torchlight barely illuminated the river water that flowed past him. He knew that somewhere, in that darkness, on the opposite bank, death was still there; still pacing restlessly.

Tushema gave up his attempt to see across the Mara. He turned back inland to where the farmers and five warriors had gathered for their evening meal. They sat around a small campfire and talked as they ate. Tushema planted the end of his torch into the sand. It was clear he intended to use it again. He joined the group sitting on a log between Lobarra and Elder Zekke. Lobarra handed him a bowl of hot lentils.

"Thank you, Sacred Woman."

"We were just wondering," Elder Zekke began, "to whom do we recommend warriors for promotions? We farmers think the Orange Warrior Wema and the Red Warrior Nienko deserve promotions for their actions."

"Yes," agreed Lobarra. "If not a promotion, then at least some honored recognition."

Tushema opened his mouth to answer, but the Orange Warrior Wema spoke to Zekke first. "Great Creation, we only did what Mfalme Ameh Jobabwe asked us to do."

"Yes, but you risked your lives just to deliver a warning. You saved us from that demon."

"We did not save you, Great Creation." Wema was not being modest. He was trying to be honest. "It was the grace of the Supreme Spirit that saved you. If the truth be known, that demon outpaced the Red Warrior and me. We did not reach you until it was already too late."

"Yes," agreed Nienko. "Before that thing killed everything on the savanna, we lost at least two or three hours just waiting for the herds to move past us."

"If things had gone as planned," Wema continued, "we would have reached you long before you reached the Mara. But you were here before us. By the grace of the Supreme Spirit, you had not crossed over yet."

"Looking back," Elder Zekke chuckled as he recalled the incident under the acacia tree yesterday, "In this case, the Supreme Spirit's saving grace came as those lions. Those five lions in our pathway delayed our travel. I suppose they served a divine purpose in doing so."

"Yes, they would have," the Gold Warrior Oghani agreed, "but not completely. The Lions threw our schedule off. You must remember. We still reached the Mara before the demon did."

"I must take the blame for that," Tushema said. "After the lions delayed us, I tried to recover our schedule. I was the one who pushed everyone to reach the Mara. I was the one who did not recognize the Supreme Spirit's saving grace and overcompensated. I must apologize for that. Still, She prevailed. She gave us another divine reason for not crossing the Mara sooner."

"What reason was that, Great Creation?" Zekke wanted to know.

Tushema looked to his left. He gestured toward Tutapona. Tutapona was sleeping on his stomach across his mother's lap. "If you recall, the Little Creation was hungry and in his way, demanded to be fed. If the Sacred Woman Lobarra had not been given the time to feed him, we would have crossed the river just moments before the demon first appeared."

Lobarra looked down at Tutapona. She smiled as she gently patted his back. "The Supreme Spirit's grace is more complex than ever imagined. It comes in so many unexpected ways."

"I like to think that Her grace is always available," Zekke commented. "And sometimes, it is forced upon us before we recognize it for what it is and act as we should."

"I could not have said it better myself, Great Creation." Tushema acknowledged his lesson learned. He tasted his hot lentils. After a thoughtful moment, he turned to Lobarra. "Sacred Woman, I must admit, I thought bringing the Little Creation on this trip was bad. Now, I am very glad you did."

"Thank you, Great Creation."

"In hindsight, I was wrong to push everyone so hard to reach the Mara. I truly felt bad about doing it. I suppose the feeling marked the mistake I was making. But the Little Creation Tutapona helped all of us by correcting my mistake. When we return to the valley, I will ensure he receives his due recognition." Tushema gestured toward the warriors Wema and Nienko. "As for the two of you, your

Blue Warrior, Obe Bendabe, and Mfalme Jobabwe will learn of the honorable things you have done."

"Thank you, Tushema." The Red Warrior Nienko spoke just above a whisper. He gave a weak smile. He looked down into his bowl of lentils, stirring them slowly. Without an appetite, he was not eating. He appreciated the Green Warrior's intent to give him honors. It was a good feeling, but he felt it was pointless. "The Blue Warrior Obe Bendabe is probably dead. And so is the Blue Warrior Dabete Ehkili, and Mfalme Ameh Jobabwe. By now, the entire valley is dead."

The heavy silence that followed made Nienko look up from his bowl. Everyone was looking at him. "I am sorry. Forgive me for being so insensitive. According to the rumor, the demon promised to kill everyone in the valley in two days. Those two days have passed. When we return, we will find a dead valley."

That statement made the silence linger even longer. No one could refute the possibility. The Green Warrior Tushema was the first to react. He set his bowl of uneaten lentils beside him as if he had also lost his appetite. He got up and stepped over the log he was sitting on. With frustration, he grabbed up the torch he had planted. Compelled by the urge to take another look at the demon on the other side, Tushema took two steps toward the river.

"Tushema." Elder Zekke called the Green Warrior's name. "All evening long, you have stood at the river's edge, sizing up that thing on the other side. You are eager to confront it. And, after hearing the Red Warrior Nienko's concerns, I do not condemn your behavior. Such an initiative has justified your green cloak. But, does that cloak give you useful insight? What are we to do now?"

"Yes, Elder Zekke. Yes, it does." Tushema sighed. He lowered his torch. He turned and walked back toward the group. Tushema stepped over the log and returned to where he sat. He tossed the torch into the campfire. "Unfortunately, for the next few days, the demon is not our concern now."

"What do you mean, Great Creation?" There was a serious look on Elder Zekke's face. "The warriors Wema and Nienko tell us that the demon has probably killed all the people in our valley. Now it has come looking for us. You say, it is not our concern! How can you say that?"

"Great Creation, I earned this green cloak and shield because I know where my responsibilities lie. One of my greatest responsibilities lies with you and the other farmers. And, for now, I answer to the Mfalme Ameh Jobabwe." Tushema thought a moment before he explained the rest of what was on his mind. "Tomorrow morning, we will return to the Kiwane Village."

Zekke looked around at the other farmers who sat around the campfire. He could see in their faces that they felt the same. He set down his bowl of lentils and turned to face the Green Warrior. "But Great Creation, we prefer not to return to the Kiwane Village. We want to go home."

"Elder Zekke, I cannot and will not lead you into death's hand. If that thing possesses the power described by Wema and Nienko, then I have no choice. I must return you to the Kiwane Village."

"You answer to Mfalme Ameh Jobabwe, but what if the Mfalme is dead, as the Red Warrior suspects?"

Tushema picked up his bowl of lentils again. Still without an appetite, he poked at his food as he considered Zekke's question. "You are the senior farmer here. You are a tribal elder. If the Mfalme is dead, I must answer to you and your wishes. But I do not know that Mfalme Jobabwe is dead. Regarding the Red Warrior Nienko, I prefer to think that Mfalme Jobabwe is not dead. And, until I know otherwise, I assume that he is not. We are returning to the Kiwane Village."

"Great Creation, you must understand," Zekke said. "We want to go home. Before it is too late, soon, there will be no one left."

"I am sorry, Great Creation. We will go home when we receive word it is safe to do so."

"Receive word from whom?" Elder Zekke argued. "Who knows when that might be? If the Mangoni houngan summoned that demon to kill all of us, our valley may be just another hole in the ground. Word may never reach us."

"I am sorry, Great Creation. I find it difficult to believe all our people will soon die. I do know that death awaits us on the other side of this river."

There was another long and awkward silence. Elder Zekke was in charge of the farmers. But the Green Warrior Tushema had charge of all their security. Under the circumstances, it was Tushema's decision. Zekke understood and respected this protocol. He accepted Tushema's leadership. He chose not to say anything more. "So be it."

The Sacred Woman Lobarra finally disrupted the awkward moment when she redirected everyone's attention. She turned to the warriors Wema and Nienko. "If we could return home, tell us what we could expect. Do you think that everyone is dead? What were the conditions in the valley when you left?"

The Orange Warrior Wema set his empty lentil bowl aside. He collected his thoughts. "Well, I need not tell you. Tremendous sadness covers the valley. When we left, we estimated that there had been well over two hundred deaths throughout the valley."

Wema reviewed all the deaths that the Red Warrior Nienko had already mentioned. He highlighted each major incident according to the details he had heard. He described how the demon killed the people of the Pogobi kraal with a blanket of putrid black smoke. Wema described how the warriors of the Obentawni kraal and the warriors of Npatuzi's sentinel army all died in the darkness as they entered the Obentawni kraal to rest. He told everyone how the people of the Butetwa kraal died in their sleep as they waited for death to make its deadly appearance, and how the people of the Mempa kraal died trying to defend themselves with knives, rakes, and scythes.

"So many deaths, so fast." Lobarra put her hand to her mouth as if to hold back fresh tears. "What are we to do?"

"What can we do?" Elder Zekke commented. He was still somewhat disappointed over Tushema's decision. "Since we will not be there, we cannot even bury our dead."

"Burial rituals began this morning, Great Creation." Wema tried to take the sting out of Zekke's sarcasm. "If all had gone as planned, during this day, the Favored Tribesman had planned to release at least half those who had died to the Supreme Spirit."

74

NO REGRETS

Mfalme Abul-Gwan woke with a ray of the morning sunlight shining directly into his face. He opened his eyes but squinted from the intense brightness. In his sleep, he had fallen into a very uncomfortable position. He forced himself to sit upright. He wiped the sleep from his eyes. His joints and bones snapped as he stretched the stiffness from his body.

In the middle of his stretch, he suddenly remembered the two Aukmondi Blue Warriors who encroached on his camp two evenings ago. He had awakened to find the warriors standing over him. It was a frightening moment, especially when he saw his own guards gagged and bound against the tree behind him. Abul-Gwan rubbed his eyes again and looked around, searching. He relaxed when he saw Goh-Jumaane in the distance, standing guard at his usual post.

Further over, in an isolated location, beneath a cluster of acacia bushes, Abul-Gwan saw the body of the other worker warrior. The body of Kum-Bufu now lay with the other dead warriors, with a goatskin veil covering the face and arms folded across his chest.

As Abul-Gwan recovered from his interrupted stretch, his eyes came to rest once more on the body of Abul-Tess. He clung to the last spark of hope that she was only asleep. He reached over and gently touched her shoulder. "Abul-Tess, please, wake up. You have slept long enough."

When Abul-Tess did not move, Abul-Gwan slumped and fell back against the tree. He seemed to realize the futility of his hope. The terrible pain of sadness that shot through his heart intensified when he could not find the usual glow in Abul-Tess's cheeks. He saw sunken jaws. He saw ashen, dry, and cracked lips. Flies crawled at the corners of her eyes and mouth.

Abul-Gwan leaned forward. He waved his hand over Abul-Tess's face to run the flies away. "Abul-Tess, I know you want to return. What stops you?"

As if blaming the Vodun houngan for not doing all he could, Abul-Gwan shifted his stiff body toward the ritual *veve*. He noticed that the *veve* was unusually quiet. The boom-boom of the ritual drums had stopped. Onu-Vey's two vessel warriors lay sprawled out upon the ground, and neither had moved since Onu-Vey had taken the limbs from their hands. Abul-Gwan assumed that they slept, exhausted from the constant drumbeats that started over two evenings ago.

Onu-Vey did not appear too healthy either. Abul-Gwan struggled to his feet to get a better view of the Vodun houngan. He used one hand to brace himself against the Marula tree as he stood. His other hand held the blanket tightly in place over his shoulders. He took an unsteady step closer toward the *veve* to improve his view.

Abul-Gwan could see Onu-Vey sitting with his legs crossed, in his usual spot within the *veve*. His overturned cauldron lay next to him. Where his ritual fire once burned, a pile of dirt surrounded a hole in the ground. The same pile of dirt once covered the black crystal, Onu-Vey's *azima*.

Abul-Gwan attempted to focus on the pouch in which Onu-Vey had dropped the crystal. He could not see it. Onu-Vey continued to clutch the pouch tightly in both of his hands. The houngan rocked back and forth. He chanted with his eyes closed. Most of the ritual words that Abul-Gwan heard were unrecognizable. The words came out of Onu-Vey's mouth so fast that Abul-Gwan wondered how the houngan could breathe.

"He cannot continue like that too much longer," the Mangoni worker warrior, Goh-Jumaane, said. The warrior had come up from the guard post when he saw Abul-Gwan moving.

"What?" Abul-Gwan whirled around with a jolt, startled to hear someone speaking to him. He did not hear Goh-Jumaane's approach. In his weakened condition, he almost fell.

Goh-Jumaane caught him. He helped him back to his seat next to the tree. He eased him down. "I am sorry. I did not mean to startle you, Mfalme."

Abul-Gwan did not acknowledge the apology. He made himself comfortable against the tree. The cool morning air made him tug the blanket tighter over his shoulders.

Goh-Jumaane stood back. He looked down at Abul-Gwan with concern. Instead of expressing his concern, he repeated his original comment about Onu-Vey. "I said, he cannot continue like that too much longer. He has done that throughout the night."

"Since I have known Onu-Vey, I have seen him perform hundreds of rituals. I have seen him approach the threshold of death once or twice. But each time, he recovered. He always knows what he is doing." Abul-Gwan craned around to study the houngan again. "This time, I am not so sure."

Instead of returning to his guard post, Goh-Jumaane sat between Abul-Gwan and Abul-Tess's burial litter. He removed a pouch that hung by a strap across his shoulder. He made himself comfortable and pulled a small knife from its casing at his waist.

"What are you doing, Goh-Jumaane?" Abul-Gwan asked. No one, not even Onu-Vey, has ever sat next to him without asking first.

"Forgive me, Mfalme." Goh-Jumaane pulled a huge strip of dried goat meat from the pouch. He cut a small piece off with the knife. "Are you hungry?"

"No."

"Under the circumstances, I am the only one capable of preparing food. This is all we have to eat. I have not had the opportunity to prepare anything else."

"No," Abul-Gwan repeated. "Thank you."

Goh-Jumaane had cut the piece of meat off for Abul-Gwan. Since Abul-Gwan did not take it, the warrior bit off half of it himself. He chewed just long enough to moisten the dried meat. "Did you sleep well, Mfalme?"

"I slept. I slept all night. But, I am still tired."

"There is no wonder. To sleep against that tree cannot be comfortable." Goh-Jumaane put the other half of the meat into his mouth. He cut another piece from the strip. Without asking, he offered it to Abul-Gwan again.

"I said I am not hungry."

"You should eat something, Mfalme."

"I will eat later."

Goh-Jumaane put the cut-off piece and the entire strip of goat meat back into his pouch. He cleaned the blade of his knife with his hand and then inserted it back into its casing. As he was getting up, Goh-Jumaane glanced down at the body of Abul-Tess. He took the liberty of waving the flies away from her face.

The concerned expression on the warrior's face prompted Abul-Gwan to push the warrior aside. Abul-Gwan had taken offense at Goh-Jumaane's efforts. The offense seemed just enough to force Abul-Gwan to accept Abul-Tess's death. He unfolded the veil that was lying on Abul-Tess's chest. As if burning the memory of her face into his mind, Abul-Gwan slowly, delicately covered Abul-Tess's face.

"I am sorry, Mfalme. I meant no offense."

"Onu-Vey cannot bring her back." Abul-Gwan gently smoothed the veil out. He tugged at each corner to remove every wrinkle in the veil. "As powerful as his magic is, he cannot bring her back."

"When the Wabanga died, up on the north rim, Onu-Vey told you then that 'dead is dead'. That applies to everyone. Once the loa appears and takes a life, Onu-Vey cannot change that."

Abul-Gwan twisted around toward the *veve* and Onu-Vey again. "Then what is he doing? Look at him! Obviously, he thinks he can do something."

Goh-Jumaane studied Onu-Vey, too. The chants seemed to get stronger despite the houngan's labored breathing. "I think he is trying to fix the damage done. Look at him and how he holds his *azima*."

"Damage? What damage?"

"Listen, Mfalme. What do you hear?" Goh-Jumaane cocked his head as if to listen again himself. "The whole valley is quiet, and the Aukmondi drums are silent. The loa is out of control. It is killing everything. This silence suggests most, if not all, of the Aukmondi are dead."

"Do I hear regret in your voice, Goh-Jumaane?"

"May I speak freely, Mfalme?"

"Speak," Abul-Gwan said tersely.

The single word wasn't permission to speak freely. Goh-Jumaane paused to reconsider what he was about to say. He went ahead. He spoke his mind from his heart. "Mfalme, if all the Aukmondi are gone, then Africa has suffered a great loss."

"What makes you say that?"

"I do not think they deserve what the loa has done to them. These are some brave and noble people. A day and a half ago, Kum-Bufu and I stood on the pathway that leads up here to the peak. We saw the loa wipe out part of an Aukmondi regiment."

"So?"

"The death of those warriors occurred after an obvious, sacrificial tactic. As Kum-Bufu and I watched, a little Aukmondi boy came walking up the pathway. For what reason, I do not know. But before he reached us, a warrior stopped him. That is when the loa appeared. An Aukmondi regiment came to their rescue. Part of the regiment gave their lives so that the boy and the rest of the regiment could escape. The most fascinating thing about the incident was that … this partial regiment seemed to know they would die. They stood ready to face the loa, knowing they could do nothing. It was one of the most heroic things I have ever seen."

"Yes, well, it probably was not as heroic as you might think. This little Aukmondi boy was about 138 centimeters tall, weighing about 32 kilograms?"

"Yes, Mfalme."

Abul-Gwan chuckled. "You saw such a heroic sacrifice, Goh-Jumaane, because that little boy is the new Aukmondi Mfalme."

This news impressed Goh-Jumaane. "Then it was noble of him to approach as he did. Even as a boy, he took it upon himself to confront all that had happened."

"So, it is admiration you feel?"

"I am a warrior, Mfalme. I recognize bravery. It takes bravery for one as young as he to assume the doomed mission of his father. It takes bravery for warriors to do as they did."

"What are you saying, Goh-Jumaane?"

"Only, that it is a shame that such brave people must all die."

Abul-Gwan laid his head back against the tree again. He closed his eyes. "I will not miss them. And once they are all dead, I will have no regrets."

"Onu-Vey says it will come for us when the loa finishes with the Aukmondi. What will become of the Mangoni?"

Abul-Gwan said nothing at first. He looked about as if searching for an answer to Goh-Jumaane's question. His searching eyes finally came to rest on Abul-Tess's body. "I do not know, Goh-Jumaane. I do not care."

"Mfalme, your answer disturbs me."

"When I became Mfalme, I pulled all the warring clans together. We are a stronger, united people now. The Mangoni will, somehow, survive. But I am tired. I have given all I can give. Whatever future that the Mangoni people have is in the hands of Onu-Vey now."

Goh-Jumaane looked toward the ritual *veve*. The houngan had gone deeper into his ritual. Goh-Jumaane could easily see that, besides the rocking motion, the houngan now shivered. "If our future is in Onu-Vey's hands, it does not look good."

75

COME WITH ME

Shortly after mid-morning, Abul-Gwan woke up from another of his depression induced naps. He had a strip of goat meat in his hand. He had told the Mangoni warrior Goh-Jumaane that he would eat later, that he was not hungry. It was not the truth. Just before Goh-Jumaane left to return to his guard post, a mild hunger pained Abul-Gwan's stomach. Abul-Gwan finally asked for a small piece of the sun-dried meat. Goh-Jumaane cut a sizable piece off for his Mfalme. Abul-Gwan accepted the meat, but before he could take his first bite, a melancholy moment prompted Abul-Gwan to take Abul-Tess's hand. Shortly after doing so, he drifted off to sleep. The morning temperature had climbed to a comfortable level, perfect for napping.

Abul-Gwan had slept for over three hours. When he finally woke again, he opened his eyes and suddenly remembered the meat in his hand. He looked down at it, only to find flies crawling on it. Abul-Gwan flipped it over, examining it before tossing it aside. He didn't want it anymore. It wasn't because of the flies. He was not hungry. He had no appetite.

During his nap, Abul-Gwan had slumped over again. He experienced no stiffness in his neck and back, like when he sat upright. His bones did not snap when he raised his arms above his head and stretched. Abul-Gwan almost smiled as he realized how good he felt. He could not remember the last time he felt so relaxed and refreshed.

Abul-Gwan noticed that Nagorda's crosswind had increased. It had always been windy atop Nagorda Peak. Abul-Gwan felt a heightened charge of energy in the air. The current breeze rolled across the peak much more strongly than usual. Abul-Gwan also observed that it was unusually dark for this morning. He rubbed his eyes and glanced skyward. Thick gray clouds completely obscured the sun.

Abul-Gwan assumed that Onu-Vey had re-ignited his ritual fire and was performing another very smoky ritual. He twisted around toward the summit and the ritual *veve* to confirm his assumption. But before he could get into position, the horizon caught his attention. The sky was completely black with clouds. A whirling maelstrom was bellowing in his direction. A storm was rapidly approaching.

At once, Abul-Gwan's thoughts turned to the body of Abul-Tess. Something had to be done to protect her body from the coming stormy elements. When Abul-Gwan looked toward Abul-Tess's burial litter, he froze. His heart skipped a beat. The burial litter was empty. Abul-Tess's body - gone.

The Mangoni Mfalme forced himself quickly to his feet. "Abul-Tess!" He called out. He looked around, on the verge of panic. The first thought that came to his mind was that Onu-Vey had taken her body. Various people, including Onu-Vey, had long ago insisted on a proper burial. Abul-Gwan assumed that Onu-Vey had ignored his wishes and had taken her body to begin burial preparations. Abul-Gwan's alarm suddenly shifted to raw anger.

Despite a strong wind blowing against him, Abul-Gwan made several hurried and unsteady steps toward the ritual *veve* to confront Onu-Vey. The houngan was due for a royal reprimand. The wind and dust grew so much at that moment that Abul-Gwan slowed to a standstill. He shielded his face with his arm as another powerful gust of wind and thick dust moved rapidly across Nagorda Peak and the *veve*. Abul-Gwan peered ahead, only to realize that he had lost sight of Onu-Vey and the ritual *veve*.

Abul-Gwan suddenly saw the three bowls that once held Onu-Vey's colored ritual powders tumble past him, carried by the wind. The bowls clanged and clacked as they rolled upon the ground. Onu-Vey's cauldron rumbled not far behind the bowls. It rolled past the Mfalme, missing his feet by a few centimeters.

Abul-Gwan turned his back as the wind and the dust enveloped him. The comfort blanket he wore over his shoulders flapped. He pulled it up over his head for protection. The wind yanked it from his fingers. The blanket flew away and disappeared in the wind and a cloud of dust.

Abul-Gwan held his hand up to his nose to avoid breathing the dust. He covered his face with his arm again. Dust found its way into his eyes anyway. Abul-Gwan cleared his vision just in time to see Abul-Tess's empty burial litter take flight, caught by the wind. With snaps and cracks, the litter tumbled away, down the hillside. Abul-Gwan ran after it. After only a few steps, he lost sight of the litter. Like the blanket, it disappeared in a rolling dust bank.

"Abul-Tess!" In a full panic now, Abul-Gwan called out. The blowing wind muffled his voice. "Abul-Tess!"

In a gimpy, half-run and half-walk, Abul-Gwan rushed toward the guard post where he knew the Mangoni warrior, Goh-Jumaane, stood guard. He needed his help. If nothing else, Goh-Jumaane could explain what had happened to Abul-Tess's body.

Abul-Gwan made it less than a quarter down the hill when another strong wind blew the Mfalme sideways off his feet. He fell to the ground hard. He struggled against the wind and the dust to return to his feet. By the time he stood again, thick dust obstructed his vision. He could not see beyond a meter in any direction. Disoriented, he turned in a circle, making his predicament worse.

"Goh-Jumaane!" Abul-Gwan called out to the warrior several times. He got no response. The wind completely reduced his voice to nothing. Dust flew down his throat, making him double over in a spasm of coughs. He took several moments to recover.

As Abul-Gwan rose and peered over his arm. He looked around in several directions, trying to get his bearings. The black dust was impenetrable. He had experienced nothing like this. Abul-Gwan stood for a moment, wondering where such a storm had come. He wondered how long it would last. He wondered if his situation was as hopeless as it seemed.

Just then, Abul-Gwan heard the faint sound of a galloping horse. Abul-Gwan stood erect despite the wind. He tilted his head, focusing on the sound. The sound was getting closer, stronger. It was the unmistakable sound of a galloping horse.

The thought occurred to Abul-Gwan that it might be the horse from among the Mangoni pack animals. He could not remember how many pack animals had survived the rampage by the loa yesterday. But, because of the Arabian stallion's compelling beauty, he remembered seeing the horse among them. Abul-Gwan remembered the horse's triumphant escape as it galloped down the hillside, away from the loa's wrath. Abul-Gwan listened. Maybe the horse found its way back to the corral. Maybe the horse struggled now to escape the storm.

Abul-Gwan turned in the direction he thought the sound was coming from. He pushed against the wind again, taking measured steps toward the sound. He hoped that the sound would lead him back toward the corral. If he could reach the corral, he would at least understand where he was. He seemed to be walking uphill, a good sign that he was walking in the right direction.

The walk was difficult. But the hill's incline presented less of a problem than the wind. Abul-Gwan walked against a relentless and oppressive wind. It seemed to take him forever to cover a few meters. Covering his face again with his arm, Abul-Gwan angled his body and pushed ahead.

Abul-Gwan could hear the sound of the galloping horse getting closer. He still could not see anything. The dust continued to blind him. But the horse was close, only a few meters away. He could hear the horse's snorts, matching its rhythmic gallop.

Suddenly, up ahead, Abul-Gwan saw a horse gallop out of a dust bank. Abul-Gwan recognized the beautiful, pale gray Arabian stallion. Abul-Gwan could also see a rider on the horse's back as the horse cleared the dust bank. He rubbed the dust from his eyes. A smile spread across his face when he recognized the rider. It was Abul-Tess.

Abul-Tess was very much alive. She rode the horse bareback, leaning forward and holding the horse about its neck. She looked as though she might fall. But she wasn't frightened. She laughed. She seemed thrilled by the ride.

Abul-Gwan almost jumped with elation. He forgot about the wind and the dust. Like a child, he ran to meet Abul-Tess. He called out her name again and again. He held out his arms as if to perform the impossible task of catching the horse. Fortunately for him, the horse's gallop slowed to a graceful prance. The horse finally stopped next to the Mangoni Mfalme.

Abul-Tess seemed just as pleased to see Abul-Gwan. There was a wide smile on her face. When the horse came to a stop, she slid from the horse's back into Abul-Gwan's open arms. Abul-Tess's feet never touched the ground. Abul-Gwan caught her. He embraced her tightly, whirling her in a circle.

"Abul-Tess! Oh, Abul-Tess, my precious love!" There were tears of joy in Abul-Gwan's eyes. "You came back to me. I knew you would. No one believed me, but I knew you would. You came back!"

"I never left you." Abul-Tess held Abul-Gwan just as tightly. She buried her face in his chest.

When Abul-Tess's words finally registered, Abul-Gwan eased her down, allowing her feet to touch the ground. He cupped her face in his hands. The smiling expression on his face changed to one of puzzlement. "What do you mean, you never left me? You left me. For three days, you were … You were …"

He could not say the word 'dead'. Instead, he held his mate back. He looked down at her waist. She wore a sheer, all-white, ankle-length, loose-fitting garment. The wind pressed the garment tightly against her body. The form of her body suggested a divine beauty.

Abul-Gwan searched the area where the spear had pierced Abul-Tess's side. He saw no sign of the fatal injury. Not trusting his eyes, he reached down to touch the area. Abul-Tess took his probing hand and slid it around to her back, forcing him to take her into his embrace again. Abul-Gwan did not resist.

"So much has happened. I am sorry for all of it." Abul-Gwan said as he held Abul-Tess, gently swaying from side to side in the wind.

"I did not mean to put you through such horrors. From this moment forward, things will improve. I will do better. I promise."

"As Mfalme, you did what you needed to do. And I wanted to be with you. You owe me no apology, Abul-Gwan. And I shall not hold you to any promises."

"You deserve so much better." Abul-Gwan looked into Abul-Tess's eyes. "I am taking you home."

"Home?"

"Yes, home. I am through traveling. I am taking you back to our village. I want to go home where we can relax, enjoy your companionship, and love you like you should be loved."

"Wait." Abul-Tess gently broke from Abul-Gwan's embrace. She took his hand and led him toward the horse. With her other hand, she stroked the horse's muscular shoulder. The horse seemed pleased by the attention. Abul-Tess reached up and gently patted the horse's back. "Please. Help me up."

Abul-Gwan hesitated for only a moment. He was about to ask her why, but realized he did not care why. Abul-Gwan swept Abul-Tess off her feet. He held her for a long, loving moment, then swung her onto the horse's back.

Abul-Tess made herself comfortable. She reached down and offered Abul-Gwan her arm to help him onto the horse. "Come with me. I want to show you something."

"In this storm? Should we not wait until the storm passes?"

"This storm is in the darkness. What I want to show you … is beyond the storm."

Abul-Gwan took Abul-Tess's arm. He hopped onto the horse's back behind his mate with renewed energy. He snuggled close to her, holding her tightly around her waist. He made himself comfortable as he buried his face in the crook of Abul-Tess's neck. The fragrance she wore was one of the many simple things he had missed. Even the feel of the fine, soft hair on the back of her neck almost brought tears of joy to his eyes.

Abul-Tess gave one gentle kick with her heels. The horse took off with a jolt. It pranced about in a wide circle. Abul-Gwan and Abul-Tess bounced up and down as the horse's prance gradually developed into a strong gallop. They plunged directly into one of the rolling dust banks.

"I cannot see!" Abul-Gwan yelled over the thunder of the horse's hooves.

"Trust the horse," Abul-Tess shouted back just as the horse seemed to leap over some unseen object.

"Where are we going?"

"You will see. Just hang on."

76

IN THE COMPANY OF ABUL-TESS

Since yesterday evening's rampage of the Loa of Death, the worker warrior, Goh-Jumaane, has stood at the guard post at the entrance of the Mangoni camp. Currently, he is the only Mangoni warrior capable of standing guard. Kum-Bufu, the other worker warrior, lay with the rest of the dead Mangoni warriors. The two vessel warriors remained within the ritual *veve*, exhausted and incapacitated.

Throughout last evening and all night, Goh-Jumaane took a few breaks from his guard post. The only breaks came during the short respites Goh-Jumaane took when he walked up toward the summit and checked on Mfalme Abul-Gwan. Under the midday sun, Goh-Jumaane looked forward to his next break. He could see to the Mfalme's needs and enjoy a few moments in the shade of the huge Marula tree.

When Goh-Jumaane looked up toward the summit, he caught sight of the two vessel warriors approaching him. Halfway between him and the Marula tree, he saw Makoso-Kin struggling to aid Metwe-Ngu. The two staggered down the hillside. Goh-Jumaane abandoned his post and ran to help. When he reached the two warriors, he threw Metwe-Ngu's arm over his shoulder and supported him around his waist.

"Water!" Metwe-Ngu spoke with a raspy voice.

"Come," Goh-Jumaane forced Metwe-Ngu to continue walking. "I have water at the guard post."

"How long were we … asleep?" Makoso-Kin asked.

"You have been unconscious since yesterday evening."

Makoso-Kin glanced up toward the sky to judge the time. The midday sun beamed bright in his eyes. Makoso-Kin covered his eyes with his free hand. "Why did you not revive us, Goh-Jumaane?"

"The two of you … needed the rest." Goh-Jumaane tried to answer with a half-truth. He thought for a moment before revealing the whole truth. "I stood at the edge of the *veve* and called your names several times. Neither of you heard me. I thought you were dead. I considered moving your bodies with the other dead warriors, but I recalled Onu-Vey's warning. I did not dare to enter the *veve* uninvited. I could have died, too."

"No harm would have come to you. Onu-Vey has ended the ritual." Makoso-Kin clearly remembered when Onu-Vey snatched the limb from his hands. He remembered when the houngan pushed the ritual cauldron over and the bubbling goat's blood extinguished the ritual fire. He remembered the loa's rampage, the unexpected killing of Kum-Bufu, and most of the Mangoni pack animals. "The circle is no longer a *veve*."

Goh-Jumaane escorted the vessel warriors to the guard post and made them comfortable on the ground. Metwe-Ngu seemed to be the most dehydrated. He gave the warrior his water pouch as he glanced back toward the summit.

"If the circle is no longer a *veve*, then why does Onu-Vey sit within, clutching his *azima*, and chanting?"

All three warriors studied the houngan. In the distance, they could see Onu-Vey sitting with his legs crossed, slumped forward, as if looking down at his *Azima.* He continued to clutch it with both hands. Makoso-Kin recalled that moments ago, when he and Metwe-Ngu stepped from the former *veve*, Onu-Vey's body trembled with brief convulsions.

"The houngan is no longer chanting," Makoso-Kin said. "I think Onu-Vey may be finished with whatever he was doing."

"I hope he is finished. He cannot stay much longer under this sun. We must convince him to move."

The warrior Metwe-Ngu nodded in agreement. He took another swallow of water and handed the pouch back to Goh-Jumaane. "How about the Mfalme? How is he doing?"

"I finally got him to accept something to eat early this morning. On the surface, the Mfalme seems better. But his attitude and spirit are darker." Goh-Jumaane looked toward the summit again. In the distance, he could see Abul-Gwan asleep, as usual, against the Marula tree. "Speaking of the Mfalme, it is time I checked on him again."

"Do you need help?"

"I may need your help to convince Onu-Vey to move." Goh-Jumaane handed his water pouch to Makoso-Kin. He picked up his shield and spear and got to his feet. "You two rest a moment more. I will check on the Mfalme first. Then we will see about the houngan."

*****

The Mangoni Warrior Goh-Jumaane climbed the pathway from the guard post up toward the summit of Nagorda Peak. The midday sun was high overhead. Goh-Jumaane had looked forward to this moment. And now that Makoso-Kin and Metwe-Ngu were recovering, he considered spending a few more precious moments in the shade of the Marula tree with Abul-Gwan.

Goh-Jumaane stepped off the pathway. From this closer distance, he could easily see that the Mangoni Mfalme was soundly asleep again, slumped over as usual. Only this time, the pathetic Mfalme was asleep, holding Abul-Tess's hand.

Goh-Jumaane stopped walking. Something about Abul-Gwan's position told him that the Mangoni Mfalme was not just sleeping. Fearing the worst, Goh-Jumaane increased his pace to a run. He came to a stop at the foot of Abul-Tess's burial litter. The Mangoni warrior knew that Abul-Gwan was dead long before he kneeled at his side. He slowly reached over to touch him, hoping his suspicions were wrong.

"Makoso-Kin! Metwe-Ngu!" Goh-Jumaane called out. "Come, quickly!"

By the time the two vessel warriors climbed the pathway, Goh-Jumaane had laid the body of Abul-Gwan out on his back as if to make him comfortable. As a subconscious act of kindness, he did not separate Abul-Tess's hand from the Mfalme's frozen grasp.

"What happened to him?" Metwe-Ngu asked. "Did the Aukmondi somehow do this?"

"No. No, I do not think so. Since last evening, the loa has destroyed most, if not all, of the Aukmondi." Goh-Jumaane quickly examined Abul-Gwan's body. "There are no injuries. He is just … dead."

"How can this be? The Mfalme took Abul-Tess's death hard, but the last time I saw him, he was still strong and healthy. Are you sure?"

"Yes. I am sure."

"If the Aukmondi did not cause this … was it …?" Makoso-Kin hesitated. He recalled the last time he saw the loa and the level of rage the loa expressed.

Goh-Jumaane was thinking along the same line. He completed Makoso-Kin's question for him. "Was it the loa? No. I think not. It looks like the Mfalme died of some natural cause."

Makoso-Kin sighed, trying to make the sadness feel more acceptable. "He finally got what he wanted. He is … he is in the company of Abul-Tess now."

"But how is this possible?" Metwe-Ngu had a harder time accepting the Mfalme's death. "If neither the Aukmondi nor the loa caused this, how did the Mfalme die?"

"It was love, Metwe-Ngu." Goh-Jumaane looked at the way Abul-Gwan held Abul-Tess's hand. He wondered. Did the Mfalme know he was dying when he took her hand? Goh-Jumaane rose to his feet again. "Mfalme Abul-Gwan loved that woman. I could see their bond for as long as I can remember. After Abul-Tess's first mate, Kosi-Jawma, was killed, I could see the bond between Abul-Gwan and Abul-Tess grow into love. I have never seen a stronger love."

"You do not die from love."

"No. No, you do not. But you can die from the loss of it." Goh-Jumaane looked up toward the ritual *veve*. "The houngan has to be told."

"If he is not finished, dare we interrupt him?"

Goh-Jumaane turned to face Metwe-Ngu. "Abul-Gwan is dead. He had no sons. He had no brothers. By written decree, Onu-Vey is now Mfalme of the Mangoni. Yes. We interrupt him."

The three warriors took a few minutes to cover the bodies of both Abul-Gwan and Abul-Tess. Under the circumstances, there was no rush. When they had finished, they took the few steps up to the summit of Nagorda Peak.

As the three warriors approached Onu-Vey, they could see that the houngan sat perfectly still. He had not moved since Makoso-Kin and Metwe-Ngu left the ritual *veve*. His chanting had stopped. Makoso-Kin also noticed that the houngan's body no longer trembled and convulsed. Goh-Jumaane kneeled in front of Onu-Vey for a closer look. He could see that Onu-Vey's eyes were open. They were dry, red, and unblinking. Goh-Jumaane sensed something was wrong. He looked up at the other warriors at his side. He turned back to the houngan.

"Onu-Vey!" Goh-Jumaane spoke softly. There was no response. He spoke louder. "Onu-Vey! Please hear me! Abul-Gwan is dead. You are Mfalme now." There was still no response from Onu-Vey.

Makoso-Kin kneeled at Goh-Jumaane's side. "I do not like this. He is entranced deeper than I have ever seen. Is it safe to pull him out of such a trance?"

"We have no choice." Goh-Jumaane was about to reach into the former *veve* to touch the houngan when Makoso-Kin caught his hand and directed his attention to the other side of the *veve*.

Not far away stood the Loa of Death. It stood watching the three Mangoni warriors. After a moment, it paced back and forth like a caged animal. The expression on its bony face was a mixture of anger, frustration, and panic. Each time the Loa turned to glide in the opposite direction, it glanced toward the warriors.

"What is it wrong with it? What is it doing?" Metwe-Ngu asked.

Goh-Jumaane stood. "Yesterday, before Onu-Vey went into this trance, he said the loa will kill all the Aukmondi. And when it finishes with the Aukmondi, it will return to finish us. The loa has returned."

"We have to get the houngan's attention. He has to stop this thing."

"Onu-Vey is powerless over the loa. He cannot stop it." Goh-Jumaane adjusted his shield and raised his spear, although neither would do him any good. Makoso-Kin and Metwe-Ng had no shields or spears. They wore nothing but loincloths, just as Onu-Vey had instructed them to dress over two and a half days ago. But as warriors, the two crouched, ready to battle with their bare hands.

Makoso-Kin studied the loa. He recalled the way the Loa of Death had looked back at him. This time, things seemed different. The loa's threatening look seemed desperate. It behaved like a desert scorpion, ready to sting for the sake of stinging. But it only paced, reluctant to attack.

The loa stopped pacing. It raised its bony hands and moved closer toward the three warriors. The anger and desperation in the loa's eyes intensified. That is when Makoso-Kin noticed something else about the loa he had not seen. He moved closer to Goh-Jumaane's side. "What is happening to it?"

Goh-Jumaane focused on the loa. He could see through him. He realized that the loa was fading. The expression on the loa's face was one of utter distress. "Is Onu-Vey making him fade like that?"

Makoso-Kin looked down at the houngan. Onu-Vey sat unmoved. "I do not know. Perhaps. But you said Onu-Vey lost his control over this thing."

"I did. But it seems, Onu-Vey is doing something to it."

"Should we wait to see what happens? We have but minutes before the loa completely fades from existence."

The loa slowly moved closer and closer. The three Mangoni warriors considered and reconsidered the pros and cons of waiting. If Onu-Vey is causing the loa to fade, they must take their chances and wait. If Onu-Vey had nothing to do with the loa's condition, then waiting meant the loa would be upon them in seconds.

Fate decided for them. At that very moment, Onu-Vey fell over on his side. All three warriors kneeled by the houngan to learn why. At that same moment, whatever held the loa back released him and all his rage. A cloud of dust and debris flew up in the tailwind of the loa as it glided directly across the former *veve* toward the three warriors. It reached Goh-Jumaane first. It grabbed Goh-Jumaane by the neck and lifted him high off the ground. There were mutual looks of horror on both Goh-Jumaane's and the loa's faces.

Goh-Jumaane dropped both his shield and spear. He pulled at the loa's bony fingers around his neck with both hands. He struggled with all his strength to loosen the loa's grip. He kicked as his feet dangled in the air. All of his efforts to free himself were useless. Death was imminent. Then it occurred to Goh-Jumaane that he should have been dead the moment the loa touched him. But he wasn't.

The loa seemed just as horrified by its ineffective death touch. It shook Goh-Jumaane several times. With both hands, it shook Goh-Jumaane hard as if to fortify its touch. Its large, living eyes grew wider as the loa seemed to panic from its failure.

The loa instantly transformed into a column of thick black smoke. Goh-Jumaane fell to the ground as the loa's physical form dissipated. Makoso-Kin had retrieved Goh-Jumaane's spear. He jabbed and swiped at the column of smoke with the spear. His defensive efforts only created a swirling eddy of smoke. Nagorda Peak's crosswind caught the eddy and carried it away.

Makoso-Kin threw the spear aside and rushed to help Goh-Jumaane. Goh-Jumaane was coughing and trying to catch his breath. As he attempted to rub the pain away from his neck, he waved Makoso-Kin away. There was a more urgent priority. The two worker warriors turned their attention to Onu-Vey. They joined Metwe-Ngu at Onu-Vey's side.

Onu-Vey had stopped breathing. His eyes were wide open. Metwe-Ngu held the houngan's shoulders up as Goh-Jumaane raised his head. Goh-Jumaane dared to slap the houngan's face several times to bring him out of his trance.

"Onu-Vey! Onu-Vey! Can you hear me?"

Onu-Vey's arm flopped to his side. His hand hit the ground with a thud. His head fell back. The three Mangoni warriors looked at each other when they realized Onu-Vey was dead.

— **77** —

THE DEMON ONLY HIDES TO AMBUSH

Twenty-six kilometers away, the strange and gruesome specter of death had become almost commonplace on the south bank of the Mara River. Since first seeing the demon yesterday evening, all the farmers and warriors had become used to seeing death pacing up and down the opposite bank. Even death's occasional beckoning gestures sparked little emotion and were easily ignored. Everyone felt comfortable with the Mara River as the natural barrier that proved strong enough to hold death back.

By midday, the farmers and warriors had made a semi-permanent camp on the north bank. They could go no farther. They had no idea when they would receive word that it was finally safe to return to the valley. Everyone knew it would never be safe if the gruesome specter occupied the south bank.

The Green Warrior Tushema made a command decision. If the farmers and warriors could not cross the Mara by sunrise on the third day, they would return to the Kiwane Village. They could not stay on the Mara bank or the nearby plains, as migrating herds also made these areas unsafe.

Since the group would be here a while, the Green Warrior Tushema had divided the farmers and the warriors into three or four practical groups. The Sacred Woman Lobarra was one of the groups responsible for preparing food for everyone. Lobarra searched the bank, collecting firewood to cook with this evening. With Tutapona bundled in the kanga on her back, the Sacred Woman added one more piece of driftwood to her arm. She sang Tutapona's favorite lullaby as she turned and walked back along the bank toward the pile she had already collected. Lobarra glanced across the Mara when she turned. She saw a stray wildebeest calf galloping upstream. She saw the calf as just an unfortunate youngling that had separated from the herd. At least, it had the instinct to move upstream toward the Kiboko Passage.

Lobarra dropped her load of firewood onto her collected pile. Just then, it occurred to her that the lone wildebeest was the first living thing she had seen on the opposite bank since the Orange Warrior Wema crossed yesterday. The more she thought about it, the more she realized its significance. She looked across the Mara again. She searched for the demon, but saw no sign of it.

Lobarra looked downstream and saw nothing. She turned and looked upstream. She saw only the wildebeest calf prancing toward the Kiboko Passage. This significant development excited Lobarra. She had to tell someone. She turned to the nearest person to her, Elder Zekke. He worked a few meters inland, grooming one of the pack animals with a brush.

"Great Creation," Lobarra said as she rushed toward Zekke. "Have you seen the demon lately?"

"Yes, I have, Sacred Woman." Zekke rose from his work. He pointed farther downstream with his brush. "It is …" Zekke did not see the demon where he last saw it. He dropped the brush to his side. "Well, it stood there just a moment ago. It was trying to beckon the Gold Warrior Oghani across the river."

"I think it is gone, Great Creation."

"Gone?" Zekke walked out toward the river. Just as Lobarra had done, he stood at the water's edge and looked upstream and downstream. He focused on the areas on the opposite side of the river, directly across from where the other farmers and warriors had gathered. He saw no sign of the demon. "The Green Warrior must be told."

"Where is he?"

"I have not seen him since mid-morning, Sacred Woman."

Lobarra rushed downstream toward the Gold Warrior. "Oghani, Great Creation, where is the Green Warrior?"

Oghani pointed behind him. "He is helping to scout the plains beyond the bank. Why? What is wrong, Sacred Woman?"

Lobarra pointed to the other side of the Mara. "Look! The demon is gone."

Just as Lobarra and Zekke had done, the Gold Warrior looked upstream and downstream. Even though he was standing guard, Oghani had ignored the demon so categorically that he did not notice that the south bank was clear. He turned to the White Warrior Kibwe, who stood guard a few meters farther downstream.

"Kibwe, Great Creation, summon the Green Warrior."

*****

Moments later, the Green Warrior Tushema came from over the crest of the north bank plain. He ran down the bank to where Oghani, Zekke, and Lobarra stood. Several other warriors were close behind him. The White Warrior Kibwe had already shared with him the significant observation that Oghani, Zekke, and Lobarra had made. As the warrior in charge of everyone's safety, Tushema felt responsible for confirming the news. He walked several steps upstream to study the opposite bank. He turned and walked several steps downstream to study the downstream bank. The Green Warrior saw no sign of the demon.

"Great Creation," Tushema addressed the Gold Warrior Oghani. He never took his eyes off the opposite side of the river. "Is everyone accounted for?"

Oghani quickly studied the surrounding faces. Since the farmers and warriors worked in practical groups, Oghani easily recognized if anyone was missing. "All are accounted for, Great Creation."

As a tactical warrior, Tushema considered that the demon could have disappeared in pursuit if someone was missing. But, since everyone was here, the demon had lost interest, unless…

"Would the demon be in hiding somewhere?" Tushema asked. "Would it deceive us, making us think it is gone?"

The Orange Warrior Wema worked to the forefront of the group, standing around Tushema. He addressed the Green Warrior. "The demon only hides to ambush. Openly beckoning is the only way it knows how to lure people. Great Creation, the demon of death is gone."

"You sound confident, Great Creation."

"I am confident. The demon is gone."

The old farmer, Elder Zekke, stood beside Wema. "Are you as confident about the demon as you were about that crocodile?"

"If you must know, Great Creation, I feel more confident about this."

The Red Warrior Nienko hobbled between Wema and Zekke. He also addressed the Green Warrior. "Great Creation, the Mangoni houngan summoned the demon to destroy all of us. No one is to remain alive. Because the demon is so persistent, it would do it if it could kill any of us. Wema and I have witnessed its persistence over and over again. I think the demon has given up. I, too, think it is gone."

The Green Warrior Tushema looked at both Wema and Nienko. He considered what they had just told him. There was convincing validity, but it needed to be tested. "There is one way to be sure." The Green Warrior turned toward the river. He made a quick assessment of the flow and waded out into the water.

"Great Creation," the Gold Warrior Oghani called out. "What are you doing?"

"If I encounter some misfortune, Oghani, you are in charge. Make sure everyone gets back to the Kiwane Village."

"Tushema!" Oghani called out again.

The Green Warrior ignored the Oghani. He waded farther out into the water. The river in this area was deeper. The water level came up to Tushema's waist. He held his shield and spear over his head as he pushed forward. The current was stronger, making it more difficult for the Green Warrior to navigate the rocky river bottom. But he did it.

Tushema emerged onto the bank on the other side. It was a daring thing he did. It was a symbolic victory that made the people on the north bank cheer. But the 'No Nonsense Creation' never cracked a smile. With a look of total seriousness, he studied the downstream bank. He turned and walked several meters upstream.

This time, the farmers and the other warriors paralleled Tushema's walk. They followed him every step of those several meters. The Red Warrior Nienko brought up the rear of the group. He hobbled with a makeshift crutch under his arm.

With his spear and shield held tightly, the Green Warrior walked on the demon side of the river. He looked from side to side, looking for places the demon might hide. Once or twice, he turned in a complete circle as he searched for any sign of the demon. He found nothing. It convinced him that the south bank was clear of demons.

With less difficulty, Tushema re-crossed the river to the north bank. Still dripping with river water, he walked up to the old farmer. "Elder Zekke, Great Creation, gather your things. Ready your pack animals. We are returning to the valley. If we leave now, we can be in the Aukmondi Valley by sunset."

— 78 —

MORE ALIVE THAN EVER

Just as Abul-Tess had promised, the storm passed. The whirling dark clouds broke up and drifted apart. The edges of the clouds glowed with the sun's intense light behind them. Hundreds of brilliant rays poked through the clouds. Like spears of pure energy, they reached for the ground. They grew broader and brighter as the dark clouds surrendered to the sunlight. The few clouds that remained in the sky turned flawlessly white. In moments, the golden sun illuminated the sky, the surrounding landscape, and distant hillsides. The crisp, clear colors of the trees and hills created a beautiful, inspiring sight.

Abul-Gwan and Abul-Tess continued to ride upon the back of the Arabian stallion. The wild but graceful ride moved at tremendous speed. The horse galloped with remarkable agility up and down rolling hills and valleys. It galloped around small bushes and trees. It leaped over small boulders and ditches. Abul-Gwan held his arms tightly around Abul-Tess, but not out of fear of falling. He enjoyed the ride, enhanced by the magic of Abul-Tess's closeness.

Abul-Gwan heard only the rhythmic thunder of the horse's hooves on the ground and Abul-Tess's screams and laughter. The sounds struck his ears like inspirational drums and songs. The smile on his face reflected the joy he felt in his heart. Abul-Gwan did not want it to end.

"Where are we?" Abul-Gwan yelled out.

"Do you not recognize it?"

Abul-Gwan looked to his left and his right, studying the surrounding landmarks. He noticed that they raced across an endless grassland plain. He saw a few shrubs and acacia trees growing in various locations as far as he could see in both directions. Abul-Gwan tried to look to the rear. A cloud of dust raised by the horse's hooves on the ground obscured his view. When Abul-Gwan turned ahead again, the horse had dipped into a small depression. It galloped toward the crest of the hill on the other side.

At the top of the crest, Abul-Gwan beheld a breathtaking sight. The Arabian stallion suddenly angled its gallop to the left and merged into one of the largest herds of wildebeests and zebras that Abul-Gwan had ever seen. Hundreds of them thundered across the plain, raising their own cloud of dust. The Arabian stallion matched the speed of the wildebeests and zebras. It carried Abul-Gwan and Abul-Tess deeper into the herd.

Abul-Gwan was amazed beyond words to travel in the very center of the herd. He looked left and right again. On both sides, the wildebeests, zebras, gazelles, and a scattering of other ungulate animals moved so close that Abul-Gwan knew he could reach out and almost touch them.

"Abul-Tess!"

"What is it, my love?"

"How did we get here?"

"Does it matter? It is where you want to be."

Abul-Gwan held Abul-Tess tighter. The affectionate impulse came just in time. Abul-Gwan and Abul-Tess suddenly rose above the herd, rising higher and higher. The cloud of dust the herd raised, and the rumbling thunder fell away. Abul-Gwan looked left and right again. Huge wings stretched out beneath him on both sides. Carried by the wings, he and Abul-Tess floated smoothly upon currents of warm African air. Abul-Gwan and Abul-Tess no longer rode upon the Arabian stallion. They sat upon the back of a gigantic African fish eagle. Abul-Gwan recognized the huge black wings and the distinctive eagle's cry.

"Abul-Tess, how is this possible?"

"In love, all things are possible."

"I do not understand." Abul-Gwan swayed from side to side as the eagle's flight rocked gently back and forth. He continued to hold tightly to Abul-Tess. "Am I dreaming?"

"No, my love. This is no dream."

The eagle seemed never to flap its wings. Although the wind rushed by, the eagle's flight seemed almost motionless as it sailed smoothly in a wide circle. The Mangoni Mfalme craned his neck to look down. He and Abul-Tess now glided at least a kilometer high in the sky. The herd far below appeared to be one huge, black mass flowing across the African grassland.

Abul-Gwan's stomach suddenly felt weightless as the eagle banked hard and darted toward the ground. This time, Abul-Gwan screamed in unison with Abul-Tess.

The eagle flew toward a large body of water. It soared in a steep dive. The water surface seemed to come up toward Abul-Gwan fast. Impact seemed imminent. But Abul-Gwan did not fear the impact. He closed his eyes at the last second, only to feel the eagle flare to a level flight just above the water's surface. He opened his eyes to see the water's surface streaking only centimeters below him.

Suddenly, a spray of water rained on Abul-Gwan and Abul-Tess. In front of the eagle, several large fish leaped from the water as if to take flight themselves. Each time they fell back into the water, the splash created a misty shower that filled the air. Both Abul-Gwan and Abul-Tess quickly became soaking wet. The ambient temperature of the water felt good.

Without notice, the eagle dipped. True to its nature, it had grabbed a fish in its sharp talons. The sudden dip caused Abul-Gwan and Abul-Tess to fall backwards. They held tight to each other as they rolled off the eagle's back. Both of them screamed again. They closed their eyes as they tumbled from the eagle's back, prepared to splash into water.

The fall was a short one. And it wasn't water where they fell. Instead, they fell gently into a huge nest of leaves and branches. They now lay in a forest area, with a canopy of trees and other foliage overhead. Abul-Gwan had lost his embrace of Abul-Tess, but he quickly recovered and rushed to her side.

"Are you alright?"

"I am fine." Abul-Tess rested on her knees. She moved to find a more comfortable sitting position.

"What happened? Where are we?"

"I do not know." Abul-Tess pointed behind Abul-Gwan. "Maybe, we should ask them."

Abul-Gwan turned. He discovered a family of mountain gorillas behind him. Baby gorillas frolicked about as children do. Some tumbled and wrestled on the ground. Others, up in the trees, chased each other from limb to limb. Several adult females and a few young males lounged about beneath the trees. Most of them picked and nibbled on leaves, twigs, and berries. A huge silverback sat only two meters in front of Abul-Gwan. A well-chewed twig hung from his mouth. The huge silverback, the obvious patriarch of the family, watched over the other gorillas.

The Mangoni Mfalme huddled close to Abul-Tess. "Are you afraid?"

"No, not at all."

"Me either." Abul-Gwan felt excited, but also at peace. He felt he was where he should be.

Abul-Gwan and the silverback looked at each other. They locked stares - eye to eye. Abul-Gwan could almost sense the big silverback's thoughts. He felt nothing specific. But he sensed a beautiful intelligence behind those coal-black eyes, proud, protective, peaceful, and very human. The life behind those eyes valued the simple things that Abul-Gwan had always valued. Abul-Gwan broke his stare. He looked down as a respectful, submissive act. He felt humbled before this wonderful and majestic creature.

The silverback slowly rose and walked off on all fours. With grace, it seemed to accept Abul-Gwan's compliment. He glanced back at Abul-Gwan as if to say, *"You and your mate may stay as long as you like. Just behave yourselves while you are among my family."*

"Did you see that?" Abul-Gwan whispered to Abul-Tess. "What a magnificent animal!"

"This is only the beginning, Mfalme," a voice behind them said.

Both Abul-Gwan and Abul-Tess recognized that voice. They turned to see Kosi-Jawma before them, the former leader of Abul-Gwan's hunter warriors and Abul-Tess's former mate.

Abul-Gwan stood with his mouth open, unable to find a word for his dearest friend. Abul-Tess fought an overwhelming impulse to rush over and embrace her former mate. With a tearful smile, she inched forward, resisting a natural impulse.

Abul-Gwan rushed over, thrilled to see his old friend. Not believing his own eyes, he groped Kosi-Jawma from his shoulders to his forearms. The last time Abul-Gwan saw Kosi-Jawma, the hunter had bled to death after a Wabanga severed one of his arms. Abul-Gwan's eyes volley between both of Kosi-Jawma's arms. He finally looked into Kosi-Jawma's face. "How is this possible?"

"Mfalme, you already know how this is possible. Think about it."

While Abul-Gwan wrapped his mind around all that had just happened to him, Abul-Tess wiped away the tears of joy from her face. She stepped forward to express her pent-up feelings to Kosi-Jawma. She gave in to her impulse and fell into Kosi-Jawma's arms. "I have missed you. I found everything so difficult at first. Abul-Gwan understood more than anyone. He became a great comfort after you left."

"I knew that he would be. I knew him long before you did. I also knew of his love for you."

"And your children, they miss you too. You should see Kosi-Yabo. He has grown to be one of the most honored warriors in the tribe."

"I know."

"And Kosi-Uteri, she is a healer now."

"I know."

"As for Kosi-Tem, now that is another story. He is a handful. I have almost given up on him."

"Kosi-Tem will be fine. He will take Mok-Sutanni as his mate. His new family will become the focus of his life and settle his restless nature. Kosi-Tem and Mok-Sutanni will make you a grandmother before the next harvest."

Abul-Tess looked up into Kosi-Jawma's face. "You know about Kosi-Tem and Mok-Sutanni?"

"Yes. I have been keeping an eye on all of you, especially you. The Supreme Spirit's divine will is the only reason you are here."

"Kosi-Jawma," Abul-Gwan finally found his voice. "We are … we are all dead! Are we not?"

"Mfalme, we are more alive than ever."

Abul-Gwan examined his own body. He touched his face, his chest, and his arms. He looked at his hands. "I am dead? I do not remember dying."

"You probably do not remember being born either."

"But I do not feel dead. I feel … I feel good!"

"We often cry after birth. We rejoice after death."

It was true. Abul-Gwan felt so good that he took Abul-Tess in his arms and spun around with her. They laughed like playful children when Abul-Gwan lost his balance and fell against Kosi-Jawma. The noise and merriment the three made caused Silverback, the gorilla patriarch, to walk back into the area. Silverback stood erect and pounded on his chest as if to impart a warning.

"I think we have overstayed our welcome here," Kosi-Jawma said. "Come with me. I have much to show you."

79

HYENAS AND JACKALS

The returning farmers and escorting warriors crossed the Mara River with no major difficulties. They climbed the winding gorge and the trail of the Kiboko Passage with only a few minor struggles to negotiate the rocks, crevasses, and a few animal carcasses. They emerged onto the grassy plain on the south side of the Mara. After only an hour of walking across the plain, the farmers and warriors had put the river, the passage, and almost five kilometers behind them.

A half kilometer behind the farmers, the Red Warrior Nienko hobbled alone. Bandages and a wooden splint held his broken leg unbendable. He walked with a single crutch made from a sturdy tree limb and padded at the top to fit under his armpit. At his slow pace, Nienko lagged farther and farther behind the farmers.

Before the group crossed the Mara, the Green Warrior Tushema had offered to sacrifice two warriors to carry Nienko on a litter. Nienko refused the offer. He had seen enough bodies carried on litters in recent days. The Red Warrior wanted no part of being carried on one. He fell back on the pride of being a Red Warrior, willing to make the journey home on his own. With one hand holding his spear and shield, he leaned heavily on the crutch with his other hand. For the first five kilometers, Nienko made good progress. But that didn't last.

Nienko learned that his youthful stamina had its limit. The Red Warrior had become tired. His armpit throbbed. He stopped walking momentarily to rest and shake the muscle kinks from the arm across his crutch. He wiped the sweat from his brow. Discouragement intensified when he realized the remaining twenty to twenty-one kilometers home would not get any easier.

Nienko savored his moment of rest. He took the time to study his surroundings. He saw hundreds of dead animals: wildebeests, zebras, and gazelles. Carcasses lay scattered in every direction. He had seen this devastation when it first occurred yesterday afternoon. The horrendous sights retained their original impact. Even now, Nienko could not get used to seeing it. He looked ahead, wondering how the farmers reacted to all of this. He knew they saw this sea of dead animals for the first time.

Nienko pulled himself together when he noticed that the distance between him and the farmers had grown much broader. He could see that the farmers walked far ahead of him now. They shimmered in a pool of quicksilver. Nienko resumed his hobbled walk. He ignored the painful crutch under his arm. He forced himself to move along faster than was wise or necessary. The effort to catch the farmers had already become hopeless. The distance between Nienko and the farmers grew as the Red Warrior frequently stopped to rest.

During one of Nienko's stops, he glanced ahead only to discover that he had lost sight of the farmers. He saw only the pool of quicksilver, shimmering across the horizon. Nienko shrugged off his discouragement. He resumed walking but at a much slower pace. He rationalized that the farmers walked at a faster pace anyway. Two kilometers ago, before they got so far ahead, Nienko had noticed that even Elder Zekke, with his unique walk, rocked back and forth stronger than ever.

Nienko did not blame them. They were eager to reach the valley, to learn the fate of their families, not that he felt any less eager. Concern for his mother and sister continued to gnaw at him. He attempted to follow his mother's advice, focusing on his mission and forcing worry from his mind. It came easier than he expected. His effort to walk demanded most of his concentration.

Under the afternoon sun, Nienko, once again, became thirsty. Since he walked with his shield and spear together in one hand and supported himself on his crutch with his other hand, he could not easily reach for his water pouch. The Red Warrior needed to stop walking to take a drink of water. He noticed a small acacia tree nearby and hobbled toward it. He felt that if he must stop, he would take advantage of the meager shade that the tree provided.

Nienko altered his course to go around a wildebeest's carcass and hobble toward the tree. In the shade of the tree, the Red Warrior dropped his spear, shield, and crutch to the ground. He stood on his good leg as he removed his water pouch from around his shoulder. He took a measured drink. The ambient water was not refreshing, but it abated his thirst, for the moment.

Nienko replaced his water pouch. He looked ahead. It was another hopeful attempt to catch sight of the farmers. But they had outdistanced him. At their pace, Nienko assumed the farmers would reach the valley before sundown. At his pace, he would not reach the valley until tomorrow morning, even if he continued walking throughout the night. Spending the night alone on the open grassland was also a concern, but it was not a real problem. He had done it several times as a young warrior.

With an unbending leg and extreme awkwardness, Nienko eased himself to sit on the ground. He intended to sit for a short while, just long enough to rest while the shade lasted. The shade of the acacia tree just barely covered him. He looked up toward the tree's branches to study the tree's shadow and judge how long the shade would last.

A yellow-billed oxpecker caught Nienko's eye. The small bird flew from a branch and landed on the side of a wildebeest carcass nearby. It searched half-heartedly for insects before discovering the warrior sitting less than five meters away. The frightened bird took flight again. It landed on another carcass farther away.

Nienko recalled the memory of yesterday when he and Wema came upon a zebra trampled to death by the stampeding herd. A horde of squawking buzzards ravaged through the zebra's remains. With so many other carcasses nearby, the buzzards concentrated on that one unfortunate zebra. Nienko thought it was strange. Wema had suggested that it was Mother Nature's way of cleaning up the ugliest messes first. The other dead animals could go nowhere. Scavengers would clean their bodies in time. Nienko accepted the explanation.

It occurred to Nienko that the frightened little oxpecker was the first creature, other than the buzzards, to take an active interest in the dead animals. And stranger yet – the oxpecker wasn't even a scavenger. It was looking for insects. Nienko looked toward the sky. Hundreds of the true scavengers still circled overhead on huge wings. The birds gently and patiently glided through the air. But unlike the oxpecker, none of them landed. None of them dared to get close enough to any of the dead animals to see just how dead the animals were.

"Little bird," Nienko said to the oxpecker, "it looks as though you are alone. You must clean up this mess by yourself. The big birds cannot seem to generate enough interest."

Nienko looked skyward again. He thought of the buzzards' strange behavior. He sat for a long while, enjoying the effortless flight of the huge birds – so beautiful, relaxing. A loud grunt, not far away, startled the warrior and shattered his relaxing moment. Nienko jumped. He looked about, searching the nearby landscape for the noise source. He reached for his shield and spear in a natural warrior's reflex.

"What was that?" Nienko asked the oxpecker, but speculated on possible answers himself. It occurred to him that the big birds in the sky were not the only scavengers. There are land-bound scavengers too, like striped hyenas and jackals. With more awkwardness, Nienko forced himself to stand on his good leg. He adjusted his shield and spear. With several gentle hops, Nienko turned in a complete circle. He saw no sign of hyenas, jackals, or any such animal.

Perhaps it was something smaller; something less visible, Nienko thought. But then, it also occurred to him that nothing small could have made the noise he heard. Nienko made another sweep of his surroundings. He scrutinized all the dead carcasses around him. He tried to see if some sizable but unseen animal had begun what the buzzards would not.

Nienko focused on one of the nearby wildebeest carcasses. It suddenly caught his attention. With a measure of doubt, the Red Warrior thought he saw the animal's tail move. The doubt, however, was not strong enough to dismiss the impossible occurrence. He had to satisfy his curiosity. Nienko hopped closer to the carcass without the aid of his crutch. He stood over the animal momentarily and studied it from head to tail. The tail curled onto the animal's hindquarters like it had just swatted away a fly.

Nienko gathered his shield and spear in one hand and kneeled to place his other hand on the animal's side. He kept his hand there for a long while, long enough to remove any doubt that the animal was breathing. Nienko stood back up, convinced that the animal was dead. Before he turned away, he made one more study of the carcass, from head to tail. This time, however, the animal's tail was no longer curled up on its hindquarters.

Nienko did not see the tail move. But he knew movement had occurred. Did the tail slip from the hindquarters naturally? He kneeled again to touch the animal's side. He had to confirm that the animal was dead. Again, he felt no breathing. He did, however, feel a gentle, muscular tremor. Nienko jerked his hand back, startled. He forced himself to stand again.

"It is alive," Nienko said to himself. "Is this possible?" He looked around at the other dead animals. Could there be others? Nienko quickly hopped over to another wildebeest carcass. He kneeled and placed his hand against the animal's side. He felt no breathing or muscular tremor. Nienko stood up and glanced back at the first wildebeest carcass, making a comparison. Had he made a mistake?

Nienko did not want to jump to an unsubstantiated conclusion. He considered the possibility that the death of these animals was a slow process. Once the animals fall, they die after several hours or days. Nienko looked skyward again at the circling scavenger birds. If his suspicions were correct, it would explain why the big birds were so slow approaching the animals. Buzzards will not approach an animal as long as the animal is alive. The big birds knew it takes some time for these animals to die.

Nienko looked across the sea of dead animals again, studying them with a new perspective. He searched his memory from the moment he had seen his first fallen animal, trying to recall if he had overlooked any other signs that would support his suspicion that these animals were not dead yet.

And then it occurred to Nienko. He had already reached an incorrect conclusion. Maybe he was wrong that these fallen animals were slowly dying. There was another incident. Nienko remembered an incident suggesting that these fallen animals were not dying. They were waking up from a deep sleep.

Earlier today, when Nienko and the farmers climbed the Kiboko Passage, the Red Warrior was the last to enter the gorge because of his broken leg. Just after he entered, he heard something behind him. It sounded like a large splash. It sounded like something big fell into the Mara River. Curiosity got the best of him.

Nienko stopped his ascent of the Kiboko Passage. He turned back toward the river. The farmers and warriors continued up the passage, but he alone hobbled back out onto the bank of the Mara.

On the bank, Nienko saw nothing that caught his eye as unusual. But then, after several moments, he noticed that Wema's crocodile was missing. He saw no sign of it. He hobbled farther out onto the bank to improve his view. The crocodile should have been lying, belly up, against the embankment where the demon had flung it. But it wasn't there. It was not anywhere that Nienko looked.

A frightening thought popped into his head since Nienko did not see the crocodile. He suspected that the crocodile was not dead. Fear afforded him only a quick, visual search. A physical search was next to impossible. By then, Nienko's imagination had gotten the best of him. He envisioned the crocodile moving about on the bank. Or even worse, the demon had returned. Crocodile or demon, Nienko knew he had no chance of outrunning either one. At once, he turned and quickly hobbled back toward the gorge's entrance.

Nienko had forgotten about the splash he heard and the unexplained disappearance of the crocodile. The horrendous climb up the gorge and the five-kilometer walk across the grassy savanna demanded most of his attention. He had dismissed the whole splashing incident until just now. Now, it made perfectly good sense. Wema's crocodile had to be alive.

Nienko hopped on his good leg and turned in a complete circle. He studied all the dead animals around him. The Red Warrior strongly suspected that all these animals, although they appeared to be dead, were very much alive. He could not explain it. It did not matter at the moment. An explanation will come later.

With his broken and split leg held high, Nienko quickly hopped back to his crutch. He grabbed it up. He tucked it under his sore harm pit and ignored the pain. The Red Warrior hobbled out across the grassland faster than ever. He had to catch the farmers before it was too late. They had to know what he knew.

80

WE TIPPED THE BALANCE

After a brilliant and blinding flash of light, Abul-Gwan, Abul-Tess, and Kosi-Jawma stood in the middle of a vast grassy plain. The three seemed so small amid their surroundings. They appeared to be stranded in the middle of nowhere. Knee-deep grass stretched for several kilometers in all directions. Scattered acacia trees and clusters of brushwood grew nearby. A detached herd of wildebeests and zebras grazed far in the north. Toward the east, a pair of giraffes nibbled on the leaves of one of the acacia trees.

"This is beautiful." Abul-Tess turned in a slow circle. "It is remarkable. It looks so barren, yet you can feel life all around you."

"The surrounding life may be closer than you know, Abul-Tess." Kosi-Jawma stretched out his arms to embrace both Abul-Gwan and Abul-Tess. He pulled them in closer to his sides. He did it, not out of affection. Kosi-Jawma did it to protect them.

Abul-Tess saw the reason for Kosi-Jawma's behavior in just enough time to react. She squealed and quickly huddled between Kosi-Jawma and Abul-Gwan. With her hands over her face, she saw between her fingers a herd of gazelles racing toward her. The herd had suddenly appeared out of nowhere. Within seconds, about fifteen to twenty gazelles leaped and galloped past her, Abul-Gwan, and Kosi-Jawma at blinding speed. One gazelle leaped over their heads.

When the thunder of hooves died away, Abul-Gwan, Abul-Tess, and Kosi-Jawma stood in the center of a cloud of dust. The tailwind behind the fleeting gazelle soon cleared the dust. Abul-Tess slowly raised her head. She continued to peek between her fingers. She came out of the huddle, but ducked again as a tawny-yellow and black image streaked past her. It was a cheetah in pursuit of the gazelle. The cat flew by so fast that Abul-Tess did not recognize it as a cheetah until it had passed her, creating its dusty tailwind. Abul-Gwan, Abul-Tess, and Kosi-Jawma turned to watch the outcome of the pursuit.

With phenomenal agility, the cheetah closed in on one gazelle. The gazelle made one last desperate leap into the air to escape. The cheetah made the same leap. It snatched the gazelle out of the air. They fell back to the ground, into the knee-deep grass. Moments later, the cheetah raised its head. It looked about the grassy plain to reassess its surroundings. The gazelle hung in the cheetah's mouth, dead.

"That poor thing," Abul-Tess said.

"It is not just the gazelle you should pity, Abul-Tess. Pity the cheetah, too." Kosi-Jawma followed his comment with an explanation. "A day approaches. We will see no more cheetahs."

Abul-Gwan watched the cheetah drag the gazelle away and disappear in the tall grass. He turned to look into the face of the former leader of his warriors and his friend. "Kosi-Jawma, you died almost three harvests ago. Have you spent all that time here?"

"Most of the time. But you must realize, the passing of time has no meaning here."

"So, what were you doing? Watching things like this?" Abul-Gwan pointed in the direction of the cheetah.

"Yes. It is a choice that the Divine Spirit has allowed me to make. I have been right here when I am not communing with ancestors or watching my loved ones. I have been attempting to restore some of the damage I..." Kosi-Jawma looked at Abul-Gwan and then corrected himself, "we have done."

"Damage? What damage?"

"Mother Nature has a grand design, Mfalme. And in that grand design, there is a balance between life and death as you know it. The business of the Mangoni has been severely upsetting that balance."

"What do you mean? We were only harvesting the natural resources all around us."

"Mfalme, they are not our resources to harvest."

"But Kosi-Jawma, the Mangoni have harvested and traded these resources for a long time. Before you and I came along, our tribe was only a chaotic group of warring clans. The harvesting and trading of animals and other resources have pulled us all together. Harvest after harvest, we did it and never caused any serious harm."

"Thanks to your leadership, Mfalme, our tribe grew together. We grew stronger. But we did it, causing great harm. Now, our tribe must move in a different direction."

*****

In a brilliant flash, Abul-Gwan, Abul-Tess, and Kosi-Jawma stood at the base of a huge baobab tree. In a hollow cavity of the tree, the cheetah's den lay filled with twigs and other natural debris. Abul-Gwan, Abul-Tess, and Kosi-Jawma peered into the cavity. Deep inside, three cheetah kittens squirmed over each other.

"In the distant past, Mfalme, hundreds of thousands of cheetahs roamed Africa and Asia. The beautiful animals are unquestionably the fastest land creatures in existence. Because they are such unique cats, the pelts of the adults are prized possessions. The cheetahs are hunted relentlessly. As a result, the population of cheetahs shrinks each day. The business of the Mangoni has not helped their survival. In the areas where the Mangoni hunt, only 500 cheetahs remain."

"Were we really making such an impact?"

"Yes, we were. This is but one example."

In another brilliant flash, the three stood on the bank of a small pond.

"When was the last time you saw a black rhinoceros, Mfalme?" Kosi-Jawma pointed across the pond. Abul-Gwan and Abul-Tess turned to see a huge, armored animal on the other side of the pond. Its massive body was over three meters long. The rhinoceros drank the warm pond water as it ignored the small cluster of egrets upon its back.

"It has been so long." Abul-Gwan marveled at the creature. He was searching his memory. "I cannot remember the last time I saw one."

"I have never seen one." Abul-Tess studied the animal's forward horn. It curved up over its head almost 135 centimeters.

"Black rhinoceroses are extinct in the Mangoni area. Mangoni hunters killed the last one in our area over seven harvests ago."

*****

In a series of brilliant flashes, Kosi-Jawma took Abul-Gwan and Abul-Tess from one magical spot to the next, providing them with visual examples of other endangered or near-extinct animals.

There was the African elephant. Abul-Gwan knew that hundreds of thousands of these gray giants existed all over sub-Saharan Africa. He had felt comfortable with that common fact on the other side of life. On this side of life, he learned that only 95,000 remained. The elephant population was dropping rapidly because of the animal's prized tusks, over 2500 each harvest. When Abul-Gwan learned how closely tied the Mangoni people were to the elephants' decline, the falling population of the gray giants was unnatural.

After several flashes to locations across eastern Africa, Abul-Gwan saw several prides of the proud and majestic lion. He learned that, despite the vast number of prides, there were not enough breeding pairs in each pride to continue the species. The king of beasts was gradually dying out.

Abul-Gwan and Abul-Tess saw several species of monkeys, birds of prey, antelope, crocodiles, and unique vegetation. All the species were living their last days in existence.

*****

Kosi-Jawma brought Abul-Gwan and Abul-Tess back to the gorilla nest in another brilliant flash. He gestured toward the proud patriarch sitting at the nest's edge. "There was a time, Mfalme, when Silverback, his family, and other mountain gorillas like them covered central Africa. Today, there are fewer than 700. This includes Silverback and his family."

A baby gorilla, just barely big enough to be semi-independent, ran up to Abul-Gwan. It picked up a small bunch of berries off the ground at Abul-Gwan's feet. The baby gorilla sat back and nibbled the berries from the bunch one by one. It stared up at Abul-Gwan while it chewed.

"I had no idea it was this bad." Abul-Gwan knelt to be closer to the baby gorilla. He reached out to stroke its head. To his surprise, the gorilla crawled into his lap. He took the little gorilla into his arms. "I realize now, my attitude about all this has been rather selfish."

"In our narrow way of thinking, we profited from creatures like the cheetah, the black rhinoceros, and the mountain gorilla. We were happy. People who traded with us were happy. We assumed that everybody involved was happy."

"We were only destroying all these animals, jeopardizing their chances of recovering."

"Yes, Mfalme. A few have no chance. Extinction is inevitable."

A ruckus between Silverback and a young male drew everyone's attention. Silverback was exercising another disciplinary action. Abul-Gwan and the others watched until the young male surrendered to Silverback and scurried away, up a nearby tree.

"What about Silverback?" Abul-Gwan asked. "What chances does he and his family have to recover?"

"It is too late for them, Mfalme. They will not recover. The impact of their loss is strong, affecting areas where Silverback and his family do not even live."

"We overdid it, did we not? We tipped the balance." Abul-Gwan looked at Silverback again. "I suppose that would explain why the longer I looked into his eyes, the guiltier I felt. Do you think Silverback blames me for the demise of his family?"

"The demise of Silverback's family is not solely your fault, Mfalme. And I think he knows that. When you stared into Silverback's eyes, he stared back. Could it be, he was wondering? Since you are here, what are you prepared to do about all the damage done?"

"What am I prepared to do? Kosi-Jawma, I am dead. What can I possibly do now?"

"Mfalme, please let none of our ancestors hear you ask such a question. When you were among the living, how often did the wishes and dreams of the dead influence you? You heard their guiding voices all the time. Now, you are among the dead. You can be a guiding voice too. And, if you care, you can do unimaginable things."

"Believe me, Kosi-Jawma. After seeing all that you have shown me, I care."

Abul-Tess reached over to offer the baby gorilla another berry in Abul-Gwan's arms. With complete trust, the baby took it and put it into its mouth. "We only need to see these creatures as part of us in their natural habitat. Do this and you have to care."

"Unfortunately," Abul-Gwan shrugged, "among the living, there are a lot of hearts and minds encased in thick, hardened calluses. Many more are indifferent and unreachable. Personal profit is all that matters. I ought to know because I was one of them. The Kiwane, Rimoza, and Aukmondi tribes, in their way, all tried to enlighten me. But my perspective was different. I did not want to see or hear it. I saw the Kiwane, Rimoza, and Aukmondi as … just ignorant. As Mfalme, I was protecting the strength of the Mangoni Tribe."

"Your true intention was clear, Mfalme. No one can fault you for that."

Abul-Gwan put the baby gorilla back on the ground and stood up. "Unenlightened people like me live with our minds asleep. We live our lives thinking we are doing the right things. What does it take to reach us?"

"It varies from person to person. Different people are touched in different ways. Some only have to be told. Others will need a serious consequence to wake them up."

"Yes." Abul-Gwan paused a moment to recall what it took to wake him. "In my case, I suppose it took the destruction of a whole tribe of people to feel the impact of unrelated lives lost."

Abul-Tess looked at Abul-Gwan with confusion on her face. "What do you mean by that, Mfalme? What did you do?"

Abul-Gwan looked at his mate, but the guilt and sorrow made him speechless. When he finally spoke, he still could not confess any details. "I have done something horrible enough that I do not think it can ever be fixed."

"Come," Kosi-Jawma said. "There is another recent arrival to this side of life. We know him well. He may give some insightful advice."

81

WE CAN GO BACK

Abul-Gwan, Abul-Tess, and Kosi-Jawma were transported to a wooded area in a brilliant flash. They stood at the rear of a large, camouflaged wooden platform high in a tree. The ground was almost five meters beneath their feet. The Vodun houngan, Onu-Vey, stood beside them on the platform. Finding themselves situated high in a tree surprised Abul-Gwan and Abul-Tess. Seeing Onu-Vey standing beside them was a greater surprise.

"Onu-Vey!" Abul-Gwan walked up to the houngan and touched his shoulder as if to confirm that the houngan was there. He did not know whether to show joy or sorrow. "You too?"

"Yes, Mfalme, me too." There was a rare smile on Onu-Vey's face and an even rarer twinkle in his eyes.

"Why are you here?" Abul-Tess asked. "I mean, what happened to you?"

Onu-Vey shrugged. "I am not sure what happened. On the other side, I summoned a dark spirit. When I lost control of it and saw what I had done, I tried to perform a ritual to take the energy and the life out of that spirit. I may have been concentrating too hard. I went too deep into my trance. It took more from me than I had to give. Believe me. My presence here is unintentional."

"I am sorry, Onu-Vey."

"Do not be. Since I am here, I am enjoying myself." Onu-Vey gestured toward the front of the platform. "Look."

Abul-Gwan and Abul-Tess turned to see two Australian and two Kenyan hunters at the front of the platform. They sat with their backs to the Mangoni. Their legs dangled over the forward edge as they patiently waited for something. They kept a watchful eye on the forest and the well-trodden pathway that trailed past the platform. Each of them held primed and ready 54-caliber, flintlock, Jaeger rifles. The four of them were unaware of the ghostly spirits behind them.

Liam, the younger of the two Australian hunters, released the cock on his rifle. He laid the rifle down beside him and got up off the edge of the platform. He seemed to be tired of sitting and needed to stretch his legs. "Just how much longer must we wait here, Ethan? It's been what? Four days now? I must say. I've had enough of this. If we don't …"

"Would you keep your voice down?" Ethan shot back. "Why don't you just shut up? These beasts can hear you two kilometers away. I swear to god, Liam, if you frighten away my kill, I'll put you out of your misery."

"Well, I'll tell you what! You'd be doing me a big favor, you would. This place has given me the creeps since we got here." Liam shook his shoulders as if to shake loose the eerie feeling he had. He sat down again. Before sliding to the platform's edge, he spoke directly to the two Kenyan hunters. "Magogi, Jemba, the two of you are quiet. Am I the only one to suffer this weird feeling that something's wrong?"

Magogi glared at the young hunter. "I tell you what is wrong, Liam. It is you. I agree with Ethan. You need to settle down. You need to shut up. That talk-talk-talk! It must stop. Just being around you … makes me nervous."

Liam dismissed Magogi's criticism. He turned his full attention to the other Kenyan. "What about you, Jemba? You know what I am talking about, don't you? You feel nervous, too? Am I the only one to feel like we're being watched?"

Jemba shrugged as if to appear indifferent. When he spoke, frustration affected his thick, accented voice. "I will tell you the truth, Liam! We are poaching. We are all feeling guilty about it. Just what did you expect to feel? Yes, I am nervous. And, like you, I feel … dirty. But … it is a living. Unlike you, I am not fool enough to complain myself out of a job."

Liam ignored Jemba. He scooted out to the edge of the platform. He picked up his rifle and returned the flint to the half-cocked position. "I don't like this place."

"You did not like the last place we camped." A touch of anger made Jemba's voice an octave higher. "You are always complaining about something. It is not the place we are in, Liam. It is you!"

"No. It's not me. I don't like how I feel here. I tell you, this damned place is haunted. Mark my word."

"All of you, shut up!" Ethan snapped. "I don't want to hear another word from you."

*****

"What are they waiting for?" Abul-Gwan whispered.

"You may speak freely, Mfalme. They can neither see nor hear us." To prove his point, Onu-Vey walked up and waved his hand in front of Liam's face. "This one may be an exception. As you can see, he is sensitive. But he has not discovered his gift yet."

"He seems to know we are here."

"If he puts his mind to it, I know, he could sense our presence." Onu-Vey rejoined the others at the rear of the platform. He turned to face the hunters again and finally answered Abul-Gwan's original question. "These are elephant poachers, Mfalme. They have learned that three elephant cows come along the pathway below every four or five days to a watering hole up ahead. The poachers built this platform to watch for the elephants and to ambush them when they come. They have been waiting here for four days now. Ethan, the tall one on the end, is confident that today is the day they will finally make their fortune."

"From the tusks?" Abul-Gwan already knew what gave the elephants their primary value. The fact also created some confusion. "But there are only four of them. It will take the four of them to carry one elephant tusk away."

"This group of four is only part of a larger organized group, Mfalme. Once these four kill the elephants, others will harvest the tusks."

Abul-Tess crept toward the front of the platform. She was still assessing the magical phenomena, that she could not be seen or heard. Abul-Tess stood between the hunters, Jemba, and Ethan on the platform's edge. She looked up and down the pathway. "I think poacher Ethan is right. I can see elephants coming."

Abul-Gwan, Onu-Vey, and Kosi-Jawma joined Abul-Tess near the front of the platform. In the distance, through the trees, they could see the three gray giants coming down the pathway. The elephants walked in a single file at a slow and leisurely pace. None of them suspected the danger ahead.

Kosi-Jawma studied the gray giants. "Those are forest elephants coming. It looks like a mother and two of her offspring. Their tusks are smaller but much more valuable. Because of their tusks, forest elephants decrease by 500 each harvest. At that rate, after twenty to twenty-five harvests, we will see the last of the forest elephant."

Abul-Gwan looked down to his side. The four hunters had also spotted the elephants coming. All four of them had scrambled to reposition themselves on the platform. Each of them lay on their stomachs and quietly prepared their rifles. Abul-Gwan expected the inevitable. "Considering what you just told us, Kosi-Jawma, can we do anything to stop these hunters – these poachers?"

"It is taken care of, Mfalme." Onu-Vey was smiling again.

"Onu-Vey, what have you done?"

"Liam, the gifted one, is right. This place is haunted … by me. I influenced certain things through Liam. I have enhanced the natural bond between each hunter and his gun."

"What do you mean?"

"It is well known that every gun-owner has a natural bond with their gun. That may not sound like much, but that bond is stronger than one might realize. Because of that simple bond, the gun must be handled regularly. It must also be fired. The need to handle and fire the gun is an energy that grows upon itself. Often, it becomes almost irresistible." Onu-Vey stepped into the middle of the four hunters. He reached over and delicately stroked the barrel of each of their rifles.

None of the hunters felt his ghostly touch. "These four poachers must now fire their guns, even when they least expect it."

Liam put his rifle flint in the full-cocked position. He rested on his elbows. The young poacher planted the butt of the rifle against his shoulder. He braced his elbows on the platform, preparing to aim. Then suddenly, before his aim was good, he heard a loud bam! Liam's rifle fired with a puff of acrid smoke. All four of the hunters jumped.

The three elephants also heard the loud bang. Each raised its trunk and trumpeted. Their leisurely pace turned into a rapid walk. They left the pathway and moved away from the platform.

Ethan, Magogi, and Jemba all looked at Liam. Liam sat stunned. He stared at his rifle with his mouth open. Liam could see that his rifle had fired. If Liam's life depended on knowing why, he would be dead.

"Dammit, Liam! What, the hell, are you doing?"

Liam said nothing. He continued to stare at his rifle.

Ethan slammed his rifle down on the platform and got up off his stomach. Frustrated and angry, he turned in a tight circle with nothing to lash out at. He removed his hat and slammed it down on the platform, too. "Son of a bitch! You lousy, rat-ass, son of a bitch! You just ruined everything!"

"I'm sorry, Ethan. The flint must have slipped. It was an accident. I swear!"

"An accident? An accident? Liam, we spent four goddamn days setting up this site, and you ruined it all in an instant. Look at that!" Ethan pointed toward the elephants. The elephants had already moved over ninety meters away and beyond the accuracy range of the rifles.

"They'll be back, Ethan." Liam tried to appease Ethan's anger. "You'll see. They're dumb creatures of habit. They'll be back."

"Yeah, in four or five days. Are you willing to wait? I ought to …" Ethan clinched his fist and drew it back.

Magogi and Jemba saw it coming. They scrambled and caught Ethan's arm before he could swing at Liam. They held him until he calmed down.

Ethan shook himself loose. He glared at Liam. He grabbed his hat from the platform and jammed it on his head. After another intense glare at Liam, he reached down and picked up his rifle.

Bam!

The flint on Ethan's rifle had slipped, causing the rifle to fire, too. The pellet ricocheted off a nearby tree and sent splinters flying. Once again, all four of the hunters jumped. Jemba jumped so hard that he dropped his rifle. It tumbled over the edge of the platform. Jemba scrambled to catch it. The rifle slipped from his fingers and fell the five meters to the ground. Upon impact, it also fired. Bam! The pellet from his rifle flew up through the bottom of the wooden platform, right between Liam and Ethan. More splinters flew.

By now, the four hunters crouched in tight fetal positions. All four hunters wrapped their arms about their heads. It was a protective response to all the gunfire. They remained still for several long moments. Liam was the first to unfold from his protective huddle. "There! Do you see? Now, do you believe me?"

Jemba unfolded his arms from around his head. He slowly leaned out over the platform's edge, looking for his rifle as if it might fire again. When Magogi unfolded his arms around his head, he seemed to realize he held only the unfired rifle. He released the flint to prevent it from slipping. He delicately placed the rifle down on the platform and moved back.

Ethan unfolded his arms from around his head. He glared at Liam again. His glare was still angry but tempered by a hint of respect – the respect that comes from credibility. *This stupid fool seems to know what he's talking about.* Ethan rose to his feet. "Alright. We're done here. Everyone, pack up your gear. We've been here long enough."

"What? We are breaking camp?" Magogi was glad to hear the news, but it surprised him. "But Ethan, we have nothing to show. After four days of hunting, we have nothing! Others will not understand. How do we explain this?"

"Hell, if I know." Ethan walked away. He threw the carry-strap of his rifle across his shoulder and started down a ladder at the platform's edge. "We'll let that rat-ass, son of a bitch explain why we don't have a kill."

*****

Onu-Vey watched the poachers at the back of the platform with a prideful twinkle in his eyes. Abul-Gwan stood next to him, laughing. "Onu-Vey, I always knew you had a mischief nature about you. I can tell. You truly are enjoying yourself."

"That was horrible, Onu-Vey," Abul-Tess commented, trying to suppress her laugh. "You could have killed someone."

"No, Abul-Tess. On this side of life, I do not have the power to influence anyone's moment of death. This curse will cause no direct harm to anyone. These poachers will join their friends. They will spread my curse. In time, other poachers will avoid them, unwilling to hunt with any of them. Their whole hunting organization is doomed. Because of these four, their organization will soon become known as Africa's most incompetent group of poachers."

"That is brilliant, Onu-Vey." Kosi-Jawma watched the three discouraged poachers gather their gear and follow poacher Ethan down the ladder.

"Like you, Kosi-Jawma, I must now do what I can to help fix the damage the Mangoni have done."

"Your intention is heartfelt, Onu-Vey. But I am afraid the damage that the Mangoni have done cannot be fixed so easily." The smile on Abul-Gwan's face disappeared altogether. He still felt tremendous guilt after having so many Aukmondi people die by death's direct touch. "After what I have done, it can probably never be fixed."

Onu-Vey completely understood Abul-Gwan's guilt. His prideful smile gradually disappeared, too. "I must share some of that blame, Mfalme. I summoned the loa. By my design, I narrowed the loa's focus to the Aukmondi people."

"No, Onu-Vey. You did it because, as your Mfalme, I told you to do it. I remember. You tried to talk me out of it several times. But I would not listen to you. No. The blame belongs to me. And no amount of influence can fix it."

"Why? What are you and Onu-Vey talking about?" Abul-Tess asked. "What have you done?"

Abul-Gwan turned to his mate. He realized she came to this side of life before the death curse began. He held her by the shoulders. "Out of grief, anger, and bad judgment, I have done a horrible thing, Abul-Tess. I owe you an explanation. But where do I begin?"

"Begin where all the death and dying started, Mfalme," Kosi-Jawma suggested.

Abul-Gwan looked at the former leader of his warriors. In his opinion, starting at the beginning was almost impossible. "Kosi-Jawma, the death and dying started long before my birth."

"Then start with your earliest memory, Mfalme."

"It seems death and dying surrounded my whole life." Abul-Gwan took a moment to review his life, dating back to his childhood. When he spoke again, he tried to put everything into perspective.

"You must understand. Until the moment I became Mfalme, clan warfare was normal. I saw nothing unusual about all the fighting and killing. I became involved in all the bloodshed on the day I became a warrior in the ruthless Kold-Johan army. Like all young warriors during those days, I thought I was doing my duty. I joined his tyranny, not knowing that such a way of life was not normal. I believed all the misfortunes of the people we encountered were their own doing. I believed all of their poverty, their hunger, and all their suffering resulted from their own ignorance and self-centered, undisciplined, rebellious behavior."

"But Abul-Gwan," Abul-Tess placed her hand on Abul-Gwan's chest, over his heart, "that does not sound like you. I refuse to believe your heart was ever so cold."

"My love, the Abul-Gwan you now know evolved many harvests later. Over time, I rose higher and higher through the ranks of Kold-Johan's army. I gained command of my regiment. With more and more responsibilities and authority, I worked closer and closer with Kold-Johan."

Abul-Gwan placed his hand on top of Abul-Tess's. He squeezed her fingers gently. "Unfortunately, it was not until Kold-Johan had conquered most of the clans and I had gained a prominent rank in his army that I finally realized the truth. Kold-Johan was not just a ruthless leader as I had always seen him. He was evil. All the tyranny and most of the bloodshed were unnecessary. All of it had happened because of Kold-Johan's sick thirst for ultimate power and control."

Abul-Gwan turned to Onu-Vey, "Then came the day that Kold-Johan took your people – the Balba clan. On that day, when Kold-Johan learned that your mother was dead, he considered allying with him and your powerful magic."

Onu-Vey acknowledged the memory with a nod. "And you wanted no part of it."

"No. With such an arrangement, I knew that darker days would follow. I had to end the senseless killings."

"How?" Abul-Tess asked.

"I assassinated Kold-Johan. The idea to do so occurred shortly after Onu-Vey promised to serve Kold-Johan until the day he died. On the day that Kold-Johan captured Onu-Vey and the Balba people, Onu-Vey had known me for but a few hours. Yet, to this moment, he knew my mind and heart so well. He knew that by then, I had had just about enough of Kold-Johan. He knew that I was willing and fully capable of killing him."

"I only knew that you would rather see him dead than serve him any longer," Onu-Vey explained. "I knew that you were one of the few who could have ended his life without consequences."

Abul-Gwan chuckled again. "Then, I wish you had known me well enough to tell me I was only ending his reign of killing to begin one of my own."

"When you became Mfalme, all the clan warfare ended." Abul-Tess continued to see only the positive qualities of her mate. "All the clans of the Mangoni tribe have known peace ever since."

"Yes. I stopped all the tyrannical killings. I took the people down a different path. Initially, it wasn't easy, but I gave the clans a common cause. I gave them our 'so-called' natural resources. The clans banded together and reached out to other tribes. We reached other nations. We were so successful that we could reach out beyond the boundary of Africa itself."

"What you did, Mfalme, was a vast improvement, especially compared to what Kold-Johan had done." Abul-Tess tried to sound reassuring.

"Maybe. I provided for all the Mangoni people with reduced poverty, hunger, and suffering. I realized, day after day, harvest after harvest, our new enterprise had bonded the Mangoni people tighter than any other time in our history."

"So how can such accomplishments end one reign of killing and begin another?"

"As we harvested the natural resources around us, as you have just witnessed, we overdid it. Under my leadership, the Mangoni continued to destroy Africa's precious life. We destroyed life to such a level... some of it cannot recover. I now realize that, under my leadership, we may have destroyed more than all the lives lost during the clan wars."

"But you achieved one of the greatest single accomplishments in Mangoni history, Mfalme." Abul-Tess tried to make Abul-Gwan see the good in what he had done.

"But at what cost, Abul-Tess? In hindsight, I wish I had taken the people down a different path."

"Because of the Loa of Death?"

"In part." Abul-Gwan took Abul-Tess's hand. "I made the whole tragedy worse when I thought I had lost you. I pulled many things together for the Mangoni people. But I also did a lot of it, hoping to impress you. I saw an incredible, magical aura about you for most of my adult life. To behold it, you inspired and influenced me more than anything. And this truth existed long before Kosi-Jawma took you as his mate."

Abul-Tess glanced at Kosi-Jawma before turning back to Abul-Gwan. "When I accepted Kosi-Jawma's offer to become his mate, it must have disappointed you."

Abul-Gwan shrugged. "It was painful, at first. But I could still see that incredible beauty about you, and that magical aura you have. And you must remember. Kosi-Jawma was a lifelong friend. I knew him long before I knew you. I knew his heart. I knew he loved you and meant the best for you. To stay near you, I could accept that compromise. Most importantly, I saw how happy he made you. When you are happy, you radiate a spiritual beauty I could not help but love. I felt good just knowing you were nearby and happy."

"You loved me that much?"

"Yes, I did. For many harvests, I loved you from a respectable distance. As long as you and Kosi-Jawma were happy, I was happy. I was comfortable with that. I found it easy to cherish the relationship that the two of you had. And then, after Kosi-Jawma died, I suffered his loss too. As my lifelong friend, I missed him. But the pain of his loss did not hurt as badly as the sadness you seemed to experience. I felt you did not deserve such sadness. For some selfish, unexplainable reason, I felt I was the only one able to step in and to fix that."

"That selfish, unexplainable feeling, Mfalme," Kosi-Jawma began, "I think that was my doing. I hated that I had to leave Abul-Tess so suddenly. I felt her sadness too. From this side of life, I needed you to help me do something about it. As my friend, I knew you were the only one who could restore her happiness."

"Then, I am grateful for your spiritual support. I knew that I could not replace the love you gave her. It would not have been very smart to try. But I knew I could make her happy again. I had the determination to try in my way."

"You succeeded, Mfalme." Abul-Tess smiled. "I was not just happy. I could love again. The differences in the love that Kosi-Jawma gave me cannot be compared. You are as different as morning and evening. Between the two of you, I have enjoyed a full day, unwilling to give up either half. I am a fortunate woman."

Abul-Gwan gave Abul-Tess a gentle squeeze. "My biggest mistakes came after I thought I had lost you for good. After less than one harvest, fate took you away from me. I felt it was so unfair. I could not think anymore. Like a fool, I jeopardized everything to get you back."

Abul-Tess looked up into Abul-Gwan's eyes. "You took it out on the Aukmondi."

"Yes. All the Guardian Spirits know, I felt so angry. It was a crippling madness that would not allow me to listen to reason. I asked Onu-Vey to summon the Loa of death. He resisted, but did it out of respect. The loa came. And when it came, it came without mercy. As far as I know, hundreds of innocent people have died. All things considered, what I did makes me no better than Kold-Johan."

"That is not true, Mfalme. The fact you could wait so long to take me as your mate proves you have a kinder, gentler, and nobler heart." Abul-Tess embraced Abul-Gwan. She laid her head against his chest. "You said it yourself. You made a mistake with the Aukmondi. What you did was unintentional."

"Yes, it was a horrible mistake, Abul-Tess. But no, it *was* intentional. I may have ended Kold-Johan's reign and pulled my people together. But my legacy will be the Mfalme who destroyed several species of African life and a whole tribe of people."

"And now, we must work to fix that, Mfalme," Kosi-Jawma said.

"How, Kosi-Jawma? Tell me, how can we fix such a thing? How do we find redemption after what I have done?"

Kosi-Jawma thought for a moment. "We begin by leading the Mangoni down a new path. You did it before. You have already proven that it can be done. Mfalme, you can do it again."

"I had different circumstances on that side of life. I had you and your massive army behind me on that side of life. I had Onu-Vey and his powerful influences beside me."

"You still have Onu-Vey and me, Mfalme. And on this side, we have more. We have the spiritual influences of an army of ancestors on our side. We must use our spiritual influences to take the Mangoni people and the descendants of the Mangoni people on a new course."

"And what new course might that be?"

"Well, the Mangoni must no longer hunt and sell our natural resources as we have done in the past."

"Obviously," Abul-Gwan agreed.

"Instead, we must become guardians of life; we must become protectors of all life, man and beast. We must influence all our people to hold the same high respect for life as the Rimoza, Kiwane, and Aukmondi do."

"All of that sounds good. But that is not enough." Abul-Gwan looked at Onu-Vey as if seeking confirmation of his doubt.

"No, it is not enough," Onu-Vey said. "But I agree with Kosi-Jawma. It is a beginning. It offers the best chance to rebuild your legacy, Mfalme. And it offers the best chance for the Mangoni people's salvation."

"Do you believe that the Mangoni can achieve salvation?"

"Yes, Mfalme." Onu-Vey paused momentarily as he pondered what he knew would be the greatest obstacle. "Unfortunately, none of it can be done … without the support and forgiveness of the Aukmondi people."

"Then, we can forget it. It is impossible. The Aukmondi will never forgive me for what I have done. Protection and guardianship of life are dear to the Aukmondi. I know that if we adopt such an attitude, we may someday, in the distant future, gain the support of the Aukmondi. But forgiveness? It cannot be done, even with our spiritual advantages on this side of life."

"Our spiritual ability to influence the living is probably one of our greatest tools on this side of life." Onu-Vey tried to offer encouragement. "We do not know what we can accomplish until we try. We only need to apply our hearts and minds."

"You make it sound so easy, Onu-Vey. You have personal reasons to feel confident. The rest of us lack your magical talents."

"On this side of life, a sincere effort from the heart is all the magical talent you need, Mfalme. On this side of life, your ability to influence flows with the same effectiveness as mine."

Abul-Tess raised her head from Abul-Gwan's chest. "We must try. What do we have to lose? If we receive only dispassionate support from the Aukmondi, our people gain even in the distant future."

Kosi-Jawma held up his finger as if to make a final point. "I do not want to deemphasize the power of spiritual influences, nor do I intend to show a lack of confidence in Onu-Vey's remarkable powers. If forgiveness is impossible to obtain, we may be more successful if we ask for it directly. At least one of us must go back among the living."

Abul-Gwan and Abul-Tess looked at Kosi-Jawma. Even Onu-Vey looked at the warrior with amazement. The warrior had just presented a possibility none of them ever imagined. Abul-Gwan asked what was on all their minds. "What do you mean? Go back among the living? We can go back?"

"Sometimes … yes."

82

THEY ARE NOW THE GATEWAY

After the usual and brilliant flash of light, Abul-Gwan, Abul-Tess, Kosi-Jawma, and Onu-Vey suddenly stood under the lone Marula tree on Nagorda Peak. It was early afternoon. The shadows upon the ground suggested only one or two hours had passed. Abul-Gwan slowly looked around as if seeing the area for the first time. Seeing both sides of life from his perspective was an eerie feeling. He could see that little had changed since he had taken Abul-Tess's hand and fallen asleep.

The physical bodies of Abul-Gwan and Abul-Tess still lay covered, next to the tree, just as the Goh-Jumaane had placed them. Their hands protruded from beneath the coverings, still interlocked. The worker warrior had also placed Onu-Vey's physical body next to the tree. A covering over the houngan's body protected it from the afternoon sun.

Abul-Gwan could now see that Goh-Jumaane and the two vessel warriors, Makoso-Kin and Metwe-Ngu, were working in the animal corral not far away. The three warriors appeared to be covering the carcasses of animals killed by the rampaging Loa. Rather than bury the animals, the warriors had piled the ox, the one remaining goat, and two sheep together. The pile arrangement suggested that some animals' remains would be salvaged later. The warriors used branches, leaves, and anything else they could find to cover the carcasses completely, to protect them from the sun and the hordes of scavenger birds that circled overhead.

"Kosi-Jawma, are we back?" Abul-Gwan asked.

"Only our spirit forms are back, Mfalme. We can return to our physical bodies only if the body is capable of re-accepting the spirit.

Unfortunately, Mfalme, only your bodies and Onu-Vey's are suitable among the four of us."

"What do you mean?" Abul-Gwan glanced at Abul-Tess. He reached over and pulled her closer to him as if to suggest there would be no splitting them up again. He turned back to Kosi-Jawma. "Why can you and Abul-Tess not return?"

"I cannot return because my physical body no longer exists." Kosi-Jawma turned to his former mate. He smiled as he took her hand. "As for you, Abul-Tess, your physical body sustained great damage. You cannot reclaim any quality of life among the living. You could go back. But your body cannot sustain your spirit. Life will not hold."

Kosi-Jawma walked over and stood between the physical bodies of Abul-Gwan and Onu-Vey. He kneeled and gestured toward Abul-Gwan's body. "Mflame, while your spiritual heart has grown on this side of life, your physical heart suffered severe stress on the other side of life. You took Abul-Tess's death hard. You can return to your body. But you will live with the burden of poor health. If you return, your body will support your spirit with great difficulty."

"I remember the pain of loss I felt, especially in those last few moments, when I took Abul-Tess's hand. I felt terrible. If that suggests how I might feel, then I am unsure how long I could endure."

"You probably would not want to for very long, Mfalme. Only the Supreme Spirit knows your determination to live." Kosi-Jawma swiveled in the opposite direction and gestured toward the houngan's physical body. "And you, Onu-Vey, your body is dehydrated. During your ritual, you hyperventilated and stopped breathing. Life-giving air and water failed to reach vital portions of your body. If you return, air and water must be forced into your body immediately, or your return would probably be shorter than the Mfalme's. Those are the circumstances. The choice to return … remains as yours to make."

"Mfalme," Onu-Vey stepped closer to Abul-Gwan, "because Abul-Tess cannot go back, I already know your decision."

"It does not require a houngan's skills to know that. Does it?" Abul-Gwan drew Abul-Tess closer to him again. He tapped his chest. "My heart beats better here."

"Then, if someone must go back, that leaves me. In all honesty, I would love to stay. The urge to stay is compelling. But I have inherited an obligation to our people."

"You have inherited an obligation to our people and to fulfill your destiny, my son." It was the voice of Mama Kinsi.

Everyone turned to see the old woman stepping from the other side of the Marula tree. She was smiling and dressed in all white, reflecting the brilliance of the afternoon sun. Only Abul-Tess did not recognize the old woman. Everyone, including Abul-Tess, recognized her as a Mangoni High Priestess. They surrendered their unconditional respect and kneeled.

Onu-Vey recognized her not as a High Priestess but as his mother. To him, she did not look a single day older than the day she disappeared over forty harvests ago. His thought was to kneel, too. But the love between son and mother forced him to approach her and embrace her instead.

"Mama!" Onu-Vey said as he held her tightly in his arms. "Mama, my mind and heart have held you close above all else. All my life, the memories of you have sustained me."

"As they should, my son. I found comfort in your memories of me, too."

Onu-Vey seemed to remember his manners. Still embracing his mother about the shoulders, he turned to introduce the others kneeling behind him. He gestured first toward Abul-Gwan.

"Mama, this is the Mangoni Mfalme …"

"I know, Mfalme Abul-Gwan."

Abul-Gwan rose to his feet. "Mama Kinsi. I am honored to meet you. I have heard so much about you. I must admit, there was a time when mentioning your name made me tremble with fear."

Mama Kinsi gave Abul-Gwan a gentle smile. "Yes. But no time greater than the day you and Kold-Johan took the village of the Balba clan. You thought I would be there."

"I am so glad you were not. I thought I knew what Kold-Johan came to do that day. I feared that your great powers would transcend death. To make an enemy of you, living or dead, frightened me."

"Instead of making me an enemy, you made an ally of my son on that day. On that day, you set your intertwined destinies into motion. Your destiny, Mfalme Abul-Gwan, is completed. The Mangoni live now and forever as a united people. But we live with a tarnished legacy." Mama Kinsi turned to face Onu-Vey. "As for my son, his destiny continues. He must restore that legacy."

Abul-Gwan almost stepped back to take a broader look at the amazing woman standing before him. He was speechless. "You knew! You knew all along that all of this would happen. On the day I met Onu-Vey, I never realized I would take him into my confidence. It never occurred to me to treat him like the son or brother I never had. But I did."

Mama Kinsi smiled at Abul-Gwan again. "Like Onu-Vey, I know your heart, Abul-Gwan. I knew you would be the one to bring the Mangoni together. I knew you would wait an unendurable time to take Abul-Tess as your mate. In the short time the two of you would be together, I knew she would bear you no sons, and you would have no heirs. I can explain many ups and downs in your life. If you wish, we can discuss these things later. For now, Onu-Vey must go back among the living."

"Mama?" Onu-Vey took his mother by the shoulders again. "Did you know I would go back among the living?"

"I never expected you to come here, my son. I expected you to fulfill your destiny on the other side, to lead the Mangoni people toward the destiny Kosi-Jawma has suggested. It can still be done. But first, the Aukmondi people need you. They are now the gateway."

"The Aukmondi?"

"Yes. Because of Abul-Gwan's grief, they are damaged people, too. Their condition is severe and rapidly deteriorating. Without you, they have only a small chance of recovery. If they do not recover, then neither will the Mangoni."

"What can I do for the Aukmondi?"

"For the Aukmondi, you must surrender to them. You have already put into motion a force of nature that must run its course. The Aukmondi cannot survive or benefit from that force if you are not there."

"What about the support and the forgiveness we need from the Aukmondi? Do we not still need these things?"

"Yes, we do. Support from the Aukmondi is the easiest of the tasks before you. The Aukmondi live as supportive and giving people. It is their nature. Support from them can easily be achieved from this side of life. Forgiveness, however, is the most difficult. Even if we ask for forgiveness directly, there is still no guarantee the Aukmondi will give it."

"Is there anything we can do, Mama Kinsi?" Abul-Gwan asked.

"As I said. Onu-Vey must surrender to them. Allow nature to run its course. Only then will the Aukmondi find the heart to consider forgiveness."

"This force of nature you mention. What is this force of nature?" Onu-Vey wanted to know.

"You will recognize it when you see it. You only have to be there."

"If this force is natural, will it not continue to affect the Aukmondi, whether I am there or not?"

"Yes, it will, my son. As with any force of nature, it cannot be stopped."

"*Nguvu ya asili haiwezi kusimamishwa.*" Abul-Tess spoke the Swahili phrase as she first heard it from Rwuva. When she saw Abul-Gwan look at her, she explained. "The Aukmondi Principle, Mate, Rwuva, spoke those words just before I came to this side of life. A force of nature cannot be stopped. She used the phrase in a different context when she referred to the bond that united Abul-Gwan and me."

"Your hearts, minds, and circumstances came together and created a powerful force of nature," Mama Kinsi explained. "You and Abul-Gwan recognized it as love. As for the Aukmondi, Onu-Vey has set a different force into motion. It, too, cannot be stopped. The Aukmondi may not survive it if Onu-Vey is not there to explain it. If they do not understand what has happened, their gracious spirit will die with their people. And they will never consider forgiveness. If they do not consider forgiveness, hope for the Mangoni dies."

"Mama Kinsi," said Abul-Gwan, "that is a lot of 'ifs'."

"And none of those 'ifs' will ever occur if Onu-Vey does not surrender to the Aukmondi." Mama Kinsi turned to Onu-Vey. "Embrace your destiny, my son. Whatever happens, I will be near as always. Now please… go."

With tremendous reluctance, Onu-Vey released his embrace of Mama Kinsi. "So be it, mama."

The Vodun houngan walked over and kneeled next to his physical body. He could see that Goh-Jumaane and the two Mangoni vessel warriors had covered his body from head to toe with a thin garment. Onu-Vey waved his hand over his physical body. Like magic, one of Nagorda Peak's crosswinds suddenly picked up. It rustled the leaves of the Marula tree and the edges of the thin covering. The crosswind did not die down until the covering peeled away.

Onu-Vey leaned close and peered into his physical face. "The warriors gave up on me too soon. They could have revived me had they continued. But there is not much time left. If I am to return to this body, I must go now."

"Do you know how?" Abul-Gwan's spirit stood over Onu-Vey's shoulder.

"We go where our minds take us, Mfalme." Onu-Vey stood up and faced Abul-Gwan, Abul-Tess, Kosi-Jawma, and Mama Kinsi. "Are there any messages that any of you wish me to deliver to the living before I leave?"

After a thoughtful moment, Abul-Tess stepped forward. She glanced at her former mate, Kosi-Jawma. "Tell my children that their father and I love them. And remind them to know we will always watch over them."

"So be it, Abul-Tess."

"Onu-Vey," Abul-Gwan spoke up. "Since the day I met you, you have served me well. But my narrow mind and callused heart have left me and my people with an ugly legacy. Despite Kosi-Jawma's confidence, it is hard to see how this could ever be fixed. But he has been on this side of life longer than I. I must accept his judgment. In case he is in error, I must ask for your help and support again, my friend."

"I am still in your service, Mfalme."

"Tell our people I always meant the best for them."

"I am sure they understand this already, Mfalme."

"But I have hurt them. For their sake, I express my sorrow to the Aukmondi. Let the Aukmondi know, I beg their forgiveness."

"It has always been my intention to serve you as I know you wish to be served, Mfalme. When you asked me to place the curse of death upon the Aukmondi, I knew you did not mean it. I will try to make the Aukmondi understand that."

"Thank you, Onu-Vey. With your awesome power of influence, I know you will succeed. I feel better already."

"The pleasure has been mine, Mfalme."

"You keep saying that, Onu-Vey. I believe you mean it."

"Do you doubt my sincerity?"

"I do not doubt that you are sincere." Abul-Gwan smiled as he stepped forward and touched Onu-Vey's shoulder. "But I must confess, after today, I think the true pleasure has been that of Mama Kinsi."

Abul-Gwan glanced at Mama Kinsi. He tried to read her face. Nothing confirmed or dismissed his suspicion.

"Though we decreed in writing long ago, the Mangoni people fall into your hands now. Since I have no sons and no brothers, upon your return among the living, our people will recognize you as Mfalme."

"If this was by her design, Mfalme, do you regret it?"

"No. I can think of no one else I would rather leave my people to, Onu-Vey. If anyone can put them on the right path and lead them on a proper course, you can."

"I will do it in your honor, Mfalme."

"Oh! And one other thing." Abul-Gwan stepped closer to Onu-Vey. "Tell the Aukmondi Principal, Mate, Rwuva, that she was right."

"Right about what?"

"The bond between Abul-Tess and me is a force of nature that even death could not stop."

"I will tell her." Onu-Vey took one last good look at Abul-Gwan, Abul-Tess, Kosi-Jawma, and Mama Kinsi. For a moment, it seemed he was at a loss for words. "I cannot say goodbye. Across the boundaries of life and death, we will talk again, soon."

Onu-Vey stepped aside and looked up into the Marula tree as another Nagorda Peak crosswind picked up. This time, it blew strong enough to cause a one-meter limb to break loose from the tree. It fell to the ground, but not before striking Onu-Vey's physical body in the stomach. Trapped air from deep in Onu-Vey's physical body rushed out. It came out so fast that the body made a loud guttural noise.

*****

At the animal corral, Goh-Jumaane and the two vessel worker warriors made final adjustments to the branches on top of the dead animals. They arranged the branches to block the sunlight from animal carcasses. All three of the warriors heard the guttural noise behind them. Goh-Jumaane suddenly turned toward the Marula tree, searching. "What was that? Did you hear that?"

Makoso-Kin searched too. He saw that the covering over Onu-Vey's body had blown back. A sixth sense told him the exact source of the sound. "The houngan!"

Goh-Jumaane, Makoso-Kin, and Metwe-Ngu tossed aside the branches they held. They rushed over to Onu-Vey's body. They stood for several precious moments, looking down at the body. Goh-Jumaane noticed the fallen tree limb lying next to the body. He picked it up and looked up into the Marula tree. The warrior quickly realized what had happened. He threw the limb aside and knelt beside Onu-Vey's body. He studied the houngan and gave in to his impulse to see if he could duplicate what he thought had happened. With a curious caution, he pressed Onu-Vey's stomach.

Another guttural noise escaped from Onu-Vey's body. It sounded like a growl this time. The noise frightened the warriors. All three of them jumped back.

Onu-Vey's spiritual body hovered over the three warriors. "Again, Goh-Jumaane. Do it again!"

As if Goh-Jumaane had heard the ghostly plea, he pressed Onu-Vey's stomach again.

The spiritual Onu-Vey felt a powerful pull at his entire being. He was losing consciousness. The surrounding area spun under his feet, and a powerful whirlpool of energy sent him tumbling out of control.

*****

In a brilliant flash, Onu-Vey fell into his physical body. The next thing Onu-Vey knew, tremendous pain racked his entire body. He rose to a half-sitting position, coughing and gasping for air. He could feel the three warriors grabbing his body, trying to help him.

Onu-Vey rolled over on his side. He forced the words out of his mouth with a dry, raspy voice. "Water! Water, please!"

Metwe-Ngu quickly offered the houngan his own water pouch. Onu-Vey grabbed it and turned it up. More water ran down his chin than down his throat. He knew not to drink too much too fast. Onu-Vey tossed the water pouch aside. The pain and the coughing had subsided, but he was still gasping for air. As painful as it was, it felt good to be breathing again.

Onu-Vey sat up. He held up his hand. It was his way of telling the three warriors he no longer needed their help. He forced himself to speak again. "Please. Give me a moment. I will be fine."

When Goh-Jumaane and the two vessel warriors saw that Onu-Vey was recovering, they scrambled to their feet. The warriors knew of the Mangoni written decree.

"Onu-Vey, Mfalme!" Goh-Jumaane bowed. "We thought … we thought you were …"

"Dead?" Onu-Vey rubbed his face with both his hands as if waking up. "Yes, Goh-Jumaane. I *was*."

83

WEMA'S CROCODILE

Nienko hobbled across the grassland with a strong and steady pace. His armpit, which supported most of his weight on his crutch, throbbed with every other step. His broken and splinted leg had produced most of his pain at one time. But now, compared to his armpit, his painful leg meant nothing. Nienko did his best to ignore his pain. He focused on reaching the farmers. He had to tell someone what he knew about Wema's crocodile.

Nienko ignored his thirst, too. He had almost no choice. Since he started his determined walk across the grassland, he allowed himself to stop only once. About a half kilometer back, he stopped to drink from his water pouch. He turned the pouch up, begging the last of his water out. The meager dribble just barely abated his thirst. He felt thirsty again, stronger this time. But he could do nothing about it.

The Red Warrior wiped a trickle of sweat from his forehead before it ran into his eye. Sweat covered his chest and back, soaking through to his red cloak. As uncomfortable as it was, the sweat was a good sign that he had not yet become too dehydrated. Nienko knew that the Aukmondi Valley was only a few kilometers ahead. And somewhere between him and the valley were the farmers. He hoped he could hold out until he reached one or the other.

Nienko hobbled ahead for several more meters. He watched the ground and his steps with great care. An unseen rock, vine, or hole in the ground could mean a painful fall. Nienko walked around fewer and fewer animal carcasses along the way. He expected this as he got closer and closer to the valley. He had left the main, northbound migration routes several kilometers ago. This was no guarantee he would see fewer carcasses. In the past, some migrating herds moved past the valley as close as the valley rim. The possibility of seeing carcasses stretched all the way home.

Nienko did not expect to see a small herd of live wildebeests. He did not see the animals until he hobbled to the top of a moderate incline. A quarter of a kilometer, directly ahead, Nienko saw about twenty to thirty grazing wildebeests. He allowed himself to stop for the second time since he began his determined walk. He stood and watched the refreshingly normal sight.

With gentle hops on his good leg, Nienko turned. He looked in the direction he had come. Hundreds of dead wildebeest still lay scattered behind him. Nienko looked toward the grazing wildebeest again. He assumed that this herd had just arrived from regions farther south. This herd was fortunate enough to enter this area long after the death demon struck.

Nienko looked southward. He saw more wildebeest there. They seem to confirm his assumption that these were new arrivals. Nienko saw that more animals slowly appeared from over the rolling hills. Some of the animals seemed focused on grazing. Most of them, however, continued to move in his direction. This wasn't good. It occurred to the Red Warrior that if the animals continued to move like that, his path would soon become blocked.

The Red Warrior was in no immediate danger. But he tried to improve his situation before it got too late. He turned east to resume his hobble homeward. He secured his shield and spear in one hand. He adjusted the padded end of his crutch under his sore arm with his other hand. He forced himself to recover his strong and steady pace. He was careful not to frighten any animals standing directly ahead.

Nienko had covered about a quarter of a kilometer without incident. The animals ahead parted as if to give him clearance. When Nienko glanced southward, he saw the animals there had become more restless. None of them grazed anymore. Most of them still moved rapidly in his direction. This was not good at all. Nienko hobbled faster, trying to double his awkward gait. He raced to stay clear of the approaching animals.

While meeting the returning farmers, Nienko recalled the stampede that trapped him and the Orange Warrior Wema. The two warriors were fortunate to find safe refuge behind a baobab tree. Nienko saw no baobab trees this time. There were a few thin acacia trees here and there. None was large enough to provide him the protection he might need. The open grassland surrounding Nienko made him feel exposed and vulnerable.

Nienko looked at the approaching herd again. He realized that it was just a matter of moments before it overtook and blocked him. Since he could not run and hide, Nienko had no choice but to yield to the herd. He stopped his hobble. He stood where he was. His heart raced. Nienko turned to face the approaching herd. An impulse to make a noise to frighten the animals back or alter their course crossed his mind. He thought better of it. He feared he might frighten them too much and cause them to stampede. Instead, Nienko placed his shield between himself and the approaching herd. The shield was no baobab. Under the circumstances, it had to fulfill the same purpose.

To Nienko's great relief, the herd moved past him without incident. Nienko peeped out from either side of his shield to see that these animals also gave him some clearance. It was as if they knew he was there and respected his presence. Nienko noticed, however, that the herd's momentum continued to increase. As the speed of the animals increased, the animals moved closer toward him.

Nienko waited patiently for endless moments as the herd strolled past him. He watched the awesome animals up close – some less than three meters from where he stood. Nienko was a Red Warrior who had seen and experienced many things the average tribesman could only imagine. This was one of those special experiences. He had never been this close to live wildebeests. The chorus of bellows and grunts around him was almost deafening. But Nienko enjoyed what was happening. The experience frightened him at first. But it had transformed into an exhilarating event. Nienko's spirit soared. He smiled.

As Nienko continued to study the passing herd, he glanced eastward again. In the distance, about a kilometer away, Nienko saw something else that made his spirit soar higher. Two warriors – Aukmondi warriors emerged from the shimmering quicksilver, coming his way. One warrior wore an orange cloak.

"Wema?" Nienko spoke the name aloud. He would have jumped for joy if he could. He stifled the impulse but realized the mistake he had just made. Nienko quickly looked to his left and right, to see if his vocal outburst disturbed any passing wildebeests. Several of the animals appeared to be frightened. They suddenly altered their course to give the Red Warrior a wider clearance. In its haste to scurry away, one wildebeest darted around another, but had to cut in front of yet another to do so. It bumped the Red Warrior.

Nienko fell to the ground. He fell hard enough to hit his broken leg. Pain, unbearable pain, shot through his leg and seemed to seize his whole body. The Red Warrior was thoughtful enough not to cry out. With eyes closed tight, tears still poured from his eyes. With his teeth clamped together even tighter, Nienko moaned loud enough to frighten more animals. Nienko heard the stampede before he saw it. When he finally opened his eyes, the last thing he remembered seeing was a blur of animals racing, not just past him, but over his head.

*****

A kilometer away, Wema and the White Warrior Kibwe also heard the stampede before they saw it. The rumble of thundering hooves caught their attention and made them rush over the crest of the hill. Since leaving the Kiboko Passage, the two warriors had seen nothing but the carcasses of dead animals. They stood in awe when they saw the herd of living animals, like Nienko. Like Nienko, they assumed these animals were new arrivals to the region, never affected by the demon of death. The sight of the living, animated animals was refreshing to see. The two warriors stood on the hillside and watched the animals rush northward.

Just minutes earlier, the farmers and their complement of escorting warriors, which now included the Orange Warrior Wema, took a break in their journey home. The eerie and unsettling part of their walk was behind them now. The sea of carcasses had become scarce, and the hordes of scavenger birds that circled overhead thinned. Best of all, the farmers and warriors had come within six kilometers of the valley. They tolerated their surroundings long enough to take a short break and prepare for that final stretch home. That was when Wema approached the Green Warrior Tushema to ask a special favor.

"With your permission, Great Creation, may I go back? I want to find the Red Warrior Nienko, to see if he needs help."

Tushema had offered the Red Warrior help long before the crossing of the Mara. Nienko declined the offer. Tushema respected the warrior's pride and did not force help on Nienko. Tushema saw Wema's appeal as an opportunity to give Nienko something he should have had. The Green Warrior's answer came at once.

"Of course, Great Creation." He nodded toward one of the junior members of his detachment. "And take the White Warrior Kibwe with you. If Nienko has to be carried upon a litter, it will require two of you."

The distance between where the farmers had stopped and the hill crest where Wema and Kibwe now stood was just over three kilometers. The two able-bodied warriors covered the distance in less than twenty-five minutes. They stood on the hillside, watching the herd run by for another two to three minutes. They watched until they spotted something unnatural.

Almost any Aukmondi warrior knows that red is one of the magical colors seen over the farthest distance and in the most complex of patterns. This proved true when the White Warrior Kibwe saw a red object upon the ground amid the stampeding herd. Despite the beautiful panorama of the herd, Kibwe saw nothing but the red object. A young warrior's instinct made it unnecessary for Kibwe to guess the red object.

"Wema!" Kibwe pointed, but realized the Orange Warrior was well ahead of him. Wema saw the bright red spot just seconds before Kibwe did. The two warriors raced down the hillside toward what they knew to be Nienko's red cloak.

Wema estimated that the entire stampeding herd comprised about two to three hundred animals. He feared the worst as he and Kibwe watched the last of the herd run past Nienko. The herd left a cloud of thick dust behind it. The cloud was dense enough to obscure Nienko. When the dust cleared several moments later, Wema and Kibwe saw Nienko, dazed and attempting to sit up. They reached the Red Warrior just in time. Nienko fell back. Both Wema and Kibwe caught him before he hit the ground.

"Nienko, Great Creation," Wema eased the warrior down. "Do not move. Be still."

"Water," Nienko spoke just above a whisper. He tried to look up at the Orange Warrior. Only one of his eyes would open. Severe swelling around the other eye held it closed. A swollen lower lip distorted his words. "I need … water."

The White Warrior Kibwe searches for Nienko's water pouch. He found it lying a meter away, obscured by Nienko's torn and tattered shield. The pouch was empty. Kibwe gave Nienko his own water pouch.

With trembling hands, Nienko turned the pouch up to his mouth. To take measured swallows of water never crossed his mind. Wema grabbed the pouch and eased it away from Nienko's mouth before the Red Warrior could drink too much too fast.

In the meantime, Kibwe took the liberty to examine Nienko's body. Sensing what he could with just the feel of his hands, Kibwe gently examined Nienko's head, shoulders, arms, sides, legs, and feet. Although Kibwe was only a White Warrior, his knowledge and experience allowed him to reach a firm conclusion. He sighed before moving up to face the Red Warrior.

"Great Creation," Kibwe addressed Nienko, attempting to get his attention. Nienko appeared to be only half conscious and did not respond.

Wema responded instead. "What is it, Kibwe?"

"Besides a few lacerations, a bruised rib, and some swelling, I am afraid, the Red Warrior has a broken leg."

Wema almost smiled at the good news. He glanced down at Nienko's splinted and bandaged leg. "Then he survived the stampede well."

Kibwe saw the Orange Warrior looking at the wrong leg. "No, Great Creation. The other leg is also broken."

Wema looked at Nienko's other legs. It was not broken, but Wema accepted Kibwe's conclusion. He looked up into Nienko's face and sighed. "Then we had better set it before Nienko regains consciousness. We can set it before he knows what we are doing."

"I do not think it will be necessary to set it, Great Creation. It appears to me to be just a simple fracture."

Wema examined Nienko's leg. The more experienced warrior easily came to the same conclusion. Wema was about to compliment the White Warrior on his medical skill when the semi-conscious Nienko tugged at his shoulder.

"What is it, Great Creation?"

Wema heard Nienko mumble something, but he did not recognize a single word the warrior said. He looked over at Kibwe. "What did he say?"

"I am not sure. It sounded like he said, 'your crocodile'."

Wema looked down at Nienko again, puzzled. "My crocodile? What about my crocodile?"

"I …" Nienko still spoke just above a whisper. He weaved in and out of consciousness. "I … did not see it."

"What is he talking about?" Kibwe frowned, puzzled by Nienko's statement. "All of us saw that thing."

"It was …" Nienko's face contorted as he suppressed a wave of pain.

"It was what?" Wema asked.

Nienko's consciousness drifted out again. One unintelligible word slipped past his lips. "Gone."

Wema and Kibwe considered the Red Warrior too delirious to know what he was saying. Wema ignored Nienko's babble. He gathered the necessary material to splint Nienko's other leg. He gave Kibwe a series of instructions. "Find two strong limbs. We need to make a litter for the Red Warrior. Let us get him to where we can give him better treatment."

"I … I went back." Nienko's visible eye rolled back as the warrior tried to regain control of his drifting mind. He continued to speak in a whisper. "The bank … was clear."

"Do not talk," Wema ordered. "Lay still."

Wema continued to ignore Nienko's babble, hoping the Red Warrior would relax and rest. To his relief, Nienko collapsed, falling into complete unconsciousness.

— 84 —

TRUST OUR JUDGMENT

By sunset, the farmers and warriors began their last kilometer in their return home. They had left the grassy plain of the northern Serengeti several meters ago. They saw no more animal carcasses. Fewer scavenger birds circled overhead. The disturbing swarm had dwindled to the occasional one or two birds floating on the wind. It looked almost normal.

When the travelers finally crested their last hill and could look toward the valley, their illusion of normalcy turned out to be an illusion. Reality hit with a stunning impact. Everyone stopped walking. Conversations within the group died away to complete silence. They stood in awe as they looked toward the valley.

In the distance, in the sky over the Aukmondi Valley, hundreds of scavenger birds swarmed. The sky was almost black with birds – a maelstrom of hawks, buzzards, kites, ravens, and crows. Birds spanned across the horizon, over the entire length of the visible valley. The farmers and warriors could hear the ceaseless shrieks and caws of the birds over a kilometer away.

"Oh, Great Sacred Spirit!" Lobarra was the first to recover from the shocking sight and find her voice. All she saw took hold in her mind with a frightening significance. Tears welled up and flooded her eyes. "What has happened to our valley? Our people? This cannot be!"

"That is not an encouraging sight." The Green Warrior Tushema studied the birds. The strong-minded warrior took three steps forward as if to confront his initial shock. But the multitude of birds overwhelmed him. He had to stop walking again as he studied the maelstrom. "I did not expect to see that."

"Well … just what did you expect?" Elder Zekke moved up beside the Green Warrior. "The warriors Wema and Nienko told us what was happening in our valley. They told us of several horrible developments in our valley. So, just what did we expect?"

"Not this," Lobarra said. She wiped away the tear that finally streaked down her cheek. "And I fear, we have not seen the worst yet."

Lobarra held Tutapona in her arms. The infant stared and pointed toward the noisy swarm. He could even tell that the huge horde was not normal.

"Come," Tushema resumed walking. "This is home. We will change nothing by standing here."

After another half kilometer of walking, the farmers, warriors, and pack animals entered the Bongii Forest. The spectacle of swarming scavenger birds over the valley disappeared, blocked by a canopy of trees. The Bongii Forest was the last wooded area before finally reaching the valley rim. Although it wasn't part of the Aukmondi domain, all the farmers and warriors were familiar with it enough to consider it home.

Everyone missed the usual peace and comfort that the forest always provided. Even though the unsettling scavenger birds could not be seen overhead, the shrieks and caws were still audible. The farmers and warriors endured the noise as best they could as they proceeded along the forest pathway. No one felt comfortable enough to talk. Everyone feared what they might find, just a few meters ahead, on the other side of the valley rim.

"There is the smell of burnt grass in the air." Elder Zekke attempted to break the tension through conversation. "We are close to the clearing."

"Yes." Tushema agreed. He walked just ahead of Zekke. "According to the warriors Wema and Nienko, the whole clearing burned. I am surprised that we did not smell it earlier."

"Maybe, it is not as bad as we envisioned it." Elder Zekke was hopeful. "Maybe conditions in the valley are not as bad as we expect."

When the farmers and warriors finally emerged from the Bongii Forest onto the clearing, they found that the clearing had burned as badly as they had imagined. They saw none of the knee-deep, golden grass weaving in the wind. Burnt black grass stubble covered the entire clearing, from one side to the other. The farmers noticed, however, that wheatgrass straws covered most of the charred area. People from the valley had already begun restoration. It was an encouraging sign of communal life in the valley. It was encouraging until everyone remembered that the burning and the restoration occurred before the demon of death walked the valley.

Most of the warriors also saw the wheatgrass and the attempt at restoration. But as warriors, a more alarming observation drew their attention elsewhere.

The Gold Warrior Oghani walked up to stand between Tushema and Zekke. He spoke to the Green Warrior as he looked toward the valley's north slope. "Great Creation, no sentinels stand guard on the valley rim."

"You noticed that too?" The concern in Tushema's voice suggested that he had already noticed the abnormality. "I hoped that I was wrong."

Zekke looked across the clearing toward the tree line and the north slope. He studied the trees as best he could. He searched up and down the line for sentinels. The most noticeable thing he saw was a few scavenger birds perched atop some of the trees. "Is that not the whole point? Sentinels are not supposed to be seen."

"We see none, Great Creation," Oghani explained, "because there appears to be none out here."

As a Green Warrior himself, Tushema knew the locations of most of the sentinel posts. He also looked up and down the tree-lined valley rim. The Green Warrior hoped to see at least one overlooked sign that sentinel warriors still guarded the valley. He saw none. All the posts he could see appeared to be unoccupied. With just the gesture of his spear, he sent Oghani and a couple of other warriors of his detachment to check nearby posts.

Tushema himself started across the clearing toward the nearest sentinel post. His urgent pace developed into a run. His rapid approach and the swish-swish sound of wheatgrass straw beneath his feet caused the scavenger birds that dared to perch in the treetops to take flight again. Tushema ignored them. He focused his attention elsewhere.

Long before he reached the post, Tushema saw that it was occupied. But not in a way he wanted, he saw two Sentinel Warriors there. Both of them lay upon the ground as if dead. Tushema dropped his shield and spear to the ground. He rushed to the side of the nearest warrior, who lay upon the ground, face down. When Tushema flipped the warrior over, he recognized him as the Royal Warrior Jokere Gota.

Tushema quickly examined the Royal Warrior's body, from head to toe. He found no visible wounds. One of Jokere's Blue Warriors, Oumar Botele, lay sprawled out on his back, just a few meters away. Tushema half-scooted, half-crawled over to the warrior's body. He made a quick but thorough examination. The result was the same – no visible wounds. Both warriors, however, were dead.

By the time Tushema finished examining the warriors, the farmers and the rest of the warriors had gathered around him. Elder Zekke was the last farmer to rock his way across the charred clearing. Though he continued to hold on to the guide rope of the ox he led, he made his way to the forefront of the group. He stood at Tushema's side, looking down at the two fallen warriors.

"Are they dead?"

Tushema stood up slowly. "Yes, Great Creation."

"Great Sacred Spirit! News of something like this does not hit you until you see it firsthand." Zekke's eyes finally welled up with tears. He gestured toward the Blue Warrior's body. "That one, the Blue Warrior Oumar Botele … I knew him, almost like my own son. Until he moved to his warrior kraal, he lived most of his young life in the hut beside mine. I knew he would grow to be a remarkable warrior. I was right about him."

Zekke made the same feeble gesture toward the Royal Warrior's body. Despite watery eyes, Zekke chuckled. "This one, the Royal

Warrior Jokere Gota, I was so wrong about him. His father, the Great Creation Yakubu Gota, and I grew up together. To this day, Yakubu is a dear friend of mine. I was privileged to be among the family on the day of Jokere's birth. Yakubu was so proud of him. He said that Jokere would also grow to be a great warrior. It was a father's pride speaking. But as Jokere grew, I had my doubts. As that Young Creation grew, he loved to eat. Great Sacred Spirit, how he loved to eat. I knew that his weight would always be a problem. At his sixth harvest, he carried twice the weight he should have carried. This Young Creation could never become an agile and fit warrior. I could not find it in my heart to share my opinion with Yakubu. I just let him savor that impossible dream."

"Such dreams keep us going, Great Creation."

"Yes, they do. But both Jokere and Yakubu proved me wrong. Young Jokere held an unwavering determination to be a warrior. That was his dream. He surpassed my every expectation. As you can see, he became an exceptional warrior. I never believed he would become a Royal Warrior."

Zekke wiped away a tear that threatened to roll from his eye. He tried to pull himself together as he addressed the Green Warrior. "Since these two are dead, can we assume the other sentinels are dead too?"

Before Tushema could answer, the Gold Warrior Oghani and the other warriors who checked the other sentinel posts rejoined the group. Oghani had overheard Zekke's question. Oghani had gathered enough information to answer Zekke's question. He did not say a word. A single nod of his head toward the Green Warrior was all that was necessary.

Tushema allowed everyone a moment to react to this devastating news. He raised his voice. "Everyone, please hear me." Tushema waited another moment until he was sure he had everyone's attention. "Let us not fall apart–not now."

"If all the sentinels on the north rim are dead, does this confirm our expectations?" Zekke asked. "Is the whole valley just as dead?"

"I do not know, Great Creation." Tushema gave the questions some thought. "The signs are not encouraging."

"So, how do we proceed?"

Tushema had no immediate answer for Zekke this time. For the moment, he said nothing. Instead, he kneeled next to the body of the Royal Warrior Jokere. He lifted the body by the shoulders. "Here, help me move him out of the sunlight."

Zekke started, but the Red Warrior Rotho was closer. He discarded his shield and spear and made himself available. "Allow me, Great Creation."

Rotho knelt to get a firm grip of the Royal Warrior's ankles. He and Tushema lifted the warrior's hefty body and carried it into the shade. They placed it next to the body of the Blue Warrior Oumar. Rotho adjusted Jokere's body as if to make him comfortable. He completed the delicate task by gently folding Jokere's arms across his chest.

Tushema did the same for the body of the Blue Warrior Oumar. He crossed the warrior's arms across his chest and stood up. He gathered up his shield and spear and walked over to where Elder Zekke stood. The Green Warrior finally had an answer to Zekke's original question.

"I am not sure how we should proceed, Great Creation. Since we have finally made it home to our valley, or what is left, you are eager to go directly to your kraals. You want to learn what has become of your family and friends. For safety's sake, I am asking … I highly suggest that, for now, we all stay together."

"Stay together?"

"Yes. My mission to ensure your safety during your journey to the Kiwane Village and back is incomplete. If circumstances were normal, my mission would be complete once we crossed our valley's sentinel line. But it is clear. Circumstances are not normal. Until we learn how safe and secure our valley is, your safety will be my responsibility."

Tushema looked at Rotho. "The same holds for you, too, Great Creation. Until further notice, your primary responsibility is the safety of the Sacred Woman Lobarra and the little prince, Tutapona. Whatever we may find in the valley; whatever may happen, let nothing else stand in the way of that."

"So be it," Rotho acknowledged the Green Warrior.

"So, how long do you suggest we stay together?" Zekke asked.

"At least until we learn that the valley is safe."

"Under these extraordinary circumstances, how will we know when it is safe?"

Tushema shrugged. "I do not know. We must exercise all precautions and trust our judgment. We must trust our instincts and pray to stay in Her good graces."

Zekke thought about the Green Warrior's suggestion and nodded in agreement. "So be it. So where do we start?"

"The Royal Kraal. The first thing I must do is learn the status of the Mfalme Ramuza Ncobba." Tushema glanced at Lobarra, "And Mfalme Ameh Jobabwe."

85

OUR PATHS HAVE MERGED

The Green Warrior Tushema usually allowed very little to come before his responsibilities. It did not matter if some higher authority assigned these responsibilities to him or if he assumed the responsibility on his own after recognizing an urgent need.

With the Royal Warrior Jokere, the Blue Warrior Oumar, and all the warriors of Oumar's sentinel regiment dead, one of those moments demanded the Green Warrior's attention. No guards stood on the sentinel line of the north rim. The Aukmondi Valley lay open and vulnerable to anything that entered. Not that the deadliest of all dangers was already there, the valley still needed protection. Tushema recognized that need and could not ignore it.

Tushema was not a sentinel. After eighteen harvests, Tushema's experiences and accomplishments had elevated him to the rank of Green Warrior. Should the need arise, he could stand guard. But under the circumstances, he already had a higher responsibility: keeping the farmers safe and getting them into the valley. To protect the valley, Tushema found it necessary to break long-standing requirements and appoint non-qualified warriors to the task. And he had to select these warriors from his small detachment.

Tushema reviewed his available warriors. He had already reduced his detachment by one. When the Orange Warrior Wema asked to go back across the Serengeti to check on the Red Warrior Nienko, Tushema permitted him to do so. Tushema also sent the White Warrior Kibwe with him. This left him with only eight warriors to select from – Oghani, Anibi, Berko, Rotho, Ngosi, Nusada, Paki, and Wekesa.

After several moments of weighted considerations, Tushema chose the Orange Warrior Berko, the Red Warrior Paki, and the White Warrior Wekesa. He called each one over by name. These warriors were a long way from being qualified sentinels, but in Tushema's eyes, over the past several days, each one had shown the skills he needed. Each had the potential to earn the rank of Green Warrior someday.

Tushema waited for the three warriors to gather before him. He made a final visual assessment of each warrior before he spoke. "Listen. I have a very important two-fold task for the three of you. The rest of us," Tushema gestured toward the farmers and the rest of his detachment, "will descend into the valley. I will need all three of you to stay up here on the valley rim. Under the circumstances, you must perform the duties of sentinel warriors."

Both the Orange Warrior Berko and the Red Warrior Paki suppressed a prideful smile. With their heads held high and chests out, they seemed honored to be selected for the task. The unexpected appointment, however, made the White Warrior Wekesa throw a quick and uncertain glance at Tushema. *A White Warrior, performing the duties of a sentinel?* Wekesa turned to Tushema to express his concerns, but lost his chance when one of the other warriors spoke up first.

The Orange Warrior Berko, the most senior of the three, saw Wekesa's befuddled behavior out of the corner of his eye. He quickly spoke before the young and inexperienced warrior could talk himself out of an opportunity to learn something new. "We stand ready, Great Creation."

When Tushema spoke again, he looked directly at Wekesa. He had seen Wekesa's uncertainty, too. "I know I am asking you to do something most Royal or Blue Warriors will not allow. I am also asking you to do the impossible. The three of you cannot do what a regiment of Green Warriors usually does. But these are special circumstances. I am only asking you to do what you can as best."

"Our best is what you shall have, Great Creation," Wekesa spoke more confidently. "You said this task is a two-fold task. What did you mean?"

Tushema thought a moment, refining the instructions he wanted to give. He glanced at the bodies of the Royal Warrior Jokere and the Blue Warrior Oumar. He faced the warriors standing before him with the instructions clear in his head. "While the three of you are here on the north rim, I must ask that you also do what you can to account for the sentinels here. Out of respect, we cannot leave them where they have fallen. Find their bodies and gather them together. Sometime soon, we will plan for a proper burial."

Elder Zekke stood a short distance away. He had overheard most of the instructions Tushema gave the three warriors. Zekke finished securing the guide rope of one of the oxen and walked toward the Green Warrior. He waited until Tushema finished talking with the warriors before he approached to speak in confidence. "Tushema, Great Creation, giving the sentinels a proper burial. You do realize if these sentinels are any sign of what we might find in the valley, we could never bury all our dead."

"Yes, I know, Great Creation. If the situation is as bad as it appears, I intend to ask for help from Kiwane and Rimoza. They are good and generous people. If asked, they will come to help us bury our dead. For now, I resist moving in that direction."

"Great Creation, if you do not mind me saying so, this is unbecoming of you. I think you are only postponing something you know you must do."

"That, I cannot deny. I must confess. I have an optimistic ember that burns in the pit of my stomach. I am hoping and praying conditions are not as bad as they seem. But I must see the conditions in the valley before we send for help."

"So be it. We follow your leadership."

"Thank you. Gather your things. Let us proceed."

*****

Tushema turned his full attention back to his original task: escorting the farmers home. The Green Warrior had successfully brought the farmers from the Kiwane Village, across the northern Serengeti, and finally across the sentinel line, into the valley. But even now, he did not consider the farmers home until he secured their safety.

Tushema patiently waited for the farmers to finish gathering and preparing the pack animals. He watched as Zekke and several others each took the guide ropes of the oxen, donkeys, and then gathered the goats and sheep they would herd. Other farmers, not leading pack animals, lifted travel baskets or gourds and balanced them on their heads. Tushema marveled at the way the Sacred Woman Lobarra single-handedly secured Tutapona in the kanga and adjusted it to fit on her back.

The five remaining warriors of Tushema's detachment gathered up their shields and spears. They checked their water pouches. They checked their knives, ropes, and other belongings. Though they were only descending the north slope, into their valley, they prepared themselves like they were about to make another long trek in the open wilderness.

A single file line of warriors, farmers, oxen, donkeys, goats, and sheep took form. The order of people and animals in the line occurred at random. There were only two predetermined positions.

The Sacred Woman Lobarra is centered in one position. For safety's sake, the Sacred Woman with Tutapona on her back took her place at the center of the long line. Half the people and animals lined up in front of her and half behind her. The Red Warrior Rotho, because of his special responsibility, took a position behind Lobarra.

The Green Warrior Tushema took the other predetermined position. Once the line of people and animals was ready to move, Tushema assumed his position at the very head of the line. Just before sunset, Tushema finally led the way from the north rim onto the Pahoma pathway, which trailed down the north slope into the valley.

Normally, the downhill direction of the Pahoma pathway offered a relaxing walk between the north rim and the bottom of the valley. Several meters below the rim and for just under half a kilometer, the pathway trailed past the beautiful Pahoma Garden. The garden filled the air with an abundance of aromatic wildflower scents. To walk past the garden was always a pleasurable experience.

The pathway paralleled a small stream in another section about halfway down the slope. The stream flowed from the east and then raced down the north slope toward the Aukmondi River. For over a kilometer, the stream paralleled the pathway. It provided the gentle and soothing sounds of running water. People often climbed the north slope to spend time near this stream, to hear the relaxing sounds of the songbirds in the trees and the babbling water.

For Tushema, his detachment of warriors, and the farmer, the walk down the Pahoma pathway, past the garden and along the stream, was anything but relaxing. Any other time, the pathway is busy with people moving between the garden and the lower portions of the valley. But the pathway was empty of people; another disturbing indication that the valley's people were all dead. Besides the anxiety of walking into a dead valley, the deafening and irritating noise of scavenger birds drowned out the songbirds and shattered all elements of tranquility.

The larger birds – the buzzards and kites circled the sky above the treetops. Once in a while, a piercing bird shriek cut through the treetops, each time with startling results. The smaller birds, the crows and ravens, which were the most numerous birds, infested the trees. Hundreds upon hundreds of the boisterous black birds darted from tree to tree. They cawed loudly, fighting for available resting spaces upon the tree limbs.

The Sacred Woman Lobarra found the noise almost unbearable. At first, she walked with her hands pressed against her ears. Shortly after passing the Pahoma Garden, Lobarra's motherly instincts made her realize that Tutapona was just as uncomfortable. Lobarra shifted the kanga from her back. She took Tutapona in one arm and held him so that the side of his face and one ear pressed against her chest. She covered his other ear with her hand. With this new position, she sacrificed her comfort to ensure Tutapona did not endure too much discomfort.

The farther down the slope that the farmers and warriors went, the noise of the birds subsided. The noise soon died away to a bearable level. By the time the farmers and warriors reached the midway point of the stream that ran parallel to the pathway, the noise had dropped to near silence. The multitude of birds had thinned to but a few. The farmers and warriors heard only an occasional chirp or squawk here or there.

Everyone looked up into the trees and all around as they searched for the birds that were so abundant and noisy just moments ago. The mysterious quieting and dispersal of the birds caused such a distraction that the pace of warriors, farmers, and animals along the pathway slowed. Tushema brought the head of the line to a complete stop just after he reached the sizable opening in the pathway, the Gongeri Junction. The line transformed into a single mass gathering as the rest of the warriors, farmers, and animals poured from the pathway into the junction.

From the southeast corner of the junction, a smaller pathway continued. It trailed out in a southward direction. Then it doubled back, turning east and across the small, babbling stream. This smaller pathway was the same pathway on which the Gray Warrior Kharaambi had run after she learned of the deaths of Rwuva, Tongda, Zabiba, and Gengu. This smaller pathway was the same pathway on which the Royal Warrior Jokere had run. Almost three days ago, the hefty Royal Warrior raced toward Kon-Shambique's kraal to report the assault on the Pogobi and Obentawni kraals. Two and a half days ago, the little prince Adaulah had run along this pathway in his unsuccessful attempt to reach Mfalme Abul-Gwan on the summit of Nagorda Peak. This pathway stretched over five kilometers and was the most direct route between the Nagorda Peak and the Gongeri Junction, where the farmers and warriors now stood.

Most of the bewildered people turned in circles as they stood in the center of the junction and searched the nearby trees. They saw only a few frantic birds here and there. The birds they saw made very little noise. The only noise everyone heard was the familiar sounds of flowing water from the nearby stream.

Tushema, with increased vigilance, first heard something other than birds or running water. He heard approaching footsteps. The snap of a twig made Tushema turn quickly and focus his sight toward the smaller pathway.

Just beyond the junction, the Green Warrior saw two people coming. He knew that people crossed this junction throughout the day. They walked between the eastern and western portions of the valley, or between the north rim and places near the valley's bottom. But things were not normal. So far, the valley appeared to be dead. Despite his wish for normalcy, Tushema did not expect to see anyone. The people Tushema saw approaching were not even Aukmondi.

Tushema called out to the taller of the two approaching strangers. "Who are you? May we help you with something?"

The strangers walked into the junction and stopped. They said nothing at first as if neither had heard the Green Warrior's question. They only stood and studied the group of farmers and warriors before them.

A slight smile finally appeared on the taller stranger's face. "Our paths have merged. May we walk together?"

Tushema took a step closer and studied the stranger who had finally spoken. Tushema, a tall warrior himself, had to look up into the stranger's face. The stranger stood with unmistakable charisma. He wore very simple clothing – a woven garment tied around his waist and hanging past his knees. A full set of bracelets and anklets adorned his arms and legs. His upper torso was bare. A small pouch hung over his chest on a string around his neck.

Recognition made Tushema lower the tip of his spear toward the two strangers. "Where are you going, Mangoni?"

The stranger standing behind the taller one carried a shield and spear and was a Mangoni warrior. When Tushema lowered his spear, the Mangoni warrior stepped before the taller one.

"No, Goh-Jumaane. That will not be necessary." The tall stranger resumed his dominant position before speaking to Tushema. "I am Onu-Vey, Mfalme of the Mangoni."

Hearing this, everyone reacted. The five warriors of Tushema's detachment moved forward in front of the farmers. By the time the warriors had finished repositioning themselves, they had shielded the farmers and flanked the Green Warrior.

When Elder Zekke heard the stranger's introduction, his brow knitted with confusion. He dropped the guide rope of the ox he was leading and made his way forward. He pushed his way through the protective warriors and came to stand at Tushema's side.

"Great Creation," he began, "I suggest caution here. I sense deception."

"What do you mean?"

"Since last evening, the Orange Warrior Wema and the Red Warrior Nienko have told us several disturbing accounts of the Mangoni visitors to our valley. Among these accounts are ample descriptions of the Mangoni Mfalme and the Vodun houngan. Abul-Gwan is the Mfalme." Zekke nodded toward the tall stranger. "If this is Onu-Vey, he is the Vodun houngan."

Tushema studied the stranger again. He took another step closer. He looked at the stranger in his eyes. "The truth, please. Are you the Mfalme, or are you the houngan?"

"I am … both."

"How can that be?"

"Since we arrived in your valley, Mfalme Abul-Gwan has died. He now walks among his ancestors. I am Onu-Vey. I am a Vodun and the Tribal Houngan. But, by written decree, upon Abul-Gwan's death, I became the Mangoni Mfalme."

"Hum!" Elder Zekke grunted. He spoke to Tushema. "I do not care who he says he is. Either way, you recognize him, and it is all the same. He is behind our misfortunes here. I do not trust him."

The Gold Warrior Oghani, who stood at Tushema's right side, leaned closer to the Green Warrior. "Elder Zekke is right, Great Creation. The Mangoni assault on our people is grounds for war. Whether this Creation is Mfalme or Vodun houngan, he must answer to that."

Hearing this, the lead-warrior Goh-Jumaane tried again to step ahead of Onu-Vey. This time, Onu-Vey placed his hand on Goh-Jumaane's shoulder, restraining him. As Onu-Vey forced Goh-Jumaane back, he took the warrior's spear and shield. He did it slowly to appear unthreatening. He turned and surrendered them to the Aukmondi Green Warrior.

Tushema took the spear and shield. He passed them on the Gold Warrior Oghani. As he did so, he also recalled some of the detailed accounts of the Mangoni visitors, as Wema and Nienko told. Several of the accounts included several warriors. Tushema saw only the lead warrior standing here. He turned back to Onu-Vey. "Where are the rest of your warriors?"

"You have no reason for concern. I have two other surviving warriors. They are presently up on your Nagorda Peak. They stand guard over the remaining Mangoni visitors to your valley, who are all dead. As you must know, it is a sacred honor to stand watch over the dead. They will not forsake that duty."

Sacred honor or not, Tushema had heard enough about the Mangoni that he could not take the houngan at his word. He glanced back at the warriors of his small detachment. He singled out one of the Red Warriors. "Ngosi, go up to Nagorda Peak. Verify this."

"At once, Great Creation." Ngosi stepped past Onu-Vey and the Mangoni lead-warrior. He took the smaller pathway at a gentle run.

"I hope to gain your trust, Aukmondi." With this, Onu-Vey held both his arms forward, the palms of his empty hands turned up as a gesture of surrender. This prompted Goh-Jumaane to do the same. "I will answer to all accusations. You deserve that. I only ask," Onu-Vey glanced at the Gold Warrior Oghani, "before you react with war, please hear what I have to say."

"He is a Vodun houngan." Elder Zekke had moved back to stand with the rest of the farmers. "All the accounts we have heard suggest that we should beware of his words. The warriors Wema and Nienko have warned us, time and again, that his words have powerful magic in them."

Onu-Vey almost smiled. "Then hear these words. The heart of the Aukmondi people embraces peace. A choice of war is not wise."

The Green Warrior Tushema studied the houngan's face. He stepped forward again and looked him directly in the eyes. "We do not have to choose war to avenge what you have done to us. However, that decision … does not rest with us now."

"What are we to do with them?" Oghani asked.

Tushema handed his spear and shield to the Gold Warrior. He took Onu-Vey's arms and placed them behind the houngan's back. The Green Warrior slipped two short ropes from around his waist and quickly bound the houngan's wrists tightly together with one rope. He did the same to the Mangoni warrior with the other rope. "We will take them down to the Royal Kraal with us. There are many other necessary tasks we must take care of first. We will hold them until we can decide, in proper form, what must be done with them."

— **86** —

THE ROYAL KRAAL

With all their pack animals, the farmers and warriors formed their single-file line again. They poured from the junction of pathways to continue their journey down the north slope—the line formed as before, but with one major exception. The houngan and Mangoni warrior walked behind the Green Warrior at the head of the line. They walked with their hands tied behind their backs. And as an added measure of security, Tushema assigned the Orange Warrior Anibi to walk behind them, with her spear held ready.

The farmers and warriors encountered no one else throughout the rest of their walk down the Pahoma Pathway. Even after the line of people reached the bottom of the slope and turned left onto the north bank pathway, they saw no one. By far, the north bank pathway is the busiest in the whole valley. The farmers and warriors walked almost three kilometers along this pathway, well past the beautiful Katola Garden, another place of high attraction. They did not meet another living soul.

"So, where is everyone?" Elder Zekke spoke to himself. He asked out of increasing concern. After all the horrendous stories he had heard from Wema and Nienko, he did not expect to find anyone. But when this expectation became a reality, Zekke found it disturbing.

The Red Warrior Rotho walked in front of Zekke. He heard the Old Creation's question. "I do not know. But, I hope they are hiding somewhere safe."

Tushema, at the head of the line, saw people first. And, true to the stories and dreaded expectations, all the people he saw appeared dead. Several bodies lay along the pathway ahead. Tushema stood still for a few seconds, not believing the horrendous sight before him.

He broke from his stupor and ran ahead to investigate. His rapid pace slowed to a walk as he forced himself to bear the shock of finding, at least, twenty to twenty-five people scattered over the area. They looked to be an entire family, ranging over four generations, from great-grandparents to great-grandchildren. Tushema studied the scattered bodies. Everything seemed to suggest these people died together, all at once.

Tushema walked toward the bodies and slowly kneeled next to the nearest one. It was the body of a Young Creation. So young; Tushema guessed the Young Creation had not seen his fifth harvest yet. The Green Warrior slowly reached to touch the body, to search for signs of life. He gently placed his hand on the Young Creation's chest. Long before he finished the examination, he came to a foregone conclusion. This Little Creation and everyone here lay dead as the sentinels on the north rim. Tushema stood up and stepped back. He stared down at all the bodies as a stunned stupor reclaimed his mind.

It took tremendous inner strength to resist the sorrow and the surge of anger that consumed him. Tushema blocked it all out as best he could. He forced himself to rise above it and keep his self-control. He explained to himself. This was something the Supreme Spirit had allowed to happen. He had no choice but to accept it. It was up to him to react with his most responsible behavior.

As the farmers approached, most of them could not hold themselves together as well as the Green Warrior seemed to have done. Those who balanced gourds and baskets on their heads eased their parcels down. But distraught with so much sudden pain and anguish, many of them allowed the gourds and baskets to fall to the ground. Many of the farmers crumbled to their knees themselves and cried.

The warriors appeared to stand strong. They felt what everyone else felt. But just like Tushema, they appeared to restrain their emotions. Only the young Red Warrior Nusada had to wipe away the tears that flooded his eyes.

Tushema finally tossed his shield and spear to the ground. He turned to face the people who had gathered behind him. "We cannot leave them like this. Come. Let us move the bodies to the side, off the pathway."

The warriors Oghani, Rotho, and Nusada accepted Tushema's suggestion as their duty. They discarded their shields and spears. Only the Orange Warrior Anibi stood firm. She continued to guard the houngan and the Mangoni warrior. Anibi used her shield to nudge the two to the side of the pathway. She cleared the way so Oghani, Rotho, and Nusada could file past and disperse among the bodies.

The houngan and the Mangoni warrior seemed somewhat stupefied, too. Nudges by the Orange Warrior Anibi brought them back to the moment. The houngan stared at the bodies with a perplexed frown on his face. Even after the Orange Warrior Anibi forced him to move to the side, he stared at the bodies. He stared as if seeing the amazing handiwork of the loa for the first time. As for the Mangoni warrior, he took the nudge from Anibi as an opportunity to turn away. He stood with his back to the bodies, unable to face what the demon of death had done.

It took a moment, but each farmer pulled themselves together and responded to Tushema's direction. A sense of usefulness suppressed some of the pain and sorrow they felt. The sobbing stopped as the farmers rose from their knees. They moved toward the bodies, wiping away the tears that streamed down their faces.

The farmers and the warriors paired up over the bodies. With a natural respect for the dead, they gathered the bodies up, ever so gently, and carried them to the side of the pathway. They placed the bodies side by side, in a neat row. They took the time to position each body straight upon its back and then folded the arms across the chest. The farmers and warriors handled each body like a solemn ritual. They ended each ritual with a short prayer and promised a proper burial soon.

The warriors Oghani and Rotho gathered up the last body of the group. The body lay farther up, just before a bend in the pathway. By happenstance, the body was that of the Old Creation Kantuti, the family's patriarch. Oghani helped Rotho lay Kantuti's body out straight. Then he stood up and moved back. He allowed Rotho the privilege of folding Kantuti's arms across his chest and performing the ritual prayer over Kantuti's body.

Oghani stood watching. He remembered the death of his family patriarch, his grandfather. Over several harvests after his grandfather's death, family members slowly drifted apart as if his grandfather had been the bonding member that held the whole family together. Relatives became strangers. This sad condition lasted for several more harvests until his aunt took it upon herself to pull everyone together. She organized a series of family reunions. Thanks to her, the family became 'whole' again, bigger and stronger than ever. The family soon recognized Oghani's aunt as the family matriarch. Oghani wondered if his aunt and his family were still alive. As far as he knew, his whole family could be just as dead as Kantuti's family.

Oghani took another step back when the Red Warrior Rotho finished the brief ritual prayer. Where Oghani stood, he could see around the bend and past an outcrop of trees that extended down from the north slope. He could also see the entrance of Royal Kraal, which was only a quarter of a kilometer farther ahead. Oghani saw more bodies. At least two to three hundred bodies lay scattered over the area from just outside the kraal entrance and down to the bridge that crossed over to the south slope.

"Oh, Great Sacred Spirit!" Oghani said to himself in awe. He forced himself to break away from the disturbing sight. He turned to call the Green Warrior. "Tushema, Great Creation! You had better come see this."

Tushema gathered up his shield and spear. The alarm he heard in Oghani's voice made him hasten his pensive walk to a gentle run. The instant he could see around the bend and the outcrop of trees, Tushema's pace slowed to a standstill. Like Oghani, he also stood in awe, staring at all the bodies.

"Please tell me that my eyes deceive me," Tushema finally said.

"Our worst fears are coming true, Great Creation, and it is no deception." Oghani had turned back toward the bodies lined along the pathway behind him. "The bodies we found here and the sentinels up on the north rim are only a hint of what we must face. Our valley is dead."

"How are we to handle this, Oghani?"

The Gold Warrior had been Tushema's closest aide throughout the trip to and from the Kiwane Village. His duty had been to offer the Green Warrior his best advice or challenge him when necessary. He turned to face Tushema. "The discouragement I hear in your voice tells me you had hoped to find the Mfalmes Ramuza and Ameh, or even the Sacred Woman Kharaambi, alive in the Royal Kraal. I do not think that will happen."

"What are you saying, Great Creation?"

"On the north rim, I overheard you talking with the Great Creation, Elder Zekke. You told him you wanted to proceed one step at a time. You cannot wait, even with the greatest hope of finding our leaders alive. We cannot face this alone. I suggest you act on your word now. Send for urgent help immediately from the Kiwane and Rimoza peoples. We need them."

Tushema knew Oghani was right. It was true. Tushema had hoped to find at least one of their leaders alive in the Royal Kraal. Otherwise, the greatest responsibility of his lifetime would fall on his shoulders. How should he release all the dead to their ancestors? What is the proper way to bury so many bodies? How should he judge the houngan, the new leader of the Mangoni?

Tushema realized that, even if he found some authority alive in the Royal Kraal, someone would still have to answer these questions. Sending for help was justified. "So be it."

Tushema reviewed the remaining warriors of his small detachment to select one as a runner to the neighboring villages. He looked toward the warriors near him – Anibi, Rotho, and Nusada. Tushema thought about the three warriors up on the north rim, Berko, Paki, and Wekesa. He thought about the Red Warrior Ngosi, the warrior sent to verify the situation on Nagorda Peak. He even considered his detachment's most junior and remote member, the White Warrior Kibwe.

Tushema's thoughts singled out the Red Warrior Nusada as the most available and qualified. But before he could voice his choice, his eyes glimpsed something unexpected.

From where the farmers and warriors stood on the north bank pathway, directly across the Aukmondi River, Tushema could see a cluster of trees stretched along the opposite bank. The south bank pathway trailed behind that cluster of trees. Like the north bank pathway, the south bank pathway paralleled the Aukmondi River for several kilometers. And like the north bank pathway, the south bank pathway supported frequent travelers under normal conditions.

On the river's opposite side, behind the trees, Tushema saw something move. He stepped around the Gold Warrior. He tilted his head and focused his eyes. The Green Warrior thought he saw people. Brief glimpses confirmed that he saw many people moving up the south bank pathway.

"Come!" He ran up the pathway, toward the bridge between the north and south slopes. But even with the promise of finding living people, the responsible Green Warrior remained mindful of the houngan. He turned back to the Orange Warrior Anibi and pointed at the houngan and the Mangoni warrior. "Bring them! Keep them close to me."

The Orange Warrior Anibi had never moved more than a few meters away from the houngan or the Mangoni warrior. When she heard Tushema's order, she took pleasure in pushing them ahead. Instead of using her shield, she used the point of her spear to goad them into following the Green Warrior and to quicken their pace.

Farmers and warriors scrambled to follow Tushema, too. Oghani, Rotho, and Nusada quickly gathered up their shields and spears. They raced up the pathway behind the Green Warrior. The farmers, eager to see living people, left their pack animals, gourds, and baskets where they were. They scuttled up the pathway behind the warrior.

Just moments later, after a half-kilometer run, everyone veered off the north bank pathway. They took the trail that led over to the bridge. They gathered behind the Green Warrior, who now stood at the foot of the bridge. Everyone arrived just in time to see a crowd of forty to fifty people coming off the south bank pathway and rushing toward the opposite end of the bridge. An Old Creation led the crowd. Either from the respect that comes with age or by default of a strong pace, the Old Creation appeared to be the crowd's spokesperson.

"Tushema!" He called out. He recognized the Green Warrior. "You are back! Great Sacred Spirit, we are glad to see you. Is it safe?"

"Is it safe?" Tushema volleyed back. "We were hoping you could tell us."

"So much has happened here. We are not sure of anything anymore. It seems to be safe, on this side."

When Tushema, his warriors, and the farmers huddled at the foot of the bridge, the old farmer Elder Zekke, as usual, brought up the rear. People blocked his view. But he heard the voice of Old Creation on the other side of the bridge. He recognized the voice of his dear friend, Yakubu Gota, Jokere's father.

With the pleasure strong enough to evoke a wide smile, Elder Zekke pushed his way through the farmers and warriors to emerge out front. He waved with both of his hands. "Yakubu! Yakubu, Great Creation, it is me, Zekke. What happened here?"

Filled with the moment's emotion, Yakubu pointed twice toward the Royal Kraal before he could finally speak. "A Creation, oh so hideous in heart and mind, came to destroy us. It is said that all Creations are born of the Supreme Spirit. This Creation … to call it a bastard is a compliment. It had nothing in common with the Mother of Creation; no respect for life and growth. It knew only death and destruction."

"So what happened?" Zekke repeated.

"Is it gone?" Yakubu threw anxious glances between the Royal Kraal and the north bank pathway. He gestured toward the north slope. "Can we come across?"

Tushema looked down at the water of the Aukmondi River rushing past him. He recalled the amazing phenomenon at the Mara River, how the river had barred the demon from reaching the farmers. He realized the same phenomenon occurred here. The Aukmondi River had protected the people on the south slope from the demon's wrath.

"It is safe, Great Creation." Tushema beckoned to Yakubu and the crowd of people. "We believe the demon is gone. No one has seen it since …"

"We have not seen it since midday." Elder Zekke assumed he was among the last to see the demon. He turned to the Gold Warrior Oghani to confirm his assumption. "Remember? It was about midday today when we saw him trying to beckon you to cross the Mara."

"Yes, I remember. We have not seen it since then. But that carries no proof the demon is gone."

"Your concerns … are unnecessary," Onu-Vey spoke for the first time since coming down the north slope from the Gongeri Junction. He recalled that it was about midday when he crossed into the afterlife. Onu-Vey drew all eyes toward him as he spoke with confidence. "The Loa of Death … is no more."

Everyone stared at the houngan. Many were not sure they had even heard the houngan's voice. They cast questionable glances at each other. All eyes finally settled on Tushema to see his reaction.

Tushema stared at the houngan longer than everyone else. The houngan's statement sounded like something everyone wanted to hear. Wema, Nienko, Zekke, and Oghani had all warned Tushema to listen to the houngan's words with caution. Tushema heard what the houngan said. But he made his analysis and trusted his judgment. No one had seen the demon in over six hours. That was more convincing than the houngan's words. He turned back to Yakubu. "Come on across, Great Creation. For now, this side is also safe."

The smile returned to Zekke's face as he watched Yakubu step onto the bridge and walk toward him. Yakubu was slim and tall, completely contrasting with his hefty son, the Royal Warrior Jokere. Jokere got most of his physical traits from his mother. If there was any similarity between Jokere and his father, it was his strong steps and how he led the crowd across the bridge. The smile on Zekke's face disappeared when he wondered if Yakubu knew about his son yet.

"After this Forsaken Creation walked our valley," Yakubu was saying, "many of our families and friends fell … dead. The Sacred Women, Rwuva and Tongda, were the first two. That was over three days ago. Since then, many, many more have fallen. Even our Mfalme, the great ram, Ramuza Ncobba, is dead."

Zekke stepped forward to embrace his friend as Yakubu stepped off the bridge. The warm embrace, however, was brief. Zekke stepped back, still holding Yakubu by the shoulders. "Yakubu … Yakubu, Great Creation … I have to tell you, as we entered the valley … we saw Jokere."

Yakubu already knew what Zekke was about to say. His face tensed as he suppressed the sudden flare-up of grief. To hide the tears he could not stop, he looked away, toward the Royal Kraal. He said nothing.

"Yakubu, my friend," Zekke said, squeezing Yakubu's shoulder. "Did you hear what I just said?"

To suppress his grief, Yakubu seemed to ignore Zekke. He waved his hand toward all the bodies between him and the Royal Kraal. "The Great Creation Kon-Shambique discovered a way to undo all this."

Zekke, still holding Yakubu's shoulders, turned his friend to face him. "Is this true? All this can be undone?"

"Yes. Well … at first, it could. From the little prince Adaulah's insight, the Great Creation Kon-Shambique discovered a way to overcome the demon's effect. He discovered that the dead did not die right away. It was a slow death. He discovered if we celebrated life … if we celebrated life, we could undo death."

"But?" Zekke heard doubt in Yakubu's voice.

"We celebrated life in the Royal Kraal. It was a very special celebration. Even with burial litters scattered among us, it was one of the biggest celebrations ever. Great Creation, you should have seen it! Everyone was there. And … there were resurrections."

"Resurrections?"

"Yes! Several of the dead climbed off their litters. I witnessed two resurrections myself. And I heard rumors of others. Great Sacred Spirit! We were recovering."

"So what went wrong?"

Yakubu's shoulders slumped. "I do not know. We were enjoying ourselves too much. Our joyous attitude must have angered that

Forsaken Creation. It came back for us. It came for us like never before. Our attitude to celebrate life, I guess, was not strong enough. That thing overpowered us. Many in the Royal Kraal died immediately, including the Favored Tribesman, Kon-Shambique. And because we lack his wisdom and inspiration, I highly doubt that we will ever be able to celebrate like that again. We lost our best opportunity to recover. Many of us tried to run when we saw what was happening."

Everyone looked toward the bodies that trailed up to the entrance of the Royal Kraal. The positions of the bodies suggested people ran in desperate flight from the kraal. The huge pile of bodies at the kraal entrance suggested there was panic and chaos.

"Those of us who made it out of the kraal and across the river to the south slope survived. Everyone else was not so lucky."

Tushema glanced at the crowd of survivors behind Yakubu. "How many of you are there? Are there more?"

"I do not know the number." Yakubu also glanced at the people behind him. "There are about fifty of us here. Several enclaves are scattered on the south slope – twenty-five here, thirty there. All are in hiding. A hundred or two tried to seek refuge in the Sacred Temple, filling the Temple Gardens. Many are still there."

"Are there any warriors among the survivors?"

"A few. We have no Royal or Blue Warriors among us. A handful of Green and Gold Warriors have helped to maintain order among us. For our safety, they have warned us not to leave the south slope."

"Word must be sent to those warriors. It is safe now." Tushema glanced toward the Royal Kraal. "And I will need some of those warriors, and anyone else willing, to help recover the Royal Kraal."

"So be it, Great Creation."

Tushema turned to the Gold Warrior Oghani. "Even with the discovery of survivors on the south slope, we will probably still need the Kiwane and Rimoza. Since both Kon-Shambique and Tongda are dead, that help must also include spiritual leaders; people skilled enough to give our dead a proper burial."

"Agreed, Great Creation."

"But …" Tushema stepped away, deep in thought.

"But what, Tushema?"

"Even now, I hesitate to send a runner for that help."

"Why?"

"Oghani, I hope all of you can forgive me for my procrastination. But I must consider the recreation of a miracle first." Tushema turned to look at Yakubu. "Tell me something, Great Creation. You say you witnessed two resurrections?"

"Yes," Yakubu stepped forward to stand beside the Green Warrior. "The first I saw was the Little Creation Robuti"

"The young artisan who makes those beautiful metal sculptures?"

"Yes, he is the one. The second resurrection was that of Sacred Woman Mitma." Yakubu chuckled. "Mitma rose from her litter with the spirit that is truly Mitma."

"I can only imagine."

"I heard rumors of other resurrections, too. Over the day, rumors included stories of Nionu's Blue Warriors, the Sacred Woman Tongda, and Rwuva's guard, the Red Warrior Gengu. But that is all. By that evening, that Forsaken Creation had returned with a vengeance. It tried its best to destroy all of us. Anyone who failed to escape the Royal Kraal is dead. Even the once resurrected, Obe, Dabete, Tongda, Gengu, if they did not make it out and across the river to the south slope, they are now twice dead."

Tushema finally turned away from the Royal Kraal to look at the Mangoni houngan. He walked over and stood in front of the houngan. Tushema said nothing at first. He looked directly into the houngan's eyes. "Our Favored Tribesman discovered a way to undo what you have done here." Tushema gestured toward the trail of bodies. "Can all this still be … undone?"

The houngan slowly glanced over the multitude of bodies, as if studying each body, one by one. After a deep sigh, he finally spoke. "The Loa of Death's sole act of mercy, sometimes, is a slow, gentle, and painless departure from this life. During such times, resurrections are possible. But, it is said, when Death strikes with vengeance and without mercy, the spirit of the dead is too damaged. It has no desire to return to the body. The will to live is destroyed. During those times, death is permanent. It may be too late for the dead that lie before you."

87

ONE MORE WALK AROUND
THE ROYAL DAIS

Soon after, the survivors from the south slope received word that it was safe to come out of hiding. They wasted no time. Most of them emerged from their remote kraals, the Sacred Temple, and all their other hidden pockets of safety and security. They descended from the south slope in droves, eager to salvage their shattered lives. With their original fear of the demon pushed aside just enough to move about, they crossed the bridge over to the north slope. They headed directly for the Royal Kraal to join Tushema and the returning farmers.

Initially, it took significant effort and time to work through the bodies at the kraal entrance. People had fallen on each other in the chaotic effort to escape the demon. Just outside the kraal entrance, the bodies had piled two or three people deep. Inside the kraal entrance, a wall of bodies covered the ground.

The massive effort by the people from the south slope to move the bodies aside proved to be a hindrance. Uncoordinated efforts caused people to get in each other's way. But they quickly organized once the people broke through the wall of bodies inside the kraal. They formed efficient and practical work teams to sort the bodies by family and then to place each family as closely as possible together. Despite periodic flare-ups of overwhelming pain and sorrow, the dispirited work went smoothly. Here and there, the work stopped for a while as people, overwhelmed by emotions, broke down when they discovered the bodies of relatives and friends.

Shortly before the people broke through the wall of people at the kraal entrance, the south slope survivors agreed among themselves. The majority of them would focus their work efforts on the celebration area. The Green Warrior Tushema, his small detachment of warriors, and a few farmers, including Elder Zekke and Lobarra, also solidified their plan. They intended to reach the back of the Royal Kraal. Their primary focus and task would be to recover the remains of the Royal Family.

By late evening, Tushema and his detachment of warriors, the returning farmers, and most survivors from the south slope restored an eerie order in the Royal Kraal. Hundreds upon hundreds of bodies still occupied the celebration area. Bodies stretched from the kraal entrance and back to the royal dais and the four huts of the Ncobbas. The bodies no longer lay in disarray. Workers had repositioned the bodies in neat, uniform rows, much like the staging areas during a massive burial ritual. Each body lay upon their backs with arms folded across their chests.

*****

Just over three hours after entering the Royal Kraal, Tushema and his group had completed most of their task. They found enough time to settle down behind the royal dais for a short break and an evening meal. One of the practical teams out in the celebration area had prepared enough food to share. The team offered Tushema and his group a huge cauldron of *irio*. After an evening of hard work and hunger, the cauldron of *irio* came as a welcome relief. It was the first time Tushema and his group had eaten anything since crossing the Mara River, over eight hours ago.

Tushema was just as hungry as everyone else. But before he settled with the others to eat, he wanted to make one more walk around the royal dais. The unwavering warrior needed another look at the work he and others had done. Before he rested, he needed to see if some unfinished work required immediate attention.

On the right side of the royal dais, Tushema glanced over at the body of Kon-Shambique. The Favored Tribesman's body lay with the family of the Sacred Woman Tongda. All the bodies – Kon-

Shambique's, Tongda's, Tongda's father and aunt, and Tongda's cousin, the White Warrior Upenda, lay side by side in a neat row.

Tushema recalled that in the deliberate effort to reach the Royal Family, he and his group first came upon Kon-Shambique's body. Although Kon-Shambique was not a member of the Royal Family, he was the Favored Tribesman. The warriors Oghani and Rotho could not walk past him and do nothing. Almost as an impulse, the two warriors gathered the Favored Tribesman's body and placed it next to the royal dais. As a gesture of kindness, they also placed Tongda's body next to Kon-Shambique's. They felt that the Favored Tribesman would have wanted it that way. That infectious nature of kindness prompted the Red Warrior Nusada and some of the farmers to place the rest of Tongda's family next to Tongda's body.

At the front of the royal dais, the Green Warrior stopped his pensive walk to study twenty-one bodies in three rows. The body of the Mfalme Ramuza Ncobba lay at the head of the first row. Mfalme's mates, Rwuva, Olabisi, and Kharaambi, lay beside him. The bodies of the Mfalme Ameh Jobabwe, the little prince Adaulah, and Ramuza's oldest daughter, the Sacred Woman Omari, completed the first row. The rest of Ramuza's daughters and six warriors who had died with the Royal Family completed the other two rows.

Tushema kneeled between the bodies of Ramuza and Rwuva. He felt compelled to change a minor position of the huge black shield at Ramuza's side. As he moved the shield closer to Ramuza's body, Tushema recalled when he found the Mfalme and his Principal Mate.

*****

The Green Warrior had found the bodies of Ramuza and Rwuva near the right edge of the royal dais. By some violent action, one that Tushema could only imagine, the bodies had tumbled, along with their respective burial litters, across the royal dais and onto the ground. Ramuza's body lay face down in the dirt with his black shield and remnants of his burial litter piled on top of him.

In one of the many stressful moments of the evening, Tushema remembered rushing over to the Mfalme's body and throwing aside the remnants of the litter that covered it. By then, the Red Warrior

Rotho had also rushed over to help. Together, the two flipped Ramuza's body over on its back. Rotho held Ramuza's body up while Tushema brushed away the dirt from Ramuza's face.

When Tushema and Rotho finally lifted Ramuza's body to reposition it, Rotho assumed that the Mfalme's body belonged back on the royal dais. He took a step in that direction, but Tushema stopped him. Tushema had to remind the Red Warrior that, even in death, the royal dais is reserved for the Royal Family, Mfalme Ameh Jobabwe, and the little prince Tutapona. Tushema suggested the area directly before the royal dais with just a nod.

Tushema recalled that after he and the Red Warrior Rotho repositioned Ramuza's body, they returned to recover and reposition Rwuva's body. Rwuva's body also belonged on the royal dais, but like the Mfalme's, they took it to the area in front of the dais.

These incidents, to respect the boundaries of the royal dais, made Tushema realize something he should have noticed. Only after Rotho had folded Rwuva's arms across her chest did Tushema notice that not all the people who belonged on the royal dais were present. Several key people were missing.

From where he stood, Tushema had visually searched the area. He turned in a complete circle, searching. With increasing alarm, he saw no sign of Mfalme Ameh Jobabwe. He saw no sign of Ramuza's other mates, Olabisi and Kharaambi. He saw no sign of any of Ramuza's ten children. Tushema reasoned that if events happened as the Great Creation Yakubu described earlier, the missing bodies should be in the immediate vicinity. They were not.

Tushema ordered the farmers and all the available warriors in the area to stop repositioning bodies. Locating the missing people, part of his original focus and task, had become the highest priority again.

Everyone did a physical search of the entire area quickly, but found nothing. Even the four huts of the Ncobbas received a thorough search. These personal huts were almost as off-limits as the royal dais, but a search was necessary. Tushema, alone, entered each hut and searched for the missing people. He found no one.

Tushema emerged from the last of the four huts, Olabisi's hut. The concern on his face suggested he was completely lost on where to look next. He joined a small group of farmers huddled behind the royal dais to discuss the situation. Tushema hoped that someone among them could suggest other places to look.

The Green Warrior joined the huddle just in time to overhear Elder Zekke suggest that, maybe, the missing people had run unseen out into the celebration area. Although the suggestion conflicted with the detailed account that the Great Creation Yakubu described earlier, it was the most plausible explanation.

Word of the missing people had already spread across the celebration area. The Great Creation Yakubu had been working in the celebration area all evening. Long before Tushema thought to summon him and question him more about his account from the earlier evening, Yakubu had volunteered to walk to the back of the kraal to speak with the Green Warrior.

"They are here, Great Creation," Yakubu insisted.

"Are you sure? We have searched everywhere."

"I am positive."

Yakubu went on to explain why he was so adamant in his conviction. Like so many others, he and a neighbor had been closely following the Motobo dancers who had worked their way back to the royal dais. By then, almost everyone had learned the inspiring and magical effect the dancers seemed to have. At one point, Yakubu offered to help the neighbor move a burial litter closer to the dancers to take full advantage of the effect. He and the neighbor had to return to the kraal entrance to retrieve the litter. Fortunate for Yakubu, that is when the demon struck.

Yakubu remembered that when the demon struck, the entire royal family was still on or near the royal dais. None of them had the time to escape to any other place. They had to be here, somewhere near the four huts of the Ncobbas.

Despite overwhelming evidence that the missing people were not here, the Green Warrior could not challenge Yakubu's conviction. Instead, he insisted on a more thorough search of the area. He insisted that everyone consider both the improbable and the impossible in their search efforts. That insistence paid off almost at once.

The Red Warrior Rotho considered the unlikely and impossible chances of someone climbing the steep and impassable tree-filled slope behind the four huts of the Ncobbas. Sure enough, a few meters up the slope, behind the work area between Rwuva's and Olabisi's huts, warriors found the missing bodies. Mfalme Ameh Jobabwe, Kharaambi, Olabisi, Adaulah, nine Ncobba daughters, and six protective warriors lay in a pile. All had died together as they hid among the thick bushes and trees.

*****

On the left side of the royal dais, Tushema made one more heartfelt stop during his pensive walk. This time, he glanced down at several more rows of bodies – all warriors; about six from the Bendabe Regiment and over forty from the Ehkili Regiment. At the forefront, in the first row, the warriors Oghani and Rotho had placed the bodies of Quazzi, Nionu, and Nionu's Blue Warriors Obe and Dabete.

Tushema felt close to many of these warriors. The Blue Warrior Dabete Ehkili was his regiment commander. The Royal Warrior Nionu was his army commander. Tushema had served them since he became a White Warrior, over fifteen harvests ago. As for the warriors of Dabete's regiment, Tushema had worked with most of them for so long they were like family to him. Day after day, over fifteen harvests, Tushema interacted with each of these warriors. As they lay before him now, he saw only familiar faces. He barely noticed that no one wore any warrior's gear. Even the garments of the Motobo dancers carried little meaning.

The body of the Brown Warrior Quazzi lay next to Nionu's body. Due to a lack of a better place, Tushema suggested that Oghani and Rotho place Quazzi's body there. Quazzi had died with six warriors of Nionu's Bendabe Regiment. Oghani and Rotho found them behind the royal dais, still holding their shields and spears. The huddled position of the bodies told Tushema that these warriors attempted a diversionary tactic. Quazzi and these warriors had tried to give

Ameh, Kharaambi, and the bulk of the Royal Family time to make their desperate escape go well.

As Tushema completed his walk around the royal dais, he looked out across the celebration area. It was dark now. Tushema saw several bonfires burning throughout the area. The fires illuminated row after row of bodies that stretched back to obscurity. Tushema sighed again. He turned away. Low in spirit, he joined the group of farmers and warriors behind the dais.

— 88 —

THE SPIRIT HAS NO DESIRE TO RETURN

Behind the royal dais, Tushema joined Lobarra, Oghani, Rotho, Zekke, and the Great Creation Yakubu sitting around the steaming cauldron of *irio*. Tushema sat upon the ground between Elder Zekke and the Red Warrior Rotho. Zekke handed him a bowl of the hot, seasoned potatoes and corn mixture.

"Thank you, Great Creation."

Elder Zekke picked up his bowl and spoon. "We were just wondering."

"You were wondering what?" Tushema was not in a good mood. He still felt the depressive affect of his walk around the royal dais. He never looked up from his bowl of *irio*.

"What is next? Where do we go from here?"

Tushema poked at his food as he thought. The same questions had crossed his mind earlier, but he had other, more pressing concerns. The questions remained unanswered. "We have yet to decide those things."

"All our tribal leaders are dead."

Tushema said nothing at first. He quickly reviewed the complex line of succession. His conclusion made him glance toward Lobarra. Tutapona slept in the kanga on Lobarra's back, unaware of his new authority. "The Mfalme Ameh Jobabwe's grandson still lives."

"Forgive me, Great Creation. But that is not what I meant."

"What did you mean?"

"With due respect to the little prince Tutapona, we now have some serious decisions. We must make these decisions soon, if not right now."

The Green Warrior poked at his food again. Thoughts tumbled in his head, taking him longer to reach an answer. "You are a tribal elder, Great Creation. You must gather with the other surviving elders. Do what you must do. Reform your councils. Develop a new, guiding council if you must. With due respect to Tutapona, make your decisions. All remaining warriors and I will support your decisions."

"Excuse me, Great Creation." Yakubu sat forward. Yakubu was not a tribal elder. The only ties he had to tribal leadership were his opinions and weighted suggestions during discussions here and there. He addressed the Green Warrior and nodded toward a secluded area between Ramuza's and Kharaambi's huts. "Must a council of elders decide what to do about the Mangoni houngan? As long as he is among us, tribal leadership will be the least of our concerns."

Everyone looked in the direction that Yakubu had nodded. In the secluded area, the houngan sat upright, legs crossed, eyes closed, and head bowed. He looked to be praying toward the pouch that hung at his chest. The Mangoni warrior, Goh-Jumaane, lay upon the ground next to the houngan. The houngan and the Mangoni warrior still had their hands tied behind their backs. The Orange Warrior Anibi and the Red Warrior Nusada now stood guard over them.

The Mangoni houngan seemed aware that he was suddenly the subject of conversation. He opened his eyes and slowly raised his head. He looked directly at Tushema. The houngan stared as if waiting to hear the Green Warrior's answer.

Tushema stared back at the houngan. He could justify severe punishment for the houngan. But proper judgment by an Mfalme or tribal elders must come first. Tushema knew that if judgment were his to make, the houngan would receive the severest punishment that Aukmondi law could impose. The houngan deserved nothing less than banishment to the middle of the great deserts of the north, with but a day's ration of food and water. The houngan's life would rest in the hands of the Supreme Spirit. If he survived, it would be by Her grace.

Tushema did not get a chance to answer Yakubu's question. He broke his stare at the houngan when he heard the noise of a crowd of people behind him. Tushema sat with his back to the royal dais and the celebration area. He twisted around to see what prompted all the noise.

A large crowd approached the celebration area, about fifty meters away. Tushema saw the warriors Wema and Kibwe walking in the forefront of the crowd. They carried the Red Warrior Nienko on a litter. Tushema set his bowl of *irio* down when he noticed who walked beside Nienko's litter. On the right side of the litter walked Wekesa, the young, inexperienced White Warrior he had left on sentinel duty up on the north rim. On the left side of the litter, walked the Great Creation Kantuti, the patriarch of the family, found dead on the north back pathway. The sight of the White Warrior Wekesa, who had abandoned his post, disturbed him. But the sight of the Great Creation Kantuti made Tushema come quickly to his feet.

Tushema stared at Kantuti with amazement. He swiveled around to look back at the warriors, Oghani and Rotho. He pointed toward Kantuti. "Was he not out on the north bank pathway among the dead?"

The sight of Kantuti made everyone sitting around the cauldron of irio stand up too. Oghani and Rotho walked over to stand at Tushema's side.

"He was among the dead, Great Creation," Rotho finally answered. "I folded his arms across his chest and prayed over his body myself."

Tushema walked out to meet the crowd. With curiosity at its highest, he led the people who had sat with him. He walked quickly around the royal dais. He met the approaching crowd on the other side of the twenty-one bodies in front of the dais. Tushema focused not on the returning warriors, Wema, Nienko, and Kibwe. He now ignored the White Warrior Wekesa and the noisy crowd gathered there. He continued to study the unbelievable sight of Kantuti.

"Great Creation, you are alive!"

"How fortunate for me." There was a touch of bitterness heard in Kantuti's voice. He should have been grateful and happy, but his whole family lay dead. That overshadowed everything. "Why am I alive and my entire family lies dead? All of us ran. Why am I the only survivor?"

"I… I do not know, Great Creation." Tushema was almost speechless.

"Why did they not survive? All of us ran. They should have survived too!"

"You should have come across the bridge," the Great Creation Yakubu said out of sorrow and sympathy. "All those who crossed over to the south slope survived."

"How were we to know that?" Kantuti snapped. His eyes welled up anew with tears. Sadness replaced the bitterness in Kantuti's voice. "Too many people converged at the bridge, trying to cross. My family and I ran up the north bank pathway instead. Now … now my entire family is dead."

"No, Great Creation. I keep telling you. That is not true." The Red Warrior Nienko rose on his litter. He rested on his elbow. He seemed to have recovered some of his strength. There was confidence in his voice. "You have to believe me. They are not dead."

The warriors Wema and Kibwe had set Nienko's litter down at Tushema's feet. The Green warrior looked at Nienko for the first time. He made a quick sweep of Nienko from head to toe. The Red Warrior's swollen eye, lip, lacerations, and splinted legs made him look worse than he sounded.

Tushema expressed his pleasure at seeing the Red Warrior's safe return with a subtle greeting. "Welcome back, Great Creation."

"Thank you."

Under normal circumstances, Tushema would have asked the Red Warrior what had happened to him. However, that answer was of low priority and could come later. At the moment, the focused Green Warrior needed to get to the heart of another matter. "What do you mean, they are not dead?"

"I know you will probably find this hard to believe." Nienko gestured toward the multitude of bodies out in the celebration area. "All these people will wake up soon."

"What makes you say that?"

"I … I have seen some things."

When Tushema glanced at the Orange Warrior Wema for an explanation, Wema nodded in agreement. "You must hear what the Red Warrior says, Great Creation. Since the White Warrior Kibwe and I rescued him, out on the Serengeti, he has been telling us about some amazing phenomena. We found his stories hard to believe at first. We had our doubts, too, until we reached the north rim."

"To be honest," Nienko began, "until we reached the north rim, I had doubts."

"Why? What happened up on the north rim?" Tushema turned and directed the questions to the White Warrior Wekesa. The questions also seemed to ask Wekesa why he had abandoned his assigned post.

"Great Creation," Wekesa began. He swallowed to steady his nerves. "The warriors Wema, Nienko, and Kibwe arrived on the north rim just in time to witness … to witness my dismissal."

"Your dismissal? By whom?"

"The Royal Warrior Jokere."

Jokere's father, the Great Creation Yakubu, had stood quietly among the listeners. Like everyone, all he had just seen and heard fascinated him. When he heard about Wekesa's dismissal and the reference to his son, he pushed his way forward. "Jokere? You mean, Jokere is alive?"

"Yes, Great Creation. He is very alive. He did not seem so happy when he discovered what I was doing. He said no White Warrior would stand guard on his sentinel line even if he had to stand alone."

"Yes!" Yakubu clapped his hands, smiled, and jumped for joy. Tears of happiness lined his eyes. "Yes, that is Jokere. That sounds very much like my son."

"How can this be?" Elder Zekke asked. "Why are the Royal Warrior Jokere and the Great Creation Kantuti the only ones to survive this? Is there something special about these two?"

Everyone looked down at the Red Warrior Nienko as if Nienko were now an authority on the subject. Nienko shrugged as best he could on his elbow. "Do not ask me. Because I recognize some amazing happenings, it does not mean I can explain them. The Royal Warrior Jokere and the Great Creation Kantuti are the only ones. But I strongly feel others will wake up too."

Tushema sighed, frustrated by his confusion. He looked back toward the body of the Favored Tribesman. He wished that Kon-Shambique were available. Solving mysteries like this was among Kon-Shambique's special talents. Tushema knew that if anyone could suggest a plausible explanation, Kon-Shambique could. Personally, Tushema could only guess why this phenomenon had occurred. He knew no available person who could offer a better guess … except one.

Tushema looked toward the other side of the royal dais and into the secluded area between Ramuza's and Kharaambi's huts. His eyes came to rest on the Mangoni houngan.

Tushema turned to the Red Warrior Rotho, the nearest warrior to him. "The houngan. Bring him to me."

Just moments later, the warriors Anibi and Rotho escorted the houngan to where everyone stood. The Mangoni houngan walked between the two warriors with his head held high and hands still tied behind his back. He almost smiled when most of the crowd moved back as he approached. It showed that they still respected his power regardless of what they thought of him.

"Great Creation," Tushema came to stand directly before the houngan. "Did you not tell me earlier that this demon's wrath was permanent?"

"I said, the Loa of Death assaulted your people with a vengeance, one I have never seen. When the Loa strikes with such vengeance, the spirit has no desire to return to the body. When the spirit has no desire to return, death is permanent."

"Then how do you explain this Creation?" Tushema pointed at the Great Creation Kantuti. "And there is another, up on our valley rim, who has also overcome your demon's wrath."

The houngan turned toward Kantuti. He took two steps closer. He studied the Old Creation's face with penetrating eyes. Intimidated, Kantuti stepped back, breaking the houngan's stare. The houngan turned back to face Tushema. "I am sorry. I cannot explain it. Either the loa's wrath failed to cripple the spirit of some, or your people's will to live is remarkable. In either case, it seems … I made a mistake."

"No doubt about it, houngan," Nienko sounded confident.

The houngan looked at Nienko with his usual penetrating stare. Several moments passed before the houngan smiled at the warrior's resolve.

Nienko ignored the disarming smile as he turned to the Green Warrior. He rose from his elbow to sit upright. "Great Creation, I have reported to you as the Royal Warrior Jokere has asked me to do. May I have your permission to find my mother and sister?"

Tushema thought briefly about Nienko's appeal. "I understand your desire to find your family, Great Creation. But no. We may need you here. The Royal Warrior Jokere and the Great Creation Kantuti, returning from the dead, are strange occurrences. We need to learn why. You may have some of the answers we desperately seek. Your mother and sister are most likely among the south slope survivors. If you like, I will send for them."

"Thank you, Great Creation. I would like that."

For the moment, Tushema had no further use for the houngan. He turned to the Orange Warrior Anibi. "Take him back to the secluded area, please."

Everyone watched as the Orange Warrior escorted the houngan away. The most direct route back to the secluded area was around the left side of the royal dais and the twenty-one bodies lying out front. Few eyes saw what was happening on the right side of the dais.

No one saw when the Favored Tribesman, Kon-Shambique, slowly unfolded his arms from across his chest. Only one or two people saw Kon-Shambique sit up.

— 89 —

LIFE AMONG THE LIVING

The cascade of resurrections continued when Kon-Shambique sat up.

The simple act drew elated people toward the Favored Tribesman in a frightening rush. Kon-Shambique scooted back, in part because of the sudden convergence of so many people and in part because of his last clear memory before he fell dead. The violent wrath of the demon lingered in his head as if it had occurred moments ago—the Favored Tribesman, known for his calm demeanor, almost panicked.

'It is alright! It is safe! The demon is gone!' Calming words from familiar voices finally penetrated Kon-Shambique's fear. The Favored Tribesman exercised his amazing talent for self-discipline. He accepted help from others to get back on his feet. He gazed past the crowd across the celebration area at the rows of bodies. His only sign of weakness was the tears that flooded his eyes.

"The demon … the demon did this?"

"Yes." The Old Creation Yakubu stood at Kon-Shambique's side. "But there is hope now. Two of the dead have returned. There was no coaxing, no celebration to inspire them. They just got up on their own. And now … we have greater hope. We have you with us again."

"How long was I …?"

Yakubu knew that Kon-Shambique was about to say the word 'dead'. He finished the question with a more correct word. "Asleep? Just over a day. The demon struck early last evening."

Kon-Shambique looked out across the celebration area again. "The demon struck this time without mercy. It looks as though it tried to destroy every living thing in sight. This is just … so overwhelming. I am afraid I cannot help with any of this."

"You did it before, Great Creation. You can do it again."

"No. I feel this is different, somehow. When the demon struck before, our Great Celebration of Life gave us what we needed. It inspired people to get back to life. But with this devastation, this sea of bodies before us, how can we celebrate anything?"

"You will find a way." The Green Warrior Tushema was one of the many so jubilant to see Kon-Shambique back among the living. He had tremendous confidence in the Favored Tribesman. "I speak from my perspective, Kon-Shambique. But the words I speak express what we all feel. We welcome your spiritual guidance."

"Thank you, Tushema. Unfortunately, I am completely at a loss for what to do. Three days ago, I suggested we hang on. But, in a situation like this, just hanging on falls short." Kon-Shambique took several steps toward the celebration. He knew that the surrounding people needed something; something he felt unable to give. He was about to apologize to Tushema and everyone else for being so helpless when a ray of hope interrupted him.

Lying upon her burial litter, the Sacred Woman Tongda took a deep breath. When she exhaled, she also unfolded her arms. Since everyone stood crowded around Kon-Shambique, almost no one saw when the Sacred Woman stirred.

The Red Warrior Nienko continued to rest upon his litter in the same spot where Wema and Kibwe had set him down earlier. Unable to huddle around the Favored Tribesman as almost everyone else had done, Nienko rested alone, in open isolation. He alone saw Tongda sit up.

"There!" Nienko shouted and forced himself to sit up. He pointed at the Sacred Woman. "There is another! Tongda is back! I told you! Do you see? Tongda is back!"

Tongda's foggy mind cleared in time to see the crowd turn toward her and rush to her side. She scooted back, just as Kon-Shambique had done moments ago. She did not panic but covered her head with her arms as the people surrounded her. Tongda had gone through this resurrecting process before. She understood what was happening.

Tongda's moment of panic did not come until she turned. She made the horrifying discovery of her dead father, aunt, and cousin lying beside her. Gripped by a sudden wave of hysteria, Tongda fought through the crowd of people around her. She desperately had to reach her loved ones. But the same calming words from all the familiar voices around her, including Kon-Shambique's, gave her the reassurance she needed to quell her hysteria.

Several moments later, after Tongda had finally calmed down, Kon-Shambique attempted to offer reassuring words to the rest of the people. The Favored Tribesman admitted that he was still unsure what to do next. But he realized that the resurrections of Jokere, Kantuti, Tongda, and himself had given him hope. There was also the adamant conviction of the Red Warrior Nienko that more resurrections would occur. Kon-Shambique felt these were reasons enough to hang on. He tried to share his thoughts and feelings with the crowd.

Then, as if to give Kon-Shambique more convincing support, the cascade of resurrections continued when the fourth body of the evening came back to life. It occurred when the crowd heard Mfalme Ramuza Ncobba fight out of the darkness that wrapped around his mind.

Ramuza gave a long, animal-like growl, as if it took great physical strength to break free of the darkness that held him. The growl ended with a successful grunt as Ramuza finally opened his eyes. Unlike Kon-Shambique or Tongda, Ramuza did not just sit up. He suddenly sprang to his feet. He was ready to defend himself against the demon that, he remembered, held him by the neck.

But groggy, not fully recovered, Ramuza staggered. He did not seem to gain physical control of himself until he saw the bodies of Olabisi, Kharaambi, Adaulah, and all nine of his daughters lying nearby. The shock of seeing all his closest loved ones, together, dead, made Ramuza stop his struggle. He focused on the horrifying sight before him. His mind began a new, mental struggle to explain away what he saw. Standing on unsteady legs, Ramuza collapsed to his knees.

Ramuza's breakdown would have plummeted deeper had Kon-Shambique not rushed to his side and braced him by the shoulders. Kon-Shambique tried to shield Ramuza from the disturbing sight by repositioning himself between Ramuza and the bodies on the ground. "Mfalme, please, focus on me! Ramuza! Please! They are not dead. It is alright. They are not dead."

With adrenaline surging through his body, Ramuza easily pushed Kon-Shambique aside. Ramuza's eyes slowly studied the bodies of Rwuva, Olabisi, and Kharaambi. He remembered examining Rwuva's body when she fell dead three days ago. There was no doubt in his mind that she was dead. Now, he saw all three of his mates, all dead. The nightmare had intensified. And it didn't end there.

As Ramuza's eyes glided over the bodies of all his children, their wasted innocence seemed to be the greatest nightmare of all. Their precious lives had ended too soon. His inner turmoil showed clearly on his face. He wanted so badly to believe what Kon-Shambique was telling him. He wanted to believe none of his loved ones were dead. His memory and his eyes told him something different.

Overwhelmed, Ramuza could not talk. He gestured toward all the bodies before him, as if to ask, 'If they are not dead, then how do you explain this?'

"They are not dead, Mfalme. Please. You must believe me." Kon-Shambique repeated, emphasizing each word. "They … are … not … dead!"

Kon-Shambique's insistent words seemed to ease Ramuza's mind. The turmoil in his head cleared just enough for him to gain control and reorganize his thoughts. His top priority suddenly became his last clear mission, the probable reason for all this. "Where is Abul-Gwan?" He spoke through clenched teeth with vengeance and anger in his words.

The question made everybody who heard it think about the last time they saw the Mangoni Mfalme. The process took too long for Ramuza. Under the circumstances, he had no patience. He barked his question again, his voice louder. "Where is Abul-Gwan?"

"Mfalme." The Green Warrior Tushema made his way through the crowd of people to step forward. "We are told that Mfalme Abul-Gwan is dead."

"Dead?" Ramuza looked up into the Green Warrior's face. He looked at Kon-Shambique for verification. The expression on the Favored Tribesman's face told him that the news was just as new to him. Ramuza turned back to Tushema. "You are told this … by whom?"

Tushema nodded toward the secluded area.

Ramuza swiveled to look behind him. He saw the houngan and one of the Mangoni warriors sitting calmly in the secluded area, already bound and under guard. Ramuza quickly got to his feet. He began strong, angry strides toward the houngan. Halfway to the houngan, he pointed at him. "Stand him up!"

The warriors Anibi and Nusada caught the houngan by the arms and pulled him to his feet. Ramuza caught the houngan by his jaw with powerful fingers and forced him to face him. "Is this true? Is Abul-Gwan dead?"

The houngan endured the pain of Ramuza's powerful grip by holding his eyes tightly closed. He spoke through puckered lips. "Abul-Gwan has crossed over into the afterlife, Mfalme Ncobba. He is preparing to meet with and answer to all his ancestors."

Ramuza cared nothing about that now. His focus centered on finding accountability on this side of life. "So, who is the Mangoni Mfalme now?"

The houngan opened his eyes before answering. "I speak for all the Mangoni. I am Mfalme."

Except for the Green Warrior Tushema, Tushema's small detachment of warriors, and the farmers, everyone else heard this news for the first time. There was a wave of restless voices as everyone reacted. Ramuza reacted by slowly releasing his grip on the houngan's face. He waited for the houngan to flex his jaw muscles and look at him again.

"What about that Forsaken Creation you conjured up? Where is it?"

"The Loa of Death … is no more."

"Hear me, Mangoni. Hear me well!" Ramuza held his boiling anger to a simmer. Tension and bitterness distorted his voice. "The Aukmondi can never forget what you have done here. Never, in the history of the Aukmondi, have we found it necessary to condemn …"

"Mfalme Ncobba," the houngan interrupted. "Please. Before you condemn anyone, allow me the opportunity … to ask for… forgiveness."

"What? Forgiveness? Forgiveness?" Ramuza could not believe what he was hearing. Just hearing the word aggravated his anger. He pointed at the bodies in front of the royal dais. "You want forgiveness for that? You dare even to ask?"

"I am … obligated to ask. The request comes directly from Mfalme Abul-Gwan. I ask it now, for him, myself, and all the Mangoni. We never intended your people's involvement in our painful growth."

"And yet, it happened." Ramuza had no intention to accept the Mangoni apology. He turned away. He had heard enough. If he had to face the houngan another second, no telling what his reaction would be. He walked away to help gain control of his rage.

Ramuza took a deep breath. He wiped his face with both hands as if to wipe away the tension. Despite his anger, he knew he had other, more important things to oversee first. If there was to be any recovery, he knew his whole tribe had to be restructured and strengthened, almost at once. He turned to the Green Warrior.

"Tushema, are there any surviving Royal Warriors?"

"There is only one we know of, Mfalme, the Royal Warrior Jokere Gota. He stands guard on the north rim sentinel line with two other warriors. We are certain that the warriors on the south rim have no Royal Warriors among them. Otherwise, we would have known about it already."

"The north rim is guarded by Jokere and only two others? Is that all?"

"Yes, Mfalme. They are all that is available. Shall I summon Jokere for you?"

"No. Let him stay on the rim." Ramuza thought for a moment about revising his immediate plans. "What about surviving tribal elders?"

Elder Zekke rocked his way over to where Ramuza stood. "Mfalme, all the farm elders are here. There should be several kraal elders who found refuge on the south slope."

"Gather as many as you can find." As Ramuza walked away, he pointed to the area between Rwuva's hut and Olabisi's huts. "Have them join me in the work area as soon as possible."

"So be it, Mfalme."

"Mfalme," the Green Warrior Tushema got Ramuza's attention before he walked too many steps away. "What should we do with the houngan?"

Ramuza stopped walking. He turned to face the Green Warrior. "You do not want to ask me that question, Great Creation." Ramuza realized his thoughtless words. He suppressed the rage that had prompted his ill-tempered response with one more calming breath. He looked back at the houngan. "If I am to remain a Rational Creation, just keep some distance between me and him. The elders and I will decide what to do with him later."

Ramuza walked away again. He headed directly for his hut. He needed a few more moments of seclusion to suppress his anger and calm himself down before meeting with the elders. Ramuza made it to the entranceway of his hut. He did not make it inside the hut.

At that moment, five more resurrections occurred. One behind the other, Rwuva, Ameh, Adaulah, Kharaambi, and Olabisi stirred. They lay in proximity with each other and woke up together as if by some common outside signal. When they did, a wave of vocal restlessness erupted, followed by cheers from excited people.

Ramuza had ducked his head to move through the entrance of his hut when he heard the cheers. He pulled back out of the entrance. He turned toward the crowd just in time to see people converging on where his mates, his son, and the Chinchigwe Mfalme once lay.

Ramuza became highly curious. He rushed toward the crowd. Because he was Mfalme, it parted and moved back out of his way when he reached the crowd. He moved through it with relative ease. Because he was Mfalme, it also allowed him to coax four of the five resurrected people to their feet and into his embrace. With powerful arms and a near-tearful gratitude on his face, he pulled Rwuva, Olabisi, Kharaambi, and Adaulah as close as possible to him.

The Sacred Woman, Rwuva, squirmed in Ramuza's embrace. Her thoughts, however, were not on herself even in her foggy state of mind. As her consciousness cleared, her last memory from over three days ago came back into focus. She remembered that she and Tongda huddled on the ground and behind an overturned table in Kon-Shambique's hut; their lives were in imminent danger. The fact that she now stood in Ramuza's warm embrace told her she had survived that perilous moment. Rwuva turned, searching. "Where is Tongda? Is Tongda alright?"

"I am here, Sacred Woman." Tongda worked her way through the crowd and came to stand beside Rwuva. "I am fine. The demon and the danger are gone. We are safe now."

Rwuva accepted Tongda's reassurances and melted in a series of comforting embraces from Ramuza, Tongda, Olabisi, Kharaambi, and Adaulah.

Of the five resurrected people, the Chinchigwe Mfalme, Ameh Jobabwe, was the only one not standing yet. He had drawn his share of the excited crowd, but continued to sit on the ground. With his characteristic frown, he twisted around to look up over his left shoulder. He studied the people huddling over him. He twisted around, studying the people over his right shoulder. The frown on his face deepened as his eyes finally came to rest on Tongda. "You people look nothing like any ancestors I remember. Am I in the right place?"

"You are in the right place, Mfalme."

"I guess that means I am not dead."

"No. You are not dead; not anymore."

Ameh allowed Tongda and several others to help him to his feet. He did not see it when he turned to pick up his ever-present walking staff from the ground. Instead, he saw the Sacred Woman

Lobarra standing before him with his staff already in her hand and smiling. She stepped forward to hand Ameh the staff. Ameh accepted it. He also received one of the warmest, tightest, most loving and unexpected embraces he had ever gotten from the Sacred Woman.

It was a beautiful moment that brought a tear to Ameh's eye. And the moment did not end there. From the surrounding crowd, Ameh saw the Red Warrior Rotho emerge. Rotho carried Tutapona in his arms. Tutapona's eyes had already locked onto Ameh with more than simple recognition. Tutapona smiled, showing both of his tiny teeth. When Tutapona reached for his grandfather with both arms, that tear finally streaked down Ameh's face. He took Tutapona and Lobarra into his arms. Until this moment, it was never clearer to Ameh that the two people he held represented the center of all his happiness.

"Moments like this make life among the living worthwhile."

Ameh heard the words but was so inundated with emotion that he barely recognized Kon-Shambique's voice. He opened his eyes to see the Favored Tribesman standing before him. "I have never heard a truer word, Great Creation. I suppose we have you to thank for this? You did as you had hoped. You lifted the curse from us."

"No, Mfalme. It was not me. I did nothing this time. A few of us are waking up on our own, including me. And even though I am among the lucky few, I do not know why."

Ramuza stood not far away. He had heard the exchange between Ameh and Kon-Shambique. He peeled away from the huddle of his three mates and son and approached the Favored Tribesman. "When you say, 'a few', how many do you mean?"

"I understand, the Royal Warrior Jokere was the first." Kon-Shambique reviewed and spoke the names of the resurrected as he recalled them. "About an hour after Jokere, the Great Creation Kantuti returned. Then came me, … then Tongda… and then you, Mfalme. Just moments ago, as you witnessed, Rwuva, Olabisi, Kharaambi, Adaulah, and Mfalme Jobabwe made the last five. There have been ten resurrections, Mfalme."

"Make that twelve, Great Creation." The Brown Warrior Quazzi had overheard Kon-Shambique's tally and corrected him. He worked through the crowd from the far left with the Royal Warrior Nionu close behind him. Unseen by almost everyone, the two warriors had also rejoined the living.

The Royal Warrior Nionu was still rubbing the grogginess from his face. "We would appreciate it if we could be counted among the living, too."

Quazzi and Nionu inspired their wave cheers from the crowd, which lasted for several minutes. Ramuza had to raise his hands to regain everyone's attention. He waited until the cheers died down. When he knew he had everyone's undivided attention, he walked over to stand near the bodies of his nine daughters. In an atmosphere of dead silence, he kneeled on one knee.

"What is happening here?" Ramuza never looked up from his daughters' bodies as he posed his next questions to the Favored Tribesman. "Can we expect more resurrections? If so, when? And who will be next?"

"Mfalme, I am afraid that the answers to those questions are among the Supreme Spirit's most guarded secrets. We must accept the gift of Her grace as it comes."

Ramuza raised his head and looked out across the celebration area. In the darkness, the bonfires throughout the area illuminated row after row of bodies upon their burial litters. "Twelve of us have returned from the dead. I accept Her good graces. But, I am compelled to ask. Why?"

After another long and thoughtful scrutiny of his nine dead daughters, Ramuza stood up. He turned and walked away. He circled behind the royal dais, heading toward his hut, and disappeared inside without another word.

— 90 —

WHAT WOULD YOU HAVE DONE

The groups of people around the royal dais began to thin after Ramuza disappeared into his hut. Only a few people remained close, waiting for the urgent gathering scheduled to take place in the work area between Rwuva's and Olabisi's huts. Over half of the people, including the Great Creations Yakubu and Kantuti, only went as far as the celebration area. There, they joined with others who were already waiting and sitting in vigil around the bodies of loved ones.

The Great Creation, Elder Zekke, and all the farm elders complied with Ramuza's instructions. They spent the next several minutes coordinating activities to summon all the kraal elders. They used available warriors to get the word out quickly across the celebration area and beyond the Royal Kraal. Once done, the farmer elders slowly worked toward the work area to begin their wait. There, they joined with the Sacred Woman Rwuva and Mfalme Ameh Jobabwe, who had already settled into their places.

The Green Warrior Tushema, his small detachment of warriors, Wema, and Nienko, resettled behind the royal dais. Until Ramuza re-emerged from his hut, they had nothing else to do except wait. They held casual conversations among themselves and kept a watchful eye on the houngan and the Mangoni warrior.

The Sacred Woman Olabisi, still somewhat distraught by the bodies of the Ncobba daughters, evaded her sorrows by playing host to Tongda, Lobarra, Tutapona, and Adaulah. Until the urgent gathering started, Olabisi invited the small group to wait with her. To keep herself busy, she dismissed her surviving personal aides and made Tongda, Lobarra, Tutapona, and Adaulah comfortable on woven mats and pillows in front of her hut. Adaulah curled up on his pillow and fell asleep due to the late hour.

When Ramuza disappeared into his hut, only Kharaambi, Quazzi, Kon-Shambique, and Nionu waited near the royal dais. The four sat upon the ground along the front edge of the dais. Until Ramuza came from his hut, there was no hurry to gather in the work area. They sat quietly. None of them talked. In front of them lay the bodies of the nine Ncobba daughters as well as the six Aukmondi warriors who had died with them.

The highly sensitive Kon-Shambique was not just sitting and waiting. As a natural people-watcher, he saw the heavy silence among the four of them as a symptom that needed to be addressed. He knew where to start. He looked toward the Gray Warrior.

"Kharaambi, Sacred Woman, your silence is deafening."

Kharaambi had sat staring at the bodies before her, but was lost in her thoughts. She broke from her stupor and looked at Kon-Shambique, puzzled by his statement. "What is that supposed to mean?"

"I cannot help noticing how quiet you are now."

"We are all quiet."

"Of the four of us sitting here, your feelings are the strongest. We are all quiet because we are overwhelmed by what you are feeling. What is wrong?"

Kharaambi knew better than to debate the Favored Tribesman's observation. She sighed heavily before she spoke again. "Just before Ramuza left, did you see how he looked at his daughters? I could tell. He was hurting."

"Understandable. We are all hurting."

"Yes, but I, somehow, feel responsible. I feel I have personally failed him." Kharaambi gestured toward the bodies in front of her. "These are his daughters. I failed all of them."

"No, Sacred Woman. We failed them." The Brown Warrior Quazzi knew Kharaambi was referring to the desperate attempt to save the Royal Family. In all honesty, he felt some of the blame lay with him. "We failed them because we were in a situation with no possible way to achieve victory."

"I should have known better. To run with these children up that slope was foolish."

The Royal Warrior Nionu glanced back over his shoulder at the thick, tree-filled slope behind the four huts of the Ncobbas. Thick trees, vines, and bushes covered the steep slope. Nionu looked at Kharaambi, surprised that the leader of the Aukmondi Army would try such a hopeless thing. "What were you thinking, Sacred Woman?"

"I had no other choice. The demon was coming for us. Quazzi and a handful of warriors from your Bendabe Regiment gave us our only chance. Our only chance turned out to be a death trap."

"If you had every available chance," Quazzi agreed, "there was no way to escape the demon. It did not matter which way you ran. The result would have been the same. In the same situation, I probably would do just as you did."

"Thank you for your support, Quazzi."

"Well … not me," Nionu commented.

Quazzi looked at Nionu. He wasn't sure if the Royal Warrior was speaking with arrogance or with confidence. "Great Creation, I have said many times, you have one of the best tactical minds in the Aukmondi Army. So, I have to ask, what would you have done? Throw stones at the demon?"

"Well … maybe not that either." Nionu shrugged. "But you are right. It was a no-win situation. In such a situation, I would have done my best and left a victory up to the Supreme Spirit."

"Which is what the Gray Warrior did," Kon-Shambique said. "Everything considered, we have all done our best. The Supreme Spirit has allowed us to reach our present situation. Twelve of the dead have returned to the living. Although we cannot explain it, it suggests that the Supreme Spirit is still at work here. Our dead, including Ramuza's daughters, still have hope. Who knows? Our best tactical action may be … to wait."

"Wait? Wait?" That suggestion seemed to disturb Nionu. "I have trouble with waiting. I always have. The last two to break free of death's grip were Quazzi and I. That was some while ago. Since then, we have only waited. We can do more, besides waiting."

"Do you have a better suggestion?" Kon-Shambique nodded toward the far left side of the dais, at the forty to fifty bodies there; the Motobo dancers, warriors, and their mates of Nionu's Ehkili Regiment. "We see the result of your last impatient idea."

Nionu looked toward the left side of the dais, too. He focused on his warriors. "Well … Sometimes, even our best ideas have consequences we do not expect."

"Speaking of consequences, have you made your appeal to the Sacred Woman Rwuva about overriding her ban on the forbidden dance?"

"No, I have not. Since her resurrection, I have not had the opportunity." Nionu looked around toward the work area, searching for Rwuva. He saw her sitting in the work area, talking with other elders. He got quickly to his feet. "I suppose I should go and speak with her now, while we have the time."

"This moment may also be when you must wait, Great Creation."

"What do you mean?"

Kon-Shambique nodded toward Ramuza's hut. Everyone turned to see the Mfalmc standing just outside the entranceway. He looked rested and ready to convene his gathering.

91

ME

Mfalme Ramuza Ncobba has not held gatherings like this so late. It was almost midnight. Daylight hours provided a huge range of proper times. Even an occasional gathering during the Daily Celebration of Life was more acceptable. However, the recovery and strengthening of the tribe demanded that Ramuza act. He had to start the process at once.

Ramuza did not hold gatherings like this in the work area either. The many chores supporting the Royal Family occurred in his area, between Rwuva's and Olabisi's hut. Aides of the royal mates had pushed back all the cooking utensils, wash tubs, and storage racks to make room for the required people to assemble.

Ramuza usually conducted gatherings like this from the royal dais. He would sit upon his chieftain stool, on the dais, with all the people he needed assembled before him. Unfortunately, the royal dais was not a good place now. Bodies of the dead occupied the areas around the dais. Most of the bodies that lay directly in front of the dais were his daughters.

Ramuza sat upon a cushioned pillow near the back of the work area. He appeared to be a calmer person. He had suppressed his rage and anger to a tolerable level. As he waited for everyone to finish gathering, he conversed casually with others who waited with him. He exchanged thoughts and opinions with Mfalme Ameh Jobabwe, the Brown Warrior Quazzi, and the Sacred Woman Rwuva, who sat on his right. He did the same with the Gray Warrior Kharaambi and the Favored Tribesman Kon-Shambique, who sat on his left.

Ramuza studied the group of people who already sat before him. The majority of them were kraal leaders. Kraal elders were among the most prominent. With the highest respect, they often had the last word in most events or developments within the kraals they represented. On occasions, it took the word of Ramuza, Ameh, Kharaambi, or Quazzi to override the decisions they made.

Ramuza counted twelve of these leaders sitting before him. This was less than a third of the kraal leaders in the valley. About half of the kraal leaders, overall, were due to arrive. Kraal leaders from the Pogobi, Sokoto, Butetwa, and Mempa were among the third of the leaders who would not be coming. These leaders lay among the dead out in the celebration area.

Behind the kraal leaders, Ramuza could see the Great Creation Zekke and all the farm elders. Just as respected and no less prominent, these six tribal elders decided issues that extended far beyond their kraals. Ramuza saw that these farmers had just returned from the farmers' *mkutano* in the Kiwane Village. All of them still wore their travel garments. What seemed like so many days ago, Ramuza had looked forward to hearing what they had learned. But now he wondered. Was the trip a wasted journey? If the dead do not wake up, whatever the farmers learned might be useless to the survivors.

Ramuza glanced past the group of elders to the area behind the royal dais. Another large group of curious people had also assembled and waited. These people offered nothing constructive to the work area gathering. But Ramuza understood. They were curious. They wanted to learn, first-hand, the decisions made and the directions the tribe intended to take.

The Sacred Women Olabisi, Tongda, and Lobarra sat and quietly talked among themselves in the forefront of this huge crowd behind the dais. Both the infant Tutapona and the little prince Adaulah lay at their feet. At this late hour, and despite the constant chatter of voices around them, the two princes slept. A small campfire that burned nearby illuminated the peaceful look on their faces.

Further back, most of the warriors in the area had gathered around their small campfire. On one side of the campfire, the Red Warrior Nienko lay upon his litter with both legs propped for comfort. He talked with his mother, sister, the Orange Warrior Wema, and Wema's family. The rest of the warriors waited on the other side of the campfire, including the Royal Warrior Nionu, the Green Warrior Tushema, Oghani, Anibi, Rotho, and Nusada. They sat in a circle that surrounded the houngan and the Mangoni lead-warrior.

The Mangoni lead-warrior, Goh-Jumaane, seemed just as curious about the meeting in the work area. He sat quietly, watching everyone around him and listening to everything they said. The anxious expressions on his face suggest that he was uneasy about what lay ahead. As for the houngan, as far as Ramuza could tell, he appeared to be asleep. He lay on his stomach. He had been lying like that all evening, his hands still tied behind his back.

"That has to be uncomfortable," Ameh had noticed the loathsome way Ramuza looked at the houngan.

"Yes … Well … perhaps such comfort can fill the rest of his life." Ramuza pushed his anger back down to just below the surface. He sighed and took his mind off the houngan. He changed the subject before his anger flared up again. "Have there been any more resurrections?"

"No, Mfalme. Not a single one." Quazzi gave the question some thought. "The Royal Warrior Nionu and I were the last two. It has been over an hour now."

"You and Nionu are the last two we are aware of returning." Ameh was trying to be hopeful. "But hundreds of bodies lay out there in the celebration area. If even one of them rose, we would learn about it."

"So why have there been no more?" Ramuza asked.

"That is a very good question, Mfalme." Kon-Shambique had been trying to answer that question since the Royal Warrior Nionu brought it up earlier. In an hour or less, twelve people returned from the dead. And then suddenly, everything stopped. Why?"

"I hate to say it, but that elapsed hour makes me think there may not be any more," Kharaambi commented. "The Green Warrior Tushema spoke at length with the Mangoni houngan. He told me what the houngan said. The wrath of the demon's last attack was so severe that the results may be permanent. The houngan expected no resurrections at all."

"But you must remember, the houngan also said he was unsure." Ameh offered a hopeful perspective. "He said he could be mistaken."

"Well … the Red Warrior Nienko thinks the houngan is mistaken," Kon-Shambique recalled the Red Warrior's rebuke of the houngan earlier. "He has been telling us all evening that all the dead will rise again. He sounded confident."

Ramuza was curious. He turned to face the Favored Tribesman. "What is it the Red Warrior knows and the Mangoni houngan does not?"

"Nienko claims to have witnessed things that suggest it is just a matter of time."

"Things like what?"

"I am not sure, Mfalme."

Ramuza's curiosity piqued. He wanted to learn more. He looked out across the group of elders. "Zekke, Great Creation."

"Yes, Mfalme?"

"When do you expect the rest of the elders to arrive?"

"Unfortunately, Mfalme, many of them had returned to their respective kraals on the south slope hours ago. They were unaware of developments and did not expect a gathering at this hour. We have sent a messenger to recall them. It may be several more minutes before they can get to the Royal Kraal."

"Then so be it. We will use the time to resolve another matter." Ramuza turned to Kharaambi. "Sacred Woman, bring me the houngan and summon the Red Warrior Nienko for me, please."

"So be it, Mfalme."

Since the houngan and Nienko were just outside the work area, Kharaambi had the two brought in almost immediately. The warriors Wema and Kibwe carried Nienko in on his litter. They sat Nienko down in front of the elders on the right side of the work area. The Red Warrior Nienko seemed somewhat nervous. He did not expect to sit in such a prominent position and so soon before the Mfalme and the tribal elders.

The Green Warrior Tushema and the Red Warrior Rotho escorted the houngan into the area. The houngan walked with his head held high, his chest out, and his hand still tied behind his back. He looked well-rested, even after sleeping on his stomach all evening. The small pouch that hung around his neck dangled over his chest.

The tall, charismatic houngan ignored all the eyes that followed him into the area. He stared straight ahead until Tushema and Rotho forced him to sit on the ground, in front of the elders on the left side of the work area. Once seated, he crossed his legs, closed his eyes, and bowed his head. He ignored the proximity of the warriors Tushema and Rotho, who continued to stand close behind him.

Kon-Shambique saw the way Ramuza watched the houngan. He could easily sense the animosity that Ramuza held. It seemed to grow stronger by the second. Kon-Shambique got Ramuza's attention and requested permission to speak with the houngan first. "Mfalme, may I?"

Ramuza broke his stare at the houngan. He sat back and nodded his permission to the Favored Tribesman.

Kon-Shambique approached the houngan. He waited until the houngan raised his head and looked up at him. "Great Creation, how do you wish to be addressed?"

Ramuza returned his stare at the houngan. When Kon-Shambique asked his first question, Ramuza's eyes returned to the Favored Tribesman. Ramuza's attitude toward the houngan had fallen so low that referring to the houngan with the proper title was an unnecessary, undeserving courtesy. He glanced at the others beside him to see if the offense struck them as hard.

Kon-Shambique pretended not to notice. He hoped his attitude took some of the tension out of the air. "Shall we address you as Mangoni? Shall we call you Mfalme? Houngan? Or Onu-Vey?"

The houngan glanced at all the Aukmondi leaders and elders before returning to Kon-Shambique. "Whichever you are comfortable with. I will answer them all."

"Then … Onu-Vey," Kon-Shambique personally selected the houngan's given name. "We were wondering. You said that the last demon assault was so severe that the results may be permanent."

"Yes. It is what I said. It is my understanding of the loa's wrath. When I last saw the loa, its intention had gone far beyond the reason I called it. Its purpose was pure vengeance. The wrath of the Death Loa is usually permanent."

"Yet several of our people have returned from the dead."

"I also said the loa's vengeance and wrath failed to cripple the spirit of some of your people. Some hold an exceptional will to live."

"Only some?"

"I have learned the will to return from the dead is a personal choice. Most of the dead will not choose that option."

Ameh sat forward. "When you say a personal choice, how do you know it is personal?"

Onu-Vey hesitated before answering. He knew what he had to say would be unbelievable. But it was the truth. "I … have returned from the dead myself. On life's other side, I learned we often have a choice to return. Since I did not die as the result of the loa's vengeance or wrath, my physical body suffered no damage. My spirit held no crippling fears. I could choose to return. The choice was solely my own."

"You mean you died, too?"

"Yes, Mfalme Jobabwe."

"And you came back among the living because you wanted to?"

"It was … not that simple. My reasons for returning are great. But that is what happened. I cannot speak for your people on life's other side. Their reasons to return to the living may not be as compelling as mine are."

"If they are dead!" The Red Warrior Nienko spoke out on the other side of the work area. "I do not think they are dead."

Nienko's statements drew everyone's attention. The statements caused a wave of restless voices. Ramuza had to raise his hand, silencing the people before him. He turned to the Red Warrior. "You have something to say, Great Creation?"

"Please accept my apology, Mfalme." Out of respect, Nienko attempted to sit more erect. He suppressed the pain in his legs. "But yes. If I may, I have some interesting things to say."

Ramuza studied the Red Warrior's physical condition. "I hope you feel better than you look."

"Oh, I do, Mflame. I am fine. Thank you. I feel better than I did."

"Please continue. Tell me. Why are you convinced the dead will rise again?"

"Well,… I am not sure, Mfalme." Nienko thought before continuing. Like the houngan, Nienko knew a truth that must be told. In Nienko's case, however, this truth was beyond his understanding. The natural phenomenon defied explanation. "There is no clear way to describe what I have seen, Mfalme. I have noticed there is … a force of nature working here."

The houngan had closed his eyes and bowed his head again after everyone turned away. When Nienko used the phrase 'force of nature', it caught the Mangoni houngan's attention. He remembered the words of his mother's spirit. *'You have already put into motion a force of nature that must run its course.'* Onu-Vey raised his head. He focused his eyes on the Red Warrior and listened.

"It all started yesterday afternoon with the Orange Warrior Wema's crocodile," Nienko said.

"Wema's crocodile?" Ameh looked up at the Orange Warrior standing behind Nienko. The expression on Ameh's face showed his confusion. "You had a crocodile?"

"A crocodile almost had me, Mfalme."

"So … what makes this crocodile so special?" Ameh's eyes volleyed between Wema and Nienko, expecting one of them to answer his question.

Nienko spoke up first, eager to tell his amazing story. To answer Ameh's question, Nienko started with Wema's heroic attempt to cross the Mara River and the three-way standoff involving Wema, the crocodile, and the demon. He held everyone's attention as he continued with details of all the incidents that made him suspect that the dead were not dead. He told of the strange disappearance of the crocodile from the Mara River bank; the sudden grunt and the tail movement of an assumed dead wildebeest; and the unexpected herd of live animals that almost killed him when they stampeded around him. Nienko explained that he became completely convinced when the Warriors Wema and Kibwe finally got him to the sentry line on the north rim.

"What happened there, Great Creation?" Kon-Shambique asked.

"Wema, Kibwe, and I arrived there as the Royal Warrior Jokere had just finished reviewing the bodies of all his sentinels. It was a very unsettling, disturbing moment, not just for the Royal Warrior Jokere, but for all of us."

"In what way?"

"The Royal Warrior seemed distressed. But he was also very angry! And he took that anger out on the rest of us – Wema, Berko, Paki, Kibwe, Wekesa, and me. At one point, he became so angry with Wekesa that he dismissed the White Warrior from the sentinel line. Jokere dismissed Wekesa when he needed all the warriors and help he could get."

"Jokere's behavior was harsh and irrational, but somewhat understandable. Do you not agree? He had just learned that all his sentinel warriors were dead."

"Well… that is how Wema, Kibwe, and I saw it. We felt the Royal Warrior had a right to be angry. We did not know the whole story until the Orange Warrior Berko explained it."

"How did Berko see it?"

"According to Berko, the Royal Warrior Jokere showed distress, not because his warriors were dead, but because he was alive. Berko said that the Royal Warrior thought he had somehow survived the demon's attack when none of his sentinels did."

"Jokere did not know he was once dead?"

"No, Great Creation. I tried to explain to him what was happening. The Royal Warrior refused to listen to me. I could not make him believe me. The Orange Warrior Berko tried to help me by pointing to the vacant spot where Jokere once lay, next to his Blue Warrior Oumar."

"What happened?"

"Jokere became angrier than convinced. The warriors Berko, Paki, and Wekesa had placed the bodies in a neat and uniformed line. Everyone could see that the vacant spot where the Royal Warrior once lay spoke for itself. Before that moment, I only suspected Wema's crocodile, several wildebeests, and possibly a herd of migrating animals came back to life. But after seeing that vacant spot, I knew. The Royal Warrior once lay dead with his sentinels."

"Just seeing the vacant spot was enough to convince you?"

"After all I had seen before, yes. And there is more. It gets better. After the Royal Warrior Jokere dismissed us, the warriors Wema, Kibwe, and Wekesa carried me to the bottom of the north slope and onto the north bank pathway. There, all four of us saw our first actual resurrection. We saw the Great Creation Kantuti sat up with our own eyes."

"Did the Great Creation know he was once dead?"

"It never occurred to him. The moment he sat up, he wrestled with the frightening sight of seeing his entire family dead beside him. The Warriors Wema, Kibwe, and Wekesa subdued Kantuti, trying to calm him down. Since I had two broken legs and was confined to my litter, all I could do was shout to him. I told him many times that his family was not dead."

"Did he believe you?"

"Not at first. But the Great Creation Kantuti finally calmed down enough to hear what I was saying to him. He was easier to convince than the Royal Warrior Jokere was. He accepted the possibility and hoped I was right enough to accompany us into the Royal Kraal, where we found the Green Warrior Tushema. Since then, as you know, ten more resurrections occurred."

"Totaling twelve resurrections altogether," Ameh added. "What is so special about us twelve? Why did we return and no one else so far?"

Here was another one of those questions that fascinated the Favored Tribesman. Kon-Shambique, heavy in thought, paced slowly in front of the elders.

"Let us see," he said as he organized his thoughts and slowly named the resurrected people again. "Jokere, Kantuti … me, Tongda … Ramuza, Rwuva, Ameh… Adaulah, Kharaambi, Olabisi… Quazzi and Nionu. What is so special about us?"

Until this point, the Red Warrior Rotho stood quietly behind the Mangoni houngan and listened to all that everyone said. Like everyone present, he found all the exchanges and discoveries fascinating. He found the Mangoni houngan's claim of returning from the dead, with the personal choice to do so, incredible. He found the Red Warrior Nienko's perspective of the journey from the bank of the Mara to the Royal Kraal absorbing. His interest in everything he heard became personal when he heard the Favored Tribesman's simple question.

Like everyone in the area, Rotho asked himself that question. He reviewed each of the twelve names mentioned. He reached a surprising conclusion long before the last two names, Quazzi and Nionu.

"Great Creation," Rotho spoke up. He stepped before the Mangoni houngan to move closer to the Favored Tribesman. "You have asked a question. I believe I can answer it."

Kon-Shambique was in the middle of one of his pacing segments away from the Red Warrior. He had to turn around to face Rotho. "You can?"

"Yes, Great Creation. I do not know what makes all of you special. But each of you holds one thing in common."

"What is that?"

"Me."

"You? How so?"

"Upon the north rim, I helped the Green Warrior Tushema move the body of the Royal Warrior Jokere out of the evening sun. Then, down on the north bank pathway, I helped the Gold Warrior Oghani move the body of the Great Creation Kantuti from the middle. I performed the prayer ritual over Kantuti's body."

"This is incredible." Rotho's story captivated in Kon-Shambique. "Please continue."

"When we entered the Royal Kraal, your body was one of the first I helped to move, next to the royal dais. I also helped Oghani move Tongda's body next to yours. By then, the Green Warrior Tushema had discovered Mfalme Ncobba's body. I helped him move the Mfalme's body from beside the royal dais to the front. Tushema and I placed the Sacred Woman Rwuva's body next to Ramuza's."

"And the bodies found on the slope behind the huts?"

"For a brief period, all repositioning of bodies stopped because we could not find some of the Royal Family. But later, when we finally found the hidden bodies, many of us helped to reposition them. But it was I who helped to move the bodies of Ameh, Kharaambi, Adaulah, and Olabisi. I was privileged to reposition the final two bodies, the Brown Warrior Quazzi and the Royal Warrior Nionu. I have helped with no others. Since Quazzi and Nionu, I have touched no other bodies. Since then, no others have returned from the dead."

Kon-Shambique walked over to stand directly in front of Rotho. He smiled, studying the Red Warrior's face. "Great Creation, maybe we should not ask, what is special about us. Maybe we should ask, what is so special about you?"

92

IT IS MANGONI

The Sacred Woman Lobarra sat among the people who had nothing to offer to the work area gathering. She had listened to all the exchanges. She heard when the Mangoni houngan repeated his uncertainty that the latest wrath of the demon was permanent, and that he, too, had died and returned. She heard when the Red Warrior Nienko described all his experiences to support his belief that the dead would rise again, from Wema's disappearing crocodile to the actual resurrection of the Great Creation Kantuti. She heard about the strange circumstance, in which twelve resurrections had occurred, from the Royal Warrior Jokere to the Royal Warrior Nionu, and no more. Lobarra knew she could contribute nothing to any of it.

But a realization took hold when the Favored Tribesman Kon-Shambique asked the Red Warrior Rotho what was so special about him. Lobarra suddenly had something to offer. She felt the past three days had been very special because of Rotho. Lobarra adjusted the covering on the sleeping Tutapona. She excuses herself from where she sat next to Olabisi and Tongda. She got up and slowly walked toward the work area. Lobarra stopped at the area's edge and stood, unsure how to interrupt this important gathering.

Tongda's distracting behavior drew Mfalme Ncobba's attention. When he saw her standing at the edge of the work area, he could tell she was no longer a curious listener. As far as he could tell, Lobarra looked as though she had something she wanted to say. "Sacred Woman, please." He beckoned her to come forward.

With more confidence in her steps, Lobarra entered the work area. She smiled at the Great Creation Elder Zekke when she walked past him. She gave several other elders a few more respectful nods as she walked around them. Lobarra stood next to Kon-Shambique and Rotho, giving Ameh another smile and a silent greeting. She finally turned to Ramuza.

"Thank you, Mfalme, for allowing me to speak before this gathering."

"If you can help in any way, Sacred Woman, you belong here."

Lobarra almost shrugged. I hope I can help, Mfalme. I can tell Kon-Shambique when the Red Warrior Rotho became… special."

"You can? Then, perhaps, there is something special about you, too." Ramuza could tell by the gentle smile on Lobarra's face that his comment had made her self-conscious. "Please continue."

"As I look back over recent days, I believe the Red Warrior became special the night before the farmers left the Kiwane Village."

"And what makes you believe that?"

Lobarra thought for a moment, wondering how to tell her story. "For most of the early part of the farmers' trip to the Kiwane Village, my son, Tutapona, had been unusually fretful. His behavior was different; sometimes difficult. Several times, I considered allowing the Kiwane healer, the Great Creation Ngo Wenfundi, to look at Tutapona. But I knew that Tutapona was not sick. I wish I had left him here, as his grandfather, Ameh, suggested."

"But you did not want to break that motherly bond," Ameh said.

"No, Mfalme. And I am glad I did not. Tutapona's presence at the *mkutano* had to be part of the Supreme Spirit's grand design."

"So, what happened?"

"The night before we left the Kiwane Village, Tutapona threw one of his crying tantrums. By chance, Mfalme Modoffa Menda of the Kiwane Tribe was there among us. He saw it all. Mfalme Menda was a wonderful host during our stay. And he is a Kind, Generous Creation. To help calm Tutapona, he gave away the royal scepter he carried with him."

"Mfalme Modoffa gave *you* his royal scepter?" Ameh seemed confused about how this would calm Tutapona down.

"No, Mfalme. He did not give it to me. Tutapona seemed so attracted to the scepter that Mfalme Menda gave it to him as a gift. The Red Warrior Rotho, as the warrior assigned to protect Tutapona and me, offered to carry the scepter for Tutapona. Since that moment, Tutapona's behavior changed. His fretfulness died away. And I could easily see a special bond developing between Tutapona and Rotho."

"And you think the scepter caused these changes?" Kon-Shambique asked.

"Yes, Great Creation. I did not realize it at first. But, in hindsight, I do."

"Then, perhaps, it is the scepter that is special." Kon-Shambique turned to the Red Warrior. "Rotho, Great Creation, do you have the scepter with you now?"

Rotho gathered his shield and spear into his right hand. He reached into a pouch on his left side and extracted the 50-centimeter scepter. He gave it to the Favored Tribesman. "Beautiful, is it not?"

"Yes, it is." Kon-Shambique examined the scepter. Like everyone who saw it, the craftsmanship, intricate detail, the inscriptions, carvings, symbols, and the potbellied bullfrog perched at the top of the shaft fascinated Kon-Shambique.

When Kon-Shambique tapped the bullfrog in the palm of his hand, just like Mfalme Menda always did, Lobarra and Rotho looked at each other and smiled. The perfect balance of the scepter had its magical attraction.

Since the moment Rotho extracted the scepter from his pouch, the houngan locked his eyes onto it. His eyes grew wide, and his mouth turned dry. His heart raced. He opened his mouth to speak, but no words could express his feelings. Throughout the gathering, the houngan had sat with his legs crossed. The force that surged through his body gave him enough leg strength to rise slowly to his feet.

Tushema reacted first. He grabbed the houngan by the shoulder and pulled him back. He and the Red Warrior Rotho quickly took a protective position in front of Lobarra, their spears pointed at the houngan.

The houngan struggled to find his voice. "It … it is … Mangoni!" Although the houngan stood with his hands bound tightly behind his back, at that instant, he performed the miraculous feat of bringing his freed hands to his sides. He pointed at the scepter. "It is Mangoni!"

The houngan's statement and the unexpected freedom of the houngan's hands caused a wave of restless voices from the elders in the work area. Several of the frightened elders moved back.

Everyone realized the Mangoni houngan could have freed himself whenever he wanted. The alarming realization brought Ramuza, Kharaambi, and Quazzi to their feet.

Ramuza started toward the houngan, but the Gray Warrior Kharaambi caught him by the shoulders and held him back. "No, Mfalme."

Quazzi had also stepped in front of Ramuza to block his advances. He glanced back at the houngan's hands. "It is clear. He is no Ordinary Creation, Mfalme."

At the advice of Kharaambi and Quazzi, Ramuza stepped back. He wondered if the houngan could free his hands at will, and then how dangerous was he? He stared at the houngan, ready for any challenge.

"Please, I mean no harm," the houngan said, his voice coarse and barely audible. He pointed again. "But the scepter; it is Mangoni."

Ramuza stepped around Kharaambi and Quazzi. He walked over to Kon-Shambique instead. He took the scepter from Kon-Shambique's hands. Ramuza could not help but examine it himself before turning to the houngan. "Why do you say this is Mangoni?"

"The inscriptions, the carvings, and symbols; they are Mangoni. The design, including the figure on top, is Mangoni."

Ramuza looked closer at all the fine craftsmanship along the shaft. "This inscription, can you read it?"

"Yes."

Ramuza glanced at Kon-Shambique. Against the objections of Kharaambi and Quazzi, he moved closer to the houngan. He waited for Tushema and Rotho to move aside. The warriors resisted. Respect for their Mfalme forced them to comply. Ramuza took another step closer to the houngan and handed him the scepter. "Here. Read it."

The houngan wiped sweat from his brow before it ran into his eyes. He reached out to take the scepter. His hand was shaking. "Among my people, the frog symbolizes a return of the lost. The frog can burrow below the mud. It stays there, buried for many moons, only to surface again, alive and well. Sometimes, the frog also symbolizes resurrection of the dead."

Onu-Vey slowly ran his fingers gently over the inscriptions and symbols. "This ... writing comes from many ... many harvests ago. The scepter's creator ... wrote here, 'I fear the end. My people are taken. All we had ... all we have known ... is gone. Never ... to be seen again. But ... Hope remains. Hope will always remain ... if the heart of this scepter ... finds home.'"

"The heart? Finds home?" Kon-Shambique asked. "What is meant by that?"

"I am not sure."

Onu-Vey turned the scepter over to find more of the inscriptions and symbols. "Here ... there is more. The creator of the scepter has also written ... 'when the heart of the scepter finds home ... all the guardian spirits will rally. No man ... no force... will prevent... my people's redemption.'"

"Great Sacred Spirit!" Kon-Shambique could feel the writer's passion. It excited him. He turned to speak to Lobarra and Rotho. "Did Mfalme Modoffa Menda say where he got the scepter from? Did he know what it meant?"

"We asked him," said Rotho. "He did not seem to know."

"Yes," Lobarra quickly agreed. "He said he received it over thirty harvests ago, during his coronation. It was left among his many gifts. But that was all. He knew nothing else about it."

"This is fascinating. Whoever created the scepter and wrote those inscriptions had some very strong convictions. I would love to know the writer's inspiration." Kon-Shambique turned to Onu-Vey again. "Please continue. Is there more?"

Onu-Vey turned the scepter over again to read more of the inscriptions and symbols. "The writer's prayer ends. The rest … is a puzzle; or maybe … instructions."

"Instructions? For what?"

Onu-Vey became so absorbed by the instructions that he could not give Kon-Shambique an answer. He ran his fingers over the scepter's shaft again. He repositioned the scepter, turning it one way and then another. He seemed confused, trying to read the instructions and follow them simultaneously.

Onu-Vey turned the scepter upside down. He gripped the shaft with both hands. The beautiful scepter snapped in two with a sudden twist of his hands in opposite directions. The snap was so loud that even Onu-Vey jumped at the unexpected sound.

"Did you intend to do that?" Ameh asked the houngan. The frown on Ameh's face showed his concern. "Did you break it?"

"No, Mfalme Jobabwe. It is not broken." Onu-Vey studied the halves of the scepter he held in each of his hands. "It is the scepter's design. The instructions are clear."

Onu-Vey discarded the bottom half of the scepter. He felt comfortable committing the rest of the instructions to memory. He examined the top half with the potbellied frog at the top. The bottom end of the top half had a small wooden appendage protruding from the core of the shaft. Onu-Vey twisted, pushed, and pulled on the wood appendage with his fingers. He found it unmovable.

Onu-Vey frowned. The unmovable appendage seemed contrary to the instructions. Onu-Vey studied the top half of the scepter again. He turned it over, searching for another way to dislodge the appendage. Wondering if he had misinterpreted the instructions, Onu-Vey finally turned the top half of the scepter upright. He held it with both his hands and kneeled. To the surprise of everyone, he jabbed the wooden appendage into the ground.

With another resounding snap, the wooden appendage suddenly receded into the shaft. The entire head of the potbellied frog popped off and tumbled to the ground. Onu-Vey could see into the body, into the belly of the frog. Onu-Vey had already knelt to a squat position.

What he saw, inside the belly of the frog, made him fall to a sitting position, as if all the strength in his legs had suddenly disappeared altogether. He sat back. He covered his eyes with his hand. And to everyone's amazement, Onu-Vey cried.

Kon-Shambique made his way over to the houngan and kneeled in front of him. "Great Creation, are you alright?" He got no answer. Kon-Shambique reached over and took the upper half of the scepter from the houngan. He looked into the belly of the frog. "What is this?"

When Onu-Vey did not answer, Kon-Shambique reached into the belly of the frog to extract the object with his fingers. He realized his fingers were too big. The object rested in a perfect cavity. He turned the scepter up to dump the object into his hand. He had to shake it twice before a beautiful, brilliant, flawless crystal tumbled.

"It is … the other half … of my *azima*," Onu-Vey said.

"Your *azima*?"

"Yes. It is a charm blessed with the power to focus my will; to focus, what you call, my magic."

Kon-Shambique studied the crystal. The rainbow of colors shone with intense richness. The flashes and sparkles were blinding. He turned to the houngan again. "Onu-Vey, the writer of the inscriptions on the scepter, seems convinced. The writer believes the heart of the scepter, this crystal, must find its home first. When it does, the writer's people may find redemption. But you say this is your *azima*. Tell us. What is the connection?"

Onu-Vey suppressed his embarrassment and wiped away the tears on his face. "Over forty harvests ago, my mother, the tribe's High Priestess, revealed my *azima* to me. On that day, she died. By her own will, she crossed to the afterlife. On that day, I inherited her position."

"You became the Tribal High Priest; the Tribal Houngan."

"Yes. On that day, I realized the full power of my will. And I used it. On that very same day, the ruthless, tyrannical warrior, Kold-Johan, took our village and gained control of all the warring clans. He became the Mfalme of all the Mangoni. When Kold-Johan took our village, he took me prisoner, hoping I would deliver the High Priestess. He did not know that my mother was already dead. During his brutality to make me talk, I lost half of my *azima* that you now hold."

Kon-Shambique studied the crystal again. "You mean, you have not seen this since your mother revealed it to you?"

"No. On that day, the ruthless Kold-Johan killed many of our village warriors. He forced them to jump to their deaths from the Jabali, a rocky, 75-meter cliff at the edge of our village. In the same manner, Kold-Johan also killed a little village boy." Onu-Vey paused, overcome with emotion again as the memory of that day resurfaced. Fresh tears flowed. "The little boy's name was Moh-Saalim. Moh-Saalim had only seen his ninth harvest. He was about the same age as your son, Mfalme Ncobba. He was a gentle, innocent little boy, full of the hopes and dreams of all children."

"Why did Kold-Johan kill Moh-Saalim?"

"Kold-Johan felt that Moh-Saalim had shown him a little too much disrespect. In a deliberate and heartless act, he threw the little boy from the Jabali. I did not know, until this very moment, that Moh-Saalim had found the lost half of my *azima*. He had it with him when Kold-Johan threw him over that cliff. Unlike all the village warriors, Moh-Saalim survived that fall. I want to think that the crystal he held and cherished inspired his convictions and his survival."

Kon-Shambique held the beautiful crystal up, still fascinated by its colorful sparkles and history. "How do you know that it was young Moh-Saalim who created the scepter and encased the crystal in the belly of the frog?"

"I remember some of his earlier work. Even as a young boy, his skill was extraordinary. The artistry is Moh-Saalim's. Dreaming to be a woodsman like his father motivated Moh-Saalim's young and innocent life. I know the inscriptions on the scepter come from the heart of the young Moh-Saalim." Onu-Vey looked up at Ramuza. "Mfalme Ncobba, I am the 'home' that Moh-Saalim mentioned. I am the redeemer of Moh-Saalim's people – my people."

"Words, houngan." Ramuza kneeled next to Kon-Shambique as he looked directly into the houngan's eyes. "You speak beautiful words. People have often warned me to be wary of your words and how you use them to your benefit. The Young Creation Moh-Saalim wrote that inscription at different times and places for different people. How do we know you speak the truth?"

Onu-Vey sat more erect and crossed his legs. He took a deep breath to recompose himself. He wiped the rest of the tears from his face with both his hands. The houngan bowed his head as if to pray. He was looking down at the pouch that hung over his chest. He reached up, opened the pouch, and slowly pulled out another crystal. This crystal was abysmally black. It did not sparkle. Onu-Vey placed it on the ground before him, for all to see.

"I have lived with the dark half of my *azima* most of my life."

Kon-Shambique could easily see a connection between the abysmal black crystal and the clear crystal in his hand. He placed the clear crystal next to the black crystal on the ground. The jagged ends of each crystal came together in a perfect fit. After seeing this, no one doubted that these crystals once existed as one.

Kon-Shambique looked at Ramuza. "Mfalme, I must admit, I think the heart of this scepter ... has come 'home'."

Ramuza stood up and turned away. He found it very hard to accept what lay before his very eyes. He slowly walked back to where he had sat. Wrestling with his conflicting thoughts, Ramuza sat back down. He looked at the houngan. He stared, unwilling to accept where his thoughts were leading him. Several moments passed before he finally spoke again. "If the heart of the scepter has found home, then must we also recognize that the houngan can provide redemption for Moh-Saalim's people – the houngan's people?"

"Huh!" Ameh grunted loudly. He seemed to support Ramuza's resistance to the idea. "After what he has done? How can he redeem anybody's people?"

Kon-Shambique picked up both halves of Onu-Vey's *azima*. He still seemed fascinated by the perfect way the halves fit together. He replaced both halves on the ground as he stood up. Kon-Shambique thought about Ameh's emotion-filled questions and the only possible answer. "It is called forgiveness."

"Forgiveness?" Ramuza sounded offended. The rage behind his anger threatened to resurface. "Kon-Shambique, Great Creation, have you looked out across the celebration area? Do you need to take another look? Forgiveness is impossible."

"In this case, Mfalme, I would have to agree. Forgiveness is impossible. Some will say that, to forgive, we must be able to forget." Kon-Shambique walked over to where he sat. "I could consider forgiveness for the houngan and the Mangoni. But I must be honest. Try as I might, I cannot forget all that has happened in our valley recently."

"The guardian spirits will rally. No man, no force will prevent my people's redemption." Onu-Vey repeated part of the inscription.

"I find your words offensive, houngan." Ramuza looked over at the Green Warrior. "Tushema, Great Creation, take him back to the secluded area."

"Mfalme, please, wait!" Lobarra suddenly pleaded. After Ramuza looked her way and gave a gentle nod, she quickly knelt by the discarded pieces of the disassembled scepter. She gathered them up in one hand. She picked up the clear crystal half of Onu-Vey's *azima* in her other hand. Lobarra stood up and faced Ramuza again. She held out the pieces of the scepter first.

"Mfalme Modoffa Menda gave this scepter to Tutapona. It is only a simple gift, and it belongs to Tutapona." Lobarra held out the clear crystal. "But this, the scepter's heart, belongs to the houngan. Through it, the houngan can focus his magic – his true will. And after what I have learned about this crystal, I believe the houngan's true will is not what we should fear. It is what we need. It is our redemption, too."

"Lobarra!" It was Ameh's turn to show offense. "How can you say that? And I repeat my original question: After what has he done? We gained nothing good from that curse he placed on us. You were not here, Sacred Woman. You did not experience it like we did."

"No, I was not, Mfalme. But returning home to a valley of dead people was an experience enough. It is something I will never forget. Mfalme Abul-Gwan ordered that curse, out of hurt and anger. The Great Creation Onu-Vey, in loyal obedience, executed that curse. Out of respect to his Mfalme, he had no choice. But I feel that on the day Onu-Vey placed that curse, his true will and heart began its journey home to erase that curse." Lobarra turned to Ramuza. "And that is why, Mfalme, I suggest the crystal be returned to him."

"To what end, Sacred Woman?"

"So, he may do what must be done. The Little Creation Moh-Saalim believed that this crystal would save his people. I believe that too. But it cannot redeem the Mangoni until it saves the Aukmondi first."

"Lobarra, Sacred Woman," Ameh sighed with exasperation, "what are you talking about?"

"With this crystal, Moh-Saalim survived a 75-meter fall and successfully set it on a course to send it home. We do not know how Moh-Saalim got it into Mfalme Menda's possession. We may never know. But, somehow, he did. The whole process has to be part of the Supreme Spirit's grand design. We see a hint of Her blessed support through the recent and special abilities of the Red Warrior Rotho." Lobarra walked over to stand next to Rotho. "The Red Warrior Rotho only walked past the dead crocodile and thousands of dead animals on the savanna. That simple act brought the dead animals back to life. In the short time since Rotho returned to the valley, he touched twelve of our dead. Twelve of our dead returned to the living. If Rotho can do this without realizing what he is doing, imagine what the houngan can do with deliberate skill."

Kon-Shambique got up and walked over to Lobarra, smiling. "I love the way you think, Sacred Woman. I do not know whether to credit such beautiful thoughts to your forgiving heart or to the power of that crystal you hold in your hand."

Lobarra acknowledged Kon-Shambique's compliment with a smile. She held on to the scepter pieces but offered the crystal to the Favored Tribesman.

Kon-Shambique took the crystal and turned to Ramuza. "Mfalme, the Sacred Woman, is right. Assuming the houngan is the Mangoni redeemer, our interest is best served if we do not stand in his way."

"But can we trust him?" Ramuza asked. "Since the Great Creation, Onu-Vey has been in our valley, he has carried only half of his *azima*. Who knows what damage he could do if we give him the other half."

"Mfalme, without realizing it, the Red Warrior Rotho has proven that the clear half of Onu-Vey's *azima* is here to undo any damage done."

Ramuza glanced at the Sacred Women, Rwuva and Kharaambi, as if to sense their opinions. He received only an indecisive shrug from both of them. He looked at Quazzi and Mfalme Ameh Jobabwe. Ramuza got the same responses. He finally looked out across the faces of the tribal elders who sat before him. All of them mumble among themselves, but none offered anything decisive.

"It looks as though the decision is mine." Ramuza sighed heavily. "Then, so be it."

Decision made, Ramuza got up. He approached Kon-Shambique. He asked for the crystal with an open hand. With the crystal in his hand, he placed it gently on the ground next to the black crystal. He looked up into the houngan's eyes. "Houngan, if you harm my people again, I will make your demon's wrath look like child's play. Everyone, including my people, will consider my behavior unforgivable. Are my words clear to you?"

"Mfalme Ncobba, I am probably doomed to live the rest of my life without forgiveness from your people. But you have my word. I will not give you a reason to join me in that predicament."

After Ramuza stood up and returned to his seat, Onu-Vey closed his eyes. He took another deep breath as if to readjust his mind and his heart. When he opened his eyes, he reached out to pick up the two halves of his *azima*. Almost ceremoniously, he slowly put the halves into the pouch that hung over his chest.

"We cannot appreciate the heat," he began, "until we have known the cold. We cannot enjoy the silence until the noise assaults us. We cannot value love until we have known loneliness. We cannot appreciate peace until we have experienced war. We cannot appreciate familiarity until we become lost. But death is a transition in life. Life is forever. Its appreciation comes from living."

Onu-Vey got slowly to his feet. He turned to Ramuza and bowed. "Mfalme Ncobba, my people's redemption awaits. Please permit me to help the Aukmondi."

— 93 —

YOUR ATTITUDE HAS CHANGED

Hundreds of living and lively people filled the celebration area at this hour of the night (or morning). People celebrated the simple pleasures of being alive from the royal dais to the kraal entrance. In some areas, huge gatherings of people sang and danced together. Some people, young and old alike, played games together. In other areas, groups of people talked and laughed. In their way, all of them celebrated every simple breath they took. All across the valley, the dead had returned to the living, all at once.

Earlier, Ramuza had led Onu-Vey from the work area. Everyone else who had been in the work area, including all the elders, got quickly to their feet and followed. People who had waited outside the work area, including Olabisi, Tongda, and the warriors Nionu, Tushema, and Oghani, merged with the group. With curiosity at its highest, everyone wanted to see what the re-empowered houngan would do.

Ramuza took Onu-Vey to stand directly in front of the royal dais. He waved his arm out toward the celebration area. "Hundreds of people lie dead before you, houngan. I foresee a very long night if you must touch each one to bring them back to life. The sooner you get started, the better. But I ask that you … Please start with these." Ramuza pointed to the bodies directly in front of him.

Onu-Vey looked down at the bodies that lay there. "Many of these … are your daughters, Mfalme?"

"Yes."

Onu-Vey looked back over his right shoulder at the mothers of the daughters – Rwuva, Olabisi, and Kharaambi. He received a hopeful stare from each one. He looked down at the bodies again. "I can only imagine the pain you and your mates must feel."

"I must admit, you have a brilliant mind, houngan. Your imagination is good. You can probably imagine my pain well. If that is so, you know how urgent it is that you begin your magical touches … now."

Onu-Vey looked back over his left shoulder at the Aukmondi Red Warrior Rotho. He smiled at the young warrior carrying such a gift without knowing its power. He turned back to Ramuza. "Mfalme, you assume I will use the same blind magic your warrior used. Now that my *azima* is intact again and in my possession, the method I will use is far more efficient." Onu-Vey stepped back. "Behold."

Onu-Vey closed his eyes. He raised his arms and held his hands toward the multitude of bodies as if radiating his magical energy. His lips moved in a soundless whisper. The whisper gradually became louder and louder. Soon, Onu-Vey spat out a series of clearly audible but unintelligible words. The words became a rolling, repetitive chant.

Onu-Vey reached for the pouch over his chest as he had always done in his most powerful rituals. He raised it and pressed it to his forehead with both his hands. He forced the chanted ritual words from his mouth faster and faster. The speed of the words did not affect each word's clarity. When it seemed Onu-Vey could not speak any faster, he suddenly stopped. A long and heavy silence followed.

Onu-Vey stood still. He seemed frozen, his eyes closed, and the pouch pressed against his forehead. After a moment, which seemed like forever, Onu-Vey released the pouch and allowed it to fall to his chest again. He raised his arms and held his hands toward the multitude of bodies again. He slowly opened his eyes. As his eyes opened, the eyes of all the dead opened too. The multitude of dead bodies moved; those on the ground before him, those out across the celebration area, and beyond the Royal Kraal.

Within seconds, the noise level across the celebration area changed from dead silence to the constant roar only a crowd could make. The initial gasps of amazement transformed into a series of shouts and cheers. Many who saw this miracle rushed to welcome the once-dead back to life. Families and close friends surrounded the resurrected with overwhelming joy. They absorbed their momentary period of disorientation and confusion. The excitement and outpouring of love flowed across the area like a warm wind, setting the basis for a great and special Celebration of Life.

*****

After a leisurely and aimless walk through the celebration area, Ramuza and Onu-Vey walked back toward the royal dais. Ramuza and Onu-Vey had found walking out among the joyful people necessary. In their way, each wanted to absorb energy generated by the rejuvenated people.

The walk lasted over an hour. During that time, as Ramuza and Onu-Vey weaved between the groups of people, they received hundreds of compliments with various degrees of gratitude. Even people who still found it difficult to approach the Mangoni houngan thanked him for what he had just done.

"I know that the events of recent days will linger in the memory of the Aukmondi people for some time," Onu-Vey said to Ramuza. "In your own words, this forgiveness is impossible. Believe me. I understand the attitude and feeling of your people."

"It is good you do."

"As I walked among your people, I sensed that there is still tension and mistrust. I know it is too soon to expect a change. However, I am pleased to notice that during the exchanges with your people, Mfalme Ncobba, you referred to me as 'Mfalme'. You have not done that since your resurrection. Already, your attitude has changed. I see it as a good sign. Attitude is everything."

Ramuza had not noticed the subtle change in his behavior or his attitude. He felt grateful for the houngan's resurrection ritual. The ritual had restored the lives of his precious daughters and all his beloved people. But his basic feelings about the houngan remained unchanged. Ramuza admitted that he still carried his share of tension and mistrust. He felt that if Kon-Shambique could refer to the houngan by name, he could only refer to him by title.

Ramuza thought about Onu-Vey's comment, saying that his changed attitude suggested a good sign. To Ramuza, it sounded like a compliment. He chose not to accept it. "Because I feel this forgiveness is impossible, it does not mean I should not expect it to happen."

"Then, it is also good that you can expect change. I want you to know. In the coming days, and as impossible as it may sound, the Mangoni intend to earn the forgiveness of the Aukmondi people. Forgiveness is possible if your people and your minds are open to it."

Ramuza did not acknowledge Onu-Vey. His only reaction was a questionable glance at the houngan. After all that had happened in recent days, it surprised Ramuza that the houngan could make such a suggestion. Was he joking or serious? Whatever his changing attitude or the attitude of his people might be, Ramuza knew better than to give an open mind to the houngan. Lesson learned – it was not wise. Ramuza dismissed the suggestion. He continued walking toward the royal dais and turned his full attention to the revelry of the surrounding people.

The crowd around the dais was much larger than usual. The people stood and talked among themselves. No one sat on the ground yet. With respect, they waited for Ramuza and Onu-Vey's imminent return.

On the left side of the dais, Ramuza noticed a huge group of warriors. The Green Warrior Tushema, Tushema's entire detachment, and Wema and Nienko centered the group. The Orange Warrior Berko and the Red Warrior Paki were also there. They had come from the north rim. The Royal Warrior Jokere now had a full regiment of sentinels on the north rim and no longer needed these inexperienced stand-ins.

As a group, Tushema and his detachment held everyone's attention. Quazzi, Nionu, Nionu's Blue Warriors, Obe and Dabete, and a host of others who stood nearby, listening to them talk. Ramuza assumed the group was sharing the adventurous details of the trip to and from the Kiwane Village.

Ramuza was eager to hear the details of that trip, too. Unfortunately, the rapid unfolding of events had not allowed him to do so. He felt envious of the warriors who stood around Tushema and his detachment. They were getting a fresh account of events. Such fresh accounts are how warriors share their experiences. The exchanges were the next best thing to being there. And there was nothing like it. Ramuza had to placate his envy by accepting that he would hear their story later.

In front of the dais, in the area where the bodies of Ramuza's daughters once lay, Ramuza and Onu-Vey had to work their way around two smaller groups. A small, common campfire separated the two groups.

The returning farmers, including the Great Creation Zekke and the Sacred Woman Lobarra, comprised most of the people in the group on the left side of the campfire. Ramuza was pleased to see that, as the evening and night progressed, many of them had found the time to change from their travel clothing. Despite the late hour of the night, all of them looked refreshed as they stood and talked together.

On the right side of that campfire, Ramuza saw Kon-Shambique and Tongda standing among the people of the group there. The two talked with two Mangoni warriors. One was the Mangoni lead-warrior, Goh-Jumaane, who had been in the Royal Kraal with the houngan all evening. The other Mangoni warrior, however, had recently come down from Nagorda Peak. Ramuza remembered the warrior's face from three days ago. He was Kum-Bufu, the brash, disrespectful warrior who had placed the tip of his spear against his chest. Ramuza suppressed his lingering offense from the incident.

Judging by Kon-Shambique's, Tongda's, and Goh-Jumaane's bearing around Kum-Bufu, he had captivated all of their attention. Ramuza's lingering offense and surprise at the warrior's sudden arrival in the Royal Kraal made him curious. He had to say something. He spoke for the first time since the houngan's comment about keeping an open mind. "Another of your warriors has come down from Nagorda Peak to join you."

Onu-Vey glanced at the warrior just long enough to smile. "It appears he came to tell me he is alive and well."

"What do you mean?"

"Believe it or not, Kum-Bufu was one of the many dead. A day and a half ago, when the Loa of Death began its wrath, Kum-Bufu was its first victim. When I performed the ritual to resurrect your people, Kum-Bufu benefited too."

"I thought your demon walked my valley, searching only for my people."

"It did, at first. But it seems your people's resistance and tenacity enraged the loa. It became desperate. I soon lost my influence over it. In the loa's final moments, it killed for the sake of killing. It did not care who died."

Ramuza was about to ask the houngan how extensive the loa's wrath had been; if other Mangoni had died, but the two finally reached the royal dais. He set his questions aside for the moment.

Upon the royal dais, most of the people permitted on the dais stood waiting. They included Ameh Jobabwe, all three of Ramuza's mates, and four of Ramuza's oldest daughters. The five youngest daughters were not there. Ramuza realized that they had long ago retired to their respective mothers' hut for a good night's sleep at this hour of the night.

Ramuza's youngest child, however, the little prince Adaulah, had already slept for much of the evening. He had missed most of the exchanges during the gathering that had taken place earlier in the work area. He was wide-awake now. Ramuza knew his son well enough that the little prince resisted the natural need to sleep. Still wearing most of the garments of an Honorary Black Warrior, he stood somewhat restlessly at Rwuva's side. Adaulah had awakened just in time to witness the houngan's resurrection ritual. He intended not to miss another minute of this very special evening.

All the people on the royal dais and the nearby crowds grew silent as Ramuza stepped onto the dais.

94

THESE ARE NOT JUST WORDS

Ramuza sat down on his chieftain stool almost ceremoniously. With a gesture, he invited Ameh and Onu-Vey to take their seats too. Ameh eased himself down on his chieftain's stool on the royal dais. Onu-Vey made himself comfortable on a beautiful mat Goh-Jumaane and Kum-Bufu had spread out for him before the dais. Everyone else observed the standard etiquette of waiting until all the Mfalmes, Ramuza, Ameh, and Onu-Vey were comfortable before they settled down.

The Great Creation, Elder Zekke, made a special effort to find a seat next to Lobarra. Of all the people surrounding the royal dais, Zekke was one of the last to sit. Ramuza waited until the old farmer found his seat and coaxed his aged body to the ground.

"Elder Zekke, Great Creation, I have yet to hear the results of your trip to the Kiwane Village. I understand it was a successful trip. I must apologize to you for not asking about it earlier."

"There is no need to apologize, Mfalme. I understand. So many other things have taken precedence. Details of our trip can wait until later." Zekke finally made himself comfortable. "But if you must know, the trip was an overwhelming success. You will be happy to know, it was such a success that the member tribes have all selected the Aukmondi as the host for the next farmer's *mkutano*."

"That is good to hear!" Ramuza smiled. "We have not hosted such a gathering for several harvests now. It is about time."

"I must also add, Mfalme, the success of the *mkutano* was due in part to the Sacred Woman Lobarra. Her service and contributions there were amazing. She received special recognition there. We are all very proud of her. We are glad she accompanied us."

Lobarra gave a prideful smile this time. She remembered the final session of the *mkutano*. During that session, after receiving her honors, she hid her face. Elder Zekke had leaned over and told her she 'should have known this was coming.' This time, she did. She experienced no embarrassment. She accepted with a graceful nod to Ramuza. What she did not expect was Ramuza's compliment.

"Congratulations, Sacred Woman. I look forward to hearing about your accomplishments. If your insightful contribution during tonight's gathering is any example, it is no wonder the *mkutano* was such a success. I am personally grateful for what you did there. And for what you did here."

"Thank you, Mfalme." Lobarra placed the credit where she felt it belonged. "I think my performance there, and here, is due to the Blessed Supreme Spirit. I and my son, Tutapona, and I unknowingly followed Her guidance."

"There is no doubt about it, Sacred Woman." Ameh shifted to a more comfortable position on his chieftain's stool. "I am so glad you listened to Her and not me. Our crisis probably could have been worse. Instead, we have come to this acceptable end."

"Mfalme Ameh Jobabwe," Onu-Vey spoke, suddenly drawing everyone's attention. He waited until a stiff silence settled over the area. "This 'acceptable end' you speak of, Mfalme Jobabwe, is incomplete."

Ameh's characteristic frown deepened as he looked at the houngan. Puzzled by the statement, Ameh glanced back at Ramuza before he turned back to Onu-Vey. "What are you talking about, houngan?"

Onu-Vey made a sweeping glance at all the others on the royal dais. He looked at all the Aukmondi that sat nearby. "For the Mangoni people, an 'acceptable end' cannot come until the Aukmondi people know of Abul-Gwan's sincere apology. I must take this moment and ask for that apology, for all Aukmondi to hear. Tremendous pain and grief initiated all that has happened in recent days. Although Abul-Gwan is dead now, he wants you to know he is sorry for all of it."

Ramuza did not allow Ameh or anyone to acknowledge or accept the apology. He chose this moment to follow up on something else the houngan had said. "Mfalme Onu-Vey, you told me earlier, toward the end of your demon's assault, it did not care who died. Did Abul-Gwan die by the demon's touch? Why was he not resurrected like your warrior Kum-Bufu or the rest of us? Why does Abul-Gwan not sit before us now and make his own, sincere apology?"

"The loa did not take Abul-Gwan, Mfalme. He died in the truest sense of the word. Once he crossed to the afterlife, he decided not to return."

"If the demon did not take him, how and when did Abul-Gwan die?" Ameh asked.

Onu-Vey had not considered Abul-Gwan's specific cause of death until just now. He took a moment to consult his memory. He recalled the spirit of Kosi-Jawma's assessment of Abul-Gwan's health. "It was his heart that failed him. The loss of Abul-Tess sealed his fate. He could not endure. He died in his sleep, during mid-morning yesterday."

"Then, I am sorry." The sad nature of Abul-Gwan's death allowed Ramuza to speak with sincerity. "The Mangoni have my condolences."

A moment of awkward silence followed. Almost all the Aukmondi held negative feelings about Abul-Gwan. Despite how most of the people felt, everyone also felt that negative words were inappropriate at the moment. Ameh finally broke the silence when he found the right words to qualify Ramuza's condolences. He addressed the houngan. "You have my condolences, too, Great Creation. There is no doubt. Many will well remember Mfalme Abul-Gwan ... in one way or another."

Onu-Vey acknowledged Ameh with a nod of his head. He understood the insinuation he heard. "It has been my experience in life, Mfalme Jobabwe, when you like someone, you will always give them the benefit of the doubt. If you dislike someone, you can find fault in all they do. To forgive Abul-Gwan, you must understand he was not evil."

"How, in all Her Creation, did we get the impression that Abul-Gwan was evil?" Ameh was being sarcastic.

"Abul-Gwan was a man with very strong passions. His business and his responsibilities often blinded him. The needs of his people and Abul-Tess's happiness forced him to be single-minded and determined. After the death of Abul-Tess, the Mfalme's great passions quickly soured and turned to great pain. The horrendous events you have experienced came out of that pain. In his pain, he ordered the death of your people."

"Yes. Beware of those who grieve," Ramuza repeated the warning Onu-Vey had given almost four days ago. "That much, we already know."

"Shortly thereafter, I tried to appeal to him. I truly tried to change his mind. He would not listen to me. He was my Mflame. I had no choice but to grant his request."

"But of course." The sarcasm in Ameh's voice continued.

"I must confess." Onu-Vey thought a moment. "Developments occurred that I did not foresee. I knew the Mfalme's heart. In his ill-mannered way, I knew Mfalme Abul-Gwan cared. I knew he would live to regret his request. So, I tried to fulfill his request in such a manner that would completely satisfy him. I tried to perform a ritual in which he would witness the death of every Aukmondi. He would then move on to complete his period of grief."

"But?" Ameh sat forward, anxious to hear more.

"I deceived Abul-Gwan. He did not know I performed a ritual where all your people could easily recover. Abul-Gwan would be none the wiser. I had hoped that by the time he learned what I had done, he would have realized his mistake with no lasting harm done to your people."

"So what went wrong?"

"Two unforeseen developments occurred." Onu-Vey gestured toward Kon-Shambique. "I did not expect the genius of your medicine man. He discovered a way to revive the people before I achieved my goal."

"Well, I am sorry for foiling your plan, Onu-Vey." Kon-Shambique's fake apology came with the hint of a smile. He looked up onto the royal dais. "But if the truth be known, I must credit the seed of that discovery to the young prince Adaulah. Thanks to him, we saw behind your mask of death. We discovered no one had died by your demon's assault."

When Adaulah heard the compliment come his way, he smiled. He looked up at his mother, Rwuva, obviously very proud of himself.

"We soon learned all we needed to revive everyone," Kon-Shambique continued, "was a good dose of inspiration, one that our Daily Celebration of Life often provides. And we got a good one started. It grew into one of the grandest celebrations ever. It had the potential to be completely successful, thanks to …"

Kon-Shambique was about to give another deserving compliment. This time, he glanced toward the Royal Warrior Nionu. However, the expression on Nionu's face told Kon-Shambique the Royal Warrior was not ready to accept the credit yet. Kon-Shambique quickly shifted his eyes and the credit elsewhere. "Thanks to the determination and the strong minds and hearts of the Aukmondi people, we almost did it."

"Where would we be without such determination, strong minds and hearts?" Ameh was one of several who saw Kon-Shambique avert his eyes from Nionu. He understood why but pretended not to notice. He gave both Nionu and Kon-Shambique a subtle reprieve when he shifted all the attention back to the houngan.

"Onu-Vey, Great Creation, you said there were two unforeseen developments. What was the other?"

"As I told you earlier, I died."

"In the truest sense of the word?" Ramuza asked.

"Yes, Mfalme Ncobba. When your people overcame my ritual, the Loa of Death became frustrated and impatient. It returned to its *veve*, looking for more strength and more guidance. When I could not help it, I lost all my influence. That is when it began its rampage, killing anything and everything. I tried to recover my influence over the loa. I made the fatal error of putting everything I had into a recovery ritual. As a result, I died shortly after Mfalme Abul-Gwan died."

"And yet you sit before us." Ameh's characteristic frown deepened. "Please explain. Who stood over you and performed a ritual to bring you back?"

"As I also said earlier. Resurrection is a personal choice, Mfalme Ameh Jobabwe. Upon death, we all have a clear choice of returning among the living. For many compelling reasons, many of us do not choose to do so. We stay on the other side for many compelling reasons, despite anguished whispers and prayers from loved ones who call to us on this side."

"Why did you come back?"

"I had to. As young Moh-Saalim believed, I am the Mangoni people's only hope. On the other side of life, I learned I must fulfill my obligation to them. My destiny is incomplete. Many harvests ago, Mfalme Abul-Gwan united our warring clans into one people, but he used a business that left us with a stigma of death and destruction. Several species of life are dead or dying because of the Mangoni business. If the Mangoni business does not end, history will recognize the Mangoni people as one of the greatest threats of all time to our natural resources."

"If the Mangoni business does not end?"

"It must end, Mfalme. It is a business that grew out of control many harvests ago. The passion behind it almost culminated in the irreversible death of the Aukmondi people. Mfalme Abul-Gwan now regrets every bit of that mistake. He wants to turn it around. He has started the difficult task of recovery by asking the Aukmondi people for forgiveness. I came back among the living, Mfalme, to relay Abul-Gwan's request and complete the task before the Mangoni people."

"One moment, Onu-Vey. Let me get something straight. Are you saying Abul-Gwan asked for forgiveness … after he died?"

"Yes." Onu-Vey could see behind Ameh's characteristic frown that he still had trouble accepting this. "Mfalme Ameh Jobabwe, do you find it difficult to accept Abul-Gwan's request for forgiveness? Or do you find it difficult to accept I have come back from the dead to ask it?"

"Well, both."

Onu-Vey smiled. "The Aukmondi are among many tribes that practice the tradition of imparting wishes to the dead. You whisper your wishes into the ear of the dead to be taken to the other side to your ancestors. Can the dead impart wishes to the resurrected, to be brought back to the living?"

Kon-Shambique nodded his head in agreement. "It makes sense."

Onu-Vey could still see the skepticism on Ameh's face. "I experienced no illusion of death. I experienced the very real afterlife. I walked among the dead. I walked and talked with the spirit of the former leader of the Mangoni warriors, Kosi-Jawma. I walked and talked with the spirit of Abul-Tess and with the spirit of my mother, Onu-Kinsi. I walked and talked with the spirit of Mfalme Abul-Gwan. I bring back all their wishes. I bring directly to you Abul-Gwan's request for forgiveness."

"Since the day you set foot in our valley, Great Creation, your words have carried incredible power. Your words now fail to convince me that these things are true."

"Do you seek proof, Mfalme?"

"Forgive me for being so stubborn, but yes. So, what now? Is there proof? Are we about to hear Abul-Gwan's actual voice upon the wind?"

"You may interpret what you sense as you please. But, with greater resonance, you will feel Abul-Gwan's spirit in your hearts." Onu-Vey looked up at the dais at Ramuza's Principal Mate. "Rwuva, I look to you to provide Mfalme Jobabwe the proof he seeks. I ask you to give validity to my words."

"Me? How, Great Creation?"

"Abul-Gwan told me to tell you. You were right."

"Right about what?"

"Shortly before Abul-Tess died, you quoted a memorable phrase. You told her the love between her and Abul-Gwan was *Nguvu za asili hauwezi kusimamishwa* – a force of nature that cannot be stopped. During my experience on the other side, Abul-Tess repeated and explained that phase to Kosi-Jawma, Abul-Gwan, Onu-Kinsi, and me. Abul-Gwan wants you to know you were right."

Rwuva sat back, surprised to hear her own words, repeated back to her from such a remote place. Rwuva knew that the Sacred Woman Abul-Tess died shortly after hearing the phrase. There was no way Onu-Vey could have known the phrase or how it related to Abul-Gwan and Abul-Tess, unless Onu-Vey spoke with Abul-Tess after she died.

"Ameh, these are not just words." Filled with emotion, Rwuva spoke with tears in her eyes. "I believe the Great Creation Onu-Vey speaks the truth. I hold no doubt in my mind and heart. The Great Creation Onu-Vey brings words directly from the other side."

"Then, you feel Abul-Gwan's request for forgiveness is sincere?"

"I do."

Ameh had always held Rwuva in high regard. Her sense of judgment was usually good. He could find no reason to object to her opinion. Ameh looked back at Ramuza. He knew that Ramuza's opinion made the decisive difference. He waited for Ramuza to respond.

"So be it." Ramuza's attitude had changed once again. He looked at Onu-Vey. "I will discuss Abul-Gwan's request with the tribal elders."

"Thank you, Mfalme Ncobba."

"As I told you earlier, because this forgiveness is impossible, it does not mean I should not expect it to happen. I will also add that it does not mean we should not try. I wish you success in the Mangoni salvation."

"As do I," Ameh added. "But tell me, Mfalme Onu-Vey. You said the business of the Mangoni must end. What will your people do now? If you stop the hunting, killing, and trading of animal products and other natural resources, how will your people provide for themselves?"

Once again, Onu-Vey recalled his recent visit to the other side. "The warrior, Kosi-Jawma, envisioned the Mangoni moving along a different, brighter path. As the new Mangoni Mfalme, I intend to lead my people along that path, to compensate for our history. As we work to earn the forgiveness of the Aukmondi, it is my intention that the Mangoni people become one of the strongest guardians and protectors of all African life. It is my intention that, someday soon, people will see the Mangoni in the same light as the Aukmondi, the Kiwane, and the Rimoza peoples."

"Will this provide for your people?"

"The Mangoni will make all of Africa a natural wildlife reserve. People can visit our great land to see African life thriving in all its natural glory. If the Mangoni people can guarantee this in fair trade, we will provide for ourselves."

"You intend to guarantee this?" Ramuza asked. He found Onu-Vey's resolve strong. "I will be the first to tell you it may be easier to earn the forgiveness of the Aukmondi than to guarantee such a dream. It will require major adjustments by your people."

"It is a guarantee, Mfalme."

"You sound confident."

"You forget, Mfalme Ncobba. I am still a Vodun houngan."

— 95 —

A TACTICAL DECISION

With good reason, people continued to celebrate throughout the night. When the leading edge of the morning sun eased over the horizon, people finally quieted down and left the celebration area. For many, the coming day meant they could finally rest after a long night of merriment. For a few, the coming day meant that various chores and responsibilities still had to be done. This was the case for the Royal Warrior Nionu and his two Blue Warriors, Obe and Dabete. Almost a full day's work lay ahead of the high-ranking warriors.

Nionu, Obe, and Dabete got up from where they had sat most of the night. They gathered up their shields, spears, and other belongings. The Royal Warrior Nionu stepped closer to the dais to ask permission for him and his warriors to leave, a customary procedure.

"Mfalme," Nionu greeted Ramuza with a friendly smile, "it has been a wonderful night, but we must part now with your permission. As a special favor to Mfalme Onu-Vey, some of my warriors have volunteered to help prepare a special burial site in the valley depths. The site is for the bodies of Abul-Gwan, Abul-Tess, and the Mangoni warriors who died in our valley. My Blue Warriors and I must go make special arrangements."

"Of course, Great Creation." Ramuza acknowledged Nionu with a gentle nod. He sat back and watched the three warriors turn and walk away. All night long, Ramuza had expected at least one of these warriors would approach him on another matter. This moment told Ramuza his expectation would not happen. Before the warriors walked too far away, Ramuza took control of the moment. He called out to one of the Blue Warriors. "Dabete, Great Creation."

All three of the warriors stopped walking. Each of them could hear something unusual in Ramuza's voice. Dabete gave Nionu an anxious look and then slowly turned. "Yes, Mfalme?"

Ramuza beckoned the Blue Warrior back. He waited until the warrior came to stand at the edge of the dais. "I am curious. All last night, I noticed that many warriors of your regiment wore none of their gear."

"That is true, Mfalme."

"Was there some reason for this?"

Dabete opened his mouth to respond, but the Royal Warrior Nionu rushed back to stand at Dabete's side. He answered Ramuza instead. "There is a good explanation, Mfalme. But, with your permission, may we please discuss this with you later? It is a long walk into the valley depths. My warriors and I must get an early start to …"

"Nionu!" Kharaambi spoke the Royal Warrior's name, cutting off his explanation. The tone in her voice left no doubt that Nionu's behavior bordered on disrespect.

"Yes, Sacred Woman?"

"Those preparations you speak of … do not bother. I will assign them to another army."

Nionu already knew the answer, but he had to ask. "Why?"

"You have some unfinished business that takes precedence."

Nionu could not continue his pretense of ignorance any longer. He glanced at the Sacred Woman Rwuva. Her expression told Nionu that she knew about his transgression. Nionu suspected she knew since just after her resurrection. Nionu looked at Ramuza. His expression told Nionu that the moment of ultimate judgment was here. Ramuza had called Dabete back, knowing that Nionu would not allow his Blue Warrior to take the blame.

"I take full responsibility, Mfalme."

"Great Creation," Mfalme Ncobba sat forward, "you gave the Motobo dancers permission to dance, knowing that a ban existed?"

"Yes."

"Why?"

Nionu reviewed the reasoning behind what he did. Even now, he still felt he could justify his actions. "Remember those huge *Ngoma* drums before the Sacred Woman Kharaambi's hut?"

Ramuza looked out into the celebration area. Pieces of the drums still lay in a splintered heap. "Yes, I remember."

"The sounds from those drums were inspiring. You never heard them as we did. Those drums' sounds helped bring my Blue Warriors to their feet again. But as inspiring as the drum sounds were, I knew they were only half of the inspiration we had available. The Motobo dancers were the other half. I told the dancers to perform. The drums and the dancers created excitement and energy that caused several other people to return from the dead. It worked, just as the Favored Tribesman suggested that it would. I guess you could say that, under the circumstances, my decision to use the Motobo dancers was a … a tactical decision."

"A tactical decision," Ramuza repeated as if he could not believe the young warrior's audacity. "Great Creation, you violated a ban set by the Principal Mate and a tribal elder. You do realize such a thing cannot be tolerated?"

"I know, Mfalme. I know." Nionu dropped his head in complete resignation, but then he stood erect with his head held high and his chest out. "Mfalme, I meant no disrespect. I did what I thought was necessary. But I made a mistake. I am ready to accept whatever punishment you feel is appropriate."

Ramuza sat back. Everyone could tell he was considering what should be done about the Royal Warrior Nionu. On the one hand, Ramuza realized that the drums and the dancers inspired some resurrections. Some good came from Nionu's actions. If that was all, Ramuza felt he could be lenient.

But Ramuza also knew that the energy and excitement created sent the demon into its final, devastating rage. More harm than good resulted. Ramuza could not overlook this. A proper and just punishment was necessary.

"Wait. Wait." Rwuva placed her hand on Ramuza's arm. "Mfalme, before you judge, allow me to get something straight here." When Ramuza nodded his permission, Rwuva turned to the Royal Warrior. "Nionu, Great Creation, you told the dancers to perform, knowing that a ban existed?"

"Yes, Sacred Woman."

Rwuva sat back. She searched the crowd of nearby people. Her eyes came to rest on the Brown Warrior. "Quazzi, Great Creation, were you aware of what Nionu had done?"

Quazzi seemed surprised when Rwuva called his name and pulled him into this. He stepped forward. "Yes, Sacred Woman. I learned of his transgression soon after he had done so."

Rwuva thought about Quazzi's response for a second. She leaned forward to look at the Gray Warrior Kharaambi, who sat on the other side of Ramuza. "And you, Sacred Woman, were you aware of what Nionu had done?"

Kharaambi sat erect. "Like the Great Creation Quazzi, I learned of his deed after he had done so. I summoned him before the royal dais. But rather than punish him myself, I waited. There was strong hope that the Mfalme would soon be resurrected. Due to Nionu's transgression, I decided the Royal Warrior deserved judgment and punishment from the Mfalme."

"I see." Rwuva sensed a disturbing trend in all the answers that she had received. She looked over at the Mfalme Ameh Jobabwe.

Ameh avoided Rwuva's eyes at first. He pretended to glare at the Royal Warrior Nionu. He could not keep up his pretense. With his characteristic frown, he finally looked over his shoulder at the Sacred Woman. She did not have to repeat her question. "Yes, Sacred Woman. I knew too. And I agreed with the Sacred Woman Kharaambi. I chose not to punish Nionu because he would have to answer to the Mfalme anyway."

"I see." Rwuva looked down to the position directly in front of her, where the Little Creation Adaulah sat. She saw Adaulah discarding most garments that signified him as an Honorary Black Warrior.

As if unaware that everyone was looking at him, Adaulah was quickly undressing. He removed his wrist bracelets and dropped them aside. He took off his ankle bracelets and dropped them with the wrist bracelets. Adaulah struggled to untie the beautifully huge necklace he wore around his neck.

"Little Creation, what are you doing?" Rwuva asked.

Still, while untying his necklace, Adaulah finally turned and looked up at his mother. "The Favored Tribesman Kon-Shambique said that … if I did not want to be Mfalme anymore … the Supreme Spirit would make it so."

"What do you mean?"

"I like the Royal Warrior Nionu. Despite what he has done, please do not look to me to punish him." Adaulah finally removed the necklace and dropped it onto the pile of discarded garments. He took off his headgear and nodded toward his father. "The Great Creation Ramuza Ncobba is Mfalme. Not me."

Rwuva smiled at her son. The smile disappeared when she looked up to address everyone she had just questioned. "All of you knew that a ban on this dance existed. All of you knew that the Great Creation Nionu had told the Motobo dancers to perform. None of you punished Nionu. Instead, you passed his punishment to a higher authority. And yet … none of you … None of you used your authority … to stop the dance."

"What are you saying, Sacred Woman?" Ramuza addressed Rwuva.

"Hear me, please." Rwuva turned to Nionu again. "Great Creation, in my opinion, you are in no more trouble than Quazzi, Kharaambi, Mfalme Jobabwe, or Adaulah. Yes, you overrode my ban. They could override your … your tactical decision. But they did not. Although this dance breaks tradition, it seems to be a very popular exception. In hindsight, now I see that … it is more acceptable than I realized."

"Rwuva?" Ramuza knew what Rwuva was about to say.

"The dance should not have been banned. I was wrong to do so."

People all around reacted to Rwuva's statement. A wave of restless voices died only after Ramuza raised his hand for Rwuva to continue speaking.

"Nionu, it is my opinion. Your foresight is a gift from the Supreme Spirit. She sometimes puts us in situations we may find difficult, uncomfortable, or impossible to manage. She has a good reason. The Supreme Spirit knows that each of us, at one time or another, is the most qualified person to manage that situation. In such moments, I like to think, She is asking each of us to make a difference."

Rwuva paused. She addressed Nionu directly, but spoke for all to hear. "Great Creation, before Mfalme Ncobba passes judgment, you managed the situation as only the Royal Warrior Nionu would. And it was what we all needed. I think your deed honors you."

"Thank you, Sacred Woman."

"Then, so be it." Ramuza sat back and sighed. He stared at Nionu for a long while. He seemed thoughtful, refining his judgment. Ramuza leaned forward and pointed at Nionu as if to emphasize his words. "If you come before me for another transgression, such as this, you had better hope there is someone with greater influence than an elder to speak on your behalf. You had better hope I am feeling as forgiving."

"Yes, Mfalme." Nionu wanted to smile. He could sense Ramuza's lenient attitude. But his judgment was yet to come. Nionu stood patiently. He waited for Ramuza to say more.

Ramuza sat back again. "You and your Blue Warriors are free to go."

Nionu and the surrounding crowd suddenly erupted with a joyous cheer. The crowd began a one-word chant. Nionu! Nionu! Nionu! Nionu! Nionu's Blue Warrior Dabete Ehkili and most of the Motobo dancers swept Nionu off his feet. They carried him out toward the center of the celebration area, still chanting his name.

EPILOGUE

Many harvests ago, Moh-Saalim stood at the edge of what remained of the Balba Village, once the home of the Balba clan.

Ten harvests had passed since Moh-Saalim survived that deadly fall from the Jabali cliff. As a young man, he had matured in body, mind, and spirit. After ten harvests and a well-developed appreciation for life, he finally returned to where it all began.

Moh-Saalim stood on a hillside, outside the village. He supported all of his belongings in a large bundle on his shoulder. The golden glow of evening sunlight on the dilapidated dwellings and corrals would have been beautiful, but it only highlighted all the missing structures. Moh-Saalim shifted the bundle from one shoulder to the other as he studied the village and all its demoralizing developments. He saw that most of the village huts had collapsed into rubble. Weeds and vines had obscured the few huts that remained standing. All the animal corrals lay empty and overgrown. And worst of all, Moh-Saalim saw no people anywhere.

Moh-Saalim continued toward the village. He walked with a noticeable limp now. The limp made the bundle on his shoulder awkward to carry. But Moh-Saalim had traveled far and grown used to the awkwardness. He barely noticed his discomfort when he reached the Balba Village. At the moment, the disturbing sights before him demanded all his attention.

Moh-Saalim sighed. Despite the village's strange appearance, it held a special meaning. This was his beginning. He spent the first ten and the most formative harvests of his life here. As Moh-Saalim stepped onto the old and winding pathway that led into the village, he expected to see many things, specific places and sights. Each had the potential to awaken long-forgotten childhood memories.

Long before he walked into the village, Moh-Saalim naturally expected to find a few changes. But already, he saw things had changed so much. He barely recognized most of it. As Moh-Saalim walked through the village's outer edge, he saw only a few familiar places. He wondered if he would see anything that would still awaken fond memories.

Moh-Saalim already knew that the hut of his childhood no longer existed. The family hut had burned to the ground shortly before Kold-Johan threw him over the Jabali. Still, the memory of home pulled him deeper into the village. He had to see what remained. As he limped past the remnants of some of the other huts and corrals, a timeless quality about them finally stirred. He recalled a few fun memories of playing with the other children and his friends. He could almost hear their voices and the sound of their laughter. With a fleeting smile, he remembered their faces and their names. He wondered. Where were all his friends now?

A chopping sound, somewhere deeper in the village, caught Moh-Saalim's full attention. The sound he heard was not a memory. It was real. Moh-Saalim recognized the chopping sound. It stirred something deep within him. His eyes welled with tears before he rounded a turn in the pathway and located the sound's source.

Another hut stood in the distance, where his family's hut once stood. It was smaller, simpler, and more practical, yet built with his father's personal touch. And there, sitting upon the ground out in front of the hut, Moh-Saalim saw the hunched-over back of an old man. It was his father chopping kindling wood, as he had done almost daily. The image and the distinct sound were unique characteristics that Moh-Saalim would have recognized a kilometer away. He smiled.

Moh-Saalim rushed ahead, the limp in his walk more pronounced. After covering less than half the distance to his father, Moh-Saalim grew so overcome by emotion that he had to call out.

"Baba!" His voice echoed through the empty village. "Baba!"

The old man, Moh-Maamuni, was unsure if he heard someone call. So used to the quietness of the deserted village, he was not sure he heard a voice at all. Could it have been his imagination? He stopped chopping and listened. He twisted around slowly, listening and searching.

Over the distance, Moh-Maamuni's eyesight prevented him from recognizing the approaching person. Even the irregular gait of the person's walk gave him no clue. However, something about the person's approach seemed familiar.

"Moh-Saalim?" Moh-Maamuni threw his chopping ax aside. He forced his old body to stand. What Moh-Maamuni saw was impossible, but his heart and mind told him otherwise. "Moh-Saalim?"

Moh-Saalim dropped his bundle of belongings to the ground. He ran ahead. His limp was unnoticeable now. He collided with his father and matched his strong embrace. He held him close and tightly for a long while. When he finally pulled away to study his father's face, he saw tears in the old man's eyes.

"How have you been, baba?"

"Never better than this moment, mwana." Moh-Maamuni wiped the tears from his eyes before they streaked down his cheeks. He looked toward the Jabali, which was several meters to his right. Over the past ten harvests, the old man had found it too painful to look toward the Jabali. He had done so only a handful of times. Each time, all he saw was the memory of Kold-Johan, wiping his hands clean after tossing Moh-Saalim. Moh-Maamuni turned back to his son. "You … survived the Jabali? But … how is this possible?"

"Only the Guardian Spirits know, baba." Adrenaline and overwhelming love forced Moh-Saalim to hold his father's shoulders firmly. He looked him up and down. "It is so good to see you. You look well!"

"As do you."

"As you can probably see, I have seen my share of difficult days. But the Guardian Spirits have blessed me. And Mama? How is mama?"

"You will soon make all her ailments a thing of the past. Come! She is inside the hut." Moh-Maamuni ushered Moh-Saalim toward the hut.

Before the two men reached the hut, Moh-Amina poked her head out of the entrance. She had heard her mate talking with someone. She knew no one else was in the village and became curious. When she saw her son standing before her, ten years of growth could not hide his features. Moh-Amina threw her arms up and screamed. She rushed forward to embrace her son. She melted into his arms and cried freely out of sheer joy.

"Mama," Moh-Saalim held his mother tightly. He was thoughtful not to squeeze her frail body too hard. "I have missed you."

Moh-Amina raised her head from Moh-Saalim's shoulder. She wiped away tears and suppressed her sniffles to speak. "My prayers … all my prayers are answered. How can I ever … show the Guardian Spirits … my gratitude? This is all I could ever ask." Heavy sobs prevented Moh-Amina from saying more. She laid her head against her son's shoulder again.

"Since your disappearance," Moh-Maamuni began, "your mother has cried many times. Sometimes I thought she would never stop crying. Her tears seemed to flow from sunrise and well into the night."

Moh-Saalim relaxed his mother's embrace for the first time. He held her so he could look into her face. He used his fingers to brush away most of the tears from her cheeks. "Then I hope these tears I see are now tears of joy. No more sad tears, mama. I am home. Now, please, smile for me. You cannot imagine how much I have missed your smiles."

Still overcome with emotion, Moh-Amina attempted to stop crying. With both hands, she wiped her face dry. She stood back and studied her son from head to toe, then looked at his face again. She smiled when she realized she had to look up into his eyes. "Look how you have grown, mwana!"

Moh-Saalim now stood a head taller than his mother. "If my growth pleases you, Mama, I will do all I can and never stop."

Moh-Maamuni interrupted the loving encounter between mother and son. "Come, mwana. Sit and be comfortable. Tell us your story."

Moh-Saalim walked his mother to the area where Moh-Maamuni had chopped kindling wood. He assisted her to sit on the ground and then made himself comfortable beside her.

Moh-Maamuni sat directly in front of the two of them. He offered his son a small gourd of banana beer. "You have grown, mwana. You were too young to drink this when we last saw you."

"Thank you, baba." Moh-Saalim accepted the gourd. Despite his thirst after climbing the mountainside to the village, he took only a small sip.

"So tell us. What happened after Kold-Johan threw you over the Jabali? We want to hear everything."

Moh-Saalim looked toward the cliff. Memory of the moment before the plunge returned as clearly as if it had happened yesterday. He took another sip of the banana beer before he spoke again. "The worst of it … I do not remember. I am told I lay at the bottom of the Jabali for days. I had two broken legs, a broken arm, several cracked ribs, and a laceration down the side of my face that almost severed the bottom of my ear."

Moh-Saalim pointed to each of his injuries as he named them. Moh-Amina reached up and traced the scar on her son's face with her finger. She studied the scar as if seeing it for the first time. The scar trailed from over Moh-Saalim's right brow, down between his eyes, across his left cheek and jaw, and ended behind his left earlobe.

"By some miracle, the fall did not kill me," Moh-Saalim continued. "I have no memory immediately after the fall. I have no memory of how long I lay there dying."

"Many times, mwana," Moh-Maamuni paused as many horrible and forgotten memories flooded back. "Several villagers and I descended the mountainside. We went searching for your bodies and those of the village warriors. Day after day, we searched the rocks below. We found the remains of some of the warriors. We never found your body."

"Those were some painful days," Moh-Amina added. "Each day your father and the villagers returned from their search, I ran out to meet them. When I learned that they had not found you, it was like re-living your death over and over again."

Moh-Maamuni reached over to squeeze his mate's hand. "It got to where I hated to return from our searches. I found it harder and harder to tell your mother we had not found your body. I found it impossible to tell your mother what we found. To this day, I never told her. We found some of the warriors' bodies scattered all over the area below. The jagged rocks and boulders tore many of the bodies apart, almost beyond recognition. I felt that finding you, in one piece, seemed hopeless."

"I was fortunate," Moh-Saalim said. "I broke several bones, but my body remained intact. Although you and the villagers never found me, a traveler did. He found me just as the buzzards and scavengers moved to claim me."

"A traveler found you?"

"Yes, baba. I later learned that his name was Ngo Wenfundi. He was a medicine man. When Ngo stumbled upon me, he had no idea where I had come from. He gathered me up and took me to his camp. He later sheltered me. For several harvests, I was almost helpless, unable even to walk. With painstaking care and patience, Ngo nursed me back from the brink of death. Over time, Ngo became one of my dearest friends. I owe him my life."

Moh-Amina squeezed her son's arm. "If you owe Ngo Wenfundi your life, then he is one of the Guardian Spirits to whom your father and I owe our deepest gratitude."

"Ngo traveled a lot. He never stayed in one place long. As a gifted healer, he went wherever people needed him. But, even when I finally regained the ability to walk again, I found it difficult to keep up with him. Unfortunately, over several harvests, I lost touch with him. I just learned of his new home. He has invited me to visit him. Coincidentally, my journey has brought me back to this area. I took the opportunity to climb the mountainside to search for the two of you."

Moh-Maamuni frowned, confused by his son's wandering. "After you regained your ability to walk again, why did you not return home? Did you not miss us?"

"Yes, baba, very much. I missed you and everyone with all my heart and soul. But you must understand. I survived the Jabali. This was a miracle – a life-changing miracle. I had no doubt. I had survived the Jabali for a reason. As my body healed and my mind cleared, that reason became clear to me."

"Which was?"

"It is a long story, baba. At first, as Ngo Wenfundi nursed me back to health, and for many, many moons, I thought of nothing else but getting back to the village here. I wanted to do what I could to save you, mama, and all the Balba people from that ruthless and evil Kold-Johan. And still just a boy in mind and heart, I had no idea how I would accomplish such a feat. I just knew I had to do it somehow. I knew that all the Guardian Spirits would support me."

"You had no way of knowing, but the Guardian Spirits were already working to support your overwhelming feat. Just moments after Kold-Johan threw you over the Jabali, one of his warriors, Abul-Gwan, assassinated him."

"Yes. I learned about the assassination over a harvest after it had happened. Ngo Wenfundi told me about it. I remember the subject came up when Ngo came to talk with me one morning. As I lay upon my cot, he sat beside me. By his demeanor, I knew he wanted to discuss something on his mind since the day he found me."

"What was on his mind?"

"He came to ask me about a beautiful crystal he held up to show me. He asked me where I got it from. My vision was still poor. I could barely see beyond half a meter in front of me. At first, I did not recognize it. But then, Ngo told me I had the crystal with me when he found me. At that moment, I remembered that the crystal Ngo held before me was part of Onu-Vey's *azima*. I had completely forgotten that I had it with me."

Moh-Maamuni recalled that frightening moment when Kold-Johan struck Onu-Vey across his chest with his knife and shattered the houngan's *azima*. "Yes. I remember. Part of Onu-Vey's *azima* broke off. You mean, you found it?"

"Yes, baba. When it fell to the ground, it fell within my reach. I picked it up. No one saw me pick it up. The strange way Kold-Johan's knife chimed held everyone's attention."

"Yes. I will never forget that sound. It was one of the most extraordinary, magical sounds I have ever heard."

"More than you may know, baba. I had the crystal with me when I went over the Jabali. Looking back, I think I survived the Jabali because of the crystal. When I told Ngo where the crystal came from, he told me about Kold-Johan's fate for the first time. He told me all the details he knew about Abul-Gwan and how he had assassinated Kold-Johan. When I first heard about it, it came as no surprise that someone had killed Kold-Johan already."

"Kold-Johan was such an evil-hearted man," Moh-Maamuni commented. "He had it coming."

Moh-Saalim took another sip of his banana beer. "I suppose, the most fascinating part of the incident was that Abul-Gwan assassinated Kold-Johan immediately after something the Vodun houngan, Onu-Vey, had said."

"I will serve you until the day you die," Moh-Amina repeated Onu-Vey's now historic words.

"Everyone shares that fascination, mwana. Those words showed everyone Onu-Vey's true potential." Moh-Maamuni continued to reminisce. "With but a few choice words, Onu-Vey put the single act that changed everything into motion. At once, everyone realized the power of the new Tribal Houngan."

"When Ngo learned that the crystal was part of Onu-Vey's *azima*, he also believed that it was why I had survived the Jabali. It took little for us to realize what I needed to do. If I wanted to save you, mama, and all the Balba people, I should do all I could to get the crystal back into Onu-Vey's hands."

"So, to return the crystal to Onu-Vey became your calling."

"Yes, mama. From that moment, I knew what I needed to do. Before Kold-Johan threw me over the Jabali, I suspected Onu-Vey would be a powerful houngan. Even then, I knew he had the potential to be as great as Mama Kinsi. When I heard what prompted Kold-Johan's assassination, I realized Onu-Vey was the Balba people's greatest hope."

"It seems Onu-Vey knew what he was doing from the beginning," Moh-Amina added. "With Onu-Vey's guidance and the powerful army of Kosi-Jawma, Mfalme Abul-Gwan solidified the clans. Almost overnight, the clan wars stopped. All the clans and villages across central and eastern Africa prospered."

"Yes, but with one major exception," Moh-Maamuni chuckled at the strange irony.

"What is that, baba?"

Moh-Maamuni made a sweeping gesture toward the nearby, empty huts and corrals around him. "The Balba Village, Onu-Vey's own home, was one of the few that did not fare so well."

Moh-Saalim looked around the village. He remembered his initial shock of seeing the deserted village from the hillside. "What happened here, baba?"

Moh-Maamuni pointed toward the mountainside behind the village. The setting sun accented the patchy slope and skyline. The trees there looked scattered, skimpy, and dying. "Our most valuable resource ran out. While the mountain timber lasted, we did just fine. Regiments of Kosi-Jawma's army came through the village regularly to collect the fine timber we had harvested. But as the trees thinned, the quantity and quality of timber dwindled. After several harvests, the regiments no longer bothered to come. The village died. Most of the villagers moved on to other places."

"Baba, why did you and Mama not move on, too? Did you not see what was happening?"

"It was my fault we did not move on," Moh-Amina explained. "I did not want to leave. I had to wait."

"Wait for what?"

"For this very day. From when Kold-Johan threw you over the Jabali, I dreamed, hoped, and prayed for the day you would return to us. Since we never found your body, I always held on to the hope you would come back home someday. I had no rational reason to think you would. But my hope was so strong. I could not leave."

"I tried so many times to convince your mother to do as all the other villagers had done. She would not listen to me. I guess I was one of the few who truly understood her pain. In a dying village, I found it easier to make life comfortable here. Through the many harvests, we have done well together. With a whole village, we could grow enough food to last daily, from harvest to harvest."

Moh-Amina smiled at her mate. "For everything else that we needed, we found it in each other."

Moh-Saalim smiled at his parents. "It is as I remember."

"But what about you, mwana? Did you ever find Onu-Vey? Were you able to return his *azima*?"

"No, baba. Initially, I spent most of my time recovering from the Jabali. As you can probably imagine, the process was slow. But each day, I grew better and stronger. Many days, I could only lie in one place and make wooden carvings and sculptures. It helped me pass the time. And when I could finally get up and move about, I had to relearn to walk again."

"I noticed that you walk with a limp now."

"Yes. I am afraid this limp is permanent. Ngo Wenfundi is a good healer, but he has his limits. I am fortunate to be able to walk. All things considered, I can live with the limp. It has not limited me too much. Since I have been walking again, I have traveled too. Initially, I attempted to follow Ngo during his travels. But my primary calling continued to be locating the houngan, Onu-Vey. After all that time, I still felt it was vital I find him. With each of my steps so precious, I wasted none in my search."

"Locating Onu-Vey should not have been too difficult." Moh-Maamuni considered what he would have done. "Locate the Mfalme, Abul-Gwan, or Kosi-Jawma. Abul-Gwan, Onu-Vey, and Kosi-Jawma are now like brothers. Find one. You will find the others nearby."

"That was not as easy as it sounds, baba. Since Abul-Gwan became Mfalme, he, Kosi-Jawma, and Onu-Vey have moved about constantly, all over central and east Africa. They never remain in the same place for two or three days. Through word of mouth, I would often learned of Onu-Vey's location. But by the time I reached that location, Onu-Vey had moved on to a new location. I never made it there, even when I learned beforehand or predicted where he might arrive. My timing never put me where I needed to be for many reasons. I thought I had lost favor with the Guardian Spirits, but never gave up my search."

"You never found the houngan?"

"No, baba."

"Then, you still have his *azima*?"

Moh-Saalim set his unfinished gourd of banana beer down and got up. He limped back to where he had placed his bundle of belongings. He extracted an object wrapped in a cloth. Moh-Saalim limped back to his seat and unwrapped the cloth. As he made himself comfortable again, he peeled back the final fold of the cloth to show a beautiful scepter, topped with the carving of the potbellied bullfrog. He handed the scepter to his father.

Moh-Maamuni took the scepter delicately into his hands. He examined it from top to bottom. "Oh, Moh-Saalim, it is … magnificent. You put considerable time into this. It must have taken you a long time to do this. The craftsmanship… it is so…"

"The craftsmanship includes all the care and attention you have taught me, baba."

"Yes. But I see more here than I ever taught you. The loving care goes beyond anything I have ever seen. The wood is rich and hard, with perfect grain. And these markings, I do not recognize all of them."

"The markings are Mangoni. Since we are all Mangoni now, I felt it best to convey my wishes to the houngan using the official tribal language."

The scepter's beauty drew Moh-Amina closer. She reached over to stroke the smoothly polished wood. "So what connection does the scepter have with the houngan's *azima*?"

Moh-Saalim pointed to the carving at the top of the scepter. "The crystal is encased inside the belly of the frog. I thought carrying it would be a safe and secure way until I returned it to the houngan."

Moh-Maamuni ran his fingers gently over the shaft of the scepter, too. "Mwana, it is clear. You put your heart into this creation. And your efforts to return the *azima* to the houngan have been your focus for the past ten harvests."

"But?" Moh-Saalim looked into his father's face. After ten harvests, he still knew his father's mannerisms well. He knew his father was about to add something he did not want to hear.

"Over many harvests, I have heard countless rumors of the Vodun houngan's magical achievements. They seem to be endless. If any of these rumors and stories are true, Onu-Vey has done well with the *azima* half he still has."

"What are you saying, baba?"

"Knowing what I know about the houngan with all his power, if he never saw this half of his *azima* again, he would probably not miss it."

Moh-Saalim stared into his father's face as the truth took root. "So … do you think I should end my search for the houngan?"

"Only the Guardian Spirits can answer that, mwana. But, as powerful as Onu-Vey is, if he needed this half of his *azima*, he would have somehow repossessed it long ago."

"You are probably right. My single-minded determination blinded me. I never considered looking at this from the houngan's point of view." Moh-Saalim shook his head, feeling the initial pains of his mistake. "Ten harvests. I will regret not spending that time with you and mama. I am sorry, baba."

"Sorry? You have no reason to be sorry, Moh-Saalim. Your mother and I are happy that you have finally come home. And what you tried to do for the Balba clan makes us proud of you."

"Still ..." Moh-Saalim shrugged and looked away. His eyes welled up with tears again as he glanced around at the dead village and the pitiful, skimpy trees up on the mountainside. It was too late for the Balba clan. "I truly thought Onu-Vey could save all of this. I thought he needed half of his *azima* to do so. Perhaps, I put too much hope in the houngan and his *azima*."

Moh-Amina put her hand upon her son's chest, directly over his heart. "Do not despair, Moh-Saalim. The houngan is not finished with Abul-Gwan and the Mangoni. As for this half of his *azima*, the houngan probably no longer needs it. Maybe, it has already served its purpose."

"Maybe." Moh-Saalim held the scepter up and studied it briefly. He hoped that his mother was right. He finally laid the devalued scepter down at his side. "When I see Ngo again, he will be happy to learn I returned home. He will be happy you are safe and well."

"You must relay our gratitude to your friend," Moh-Amina said. "You must also tell him Onu-Vey's *azima* completed its purpose ten harvests ago. It kept you alive for us."

"This friend of yours," Moh-Maamuni began, "where does Ngo live anyway?"

"He lives several kilometers north of here, baba, in the village of the Kiwane."

"Do you still intend to visit him?"

"Yes, baba. Ngo has invited me there to witness the coronation of their new Mfalme, Mendoza Menda. I promised Ngo that I would be there." As an afterthought, Moh-Saalim picked up the scepter again. He looked at it with renewed value. "It is customary to bring a gift to a coronation. Do you think Mfalme Menda can use a new scepter?"